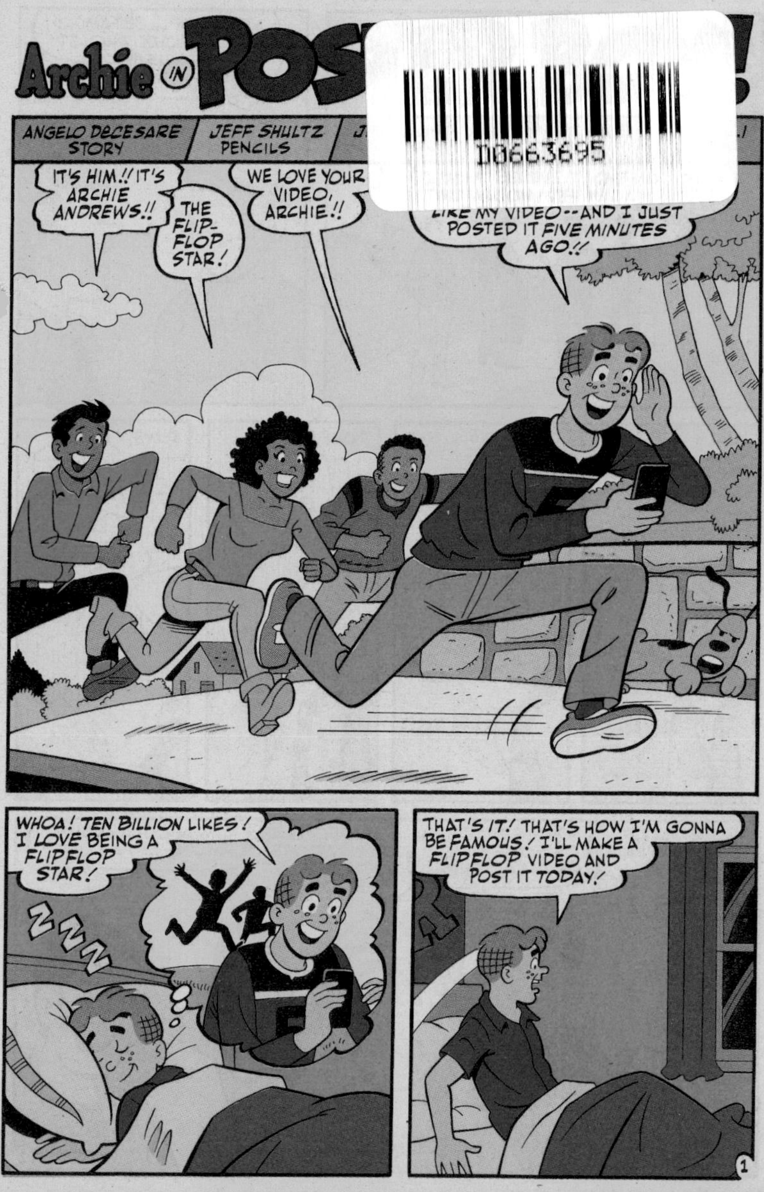
Archie IN
ANGELO DeCESARE STORY
JEFF SHULTZ PENCILS
IT'S HIM!! IT'S ARCHIE ANDREWS!!
THE FLIP-FLOP STAR!
WE LOVE YOUR VIDEO, ARCHIE!!
LIKE MY VIDEO--AND I JUST POSTED IT FIVE MINUTES AGO!!
WHOA! TEN BILLION LIKES! I LOVE BEING A FLIPFLOP STAR!
Z Z Z
THAT'S IT! THAT'S HOW I'M GONNA BE FAMOUS! I'LL MAKE A FLIPFLOP VIDEO AND POST IT TODAY!

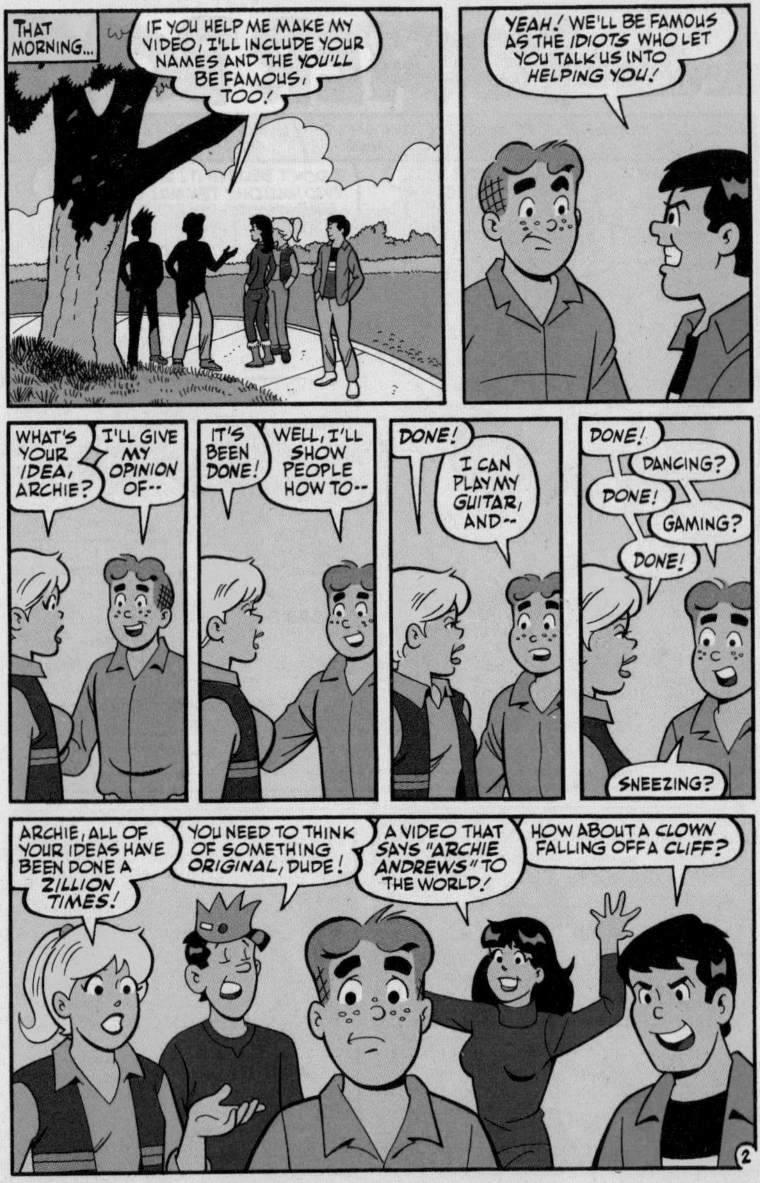
THAT MORNING...
IF YOU HELP ME MAKE MY VIDEO, I'LL INCLUDE YOUR NAMES AND THE YOU'LL BE FAMOUS, TOO!
YEAH! WE'LL BE FAMOUS AS THE IDIOTS WHO LET YOU TALK US INTO HELPING YOU!
WHAT'S YOUR IDEA, ARCHIE?
I'LL GIVE MY OPINION OF--
IT'S BEEN DONE!
WELL, I'LL SHOW PEOPLE HOW TO--
DONE!
I CAN PLAY MY GUITAR, AND--
DONE!
DANCING?
DONE!
GAMING?
DONE!
SNEEZING?
ARCHIE, ALL OF YOUR IDEAS HAVE BEEN DONE A ZILLION TIMES!
YOU NEED TO THINK OF SOMETHING ORIGINAL, DUDE!
A VIDEO THAT SAYS "ARCHIE ANDREWS" TO THE WORLD!
HOW ABOUT A CLOWN FALLING OFF A CLIFF?
2

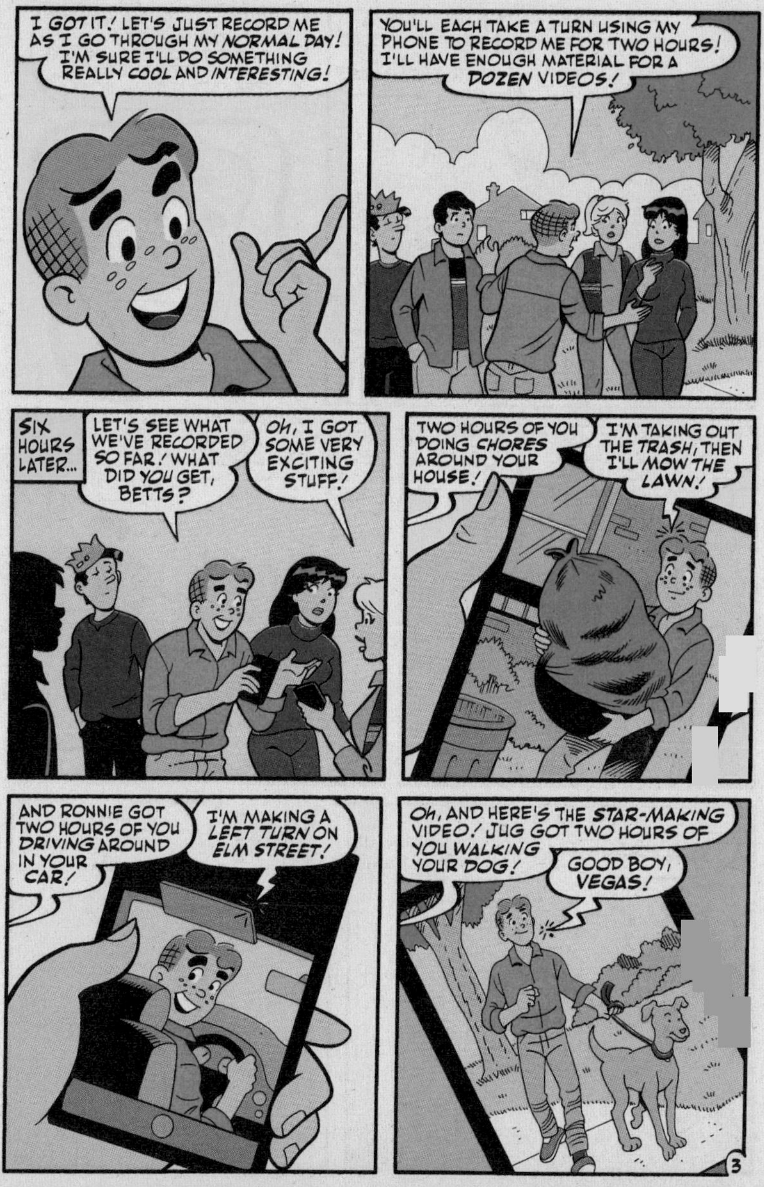
I GOT IT! LET'S JUST RECORD ME AS I GO THROUGH MY NORMAL DAY! I'M SURE I'LL DO SOMETHING REALLY COOL AND INTERESTING!
YOU'LL EACH TAKE A TURN USING MY PHONE TO RECORD ME FOR TWO HOURS! I'LL HAVE ENOUGH MATERIAL FOR A DOZEN VIDEOS!
SIX HOURS LATER...
LET'S SEE WHAT WE'VE RECORDED SO FAR! WHAT DID YOU GET, BETTS?
Oh, I GOT SOME VERY EXCITING STUFF!
TWO HOURS OF YOU DOING CHORES AROUND YOUR HOUSE!
I'M TAKING OUT THE TRASH; THEN I'LL MOW THE LAWN!
AND RONNIE GOT TWO HOURS OF YOU DRIVING AROUND IN YOUR CAR!
I'M MAKING A LEFT TURN ON ELM STREET!
Oh, AND HERE'S THE STAR-MAKING VIDEO! JUG GOT TWO HOURS OF YOU WALKING YOUR DOG!
GOOD BOY, VEGAS!

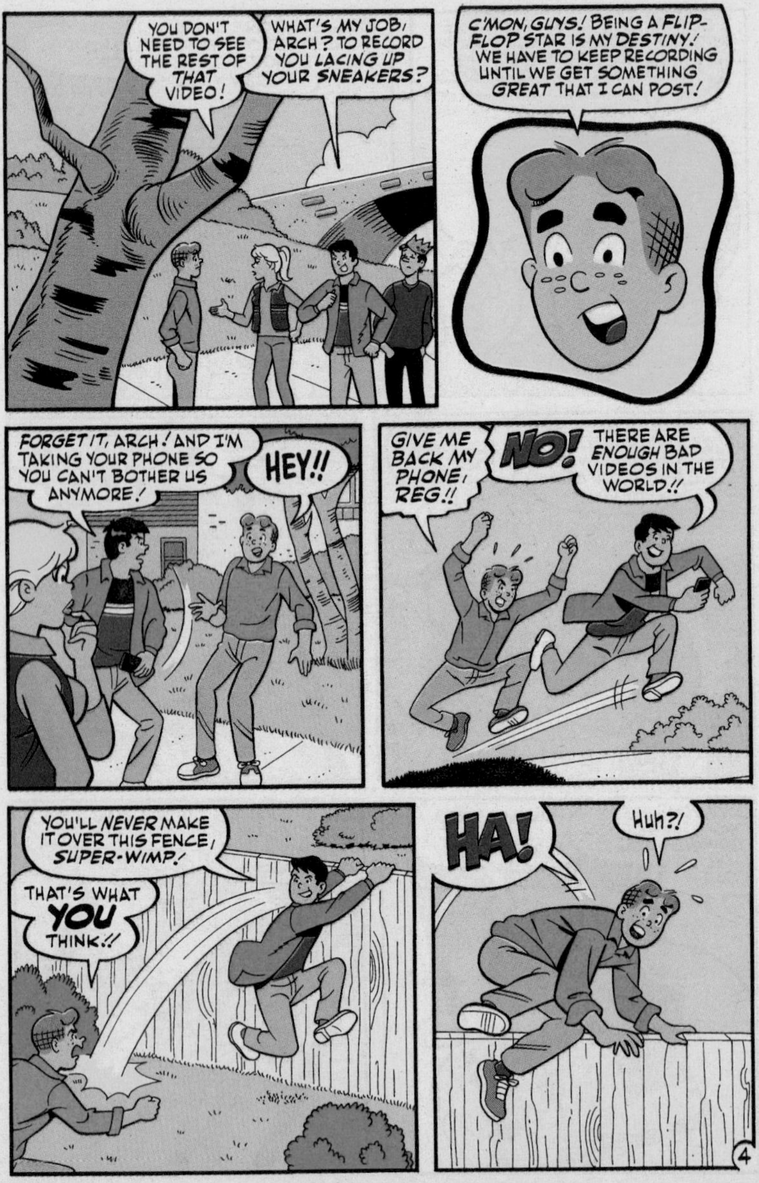

YOU DON'T NEED TO SEE THE REST OF THAT VIDEO!
WHAT'S MY JOB, ARCH? TO RECORD YOU LACING UP YOUR SNEAKERS?
C'MON, GUYS! BEING A FLIP-FLOP STAR IS MY DESTINY! WE HAVE TO KEEP RECORDING UNTIL WE GET SOMETHING GREAT THAT I CAN POST!
FORGET IT, ARCH! AND I'M TAKING YOUR PHONE SO YOU CAN'T BOTHER US ANYMORE!
HEY!!
GIVE ME BACK MY PHONE, REG!!
NO!
THERE ARE ENOUGH BAD VIDEOS IN THE WORLD!!
YOU'LL NEVER MAKE IT OVER THIS FENCE, SUPER-WIMP!
THAT'S WHAT YOU THINK!!
HA!
Huh?!
4

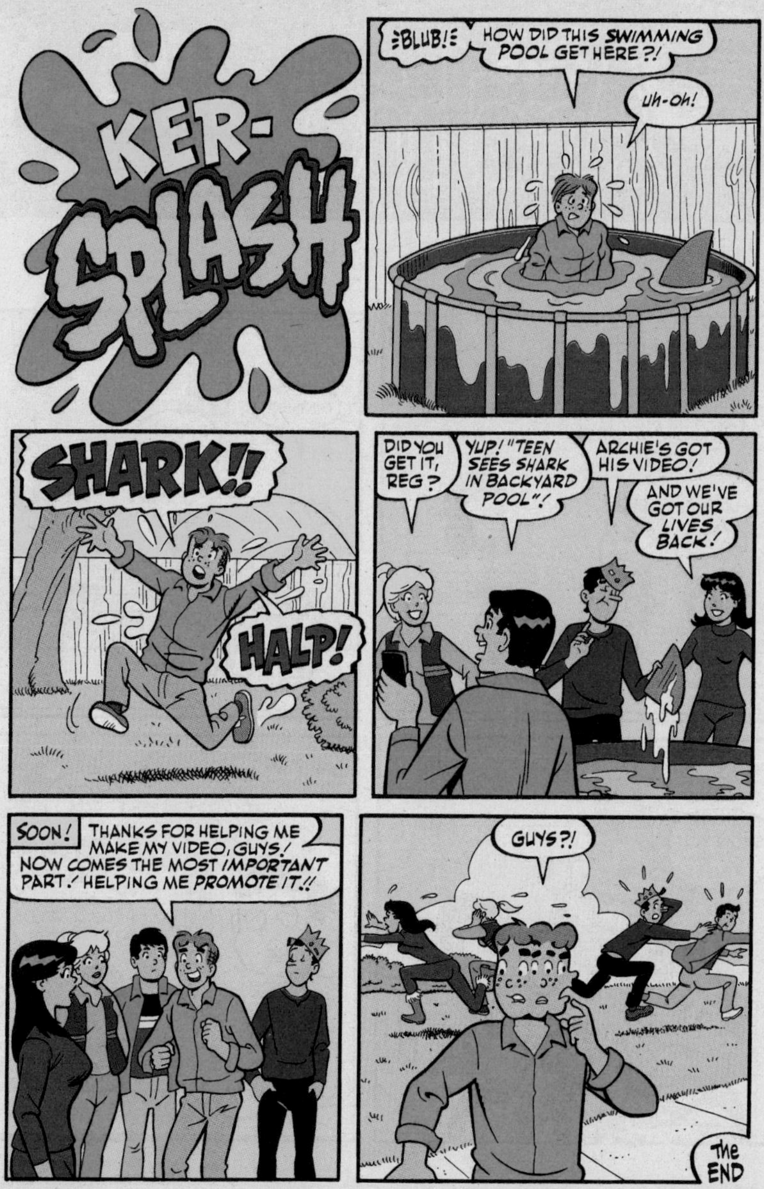
KER-SPLASH
BLUB!
HOW DID THIS SWIMMING POOL GET HERE?!
uh-oh!
SHARK!!
HALP!
DID YOU GET IT, REG?
YUP! "TEEN SEES SHARK IN BACKYARD POOL"!
ARCHIE'S GOT HIS VIDEO!
AND WE'VE GOT OUR LIVES BACK!
SOON!
THANKS FOR HELPING ME MAKE MY VIDEO, GUYS! NOW COMES THE MOST IMPORTANT PART! HELPING ME PROMOTE IT!!
GUYS?!
The END

ARCHIE'S FIRST-EVER WEBCOMIC SERIES!

Bite Sized Archie

LEFT ON READ

SCRIPT: RON CACACE
ART: VINCENT LOVALLO

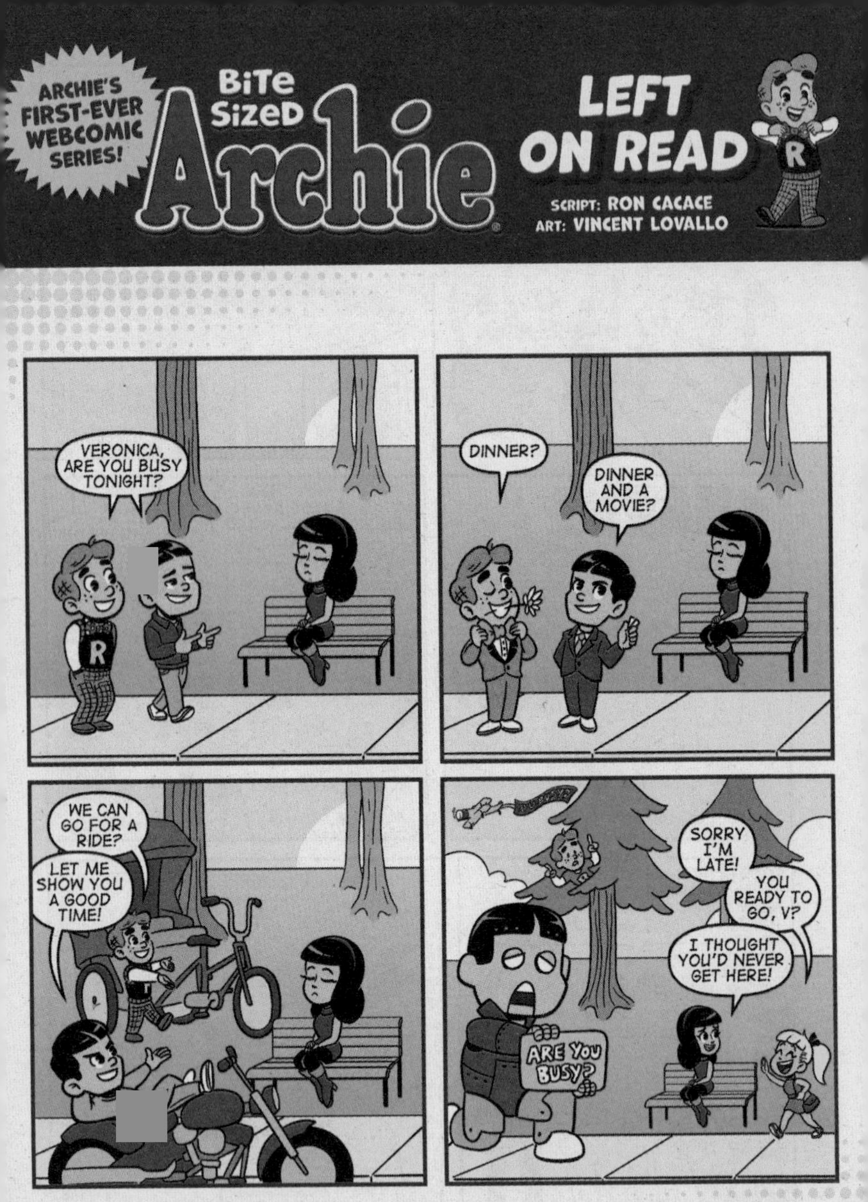

VERONICA, ARE YOU BUSY TONIGHT?
DINNER?
DINNER AND A MOVIE?
WE CAN GO FOR A RIDE?
LET ME SHOW YOU A GOOD TIME!
ARE YOU BUSY?
SORRY I'M LATE!
YOU READY TO GO, V?
I THOUGHT YOU'D NEVER GET HERE!

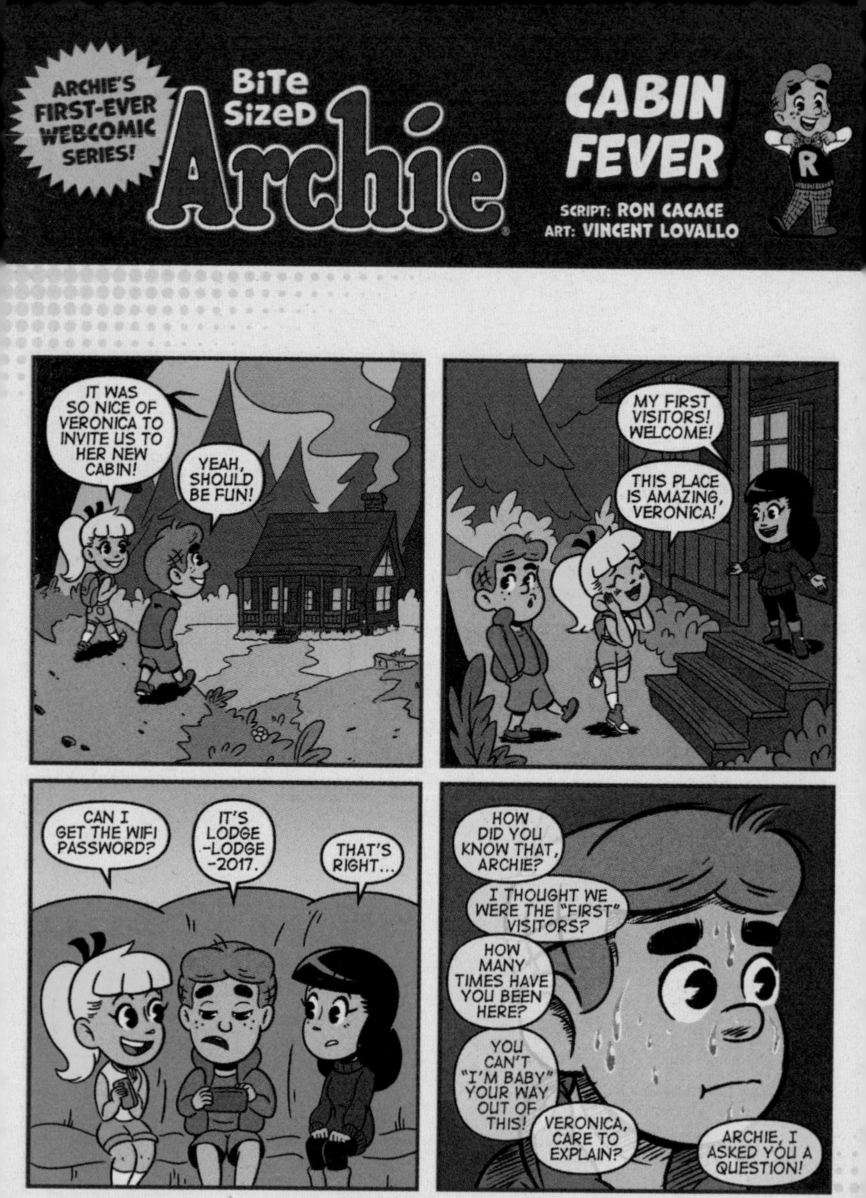

ARCHIE'S FIRST-EVER WEBCOMIC SERIES!
BITE SIZED Archie
CABIN FEVER
SCRIPT: RON CACACE
ART: VINCENT LOVALLO
R
IT WAS SO NICE OF VERONICA TO INVITE US TO HER NEW CABIN!
YEAH, SHOULD BE FUN!
MY FIRST VISITORS! WELCOME!
THIS PLACE IS AMAZING, VERONICA!
CAN I GET THE WIFI PASSWORD?
IT'S LODGE-LODGE-2017.
THAT'S RIGHT...
HOW DID YOU KNOW THAT, ARCHIE?
I THOUGHT WE WERE THE "FIRST" VISITORS?
HOW MANY TIMES HAVE YOU BEEN HERE?
YOU CAN'T "I'M BABY" YOUR WAY OUT OF THIS!
VERONICA, CARE TO EXPLAIN?
ARCHIE, I ASKED YOU A QUESTION!

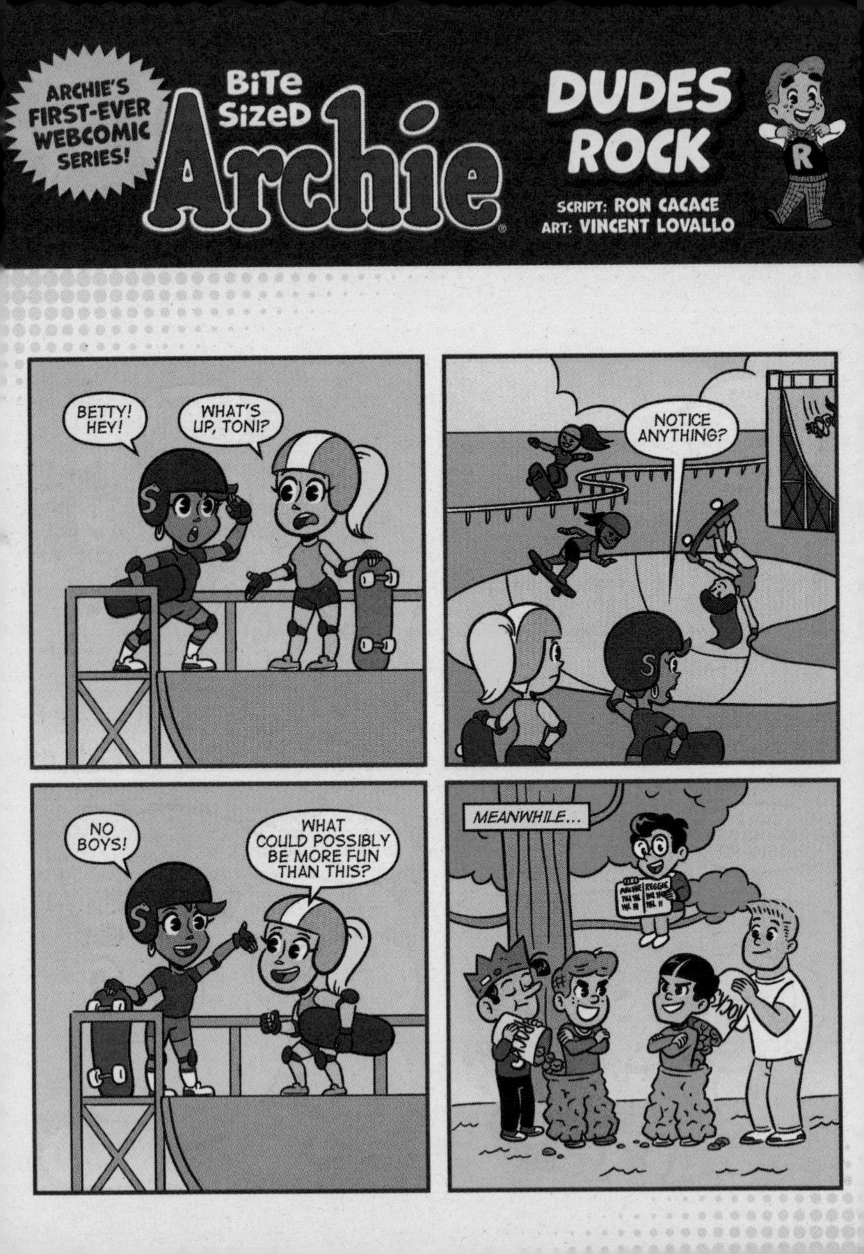
ARCHIE'S FIRST-EVER WEBCOMIC SERIES!
BiTe SizeD Archie
DUDES ROCK
SCRIPT: RON CACACE
ART: VINCENT LOVALLO
BETTY! HEY!
WHAT'S UP, TONI?
NOTICE ANYTHING?
NO BOYS!
WHAT COULD POSSIBLY BE MORE FUN THAN THIS?
MEANWHILE...
ARCHIE
RECCIE
ROCKS
ROCKS

ARCHIE'S FIRST-EVER WEBCOMIC SERIES!

Bite Sized Archie®

RIVAL SCHOOLS

SCRIPT: RON CACACE
ART: VINCENT LOVALLO

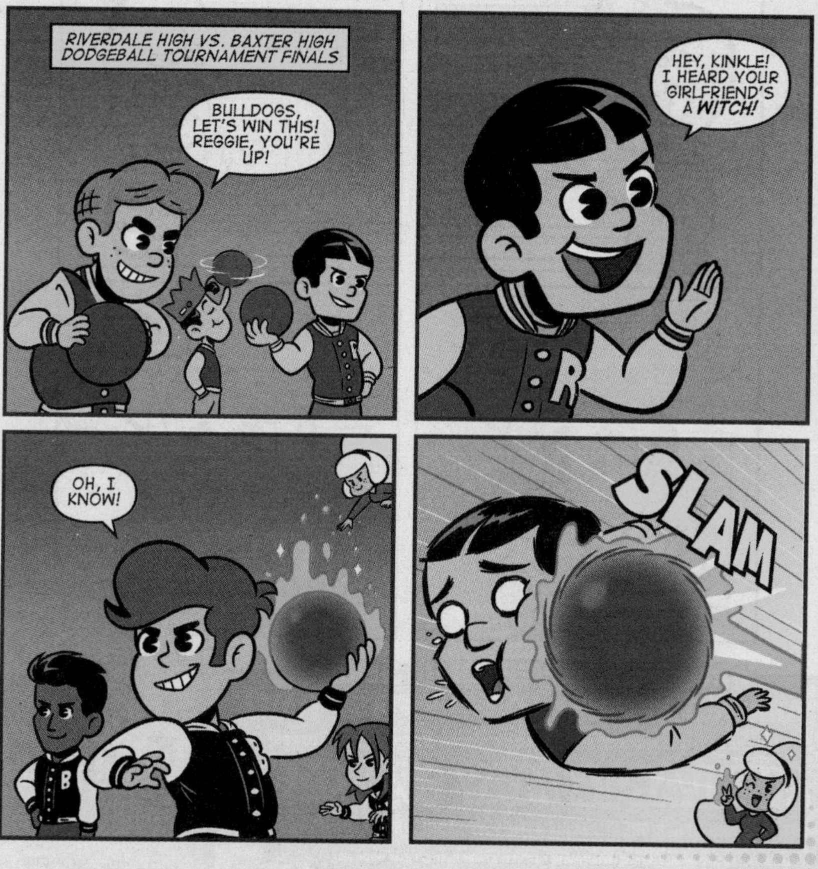

RIVERDALE HIGH VS. BAXTER HIGH DODGEBALL TOURNAMENT FINALS
BULLDOGS, LET'S WIN THIS! REGGIE, YOU'RE UP!
HEY, KINKLE! I HEARD YOUR GIRLFRIEND'S A WITCH!
OH, I KNOW!
SLAM

ARCHIE'S FIRST-EVER WEBCOMIC SERIES!
BITE SIZED Archie
THE BOY NEXT DOOR
SCRIPT: RON CACACE
ART: VINCENT LOVALLO
R

BETTY COOPER, THE GIRL NEXT DOOR.
I NEED TO FINALLY ASK HER...
ARCHIE ANDREWS. MY BEST FRIEND.
WILL HE FINALLY ASK ME?
I BROKE MY PHONE, CAN YOU TEXT VERONICA FOR ME?
RIVERDALE

BITE SIZED Archie
RON CACACE • VINCENT LOVALLO

3979D

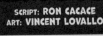

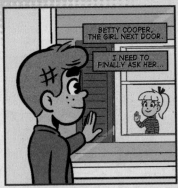

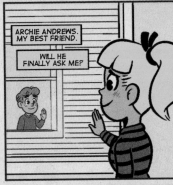

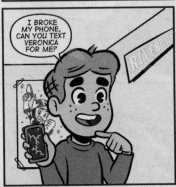

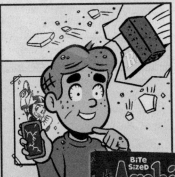

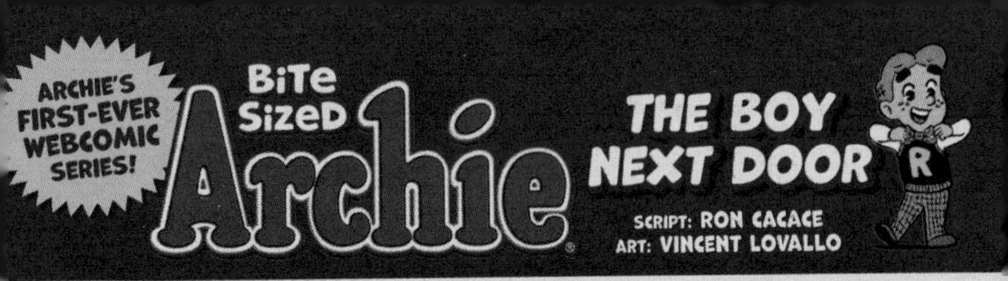

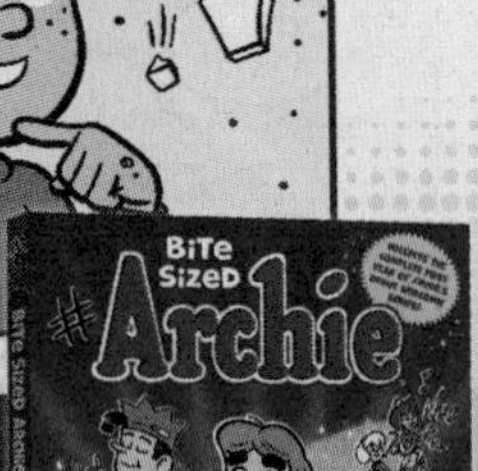

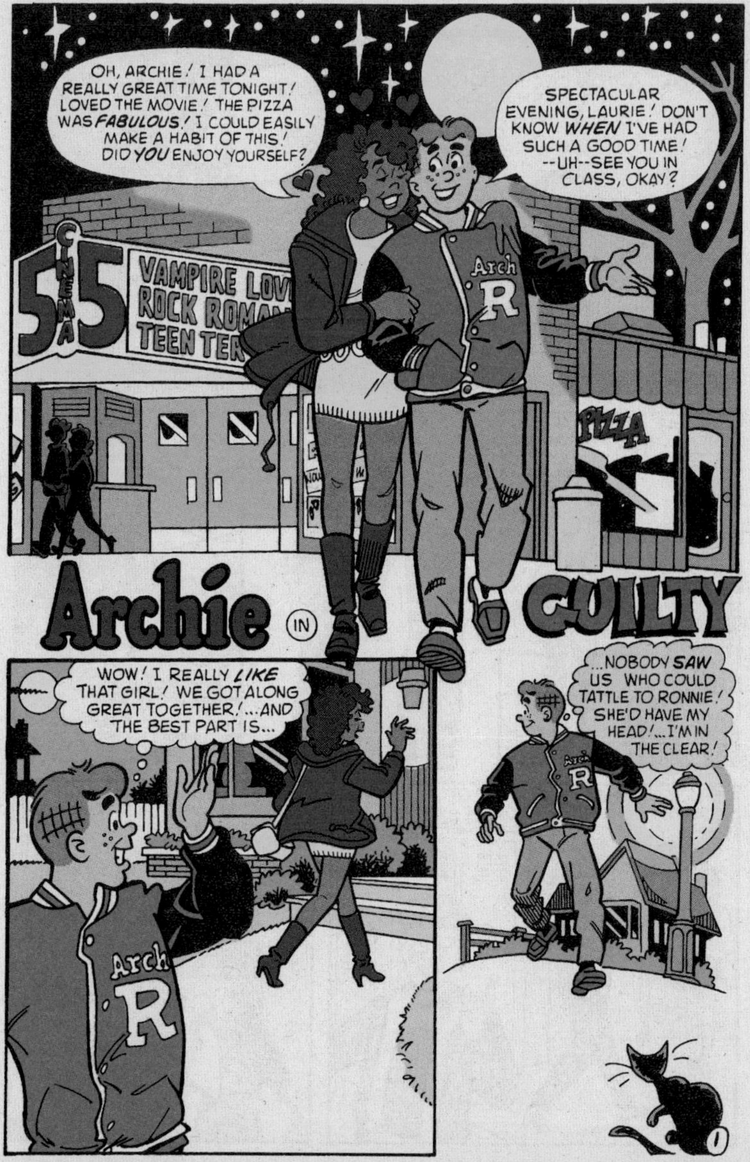
OH, ARCHIE! I HAD A REALLY GREAT TIME TONIGHT! LOVED THE MOVIE! THE PIZZA WAS *FABULOUS*! I COULD EASILY MAKE A HABIT OF THIS! DID *YOU* ENJOY YOURSELF?
SPECTACULAR EVENING, LAURIE! DON'T KNOW *WHEN* I'VE HAD SUCH A GOOD TIME! --UH--SEE YOU IN CLASS, OKAY?
CINEMA 5 5
VAMPIRE LOV
ROCK ROMA
TEEN TER
PIZZA
Archie IN GUILTY
WOW! I REALLY *LIKE* THAT GIRL! WE GOT ALONG GREAT TOGETHER!...AND THE BEST PART IS...
...NOBODY *SAW* US WHO COULD TATTLE TO RONNIE! SHE'D HAVE MY HEAD!...I'M IN THE CLEAR!
1

Script: Frank Doyle / Pencils: Stan Goldberg / Inks: Henry Scarpelli / Letters: Bill Yoshida

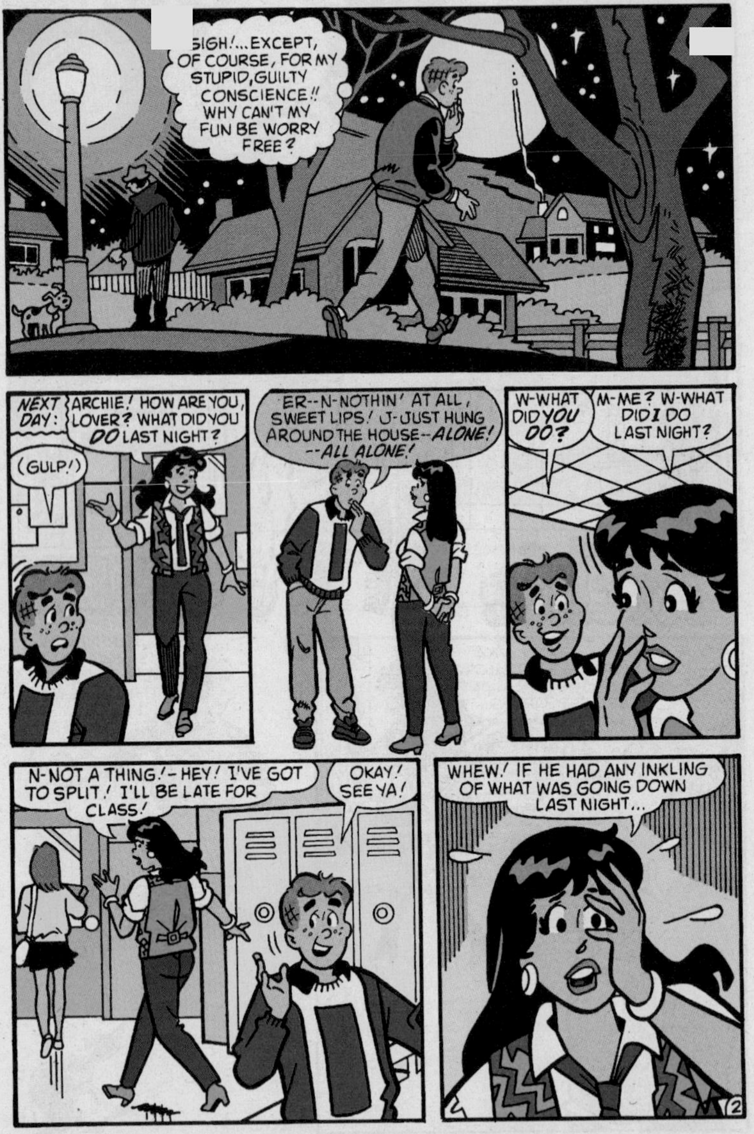
SIGH!...EXCEPT, OF COURSE, FOR MY STUPID, GUILTY CONSCIENCE!! WHY CAN'T MY FUN BE WORRY FREE?
NEXT DAY:
ARCHIE! HOW ARE YOU, LOVER? WHAT DID YOU DO LAST NIGHT?
(GULP!)
ER--N-NOTHIN' AT ALL, SWEET LIPS! J-JUST HUNG AROUND THE HOUSE--ALONE! --ALL ALONE!
W-WHAT DID YOU DO?
M-ME? W-WHAT DID I DO LAST NIGHT?
N-NOT A THING! - HEY! I'VE GOT TO SPLIT! I'LL BE LATE FOR CLASS!
OKAY! SEE YA!
WHEW! IF HE HAD ANY INKLING OF WHAT WAS GOING DOWN LAST NIGHT...
2

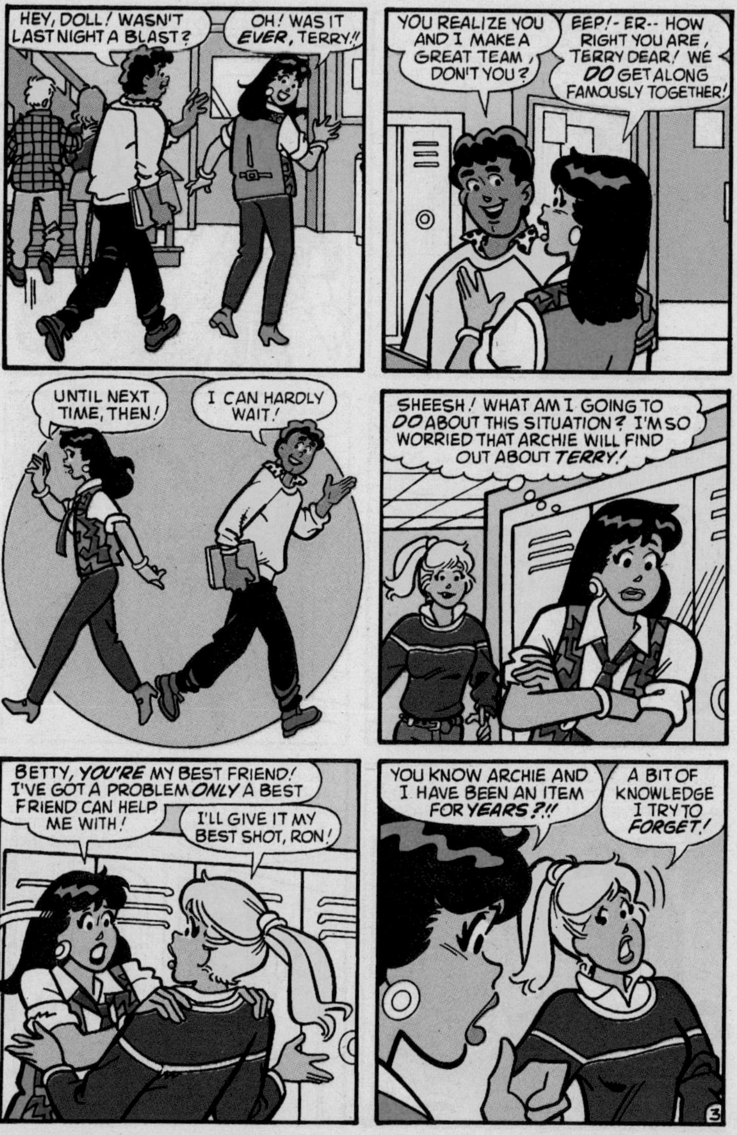
HEY, DOLL! WASN'T LAST NIGHT A BLAST?
OH! WAS IT EVER, TERRY!!
YOU REALIZE YOU AND I MAKE A GREAT TEAM, DON'T YOU?
EEP! - ER-- HOW RIGHT YOU ARE, TERRY DEAR! WE DO GET ALONG FAMOUSLY TOGETHER!
UNTIL NEXT TIME, THEN!
I CAN HARDLY WAIT!
SHEESH! WHAT AM I GOING TO DO ABOUT THIS SITUATION? I'M SO WORRIED THAT ARCHIE WILL FIND OUT ABOUT TERRY!
BETTY, YOU'RE MY BEST FRIEND! I'VE GOT A PROBLEM ONLY A BEST FRIEND CAN HELP ME WITH!
I'LL GIVE IT MY BEST SHOT, RON!
YOU KNOW ARCHIE AND I HAVE BEEN AN ITEM FOR YEARS?!!
A BIT OF KNOWLEDGE I TRY TO FORGET!
3

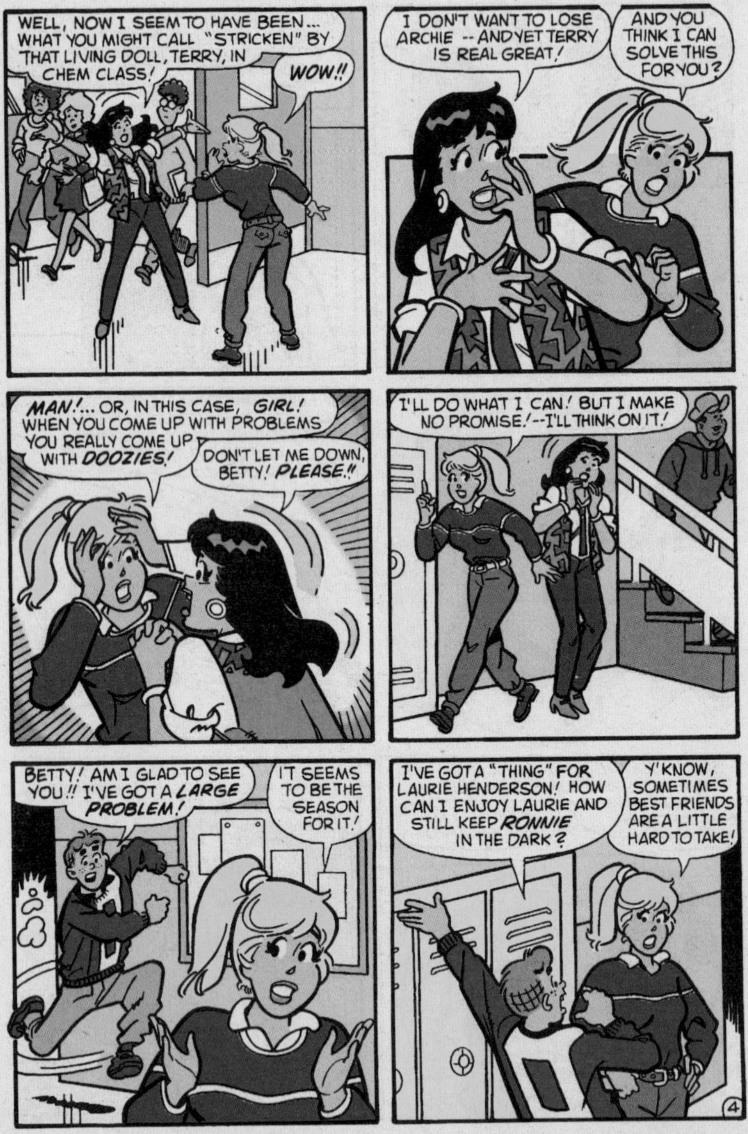

WELL, NOW I SEEM TO HAVE BEEN... WHAT YOU MIGHT CALL "STRICKEN" BY THAT LIVING DOLL, TERRY, IN CHEM CLASS!
WOW!!
I DON'T WANT TO LOSE ARCHIE -- AND YET TERRY IS REAL GREAT!
AND YOU THINK I CAN SOLVE THIS FOR YOU?
MAN!... OR, IN THIS CASE, GIRL! WHEN YOU COME UP WITH PROBLEMS YOU REALLY COME UP WITH DOOZIES!
DON'T LET ME DOWN, BETTY! PLEASE!!
I'LL DO WHAT I CAN! BUT I MAKE NO PROMISE!--I'LL THINK ON IT!
BETTY! AM I GLAD TO SEE YOU!! I'VE GOT A LARGE PROBLEM!
IT SEEMS TO BE THE SEASON FOR IT!
I'VE GOT A "THING" FOR LAURIE HENDERSON! HOW CAN I ENJOY LAURIE AND STILL KEEP RONNIE IN THE DARK?
Y'KNOW, SOMETIMES BEST FRIENDS ARE A LITTLE HARD TO TAKE!
4

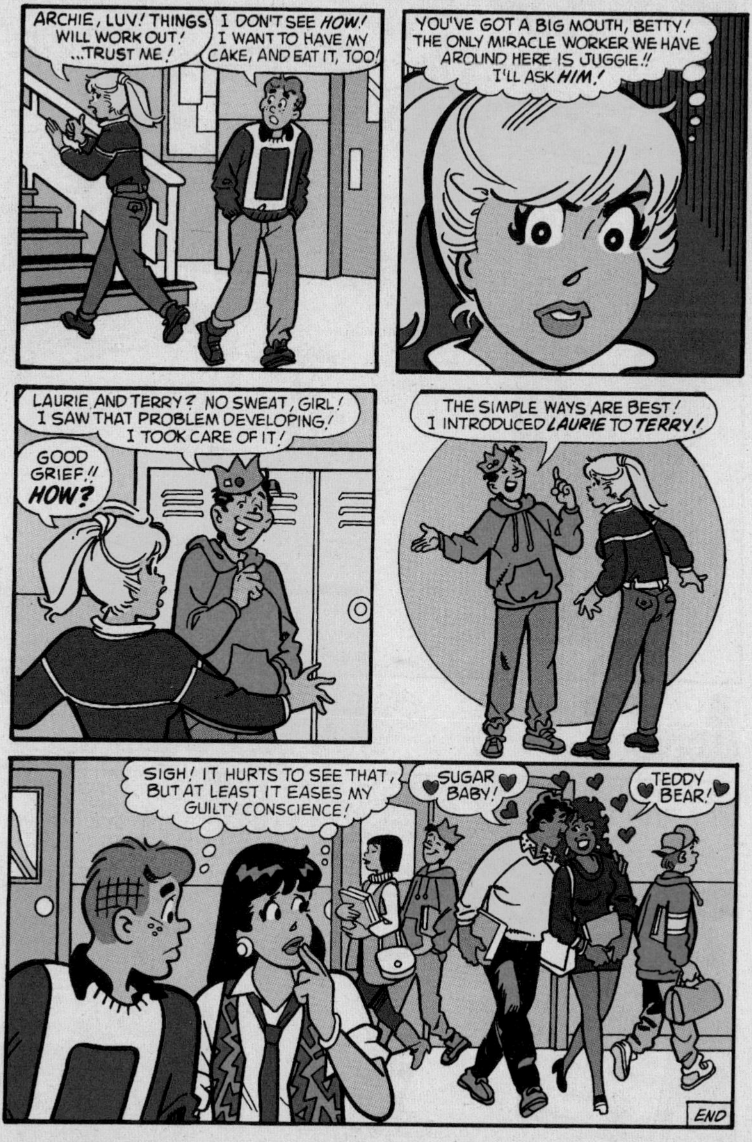
ARCHIE, LUV! THINGS WILL WORK OUT! ...TRUST ME!
I DON'T SEE HOW! I WANT TO HAVE MY CAKE, AND EAT IT, TOO!
YOU'VE GOT A BIG MOUTH, BETTY! THE ONLY MIRACLE WORKER WE HAVE AROUND HERE IS JUGGIE!! I'LL ASK HIM!
LAURIE AND TERRY? NO SWEAT, GIRL! I SAW THAT PROBLEM DEVELOPING! I TOOK CARE OF IT!
GOOD GRIEF!! HOW?
THE SIMPLE WAYS ARE BEST! I INTRODUCED LAURIE TO TERRY!
SIGH! IT HURTS TO SEE THAT, BUT AT LEAST IT EASES MY GUILTY CONSCIENCE!
SUGAR BABY!
TEDDY BEAR!
END

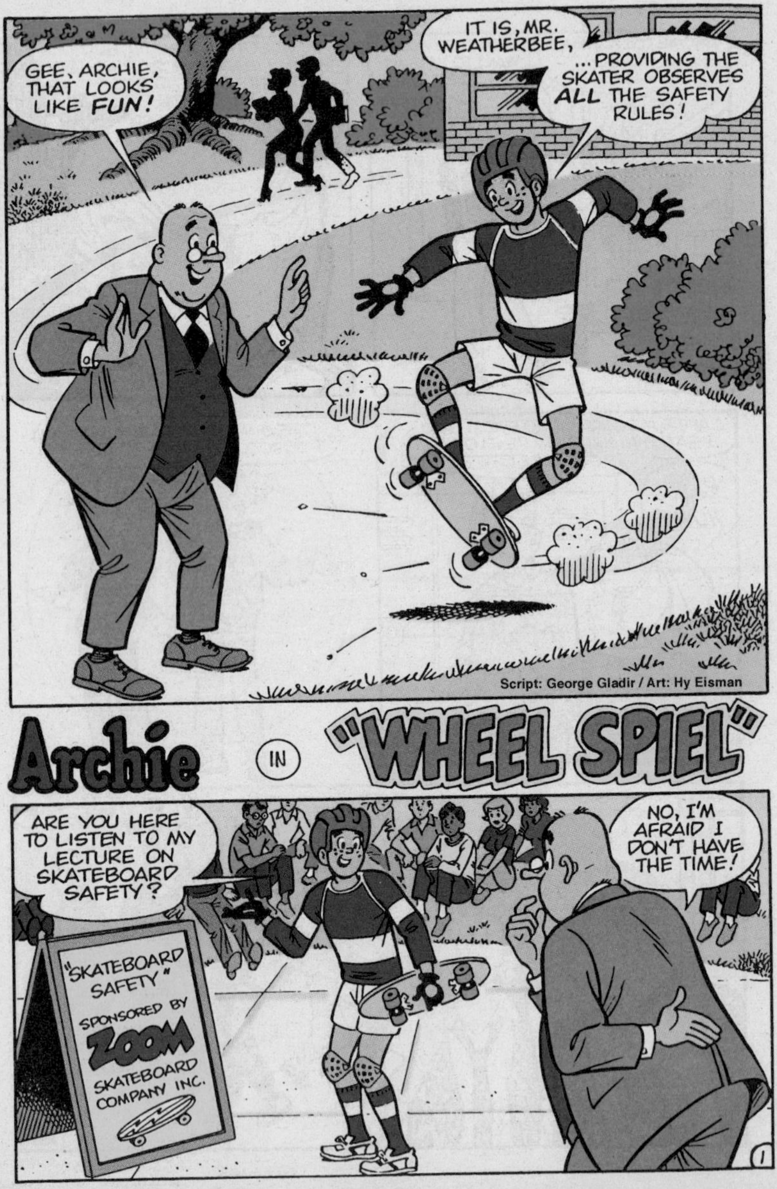
GEE, ARCHIE, THAT LOOKS LIKE FUN!
IT IS, MR. WEATHERBEE,
...PROVIDING THE SKATER OBSERVES ALL THE SAFETY RULES!
Script: George Gladir / Art: Hy Eisman
Archie IN "WHEEL SPIEL"
ARE YOU HERE TO LISTEN TO MY LECTURE ON SKATEBOARD SAFETY?
NO, I'M AFRAID I DON'T HAVE THE TIME!
"SKATEBOARD SAFETY" SPONSORED BY ZOOM SKATEBOARD COMPANY INC.
1

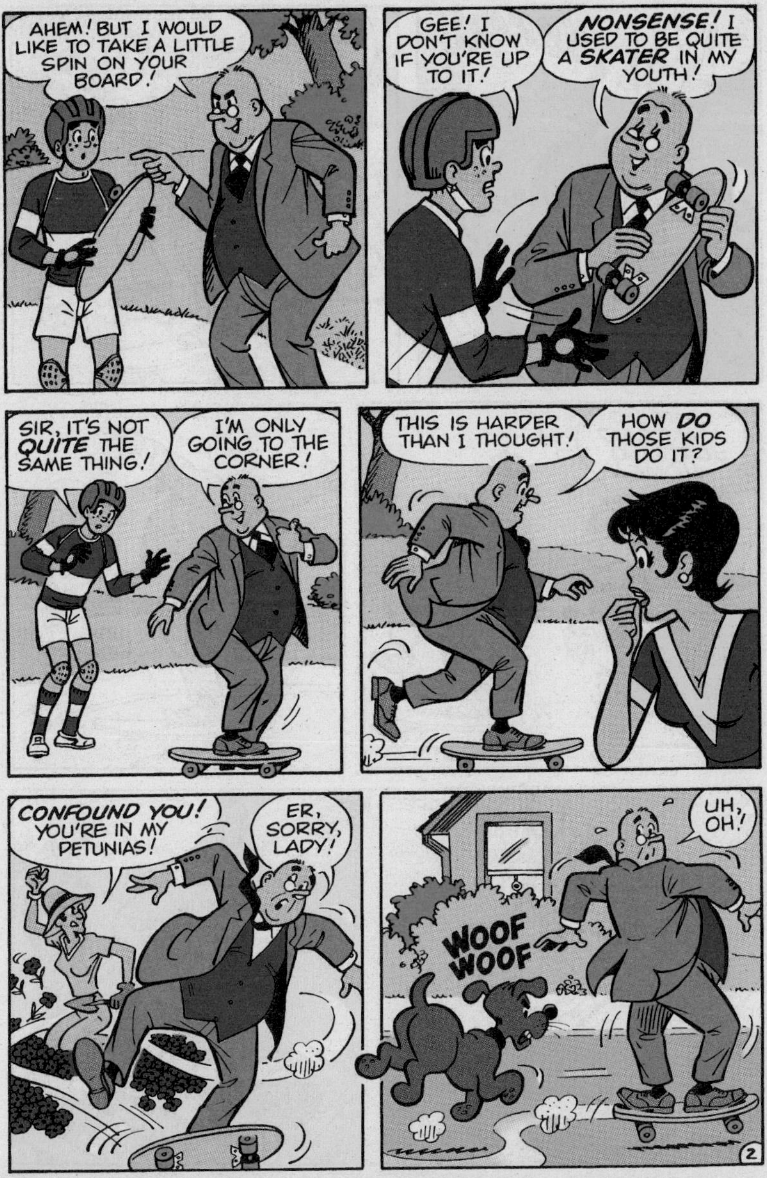
AHEM! BUT I WOULD LIKE TO TAKE A LITTLE SPIN ON YOUR BOARD!
GEE! I DON'T KNOW IF YOU'RE UP TO IT!
NONSENSE! I USED TO BE QUITE A SKATER IN MY YOUTH!
SIR, IT'S NOT QUITE THE SAME THING!
I'M ONLY GOING TO THE CORNER!
THIS IS HARDER THAN I THOUGHT!
HOW DO THOSE KIDS DO IT?
CONFOUND YOU! YOU'RE IN MY PETUNIAS!
ER, SORRY, LADY!
UH, OH!
WOOF WOOF
2

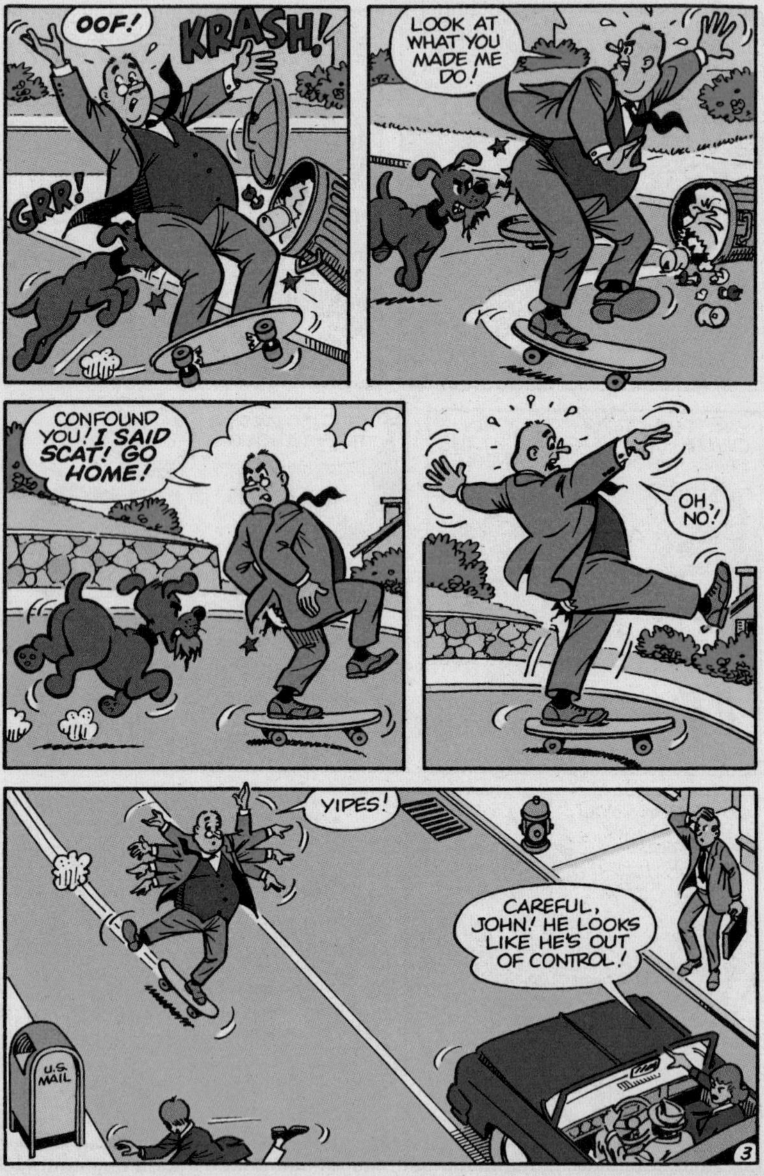

OOF!
KRASH!
GRR!
LOOK AT WHAT YOU MADE ME DO!
CONFOUND YOU! I SAID SCAT! GO HOME!
OH, NO!
YIPES!
CAREFUL, JOHN! HE LOOKS LIKE HE'S OUT OF CONTROL!
U.S. MAIL

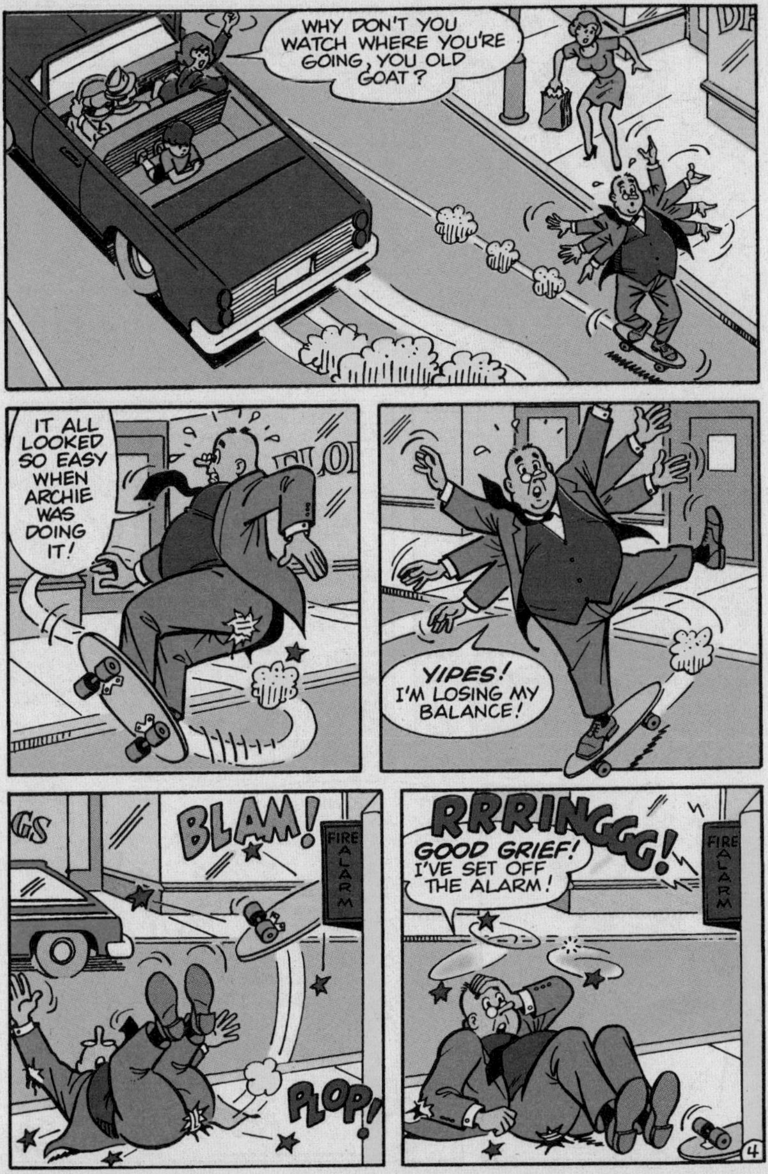
WHY DON'T YOU WATCH WHERE YOU'RE GOING, YOU OLD GOAT?
IT ALL LOOKED SO EASY WHEN ARCHIE WAS DOING IT!
YIPES! I'M LOSING MY BALANCE!
BLAM!
FIRE ALARM
PLOP!
RRRINGGG!
GOOD GRIEF! I'VE SET OFF THE ALARM!
FIRE ALARM

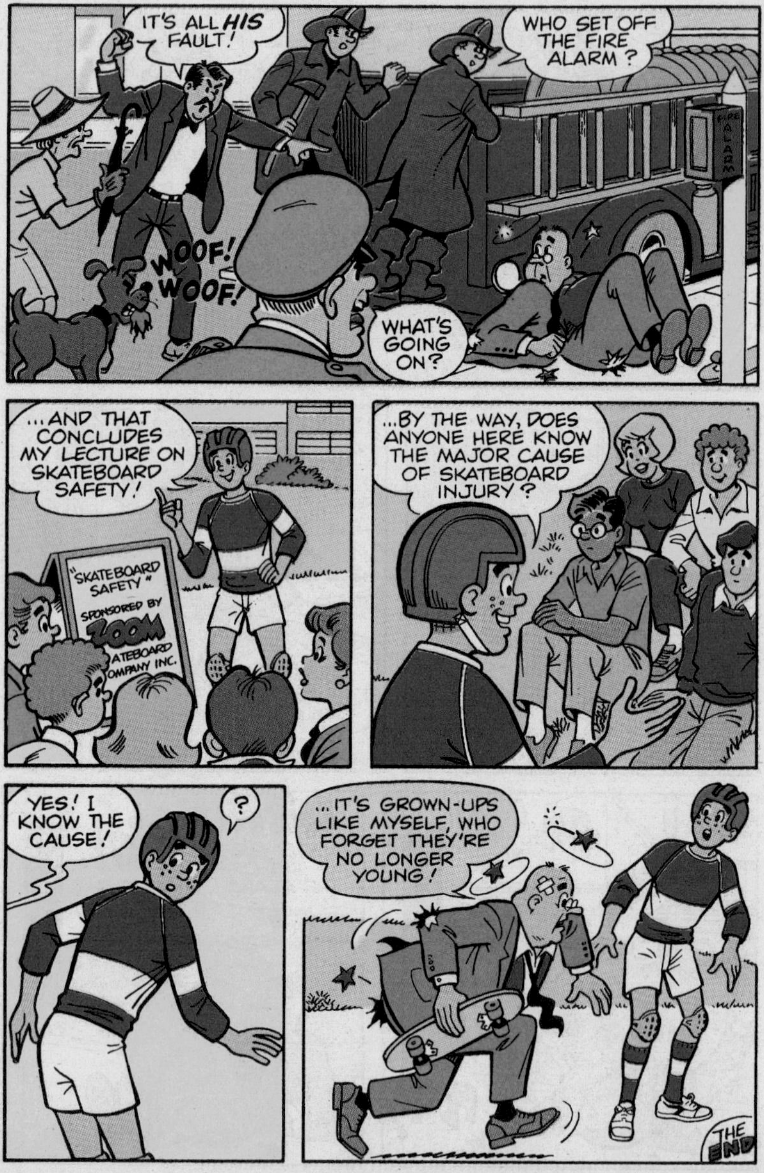
IT'S ALL HIS FAULT!
WHO SET OFF THE FIRE ALARM?
FIRE ALARM
WOOF! WOOF!
WHAT'S GOING ON?
...AND THAT CONCLUDES MY LECTURE ON SKATEBOARD SAFETY!
"SKATEBOARD SAFETY" SPONSORED BY ZOOM ATEBOARD OMPANY INC.
...BY THE WAY, DOES ANYONE HERE KNOW THE MAJOR CAUSE OF SKATEBOARD INJURY?
YES! I KNOW THE CAUSE!
?
...IT'S GROWN-UPS LIKE MYSELF, WHO FORGET THEY'RE NO LONGER YOUNG!
THE END

Archie in I GOT THE POWER!

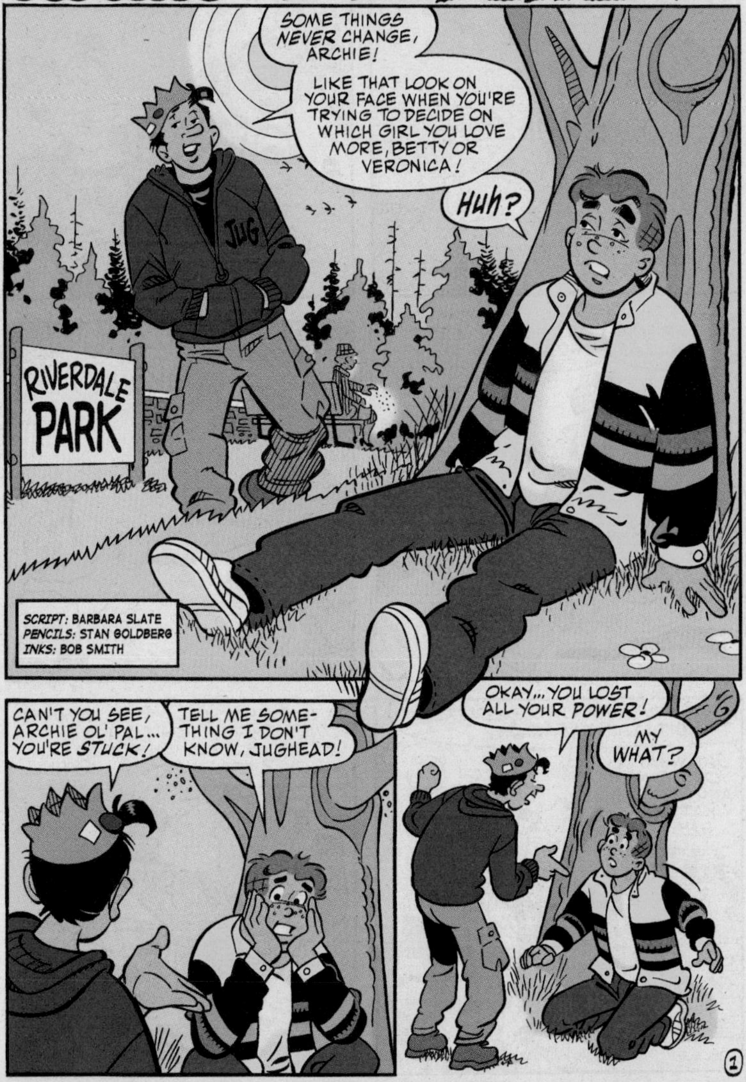
SOME THINGS NEVER CHANGE, ARCHIE!
LIKE THAT LOOK ON YOUR FACE WHEN YOU'RE TRYING TO DECIDE ON WHICH GIRL YOU LOVE MORE, BETTY OR VERONICA!
HUH?
RIVERDALE PARK
SCRIPT: BARBARA SLATE
PENCILS: STAN GOLDBERG
INKS: BOB SMITH
JUG
CAN'T YOU SEE, ARCHIE OL' PAL... YOU'RE STUCK!
TELL ME SOMETHING I DON'T KNOW, JUGHEAD!
OKAY... YOU LOST ALL YOUR POWER!
MY WHAT?

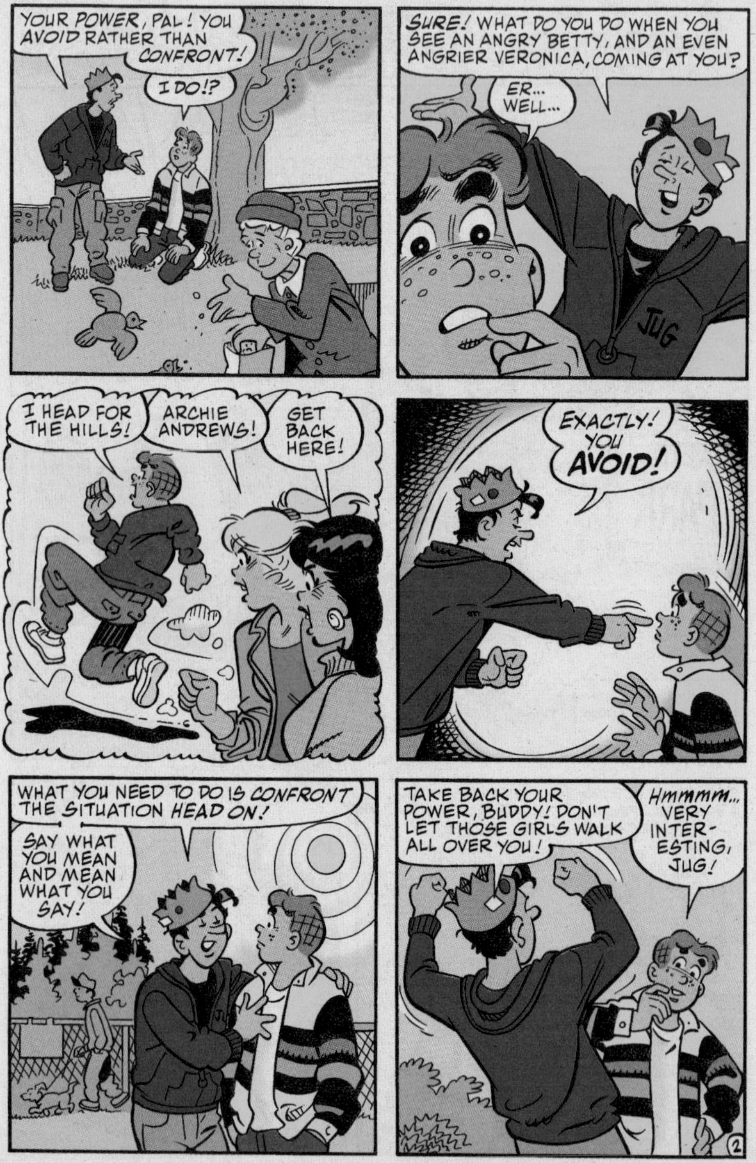
YOUR POWER, PAL! YOU AVOID RATHER THAN CONFRONT!
I DO!?
SURE! WHAT DO YOU DO WHEN YOU SEE AN ANGRY BETTY, AND AN EVEN ANGRIER VERONICA, COMING AT YOU?
ER... WELL...
JUG
I HEAD FOR THE HILLS!
ARCHIE ANDREWS!
GET BACK HERE!
EXACTLY! YOU AVOID!
WHAT YOU NEED TO DO IS CONFRONT THE SITUATION HEAD ON!
SAY WHAT YOU MEAN AND MEAN WHAT YOU SAY!
TAKE BACK YOUR POWER, BUDDY! DON'T LET THOSE GIRLS WALK ALL OVER YOU!
Hmmmm... VERY INTER-ESTING, JUG!
2

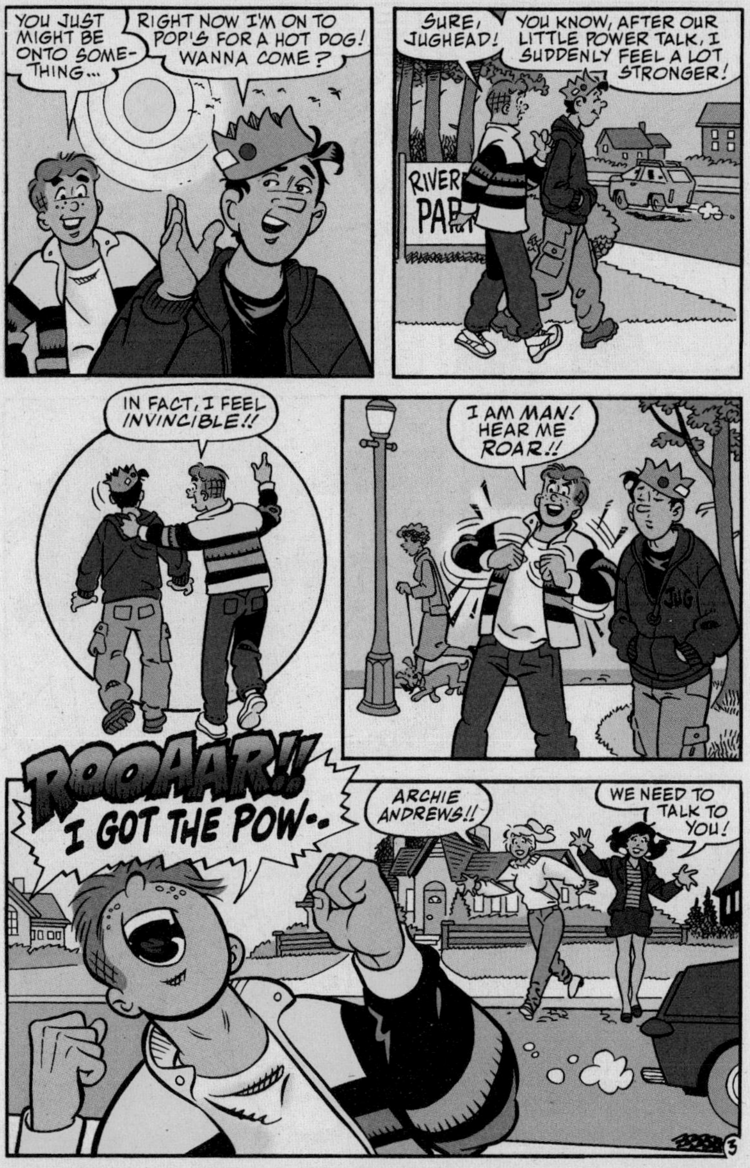
YOU JUST MIGHT BE ONTO SOME-THING...
RIGHT NOW I'M ON TO POP'S FOR A HOT DOG! WANNA COME?
SURE, JUGHEAD!
YOU KNOW, AFTER OUR LITTLE POWER TALK, I SUDDENLY FEEL A LOT STRONGER!
RIVER PA
IN FACT, I FEEL INVINCIBLE!!
I AM MAN! HEAR ME ROAR!!
JUG
ROOAAR!! I GOT THE POW-.
ARCHIE ANDREWS!!
WE NEED TO TALK TO YOU!
3

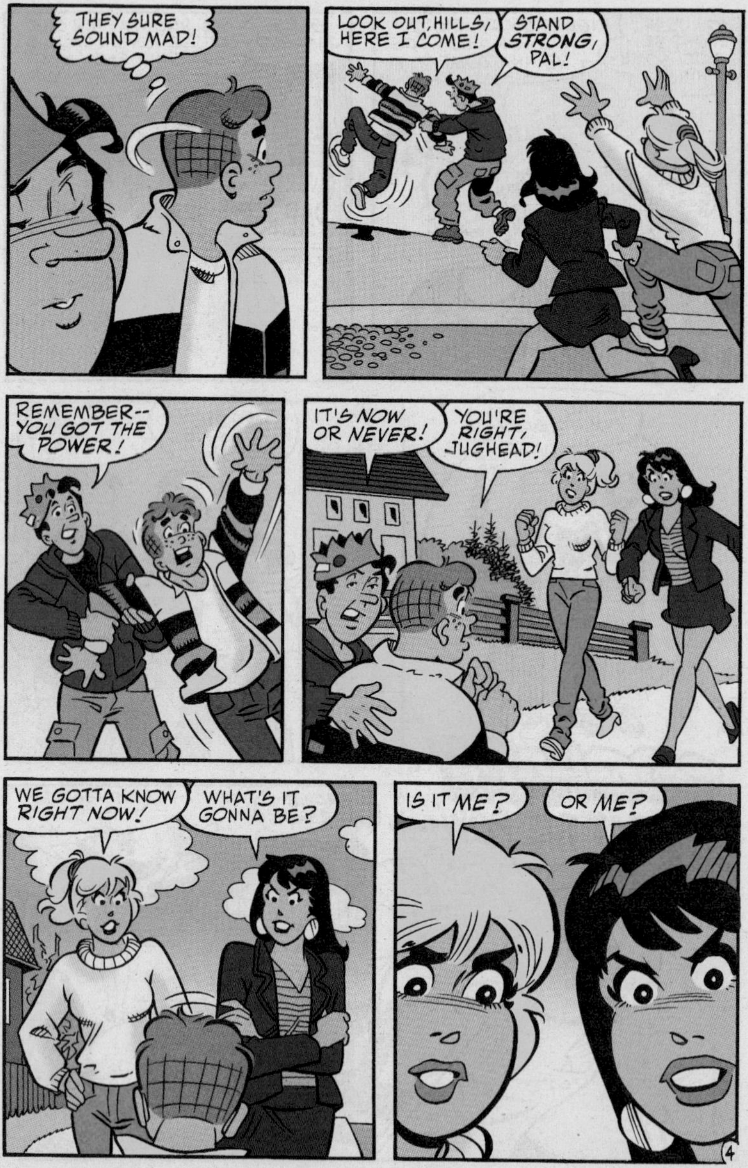
THEY SURE SOUND MAD!
LOOK OUT, HILLS, HERE I COME!
STAND STRONG, PAL!
REMEMBER-- YOU GOT THE POWER!
IT'S NOW OR NEVER!
YOU'RE RIGHT, JUGHEAD!
WE GOTTA KNOW RIGHT NOW!
WHAT'S IT GONNA BE?
IS IT ME?
OR ME?

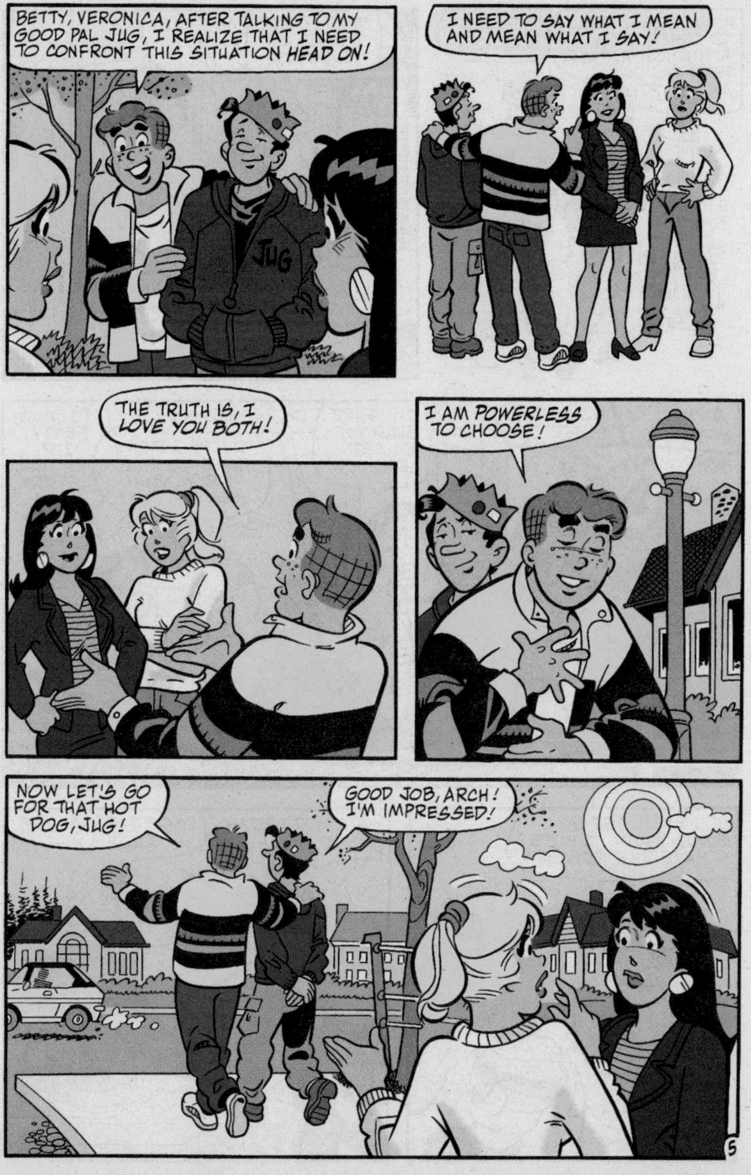
BETTY, VERONICA, AFTER TALKING TO MY GOOD PAL JUG, I REALIZE THAT I NEED TO CONFRONT THIS SITUATION HEAD ON!
JUG
I NEED TO SAY WHAT I MEAN AND MEAN WHAT I SAY!
THE TRUTH IS, I LOVE YOU BOTH!
I AM POWERLESS TO CHOOSE!
NOW LET'S GO FOR THAT HOT DOG, JUG!
GOOD JOB, ARCH! I'M IMPRESSED!
5

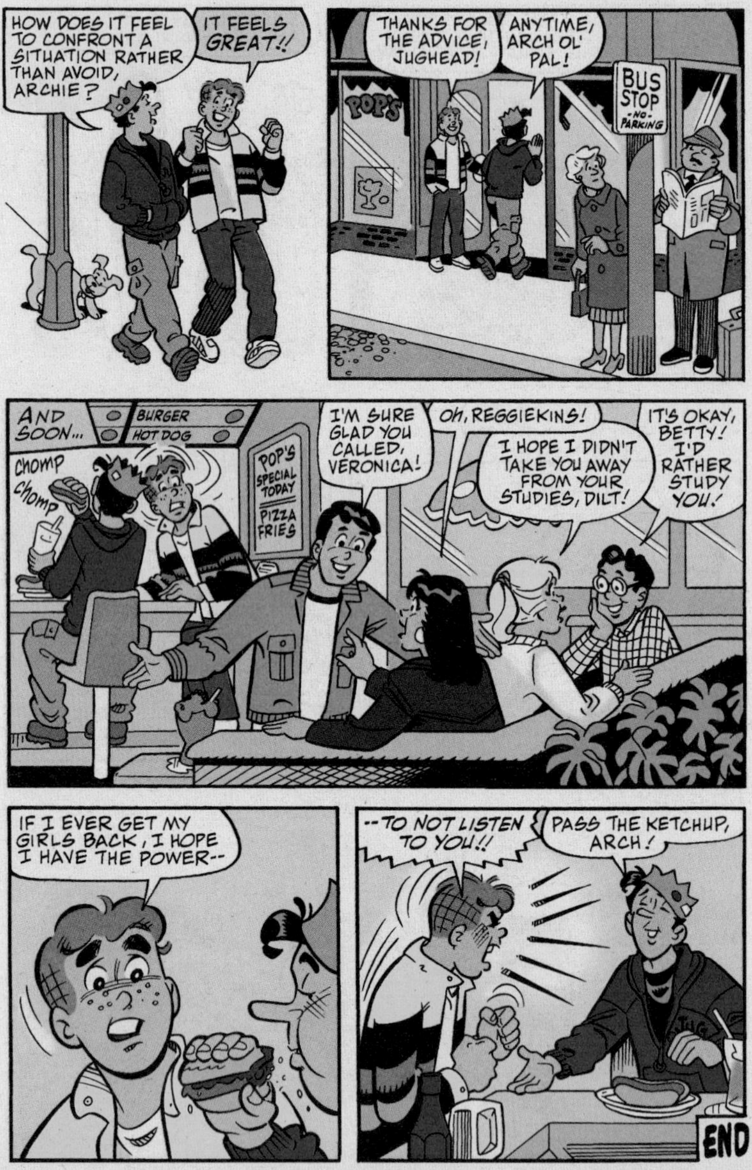

HOW DOES IT FEEL TO CONFRONT A SITUATION RATHER THAN AVOID, ARCHIE?
IT FEELS GREAT!!
THANKS FOR THE ADVICE, JUGHEAD!
ANYTIME, ARCH OL' PAL!
POP'S
BUS STOP -NO- PARKING
AND SOON...
BURGER
HOT DOG
CHOMP CHOMP
POP'S SPECIAL TODAY PIZZA FRIES
I'M SURE GLAD YOU CALLED, VERONICA!
OH, REGGIEKINS!
I HOPE I DIDN'T TAKE YOU AWAY FROM YOUR STUDIES, DILT!
IT'S OKAY, BETTY! I'D RATHER STUDY YOU!
IF I EVER GET MY GIRLS BACK, I HOPE I HAVE THE POWER--
--TO NOT LISTEN TO YOU!!
PASS THE KETCHUP, ARCH!
END

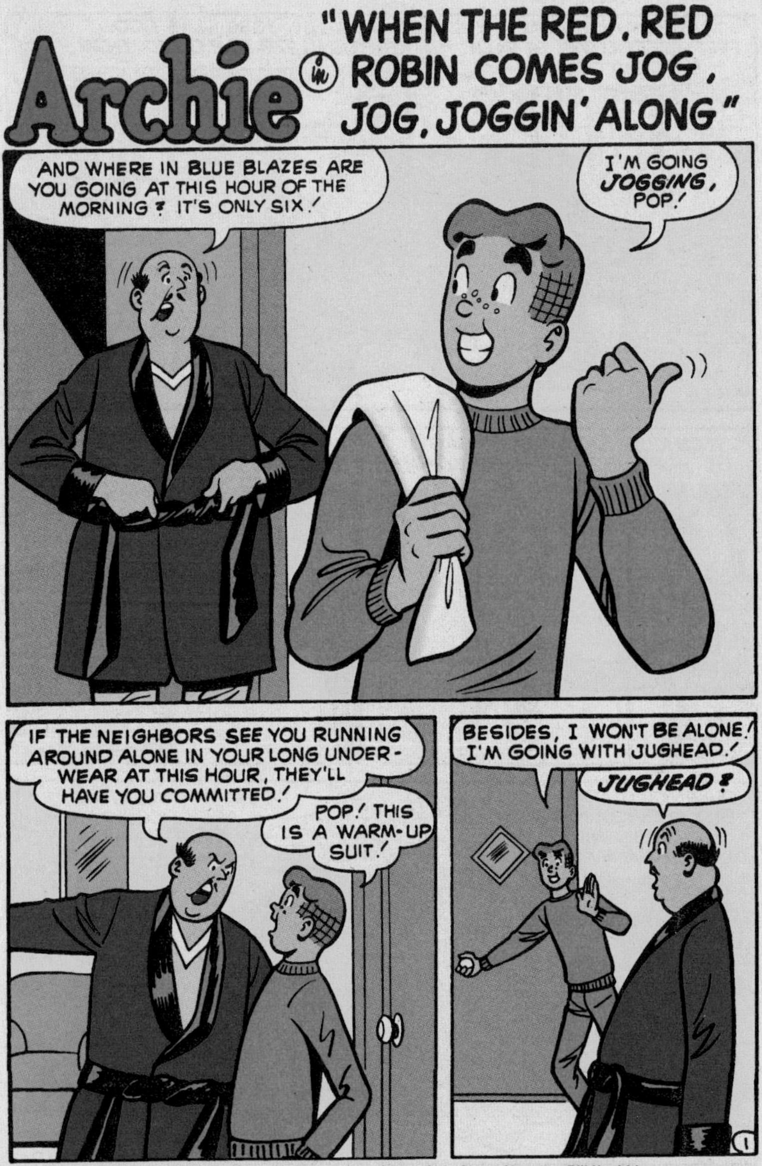

Archie in
"WHEN THE RED, RED ROBIN COMES JOG, JOG, JOGGIN' ALONG"
AND WHERE IN BLUE BLAZES ARE YOU GOING AT THIS HOUR OF THE MORNING? IT'S ONLY SIX!
I'M GOING JOGGING, POP!
IF THE NEIGHBORS SEE YOU RUNNING AROUND ALONE IN YOUR LONG UNDER-WEAR AT THIS HOUR, THEY'LL HAVE YOU COMMITTED!
POP! THIS IS A WARM-UP SUIT!
BESIDES, I WON'T BE ALONE! I'M GOING WITH JUGHEAD!
JUGHEAD?
1

Script: Frank Doyle / Pencils: Harry Lucey / Inks: Chic Stone / Letters: Bill Yoshida

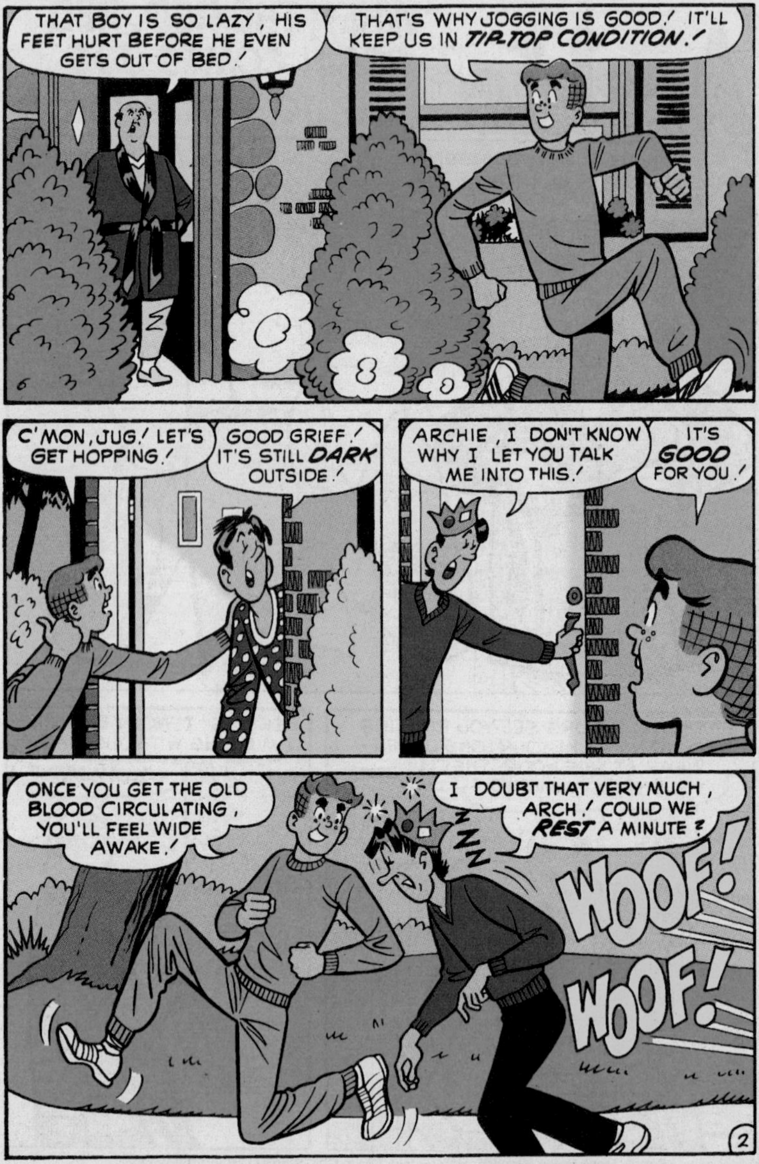
THAT BOY IS SO LAZY, HIS FEET HURT BEFORE HE EVEN GETS OUT OF BED!
THAT'S WHY JOGGING IS GOOD! IT'LL KEEP US IN TIP-TOP CONDITION!
C'MON, JUG! LET'S GET HOPPING!
GOOD GRIEF! IT'S STILL DARK OUTSIDE!
ARCHIE, I DON'T KNOW WHY I LET YOU TALK ME INTO THIS!
IT'S GOOD FOR YOU!
ONCE YOU GET THE OLD BLOOD CIRCULATING, YOU'LL FEEL WIDE AWAKE!
I DOUBT THAT VERY MUCH, ARCH! COULD WE REST A MINUTE?
WOOF!
WOOF!
2

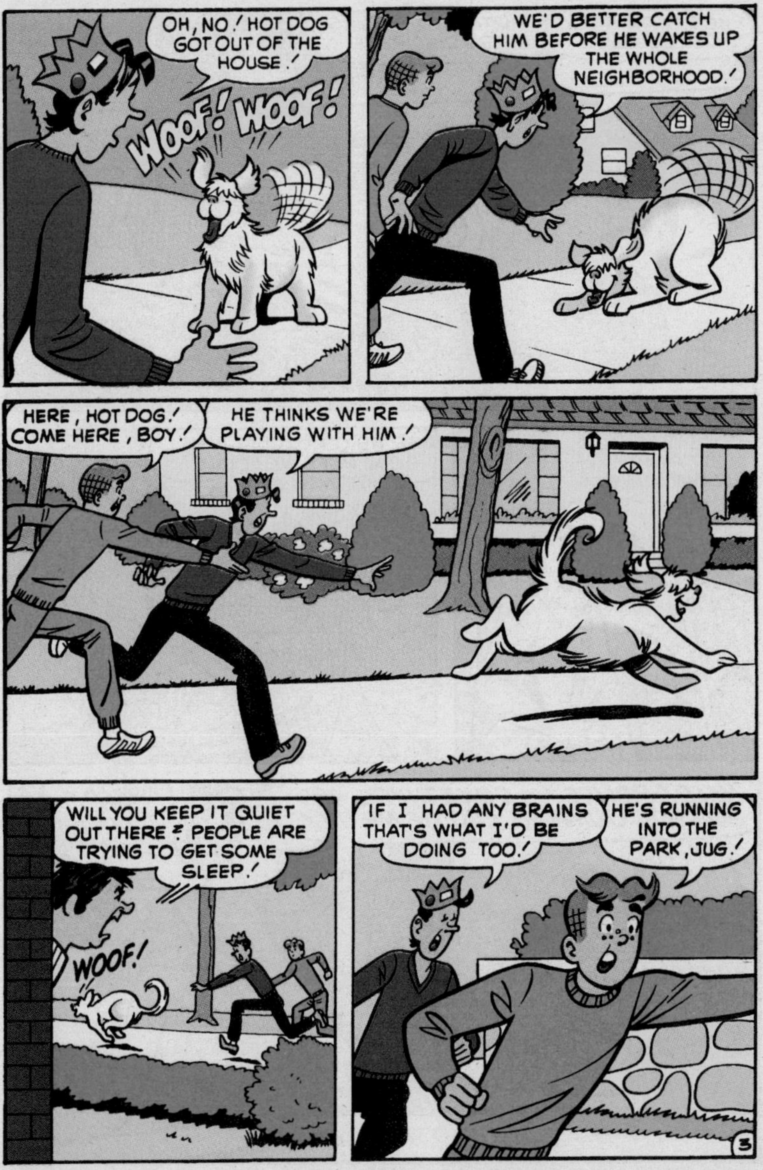
OH, NO! HOT DOG GOT OUT OF THE HOUSE!
WOOF! WOOF!
WE'D BETTER CATCH HIM BEFORE HE WAKES UP THE WHOLE NEIGHBORHOOD!
HERE, HOT DOG! COME HERE, BOY!
HE THINKS WE'RE PLAYING WITH HIM!
WILL YOU KEEP IT QUIET OUT THERE?! PEOPLE ARE TRYING TO GET SOME SLEEP!
WOOF!
IF I HAD ANY BRAINS THAT'S WHAT I'D BE DOING TOO!
HE'S RUNNING INTO THE PARK, JUG!
3

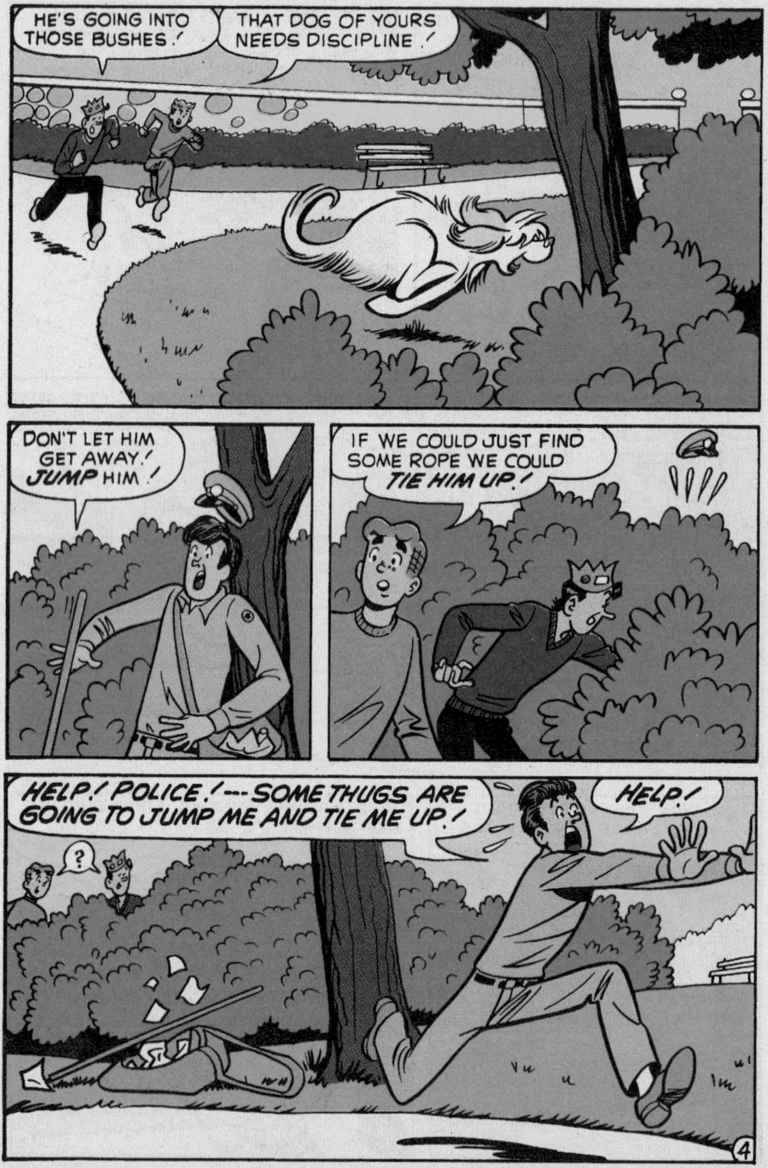
HE'S GOING INTO THOSE BUSHES!
THAT DOG OF YOURS NEEDS DISCIPLINE!
DON'T LET HIM GET AWAY! JUMP HIM!
IF WE COULD JUST FIND SOME ROPE WE COULD TIE HIM UP!
HELP! POLICE! --- SOME THUGS ARE GOING TO JUMP ME AND TIE ME UP!
HELP!
?

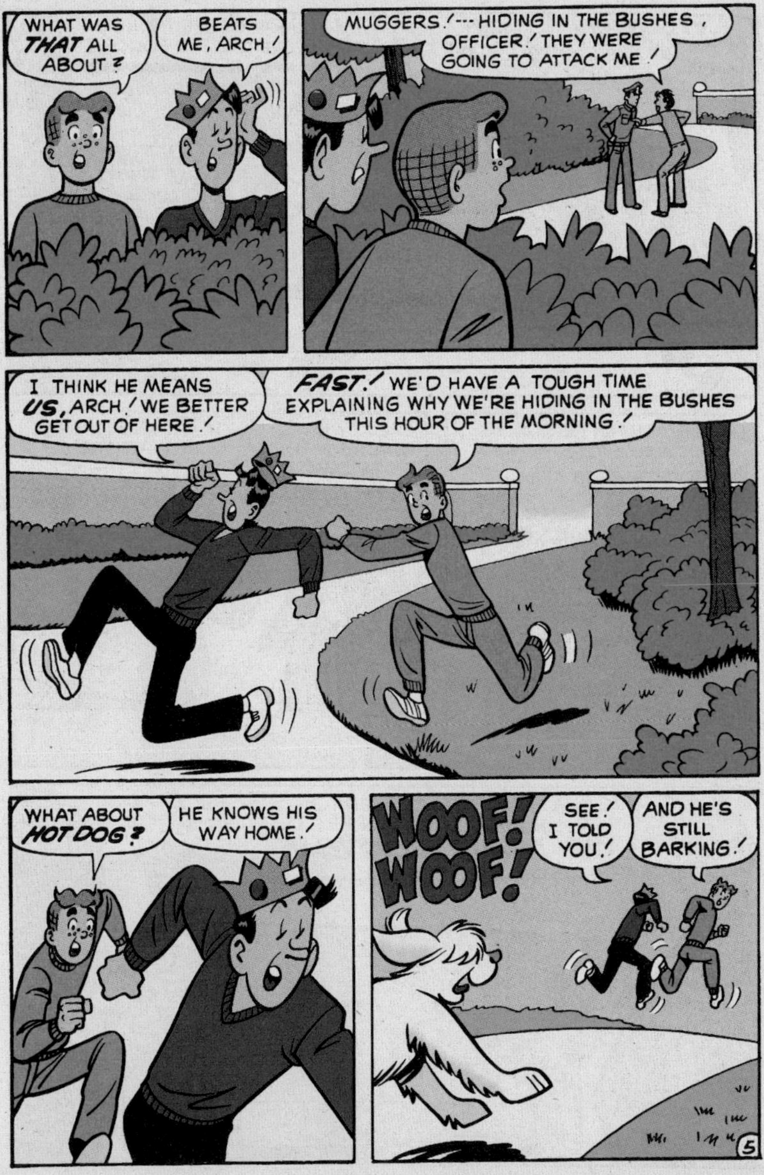
WHAT WAS THAT ALL ABOUT?
BEATS ME, ARCH!
MUGGERS!--- HIDING IN THE BUSHES, OFFICER! THEY WERE GOING TO ATTACK ME!
I THINK HE MEANS US, ARCH! WE BETTER GET OUT OF HERE!
FAST! WE'D HAVE A TOUGH TIME EXPLAINING WHY WE'RE HIDING IN THE BUSHES THIS HOUR OF THE MORNING!
WHAT ABOUT HOT DOG?
HE KNOWS HIS WAY HOME!
WOOF! WOOF!
SEE! I TOLD YOU!
AND HE'S STILL BARKING!
5

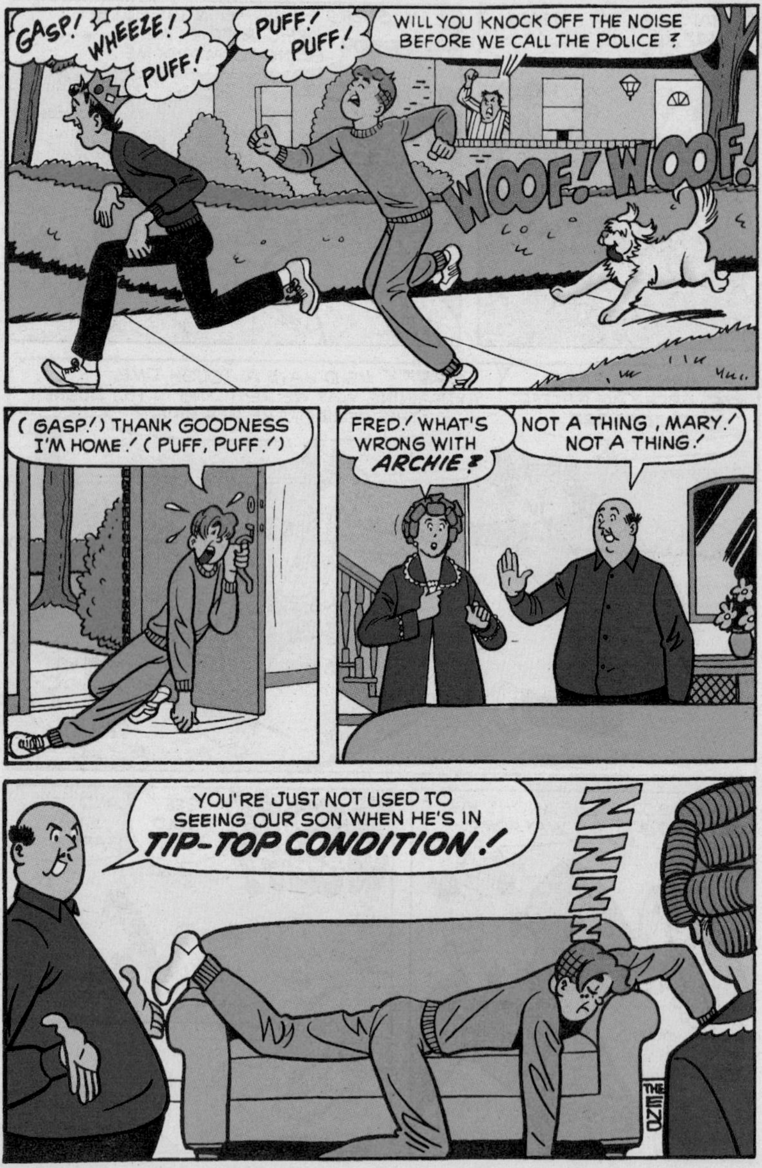
GASP!
WHEEZE!
PUFF!
PUFF! PUFF!
WILL YOU KNOCK OFF THE NOISE BEFORE WE CALL THE POLICE ?
WOOF! WOOF!
(GASP!) THANK GOODNESS I'M HOME! (PUFF, PUFF!)
FRED! WHAT'S WRONG WITH ARCHIE ?
NOT A THING , MARY! NOT A THING!
YOU'RE JUST NOT USED TO SEEING OUR SON WHEN HE'S IN TIP-TOP CONDITION!
ZZZZZ
THE END

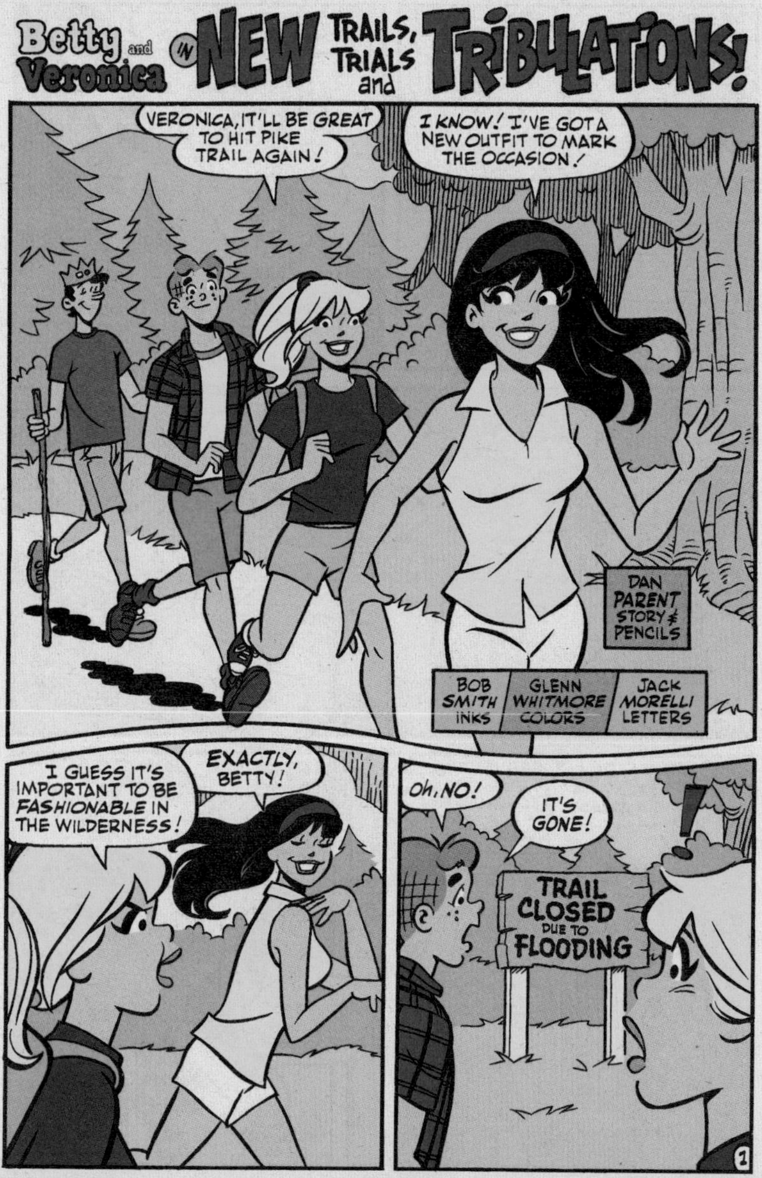
Betty and Veronica
IN
NEW TRAILS, TRIALS and TRIBULATIONS!
VERONICA, IT'LL BE GREAT TO HIT PIKE TRAIL AGAIN!
I KNOW! I'VE GOT A NEW OUTFIT TO MARK THE OCCASION!
DAN PARENT STORY & PENCILS
BOB SMITH INKS
GLENN WHITMORE COLORS
JACK MORELLI LETTERS
I GUESS IT'S IMPORTANT TO BE FASHIONABLE IN THE WILDERNESS!
EXACTLY, BETTY!
OH, NO!
IT'S GONE!
TRAIL CLOSED DUE TO FLOODING
!
1

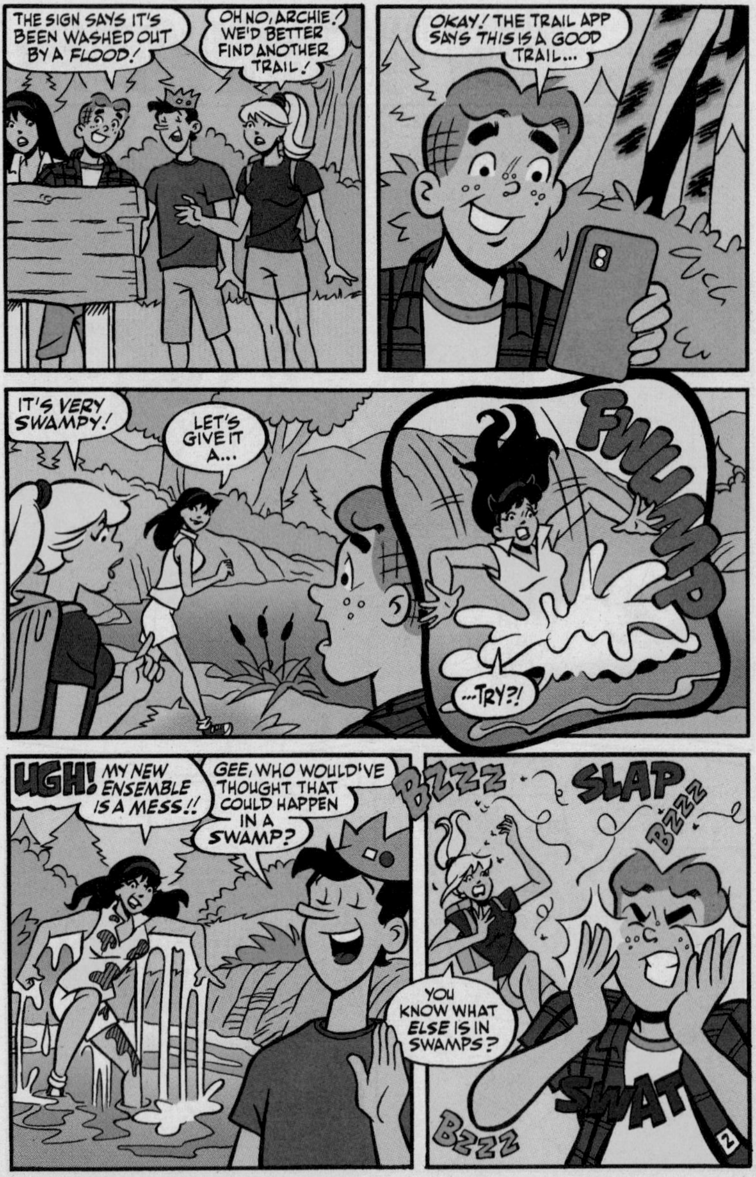
THE SIGN SAYS IT'S BEEN WASHED OUT BY A FLOOD!
OH NO, ARCHIE! WE'D BETTER FIND ANOTHER TRAIL!
OKAY! THE TRAIL APP SAYS THIS IS A GOOD TRAIL...
IT'S VERY SWAMPY!
LET'S GIVE IT A...
FWUMP
...TRY?!
UGH! MY NEW ENSEMBLE IS A MESS!!
GEE, WHO WOULD'VE THOUGHT THAT COULD HAPPEN IN A SWAMP?
BZZZ
SLAP
BZZZ
YOU KNOW WHAT ELSE IS IN SWAMPS?
SWAT
BZZZ
2

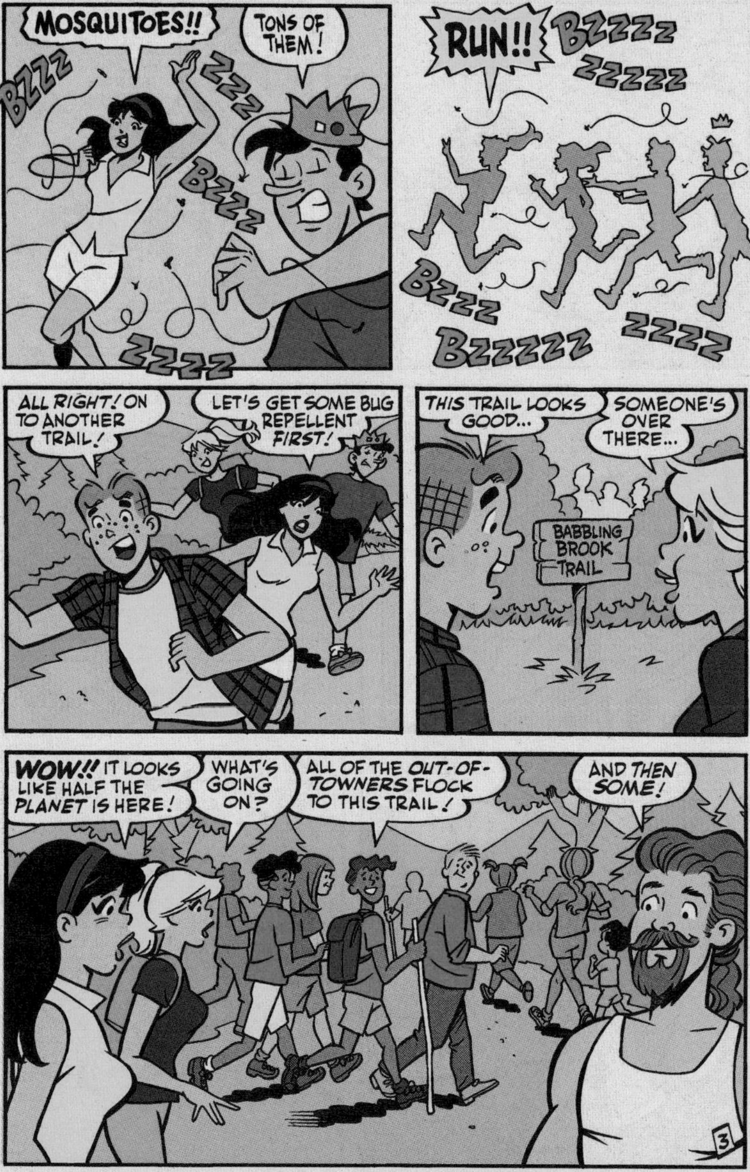
MOSQUITOES!!
TONS OF THEM!
BZZZ
ZZZZ
BZZZ
ZZZZ
RUN!!
BZZZZ
ZZZZZ
BZZZ
BZZZZZ
ZZZZ
ALL RIGHT! ON TO ANOTHER TRAIL!
LET'S GET SOME BUG REPELLENT FIRST!
THIS TRAIL LOOKS GOOD...
SOMEONE'S OVER THERE...
BABBLING BROOK TRAIL
WOW!! IT LOOKS LIKE HALF THE PLANET IS HERE!
WHAT'S GOING ON?
ALL OF THE OUT-OF-TOWNERS FLOCK TO THIS TRAIL!
AND THEN SOME!

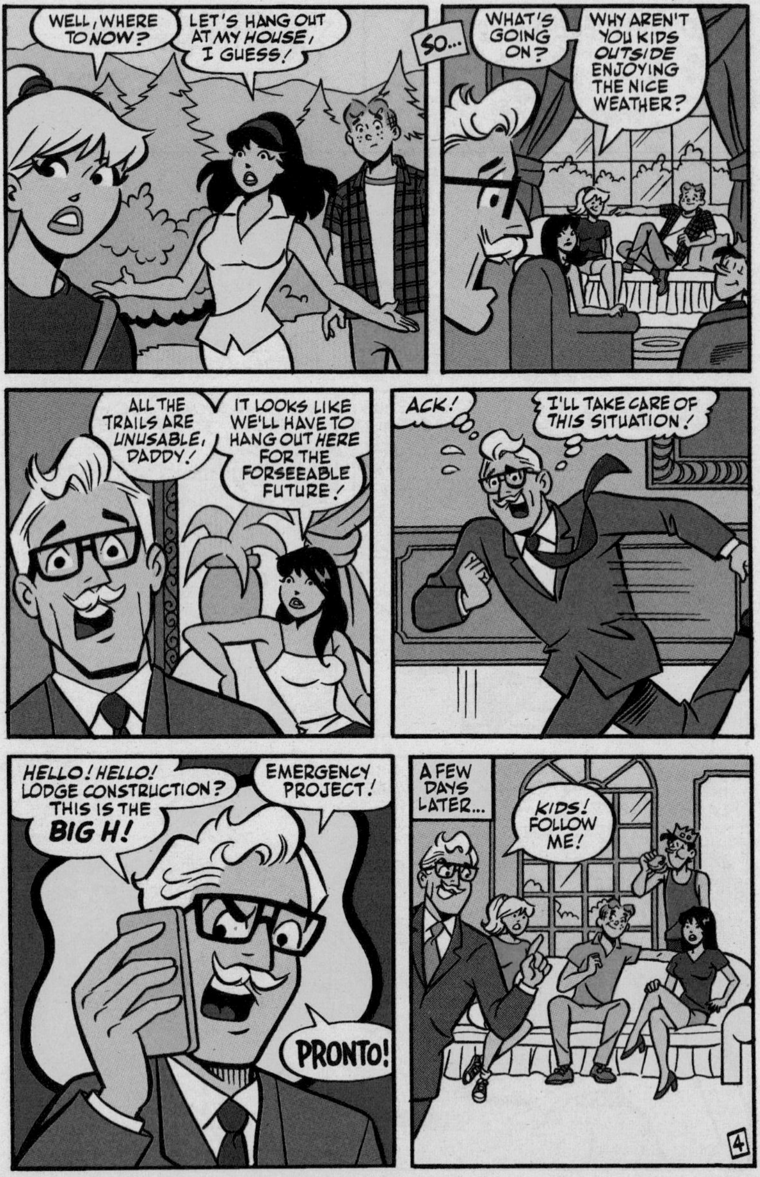
WELL, WHERE TO NOW?
LET'S HANG OUT AT MY HOUSE, I GUESS!
SO...
WHAT'S GOING ON?
WHY AREN'T YOU KIDS OUTSIDE ENJOYING THE NICE WEATHER?
ALL THE TRAILS ARE UNUSABLE, DADDY!
IT LOOKS LIKE WE'LL HAVE TO HANG OUT HERE FOR THE FORSEEABLE FUTURE!
ACK!
I'LL TAKE CARE OF THIS SITUATION!
HELLO! HELLO! LODGE CONSTRUCTION? THIS IS THE BIG H!
EMERGENCY PROJECT!
PRONTO!
A FEW DAYS LATER...
KIDS! FOLLOW ME!
4

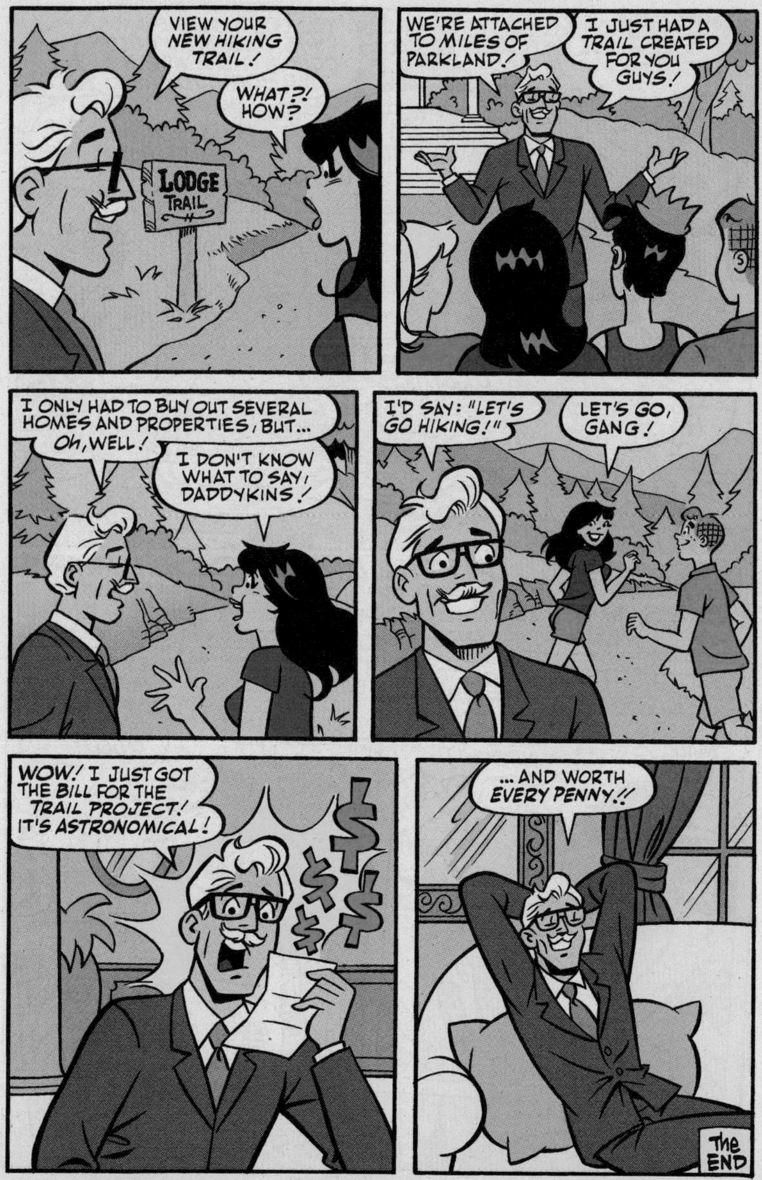
VIEW YOUR NEW HIKING TRAIL!
WHAT?! HOW?
LODGE TRAIL
WE'RE ATTACHED TO MILES OF PARKLAND!
I JUST HAD A TRAIL CREATED FOR YOU GUYS!
I ONLY HAD TO BUY OUT SEVERAL HOMES AND PROPERTIES, BUT... Oh, WELL!
I DON'T KNOW WHAT TO SAY, DADDYKINS!
I'D SAY: "LET'S GO HIKING!"
LET'S GO, GANG!
WOW! I JUST GOT THE BILL FOR THE TRAIL PROJECT! IT'S ASTRONOMICAL!
...AND WORTH EVERY PENNY!!
The END

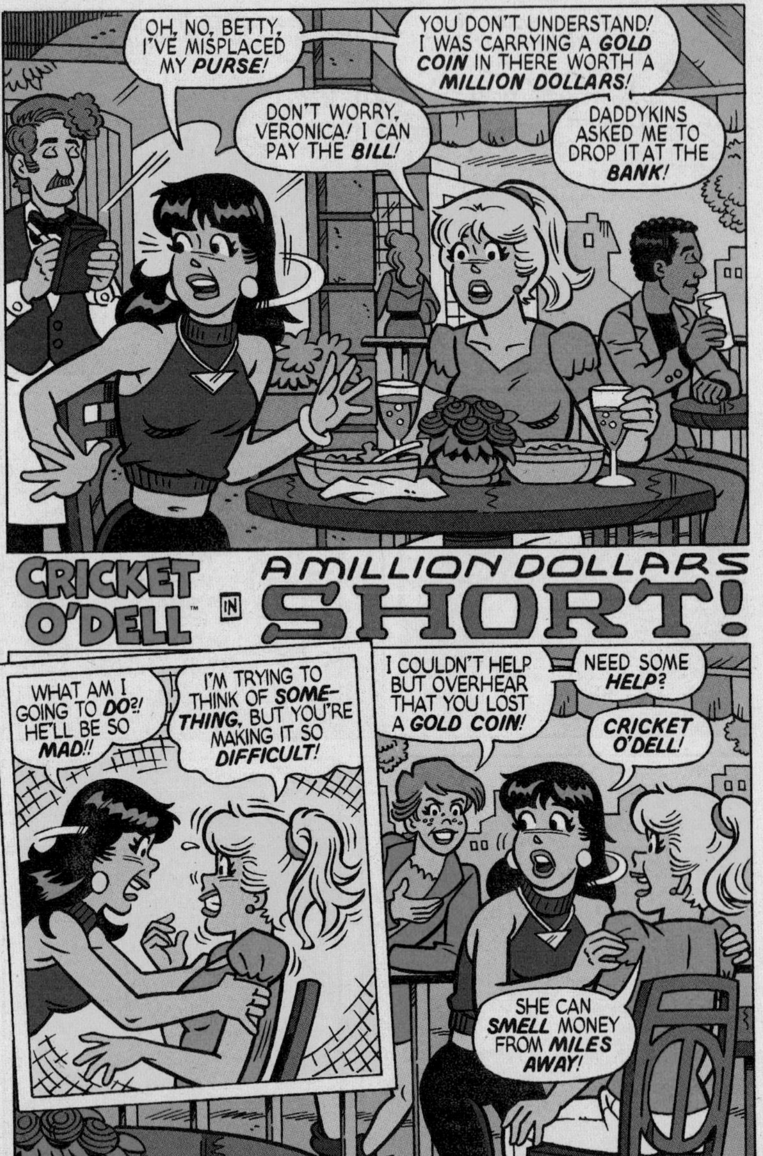
OH, NO, BETTY, I'VE MISPLACED MY PURSE!
DON'T WORRY, VERONICA! I CAN PAY THE BILL!
YOU DON'T UNDERSTAND! I WAS CARRYING A GOLD COIN IN THERE WORTH A MILLION DOLLARS!
DADDYKINS ASKED ME TO DROP IT AT THE BANK!
CRICKET O'DELL™ IN A MILLION DOLLARS SHORT!
WHAT AM I GOING TO DO?! HE'LL BE SO MAD!!
I'M TRYING TO THINK OF SOMETHING, BUT YOU'RE MAKING IT SO DIFFICULT!
I COULDN'T HELP BUT OVERHEAR THAT YOU LOST A GOLD COIN!
NEED SOME HELP?
CRICKET O'DELL!
SHE CAN SMELL MONEY FROM MILES AWAY!

Script: **Francis Bonnet** Art & Letters: **Rex Lindsey** Colors: **Glenn Whitmore**

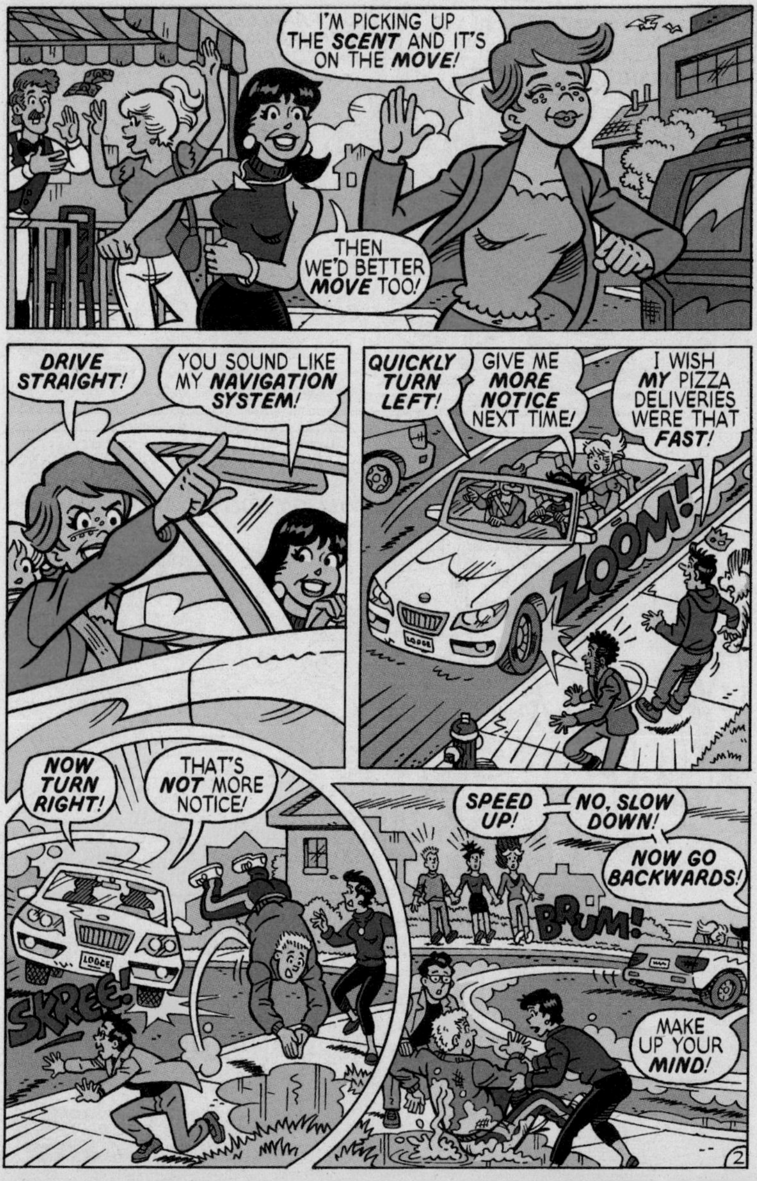

I'M PICKING UP THE *SCENT* AND IT'S ON THE *MOVE*!
THEN WE'D BETTER *MOVE* TOO!
DRIVE STRAIGHT!
YOU SOUND LIKE MY *NAVIGATION SYSTEM*!
QUICKLY TURN LEFT!
GIVE ME *MORE NOTICE* NEXT TIME!
I WISH *MY* PIZZA DELIVERIES WERE THAT *FAST*!
ZOOM!
LODGE
NOW TURN RIGHT!
THAT'S *NOT* MORE NOTICE!
SKREE!
LODGE
SPEED UP!
NO, SLOW DOWN!
NOW GO BACKWARDS!
BRUM!
MAKE UP YOUR *MIND*!

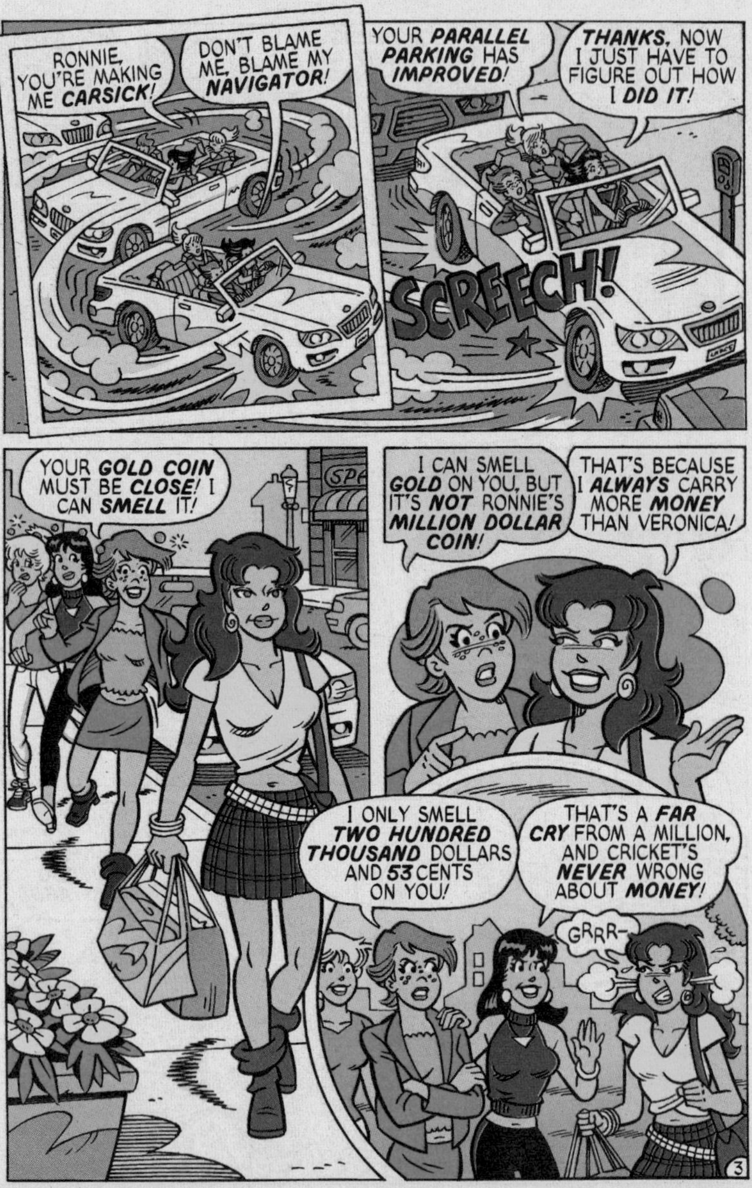
RONNIE, YOU'RE MAKING ME **CARSICK**!
DON'T BLAME ME, BLAME MY **NAVIGATOR**!
YOUR **PARALLEL PARKING** HAS **IMPROVED**!
THANKS, NOW I JUST HAVE TO FIGURE OUT HOW I **DID IT**!
SCREECH!
YOUR **GOLD COIN** MUST BE **CLOSE**! I CAN **SMELL** IT!
I CAN SMELL **GOLD** ON YOU, BUT IT'S **NOT** RONNIE'S **MILLION DOLLAR COIN**!
THAT'S BECAUSE I **ALWAYS** CARRY MORE **MONEY** THAN VERONICA!
I ONLY SMELL **TWO HUNDRED THOUSAND** DOLLARS AND **53** CENTS ON YOU!
THAT'S A **FAR CRY** FROM A MILLION, AND CRICKET'S **NEVER** WRONG ABOUT **MONEY**!
GRRR-
3

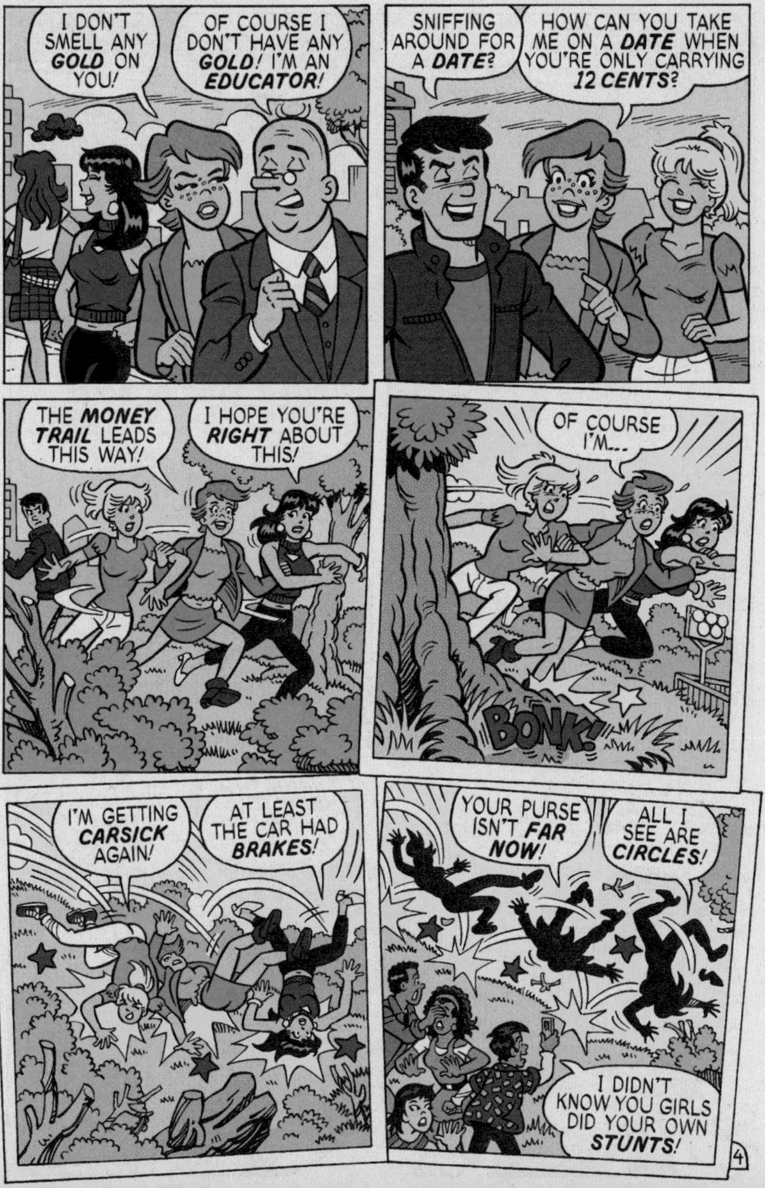
I DON'T SMELL ANY GOLD ON YOU!
OF COURSE I DON'T HAVE ANY GOLD! I'M AN EDUCATOR!
SNIFFING AROUND FOR A DATE?
HOW CAN YOU TAKE ME ON A DATE WHEN YOU'RE ONLY CARRYING 12 CENTS?
THE MONEY TRAIL LEADS THIS WAY!
I HOPE YOU'RE RIGHT ABOUT THIS!
OF COURSE I'M...
BONK!
I'M GETTING CARSICK AGAIN!
AT LEAST THE CAR HAD BRAKES!
YOUR PURSE ISN'T FAR NOW!
ALL I SEE ARE CIRCLES!
I DIDN'T KNOW YOU GIRLS DID YOUR OWN STUNTS!
4

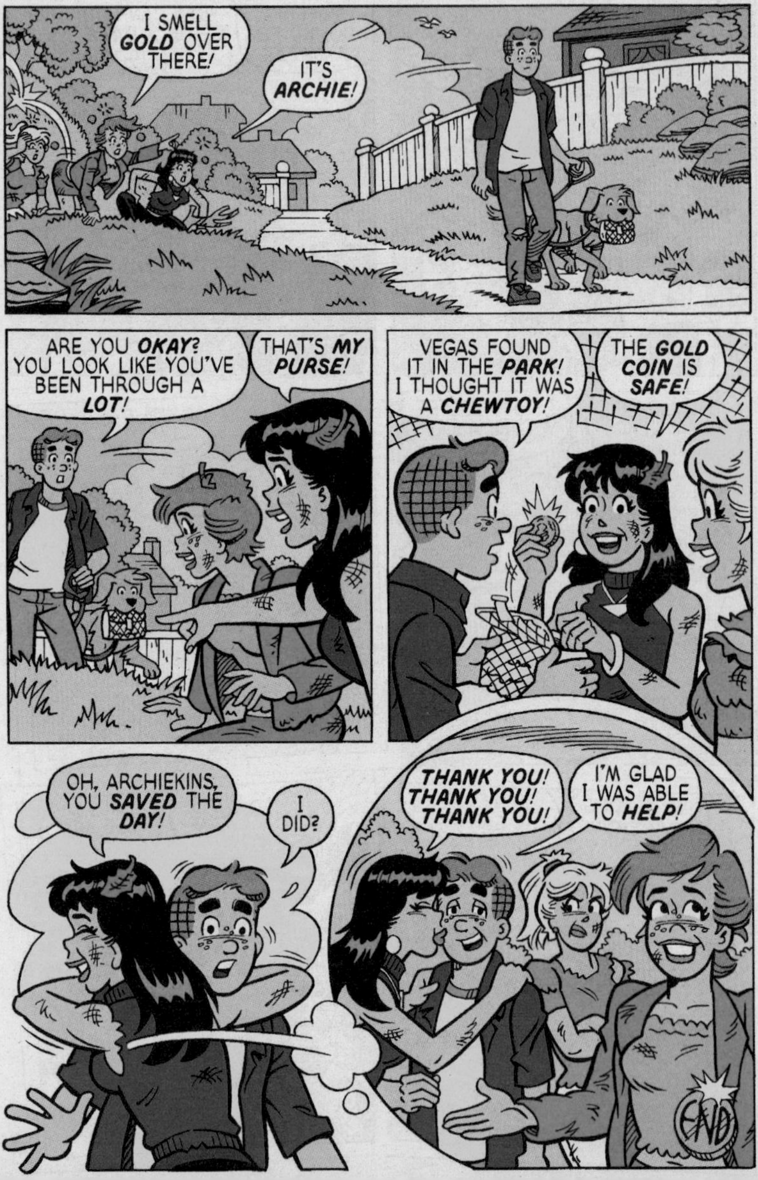
I SMELL **GOLD** OVER THERE!
IT'S **ARCHIE**!
ARE YOU **OKAY?** YOU LOOK LIKE YOU'VE BEEN THROUGH A **LOT**!
THAT'S **MY PURSE**!
VEGAS FOUND IT IN THE **PARK**! I THOUGHT IT WAS A **CHEWTOY**!
THE **GOLD COIN** IS **SAFE**!
OH, ARCHIEKINS, YOU **SAVED** THE **DAY**!
I DID?
THANK YOU! THANK YOU! THANK YOU!
I'M GLAD I WAS ABLE TO **HELP**!
END

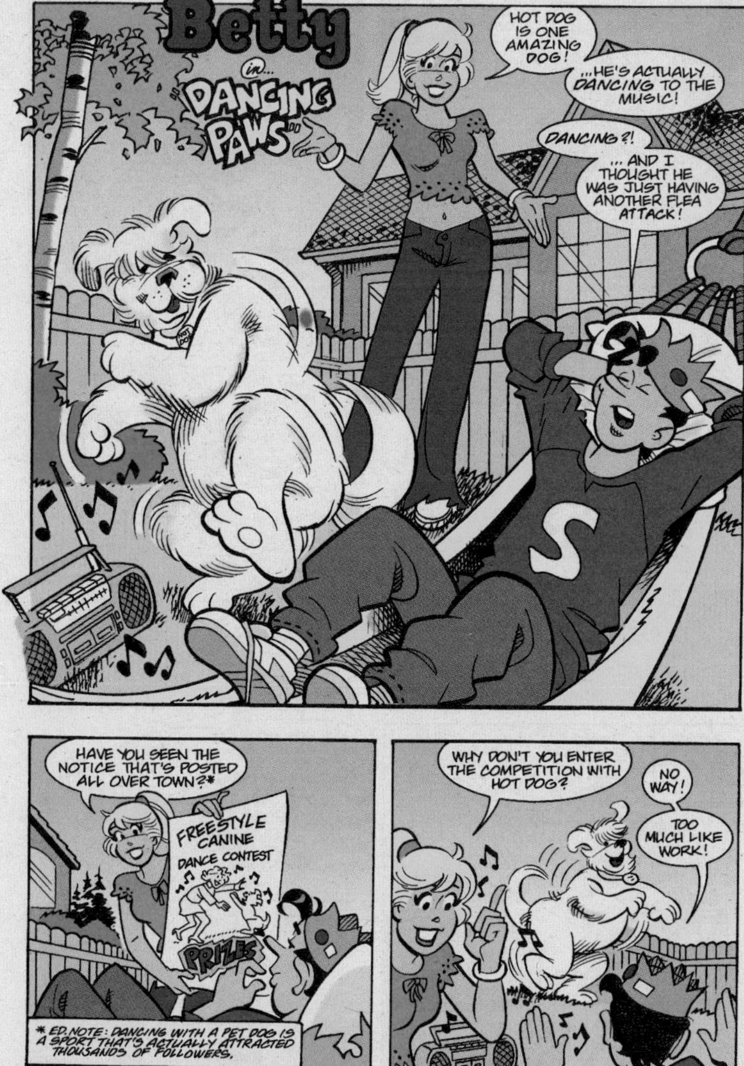
Betty in... "DANCING PAWS"
HOT DOG IS ONE AMAZING DOG!
...HE'S ACTUALLY DANCING TO THE MUSIC!
DANCING?!
... AND I THOUGHT HE WAS JUST HAVING ANOTHER FLEA ATTACK!
HAVE YOU SEEN THE NOTICE THAT'S POSTED ALL OVER TOWN?*
FREESTYLE CANINE DANCE CONTEST
PRIZES
* ED. NOTE: DANCING WITH A PET DOG IS A SPORT THAT'S ACTUALLY ATTRACTED THOUSANDS OF FOLLOWERS.
WHY DON'T YOU ENTER THE COMPETITION WITH HOT DOG?
NO WAY!
TOO MUCH LIKE WORK!

Script: George Gladir / Pencils: Stan Goldberg / Inks: John Lowe / Letters: Vickie Williams

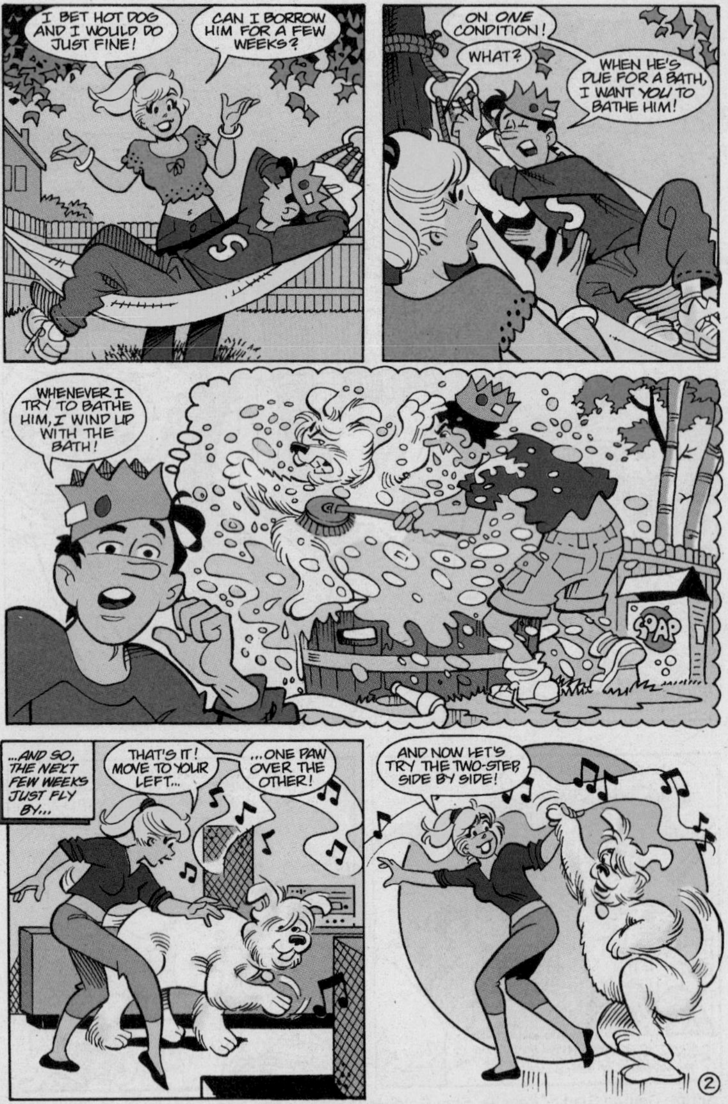
I BET HOT DOG AND I WOULD DO JUST FINE!
CAN I BORROW HIM FOR A FEW WEEKS?
ON ONE CONDITION!
WHAT?
WHEN HE'S DUE FOR A BATH, I WANT YOU TO BATHE HIM!
WHENEVER I TRY TO BATHE HIM, I WIND UP WITH THE BATH!
SOAP
...AND SO, THE NEXT FEW WEEKS JUST FLY BY...
THAT'S IT! MOVE TO YOUR LEFT...
...ONE PAW OVER THE OTHER!
AND NOW LET'S TRY THE TWO-STEP, SIDE BY SIDE!
2

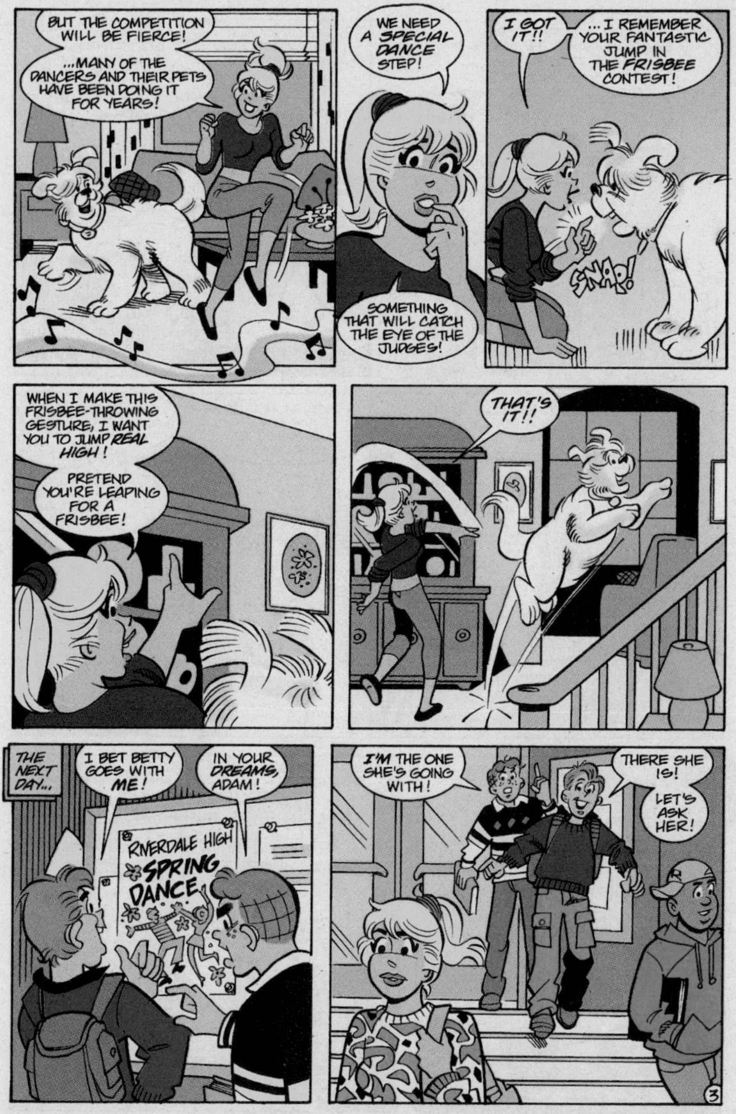

BUT THE COMPETITION WILL BE FIERCE!
...MANY OF THE DANCERS AND THEIR PETS HAVE BEEN DOING IT FOR YEARS!
WE NEED A SPECIAL DANCE STEP!
SOMETHING THAT WILL CATCH THE EYE OF THE JUDGES!
I GOT IT!!
...I REMEMBER YOUR FANTASTIC JUMP IN THE FRISBEE CONTEST!
SNAP!
WHEN I MAKE THIS FRISBEE-THROWING GESTURE, I WANT YOU TO JUMP REAL HIGH!
PRETEND YOU'RE LEAPING FOR A FRISBEE!
THAT'S IT!!
THE NEXT DAY...
I BET BETTY GOES WITH ME!
IN YOUR DREAMS, ADAM!
RIVERDALE HIGH SPRING DANCE
I'M THE ONE SHE'S GOING WITH!
THERE SHE IS!
LET'S ASK HER!

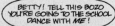

BETTY! TELL THIS BOZO YOU'RE GOING TO THE SCHOOL DANCE WITH *ME*!

SORRY, BUT I'M NOT GOING WITH EITHER OF YOU!

I'M BOOKED TO GO TO A DANCE CONTEST WITH HOT DOG!

HOT DOG?!

'SCUSE ME, BUT HOT DOG AND I STILL HAVE A LOT OF REHEARSING TO DO!

PICKING HOT DOG OVER *US*?-- SHE CAN'T BE SERIOUS!

SHE CERTAINLY SOUNDED LIKE SHE MEANT IT!

POOCH CONTEST DAY ARRIVES...

CONTESTANTS WILL HAVE THREE MINUTES IN WHICH TO PERFORM THEIR ROUTINE!

JUDGES

GOSH! THEY *ARE* FANTASTIC!

...I JUST HOPE WE WIN SOME KIND OF PRIZE!...ANY KIND OF PRIZE!

4

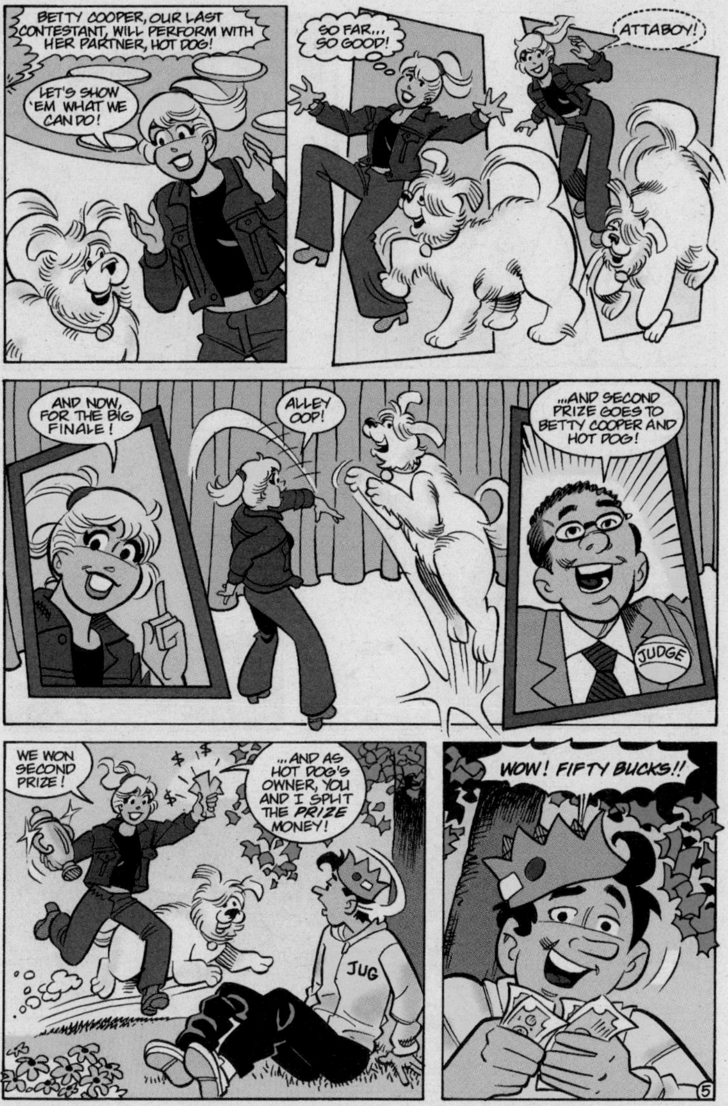
BETTY COOPER, OUR LAST CONTESTANT, WILL PERFORM WITH HER PARTNER, HOT DOG!
LET'S SHOW 'EM WHAT WE CAN DO!
SO FAR... SO GOOD!
ATTABOY!
AND NOW, FOR THE BIG FINALE!
ALLEY OOP!
...AND SECOND PRIZE GOES TO BETTY COOPER AND HOT DOG!
JUDGE
WE WON SECOND PRIZE!
...AND AS HOT DOG'S OWNER, YOU AND I SPLIT THE PRIZE MONEY!
JUG
WOW! FIFTY BUCKS!!

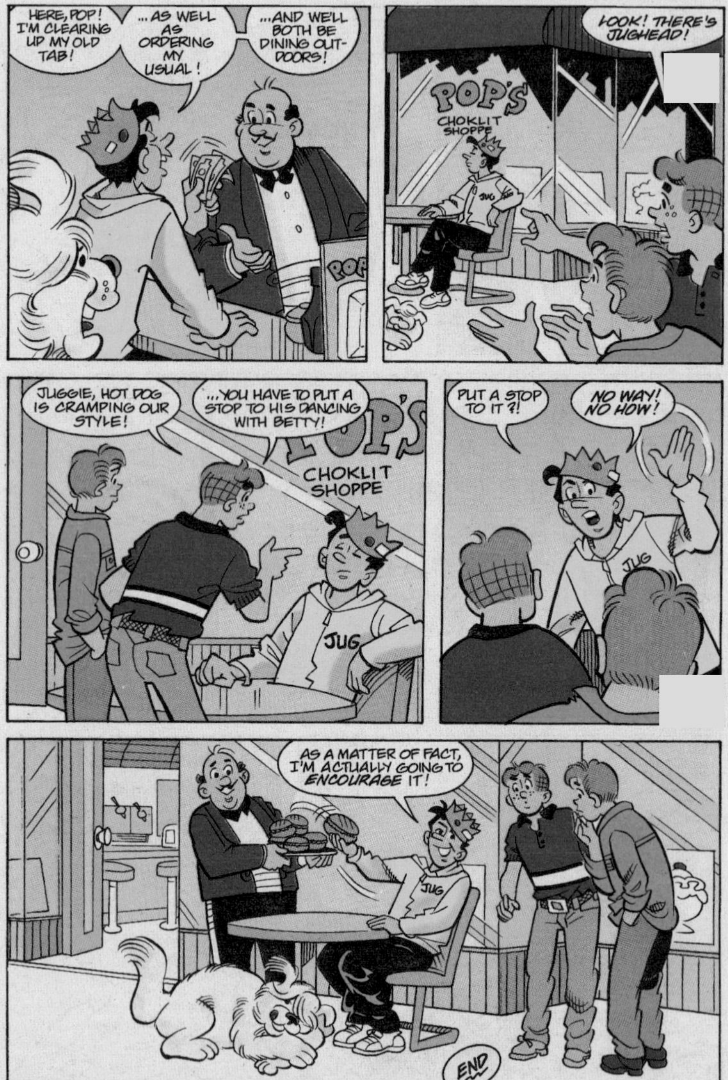
HERE, POP! I'M CLEARING UP MY OLD TAB!
...AS WELL AS ORDERING MY USUAL!
...AND WE'LL BOTH BE DINING OUT-DOORS!
LOOK! THERE'S JUGHEAD!
POP'S CHOKLIT SHOPPE
JUGGIE, HOT DOG IS CRAMPING OUR STYLE!
...YOU HAVE TO PUT A STOP TO HIS DANCING WITH BETTY!
PUT A STOP TO IT ?!
NO WAY! NO HOW!
AS A MATTER OF FACT, I'M ACTUALLY GOING TO *ENCOURAGE* IT!
END

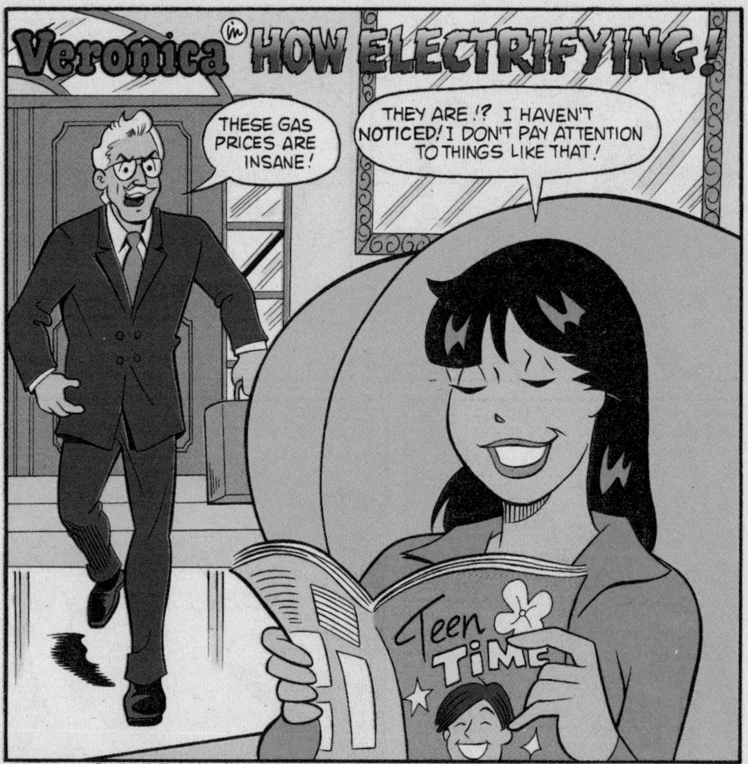
Veronica in HOW ELECTRIFYING!
THESE GAS PRICES ARE INSANE!
THEY ARE!? I HAVEN'T NOTICED! I DON'T PAY ATTENTION TO THINGS LIKE THAT!
Teen TIME

Script & Pencils: Dan Parent / Inks: Rich Koslowski / Letters: Bill Yoshida

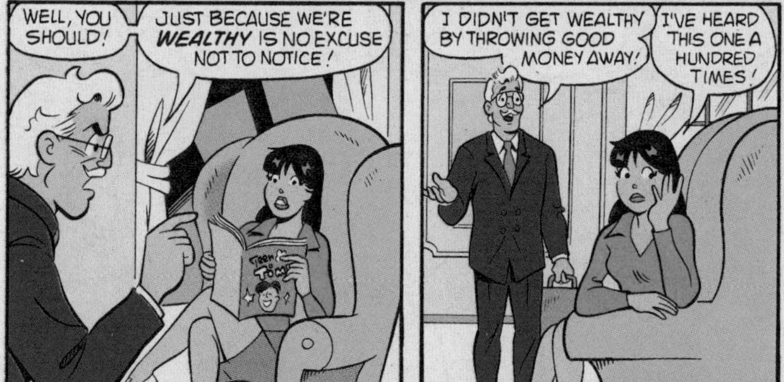
WELL, YOU SHOULD!
JUST BECAUSE WE'RE *WEALTHY* IS NO EXCUSE NOT TO NOTICE!
I DIDN'T GET WEALTHY BY THROWING GOOD MONEY AWAY!
I'VE HEARD THIS ONE A HUNDRED TIMES!

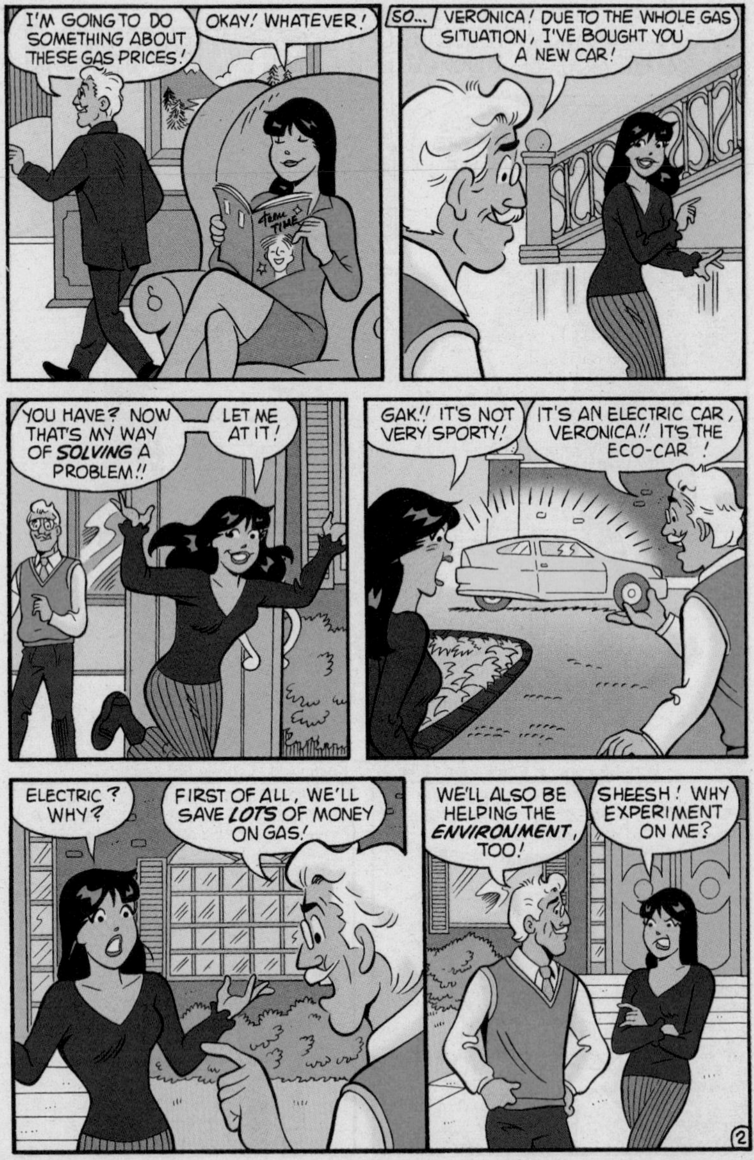

I'M GOING TO DO SOMETHING ABOUT THESE GAS PRICES!
OKAY! WHATEVER!
TEEN TIME
SO...
VERONICA! DUE TO THE WHOLE GAS SITUATION, I'VE BOUGHT YOU A NEW CAR!
YOU HAVE? NOW THAT'S MY WAY OF *SOLVING* A PROBLEM!!
LET ME AT IT!
GAK!! IT'S NOT VERY SPORTY!
IT'S AN ELECTRIC CAR, VERONICA!! IT'S THE ECO-CAR!
ELECTRIC? WHY?
FIRST OF ALL, WE'LL SAVE *LOTS* OF MONEY ON GAS!
WE'LL ALSO BE HELPING THE *ENVIRONMENT*, TOO!
SHEESH! WHY EXPERIMENT ON ME?
2

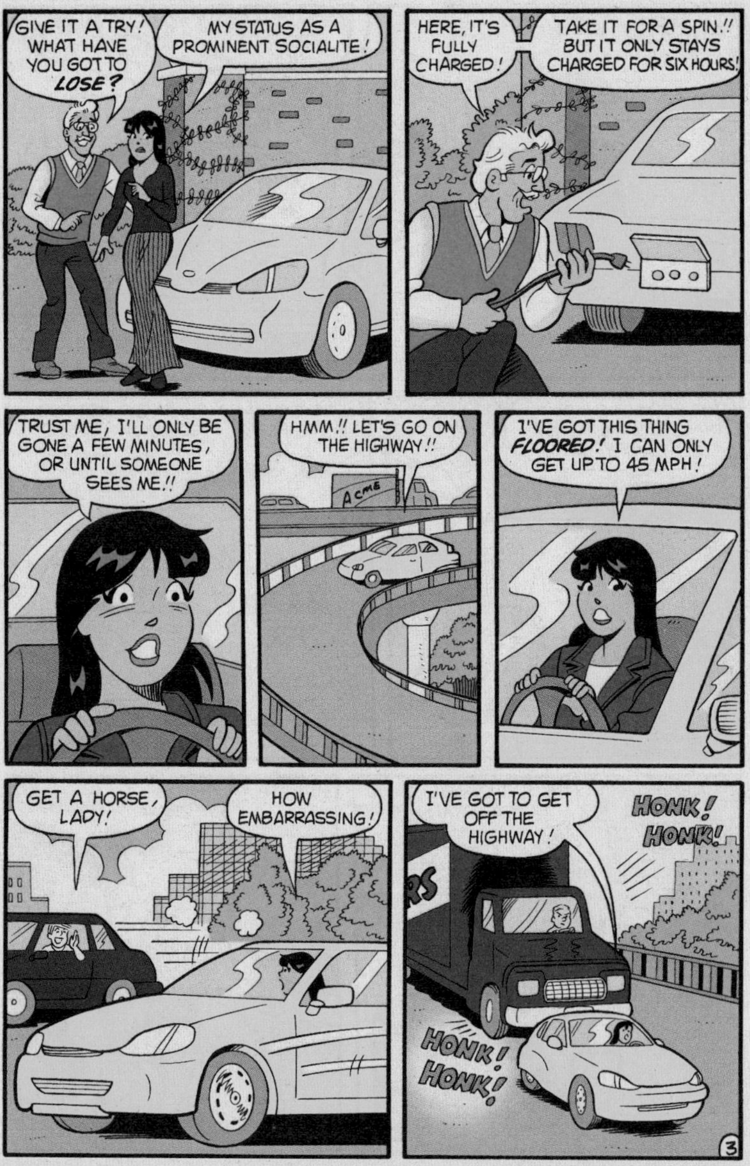
GIVE IT A TRY! WHAT HAVE YOU GOT TO LOSE?
MY STATUS AS A PROMINENT SOCIALITE!
HERE, IT'S FULLY CHARGED!
TAKE IT FOR A SPIN.!! BUT IT ONLY STAYS CHARGED FOR SIX HOURS!
TRUST ME, I'LL ONLY BE GONE A FEW MINUTES, OR UNTIL SOMEONE SEES ME.!!
HMM.!! LET'S GO ON THE HIGHWAY.!!
ACME
I'VE GOT THIS THING FLOORED! I CAN ONLY GET UP TO 45 MPH!
GET A HORSE, LADY!
HOW EMBARRASSING!
I'VE GOT TO GET OFF THE HIGHWAY!
HONK! HONK!
HONK! HONK!

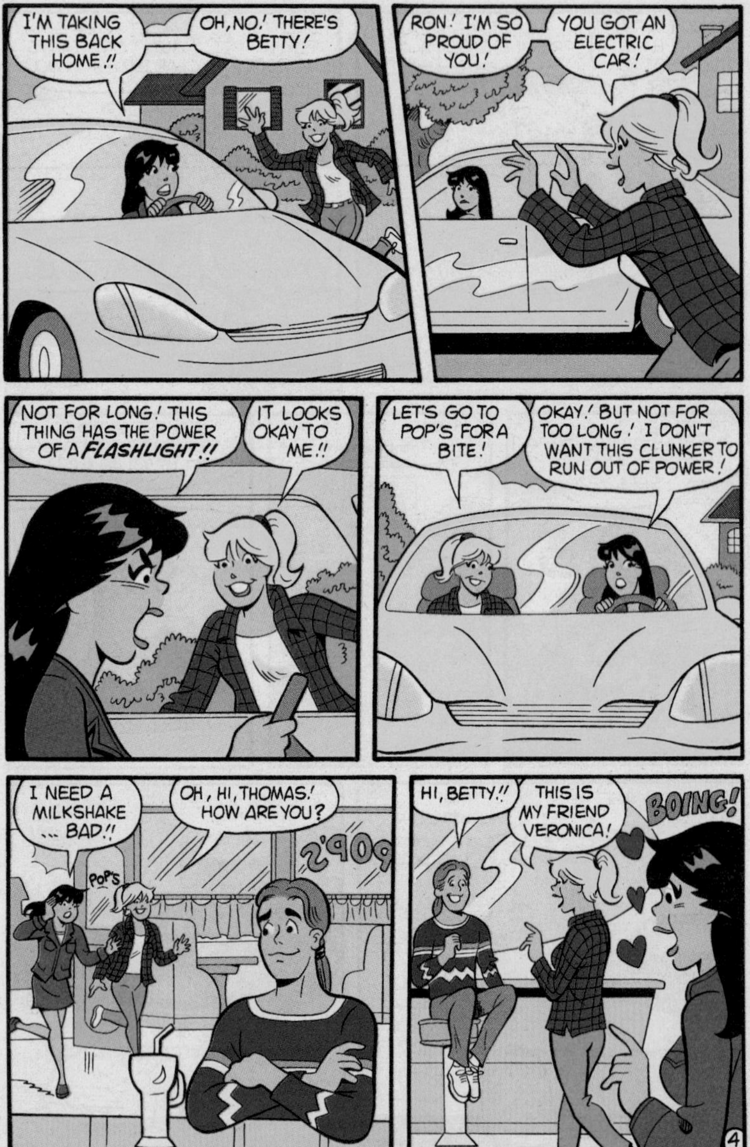
I'M TAKING THIS BACK HOME!!
OH, NO! THERE'S BETTY!
RON! I'M SO PROUD OF YOU!
YOU GOT AN ELECTRIC CAR!
NOT FOR LONG! THIS THING HAS THE POWER OF A FLASHLIGHT!!
IT LOOKS OKAY TO ME!!
LET'S GO TO POP'S FOR A BITE!
OKAY! BUT NOT FOR TOO LONG! I DON'T WANT THIS CLUNKER TO RUN OUT OF POWER!
I NEED A MILKSHAKE ... BAD!!
OH, HI, THOMAS! HOW ARE YOU?
POP'S
POP'S
HI, BETTY!!
THIS IS MY FRIEND VERONICA!
BOING!
4

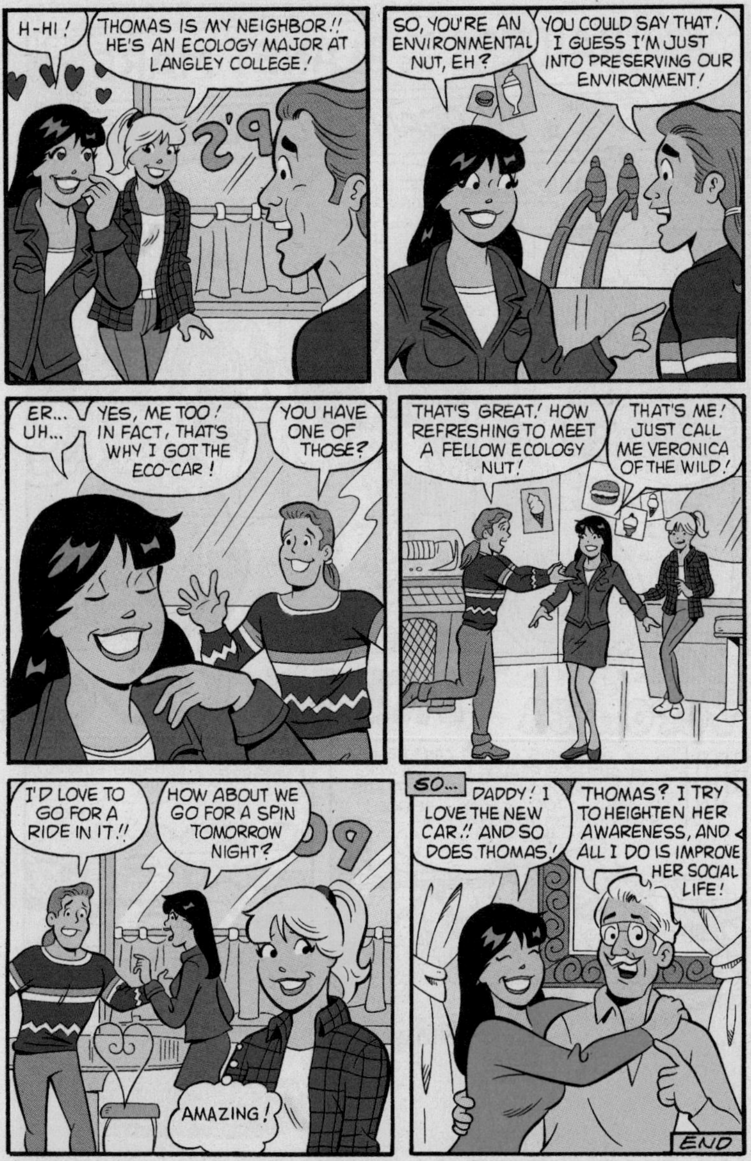
H-HI!
THOMAS IS MY NEIGHBOR!! HE'S AN ECOLOGY MAJOR AT LANGLEY COLLEGE!
SO, YOU'RE AN ENVIRONMENTAL NUT, EH?
YOU COULD SAY THAT! I GUESS I'M JUST INTO PRESERVING OUR ENVIRONMENT!
ER... UH...
YES, ME TOO! IN FACT, THAT'S WHY I GOT THE ECO-CAR!
YOU HAVE ONE OF THOSE?
THAT'S GREAT! HOW REFRESHING TO MEET A FELLOW ECOLOGY NUT!
THAT'S ME! JUST CALL ME VERONICA OF THE WILD!
I'D LOVE TO GO FOR A RIDE IN IT!!
HOW ABOUT WE GO FOR A SPIN TOMORROW NIGHT?
AMAZING!
SO...
DADDY! I LOVE THE NEW CAR!! AND SO DOES THOMAS!
THOMAS? I TRY TO HEIGHTEN HER AWARENESS, AND ALL I DO IS IMPROVE HER SOCIAL LIFE!
END

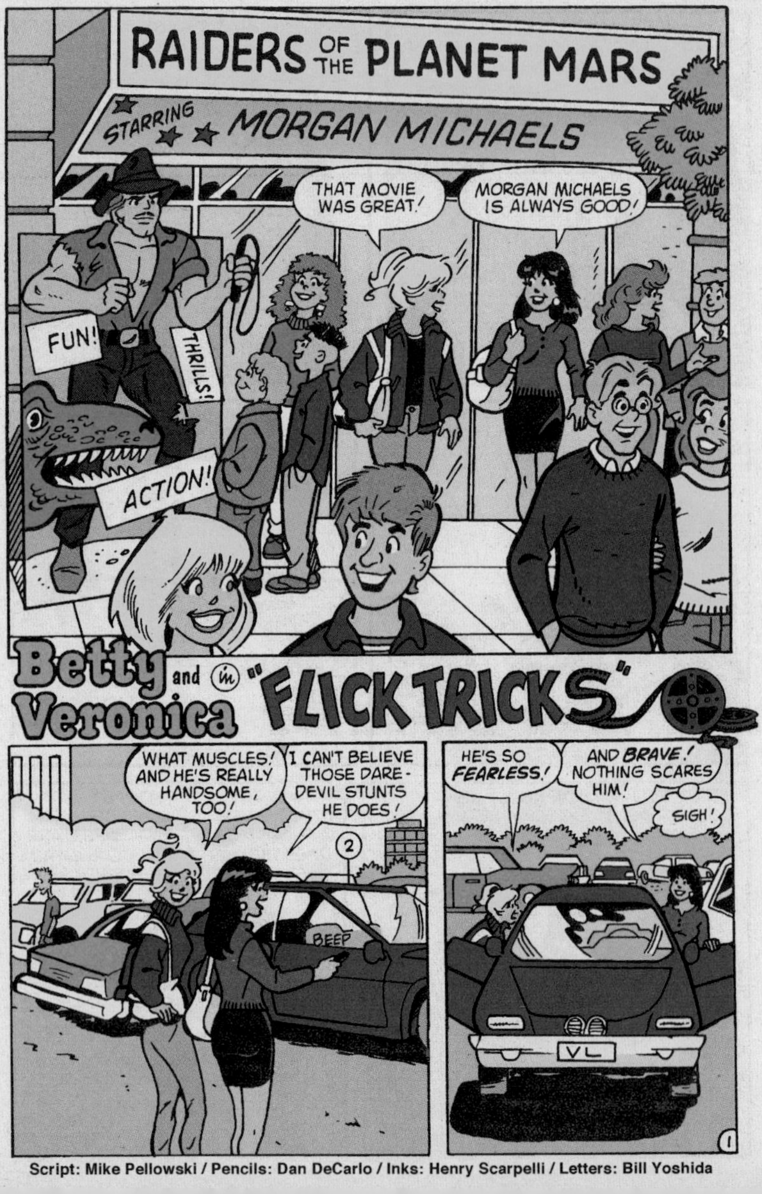
RAIDERS OF THE PLANET MARS
STARRING MORGAN MICHAELS
FUN!
THRILLS!
ACTION!
THAT MOVIE WAS GREAT!
MORGAN MICHAELS IS ALWAYS GOOD!
Betty and Veronica in "FLICK TRICKS"
WHAT MUSCLES! AND HE'S REALLY HANDSOME, TOO!
I CAN'T BELIEVE THOSE DARE-DEVIL STUNTS HE DOES!
BEEP
HE'S SO FEARLESS!
AND BRAVE! NOTHING SCARES HIM!
SIGH!
VL
1

Script: Mike Pellowski / Pencils: Dan DeCarlo / Inks: Henry Scarpelli / Letters: Bill Yoshida

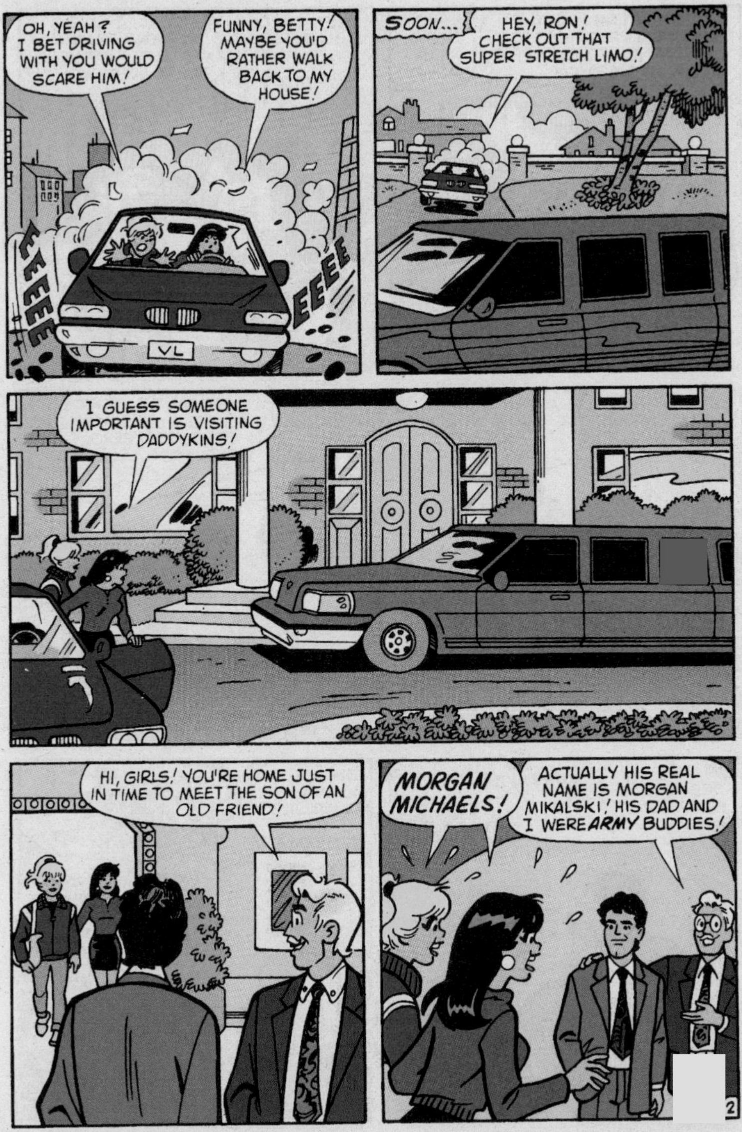

OH, YEAH? I BET DRIVING WITH YOU WOULD SCARE HIM!
FUNNY, BETTY! MAYBE YOU'D RATHER WALK BACK TO MY HOUSE!
EEEEE
EEEE
VL
SOON...
HEY, RON! CHECK OUT THAT SUPER STRETCH LIMO!
I GUESS SOMEONE IMPORTANT IS VISITING DADDYKINS!
HI, GIRLS! YOU'RE HOME JUST IN TIME TO MEET THE SON OF AN OLD FRIEND!
MORGAN MICHAELS!
ACTUALLY HIS REAL NAME IS MORGAN MIKALSKI! HIS DAD AND I WERE ARMY BUDDIES!

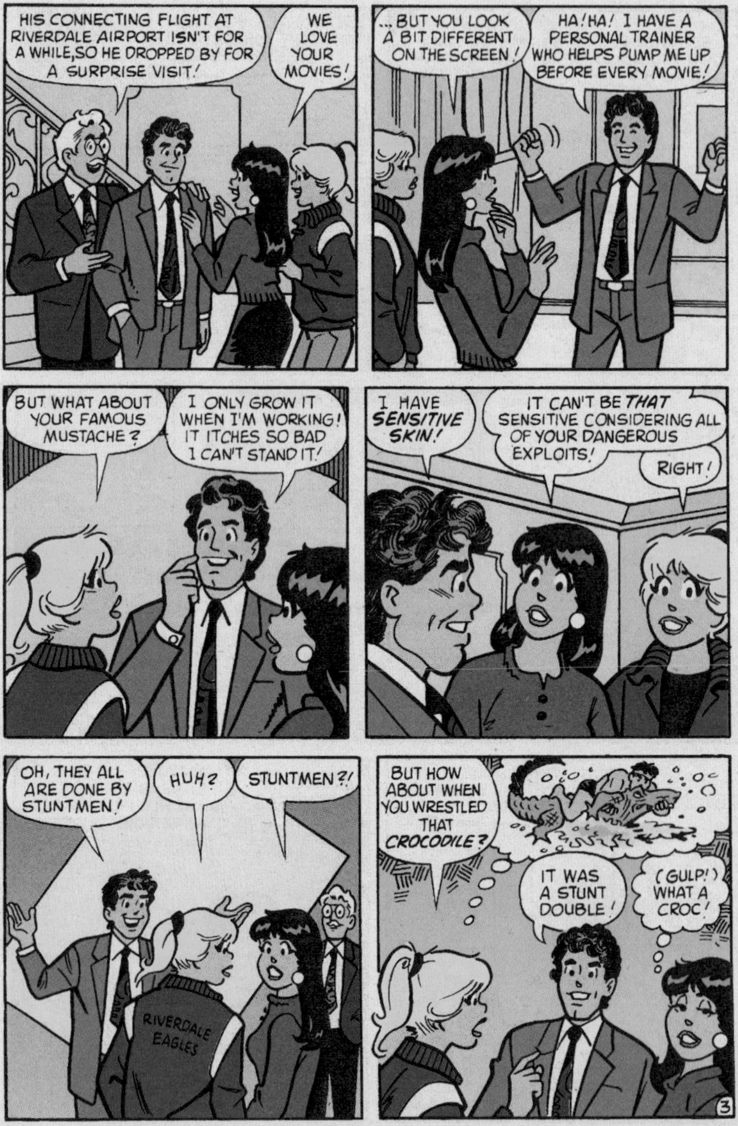
HIS CONNECTING FLIGHT AT RIVERDALE AIRPORT ISN'T FOR A WHILE, SO HE DROPPED BY FOR A SURPRISE VISIT!
WE LOVE YOUR MOVIES!
...BUT YOU LOOK A BIT DIFFERENT ON THE SCREEN!
HA! HA! I HAVE A PERSONAL TRAINER WHO HELPS PUMP ME UP BEFORE EVERY MOVIE!
BUT WHAT ABOUT YOUR FAMOUS MUSTACHE?
I ONLY GROW IT WHEN I'M WORKING! IT ITCHES SO BAD I CAN'T STAND IT!
I HAVE *SENSITIVE SKIN*!
IT CAN'T BE *THAT* SENSITIVE CONSIDERING ALL OF YOUR DANGEROUS EXPLOITS!
RIGHT!
OH, THEY ALL ARE DONE BY STUNTMEN!
HUH?
STUNTMEN?!
RIVERDALE EAGLES
BUT HOW ABOUT WHEN YOU WRESTLED THAT *CROCODILE*?
IT WAS A STUNT DOUBLE!
(GULP!) WHAT A CROC!
3

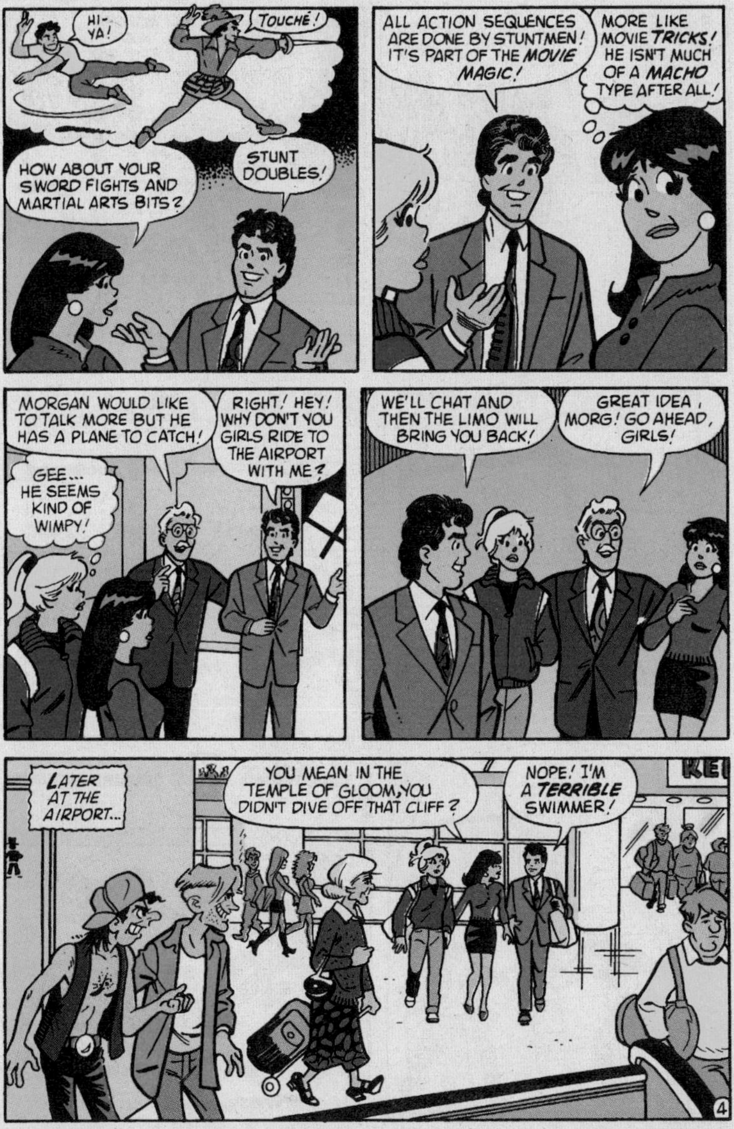
HI-YA!
TOUCHÉ!
HOW ABOUT YOUR SWORD FIGHTS AND MARTIAL ARTS BITS?
STUNT DOUBLES!
ALL ACTION SEQUENCES ARE DONE BY STUNTMEN! IT'S PART OF THE MOVIE MAGIC!
MORE LIKE MOVIE TRICKS! HE ISN'T MUCH OF A MACHO TYPE AFTER ALL!
MORGAN WOULD LIKE TO TALK MORE BUT HE HAS A PLANE TO CATCH!
RIGHT! HEY! WHY DON'T YOU GIRLS RIDE TO THE AIRPORT WITH ME?
GEE... HE SEEMS KIND OF WIMPY!
WE'LL CHAT AND THEN THE LIMO WILL BRING YOU BACK!
GREAT IDEA, MORG! GO AHEAD, GIRLS!
LATER AT THE AIRPORT...
YOU MEAN IN THE TEMPLE OF GLOOM, YOU DIDN'T DIVE OFF THAT CLIFF?
NOPE! I'M A TERRIBLE SWIMMER!
4

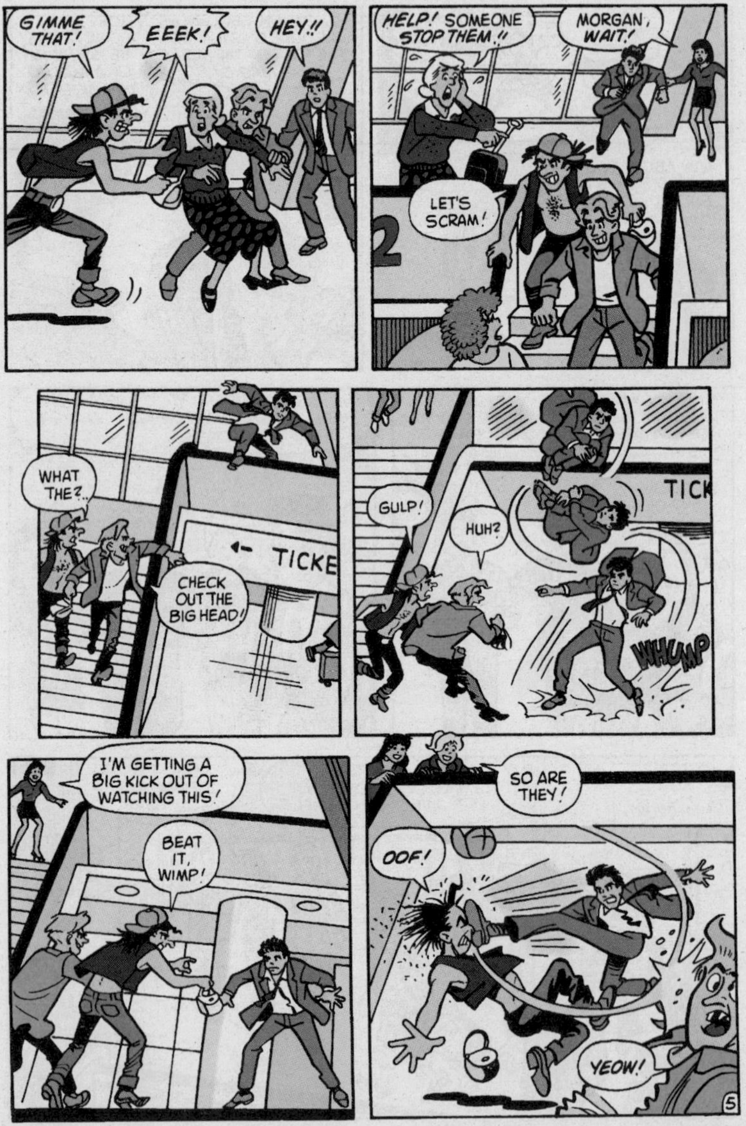
GIMME THAT!
EEEK!
HEY!!
HELP! SOMEONE STOP THEM!!
MORGAN, WAIT!
LET'S SCRAM!
WHAT THE?..
CHECK OUT THE BIG HEAD!
TICKE
GULP!
HUH?
TICK
WHUMP
I'M GETTING A BIG KICK OUT OF WATCHING THIS!
BEAT IT, WIMP!
SO ARE THEY!
OOF!
YEOW!
5

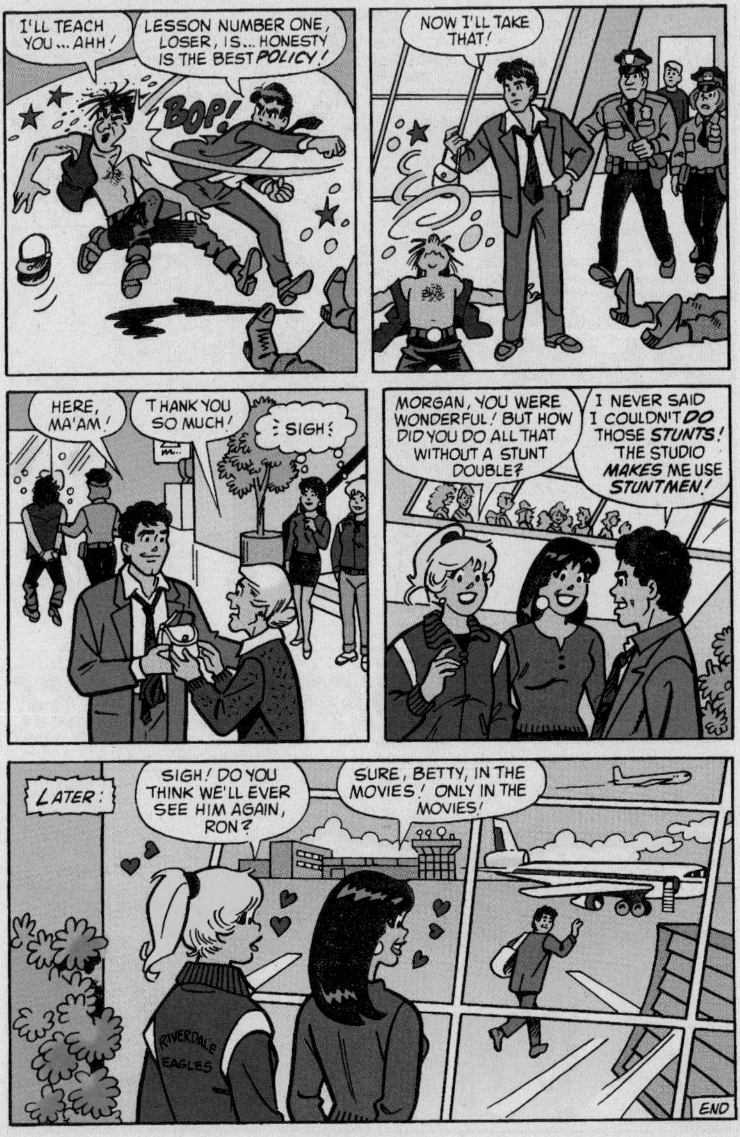
I'LL TEACH YOU ... AHH!
LESSON NUMBER ONE, LOSER, IS... HONESTY IS THE BEST POLICY!
BOP!
NOW I'LL TAKE THAT!
HERE, MA'AM!
THANK YOU SO MUCH!
SIGH!
MORGAN, YOU WERE WONDERFUL! BUT HOW DID YOU DO ALL THAT WITHOUT A STUNT DOUBLE?
I NEVER SAID I COULDN'T DO THOSE STUNTS! THE STUDIO MAKES ME USE STUNTMEN!
LATER:
SIGH! DO YOU THINK WE'LL EVER SEE HIM AGAIN, RON?
SURE, BETTY, IN THE MOVIES! ONLY IN THE MOVIES!
RIVERDALE EAGLES
END

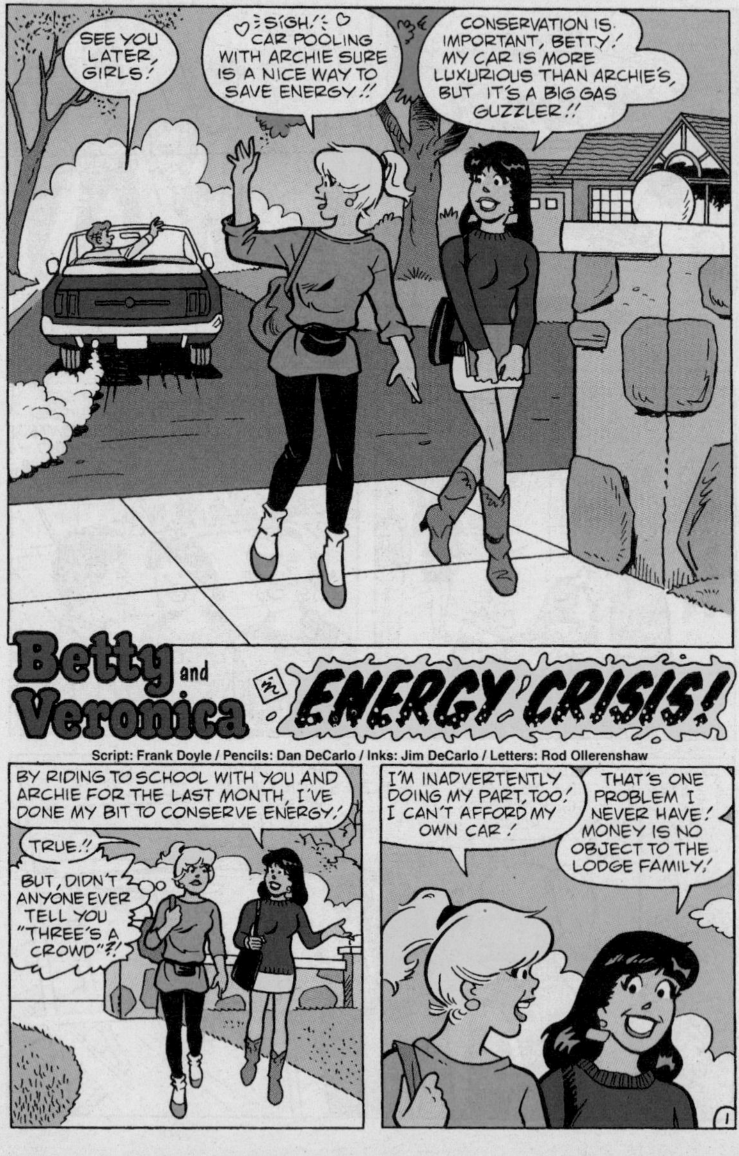
SEE YOU LATER, GIRLS!
SIGH! CAR POOLING WITH ARCHIE SURE IS A NICE WAY TO SAVE ENERGY!!
CONSERVATION IS IMPORTANT, BETTY! MY CAR IS MORE LUXURIOUS THAN ARCHIE'S, BUT IT'S A BIG GAS GUZZLER!!
Betty and Veronica
ENERGY CRISIS!
Script: Frank Doyle / Pencils: Dan DeCarlo / Inks: Jim DeCarlo / Letters: Rod Ollerenshaw
BY RIDING TO SCHOOL WITH YOU AND ARCHIE FOR THE LAST MONTH, I'VE DONE MY BIT TO CONSERVE ENERGY!
TRUE!!
BUT, DIDN'T ANYONE EVER TELL YOU "THREE'S A CROWD"?!
I'M INADVERTENTLY DOING MY PART, TOO! I CAN'T AFFORD MY OWN CAR!
THAT'S ONE PROBLEM I NEVER HAVE! MONEY IS NO OBJECT TO THE LODGE FAMILY!
1

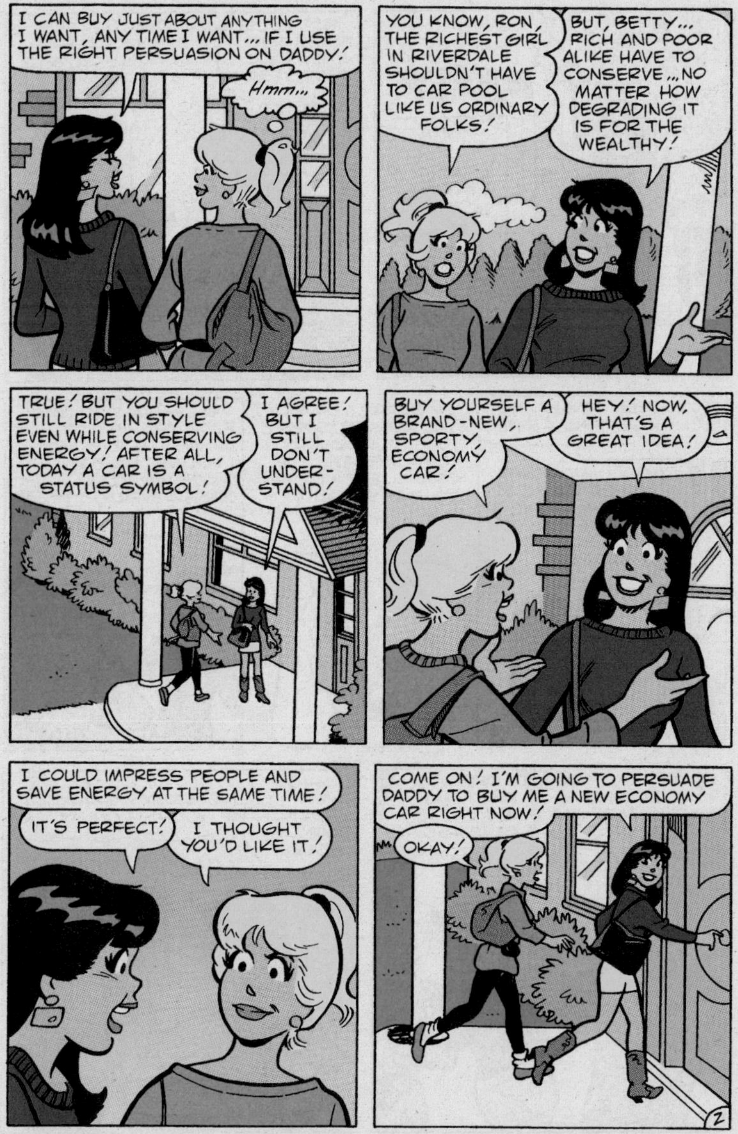
I CAN BUY JUST ABOUT ANYTHING I WANT, ANY TIME I WANT... IF I USE THE RIGHT PERSUASION ON DADDY!
Hmm...
YOU KNOW, RON, THE RICHEST GIRL IN RIVERDALE SHOULDN'T HAVE TO CAR POOL LIKE US ORDINARY FOLKS!
BUT, BETTY... RICH AND POOR ALIKE HAVE TO CONSERVE... NO MATTER HOW DEGRADING IT IS FOR THE WEALTHY!
TRUE! BUT YOU SHOULD STILL RIDE IN STYLE EVEN WHILE CONSERVING ENERGY! AFTER ALL, TODAY A CAR IS A STATUS SYMBOL!
I AGREE! BUT I STILL DON'T UNDER-STAND!
BUY YOURSELF A BRAND-NEW, SPORTY, ECONOMY CAR!
HEY! NOW, THAT'S A GREAT IDEA!
I COULD IMPRESS PEOPLE AND SAVE ENERGY AT THE SAME TIME!
IT'S PERFECT!
I THOUGHT YOU'D LIKE IT!
COME ON! I'M GOING TO PERSUADE DADDY TO BUY ME A NEW ECONOMY CAR RIGHT NOW!
OKAY!
2

HI, DADDY! HOW ARE YOU? I NEED A NEW CAR!!

HI, HONEY! FINE! **WHAT?**

BUT I JUST BOUGHT YOU A NEW CAR LAST YEAR!

I KNOW...BUT IT'S A GAS GUZZLER, AND THESE DAYS WE HAVE TO CONSERVE ENERGY!

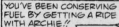

YOU'VE BEEN CONSERVING FUEL BY GETTING A RIDE WITH ARCHIE!!

HMPH! I LOOK LIKE A PAUPER RIDING TO SCHOOL IN ARCHIE'S OLD BOMB! BESIDES, IT'S NOT FAIR TO ARCHIE!

I'M SORRY, VERONICA! THE ANSWER IS **NO!** I APPLAUD YOUR CONCERN OVER THE FUEL CRISIS, BUT NOTHING YOU CAN SAY WILL CHANGE MY MIND!

WELL...OKAY! TO PAY BACK ARCHIE FOR DRIVING ME TO SCHOOL, I'LL JUST HAVE TO INVITE HIM TO DINNER EVERY NIGHT!!

GAK!

OKAY! OKAY! YOU WIN, VERONICA!! WHAT KIND OF CAR DO YOU WANT?

I TOLD YOU ALL IT TAKES IS A LITTLE PERSUASION!

I WANT A SPORTY-LOOKING ECONOMY MODEL!

I'LL HAVE A NEW ECONOMY CAR FOR YOU BY MONDAY!

3

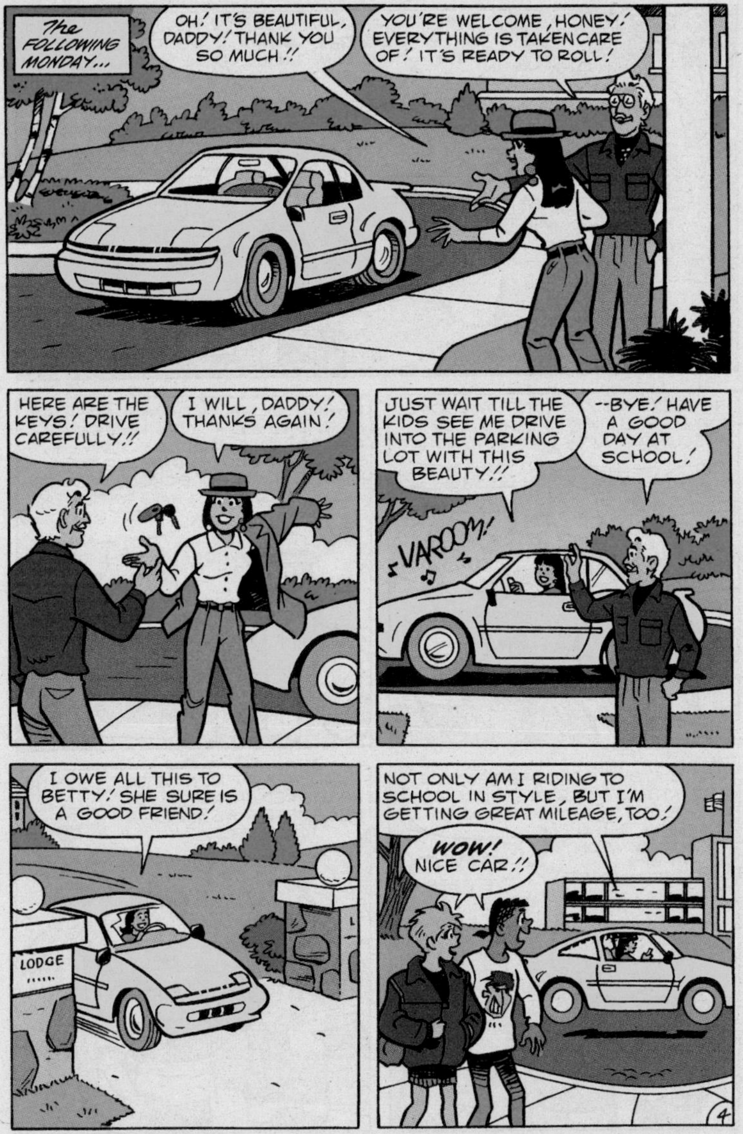
The FOLLOWING MONDAY...
OH! IT'S BEAUTIFUL, DADDY! THANK YOU SO MUCH!!
YOU'RE WELCOME, HONEY! EVERYTHING IS TAKEN CARE OF! IT'S READY TO ROLL!
HERE ARE THE KEYS! DRIVE CAREFULLY!!
I WILL, DADDY! THANKS AGAIN!
JUST WAIT TILL THE KIDS SEE ME DRIVE INTO THE PARKING LOT WITH THIS BEAUTY!!
--BYE! HAVE A GOOD DAY AT SCHOOL!
VAROOM!
I OWE ALL THIS TO BETTY! SHE SURE IS A GOOD FRIEND!
LODGE
NOT ONLY AM I RIDING TO SCHOOL IN STYLE, BUT I'M GETTING GREAT MILEAGE, TOO!
WOW! NICE CAR!!
4

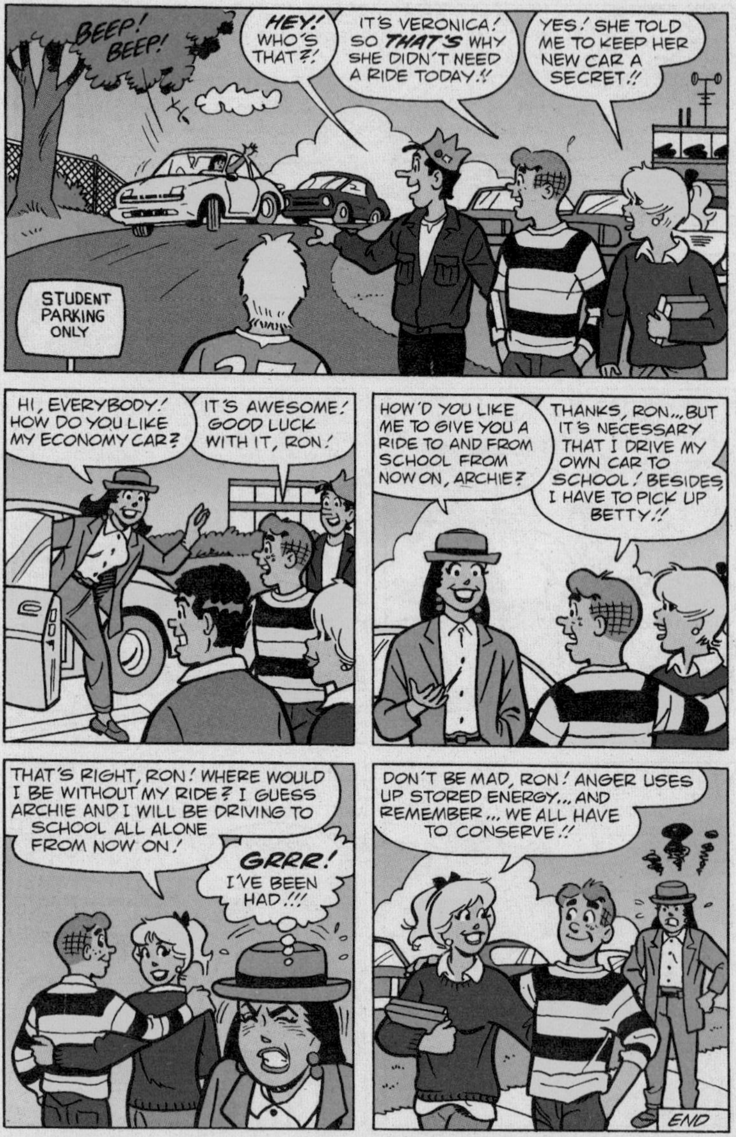
BEEP! BEEP!
HEY! WHO'S THAT?!
IT'S VERONICA! SO THAT'S WHY SHE DIDN'T NEED A RIDE TODAY!!
YES! SHE TOLD ME TO KEEP HER NEW CAR A SECRET!!
STUDENT PARKING ONLY
HI, EVERYBODY! HOW DO YOU LIKE MY ECONOMY CAR?
IT'S AWESOME! GOOD LUCK WITH IT, RON!
HOW'D YOU LIKE ME TO GIVE YOU A RIDE TO AND FROM SCHOOL FROM NOW ON, ARCHIE?
THANKS, RON... BUT IT'S NECESSARY THAT I DRIVE MY OWN CAR TO SCHOOL! BESIDES, I HAVE TO PICK UP BETTY!!
THAT'S RIGHT, RON! WHERE WOULD I BE WITHOUT MY RIDE? I GUESS ARCHIE AND I WILL BE DRIVING TO SCHOOL ALL ALONE FROM NOW ON!
GRRR! I'VE BEEN HAD!!!
DON'T BE MAD, RON! ANGER USES UP STORED ENERGY... AND REMEMBER... WE ALL HAVE TO CONSERVE!!
END

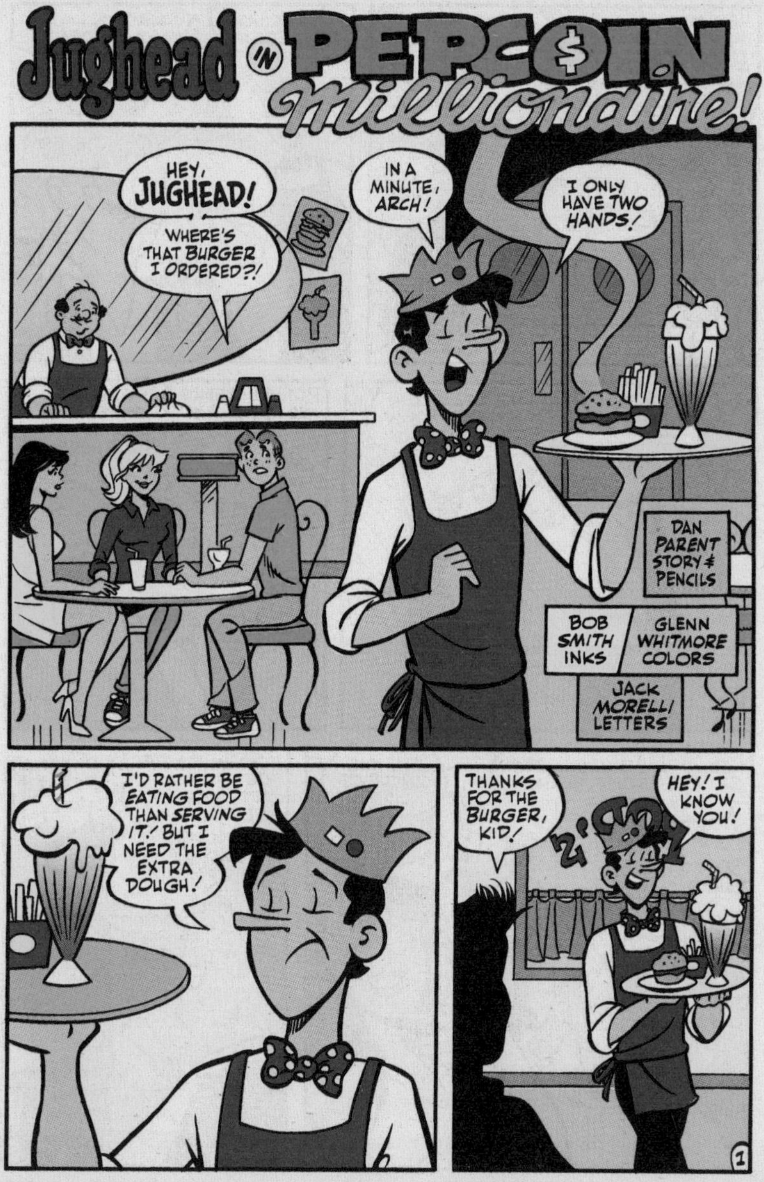
Jughead in PEPCOIN Millionaire!
HEY, JUGHEAD!
WHERE'S THAT BURGER I ORDERED?!
IN A MINUTE, ARCH!
I ONLY HAVE TWO HANDS!
DAN PARENT STORY & PENCILS
BOB SMITH INKS
GLENN WHITMORE COLORS
JACK MORELLI LETTERS
I'D RATHER BE EATING FOOD THAN SERVING IT! BUT I NEED THE EXTRA DOUGH!
THANKS FOR THE BURGER, KID!
HEY! I KNOW YOU!
POP'S
1

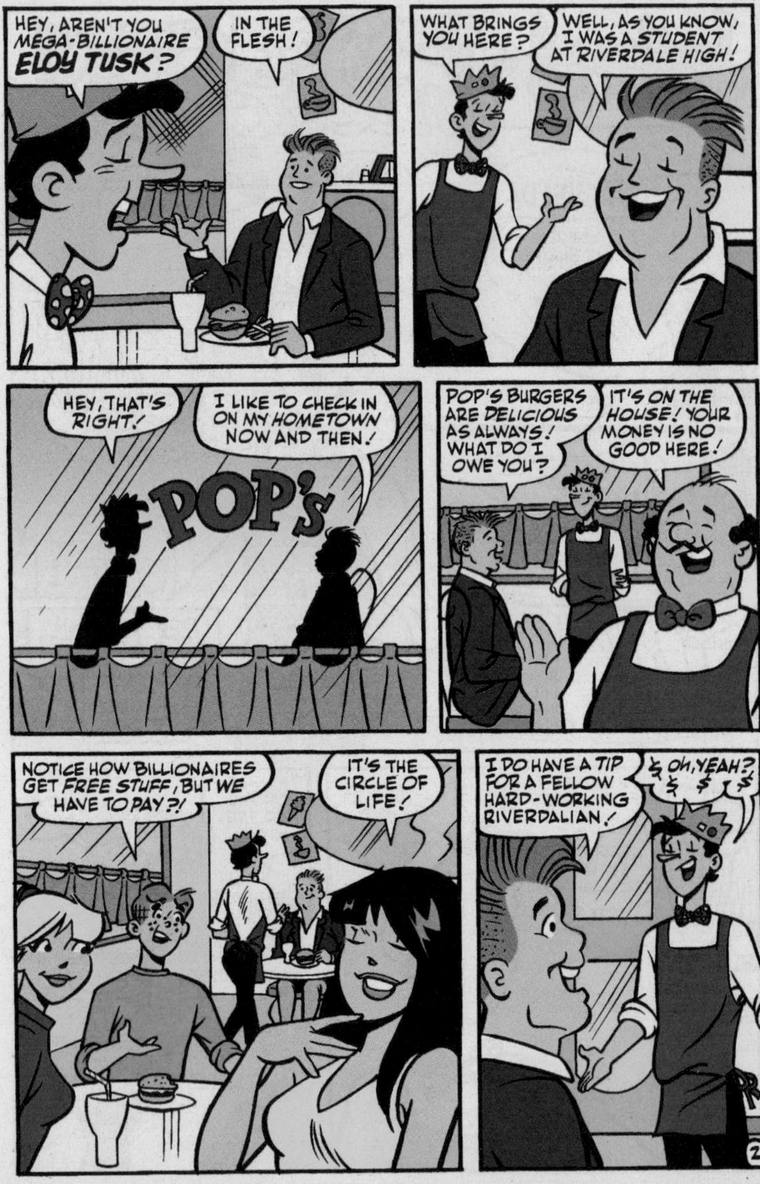
HEY, AREN'T YOU MEGA-BILLIONAIRE ELOY TUSK?
IN THE FLESH!
WHAT BRINGS YOU HERE?
WELL, AS YOU KNOW, I WAS A STUDENT AT RIVERDALE HIGH!
HEY, THAT'S RIGHT!
I LIKE TO CHECK IN ON MY HOMETOWN NOW AND THEN!
POP'S
POP'S BURGERS ARE DELICIOUS AS ALWAYS! WHAT DO I OWE YOU?
IT'S ON THE HOUSE! YOUR MONEY IS NO GOOD HERE!
NOTICE HOW BILLIONAIRES GET FREE STUFF, BUT WE HAVE TO PAY?!
IT'S THE CIRCLE OF LIFE!
I DO HAVE A TIP FOR A FELLOW HARD-WORKING RIVERDALIAN!
$ OH, YEAH? $ $ $
2

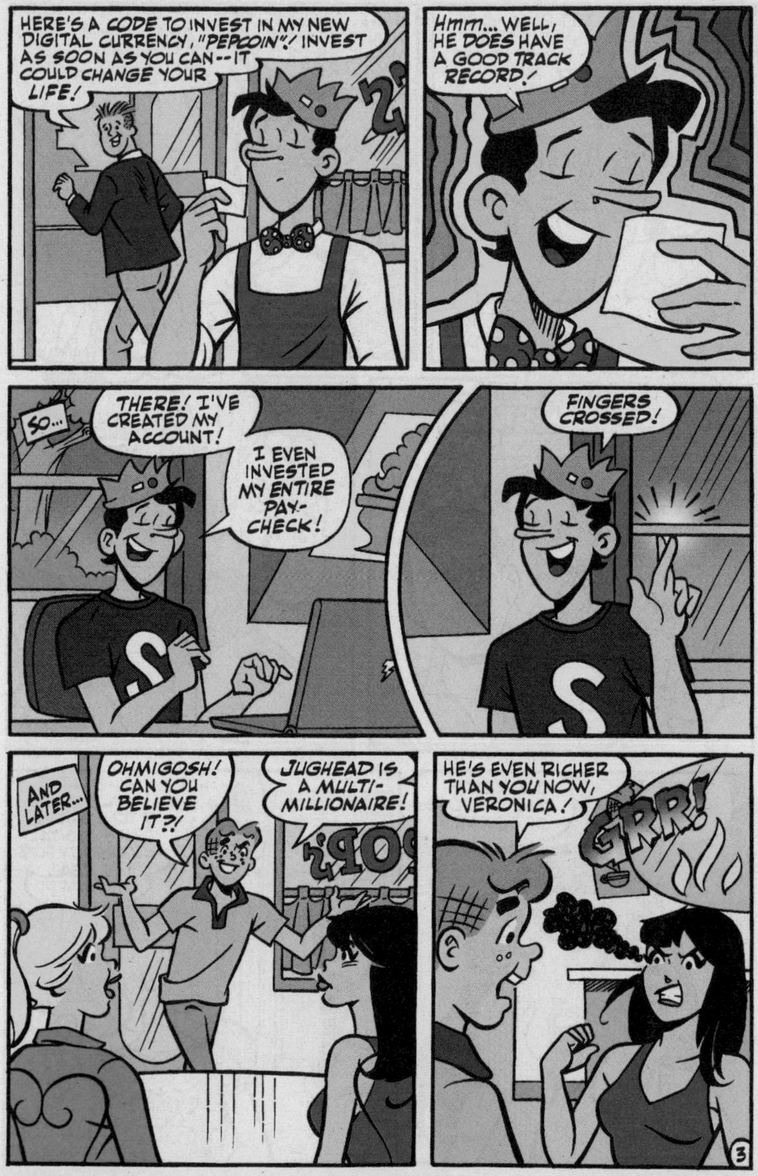
HERE'S A CODE TO INVEST IN MY NEW DIGITAL CURRENCY, "PEPCOIN"! INVEST AS SOON AS YOU CAN--IT COULD CHANGE YOUR LIFE!
Hmm... WELL, HE DOES HAVE A GOOD TRACK RECORD!
SO...
THERE! I'VE CREATED MY ACCOUNT!
I EVEN INVESTED MY ENTIRE PAY-CHECK!
FINGERS CROSSED!
AND LATER...
OHMIGOSH! CAN YOU BELIEVE IT?!
JUGHEAD IS A MULTI-MILLIONAIRE!
POP'S
HE'S EVEN RICHER THAN YOU NOW, VERONICA!
GRR!
3

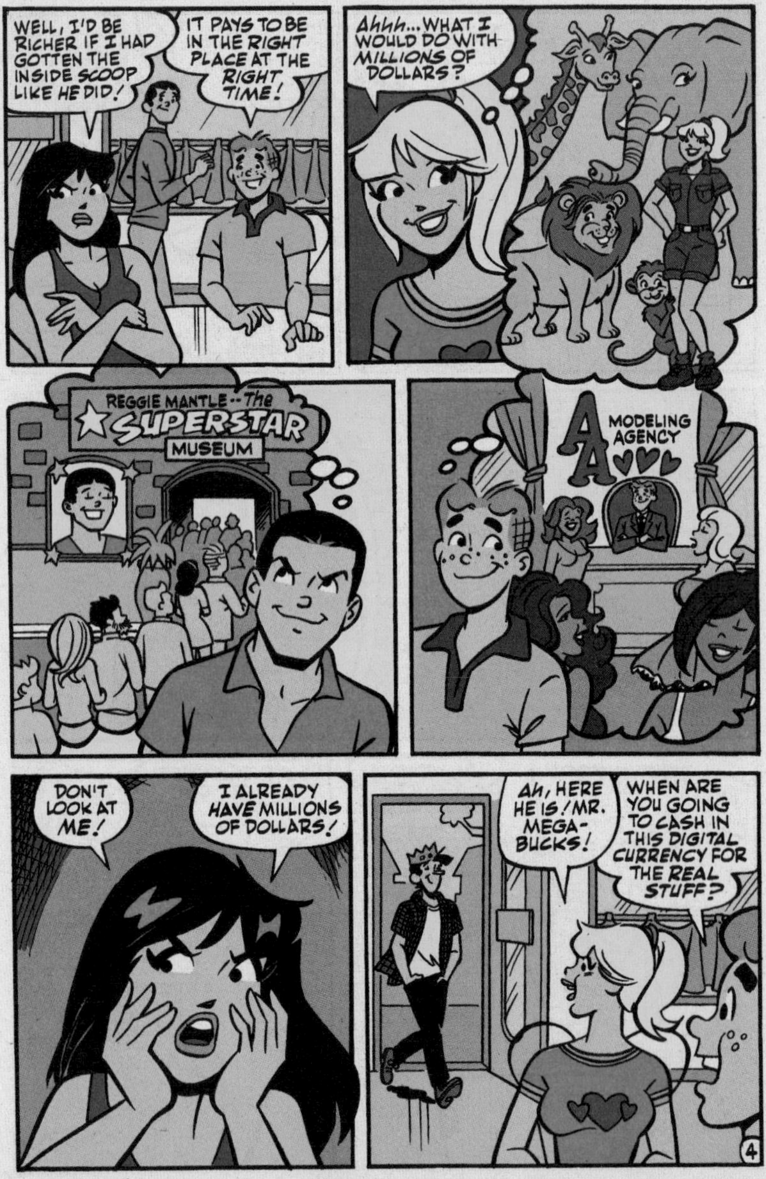

WELL, I'D BE RICHER IF I HAD GOTTEN THE INSIDE SCOOP LIKE HE DID!
IT PAYS TO BE IN THE RIGHT PLACE AT THE RIGHT TIME!
Ahhh... WHAT I WOULD DO WITH MILLIONS OF DOLLARS?
REGGIE MANTLE -- The SUPERSTAR MUSEUM
MODELING AGENCY
DON'T LOOK AT ME!
I ALREADY HAVE MILLIONS OF DOLLARS!
Ah, HERE HE IS! MR. MEGA-BUCKS!
WHEN ARE YOU GOING TO CASH IN THIS DIGITAL CURRENCY FOR THE REAL STUFF?
4

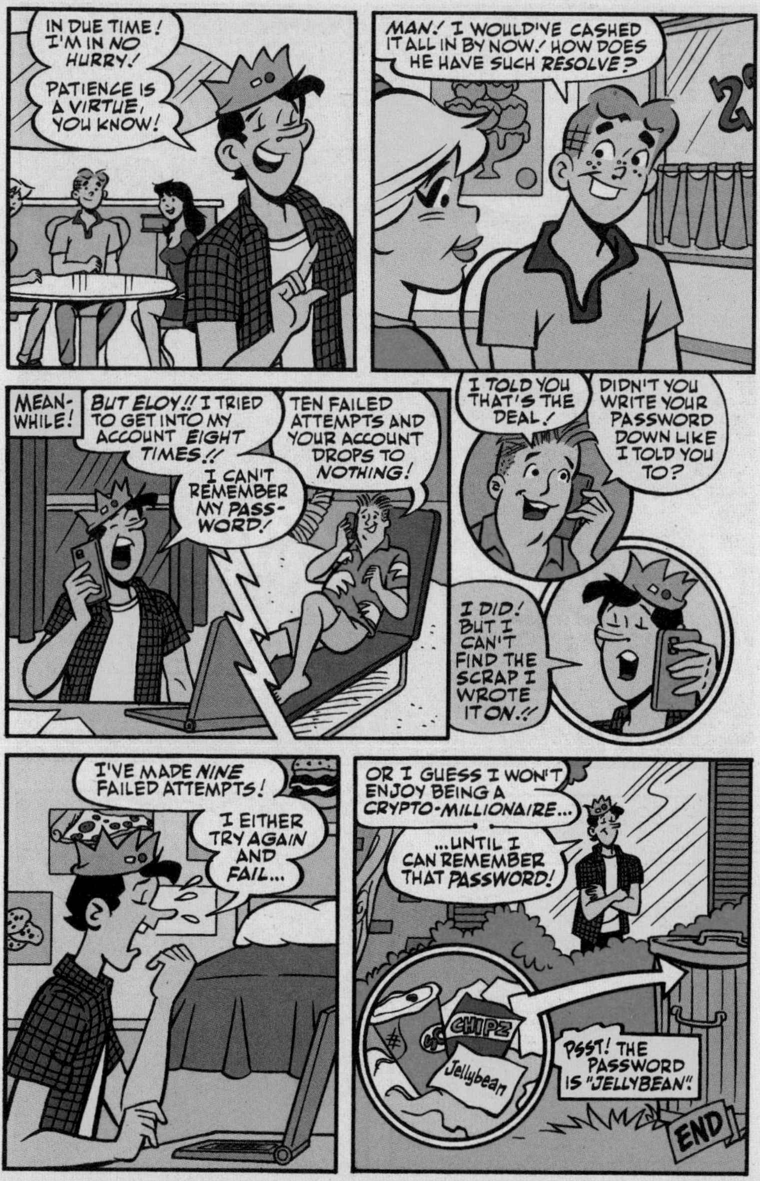
IN DUE TIME! I'M IN NO HURRY!
PATIENCE IS A VIRTUE, YOU KNOW!
MAN! I WOULD'VE CASHED IT ALL IN BY NOW! HOW DOES HE HAVE SUCH RESOLVE?
MEAN-WHILE!
BUT ELOY!! I TRIED TO GET INTO MY ACCOUNT EIGHT TIMES!!
I CAN'T REMEMBER MY PASS-WORD!
TEN FAILED ATTEMPTS AND YOUR ACCOUNT DROPS TO NOTHING!
I TOLD YOU THAT'S THE DEAL!
DIDN'T YOU WRITE YOUR PASSWORD DOWN LIKE I TOLD YOU TO?
I DID! BUT I CAN'T FIND THE SCRAP I WROTE IT ON!!
I'VE MADE NINE FAILED ATTEMPTS!
I EITHER TRY AGAIN AND FAIL...
OR I GUESS I WON'T ENJOY BEING A CRYPTO-MILLIONAIRE...
...UNTIL I CAN REMEMBER THAT PASSWORD!
CHIPZ
Jellybean
PSST! THE PASSWORD IS "JELLYBEAN"!
END

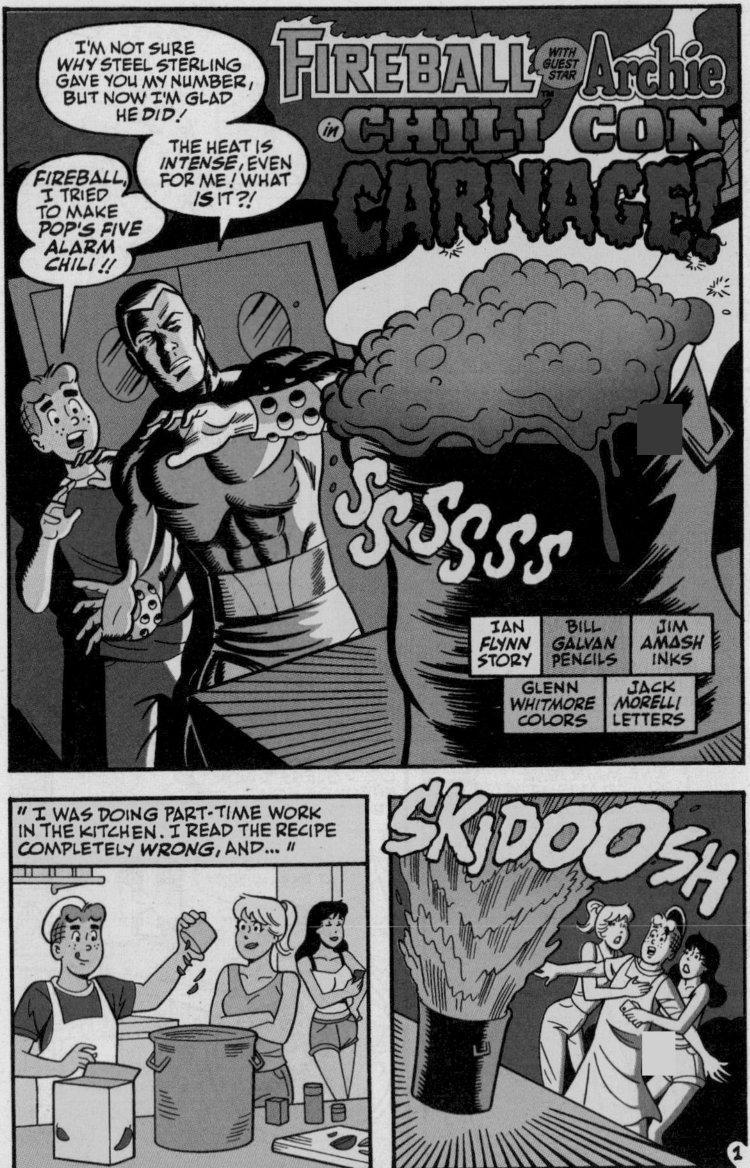

FIREBALL WITH GUEST STAR Archie in CHILI CON CARNAGE!
I'M NOT SURE WHY STEEL STERLING GAVE YOU MY NUMBER, BUT NOW I'M GLAD HE DID!
THE HEAT IS INTENSE, EVEN FOR ME! WHAT IS IT?!
FIREBALL, I TRIED TO MAKE POP'S FIVE ALARM CHILI!!
SSSSSS
IAN FLYNN STORY
BILL GALVAN PENCILS
JIM AMASH INKS
GLENN WHITMORE COLORS
JACK MORELLI LETTERS
"I WAS DOING PART-TIME WORK IN THE KITCHEN. I READ THE RECIPE COMPLETELY WRONG, AND..."
SKIDOOSH
1

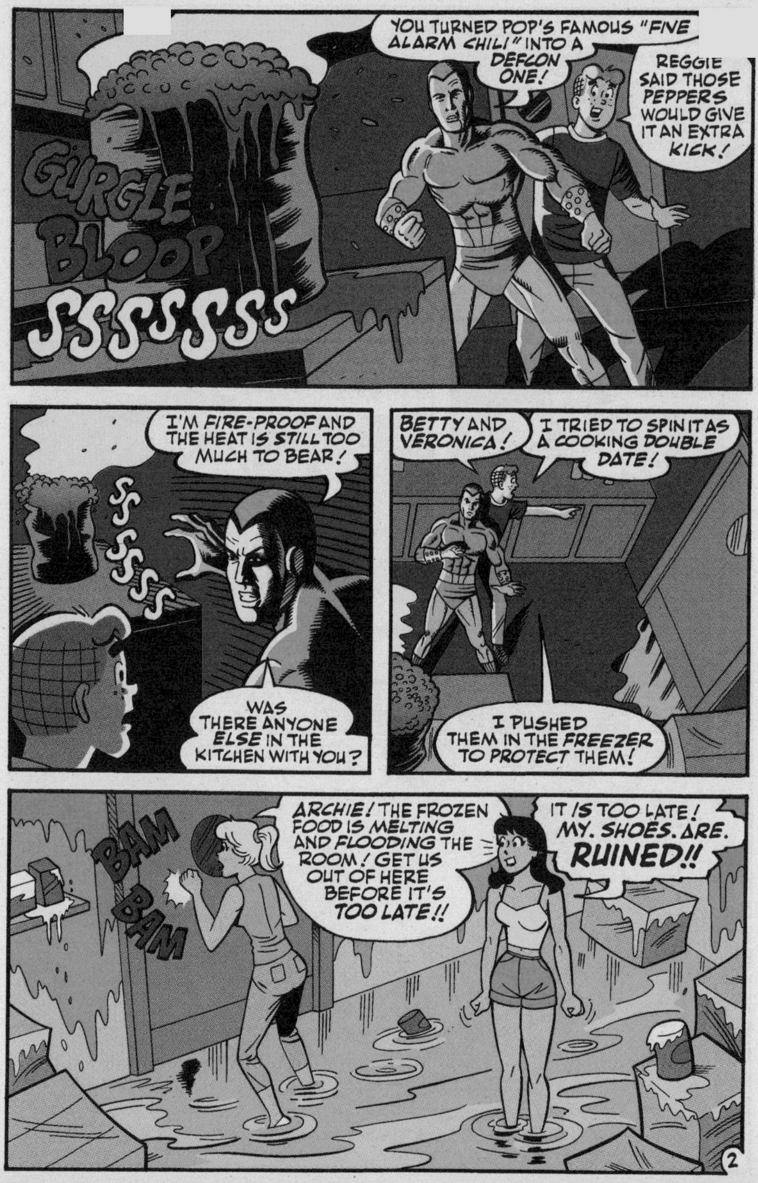

YOU TURNED POP'S FAMOUS "FIVE ALARM CHILI" INTO A DEFCON ONE!
REGGIE SAID THOSE PEPPERS WOULD GIVE IT AN EXTRA KICK!
GURGLE
BLOOP
SSSSSSS
I'M FIRE-PROOF AND THE HEAT IS STILL TOO MUCH TO BEAR!
SSSSSSS
WAS THERE ANYONE ELSE IN THE KITCHEN WITH YOU?
BETTY AND VERONICA!
I TRIED TO SPIN IT AS A COOKING DOUBLE DATE!
I PUSHED THEM IN THE FREEZER TO PROTECT THEM!
BAM
BAM
ARCHIE! THE FROZEN FOOD IS MELTING AND FLOODING THE ROOM! GET US OUT OF HERE BEFORE IT'S TOO LATE!!
IT IS TOO LATE! MY. SHOES. ARE. RUINED!!

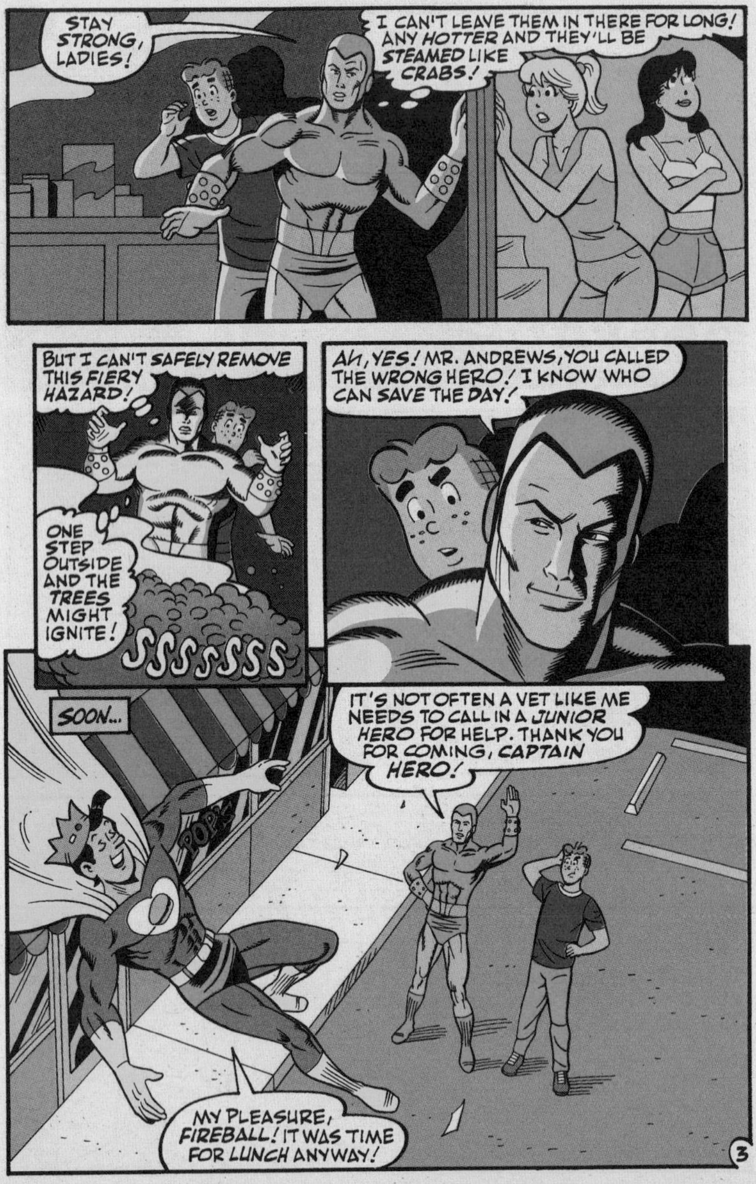
STAY STRONG, LADIES!
I CAN'T LEAVE THEM IN THERE FOR LONG! ANY HOTTER AND THEY'LL BE STEAMED LIKE CRABS!
BUT I CAN'T SAFELY REMOVE THIS FIERY HAZARD!
ONE STEP OUTSIDE AND THE TREES MIGHT IGNITE!
SSSSSSS
AH, YES! MR. ANDREWS, YOU CALLED THE WRONG HERO! I KNOW WHO CAN SAVE THE DAY!
SOON...
IT'S NOT OFTEN A VET LIKE ME NEEDS TO CALL IN A JUNIOR HERO FOR HELP. THANK YOU FOR COMING, CAPTAIN HERO!
POP'S
MY PLEASURE, FIREBALL! IT WAS TIME FOR LUNCH ANYWAY!

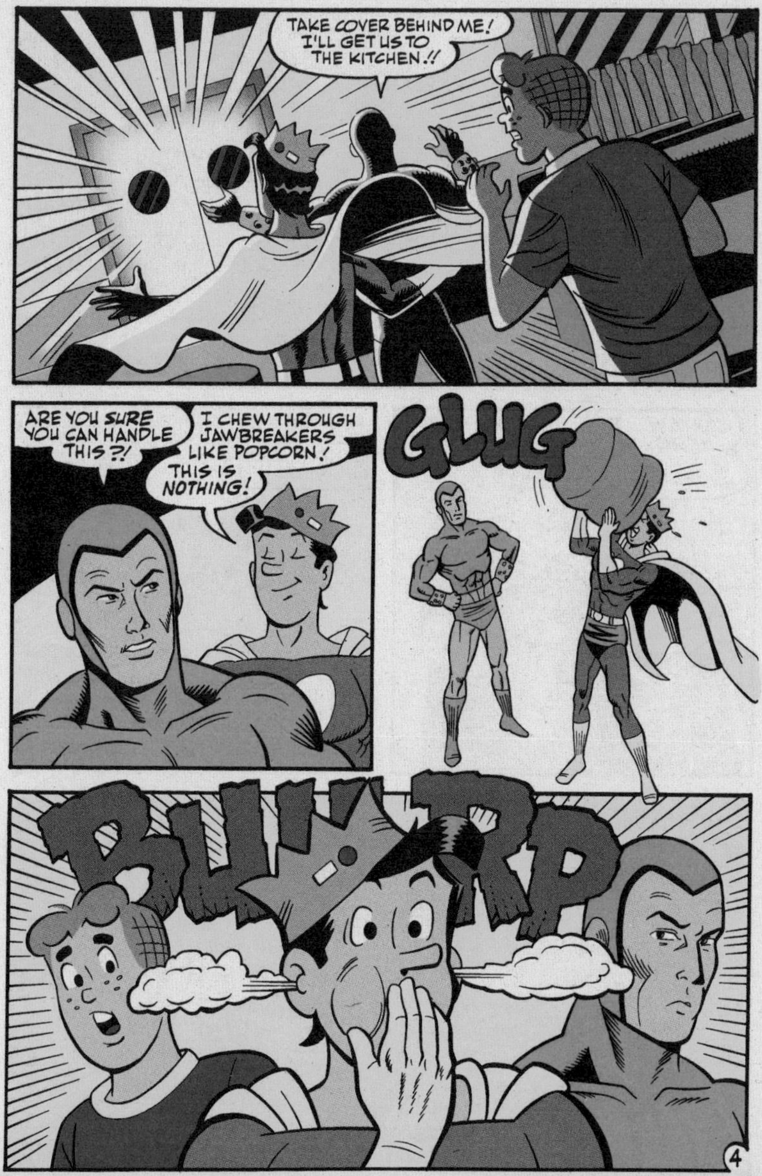
TAKE COVER BEHIND ME! I'LL GET US TO THE KITCHEN.!!
ARE YOU SURE YOU CAN HANDLE THIS?!
I CHEW THROUGH JAWBREAKERS LIKE POPCORN! THIS IS NOTHING!
GLUG
BUUURP

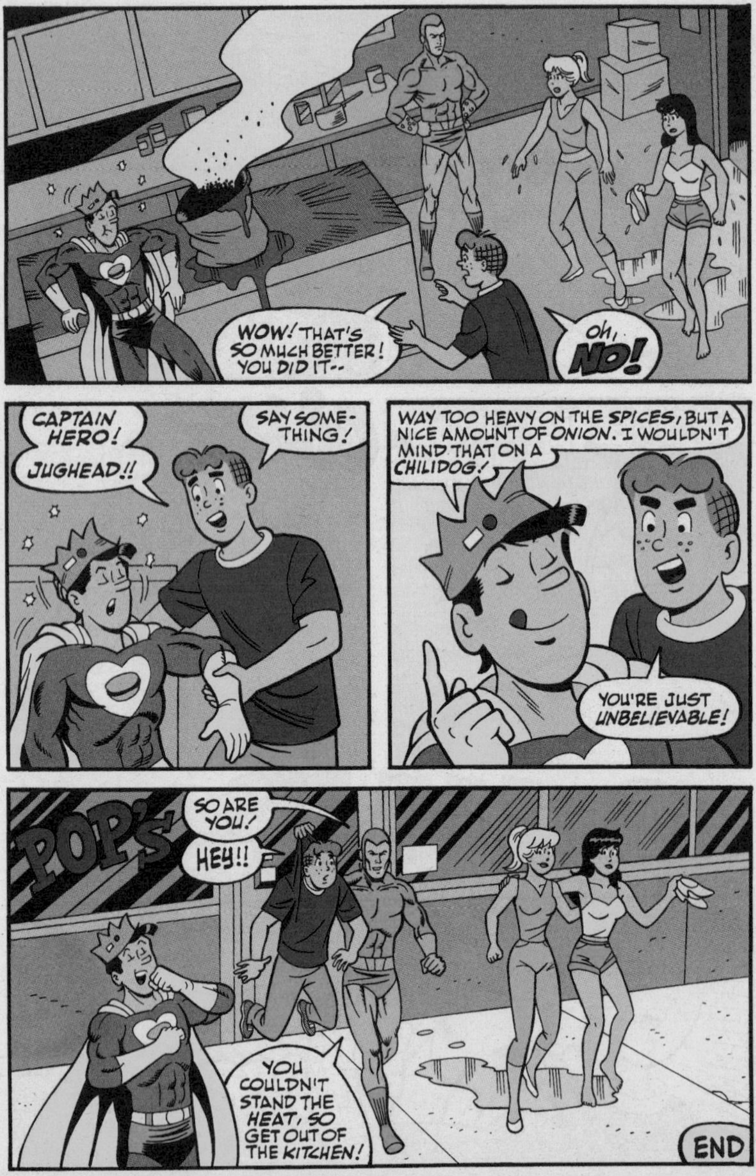
WOW! THAT'S SO MUCH BETTER! YOU DID IT--
Oh, NO!
CAPTAIN HERO!
JUGHEAD!!
SAY SOME-THING!
WAY TOO HEAVY ON THE SPICES, BUT A NICE AMOUNT OF ONION. I WOULDN'T MIND THAT ON A CHILIDOG!
YOU'RE JUST UNBELIEVABLE!
POP'S
SO ARE YOU!
HEY!!
YOU COULDN'T STAND THE HEAT, SO GET OUT OF THE KITCHEN!
END

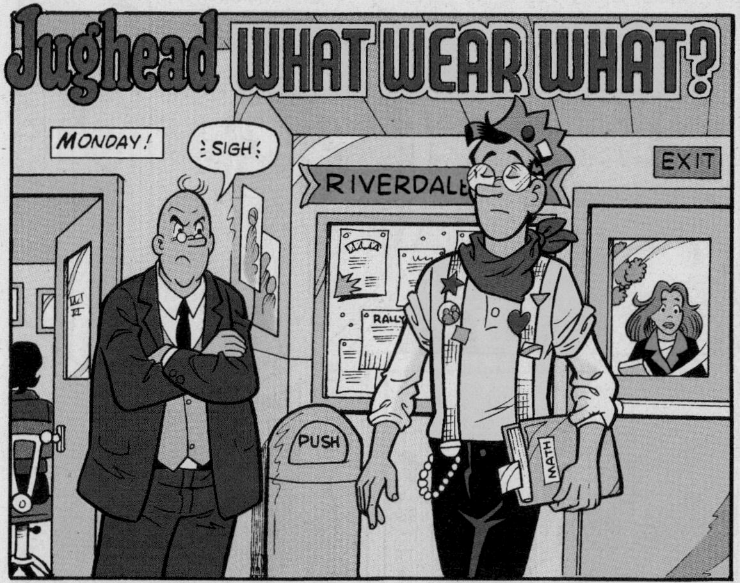
Jughead
WHAT WEAR WHAT?
MONDAY!
SIGH
RIVERDALE
EXIT
PUSH
RALLY
MATH

SCRIPT: CRAIG BOLDMAN PENCILS: REX LINDSEY INKING: RICH KOSLOWSKI LETTERING: BILL YOSHIDA COLORING: BARRY GROSSMAN

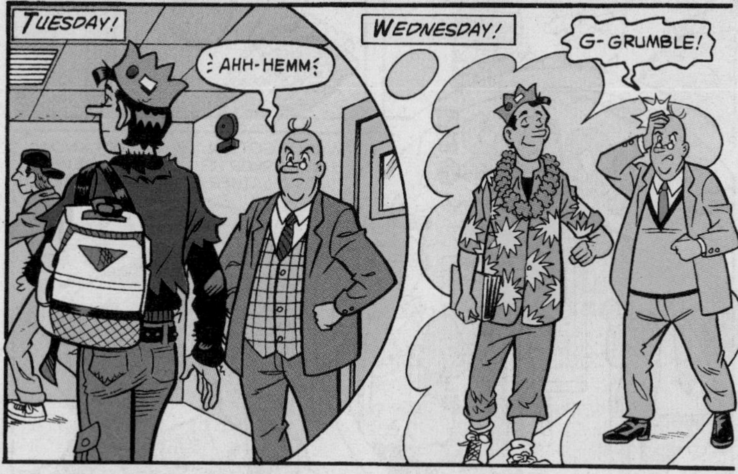
TUESDAY!
AHH-HEMM
WEDNESDAY!
G-GRUMBLE!

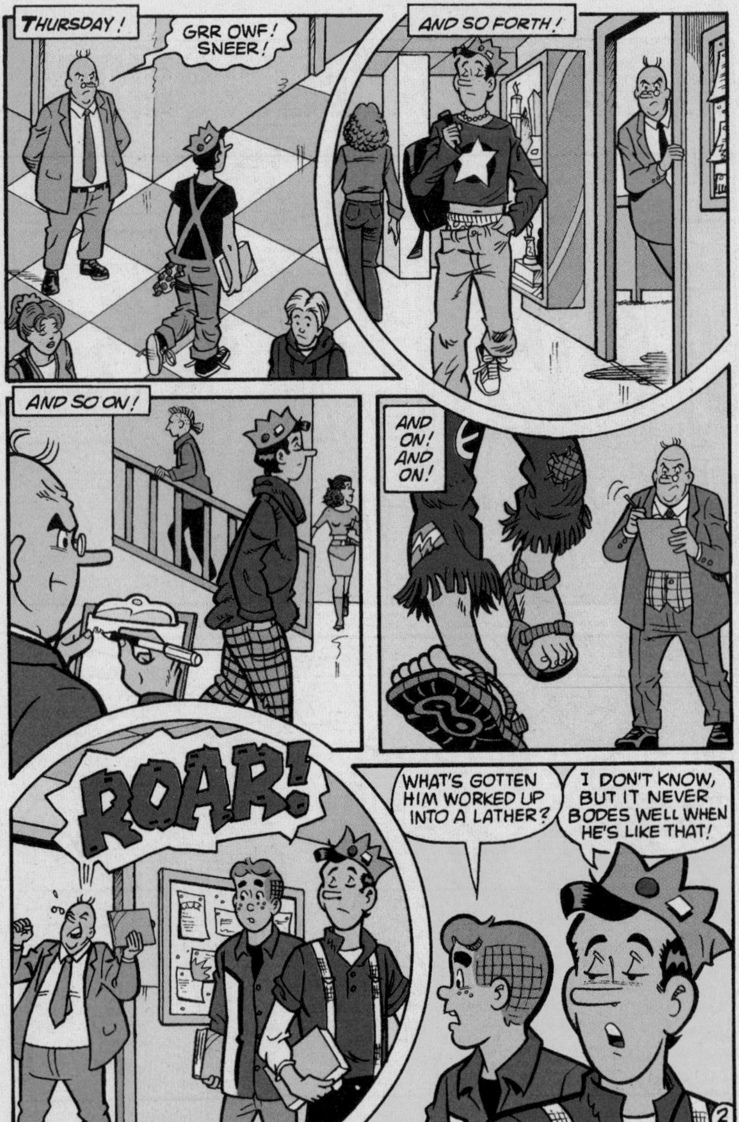
THURSDAY!
GRR OWF! SNEER!
AND SO FORTH!
AND SO ON!
AND ON! AND ON!
ROAR!
WHAT'S GOTTEN HIM WORKED UP INTO A LATHER?
I DON'T KNOW, BUT IT NEVER BODES WELL WHEN HE'S LIKE THAT!
2

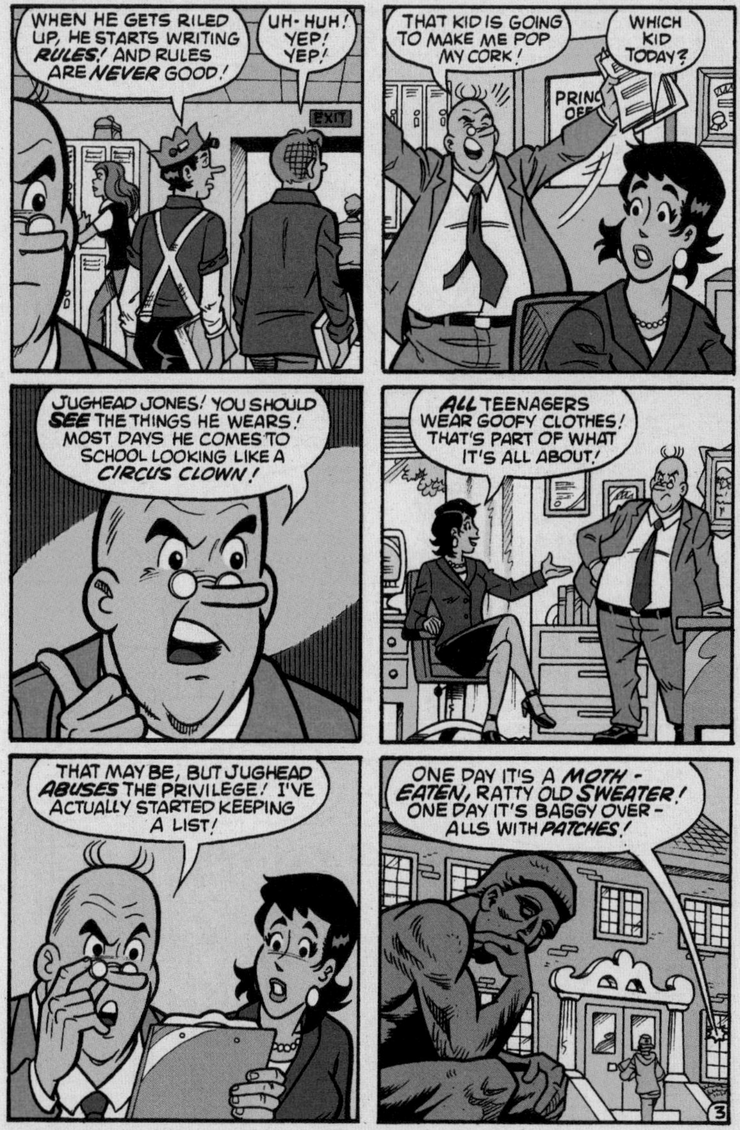
WHEN HE GETS RILED UP, HE STARTS WRITING RULES! AND RULES ARE NEVER GOOD!
UH-HUH! YEP! YEP!
EXIT
THAT KID IS GOING TO MAKE ME POP MY CORK!
WHICH KID TODAY?
JUGHEAD JONES! YOU SHOULD SEE THE THINGS HE WEARS! MOST DAYS HE COMES TO SCHOOL LOOKING LIKE A CIRCUS CLOWN!
ALL TEENAGERS WEAR GOOFY CLOTHES! THAT'S PART OF WHAT IT'S ALL ABOUT!
THAT MAY BE, BUT JUGHEAD ABUSES THE PRIVILEGE! I'VE ACTUALLY STARTED KEEPING A LIST!
ONE DAY IT'S A MOTH-EATEN, RATTY OLD SWEATER! ONE DAY IT'S BAGGY OVER-ALLS WITH PATCHES!
3

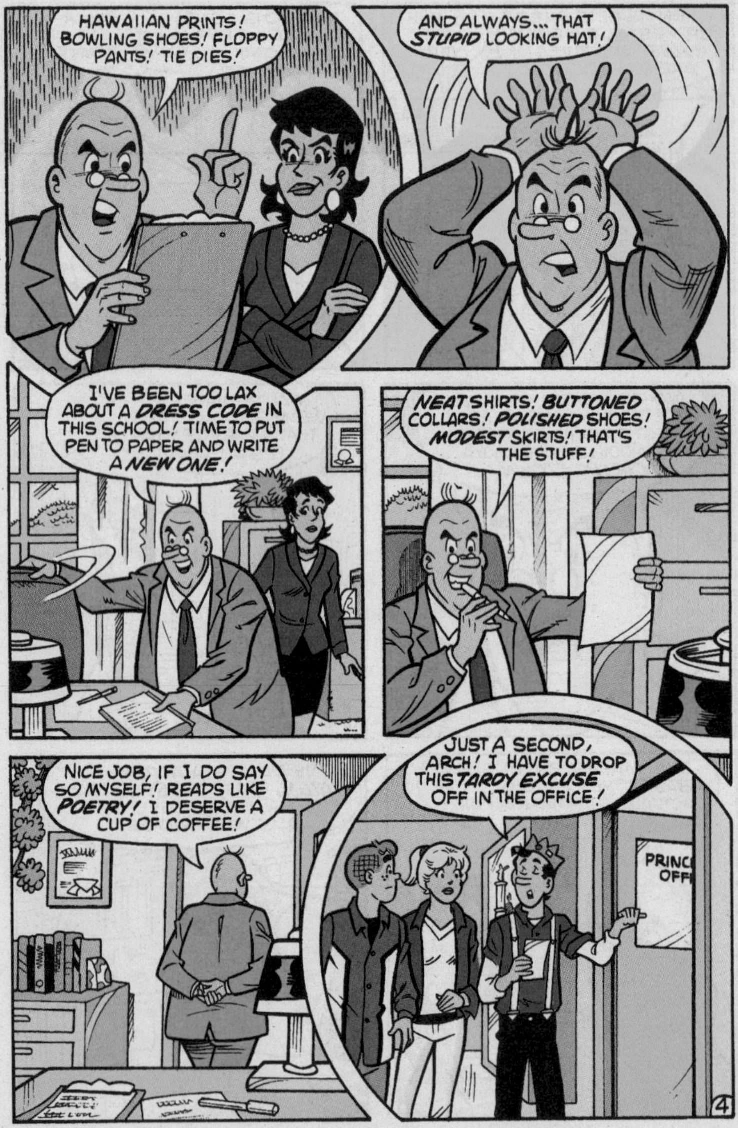
HAWAIIAN PRINTS! BOWLING SHOES! FLOPPY PANTS! TIE DIES!
AND ALWAYS... THAT STUPID LOOKING HAT!
I'VE BEEN TOO LAX ABOUT A DRESS CODE IN THIS SCHOOL! TIME TO PUT PEN TO PAPER AND WRITE A NEW ONE!
NEAT SHIRTS! BUTTONED COLLARS! POLISHED SHOES! MODEST SKIRTS! THAT'S THE STUFF!
NICE JOB, IF I DO SAY SO MYSELF! READS LIKE POETRY! I DESERVE A CUP OF COFFEE!
JUST A SECOND, ARCH! I HAVE TO DROP THIS TARDY EXCUSE OFF IN THE OFFICE!
PRINC
OFF
4

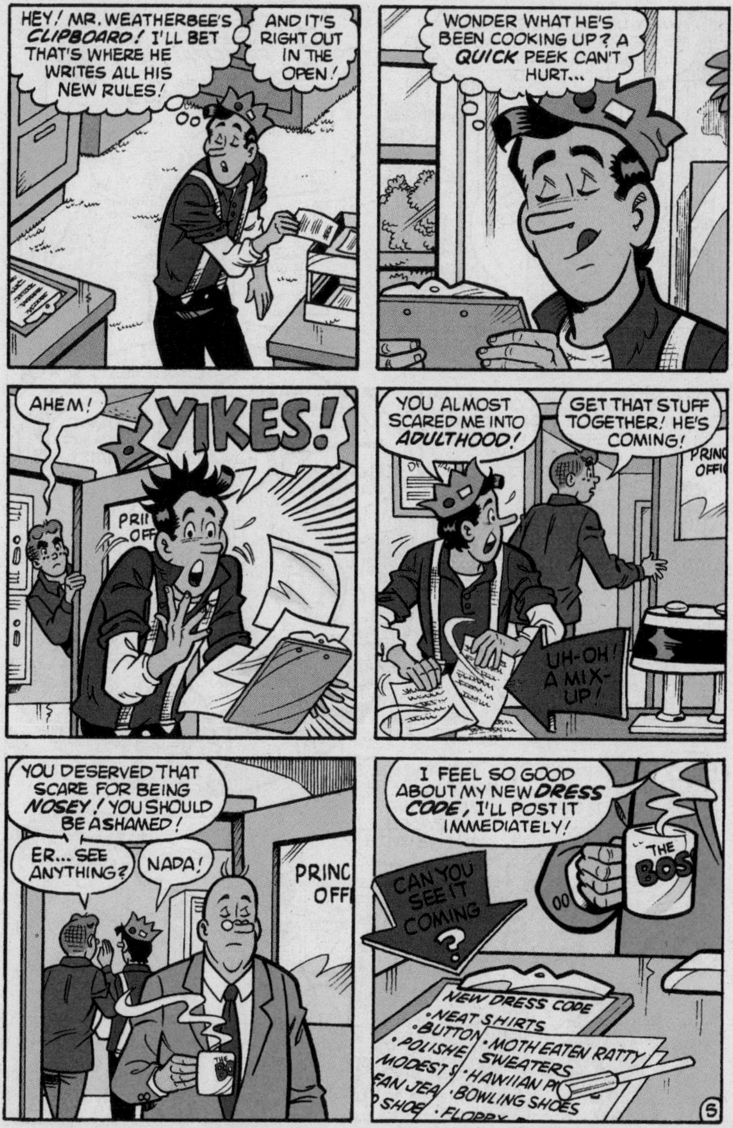
HEY! MR. WEATHERBEE'S CLIPBOARD! I'LL BET THAT'S WHERE HE WRITES ALL HIS NEW RULES!
AND IT'S RIGHT OUT IN THE OPEN!
WONDER WHAT HE'S BEEN COOKING UP? A QUICK PEEK CAN'T HURT...
AHEM!
YIKES!
PRI
OFF
YOU ALMOST SCARED ME INTO ADULTHOOD!
GET THAT STUFF TOGETHER! HE'S COMING!
PRINC
OFFI
UH-OH! A MIX-UP!
YOU DESERVED THAT SCARE FOR BEING NOSEY! YOU SHOULD BE ASHAMED!
ER... SEE ANYTHING?
NADA!
PRINC
OFF
I FEEL SO GOOD ABOUT MY NEW DRESS CODE, I'LL POST IT IMMEDIATELY!
THE BOS
CAN YOU SEE IT COMING ?
NEW DRESS CODE
•NEAT SHIRTS
•BUTTON
•POLISHE
MODEST S
EAN JEA
SHOE
•MOTH EATEN RATTY SWEATERS
•HAWIIAN P
•BOWLING SHOES
•FLOPPY
5

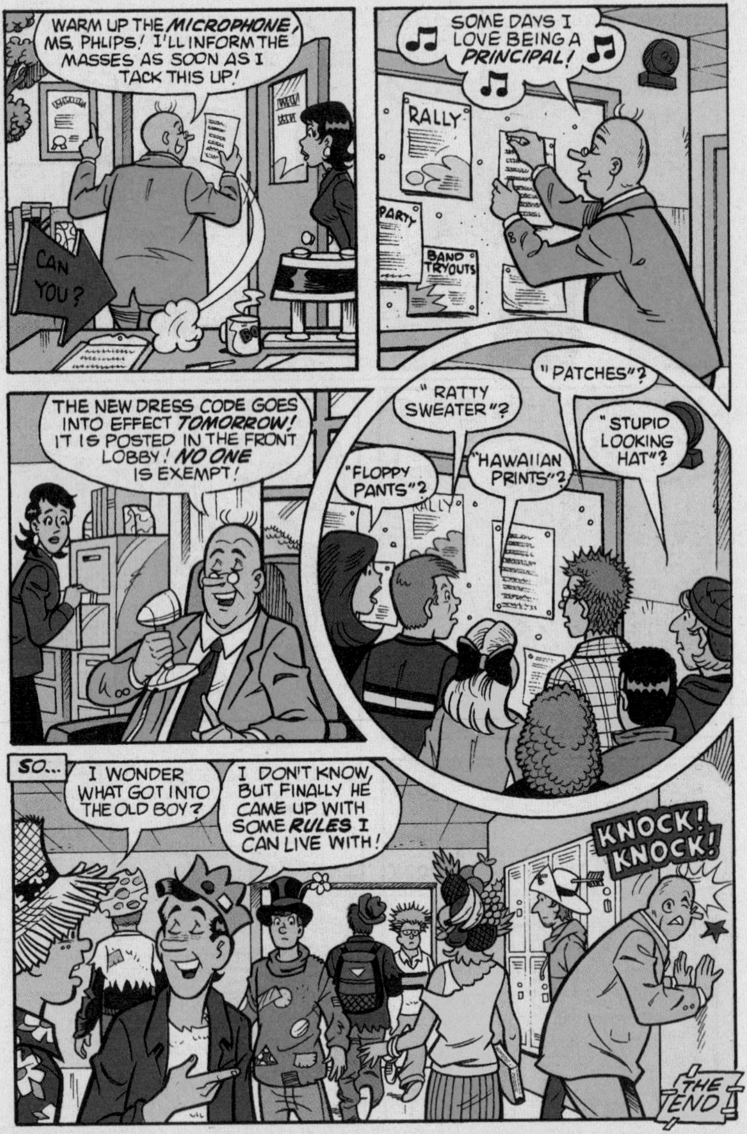
WARM UP THE MICROPHONE, MS. PHLIPS! I'LL INFORM THE MASSES AS SOON AS I TACK THIS UP!
CAN YOU?
SOME DAYS I LOVE BEING A PRINCIPAL!
RALLY
PARTY
BAND TRYOUTS
THE NEW DRESS CODE GOES INTO EFFECT TOMORROW! IT IS POSTED IN THE FRONT LOBBY! NO ONE IS EXEMPT!
"FLOPPY PANTS"?
"RATTY SWEATER"?
"HAWAIIAN PRINTS"?
"PATCHES"?
"STUPID LOOKING HAT"?
SO...
I WONDER WHAT GOT INTO THE OLD BOY?
I DON'T KNOW, BUT FINALLY HE CAME UP WITH SOME RULES I CAN LIVE WITH!
KNOCK! KNOCK!
THE END

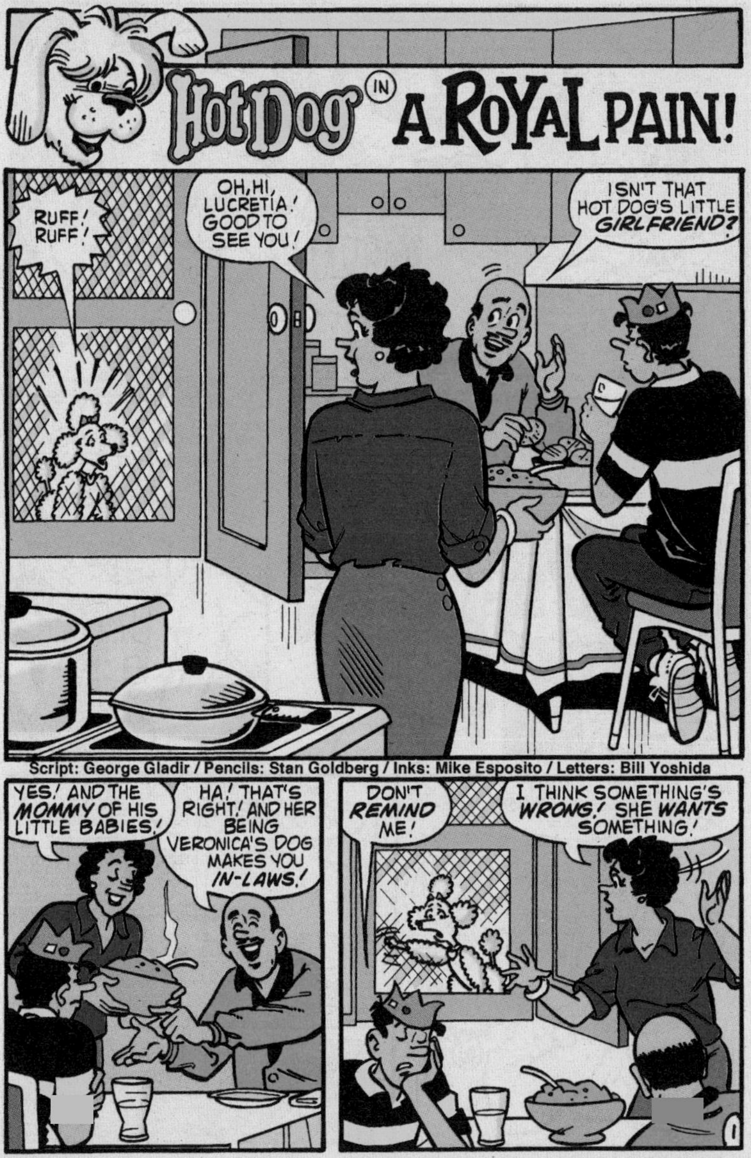
Hot Dog IN A ROYAL PAIN!
RUFF! RUFF!
OH, HI, LUCRETIA! GOOD TO SEE YOU!
ISN'T THAT HOT DOG'S LITTLE GIRLFRIEND?
Script: George Gladir / Pencils: Stan Goldberg / Inks: Mike Esposito / Letters: Bill Yoshida
YES! AND THE MOMMY OF HIS LITTLE BABIES!
HA! THAT'S RIGHT! AND HER BEING VERONICA'S DOG MAKES YOU IN-LAWS!
DON'T REMIND ME!
I THINK SOMETHING'S WRONG! SHE WANTS SOMETHING!
1

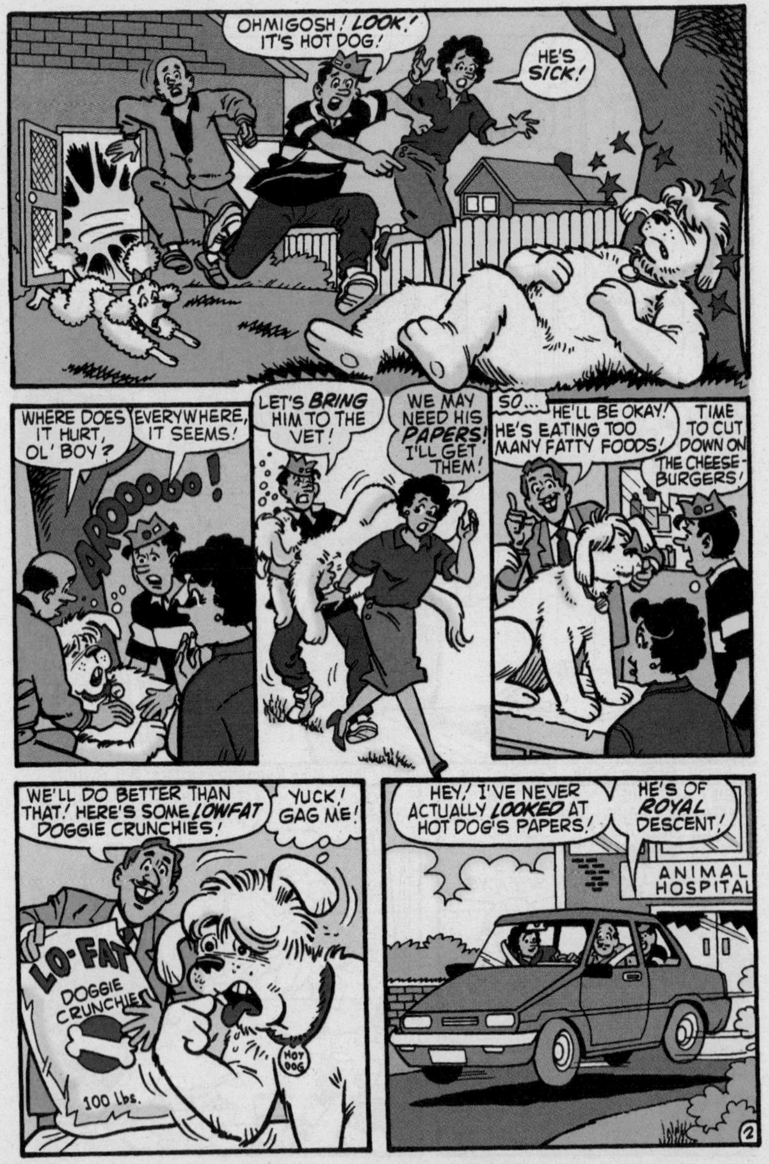
OHMIGOSH! LOOK! IT'S HOT DOG!
HE'S SICK!
WHERE DOES IT HURT, OL' BOY?
EVERYWHERE, IT SEEMS!
AROOOOOO!
LET'S BRING HIM TO THE VET!
WE MAY NEED HIS PAPERS! I'LL GET THEM!
SO...
HE'LL BE OKAY! HE'S EATING TOO MANY FATTY FOODS!
TIME TO CUT DOWN ON THE CHEESE-BURGERS!
WE'LL DO BETTER THAN THAT! HERE'S SOME LOWFAT DOGGIE CRUNCHIES!
YUCK! GAG ME!
LO-FAT
DOGGIE CRUNCHIES
100 lbs.
HOT DOG
HEY! I'VE NEVER ACTUALLY LOOKED AT HOT DOG'S PAPERS!
HE'S OF ROYAL DESCENT!
ANIMAL HOSPITAL
2

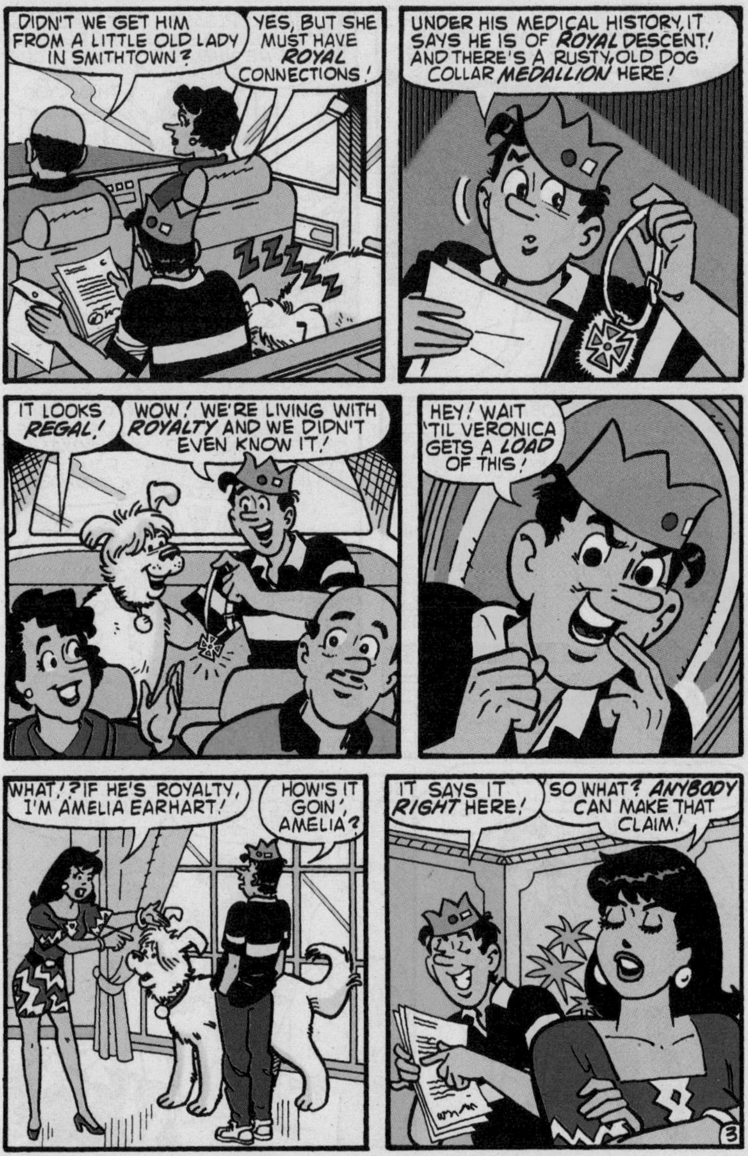
DIDN'T WE GET HIM FROM A LITTLE OLD LADY IN SMITHTOWN?
YES, BUT SHE MUST HAVE ROYAL CONNECTIONS!
ZZZZZ
UNDER HIS MEDICAL HISTORY, IT SAYS HE IS OF ROYAL DESCENT! AND THERE'S A RUSTY, OLD DOG COLLAR MEDALLION HERE!
IT LOOKS REGAL!
WOW! WE'RE LIVING WITH ROYALTY AND WE DIDN'T EVEN KNOW IT!
HEY! WAIT 'TIL VERONICA GETS A LOAD OF THIS!
WHAT!? IF HE'S ROYALTY, I'M AMELIA EARHART!
HOW'S IT GOIN', AMELIA?
IT SAYS IT RIGHT HERE!
SO WHAT? ANYBODY CAN MAKE THAT CLAIM!
3

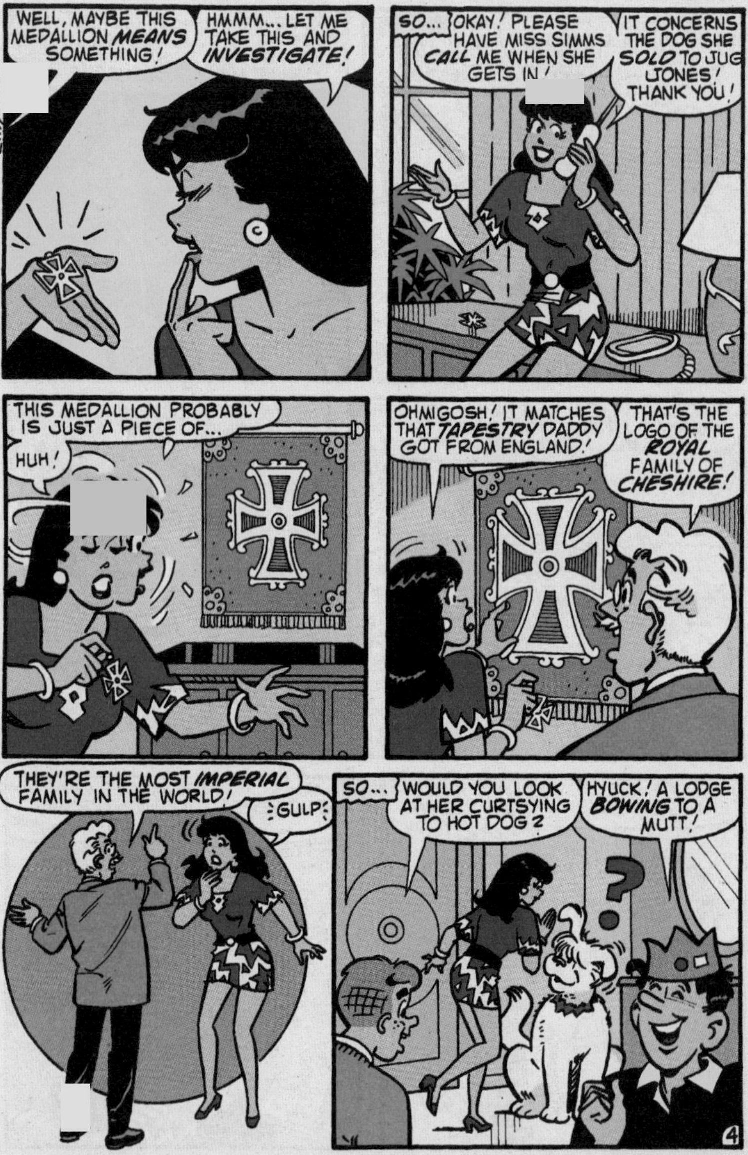

WELL, MAYBE THIS MEDALLION *MEANS* SOMETHING!
HMMM... LET ME TAKE THIS AND *INVESTIGATE*!
SO...
OKAY! PLEASE HAVE MISS SIMMS *CALL* ME WHEN SHE GETS IN!
IT CONCERNS THE DOG SHE *SOLD* TO JUG JONES! THANK YOU!
THIS MEDALLION PROBABLY IS JUST A PIECE OF...
HUH!
OHMIGOSH! IT MATCHES THAT *TAPESTRY* DADDY GOT FROM ENGLAND!
THAT'S THE LOGO OF THE *ROYAL* FAMILY OF *CHESHIRE*!
THEY'RE THE MOST *IMPERIAL* FAMILY IN THE WORLD!
GULP!
SO...
WOULD YOU LOOK AT HER CURTSYING TO HOT DOG?
HYUCK! A LODGE *BOWING* TO A MUTT!
?

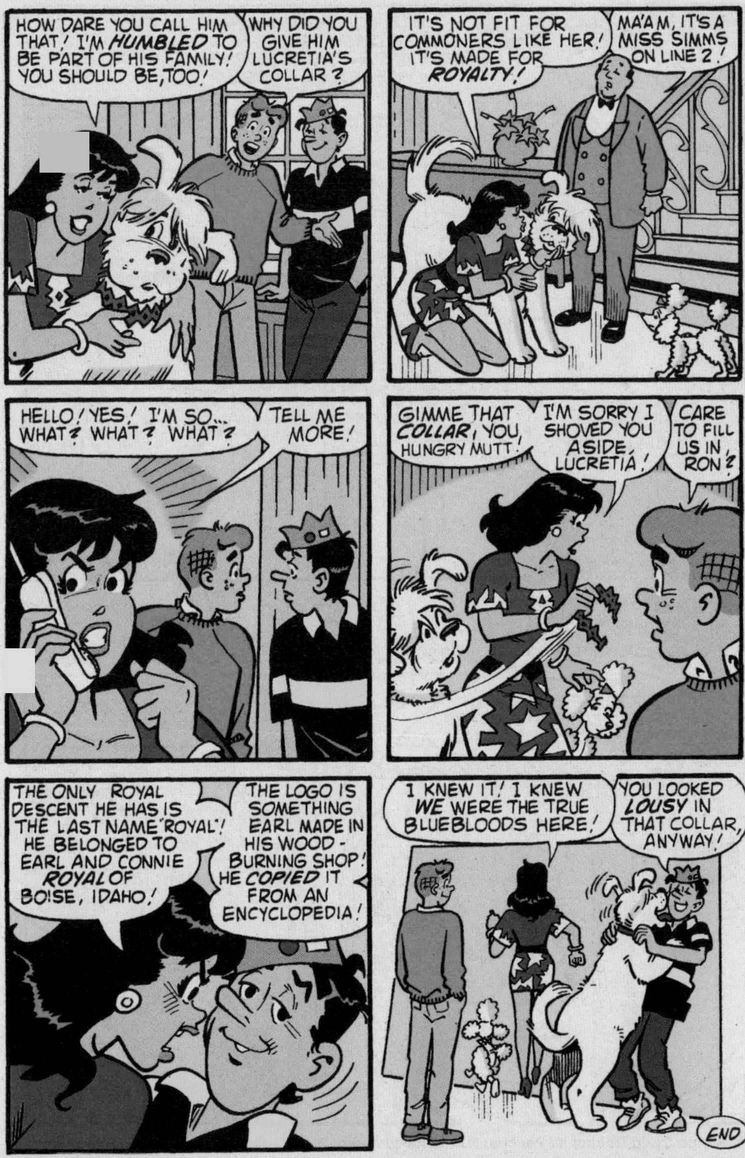

HOW DARE YOU CALL HIM THAT! I'M *HUMBLED* TO BE PART OF HIS FAMILY! YOU SHOULD BE, TOO!
WHY DID YOU GIVE HIM LUCRETIA'S COLLAR?
IT'S NOT FIT FOR COMMONERS LIKE HER! IT'S MADE FOR *ROYALTY*!
MA'AM, IT'S A MISS SIMMS ON LINE 2!
HELLO! YES! I'M SO... WHAT? WHAT? WHAT?
TELL ME MORE!
GIMME THAT *COLLAR*, YOU HUNGRY MUTT!
I'M SORRY I SHOVED YOU ASIDE, LUCRETIA!
CARE TO FILL US IN, RON?
THE ONLY ROYAL DESCENT HE HAS IS THE LAST NAME "ROYAL"! HE BELONGED TO EARL AND CONNIE *ROYAL* OF BOISE, IDAHO!
THE LOGO IS SOMETHING EARL MADE IN HIS WOOD-BURNING SHOP! HE *COPIED* IT FROM AN ENCYCLOPEDIA!
I KNEW IT! I KNEW *WE* WERE THE TRUE BLUEBLOODS HERE!
YOU LOOKED *LOUSY* IN THAT COLLAR, ANYWAY!
END

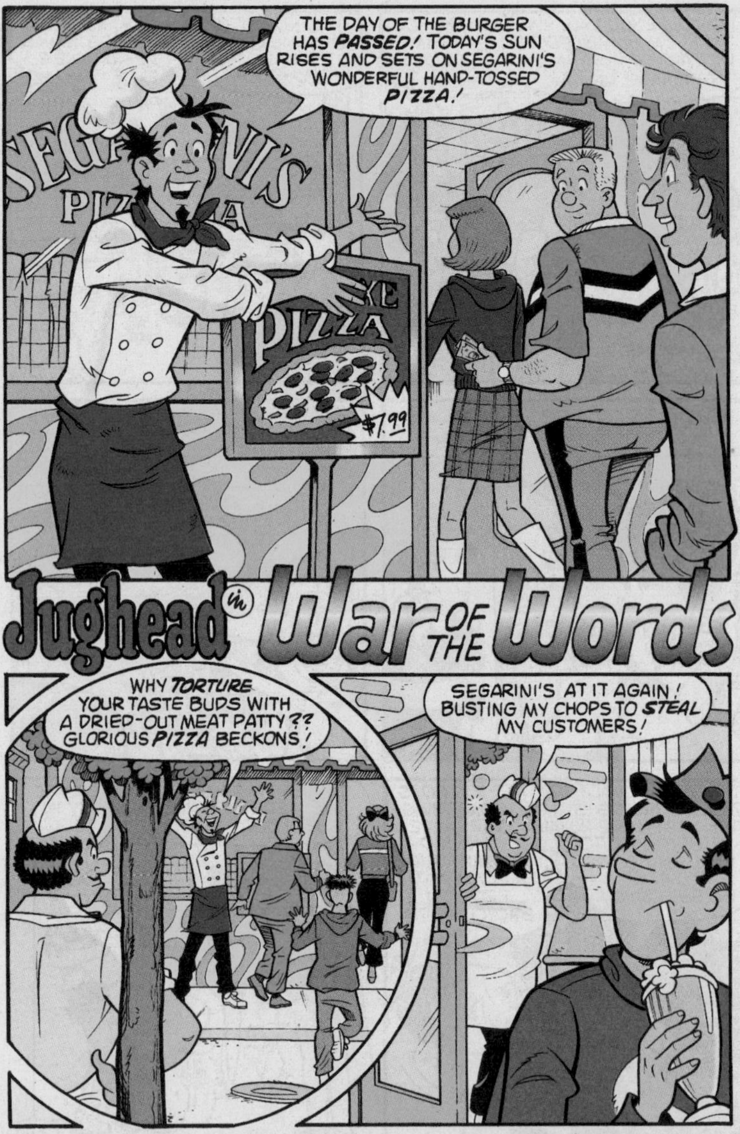
THE DAY OF THE BURGER HAS PASSED! TODAY'S SUN RISES AND SETS ON SEGARINI'S WONDERFUL HAND-TOSSED PIZZA!
SEGARINI'S PIZZA
PIZZA
$7.99
Jughead in War OF THE Words
WHY TORTURE YOUR TASTE BUDS WITH A DRIED-OUT MEAT PATTY?? GLORIOUS PIZZA BECKONS!
SEGARINI'S AT IT AGAIN! BUSTING MY CHOPS TO STEAL MY CUSTOMERS!

Script: Craig Boldman / Pencils: Rex Lindsey / Inks: Rich Koslowski / Letters: Bill Yoshida

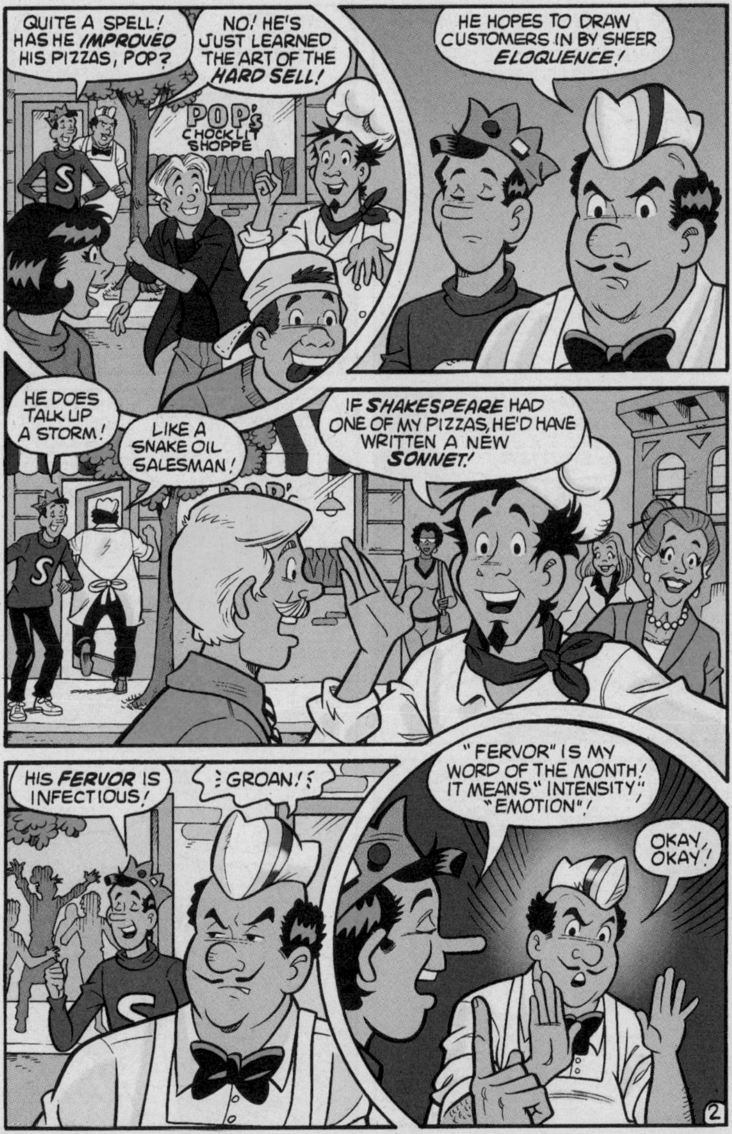

QUITE A SPELL! HAS HE *IMPROVED* HIS PIZZAS, POP?
NO! HE'S JUST LEARNED THE ART OF THE *HARD SELL!*
POP'S CHOCKLIT SHOPPE
HE HOPES TO DRAW CUSTOMERS IN BY SHEER *ELOQUENCE!*
HE DOES TALK UP A STORM!
LIKE A SNAKE OIL SALESMAN!
IF *SHAKESPEARE* HAD ONE OF MY PIZZAS, HE'D HAVE WRITTEN A NEW *SONNET!*
HIS *FERVOR* IS INFECTIOUS!
GROAN!
"FERVOR" IS MY WORD OF THE MONTH! IT MEANS "INTENSITY", "EMOTION"!
OKAY, OKAY!
2

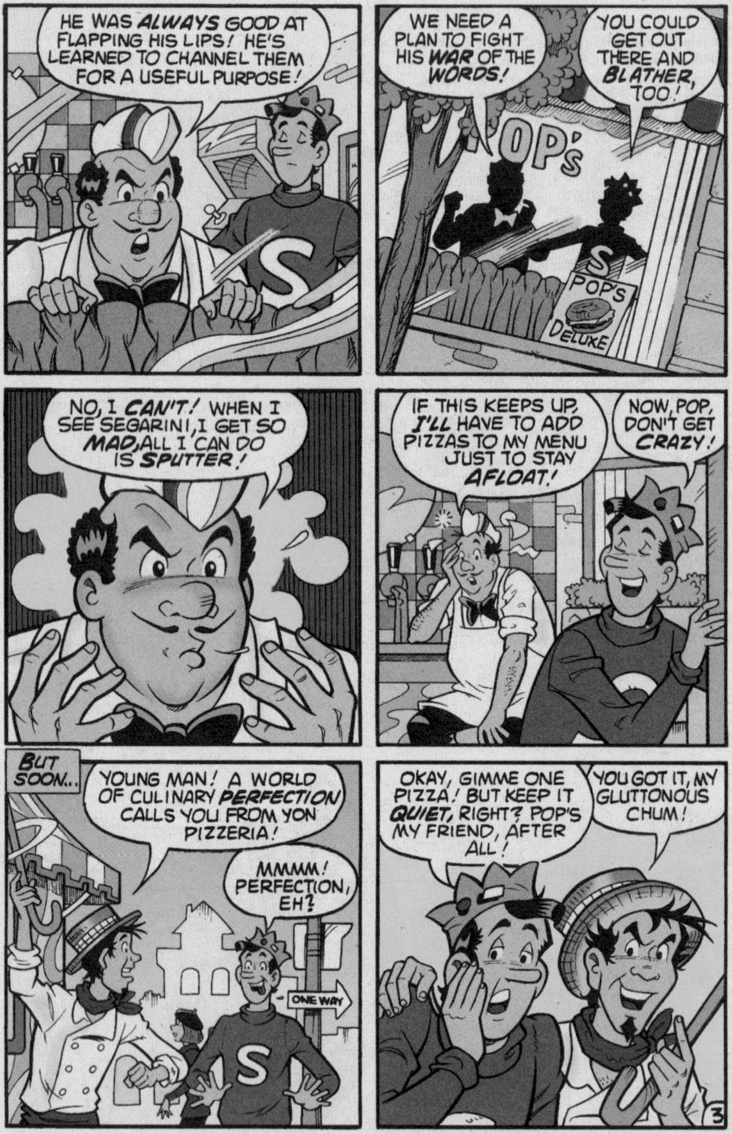
HE WAS ALWAYS GOOD AT FLAPPING HIS LIPS! HE'S LEARNED TO CHANNEL THEM FOR A USEFUL PURPOSE!
WE NEED A PLAN TO FIGHT HIS WAR OF THE WORDS!
YOU COULD GET OUT THERE AND BLATHER, TOO!
POP'S
POP'S DELUXE
NO, I CAN'T! WHEN I SEE SEGARINI, I GET SO MAD, ALL I CAN DO IS SPUTTER!
IF THIS KEEPS UP, I'LL HAVE TO ADD PIZZAS TO MY MENU JUST TO STAY AFLOAT!
NOW, POP, DON'T GET CRAZY!
BUT SOON...
YOUNG MAN! A WORLD OF CULINARY PERFECTION CALLS YOU FROM YON PIZZERIA!
MMMM! PERFECTION, EH?
ONE WAY
OKAY, GIMME ONE PIZZA! BUT KEEP IT QUIET, RIGHT? POP'S MY FRIEND, AFTER ALL!
YOU GOT IT, MY GLUTTONOUS CHUM!
3

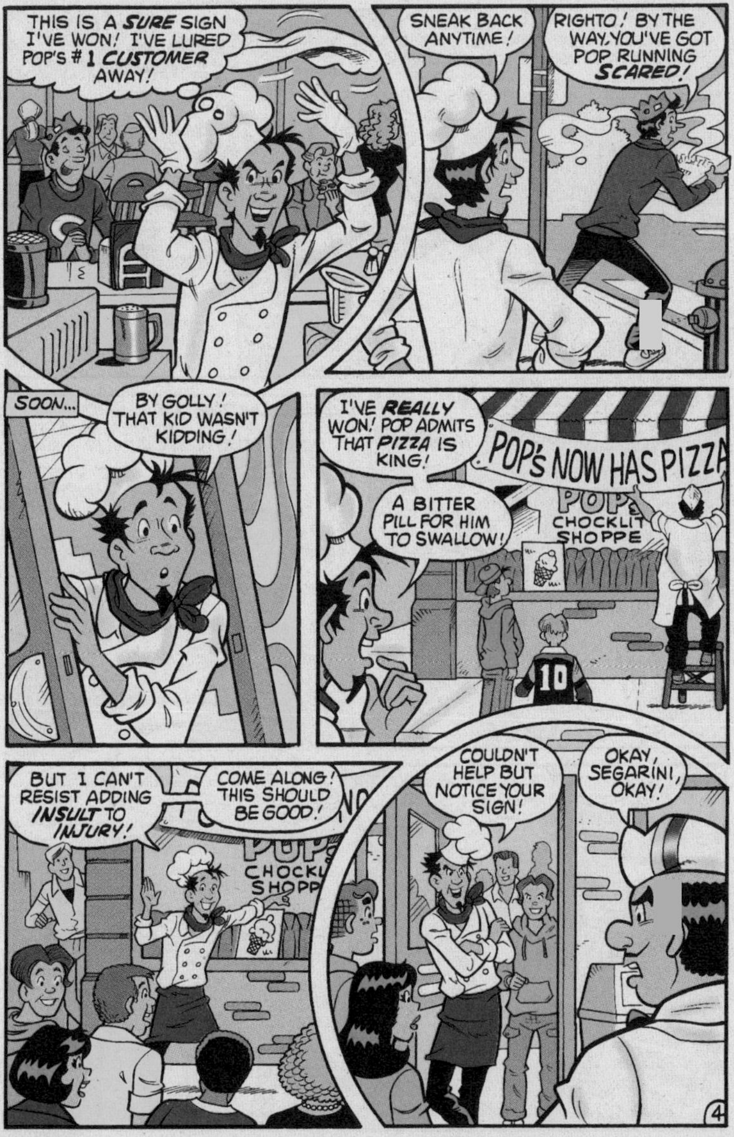
THIS IS A SURE SIGN I'VE WON! I'VE LURED POP'S #1 CUSTOMER AWAY!
SNEAK BACK ANYTIME!
RIGHTO! BY THE WAY, YOU'VE GOT POP RUNNING SCARED!
SOON...
BY GOLLY! THAT KID WASN'T KIDDING!
I'VE REALLY WON! POP ADMITS THAT PIZZA IS KING!
A BITTER PILL FOR HIM TO SWALLOW!
POP'S NOW HAS PIZZA
POP'S CHOCKLIT SHOPPE
10
BUT I CAN'T RESIST ADDING INSULT TO INJURY!
COME ALONG! THIS SHOULD BE GOOD!
COULDN'T HELP BUT NOTICE YOUR SIGN!
OKAY, SEGARINI, OKAY!

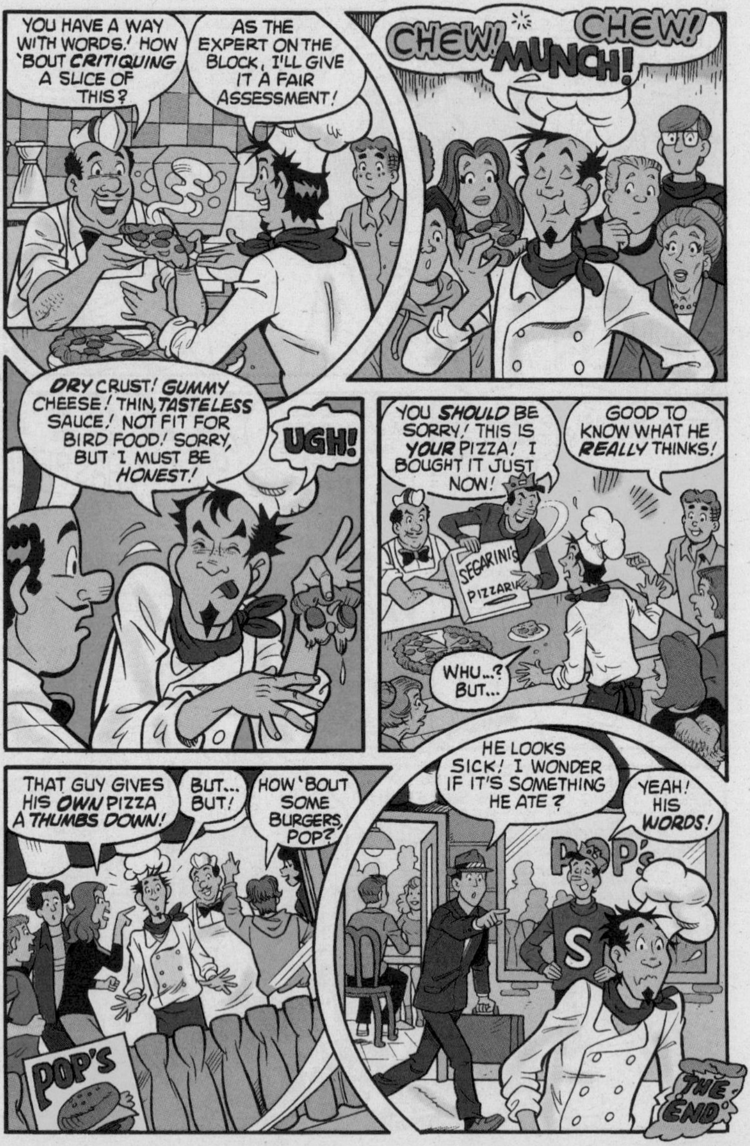
YOU HAVE A WAY WITH WORDS! HOW 'BOUT CRITIQUING A SLICE OF THIS?
AS THE EXPERT ON THE BLOCK, I'LL GIVE IT A FAIR ASSESSMENT!
CHEW! MUNCH! CHEW!
DRY CRUST! GUMMY CHEESE! THIN, TASTELESS SAUCE! NOT FIT FOR BIRD FOOD! SORRY, BUT I MUST BE HONEST!
UGH!
YOU SHOULD BE SORRY! THIS IS YOUR PIZZA! I BOUGHT IT JUST NOW!
GOOD TO KNOW WHAT HE REALLY THINKS!
SEGARINI'S PIZZARIA
WHU...? BUT...
THAT GUY GIVES HIS OWN PIZZA A THUMBS DOWN!
BUT... BUT!
HOW 'BOUT SOME BURGERS, POP?
POP'S
HE LOOKS SICK! I WONDER IF IT'S SOMETHING HE ATE?
YEAH! HIS WORDS!
POP'S
THE END

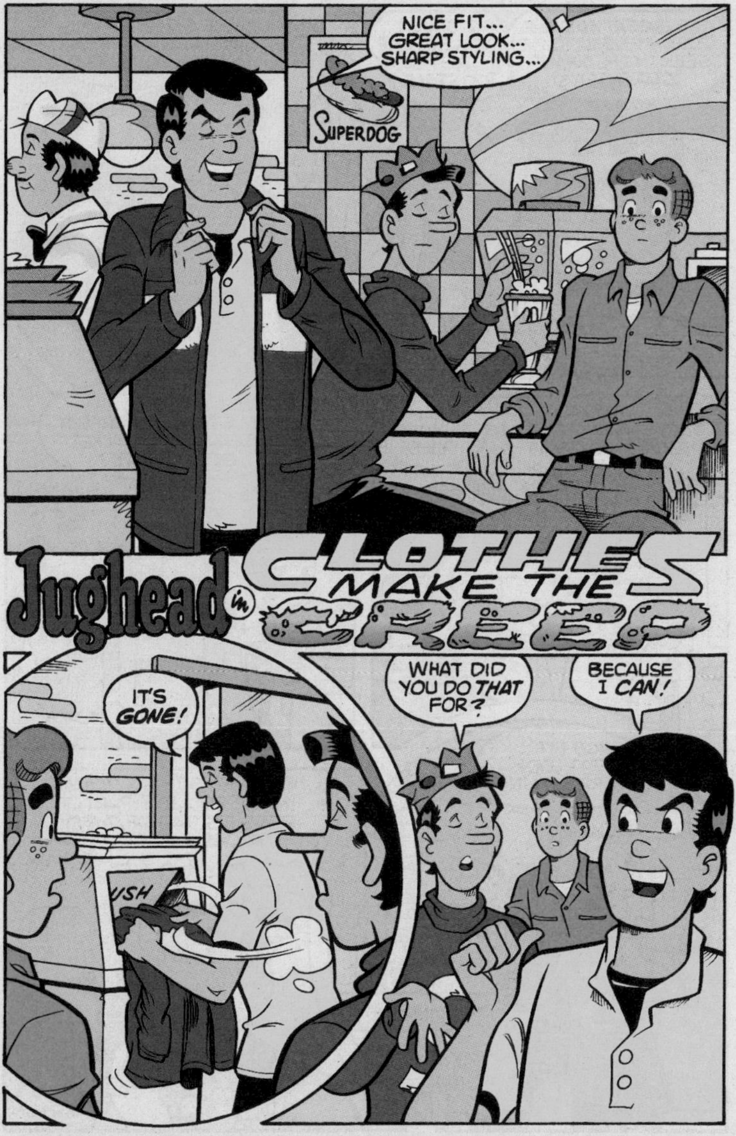

NICE FIT... GREAT LOOK... SHARP STYLING...
SUPERDOG
Jughead in CLOTHES MAKE THE CREEP
IT'S GONE!
WHAT DID YOU DO THAT FOR?
BECAUSE I CAN!

Script: Craig Boldman / Pencils: Rex Lindsey / Inks: Rich Koslowski / Letters: Bill Yoshida

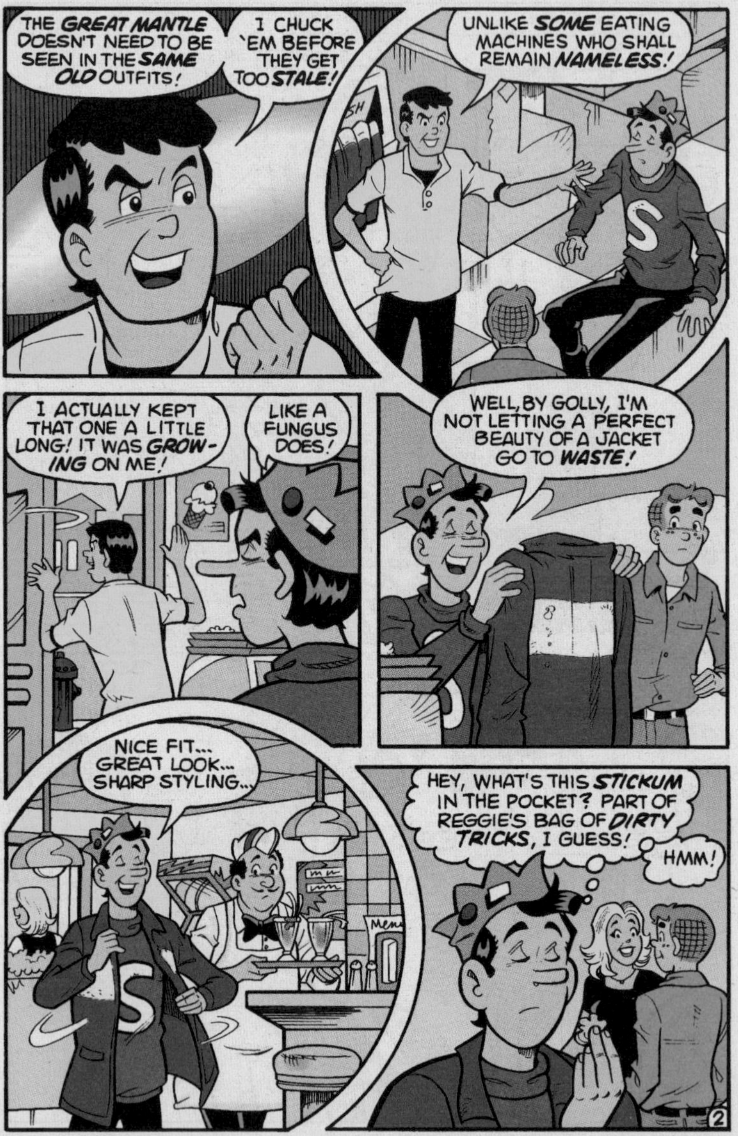
THE GREAT MANTLE DOESN'T NEED TO BE SEEN IN THE SAME OLD OUTFITS!
I CHUCK 'EM BEFORE THEY GET TOO STALE!
UNLIKE SOME EATING MACHINES WHO SHALL REMAIN NAMELESS!
I ACTUALLY KEPT THAT ONE A LITTLE LONG! IT WAS GROW-ING ON ME!
LIKE A FUNGUS DOES!
WELL, BY GOLLY, I'M NOT LETTING A PERFECT BEAUTY OF A JACKET GO TO WASTE!
NICE FIT... GREAT LOOK... SHARP STYLING...
HEY, WHAT'S THIS STICKUM IN THE POCKET? PART OF REGGIE'S BAG OF DIRTY TRICKS, I GUESS!
HMM!
2

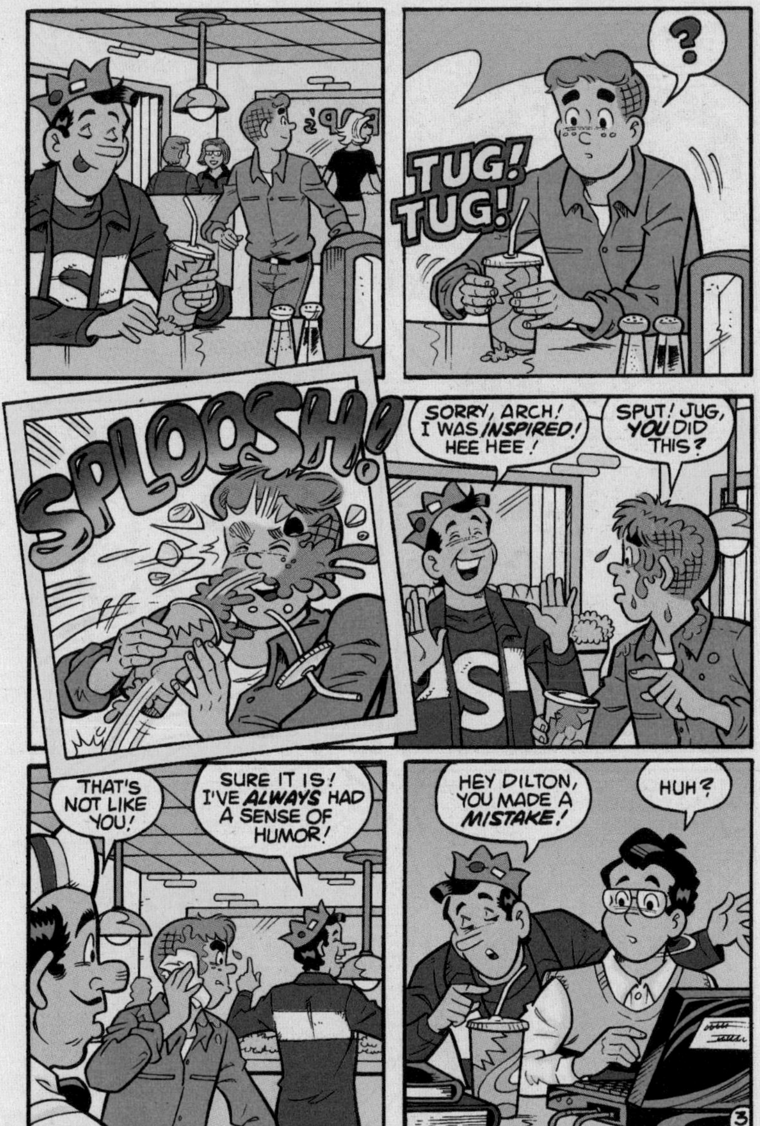

?
TUG! TUG!
SPLOOSH!
SORRY, ARCH! I WAS *INSPIRED*! HEE HEE!
SPUT! JUG, *YOU* DID THIS?
THAT'S NOT LIKE YOU!
SURE IT IS! I'VE *ALWAYS* HAD A SENSE OF HUMOR!
HEY DILTON, YOU MADE A *MISTAKE*!
HUH?

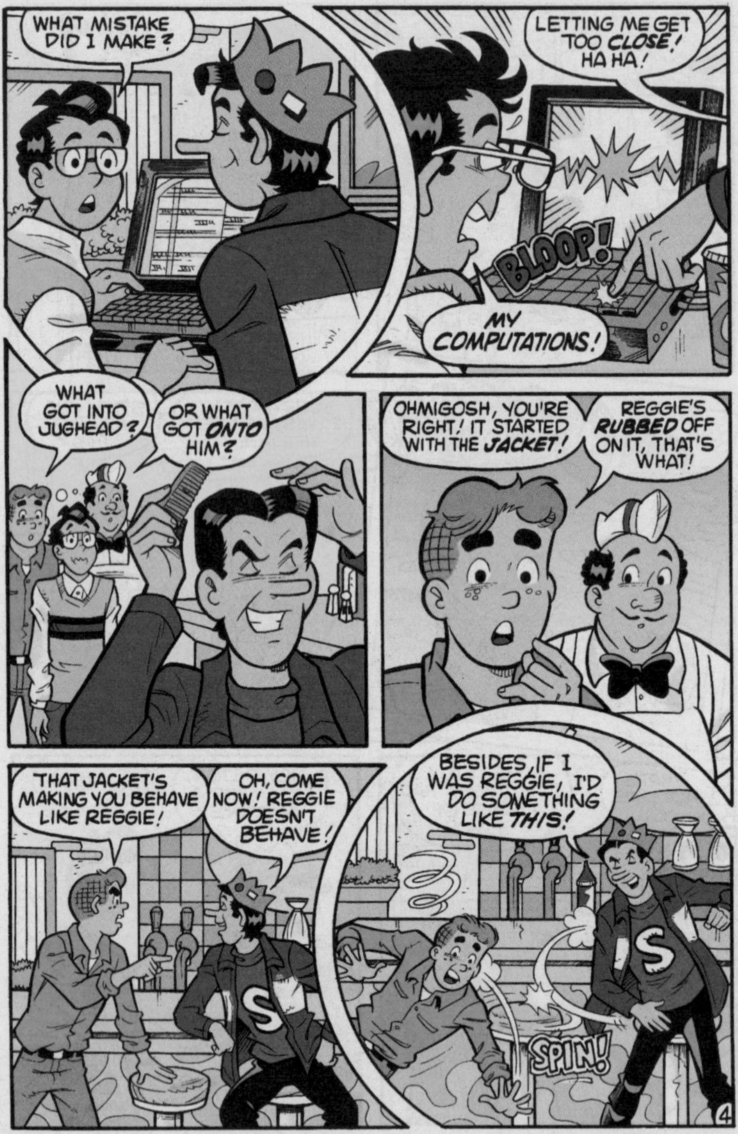
WHAT MISTAKE DID I MAKE?
LETTING ME GET TOO CLOSE! HA HA!
BLOOP!
MY COMPUTATIONS!
WHAT GOT INTO JUGHEAD?
OR WHAT GOT ONTO HIM?
OHMIGOSH, YOU'RE RIGHT! IT STARTED WITH THE JACKET!
REGGIE'S RUBBED OFF ON IT, THAT'S WHAT!
THAT JACKET'S MAKING YOU BEHAVE LIKE REGGIE!
OH, COME NOW! REGGIE DOESN'T BEHAVE!
BESIDES, IF I WAS REGGIE, I'D DO SOMETHING LIKE THIS!
SPIN!
4

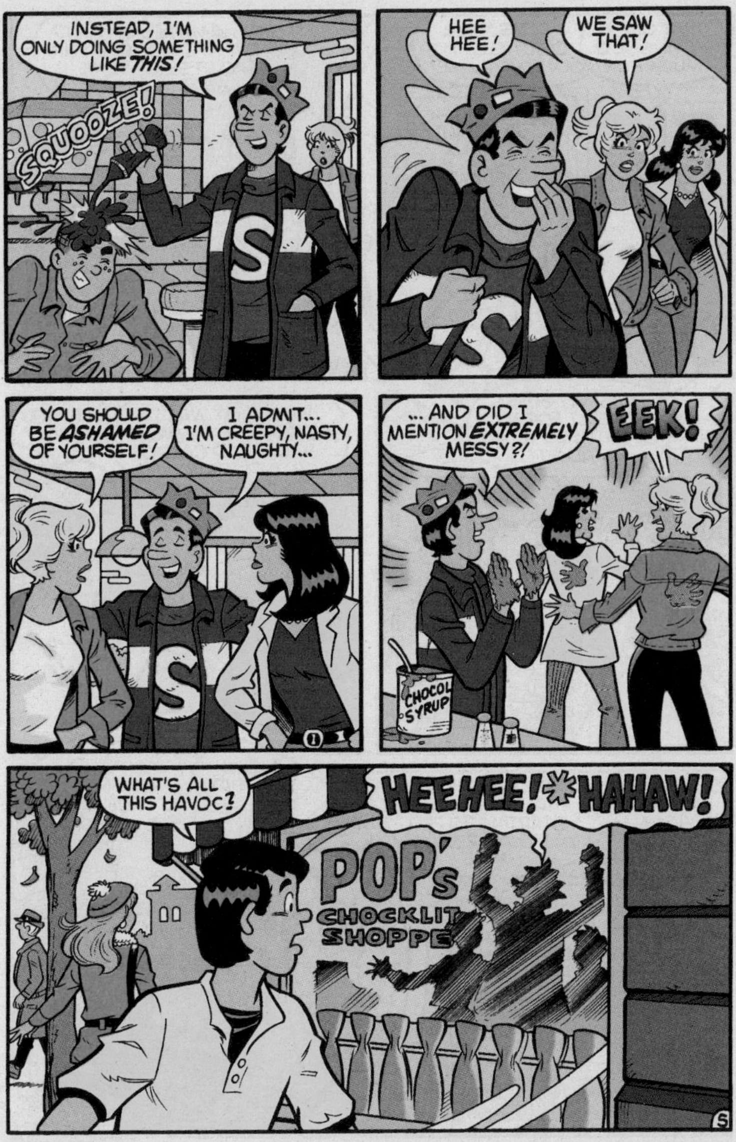
INSTEAD, I'M ONLY DOING SOMETHING LIKE THIS!
SQUOOZE!
HEE HEE!
WE SAW THAT!
YOU SHOULD BE ASHAMED OF YOURSELF!
I ADMIT... I'M CREEPY, NASTY, NAUGHTY...
... AND DID I MENTION EXTREMELY MESSY?!
EEK!
CHOCOL SYRUP
WHAT'S ALL THIS HAVOC?
HEE HEE! * HAHAW!
POP's CHOCKLIT SHOPPE
5

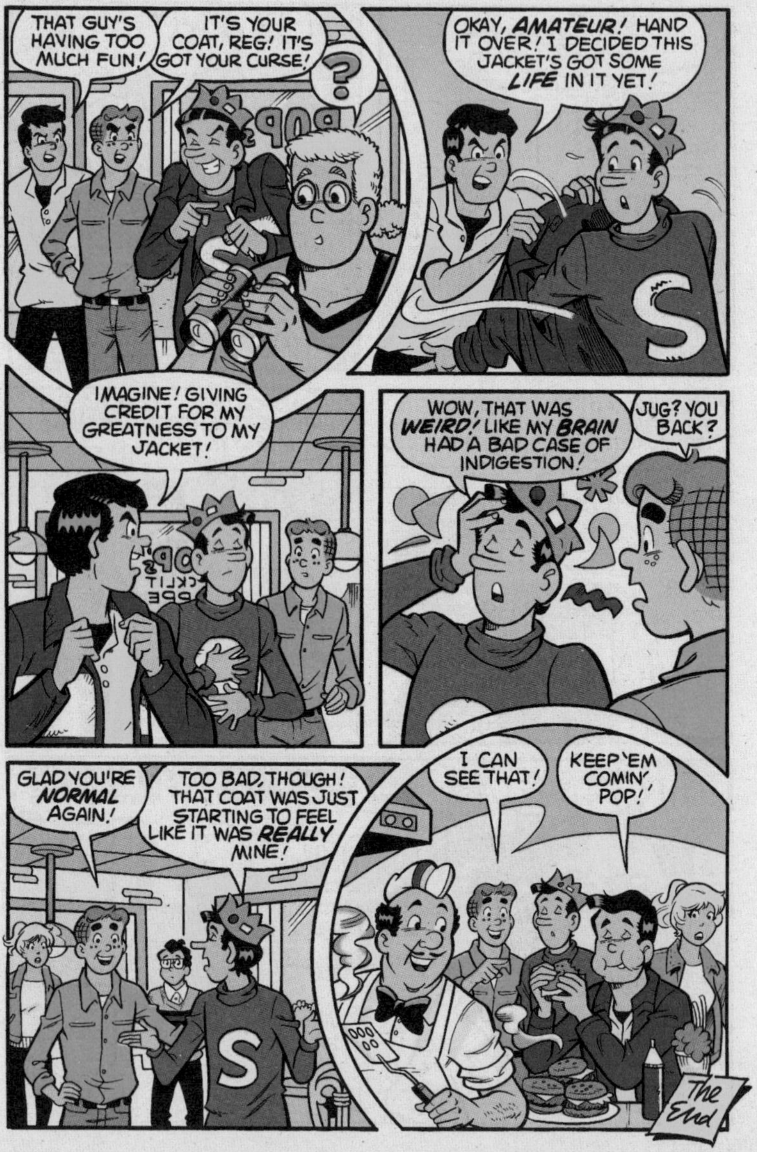
THAT GUY'S HAVING TOO MUCH FUN!
IT'S YOUR COAT, REG! IT'S GOT YOUR CURSE!
?
OKAY, AMATEUR! HAND IT OVER! I DECIDED THIS JACKET'S GOT SOME LIFE IN IT YET!
IMAGINE! GIVING CREDIT FOR MY GREATNESS TO MY JACKET!
WOW, THAT WAS WEIRD! LIKE MY BRAIN HAD A BAD CASE OF INDIGESTION!
JUG? YOU BACK?
GLAD YOU'RE NORMAL AGAIN!
TOO BAD, THOUGH! THAT COAT WAS JUST STARTING TO FEEL LIKE IT WAS REALLY MINE!
I CAN SEE THAT!
KEEP 'EM COMIN', POP!
The End

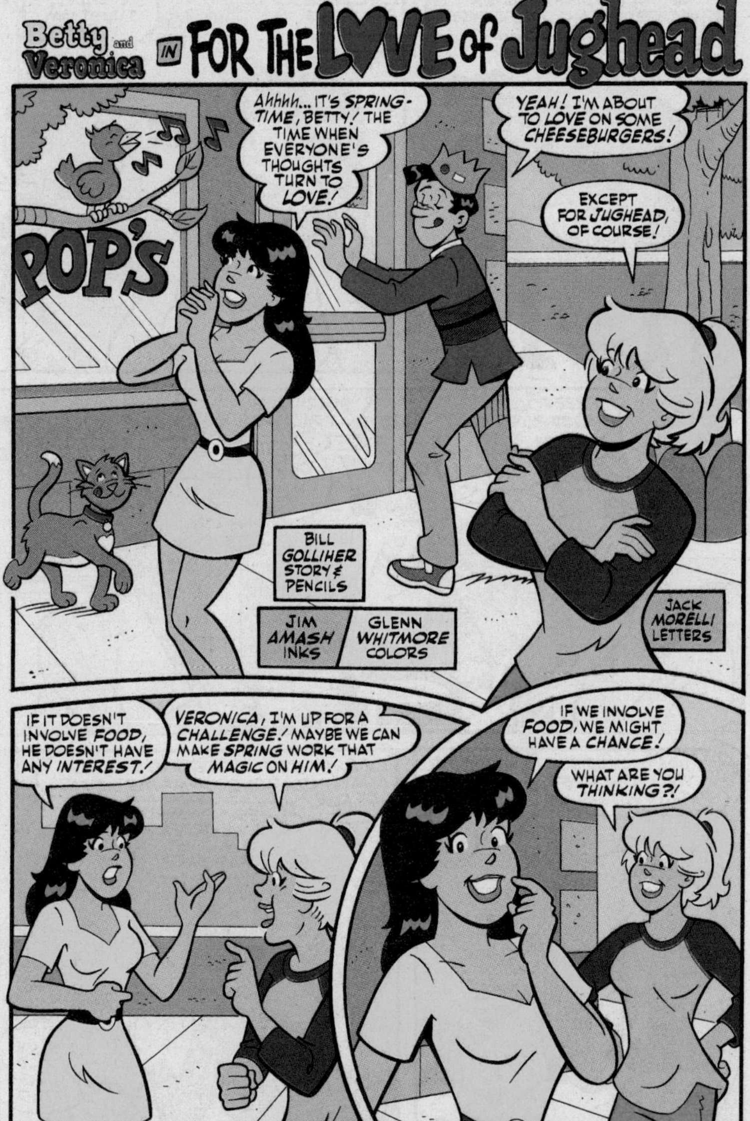
Betty and Veronica IN FOR THE LOVE of Jughead
POP'S
Ahhhh... IT'S SPRING-TIME, BETTY! THE TIME WHEN EVERYONE'S THOUGHTS TURN TO LOVE!
YEAH! I'M ABOUT TO LOVE ON SOME CHEESEBURGERS!
EXCEPT FOR JUGHEAD, OF COURSE!
BILL GOLLIHER STORY & PENCILS
JIM AMASH INKS
GLENN WHITMORE COLORS
JACK MORELLI LETTERS
IF IT DOESN'T INVOLVE FOOD, HE DOESN'T HAVE ANY INTEREST!
VERONICA, I'M UP FOR A CHALLENGE! MAYBE WE CAN MAKE SPRING WORK THAT MAGIC ON HIM!
IF WE INVOLVE FOOD, WE MIGHT HAVE A CHANCE!
WHAT ARE YOU THINKING?!
1

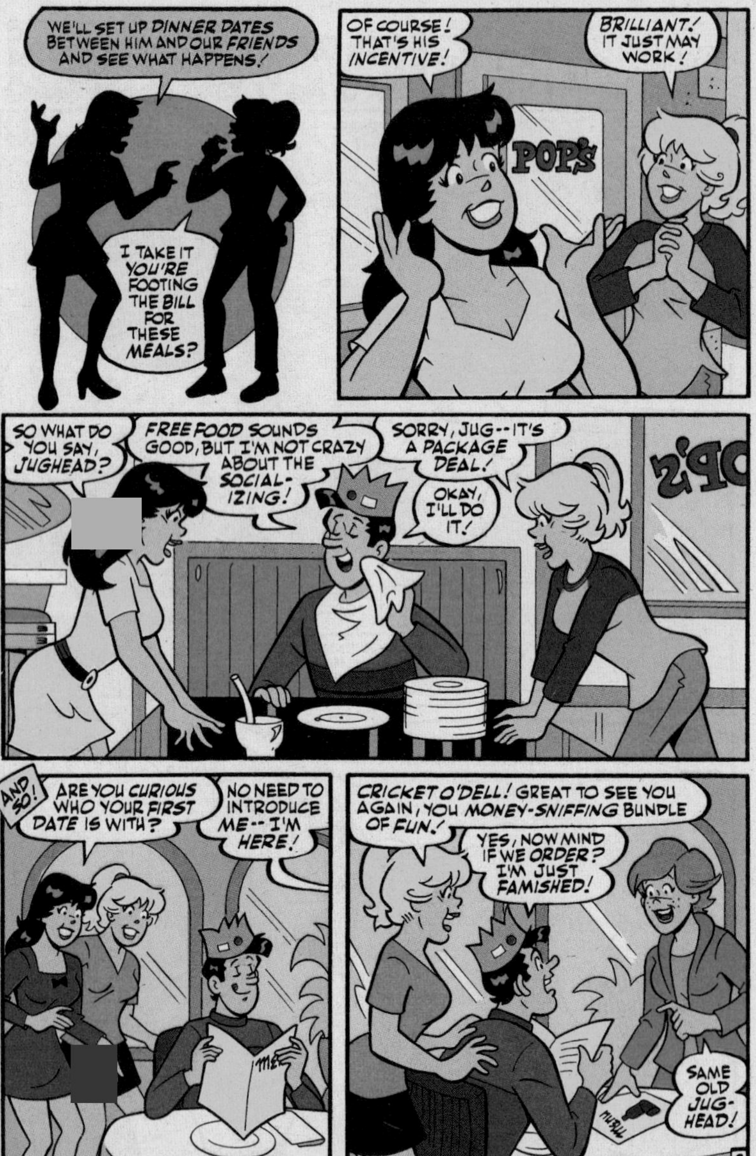

WE'LL SET UP DINNER DATES BETWEEN HIM AND OUR FRIENDS AND SEE WHAT HAPPENS!
I TAKE IT YOU'RE FOOTING THE BILL FOR THESE MEALS?
OF COURSE! THAT'S HIS INCENTIVE!
BRILLIANT! IT JUST MAY WORK!
POP'S
SO WHAT DO YOU SAY, JUGHEAD?
FREE FOOD SOUNDS GOOD, BUT I'M NOT CRAZY ABOUT THE SOCIAL-IZING!
SORRY, JUG-- IT'S A PACKAGE DEAL!
OKAY, I'LL DO IT!
AND SO!
ARE YOU CURIOUS WHO YOUR FIRST DATE IS WITH?
NO NEED TO INTRODUCE ME-- I'M HERE!
CRICKET O'DELL! GREAT TO SEE YOU AGAIN, YOU MONEY-SNIFFING BUNDLE OF FUN!
YES, NOW MIND IF WE ORDER? I'M JUST FAMISHED!
SAME OLD JUG-HEAD!
2

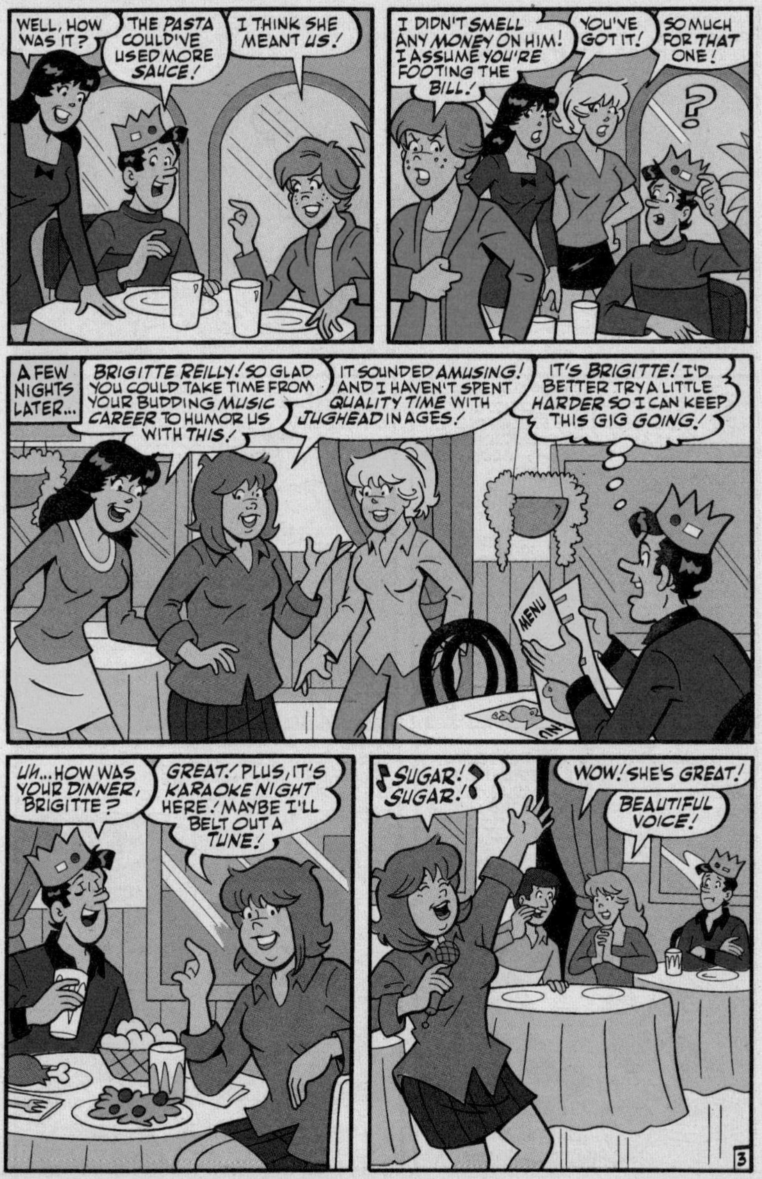

WELL, HOW WAS IT?
THE PASTA COULD'VE USED MORE SAUCE!
I THINK SHE MEANT US!
I DIDN'T SMELL ANY MONEY ON HIM! I ASSUME YOU'RE FOOTING THE BILL!
YOU'VE GOT IT!
SO MUCH FOR THAT ONE!
?
A FEW NIGHTS LATER...
BRIGITTE REILLY! SO GLAD YOU COULD TAKE TIME FROM YOUR BUDDING MUSIC CAREER TO HUMOR US WITH THIS!
IT SOUNDED AMUSING! AND I HAVEN'T SPENT QUALITY TIME WITH JUGHEAD IN AGES!
IT'S BRIGITTE! I'D BETTER TRY A LITTLE HARDER SO I CAN KEEP THIS GIG GOING!
MENU
UH... HOW WAS YOUR DINNER, BRIGITTE?
GREAT! PLUS, IT'S KARAOKE NIGHT HERE! MAYBE I'LL BELT OUT A TUNE!
SUGAR! SUGAR!
WOW! SHE'S GREAT!
BEAUTIFUL VOICE!
3

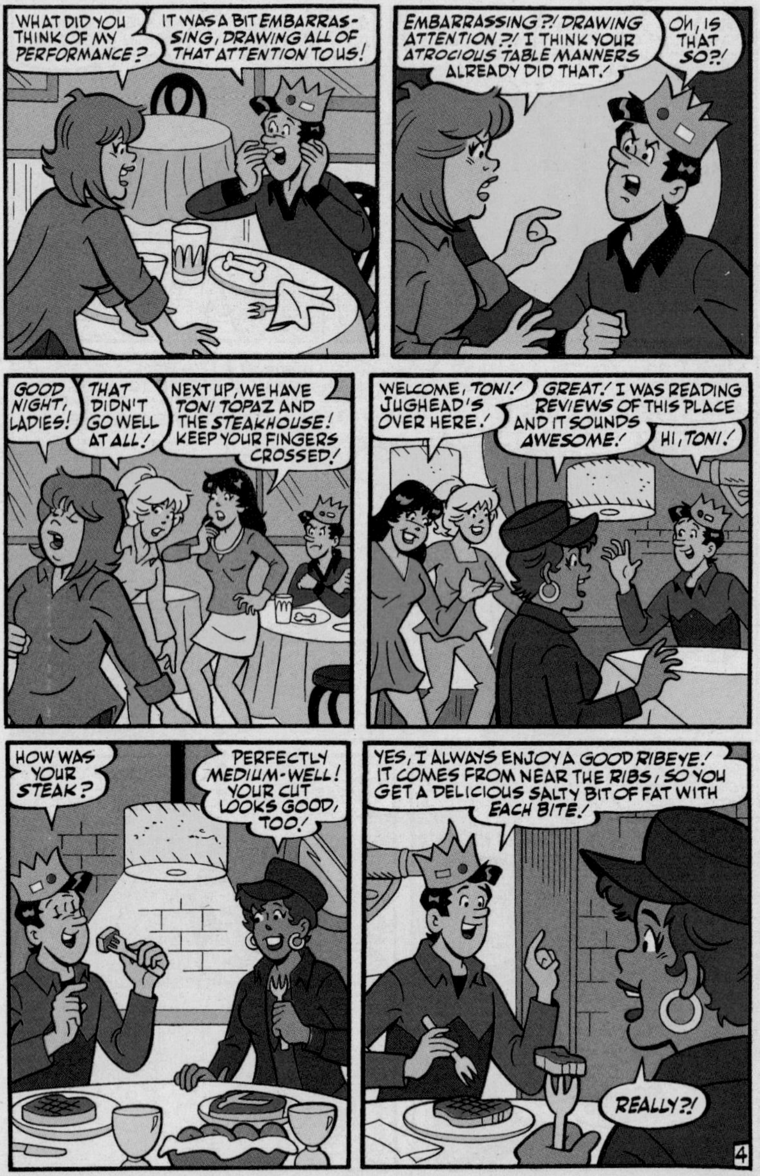
WHAT DID YOU THINK OF MY PERFORMANCE?
IT WAS A BIT EMBARRAS-SING, DRAWING ALL OF THAT ATTENTION TO US!
EMBARRASSING?! DRAWING ATTENTION?! I THINK YOUR ATROCIOUS TABLE MANNERS ALREADY DID THAT.
OH, IS THAT SO?!
GOOD NIGHT, LADIES!
THAT DIDN'T GO WELL AT ALL!
NEXT UP, WE HAVE TONI TOPAZ AND THE STEAKHOUSE! KEEP YOUR FINGERS CROSSED!
WELCOME, TONI! JUGHEAD'S OVER HERE!
GREAT! I WAS READING REVIEWS OF THIS PLACE AND IT SOUNDS AWESOME!
HI, TONI!
HOW WAS YOUR STEAK?
PERFECTLY MEDIUM-WELL! YOUR CUT LOOKS GOOD, TOO!
YES, I ALWAYS ENJOY A GOOD RIBEYE! IT COMES FROM NEAR THE RIBS, SO YOU GET A DELICIOUS SALTY BIT OF FAT WITH EACH BITE!
REALLY?!
4

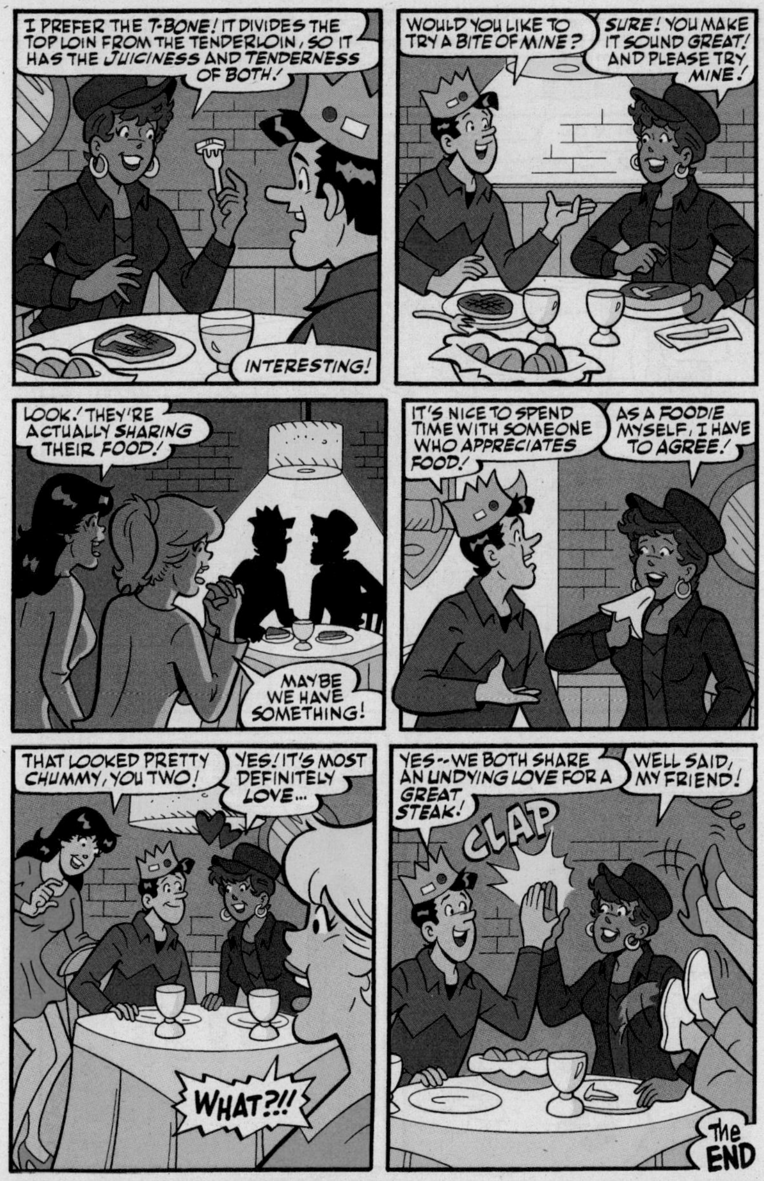
I PREFER THE T-BONE! IT DIVIDES THE TOP LOIN FROM THE TENDERLOIN, SO IT HAS THE JUICINESS AND TENDERNESS OF BOTH!
INTERESTING!
WOULD YOU LIKE TO TRY A BITE OF MINE?
SURE! YOU MAKE IT SOUND GREAT! AND PLEASE TRY MINE!
LOOK! THEY'RE ACTUALLY SHARING THEIR FOOD!
MAYBE WE HAVE SOMETHING!
IT'S NICE TO SPEND TIME WITH SOMEONE WHO APPRECIATES FOOD!
AS A FOODIE MYSELF, I HAVE TO AGREE!
THAT LOOKED PRETTY CHUMMY, YOU TWO!
YES! IT'S MOST DEFINITELY LOVE...
WHAT?!!
YES--WE BOTH SHARE AN UNDYING LOVE FOR A GREAT STEAK!
WELL SAID, MY FRIEND!
CLAP
The END

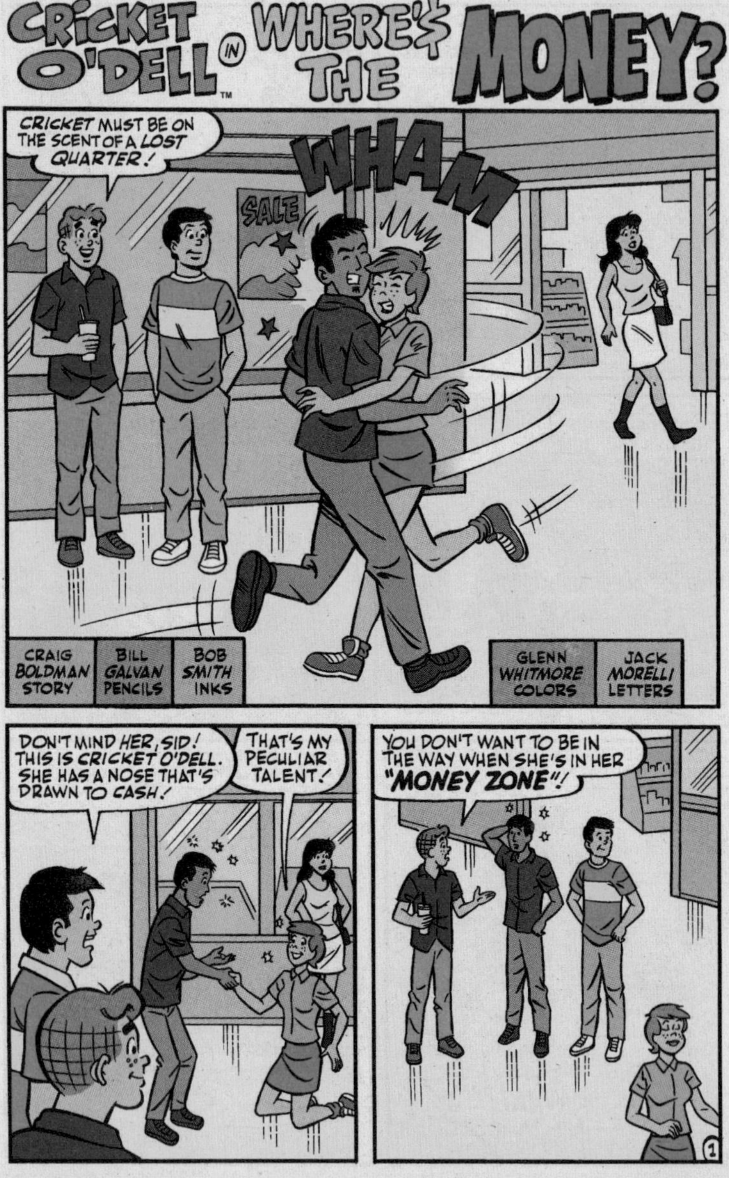

CRICKET O'DELL™ IN WHERE'$ THE MONEY?
CRICKET MUST BE ON THE SCENT OF A LOST QUARTER!
WHAM
SALE
CRAIG BOLDMAN STORY
BILL GALVAN PENCILS
BOB SMITH INKS
GLENN WHITMORE COLORS
JACK MORELLI LETTERS
DON'T MIND HER, SID! THIS IS CRICKET O'DELL. SHE HAS A NOSE THAT'S DRAWN TO CASH!
THAT'S MY PECULIAR TALENT!
YOU DON'T WANT TO BE IN THE WAY WHEN SHE'S IN HER "MONEY ZONE"!

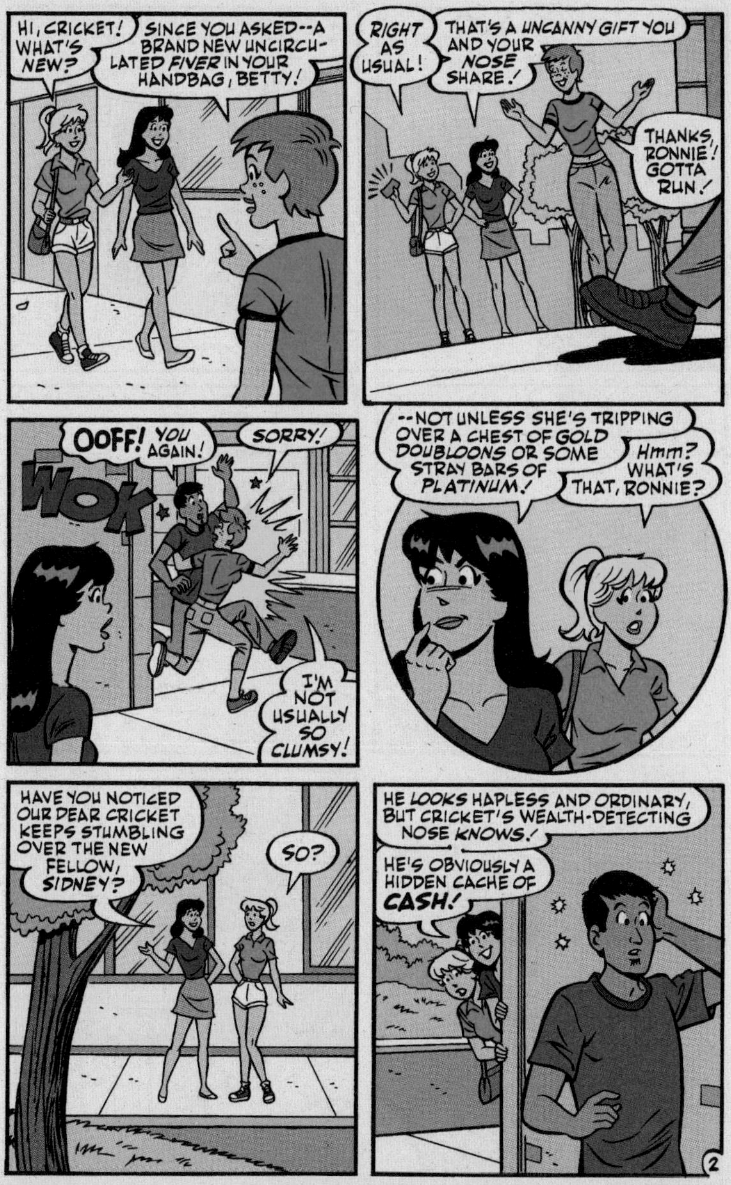

HI, CRICKET! WHAT'S NEW?
SINCE YOU ASKED--A BRAND NEW UNCIRCU-LATED *FIVER* IN YOUR HANDBAG, BETTY!
RIGHT AS USUAL!
THAT'S A *UNCANNY GIFT* YOU AND YOUR *NOSE* SHARE!
THANKS, RONNIE! GOTTA RUN!
OOFF! YOU AGAIN!
SORRY!
WOK
I'M NOT USUALLY SO CLUMSY!
--NOT UNLESS SHE'S TRIPPING OVER A CHEST OF GOLD DOUBLOONS OR SOME STRAY BARS OF PLATINUM!
Hmm? WHAT'S THAT, RONNIE?
HAVE YOU NOTICED OUR DEAR CRICKET KEEPS STUMBLING OVER THE NEW FELLOW, SIDNEY?
SO?
HE *LOOKS* HAPLESS AND ORDINARY, BUT CRICKET'S WEALTH-DETECTING NOSE *KNOWS*!
HE'S OBVIOUSLY A HIDDEN CACHE OF **CASH**!
2

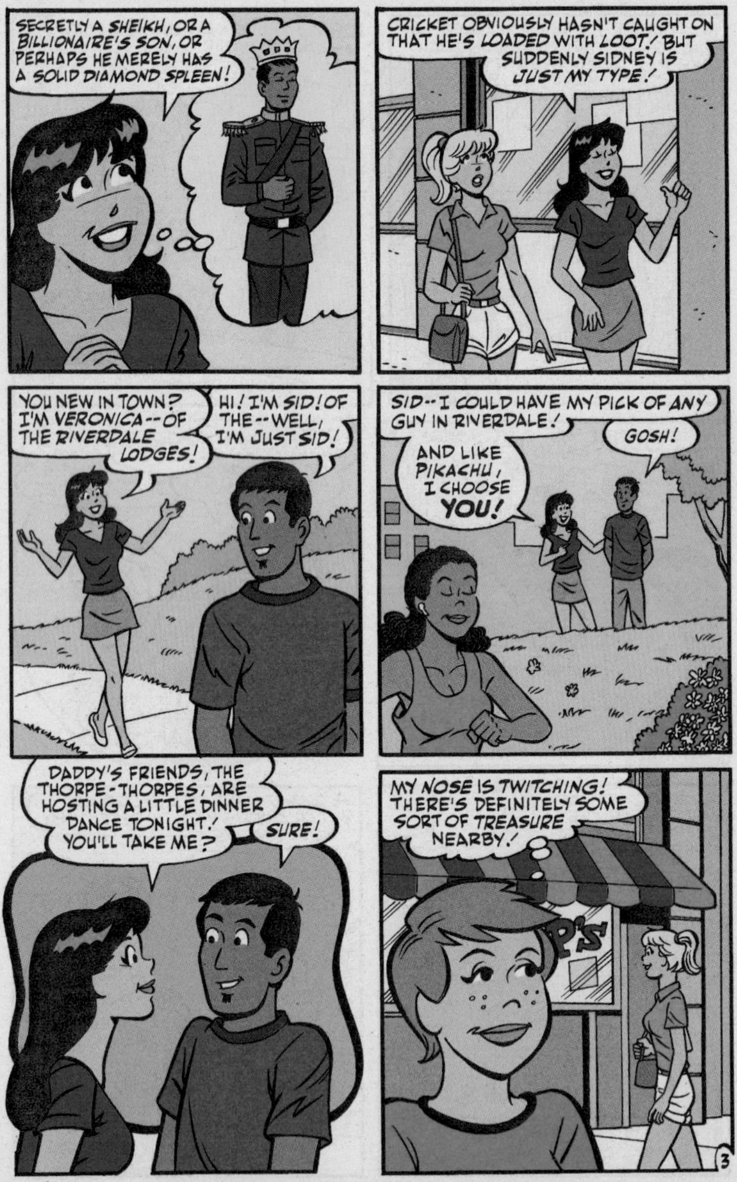
SECRETLY A SHEIKH, OR A BILLIONAIRE'S SON, OR PERHAPS HE MERELY HAS A SOLID DIAMOND SPLEEN!
CRICKET OBVIOUSLY HASN'T CAUGHT ON THAT HE'S LOADED WITH LOOT! BUT SUDDENLY SIDNEY IS JUST MY TYPE!
YOU NEW IN TOWN? I'M VERONICA--OF THE RIVERDALE LODGES!
HI! I'M SID! OF THE--WELL, I'M JUST SID!
SID--I COULD HAVE MY PICK OF ANY GUY IN RIVERDALE!
AND LIKE PIKACHU, I CHOOSE YOU!
GOSH!
DADDY'S FRIENDS, THE THORPE-THORPES, ARE HOSTING A LITTLE DINNER DANCE TONIGHT! YOU'LL TAKE ME?
SURE!
MY NOSE IS TWITCHING! THERE'S DEFINITELY SOME SORT OF TREASURE NEARBY!
P'S

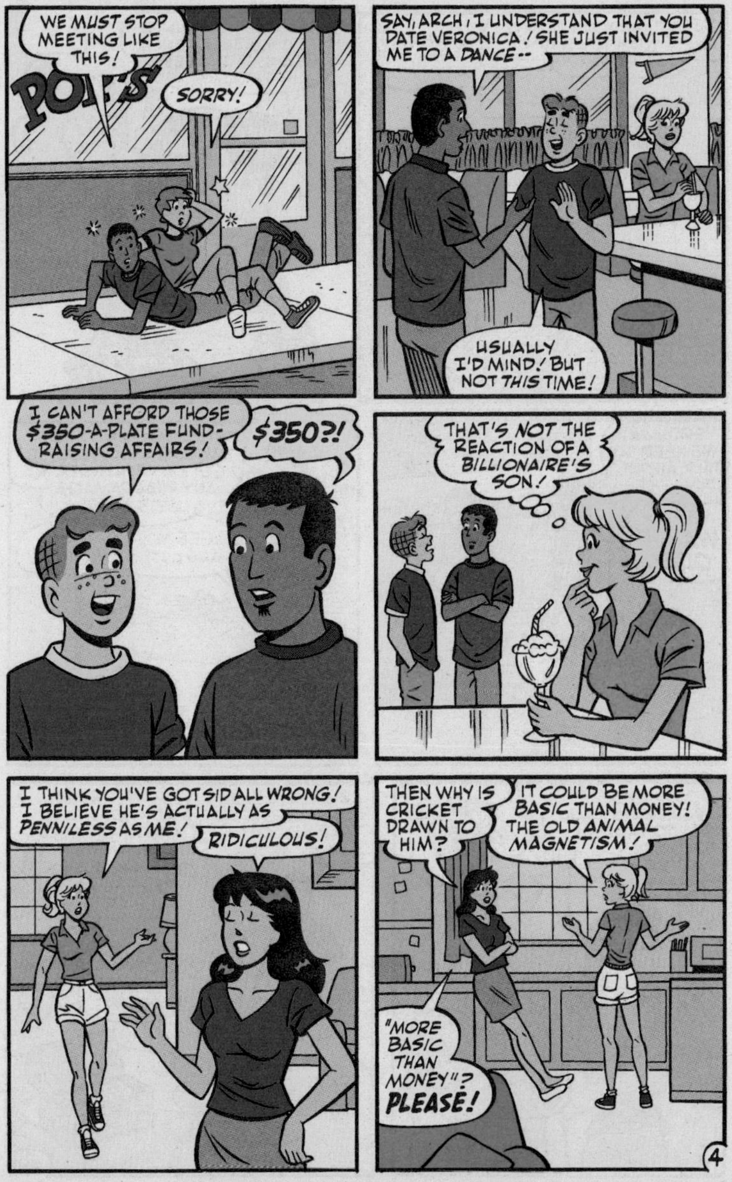

WE MUST STOP MEETING LIKE THIS!
SORRY!
POP'S
SAY, ARCH, I UNDERSTAND THAT YOU DATE VERONICA! SHE JUST INVITED ME TO A DANCE--
USUALLY I'D MIND! BUT NOT THIS TIME!
I CAN'T AFFORD THOSE $350-A-PLATE FUND-RAISING AFFAIRS!
$350?!
THAT'S NOT THE REACTION OF A BILLIONAIRE'S SON!
I THINK YOU'VE GOT SID ALL WRONG! I BELIEVE HE'S ACTUALLY AS PENNILESS AS ME!
RIDICULOUS!
THEN WHY IS CRICKET DRAWN TO HIM?
IT COULD BE MORE BASIC THAN MONEY! THE OLD ANIMAL MAGNETISM!
"MORE BASIC THAN MONEY"? PLEASE!
4

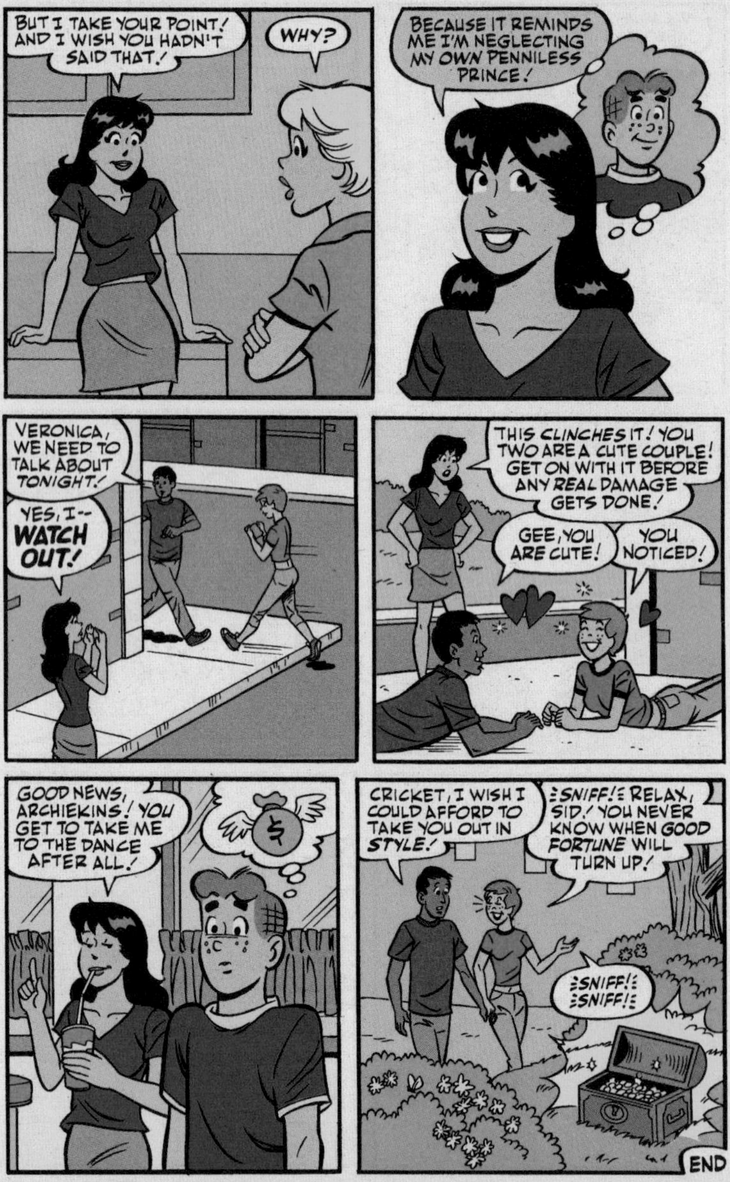

BUT I TAKE YOUR POINT! AND I WISH YOU HADN'T SAID THAT!
WHY?
BECAUSE IT REMINDS ME I'M NEGLECTING MY OWN PENNILESS PRINCE!
VERONICA, WE NEED TO TALK ABOUT TONIGHT!
YES, I-- WATCH OUT!
THIS CLINCHES IT! YOU TWO ARE A CUTE COUPLE! GET ON WITH IT BEFORE ANY REAL DAMAGE GETS DONE!
GEE, YOU ARE CUTE!
YOU NOTICED!
GOOD NEWS, ARCHIEKINS! YOU GET TO TAKE ME TO THE DANCE AFTER ALL!
CRICKET, I WISH I COULD AFFORD TO TAKE YOU OUT IN STYLE!
SNIFF! RELAX, SID! YOU NEVER KNOW WHEN GOOD FORTUNE WILL TURN UP!
SNIFF! SNIFF!
END

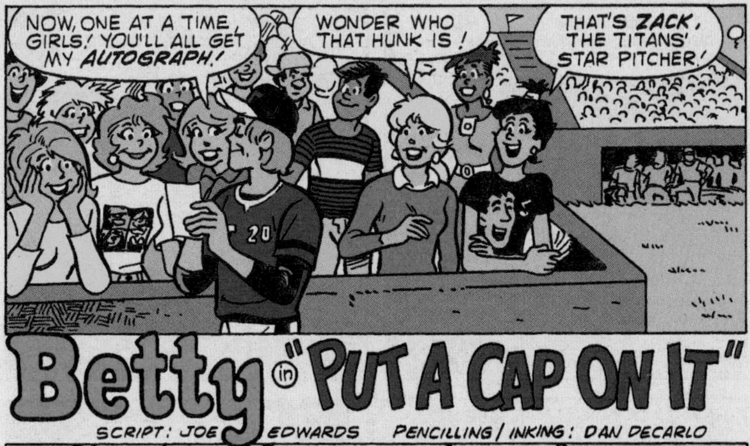
NOW, ONE AT A TIME, GIRLS! YOU'LL ALL GET MY AUTOGRAPH!
WONDER WHO THAT HUNK IS!
THAT'S ZACK, THE TITANS' STAR PITCHER!

Betty in "PUT A CAP ON IT"

SCRIPT: JOE EDWARDS PENCILLING / INKING: DAN DECARLO

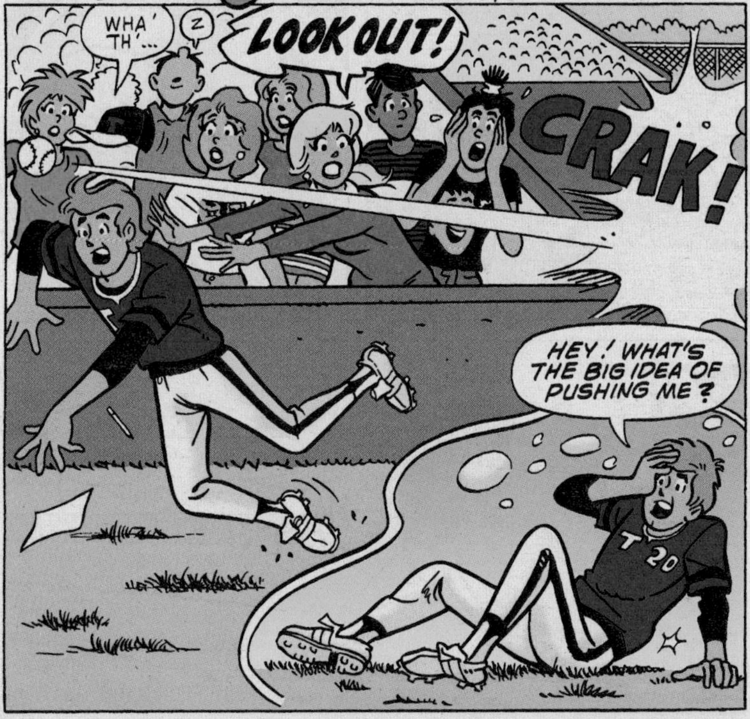
WHA' TH'...
Z
LOOK OUT!
CRAK!
HEY! WHAT'S THE BIG IDEA OF PUSHING ME?

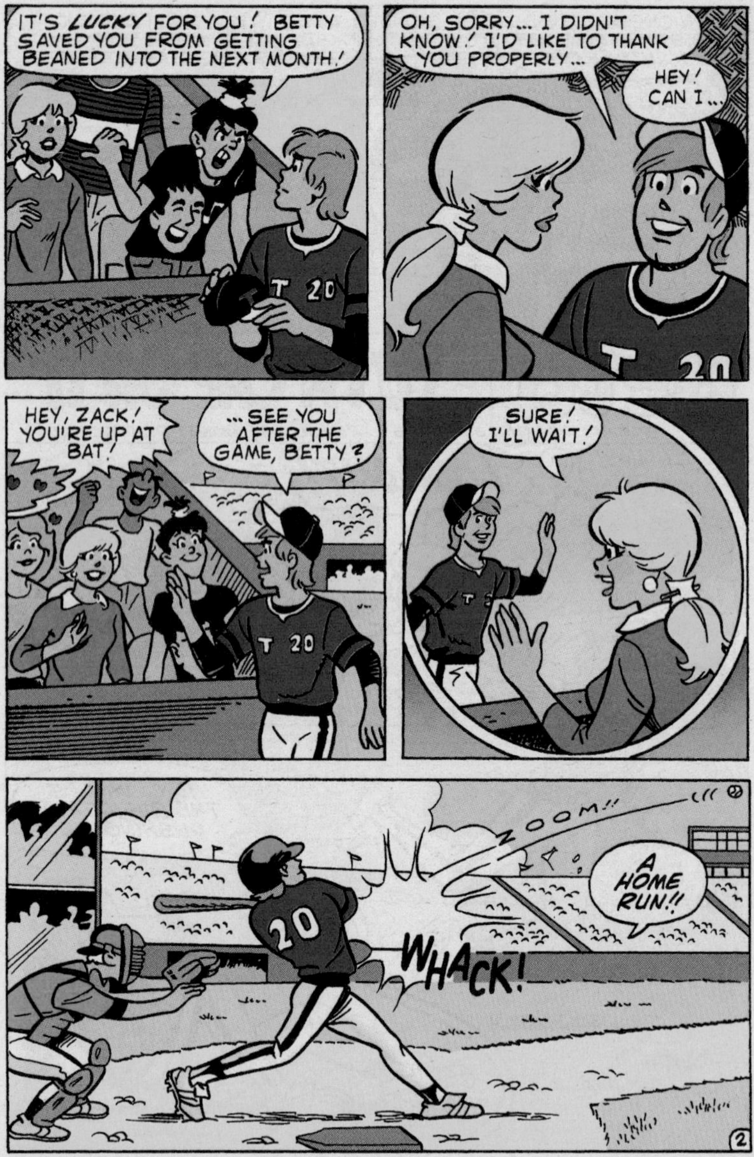
IT'S LUCKY FOR YOU! BETTY SAVED YOU FROM GETTING BEANED INTO THE NEXT MONTH!
OH, SORRY... I DIDN'T KNOW! I'D LIKE TO THANK YOU PROPERLY...
HEY! CAN I...
HEY, ZACK! YOU'RE UP AT BAT!
...SEE YOU AFTER THE GAME, BETTY?
SURE! I'LL WAIT!
ZOOM!!
A HOME RUN!!
WHACK!
2

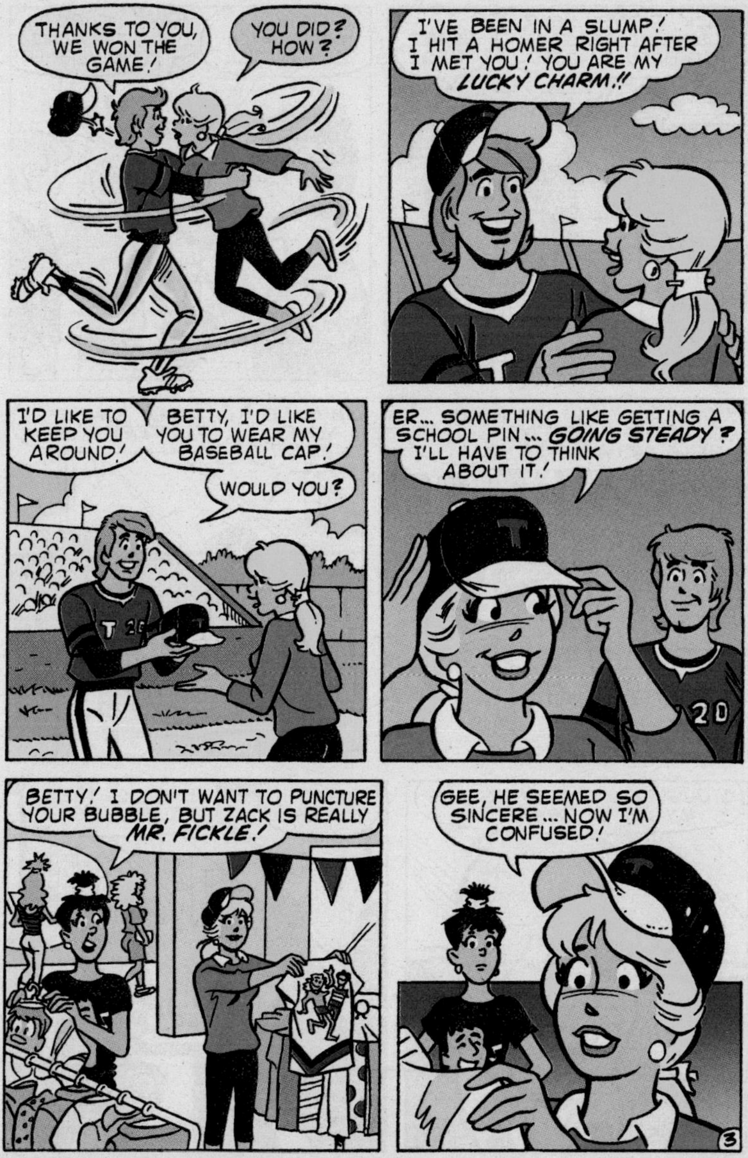
THANKS TO YOU, WE WON THE GAME!
YOU DID? HOW?
I'VE BEEN IN A SLUMP! I HIT A HOMER RIGHT AFTER I MET YOU! YOU ARE MY LUCKY CHARM!!
I'D LIKE TO KEEP YOU AROUND!
BETTY, I'D LIKE YOU TO WEAR MY BASEBALL CAP!
WOULD YOU?
ER... SOMETHING LIKE GETTING A SCHOOL PIN... GOING STEADY? I'LL HAVE TO THINK ABOUT IT!
BETTY! I DON'T WANT TO PUNCTURE YOUR BUBBLE, BUT ZACK IS REALLY MR. FICKLE!
GEE, HE SEEMED SO SINCERE... NOW I'M CONFUSED!
3

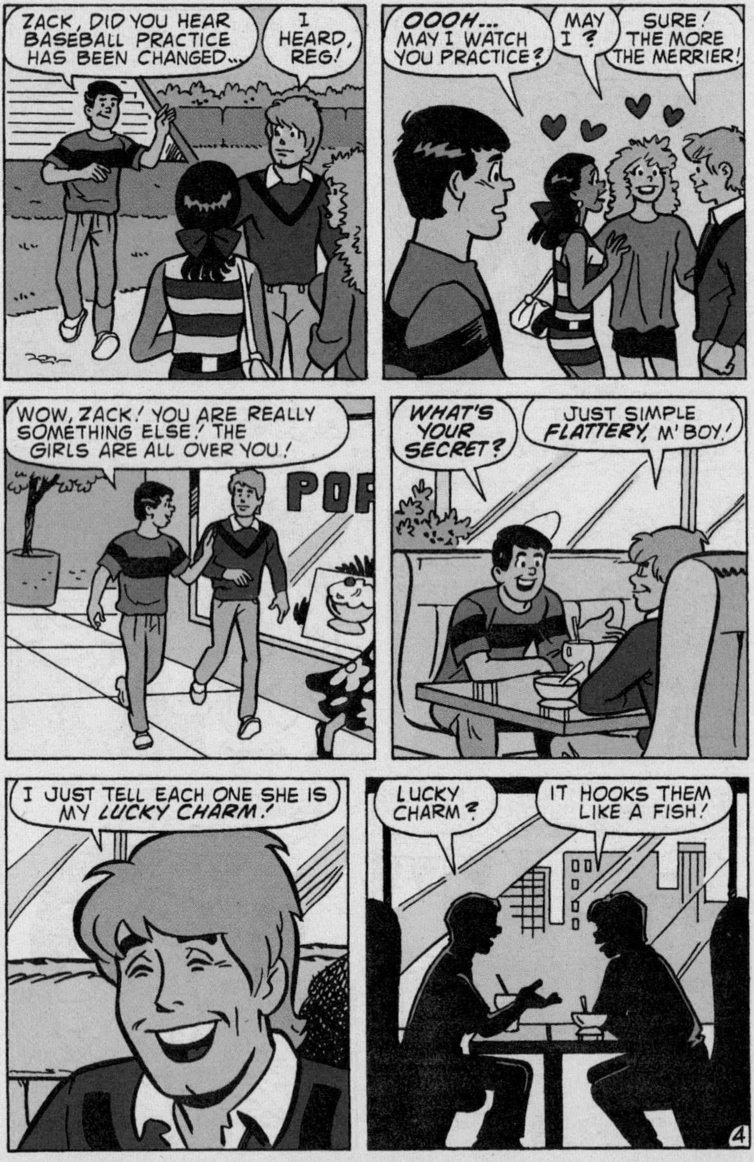
ZACK, DID YOU HEAR BASEBALL PRACTICE HAS BEEN CHANGED...
I HEARD, REG!
OOOH... MAY I WATCH YOU PRACTICE?
MAY I?
SURE! THE MORE THE MERRIER!
WOW, ZACK! YOU ARE REALLY SOMETHING ELSE! THE GIRLS ARE ALL OVER YOU!
POP
WHAT'S YOUR SECRET?
JUST SIMPLE FLATTERY, M' BOY!
I JUST TELL EACH ONE SHE IS MY LUCKY CHARM!
LUCKY CHARM?
IT HOOKS THEM LIKE A FISH!
4

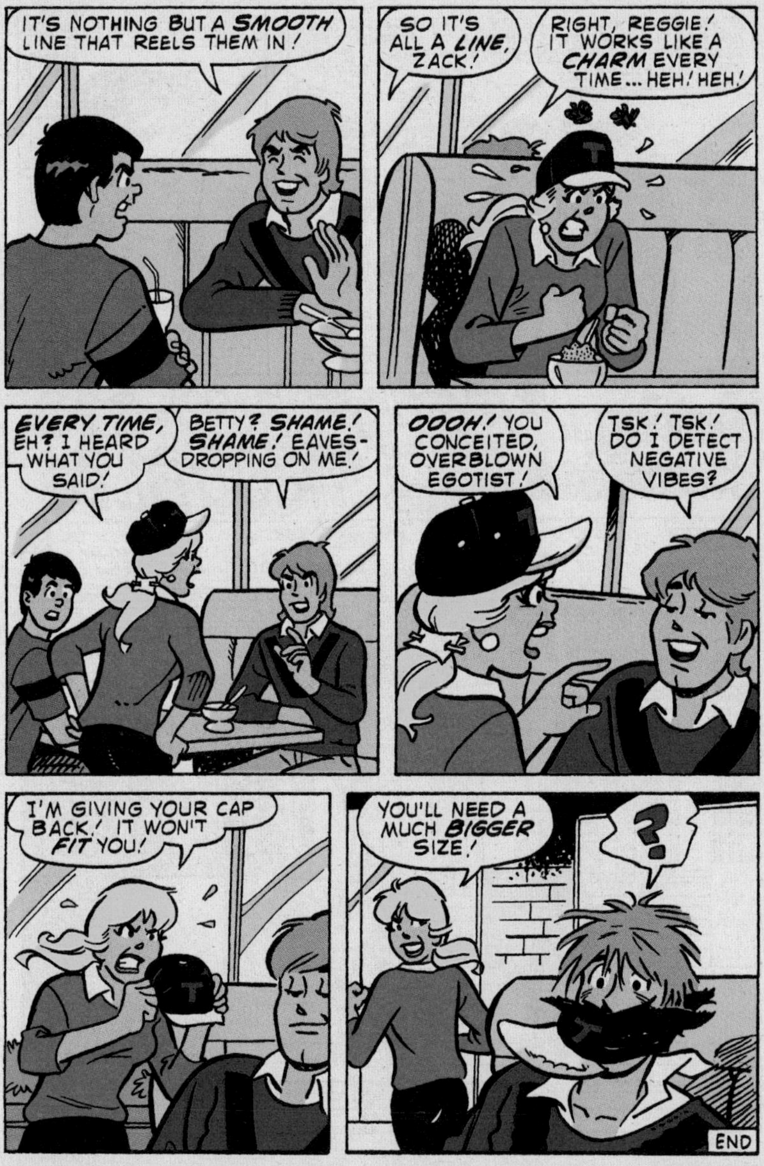
IT'S NOTHING BUT A SMOOTH LINE THAT REELS THEM IN!
SO IT'S ALL A LINE, ZACK!
RIGHT, REGGIE! IT WORKS LIKE A CHARM EVERY TIME... HEH! HEH!
EVERY TIME, EH? I HEARD WHAT YOU SAID!
BETTY? SHAME! SHAME! EAVES-DROPPING ON ME!
OOOH! YOU CONCEITED, OVERBLOWN EGOTIST!
TSK! TSK! DO I DETECT NEGATIVE VIBES?
I'M GIVING YOUR CAP BACK! IT WON'T FIT YOU!
YOU'LL NEED A MUCH BIGGER SIZE!
?
END

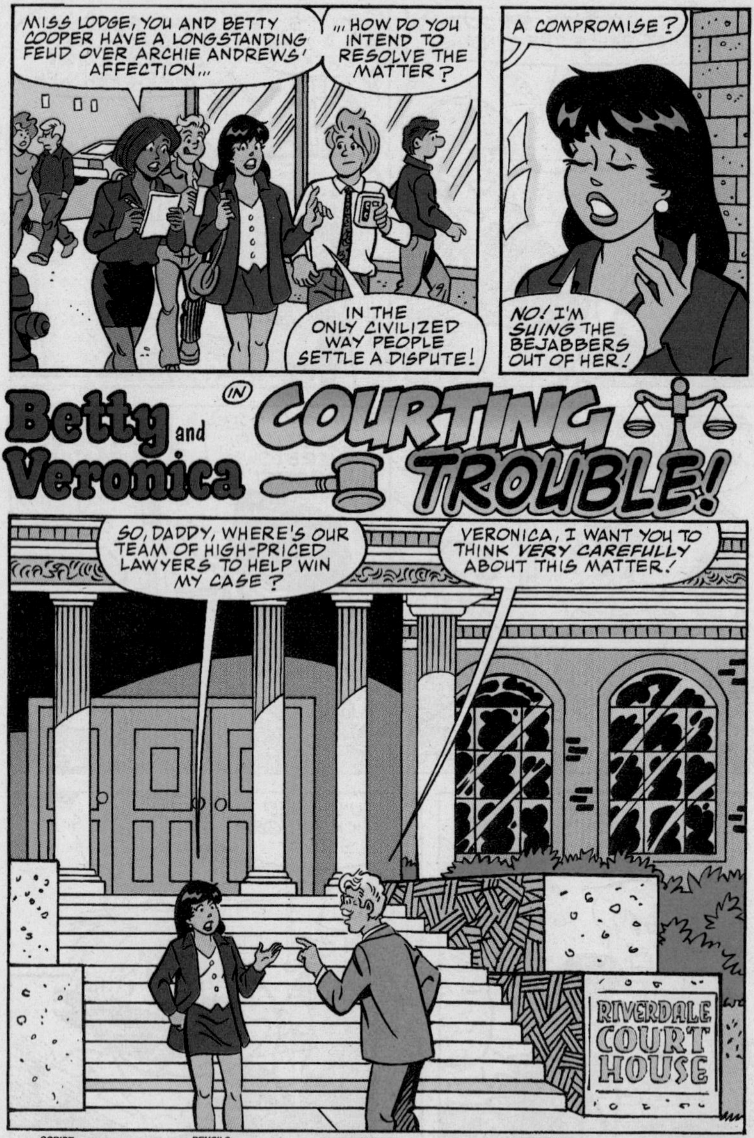
MISS LODGE, YOU AND BETTY COOPER HAVE A LONGSTANDING FEUD OVER ARCHIE ANDREWS' AFFECTION...
...HOW DO YOU INTEND TO RESOLVE THE MATTER?
IN THE ONLY CIVILIZED WAY PEOPLE SETTLE A DISPUTE!
A COMPROMISE?
NO! I'M SUING THE BEJABBERS OUT OF HER!
Betty and Veronica IN COURTING TROUBLE!
SO, DADDY, WHERE'S OUR TEAM OF HIGH-PRICED LAWYERS TO HELP WIN MY CASE?
VERONICA, I WANT YOU TO THINK VERY CAREFULLY ABOUT THIS MATTER!
RIVERDALE COURT HOUSE

SCRIPT: GEORGE GLADIR · PENCILS: JEFF SHULTZ · INKING: AL MILGROM · LETTERING: JACK MORELLI · COLORING: BARRY GROSSMAN

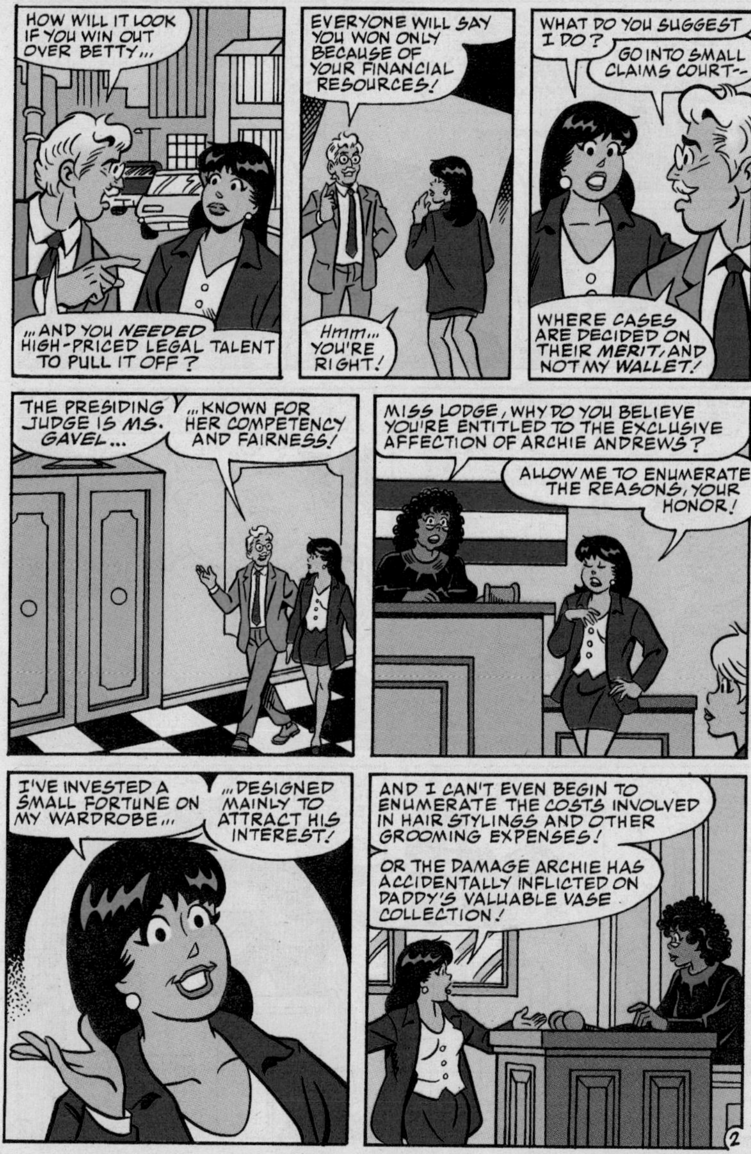
HOW WILL IT LOOK IF YOU WIN OUT OVER BETTY...
...AND YOU NEEDED HIGH-PRICED LEGAL TALENT TO PULL IT OFF?
EVERYONE WILL SAY YOU WON ONLY BECAUSE OF YOUR FINANCIAL RESOURCES!
Hmm... YOU'RE RIGHT!
WHAT DO YOU SUGGEST I DO?
GO INTO SMALL CLAIMS COURT--
WHERE CASES ARE DECIDED ON THEIR MERIT, AND NOT MY WALLET!
THE PRESIDING JUDGE IS MS. GAVEL...
...KNOWN FOR HER COMPETENCY AND FAIRNESS!
MISS LODGE, WHY DO YOU BELIEVE YOU'RE ENTITLED TO THE EXCLUSIVE AFFECTION OF ARCHIE ANDREWS?
ALLOW ME TO ENUMERATE THE REASONS, YOUR HONOR!
I'VE INVESTED A SMALL FORTUNE ON MY WARDROBE...
...DESIGNED MAINLY TO ATTRACT HIS INTEREST!
AND I CAN'T EVEN BEGIN TO ENUMERATE THE COSTS INVOLVED IN HAIR STYLINGS AND OTHER GROOMING EXPENSES!
OR THE DAMAGE ARCHIE HAS ACCIDENTALLY INFLICTED ON DADDY'S VALUABLE VASE COLLECTION!
2

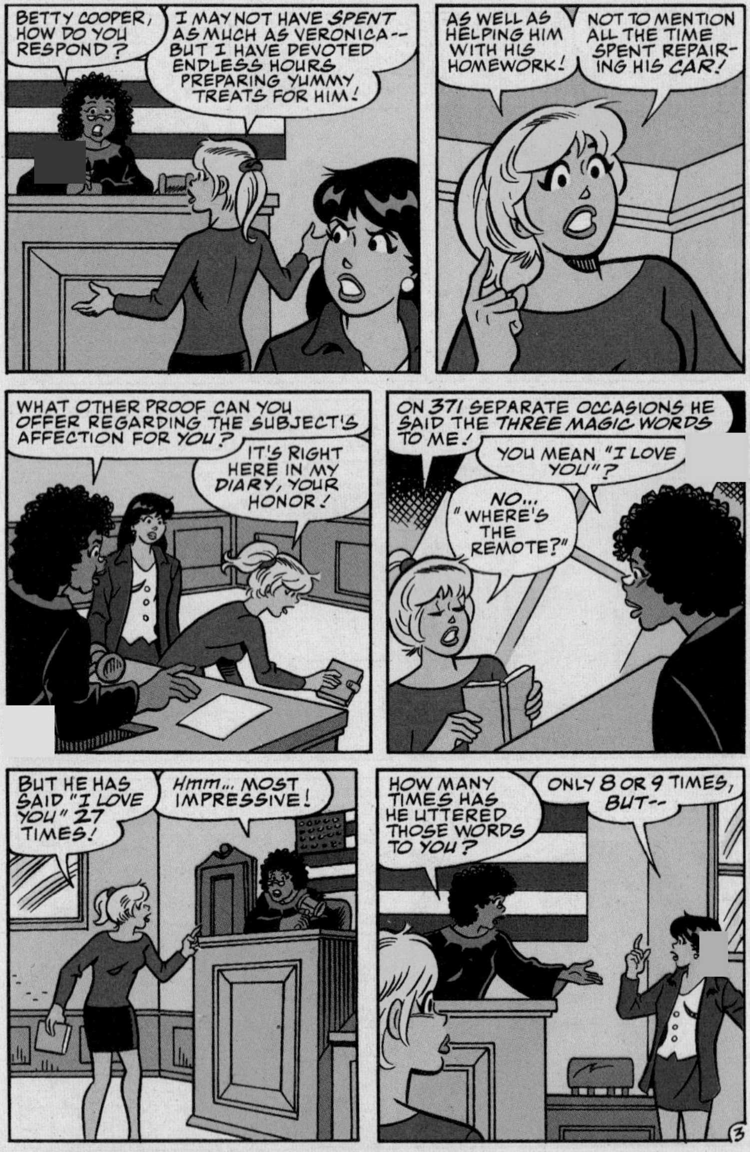
BETTY COOPER, HOW DO YOU RESPOND?
I MAY NOT HAVE SPENT AS MUCH AS VERONICA-- BUT I HAVE DEVOTED ENDLESS HOURS PREPARING YUMMY TREATS FOR HIM!
AS WELL AS HELPING HIM WITH HIS HOMEWORK!
NOT TO MENTION ALL THE TIME SPENT REPAIRING HIS CAR!
WHAT OTHER PROOF CAN YOU OFFER REGARDING THE SUBJECT'S AFFECTION FOR YOU?
IT'S RIGHT HERE IN MY DIARY, YOUR HONOR!
ON 371 SEPARATE OCCASIONS HE SAID THE THREE MAGIC WORDS TO ME!
YOU MEAN "I LOVE YOU"?
NO... "WHERE'S THE REMOTE?"
BUT HE HAS SAID "I LOVE YOU" 27 TIMES!
Hmm... MOST IMPRESSIVE!
HOW MANY TIMES HAS HE UTTERED THOSE WORDS TO YOU?
ONLY 8 OR 9 TIMES, BUT--

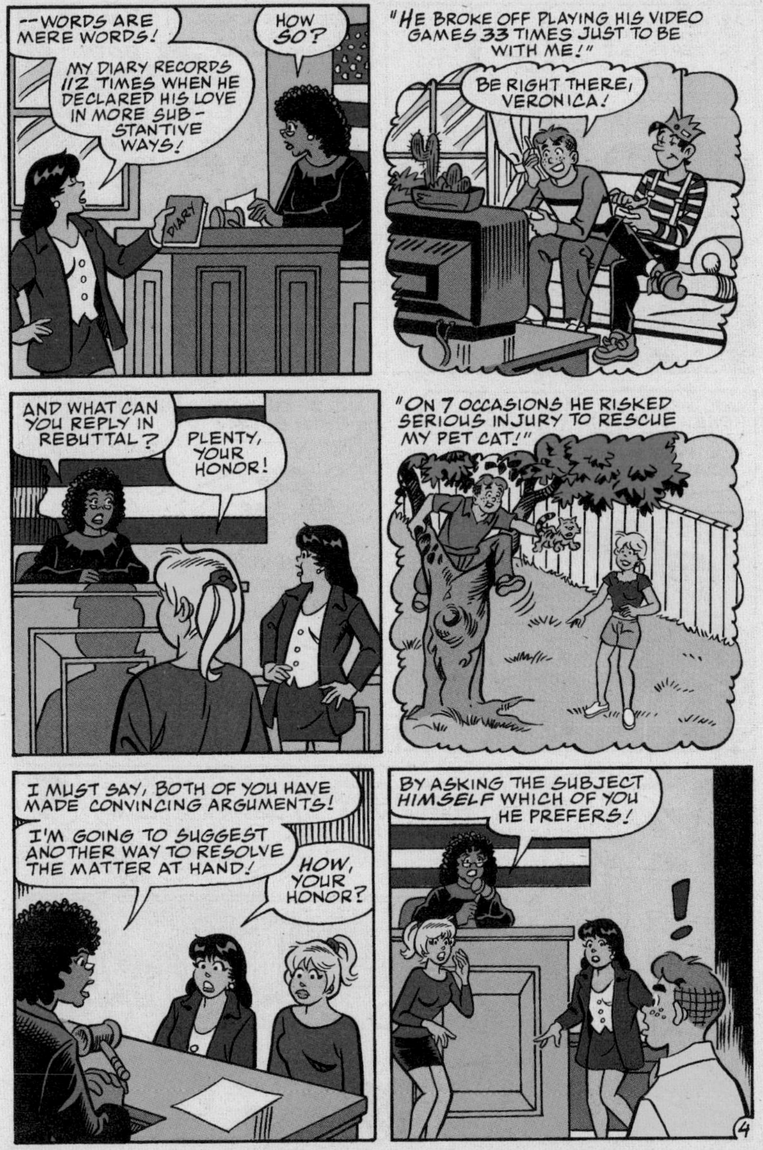
--WORDS ARE MERE WORDS!
MY DIARY RECORDS 112 TIMES WHEN HE DECLARED HIS LOVE IN MORE SUB-STANTIVE WAYS!
HOW SO?
DIARY
"HE BROKE OFF PLAYING HIS VIDEO GAMES 33 TIMES JUST TO BE WITH ME!"
BE RIGHT THERE, VERONICA!
AND WHAT CAN YOU REPLY IN REBUTTAL?
PLENTY, YOUR HONOR!
"ON 7 OCCASIONS HE RISKED SERIOUS INJURY TO RESCUE MY PET CAT!"
I MUST SAY, BOTH OF YOU HAVE MADE CONVINCING ARGUMENTS!
I'M GOING TO SUGGEST ANOTHER WAY TO RESOLVE THE MATTER AT HAND!
HOW, YOUR HONOR?
BY ASKING THE SUBJECT HIMSELF WHICH OF YOU HE PREFERS!
!
4

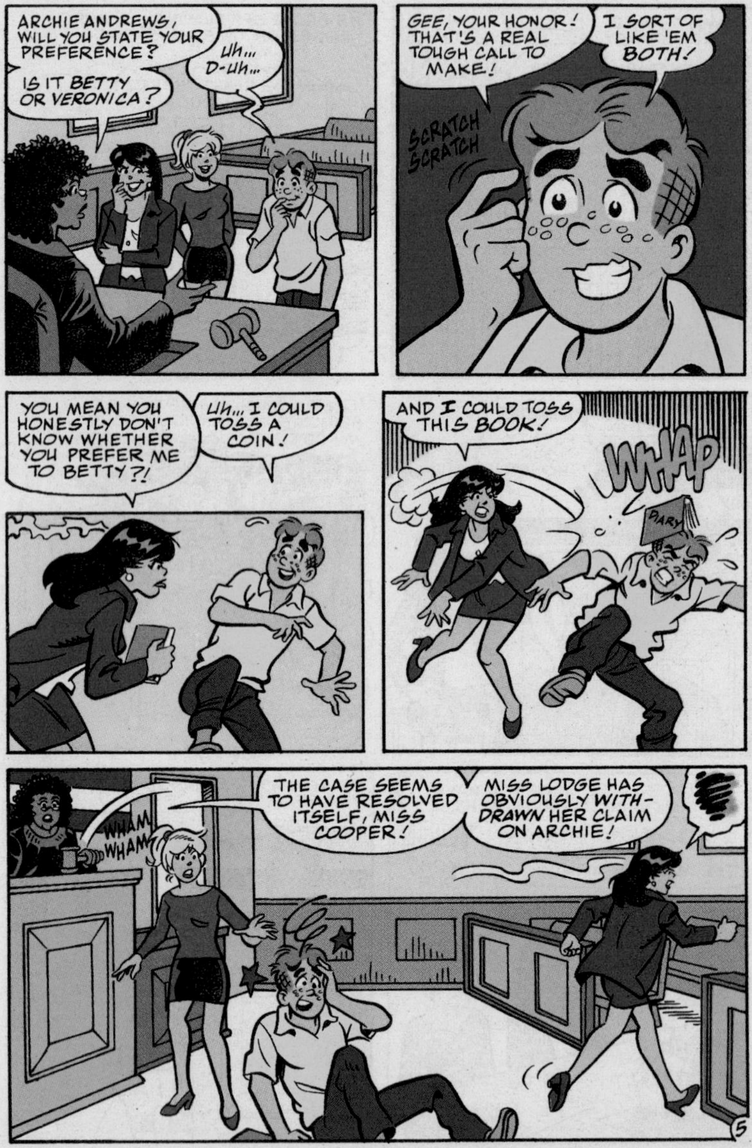
ARCHIE ANDREWS, WILL YOU STATE YOUR PREFERENCE?
IS IT BETTY OR VERONICA?
UH... D-UH...
GEE, YOUR HONOR! THAT'S A REAL TOUGH CALL TO MAKE!
I SORT OF LIKE 'EM BOTH!
SCRATCH SCRATCH
YOU MEAN YOU HONESTLY DON'T KNOW WHETHER YOU PREFER ME TO BETTY?!
UH... I COULD TOSS A COIN!
AND I COULD TOSS THIS BOOK!
WHAP
DIARY
WHAM WHAM
THE CASE SEEMS TO HAVE RESOLVED ITSELF, MISS COOPER!
MISS LODGE HAS OBVIOUSLY WITH-DRAWN HER CLAIM ON ARCHIE!
5

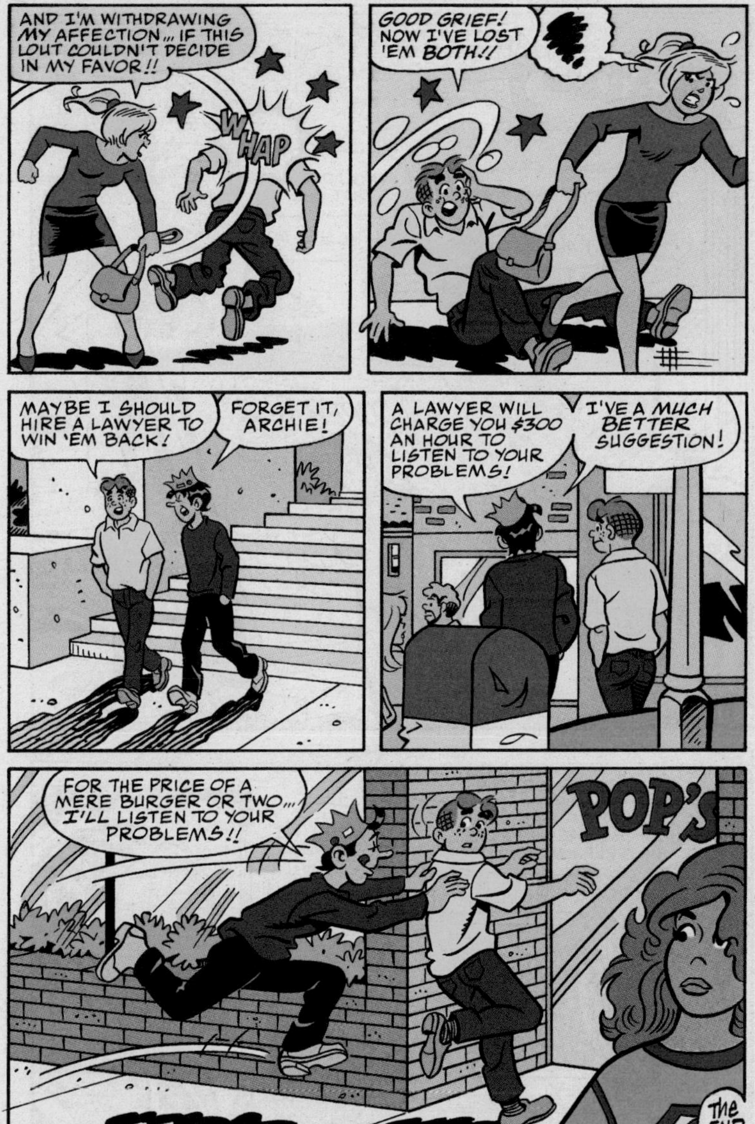
AND I'M WITHDRAWING MY AFFECTION... IF THIS LOUT COULDN'T DECIDE IN MY FAVOR!!
WHAP
GOOD GRIEF! NOW I'VE LOST 'EM BOTH!!
MAYBE I SHOULD HIRE A LAWYER TO WIN 'EM BACK!
FORGET IT, ARCHIE!
A LAWYER WILL CHARGE YOU $300 AN HOUR TO LISTEN TO YOUR PROBLEMS!
I'VE A MUCH BETTER SUGGESTION!
FOR THE PRICE OF A MERE BURGER OR TWO... I'LL LISTEN TO YOUR PROBLEMS!!
POP'S
The END

Nancy in "SUPER SAGA"
NANCY, THE KIDS AT CAMP ALL LIKE THE SUPER HERO I DRAW FOR THE CAMP PAPER!
I'M GLAD TO HEAR THAT, CHUCK!
I REALLY AM!
SUPER STAN
SANDIE
BUT I'VE GOTTEN SOME COMPLAINTS ABOUT SUPER STAN!
BECAUSE OF HIS CRIME-FIGHTING, HE NEGLECTS HIS GIRLFRIEND SANDRA!
(SIGH!) I CAN RELATE TO THAT!

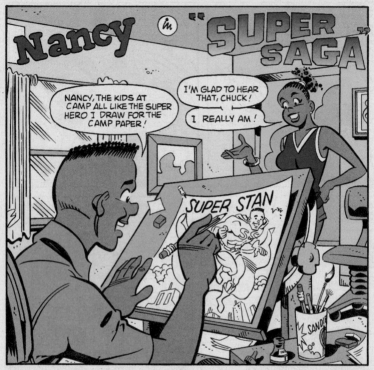

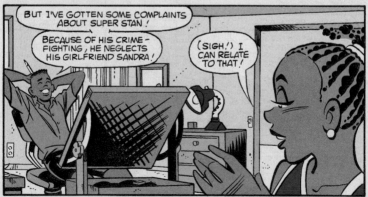

Script: George Gladir / Pencils: Al Bigley / Inks: Al Milgrom / Letters: Bill Yoshida

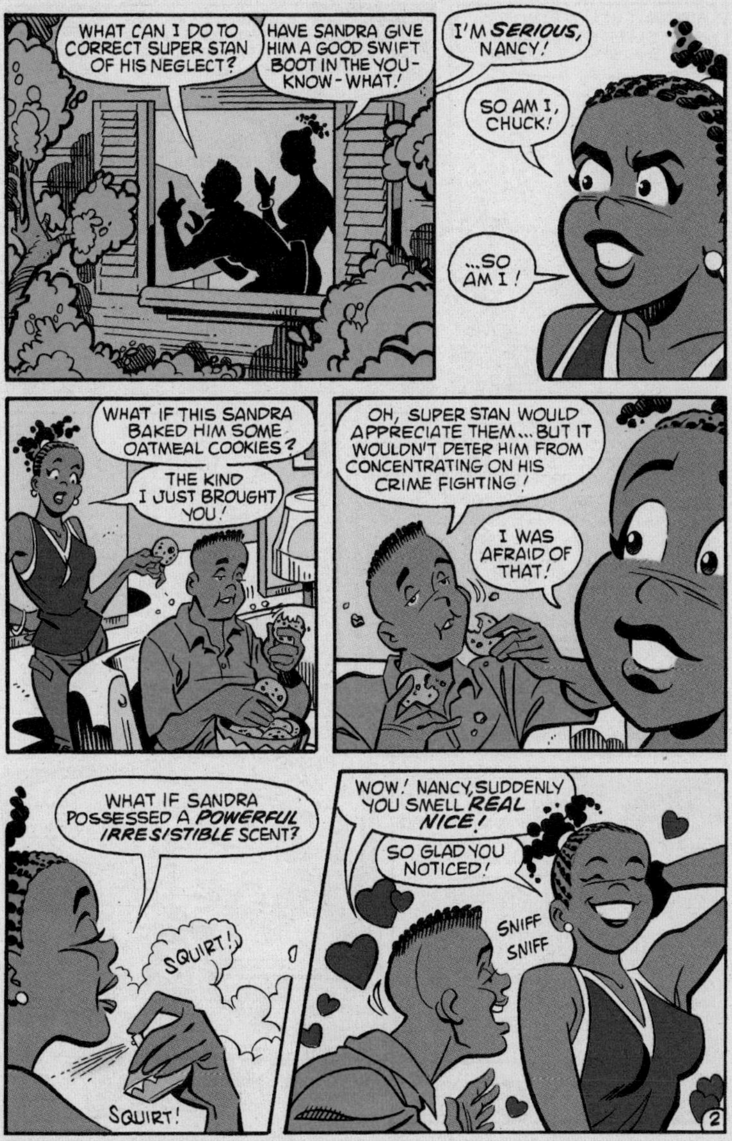
WHAT CAN I DO TO CORRECT SUPER STAN OF HIS NEGLECT?
HAVE SANDRA GIVE HIM A GOOD SWIFT BOOT IN THE YOU-KNOW-WHAT!
I'M *SERIOUS*, NANCY!
SO AM I, CHUCK!
...SO AM I!
WHAT IF THIS SANDRA BAKED HIM SOME OATMEAL COOKIES?
THE KIND I JUST BROUGHT YOU!
OH, SUPER STAN WOULD APPRECIATE THEM... BUT IT WOULDN'T DETER HIM FROM CONCENTRATING ON HIS CRIME FIGHTING!
I WAS AFRAID OF THAT!
WHAT IF SANDRA POSSESSED A *POWERFUL IRRESISTIBLE* SCENT?
SQUIRT!
SQUIRT!
WOW! NANCY, SUDDENLY YOU SMELL *REAL NICE!*
SO GLAD YOU NOTICED!
SNIFF SNIFF

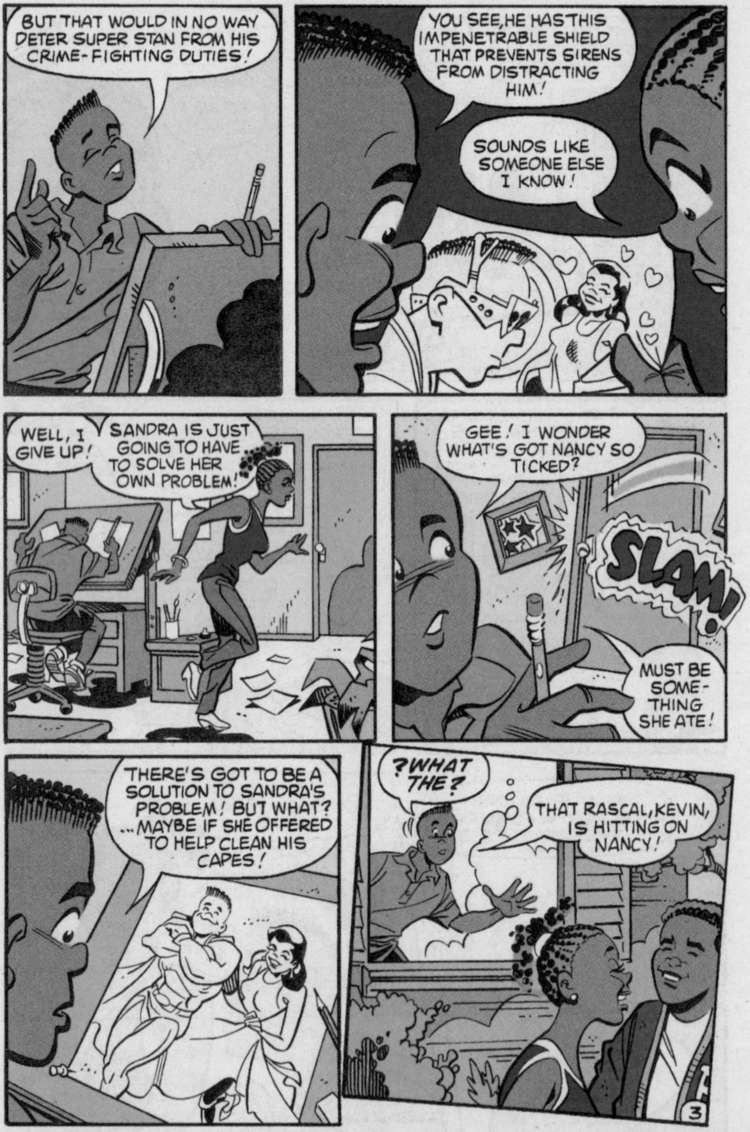
BUT THAT WOULD IN NO WAY DETER SUPER STAN FROM HIS CRIME-FIGHTING DUTIES!
YOU SEE, HE HAS THIS IMPENETRABLE SHIELD THAT PREVENTS SIRENS FROM DISTRACTING HIM!
SOUNDS LIKE SOMEONE ELSE I KNOW!
WELL, I GIVE UP!
SANDRA IS JUST GOING TO HAVE TO SOLVE HER OWN PROBLEM!
GEE! I WONDER WHAT'S GOT NANCY SO TICKED?
SLAM!
MUST BE SOME-THING SHE ATE!
THERE'S GOT TO BE A SOLUTION TO SANDRA'S PROBLEM! BUT WHAT? ...MAYBE IF SHE OFFERED TO HELP CLEAN HIS CAPES!
?WHAT THE?
THAT RASCAL, KEVIN, IS HITTING ON NANCY!
3

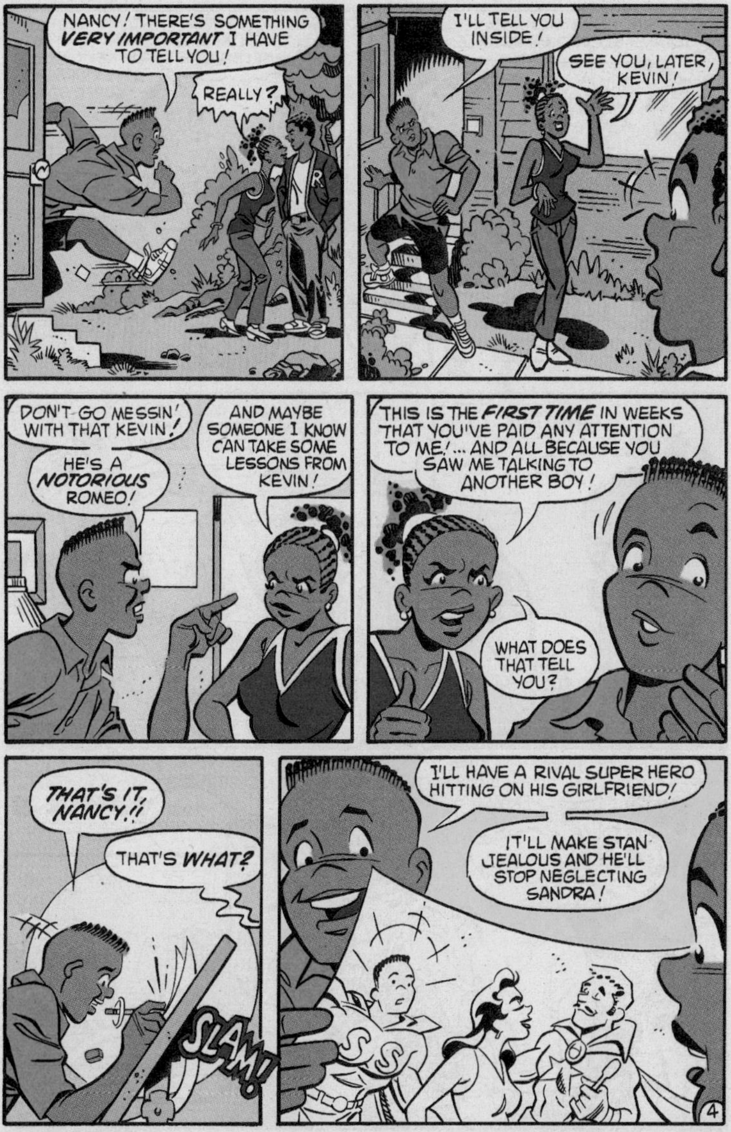
NANCY! THERE'S SOMETHING *VERY IMPORTANT* I HAVE TO TELL YOU!
REALLY?
I'LL TELL YOU INSIDE!
SEE YOU, LATER, KEVIN!
DON'T GO MESSIN' WITH THAT KEVIN!
HE'S A *NOTORIOUS* ROMEO!
AND MAYBE SOMEONE I KNOW CAN TAKE SOME LESSONS FROM KEVIN!
THIS IS THE *FIRST TIME* IN WEEKS THAT YOU'VE PAID ANY ATTENTION TO ME! ... AND ALL BECAUSE YOU SAW ME TALKING TO ANOTHER BOY!
WHAT DOES THAT TELL YOU?
THAT'S IT, NANCY!!
THAT'S *WHAT?*
SLAM!
I'LL HAVE A RIVAL SUPER HERO HITTING ON HIS GIRLFRIEND!
IT'LL MAKE STAN JEALOUS AND HE'LL STOP NEGLECTING SANDRA!
4

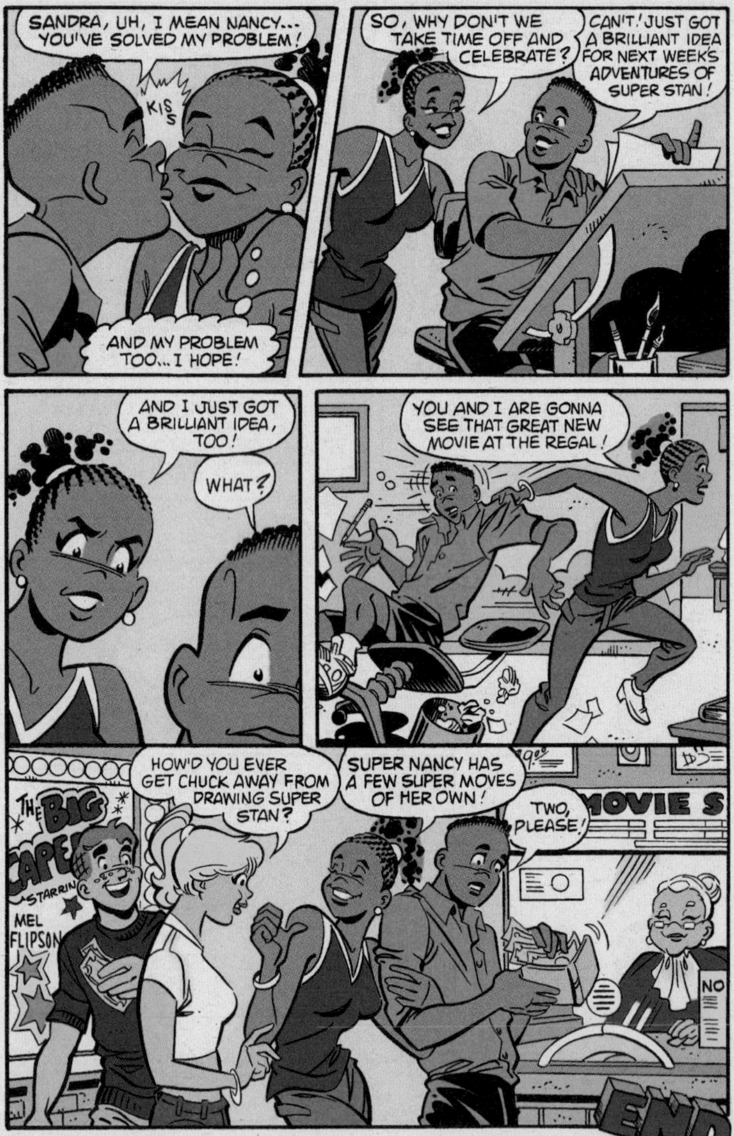
SANDRA, UH, I MEAN NANCY... YOU'VE SOLVED MY PROBLEM!
KISS
AND MY PROBLEM TOO... I HOPE!
SO, WHY DON'T WE TAKE TIME OFF AND CELEBRATE?
CAN'T! JUST GOT A BRILLIANT IDEA FOR NEXT WEEK'S ADVENTURES OF SUPER STAN!
AND I JUST GOT A BRILLIANT IDEA, TOO!
WHAT?
YOU AND I ARE GONNA SEE THAT GREAT NEW MOVIE AT THE REGAL!
THE BIG CAPER
STARRING
MEL FLIPSON
HOW'D YOU EVER GET CHUCK AWAY FROM DRAWING SUPER STAN?
SUPER NANCY HAS A FEW SUPER MOVES OF HER OWN!
MOVIE S
TWO, PLEASE!
NO
END

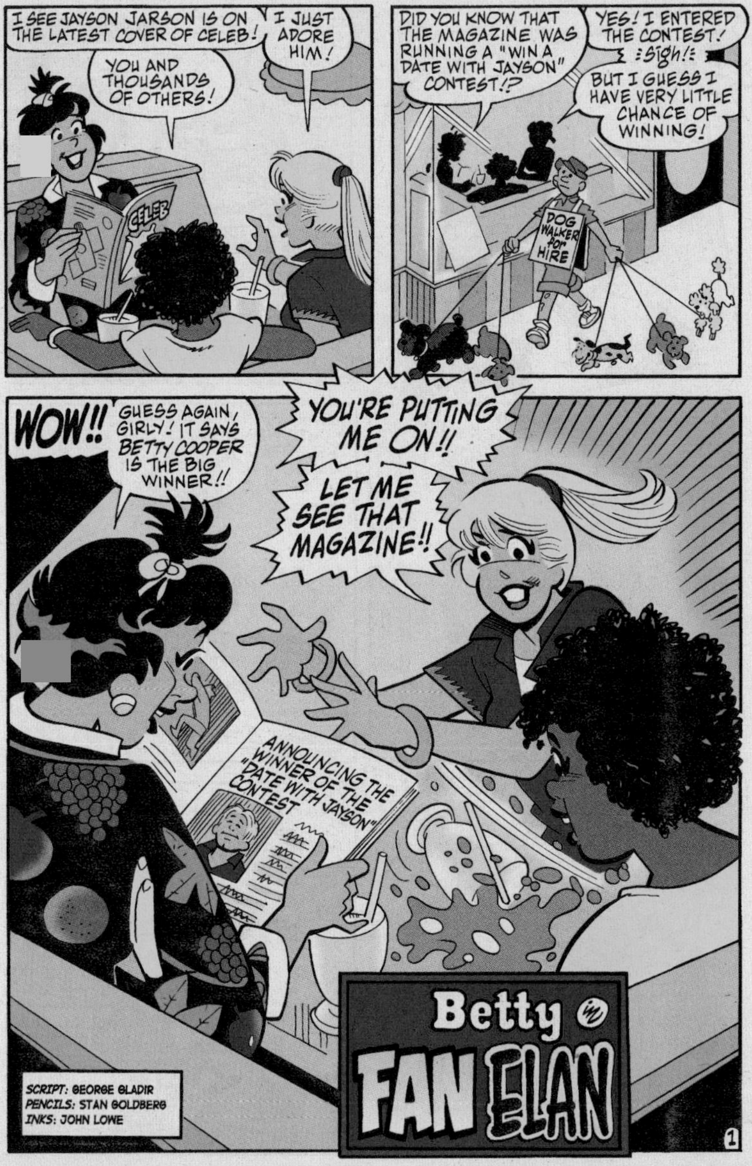
I SEE JAYSON JARSON IS ON THE LATEST COVER OF CELEB!
I JUST ADORE HIM!
YOU AND THOUSANDS OF OTHERS!
CELEB
DID YOU KNOW THAT THE MAGAZINE WAS RUNNING A "WIN A DATE WITH JAYSON" CONTEST!?
YES! I ENTERED THE CONTEST! :SIGH!:
BUT I GUESS I HAVE VERY LITTLE CHANCE OF WINNING!
DOG WALKER for HIRE
WOW!!
GUESS AGAIN, GIRLY! IT SAYS BETTY COOPER IS THE BIG WINNER!!
YOU'RE PUTTING ME ON!!
LET ME SEE THAT MAGAZINE!!
ANNOUNCING THE WINNER OF THE "DATE WITH JAYSON" CONTEST
Betty in
FAN ELAN
SCRIPT: GEORGE GLADIR
PENCILS: STAN GOLDBERG
INKS: JOHN LOWE
1

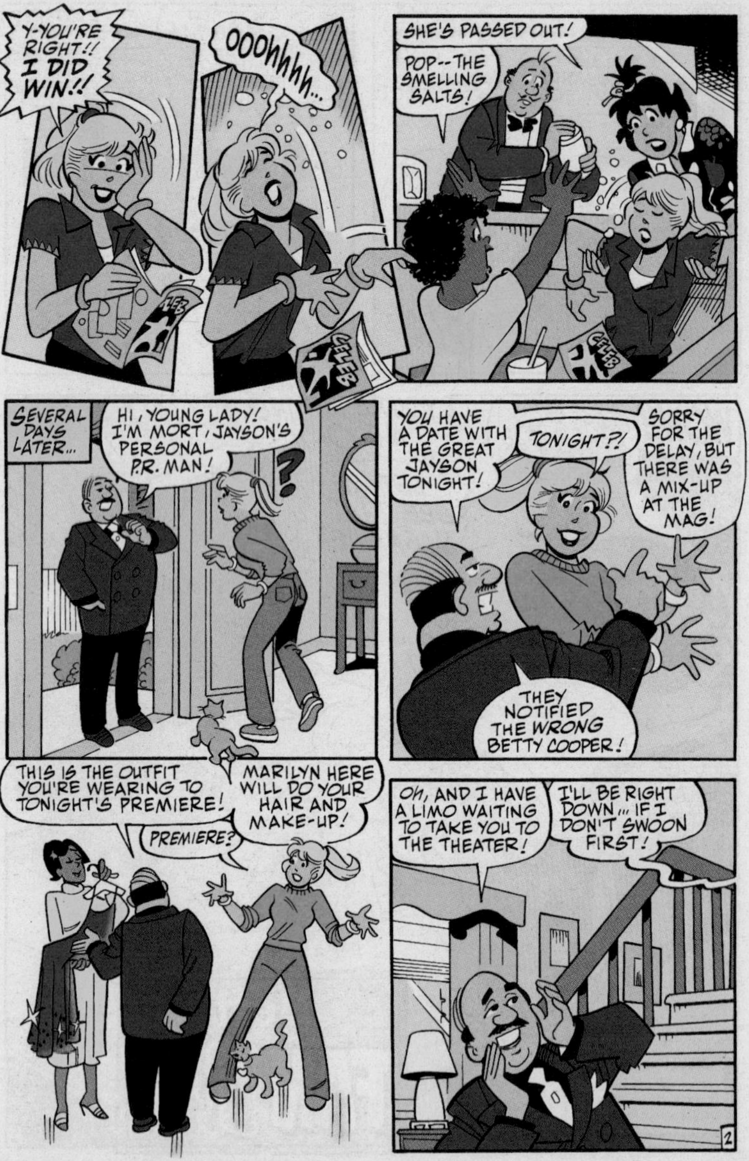

Y-YOU'RE RIGHT!! I DID WIN!!
OOOhhhh...
SHE'S PASSED OUT!
POP--THE SMELLING SALTS!
CELEB
SEVERAL DAYS LATER...
HI, YOUNG LADY! I'M MORT, JAYSON'S PERSONAL P.R. MAN!
?
YOU HAVE A DATE WITH THE GREAT JAYSON TONIGHT!
TONIGHT?!
SORRY FOR THE DELAY, BUT THERE WAS A MIX-UP AT THE MAG!
THEY NOTIFIED THE WRONG BETTY COOPER!
THIS IS THE OUTFIT YOU'RE WEARING TO TONIGHT'S PREMIERE!
MARILYN HERE WILL DO YOUR HAIR AND MAKE-UP!
PREMIERE?
OH, AND I HAVE A LIMO WAITING TO TAKE YOU TO THE THEATER!
I'LL BE RIGHT DOWN... IF I DON'T SWOON FIRST!
2

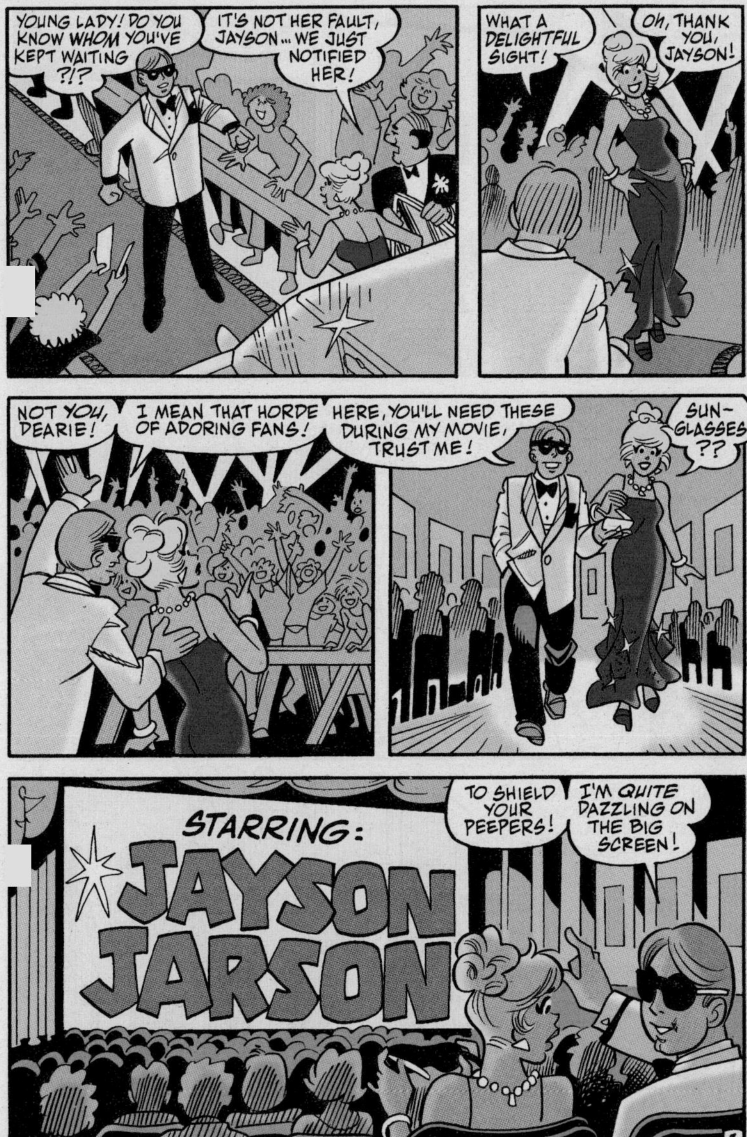

YOUNG LADY! DO YOU KNOW WHOM YOU'VE KEPT WAITING ?!?
IT'S NOT HER FAULT, JAYSON... WE JUST NOTIFIED HER!
WHAT A DELIGHTFUL SIGHT!
OH, THANK YOU, JAYSON!
NOT YOU, DEARIE!
I MEAN THAT HORDE OF ADORING FANS!
HERE, YOU'LL NEED THESE DURING MY MOVIE, TRUST ME!
SUN-GLASSES ??
STARRING:
JAYSON JARSON
TO SHIELD YOUR PEEPERS!
I'M QUITE DAZZLING ON THE BIG SCREEN!
3

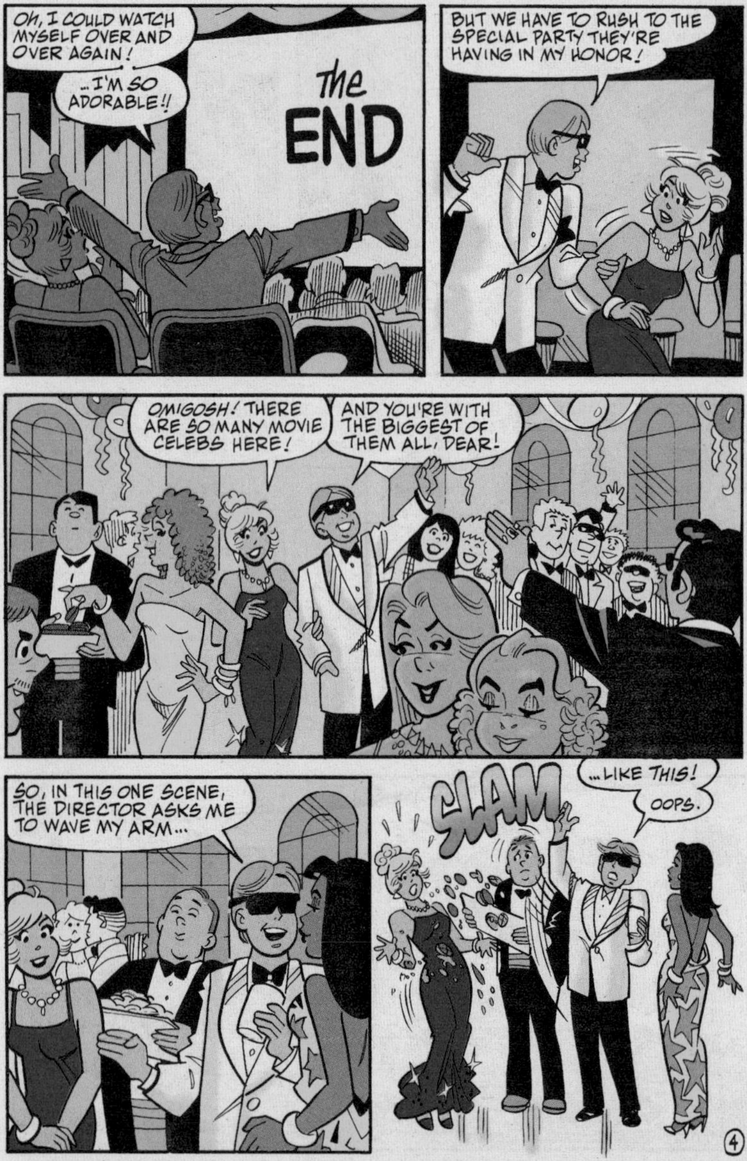

OH, I COULD WATCH MYSELF OVER AND OVER AGAIN!
...I'M SO ADORABLE!!
THE END
BUT WE HAVE TO RUSH TO THE SPECIAL PARTY THEY'RE HAVING IN MY HONOR!
OMIGOSH! THERE ARE SO MANY MOVIE CELEBS HERE!
AND YOU'RE WITH THE BIGGEST OF THEM ALL, DEAR!
SO, IN THIS ONE SCENE, THE DIRECTOR ASKS ME TO WAVE MY ARM...
SLAM
...LIKE THIS!
OOPS.

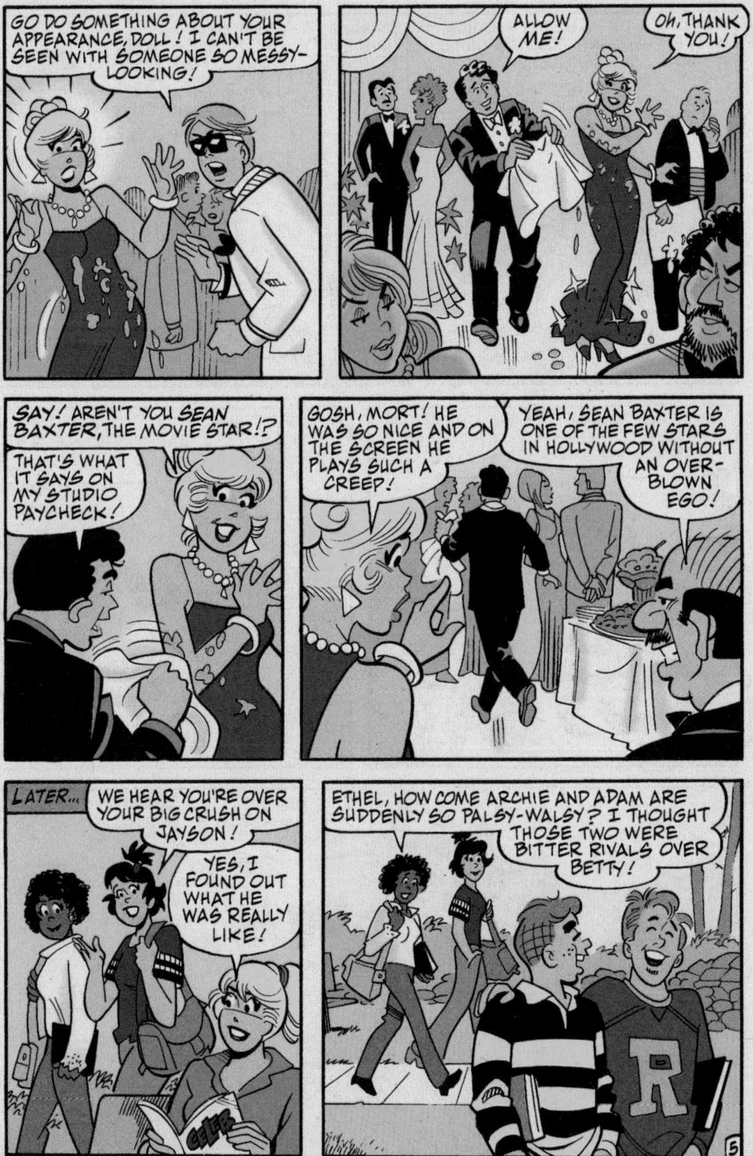

GO DO SOMETHING ABOUT YOUR APPEARANCE, DOLL! I CAN'T BE SEEN WITH SOMEONE SO MESSY-LOOKING!
ALLOW ME!
Oh, THANK YOU!
SAY! AREN'T YOU SEAN BAXTER, THE MOVIE STAR!?
THAT'S WHAT IT SAYS ON MY STUDIO PAYCHECK!
GOSH, MORT! HE WAS SO NICE AND ON THE SCREEN HE PLAYS SUCH A CREEP!
YEAH, SEAN BAXTER IS ONE OF THE FEW STARS IN HOLLYWOOD WITHOUT AN OVER-BLOWN EGO!
LATER...
WE HEAR YOU'RE OVER YOUR BIG CRUSH ON JAYSON!
YES, I FOUND OUT WHAT HE WAS REALLY LIKE!
CELEB
ETHEL, HOW COME ARCHIE AND ADAM ARE SUDDENLY SO PALSY-WALSY? I THOUGHT THOSE TWO WERE BITTER RIVALS OVER BETTY!
5

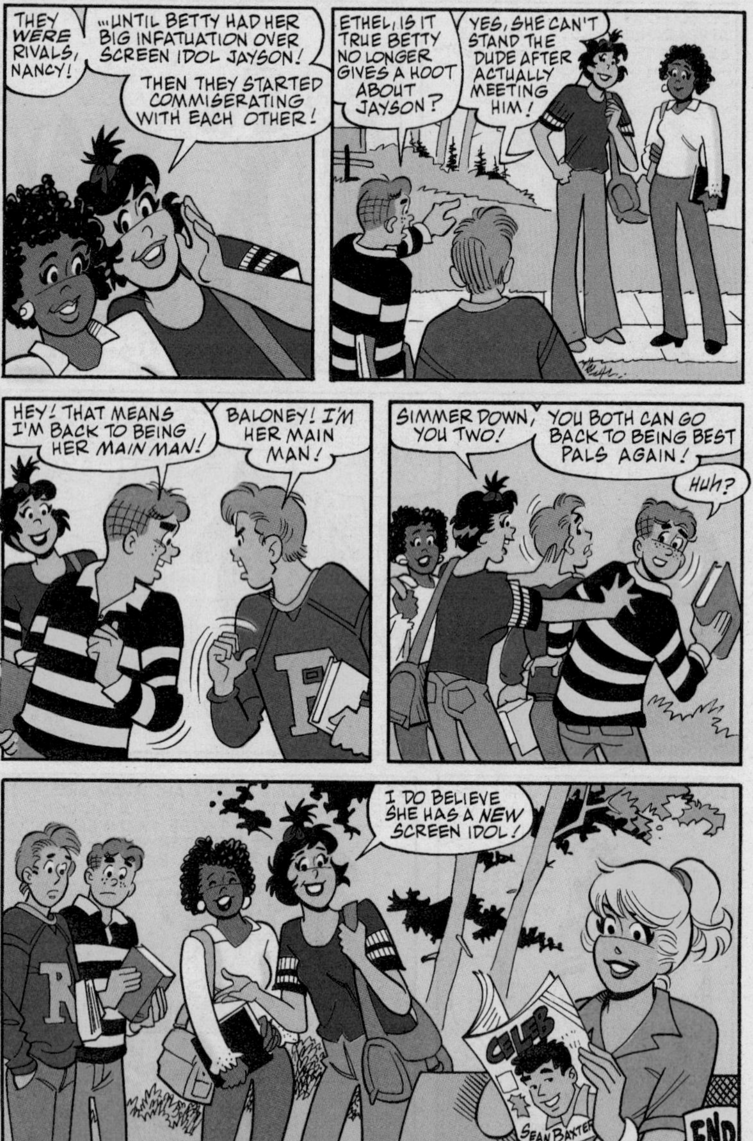
THEY WERE RIVALS, NANCY!
...UNTIL BETTY HAD HER BIG INFATUATION OVER SCREEN IDOL JAYSON!
THEN THEY STARTED COMMISERATING WITH EACH OTHER!
ETHEL, IS IT TRUE BETTY NO LONGER GIVES A HOOT ABOUT JAYSON?
YES, SHE CAN'T STAND THE DUDE AFTER ACTUALLY MEETING HIM!
HEY! THAT MEANS I'M BACK TO BEING HER MAIN MAN!
BALONEY! I'M HER MAIN MAN!
SIMMER DOWN, YOU TWO!
YOU BOTH CAN GO BACK TO BEING BEST PALS AGAIN!
HUH?
I DO BELIEVE SHE HAS A NEW SCREEN IDOL!
CELEB
SEAN BAXTER
END

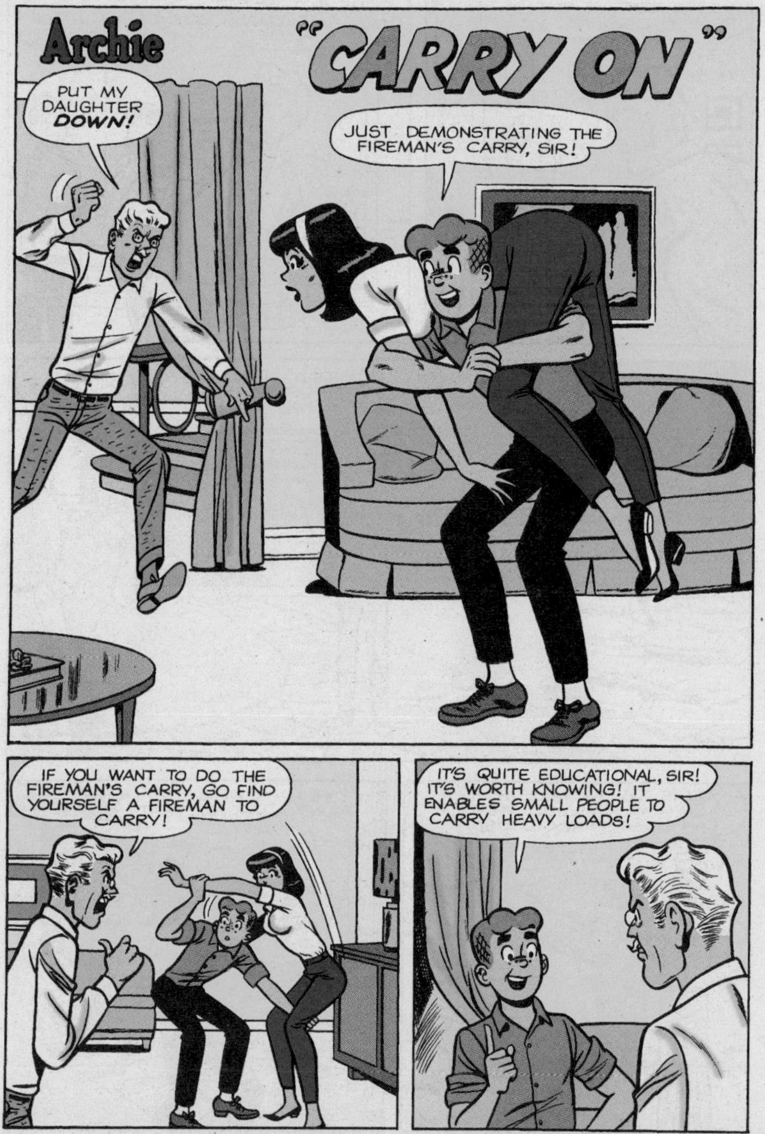
Archie
"CARRY ON"
PUT MY DAUGHTER DOWN!
JUST DEMONSTRATING THE FIREMAN'S CARRY, SIR!
IF YOU WANT TO DO THE FIREMAN'S CARRY, GO FIND YOURSELF A FIREMAN TO CARRY!
IT'S QUITE EDUCATIONAL, SIR! IT'S WORTH KNOWING! IT ENABLES SMALL PEOPLE TO CARRY HEAVY LOADS!

Script: Frank Doyle / Pencils: Harry Lucey / Inks & Letters: Mario Acquaviva

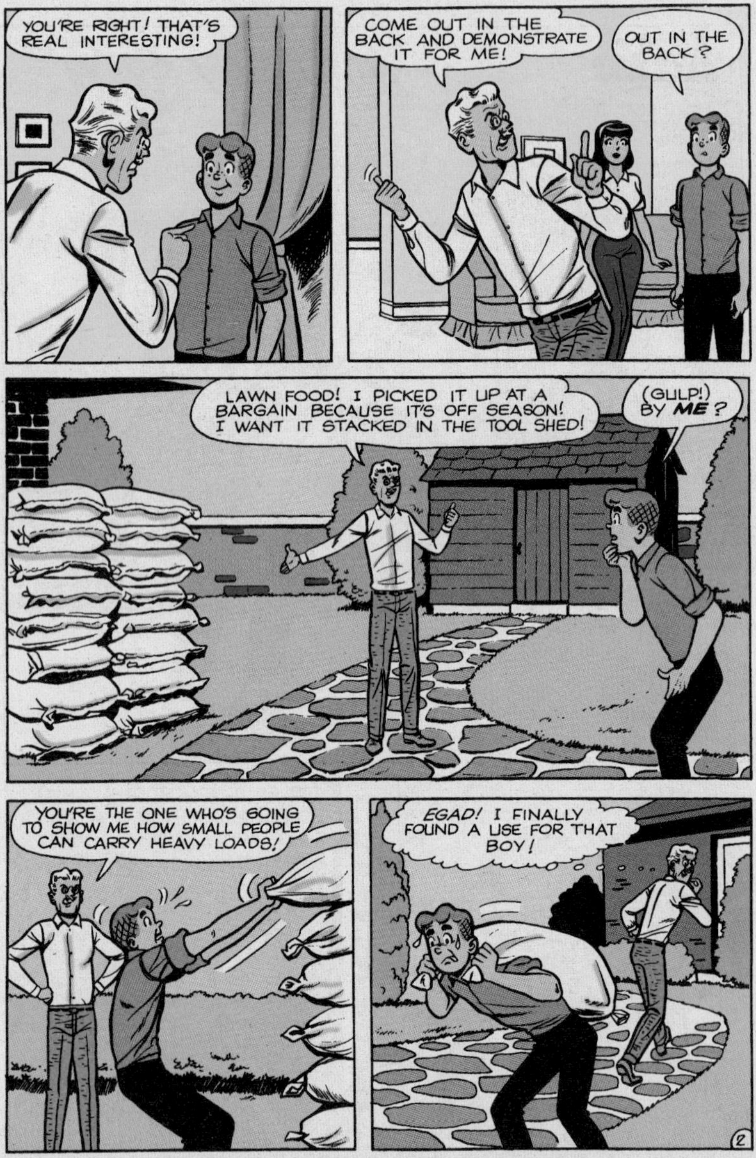
YOU'RE RIGHT! THAT'S REAL INTERESTING!
COME OUT IN THE BACK AND DEMONSTRATE IT FOR ME!
OUT IN THE BACK?
LAWN FOOD! I PICKED IT UP AT A BARGAIN BECAUSE IT'S OFF SEASON! I WANT IT STACKED IN THE TOOL SHED!
(GULP!) BY ME?
YOU'RE THE ONE WHO'S GOING TO SHOW ME HOW SMALL PEOPLE CAN CARRY HEAVY LOADS!
EGAD! I FINALLY FOUND A USE FOR THAT BOY!
2

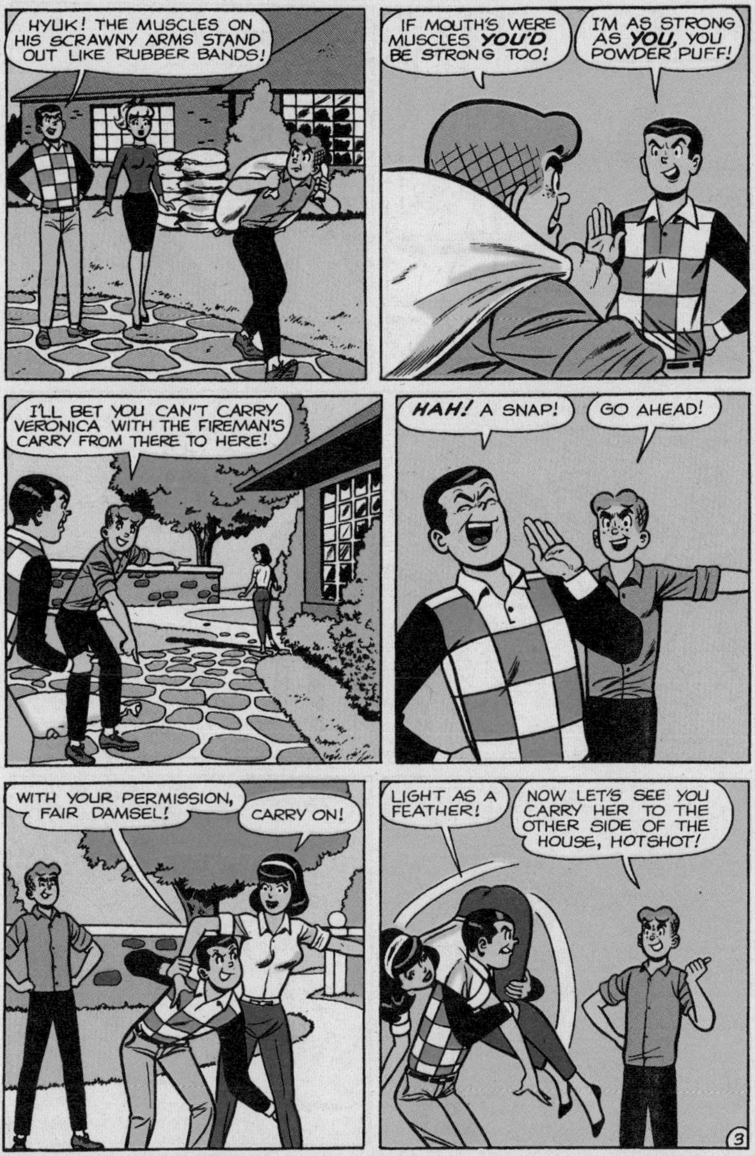
HYUK! THE MUSCLES ON HIS SCRAWNY ARMS STAND OUT LIKE RUBBER BANDS!
IF MOUTH'S WERE MUSCLES YOU'D BE STRONG TOO!
I'M AS STRONG AS YOU, YOU POWDER PUFF!
I'LL BET YOU CAN'T CARRY VERONICA WITH THE FIREMAN'S CARRY FROM THERE TO HERE!
HAH! A SNAP!
GO AHEAD!
WITH YOUR PERMISSION, FAIR DAMSEL!
CARRY ON!
LIGHT AS A FEATHER!
NOW LET'S SEE YOU CARRY HER TO THE OTHER SIDE OF THE HOUSE, HOTSHOT!
3

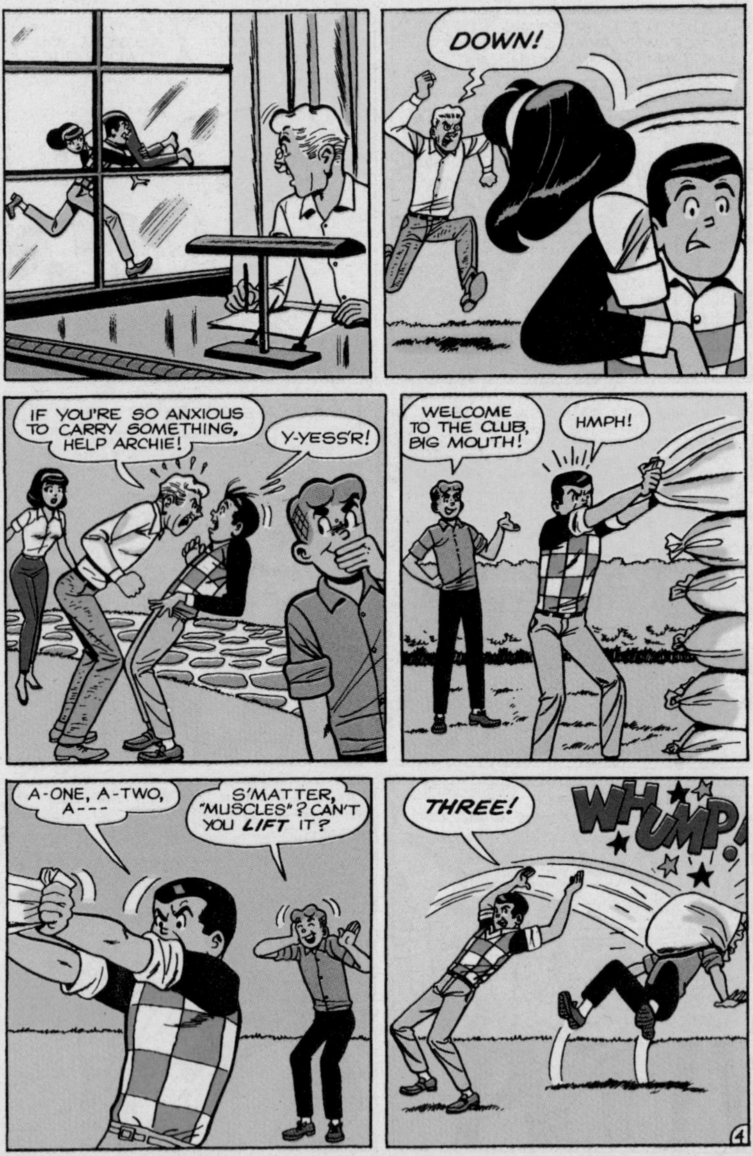
DOWN!
IF YOU'RE SO ANXIOUS TO CARRY SOMETHING, HELP ARCHIE!
Y-YESS'R!
WELCOME TO THE CLUB, BIG MOUTH!
HMPH!
A-ONE, A-TWO, A---
S'MATTER, "MUSCLES"? CAN'T YOU LIFT IT?
THREE!
WHUMP!
4

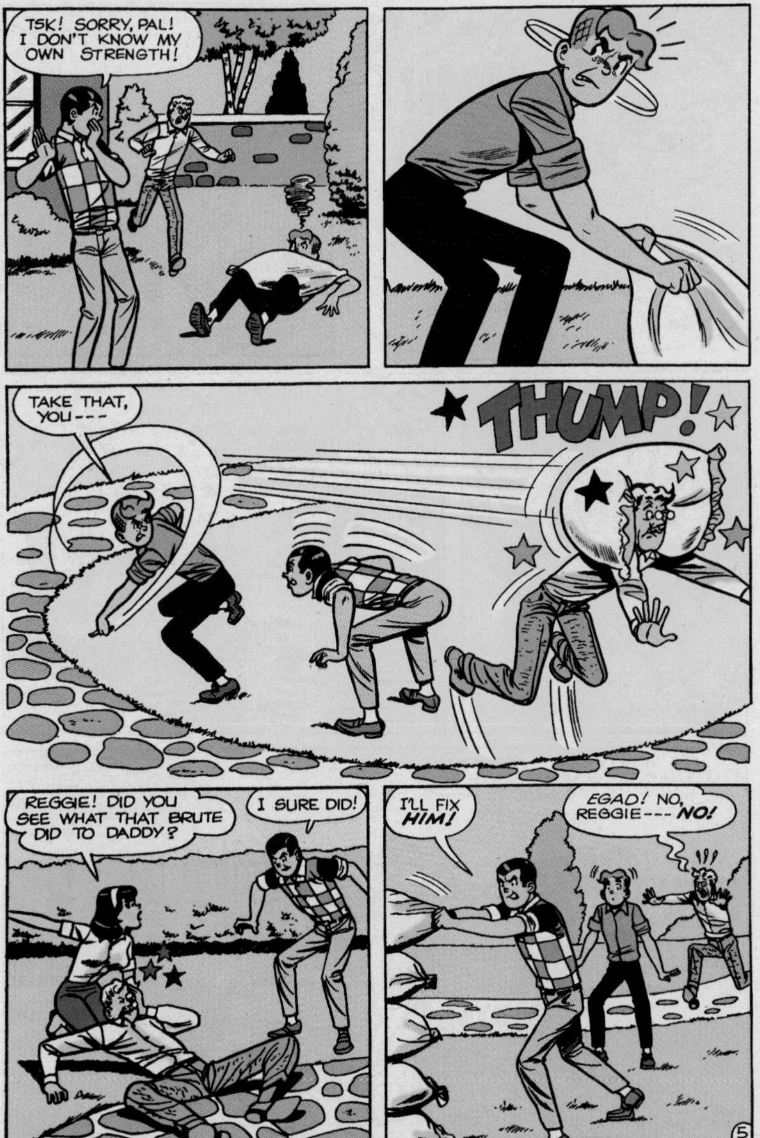
TSK! SORRY, PAL! I DON'T KNOW MY OWN STRENGTH!
TAKE THAT, YOU---
THUMP!
REGGIE! DID YOU SEE WHAT THAT BRUTE DID TO DADDY?
I SURE DID!
I'LL FIX HIM!
EGAD! NO, REGGIE---NO!
5

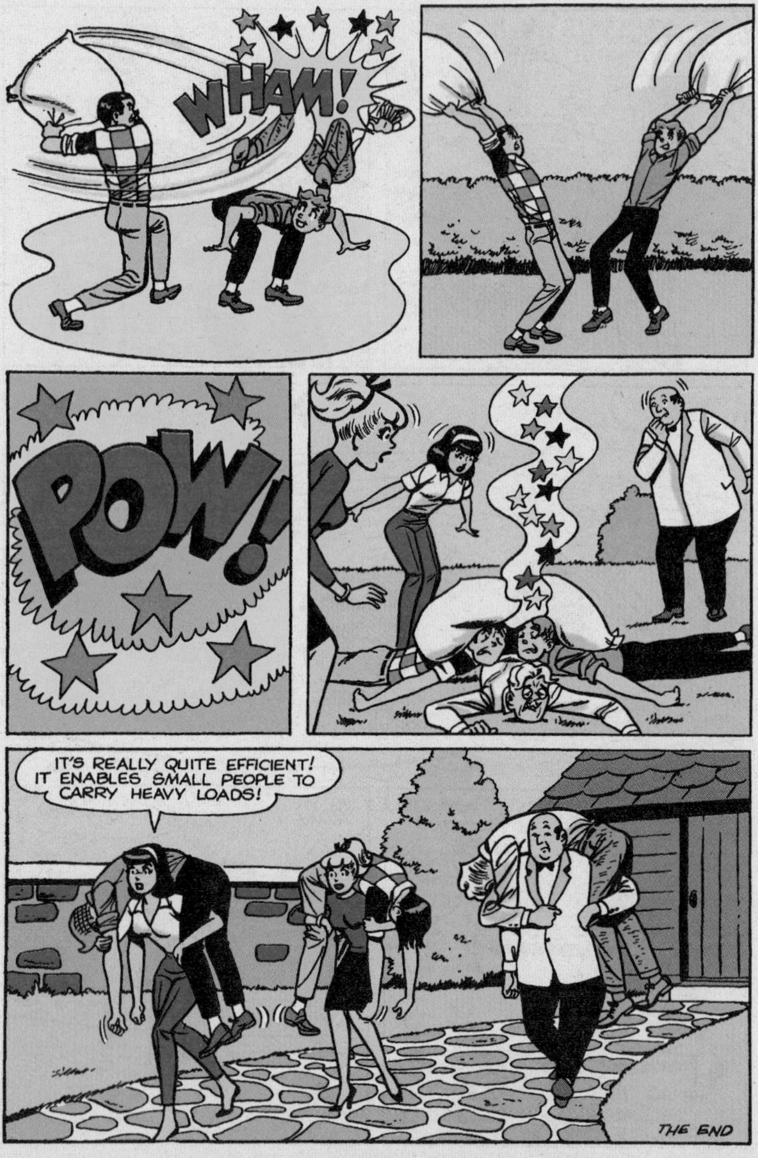
WHAM!
POW!!
IT'S REALLY QUITE EFFICIENT! IT ENABLES SMALL PEOPLE TO CARRY HEAVY LOADS!
THE END

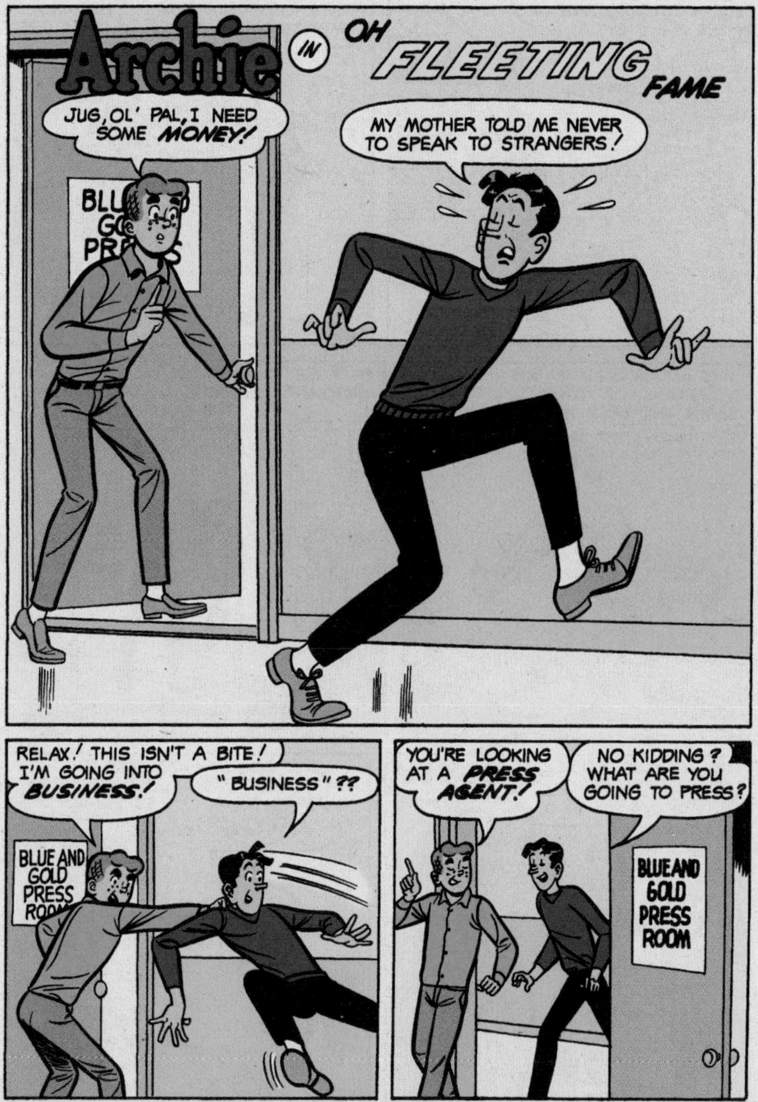
Archie
IN
OH FLEETING FAME
JUG, OL' PAL, I NEED SOME MONEY!
MY MOTHER TOLD ME NEVER TO SPEAK TO STRANGERS!
RELAX! THIS ISN'T A BITE! I'M GOING INTO BUSINESS!
"BUSINESS"??
BLUE AND GOLD PRESS ROOM
YOU'RE LOOKING AT A PRESS AGENT!
NO KIDDING? WHAT ARE YOU GOING TO PRESS?
BLUE AND GOLD PRESS ROOM

Script: Frank Doyle / Pencils: Harry Lucey / Inks: Mario Acquaviva / Letters: Bill Yoshida

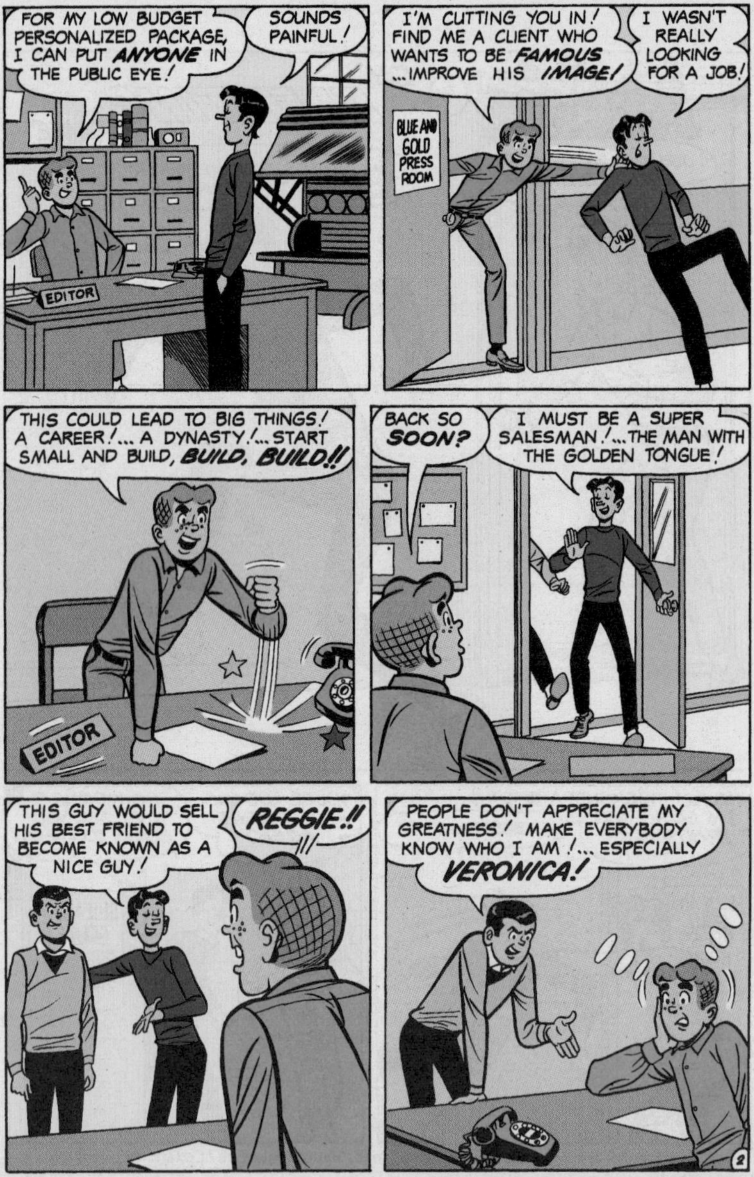
FOR MY LOW BUDGET PERSONALIZED PACKAGE, I CAN PUT ANYONE IN THE PUBLIC EYE!
SOUNDS PAINFUL!
EDITOR
I'M CUTTING YOU IN! FIND ME A CLIENT WHO WANTS TO BE FAMOUS ...IMPROVE HIS IMAGE!
I WASN'T REALLY LOOKING FOR A JOB!
BLUE AND GOLD PRESS ROOM
THIS COULD LEAD TO BIG THINGS! A CAREER!... A DYNASTY!... START SMALL AND BUILD, BUILD, BUILD!!
EDITOR
BACK SO SOON?
I MUST BE A SUPER SALESMAN!... THE MAN WITH THE GOLDEN TONGUE!
THIS GUY WOULD SELL HIS BEST FRIEND TO BECOME KNOWN AS A NICE GUY!
REGGIE!!
PEOPLE DON'T APPRECIATE MY GREATNESS! MAKE EVERYBODY KNOW WHO I AM!... ESPECIALLY VERONICA!
2

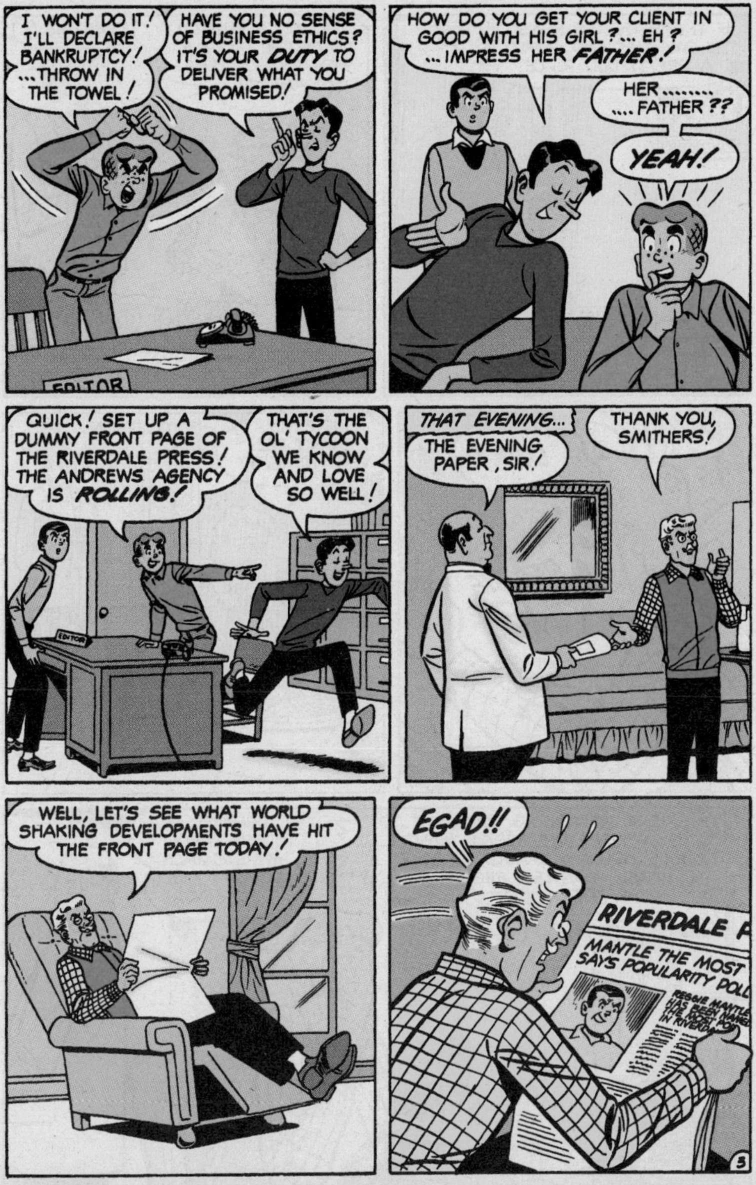
I WON'T DO IT! I'LL DECLARE BANKRUPTCY! ...THROW IN THE TOWEL!
HAVE YOU NO SENSE OF BUSINESS ETHICS? IT'S YOUR DUTY TO DELIVER WHAT YOU PROMISED!
HOW DO YOU GET YOUR CLIENT IN GOOD WITH HIS GIRL?... EH? ...IMPRESS HER FATHER!
HER .... FATHER??
YEAH!
EDITOR
QUICK! SET UP A DUMMY FRONT PAGE OF THE RIVERDALE PRESS! THE ANDREWS AGENCY IS ROLLING!
THAT'S THE OL' TYCOON WE KNOW AND LOVE SO WELL!
THAT EVENING...
THE EVENING PAPER, SIR!
THANK YOU, SMITHERS!
WELL, LET'S SEE WHAT WORLD SHAKING DEVELOPMENTS HAVE HIT THE FRONT PAGE TODAY!
EGAD!!
RIVERDALE
MANTLE THE MOST
SAYS POPULARITY
3

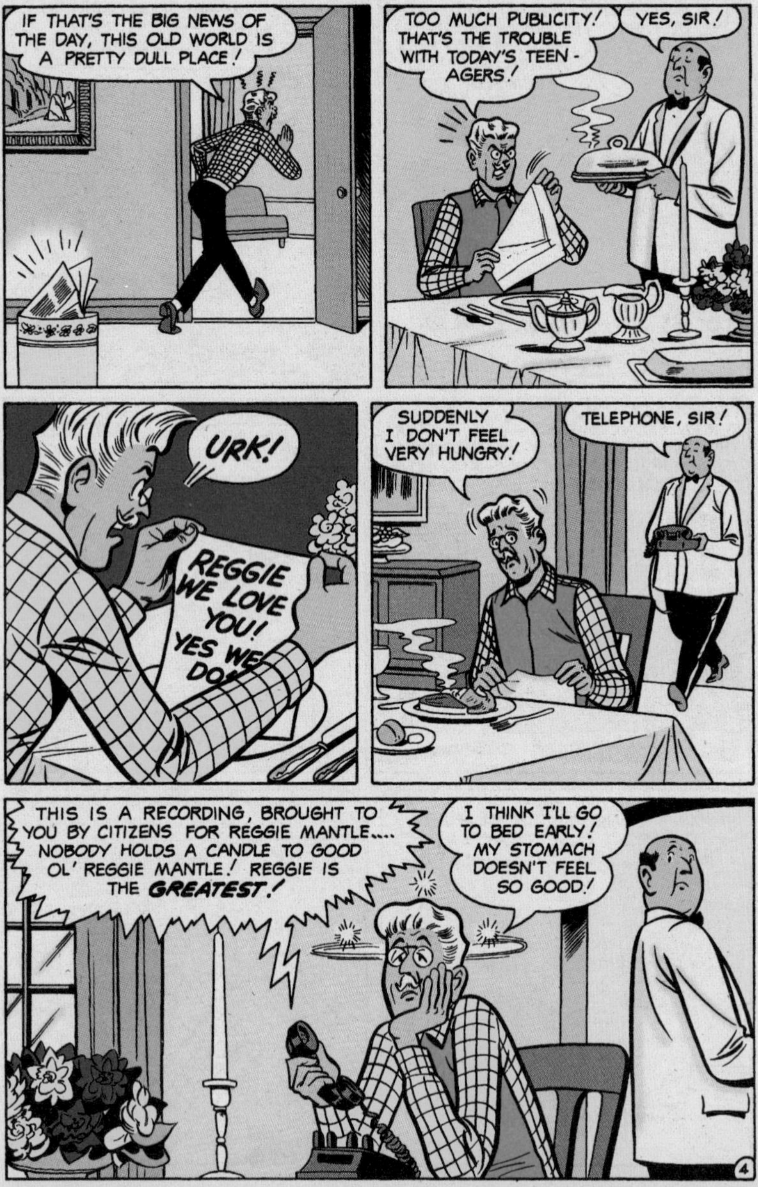
IF THAT'S THE BIG NEWS OF THE DAY, THIS OLD WORLD IS A PRETTY DULL PLACE!
TOO MUCH PUBLICITY! THAT'S THE TROUBLE WITH TODAY'S TEEN-AGERS!
YES, SIR!
URK!
REGGIE WE LOVE YOU! YES WE DO
SUDDENLY I DON'T FEEL VERY HUNGRY!
TELEPHONE, SIR!
THIS IS A RECORDING, BROUGHT TO YOU BY CITIZENS FOR REGGIE MANTLE.... NOBODY HOLDS A CANDLE TO GOOD OL' REGGIE MANTLE! REGGIE IS THE GREATEST!
I THINK I'LL GO TO BED EARLY! MY STOMACH DOESN'T FEEL SO GOOD!
4

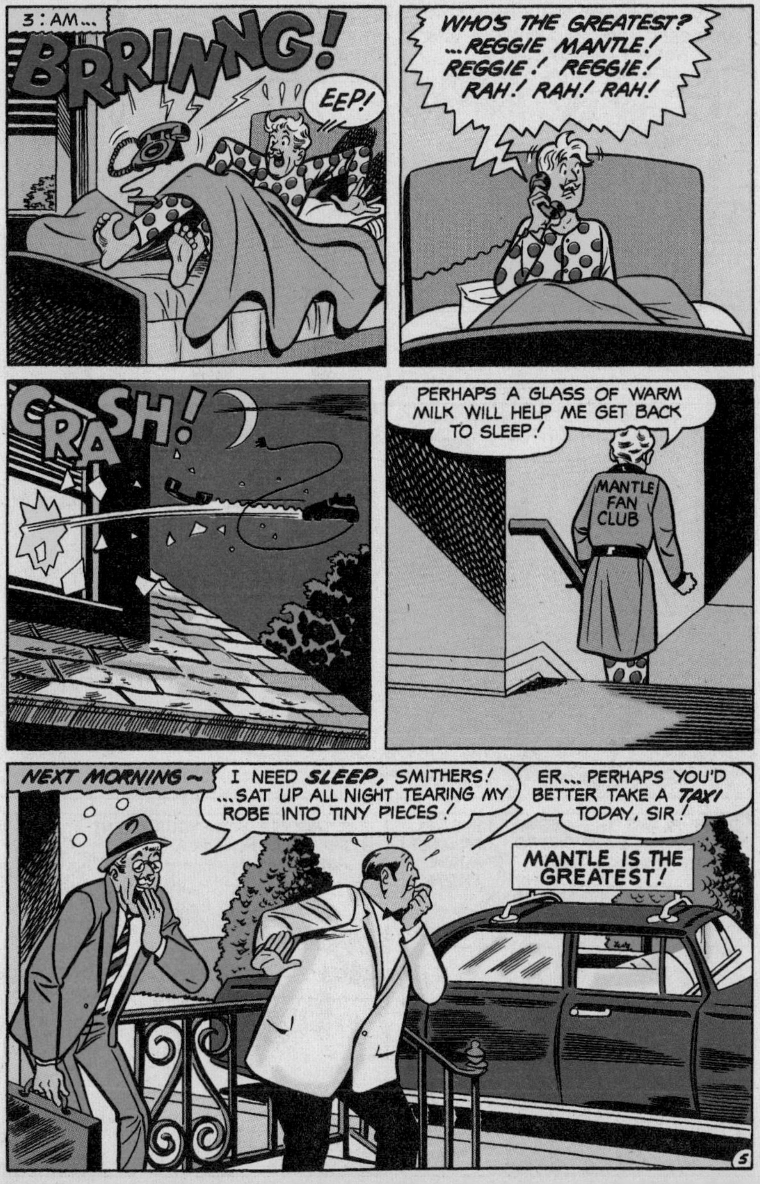
3:AM...
BRRINNG!
EEP!
WHO'S THE GREATEST? ...REGGIE MANTLE! REGGIE! REGGIE! RAH! RAH! RAH!
CRASH!
PERHAPS A GLASS OF WARM MILK WILL HELP ME GET BACK TO SLEEP!
MANTLE FAN CLUB
NEXT MORNING ~
I NEED SLEEP, SMITHERS! ...SAT UP ALL NIGHT TEARING MY ROBE INTO TINY PIECES!
ER... PERHAPS YOU'D BETTER TAKE A TAXI TODAY, SIR!
MANTLE IS THE GREATEST!
5

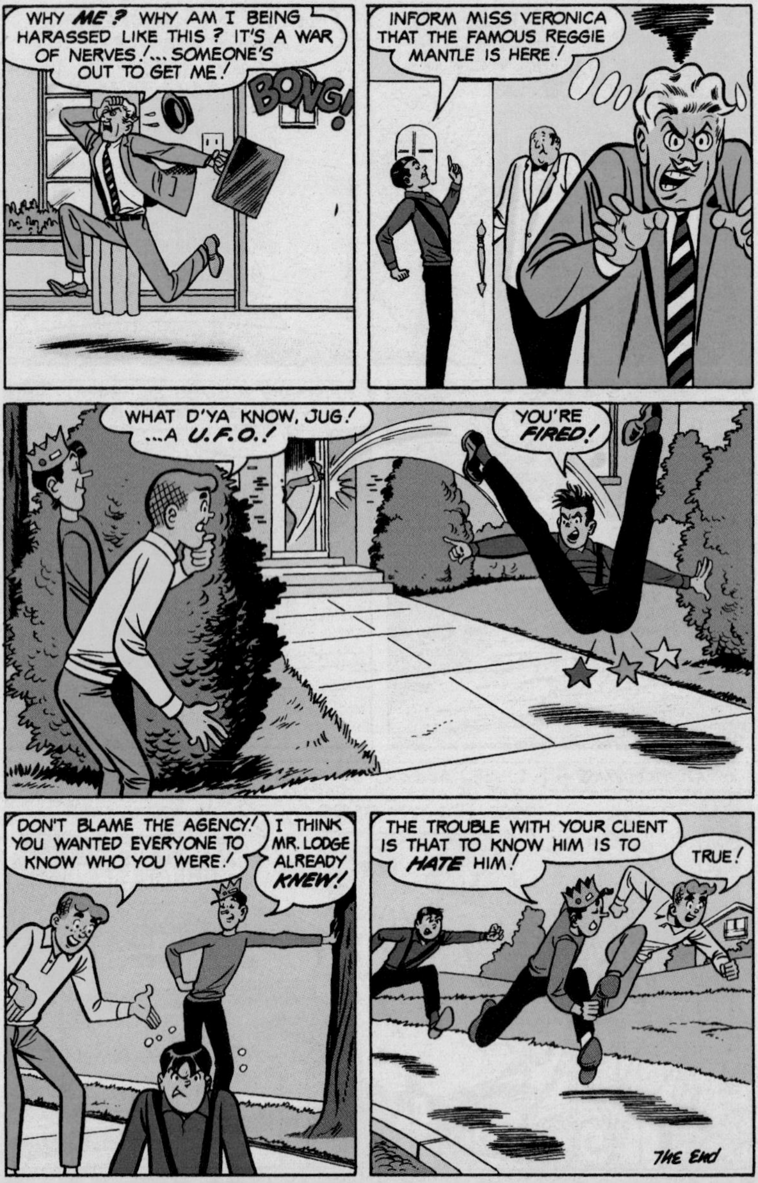
WHY ME? WHY AM I BEING HARASSED LIKE THIS? IT'S A WAR OF NERVES!... SOMEONE'S OUT TO GET ME!
BONG!
INFORM MISS VERONICA THAT THE FAMOUS REGGIE MANTLE IS HERE!
WHAT D'YA KNOW, JUG! ...A U.F.O.!
YOU'RE FIRED!
DON'T BLAME THE AGENCY! YOU WANTED EVERYONE TO KNOW WHO YOU WERE!
I THINK MR. LODGE ALREADY KNEW!
THE TROUBLE WITH YOUR CLIENT IS THAT TO KNOW HIM IS TO HATE HIM!
TRUE!
THE END

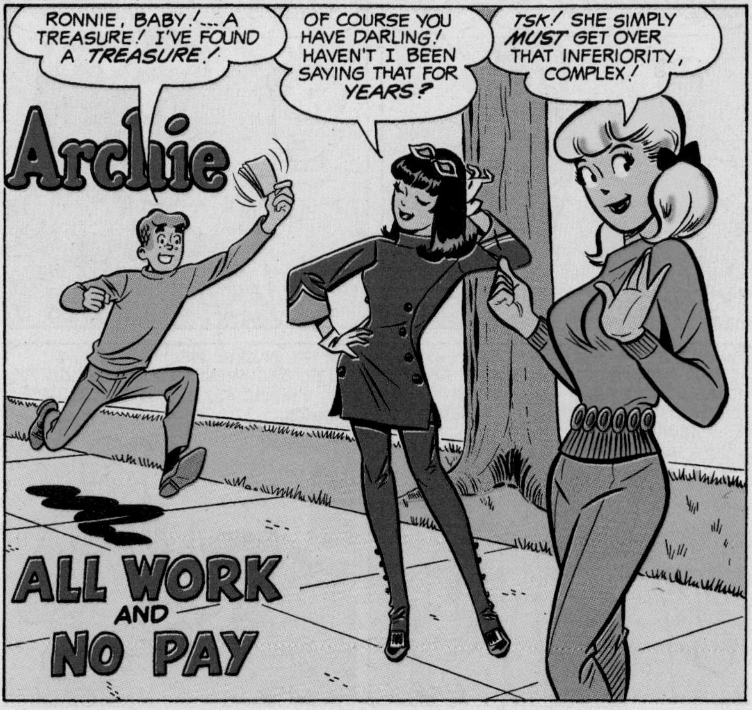
RONNIE, BABY!... A TREASURE! I'VE FOUND A TREASURE!
OF COURSE YOU HAVE DARLING! HAVEN'T I BEEN SAYING THAT FOR YEARS?
TSK! SHE SIMPLY MUST GET OVER THAT INFERIORITY COMPLEX!
Archie
ALL WORK AND NO PAY

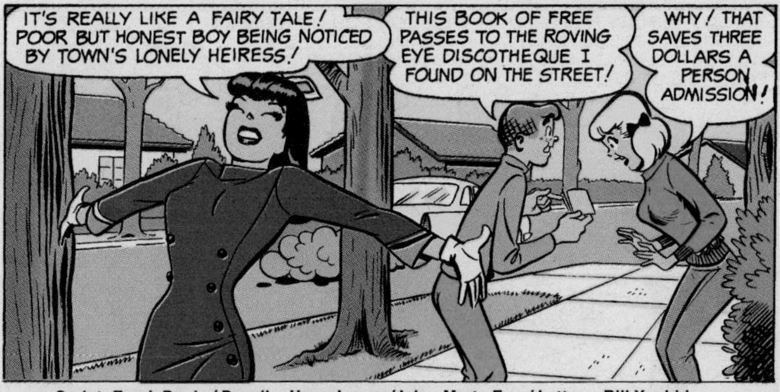
IT'S REALLY LIKE A FAIRY TALE! POOR BUT HONEST BOY BEING NOTICED BY TOWN'S LONELY HEIRESS!
THIS BOOK OF FREE PASSES TO THE ROVING EYE DISCOTHEQUE I FOUND ON THE STREET!
WHY! THAT SAVES THREE DOLLARS A PERSON ADMISSION!

Script: Frank Doyle / Pencils: Harry Lucey / Inks: Marty Epp / Letters: Bill Yoshida

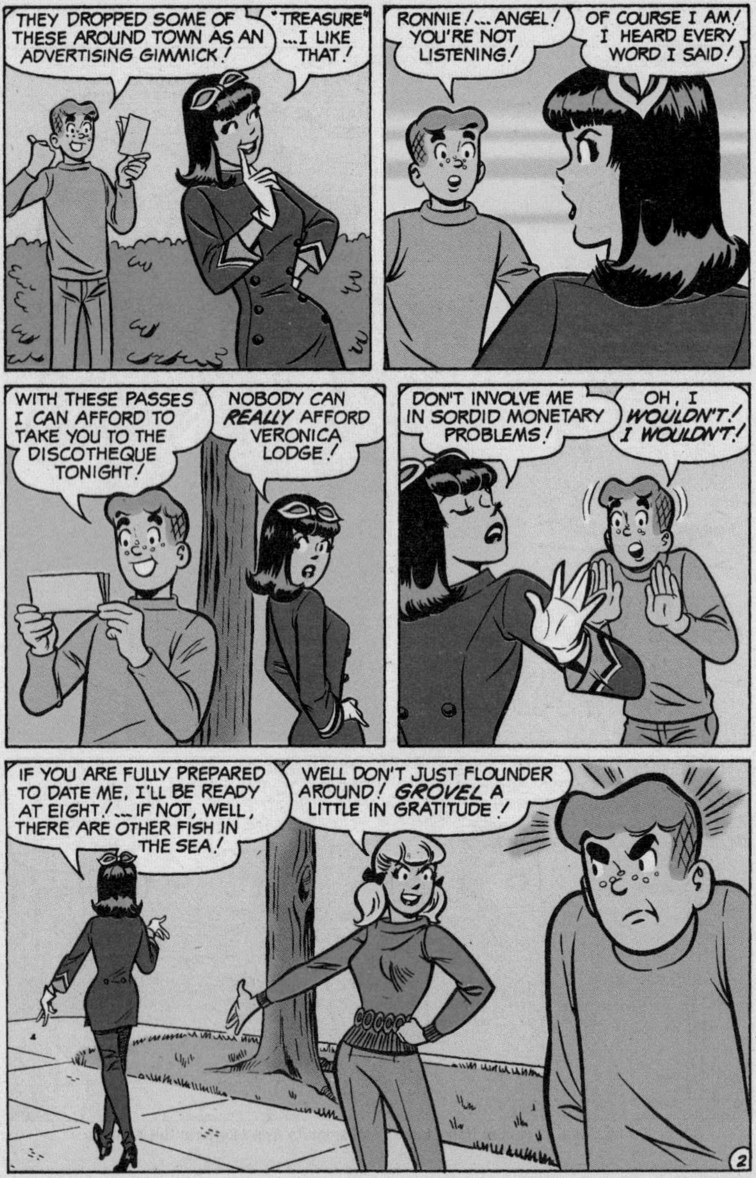

THEY DROPPED SOME OF THESE AROUND TOWN AS AN ADVERTISING GIMMICK!
"TREASURE" ...I LIKE THAT!
RONNIE!... ANGEL! YOU'RE NOT LISTENING!
OF COURSE I AM! I HEARD EVERY WORD I SAID!
WITH THESE PASSES I CAN AFFORD TO TAKE YOU TO THE DISCOTHEQUE TONIGHT!
NOBODY CAN *REALLY* AFFORD VERONICA LODGE!
DON'T INVOLVE ME IN SORDID MONETARY PROBLEMS!
OH, I *WOULDN'T*! *I WOULDN'T*!
IF YOU ARE FULLY PREPARED TO DATE ME, I'LL BE READY AT EIGHT!... IF NOT, WELL, THERE ARE OTHER FISH IN THE SEA!
WELL DON'T JUST FLOUNDER AROUND! *GROVEL* A LITTLE IN GRATITUDE!
2

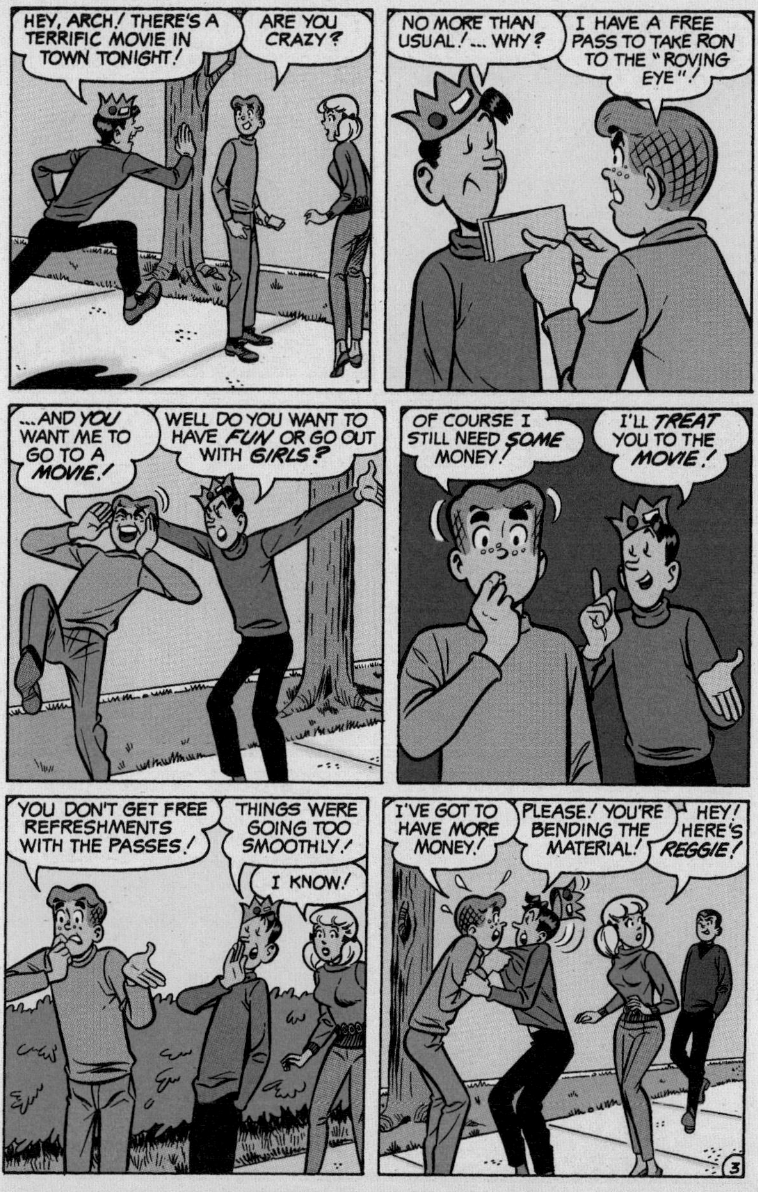

HEY, ARCH! THERE'S A TERRIFIC MOVIE IN TOWN TONIGHT!
ARE YOU CRAZY?
NO MORE THAN USUAL! ... WHY?
I HAVE A FREE PASS TO TAKE RON TO THE "ROVING EYE"!
...AND YOU WANT ME TO GO TO A MOVIE!
WELL DO YOU WANT TO HAVE FUN OR GO OUT WITH GIRLS?
OF COURSE I STILL NEED SOME MONEY!
I'LL TREAT YOU TO THE MOVIE!
YOU DON'T GET FREE REFRESHMENTS WITH THE PASSES!
THINGS WERE GOING TOO SMOOTHLY!
I KNOW!
I'VE GOT TO HAVE MORE MONEY!
PLEASE! YOU'RE BENDING THE MATERIAL!
HEY! HERE'S REGGIE!
3

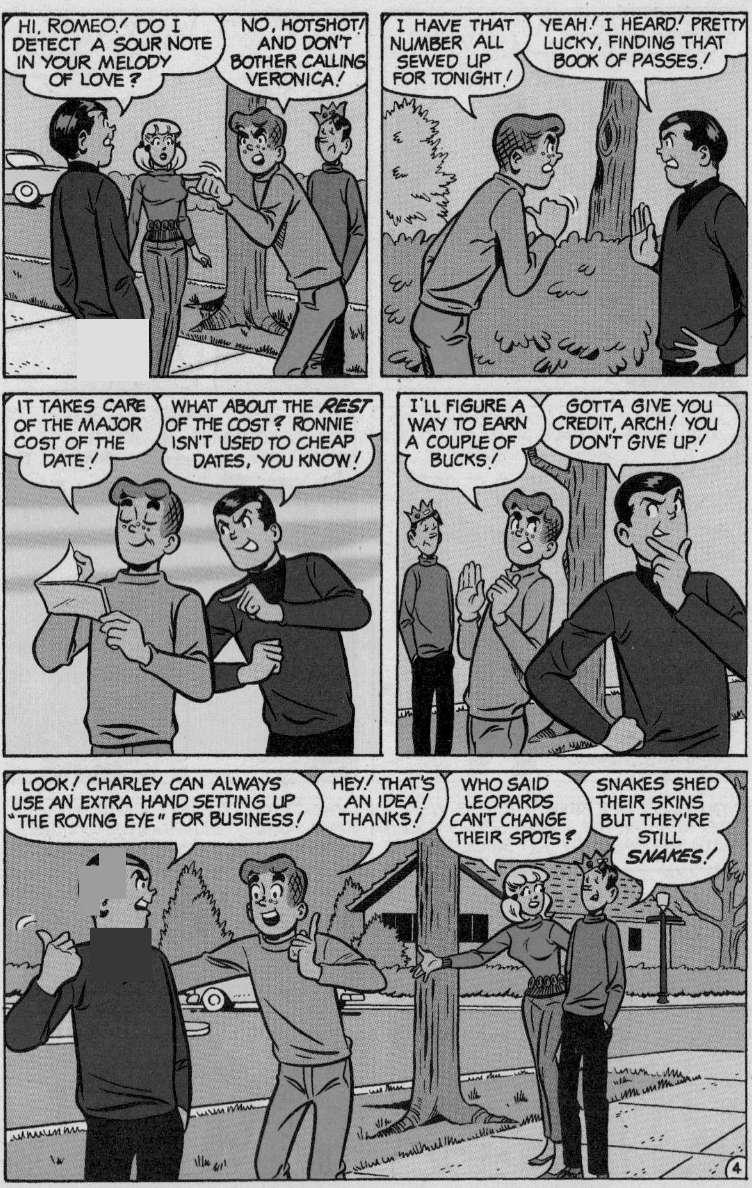
HI, ROMEO! DO I DETECT A SOUR NOTE IN YOUR MELODY OF LOVE?
NO, HOTSHOT! AND DON'T BOTHER CALLING VERONICA!
I HAVE THAT NUMBER ALL SEWED UP FOR TONIGHT!
YEAH! I HEARD! PRETTY LUCKY, FINDING THAT BOOK OF PASSES!
IT TAKES CARE OF THE MAJOR COST OF THE DATE!
WHAT ABOUT THE REST OF THE COST? RONNIE ISN'T USED TO CHEAP DATES, YOU KNOW!
I'LL FIGURE A WAY TO EARN A COUPLE OF BUCKS!
GOTTA GIVE YOU CREDIT, ARCH! YOU DON'T GIVE UP!
LOOK! CHARLEY CAN ALWAYS USE AN EXTRA HAND SETTING UP "THE ROVING EYE" FOR BUSINESS!
HEY! THAT'S AN IDEA! THANKS!
WHO SAID LEOPARDS CAN'T CHANGE THEIR SPOTS?
SNAKES SHED THEIR SKINS BUT THEY'RE STILL SNAKES!

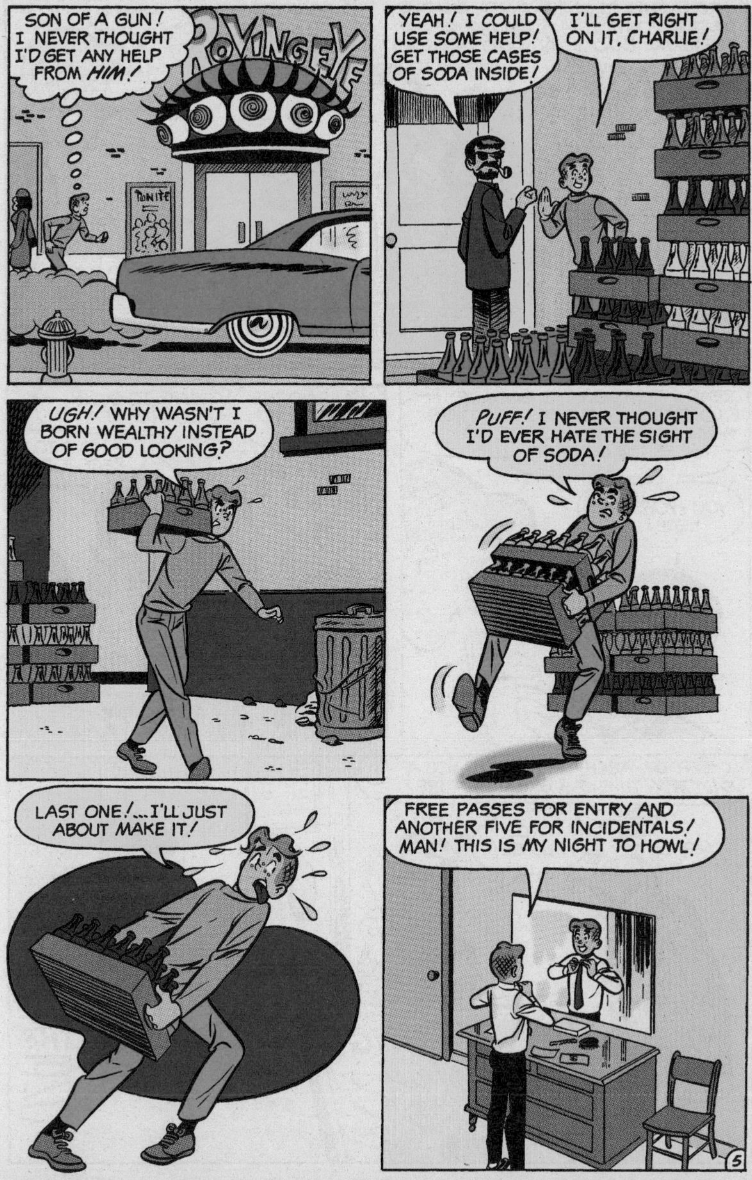
SON OF A GUN! I NEVER THOUGHT I'D GET ANY HELP FROM *HIM*!
ROVINGEYE
TONITE
YEAH! I COULD USE SOME HELP! GET THOSE CASES OF SODA INSIDE!
I'LL GET RIGHT ON IT, CHARLIE!
UGH! WHY WASN'T I BORN WEALTHY INSTEAD OF GOOD LOOKING?
PUFF! I NEVER THOUGHT I'D EVER HATE THE SIGHT OF SODA!
LAST ONE!...I'LL JUST ABOUT MAKE IT!
FREE PASSES FOR ENTRY AND ANOTHER FIVE FOR INCIDENTALS! MAN! THIS IS MY NIGHT TO HOWL!
5

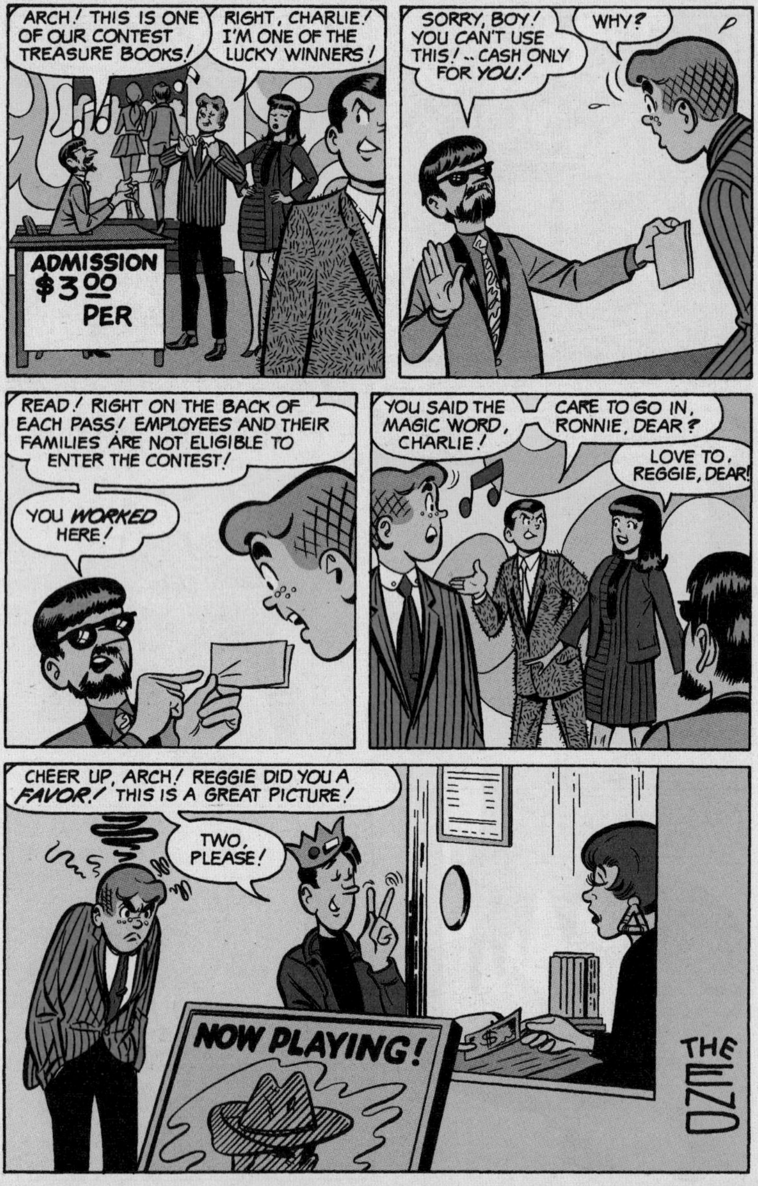
ARCH! THIS IS ONE OF OUR CONTEST TREASURE BOOKS!
RIGHT, CHARLIE! I'M ONE OF THE LUCKY WINNERS!
ADMISSION $3.00 PER
SORRY, BOY! YOU CAN'T USE THIS! -- CASH ONLY FOR YOU!
WHY?
READ! RIGHT ON THE BACK OF EACH PASS! EMPLOYEES AND THEIR FAMILIES ARE NOT ELIGIBLE TO ENTER THE CONTEST!
YOU WORKED HERE!
YOU SAID THE MAGIC WORD, CHARLIE!
CARE TO GO IN, RONNIE, DEAR?
LOVE TO, REGGIE, DEAR!
CHEER UP, ARCH! REGGIE DID YOU A FAVOR! THIS IS A GREAT PICTURE!
TWO, PLEASE!
NOW PLAYING!
THE END

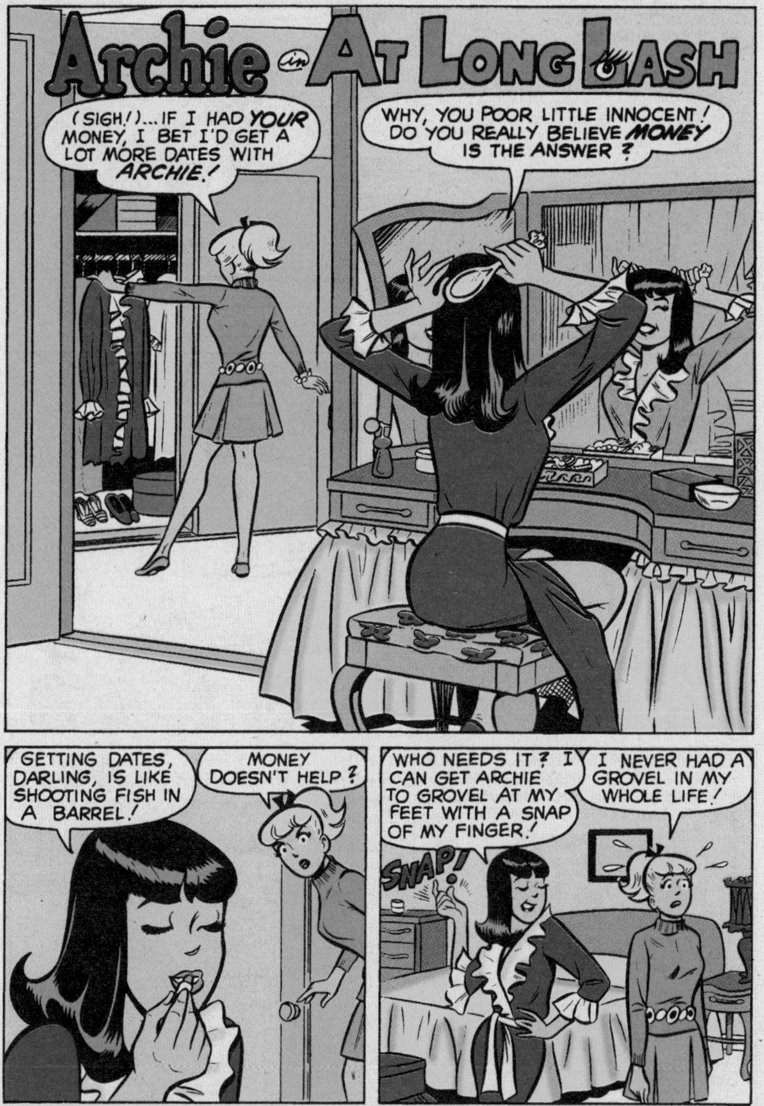
Archie in At Long Lash
(SIGH!)... IF I HAD YOUR MONEY, I BET I'D GET A LOT MORE DATES WITH ARCHIE!
WHY, YOU POOR LITTLE INNOCENT! DO YOU REALLY BELIEVE MONEY IS THE ANSWER?
GETTING DATES, DARLING, IS LIKE SHOOTING FISH IN A BARREL!
MONEY DOESN'T HELP?
WHO NEEDS IT? I CAN GET ARCHIE TO GROVEL AT MY FEET WITH A SNAP OF MY FINGER!
SNAP!
I NEVER HAD A GROVEL IN MY WHOLE LIFE!

Script: Frank Doyle / Pencils: Harry Lucey / Letters: Bill Yoshida

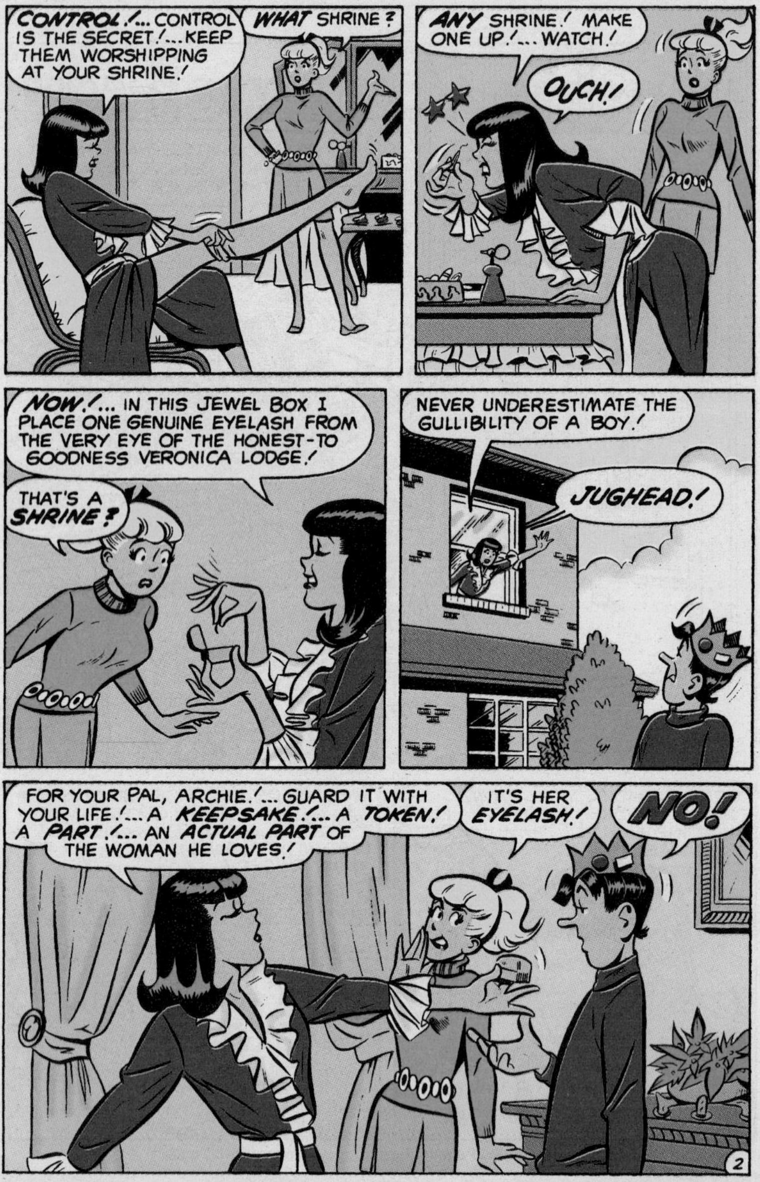
CONTROL!... CONTROL IS THE SECRET!... KEEP THEM WORSHIPPING AT YOUR SHRINE!
WHAT SHRINE?
ANY SHRINE! MAKE ONE UP!... WATCH!
OUCH!
NOW!... IN THIS JEWEL BOX I PLACE ONE GENUINE EYELASH FROM THE VERY EYE OF THE HONEST-TO GOODNESS VERONICA LODGE!
THAT'S A SHRINE?
NEVER UNDERESTIMATE THE GULLIBILITY OF A BOY!
JUGHEAD!
FOR YOUR PAL, ARCHIE!... GUARD IT WITH YOUR LIFE!... A KEEPSAKE!... A TOKEN! A PART!... AN ACTUAL PART OF THE WOMAN HE LOVES!
IT'S HER EYELASH!
NO!

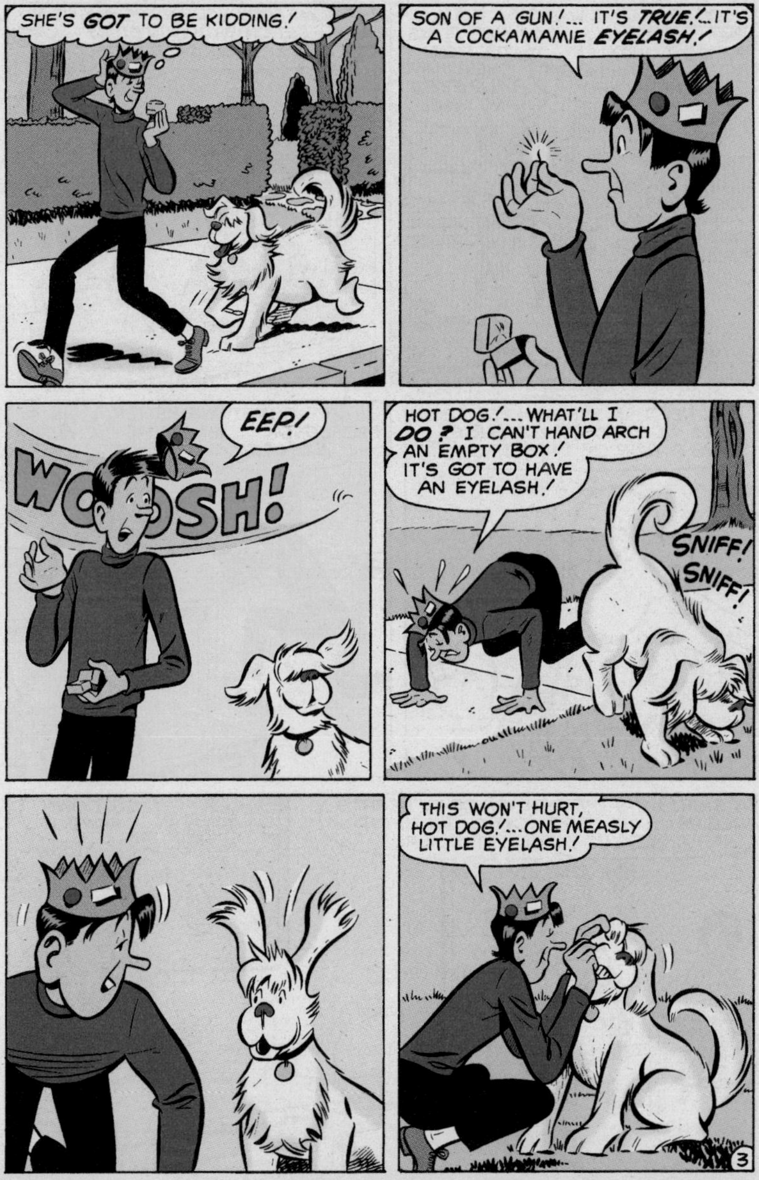
SHE'S GOT TO BE KIDDING!
SON OF A GUN!... IT'S TRUE!...IT'S A COCKAMAMIE EYELASH!
EEP!
WOOSH!
HOT DOG!... WHAT'LL I DO? I CAN'T HAND ARCH AN EMPTY BOX! IT'S GOT TO HAVE AN EYELASH!
SNIFF! SNIFF!
THIS WON'T HURT, HOT DOG!...ONE MEASLY LITTLE EYELASH!
3

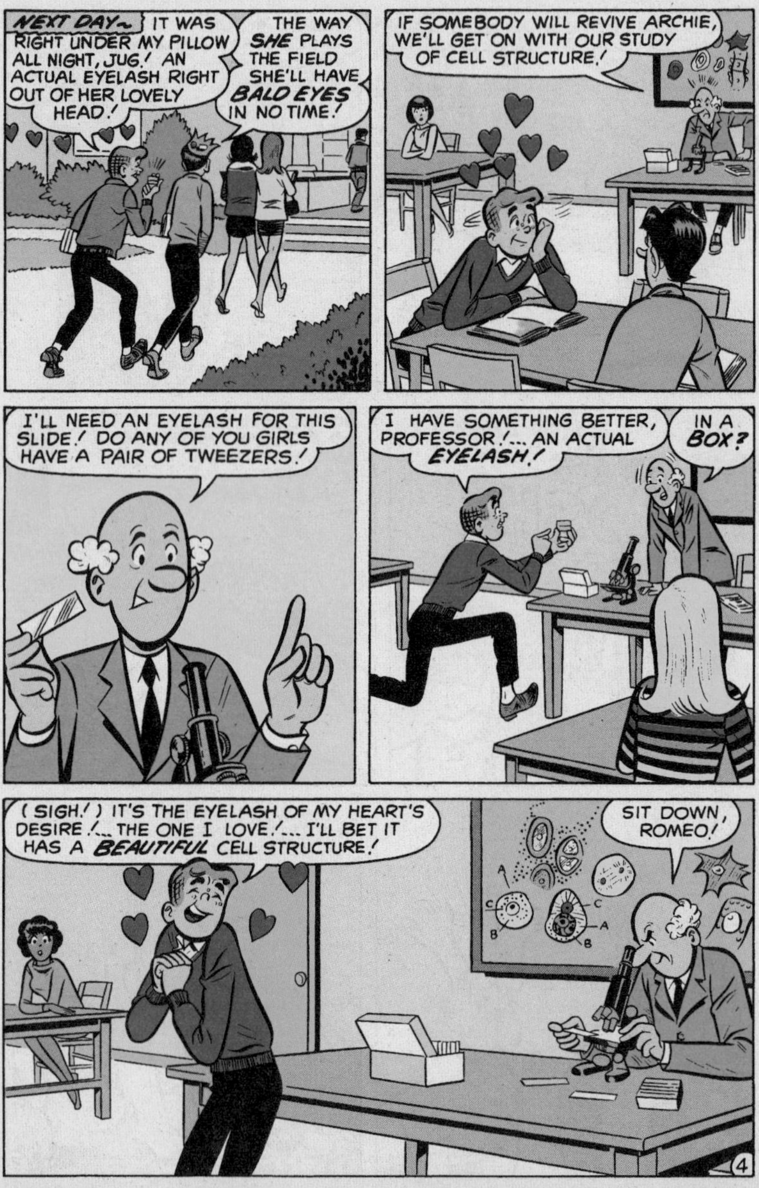
NEXT DAY~
IT WAS RIGHT UNDER MY PILLOW ALL NIGHT, JUG.! AN ACTUAL EYELASH RIGHT OUT OF HER LOVELY HEAD.!
THE WAY SHE PLAYS THE FIELD SHE'LL HAVE BALD EYES IN NO TIME.!
IF SOMEBODY WILL REVIVE ARCHIE, WE'LL GET ON WITH OUR STUDY OF CELL STRUCTURE.!
I'LL NEED AN EYELASH FOR THIS SLIDE.! DO ANY OF YOU GIRLS HAVE A PAIR OF TWEEZERS.!
I HAVE SOMETHING BETTER, PROFESSOR.!... AN ACTUAL EYELASH.!
IN A BOX?
(SIGH.!) IT'S THE EYELASH OF MY HEART'S DESIRE.!... THE ONE I LOVE.!... I'LL BET IT HAS A BEAUTIFUL CELL STRUCTURE.!
SIT DOWN, ROMEO.!
A
C
B
C
A
B

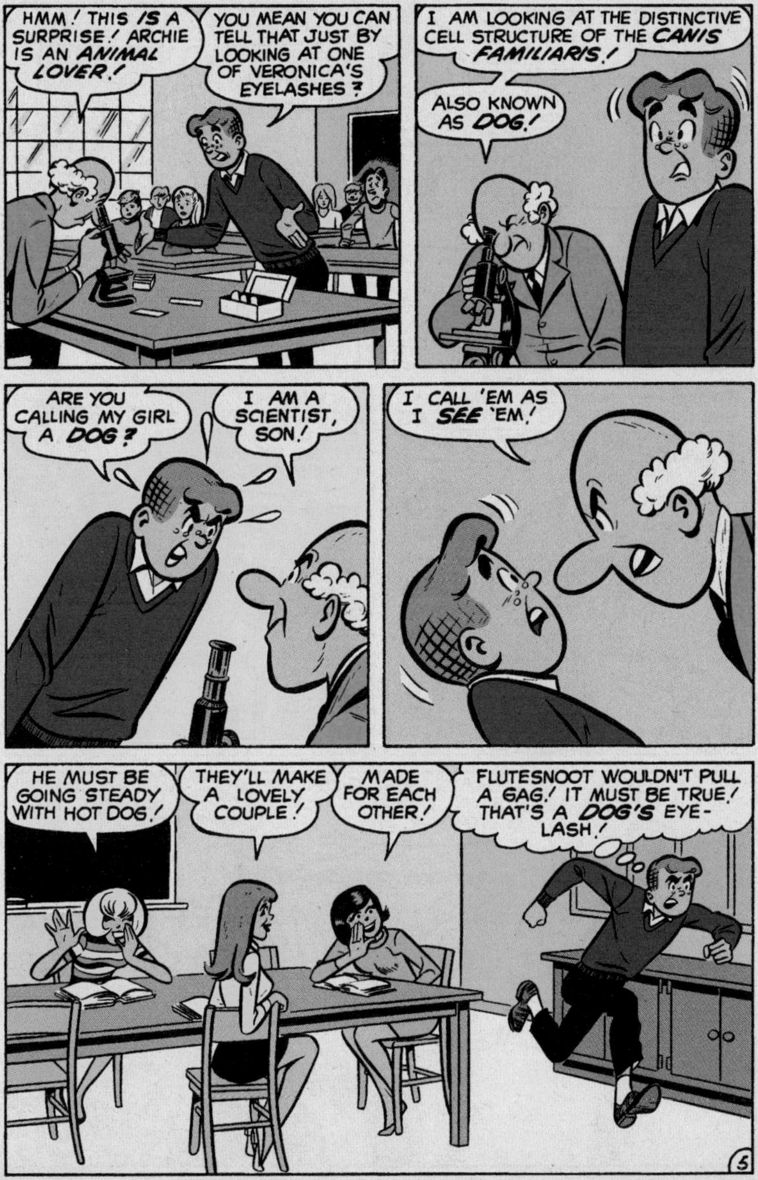
HMM! THIS IS A SURPRISE! ARCHIE IS AN ANIMAL LOVER!
YOU MEAN YOU CAN TELL THAT JUST BY LOOKING AT ONE OF VERONICA'S EYELASHES?
I AM LOOKING AT THE DISTINCTIVE CELL STRUCTURE OF THE CANIS FAMILIARIS!
ALSO KNOWN AS DOG!
ARE YOU CALLING MY GIRL A DOG?
I AM A SCIENTIST, SON!
I CALL 'EM AS I SEE 'EM!
HE MUST BE GOING STEADY WITH HOT DOG!
THEY'LL MAKE A LOVELY COUPLE!
MADE FOR EACH OTHER!
FLUTESNOOT WOULDN'T PULL A GAG! IT MUST BE TRUE! THAT'S A DOG'S EYE-LASH!
5

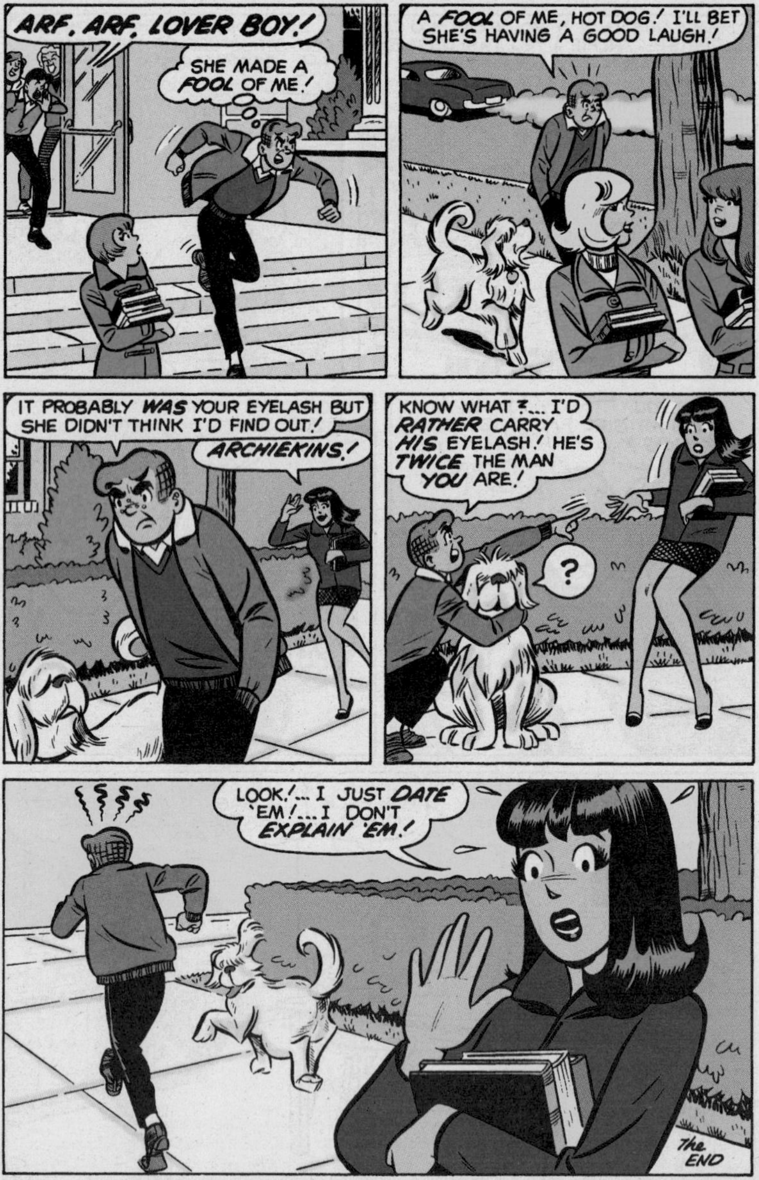
ARF, ARF, LOVER BOY!
SHE MADE A FOOL OF ME!
A FOOL OF ME, HOT DOG! I'LL BET SHE'S HAVING A GOOD LAUGH!
IT PROBABLY WAS YOUR EYELASH BUT SHE DIDN'T THINK I'D FIND OUT!
ARCHIEKINS!
KNOW WHAT ?... I'D RATHER CARRY HIS EYELASH! HE'S TWICE THE MAN YOU ARE!
?
LOOK!... I JUST DATE 'EM!... I DON'T EXPLAIN 'EM!
The END

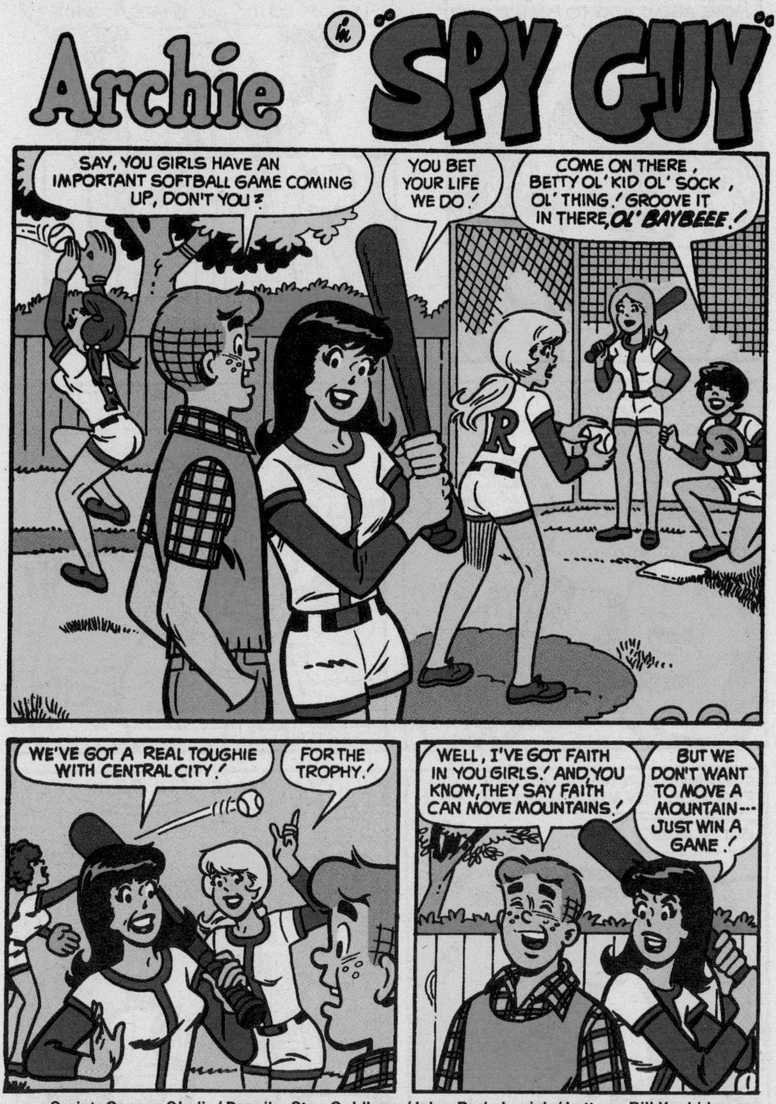
Archie in "SPY GUY"
SAY, YOU GIRLS HAVE AN IMPORTANT SOFTBALL GAME COMING UP, DON'T YOU?
YOU BET YOUR LIFE WE DO!
COME ON THERE, BETTY OL' KID OL' SOCK, OL' THING! GROOVE IT IN THERE, OL' BAYBEEE!
R
WE'VE GOT A REAL TOUGHIE WITH CENTRAL CITY!
FOR THE TROPHY!
WELL, I'VE GOT FAITH IN YOU GIRLS! AND, YOU KNOW, THEY SAY FAITH CAN MOVE MOUNTAINS!
BUT WE DON'T WANT TO MOVE A MOUNTAIN--- JUST WIN A GAME!
1
Script: George Gladir / Pencils: Stan Goldberg / Inks: Rudy Lapick / Letters: Bill Yoshida

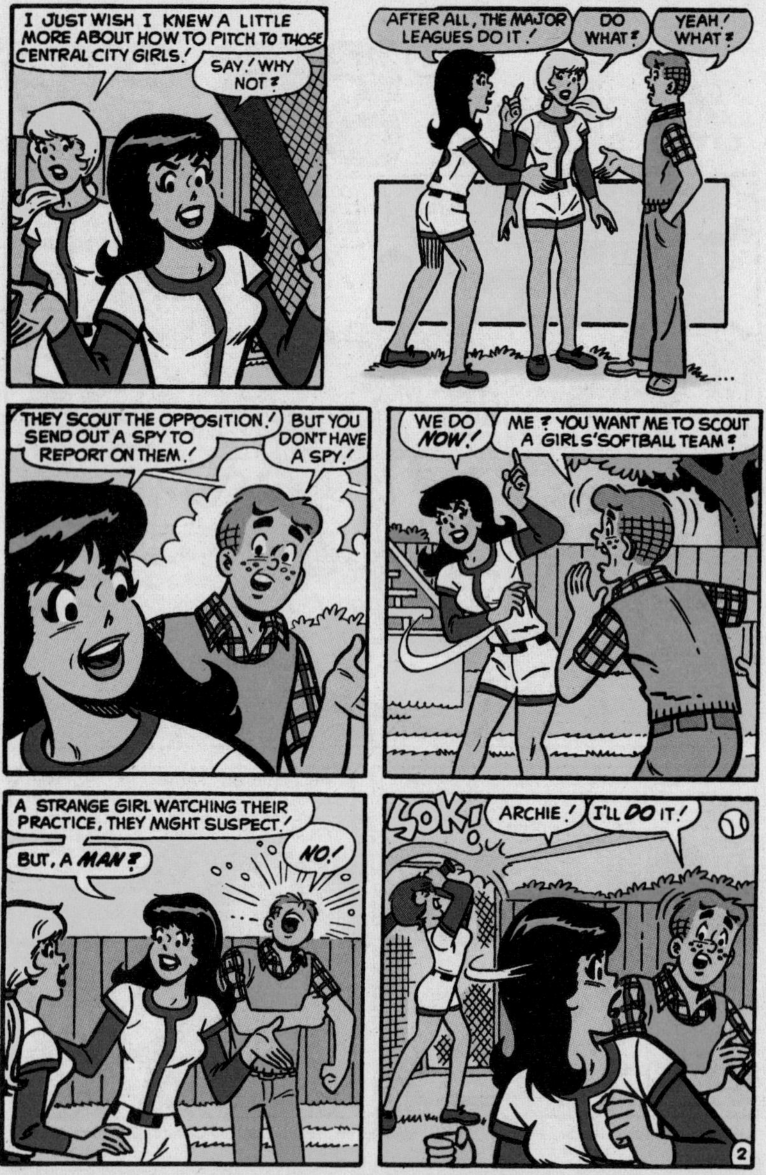
I JUST WISH I KNEW A LITTLE MORE ABOUT HOW TO PITCH TO THOSE CENTRAL CITY GIRLS!
SAY! WHY NOT?
AFTER ALL, THE MAJOR LEAGUES DO IT!
DO WHAT?
YEAH! WHAT?
THEY SCOUT THE OPPOSITION! SEND OUT A SPY TO REPORT ON THEM!
BUT YOU DON'T HAVE A SPY!
WE DO NOW!
ME? YOU WANT ME TO SCOUT A GIRLS' SOFTBALL TEAM?
A STRANGE GIRL WATCHING THEIR PRACTICE, THEY MIGHT SUSPECT!
BUT, A MAN?
NO!
SOK!
ARCHIE!
I'LL DO IT!
2

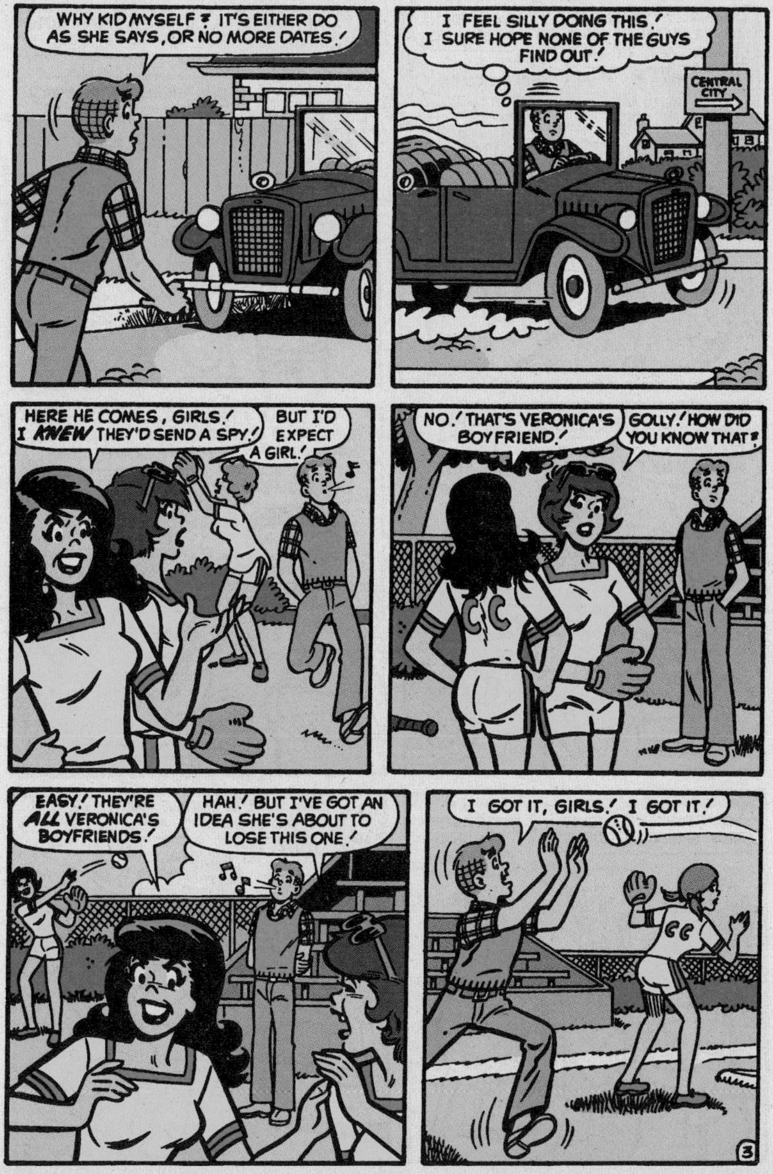
WHY KID MYSELF? IT'S EITHER DO AS SHE SAYS, OR NO MORE DATES!
I FEEL SILLY DOING THIS! I SURE HOPE NONE OF THE GUYS FIND OUT!
CENTRAL CITY
HERE HE COMES, GIRLS! I KNEW THEY'D SEND A SPY!
BUT I'D EXPECT A GIRL!
NO! THAT'S VERONICA'S BOYFRIEND!
GOLLY! HOW DID YOU KNOW THAT?
EASY! THEY'RE ALL VERONICA'S BOYFRIENDS!
HAH! BUT I'VE GOT AN IDEA SHE'S ABOUT TO LOSE THIS ONE!
I GOT IT, GIRLS! I GOT IT!
3

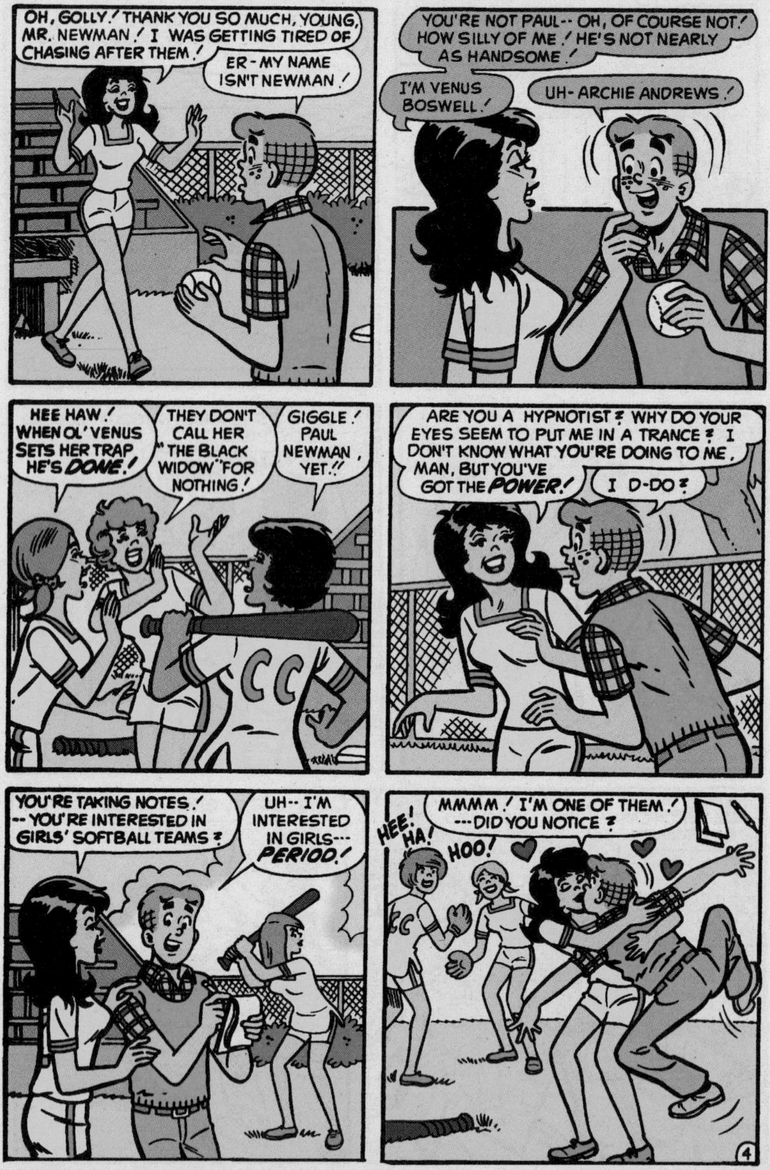
OH, GOLLY! THANK YOU SO MUCH, YOUNG, MR. NEWMAN! I WAS GETTING TIRED OF CHASING AFTER THEM!
ER-MY NAME ISN'T NEWMAN!
YOU'RE NOT PAUL-- OH, OF COURSE NOT! HOW SILLY OF ME! HE'S NOT NEARLY AS HANDSOME!
I'M VENUS BOSWELL!
UH- ARCHIE ANDREWS!
HEE HAW! WHEN OL' VENUS SETS HER TRAP HE'S DONE!
THEY DON'T CALL HER "THE BLACK WIDOW" FOR NOTHING!
GIGGLE! PAUL NEWMAN, YET!!
ARE YOU A HYPNOTIST? WHY DO YOUR EYES SEEM TO PUT ME IN A TRANCE? I DON'T KNOW WHAT YOU'RE DOING TO ME, MAN, BUT YOU'VE GOT THE POWER!
I D-DO?
YOU'RE TAKING NOTES! -- YOU'RE INTERESTED IN GIRLS' SOFTBALL TEAMS?
UH-- I'M INTERESTED IN GIRLS--- PERIOD!
HEE! HA!
HOO!
MMMM! I'M ONE OF THEM! ---DID YOU NOTICE?
4

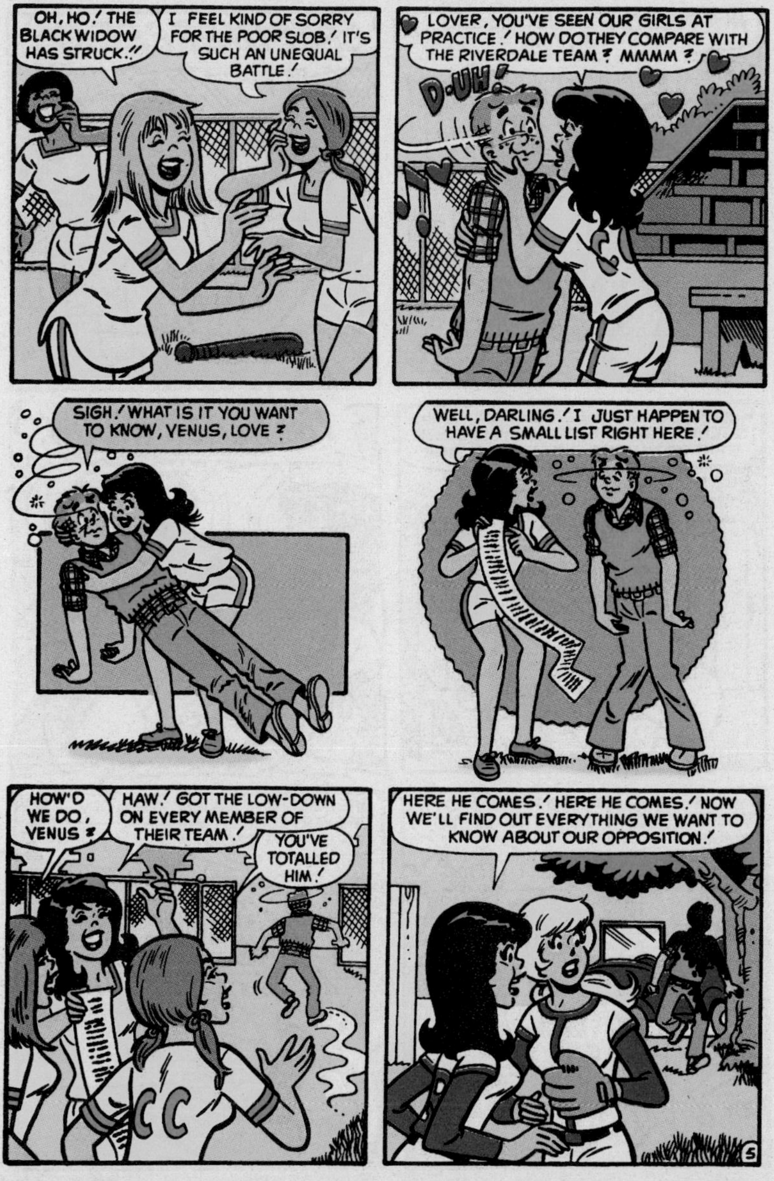

OH, HO! THE BLACK WIDOW HAS STRUCK!!
I FEEL KIND OF SORRY FOR THE POOR SLOB! IT'S SUCH AN UNEQUAL BATTLE!
LOVER, YOU'VE SEEN OUR GIRLS AT PRACTICE! HOW DO THEY COMPARE WITH THE RIVERDALE TEAM? MMMM?
D-UH!
SIGH! WHAT IS IT YOU WANT TO KNOW, VENUS, LOVE?
WELL, DARLING! I JUST HAPPEN TO HAVE A SMALL LIST RIGHT HERE!
HOW'D WE DO, VENUS?
HAW! GOT THE LOW-DOWN ON EVERY MEMBER OF THEIR TEAM!
YOU'VE TOTALLED HIM!
HERE HE COMES! HERE HE COMES! NOW WE'LL FIND OUT EVERYTHING WE WANT TO KNOW ABOUT OUR OPPOSITION!
5

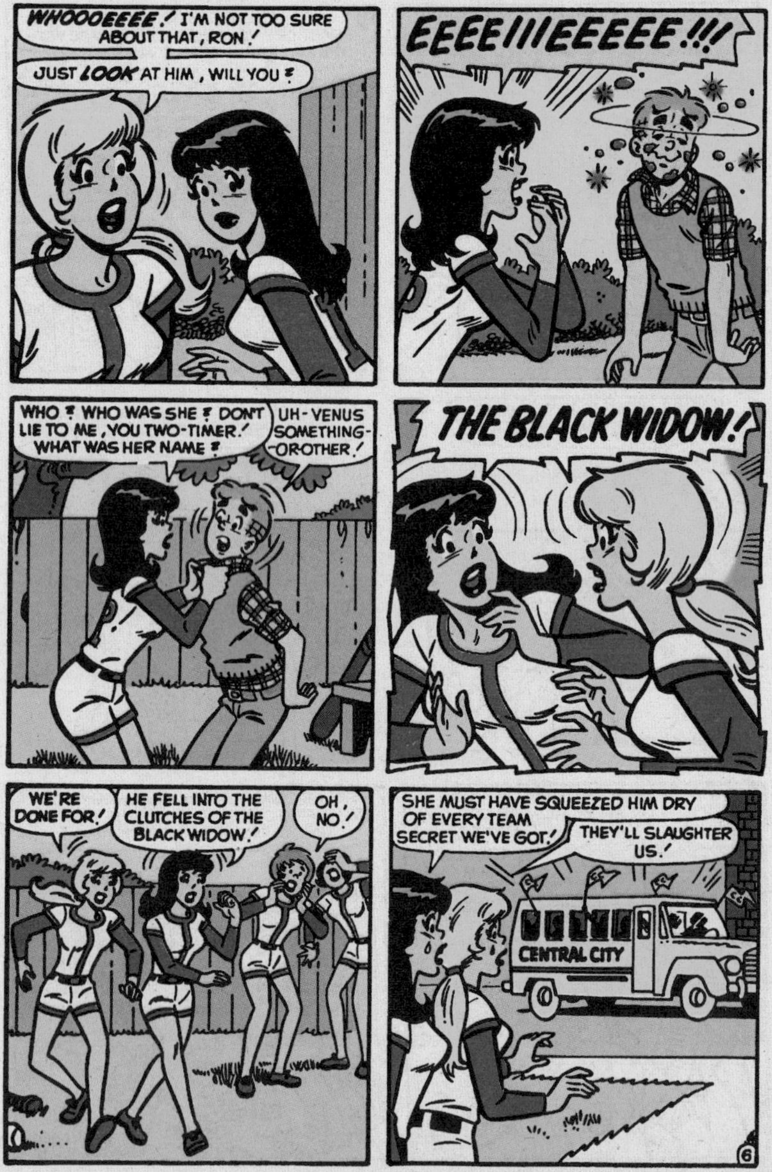
WHOOOEEEE! I'M NOT TOO SURE ABOUT THAT, RON!
JUST LOOK AT HIM, WILL YOU?
EEEEIIIIEEEEEE!!!
WHO? WHO WAS SHE? DON'T LIE TO ME, YOU TWO-TIMER! WHAT WAS HER NAME?
UH-VENUS SOMETHING-OR-OTHER!
THE BLACK WIDOW!
WE'RE DONE FOR!
HE FELL INTO THE CLUTCHES OF THE BLACK WIDOW!
OH, NO!
SHE MUST HAVE SQUEEZED HIM DRY OF EVERY TEAM SECRET WE'VE GOT!
THEY'LL SLAUGHTER US!
CENTRAL CITY
6

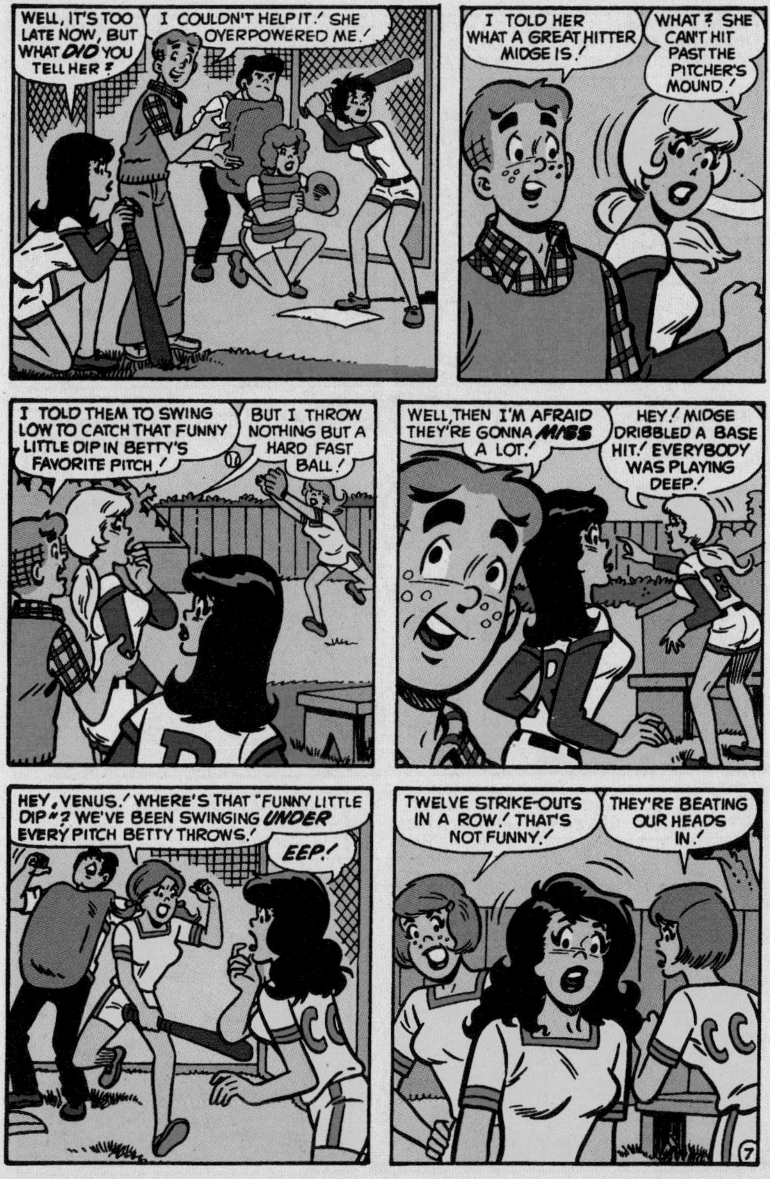
WELL, IT'S TOO LATE NOW, BUT WHAT DID YOU TELL HER?
I COULDN'T HELP IT! SHE OVERPOWERED ME!
I TOLD HER WHAT A GREAT HITTER MIDGE IS!
WHAT? SHE CAN'T HIT PAST THE PITCHER'S MOUND!
I TOLD THEM TO SWING LOW TO CATCH THAT FUNNY LITTLE DIP IN BETTY'S FAVORITE PITCH!
BUT I THROW NOTHING BUT A HARD FAST BALL!
WELL, THEN I'M AFRAID THEY'RE GONNA MISS A LOT!
HEY! MIDGE DRIBBLED A BASE HIT! EVERYBODY WAS PLAYING DEEP!
HEY, VENUS! WHERE'S THAT "FUNNY LITTLE DIP"? WE'VE BEEN SWINGING UNDER EVERY PITCH BETTY THROWS!
EEP!
TWELVE STRIKE-OUTS IN A ROW! THAT'S NOT FUNNY!
THEY'RE BEATING OUR HEADS IN!
7

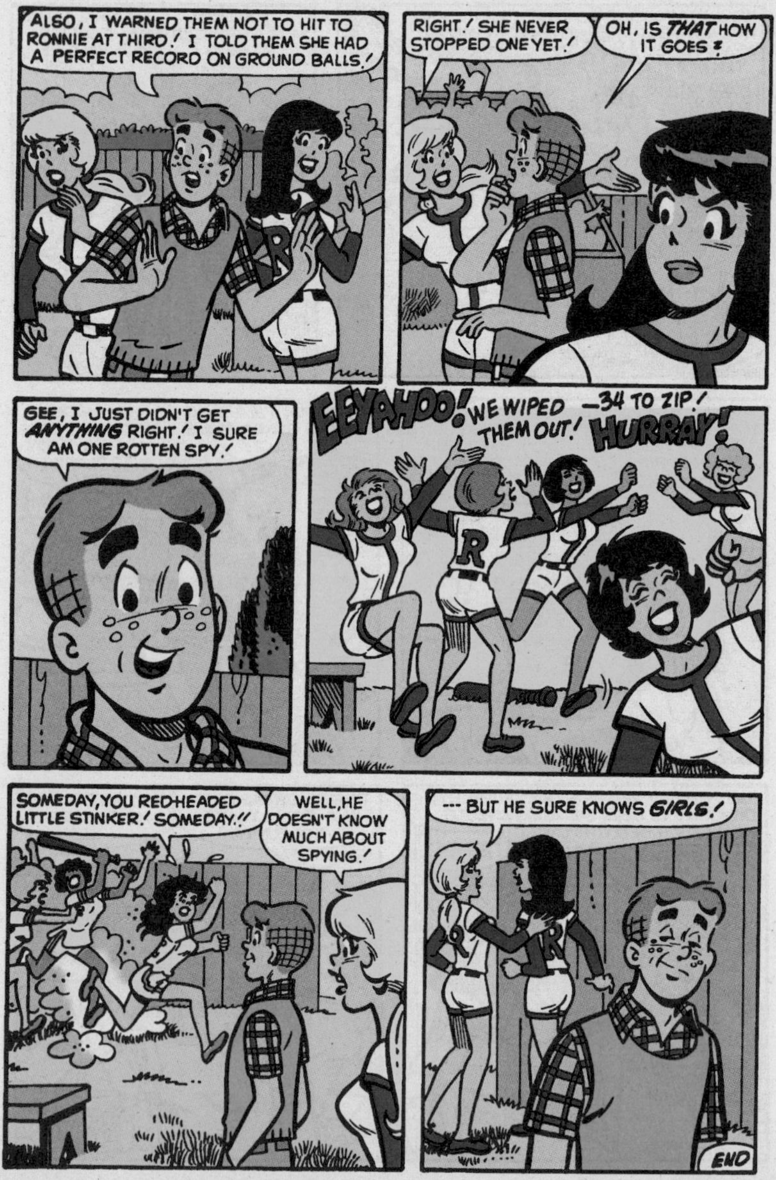
ALSO, I WARNED THEM NOT TO HIT TO RONNIE AT THIRD! I TOLD THEM SHE HAD A PERFECT RECORD ON GROUND BALLS!
RIGHT! SHE NEVER STOPPED ONE YET!
OH, IS *THAT* HOW IT GOES?
GEE, I JUST DIDN'T GET *ANYTHING* RIGHT! I SURE AM ONE ROTTEN SPY!
EEYAHOO!
WE WIPED THEM OUT!
—34 TO ZIP!
HURRAY!
SOMEDAY, YOU RED-HEADED LITTLE STINKER! SOMEDAY!!
WELL, HE DOESN'T KNOW MUCH ABOUT SPYING!
--- BUT HE SURE KNOWS *GIRLS*!
END

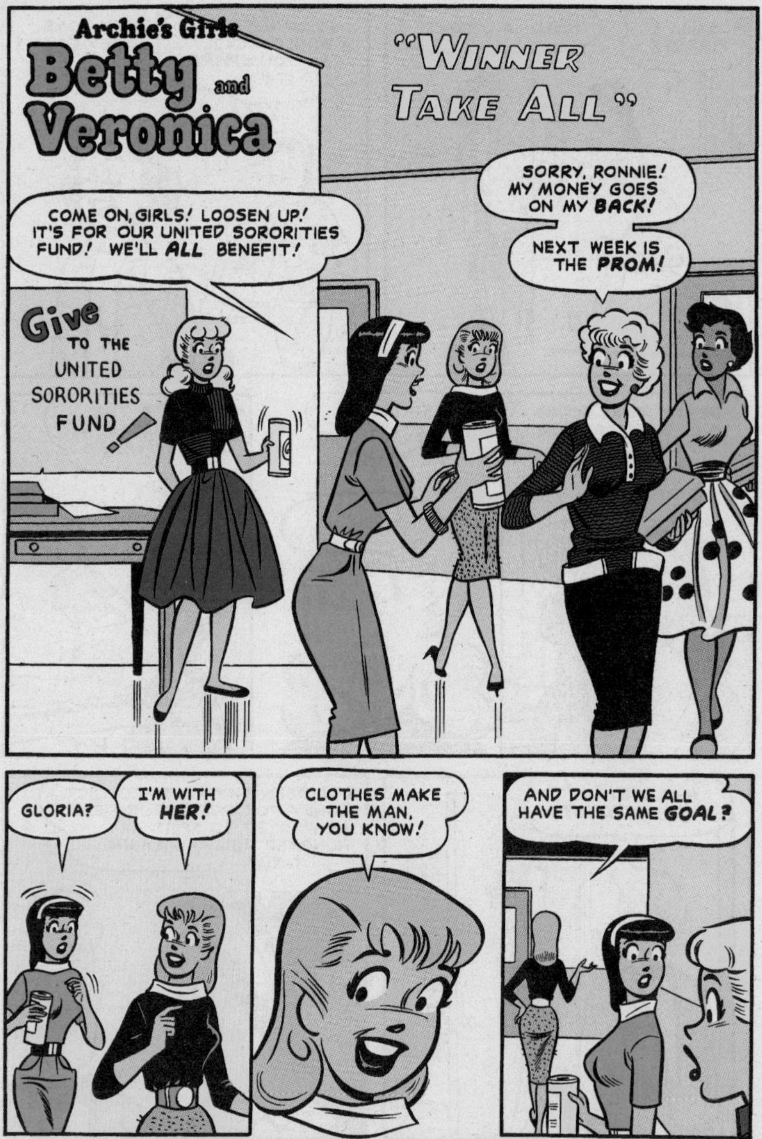
Archie's Girls Betty and Veronica
"WINNER TAKE ALL"
COME ON, GIRLS! LOOSEN UP! IT'S FOR OUR UNITED SORORITIES FUND! WE'LL ALL BENEFIT!
Give TO THE UNITED SORORITIES FUND!
SORRY, RONNIE! MY MONEY GOES ON MY BACK!
NEXT WEEK IS THE PROM!
GLORIA?
I'M WITH HER!
CLOTHES MAKE THE MAN, YOU KNOW!
AND DON'T WE ALL HAVE THE SAME GOAL?

Script: Frank Doyle / Pencils: Dan DeCarlo / Inks: Rudy Lapick / Letters: Vince DeCarlo

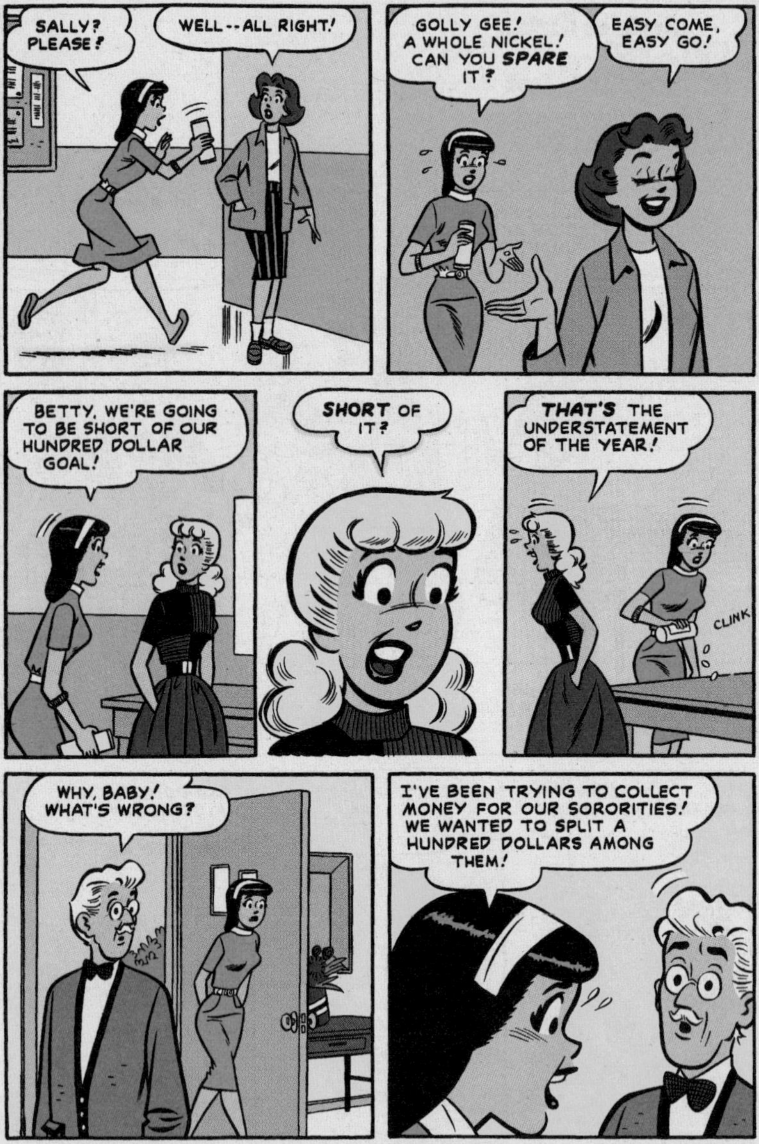
SALLY? PLEASE?
WELL--ALL RIGHT!
GOLLY GEE! A WHOLE NICKEL! CAN YOU SPARE IT?
EASY COME, EASY GO!
BETTY, WE'RE GOING TO BE SHORT OF OUR HUNDRED DOLLAR GOAL!
SHORT OF IT?
THAT'S THE UNDERSTATEMENT OF THE YEAR!
CLINK
WHY, BABY! WHAT'S WRONG?
I'VE BEEN TRYING TO COLLECT MONEY FOR OUR SORORITIES! WE WANTED TO SPLIT A HUNDRED DOLLARS AMONG THEM!

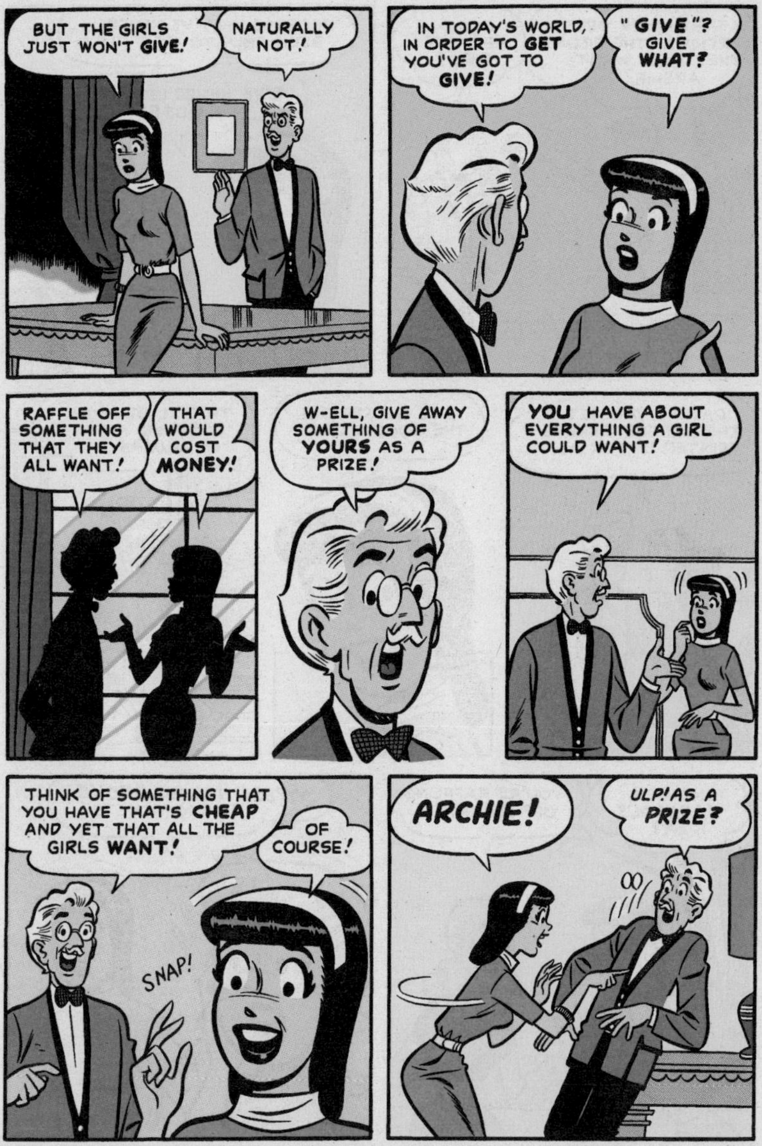
BUT THE GIRLS JUST WON'T GIVE!
NATURALLY NOT!
IN TODAY'S WORLD, IN ORDER TO GET YOU'VE GOT TO GIVE!
"GIVE"? GIVE WHAT?
RAFFLE OFF SOMETHING THAT THEY ALL WANT!
THAT WOULD COST MONEY!
W-ELL, GIVE AWAY SOMETHING OF YOURS AS A PRIZE!
YOU HAVE ABOUT EVERYTHING A GIRL COULD WANT!
THINK OF SOMETHING THAT YOU HAVE THAT'S CHEAP AND YET THAT ALL THE GIRLS WANT!
OF COURSE!
SNAP!
ARCHIE!
ULP! AS A PRIZE?

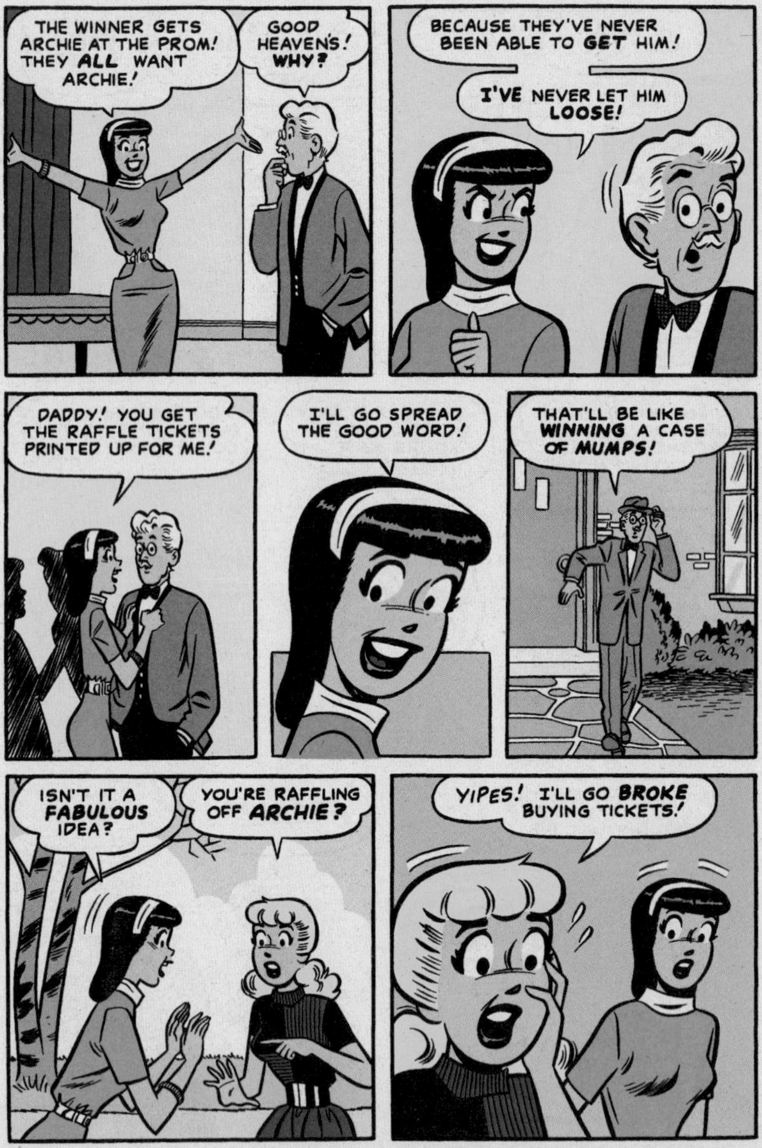

THE WINNER GETS ARCHIE AT THE PROM! THEY ALL WANT ARCHIE!
GOOD HEAVEN'S! WHY?
BECAUSE THEY'VE NEVER BEEN ABLE TO GET HIM!
I'VE NEVER LET HIM LOOSE!
DADDY! YOU GET THE RAFFLE TICKETS PRINTED UP FOR ME!
I'LL GO SPREAD THE GOOD WORD!
THAT'LL BE LIKE WINNING A CASE OF MUMPS!
ISN'T IT A FABULOUS IDEA?
YOU'RE RAFFLING OFF ARCHIE?
YIPES! I'LL GO BROKE BUYING TICKETS!

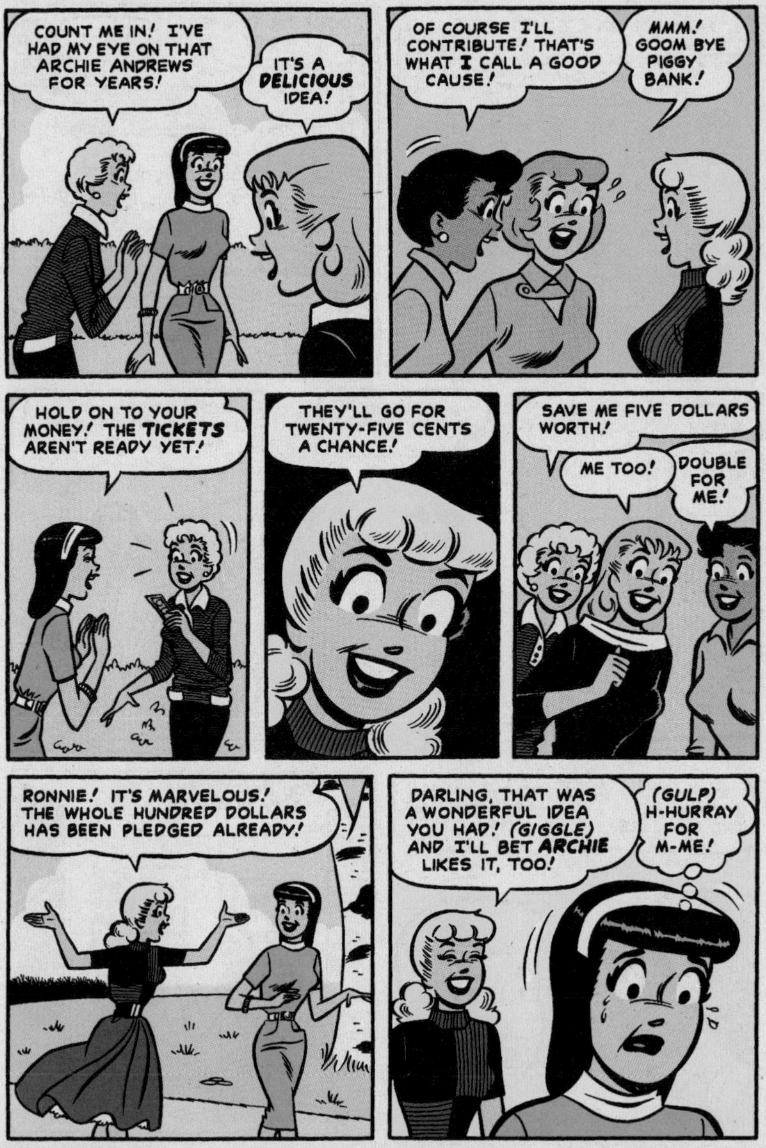
COUNT ME IN! I'VE HAD MY EYE ON THAT ARCHIE ANDREWS FOR YEARS!
IT'S A **DELICIOUS** IDEA!
OF COURSE I'LL CONTRIBUTE! THAT'S WHAT **I** CALL A GOOD CAUSE!
MMM! GOOM BYE PIGGY BANK!
HOLD ON TO YOUR MONEY! THE **TICKETS** AREN'T READY YET!
THEY'LL GO FOR TWENTY-FIVE CENTS A CHANCE!
SAVE ME FIVE DOLLARS WORTH!
ME TOO!
DOUBLE FOR ME!
RONNIE! IT'S MARVELOUS! THE WHOLE HUNDRED DOLLARS HAS BEEN PLEDGED ALREADY!
DARLING, THAT WAS A WONDERFUL IDEA YOU HAD! (GIGGLE) AND I'LL BET **ARCHIE** LIKES IT, TOO!
(GULP) H-HURRAY FOR M-ME!

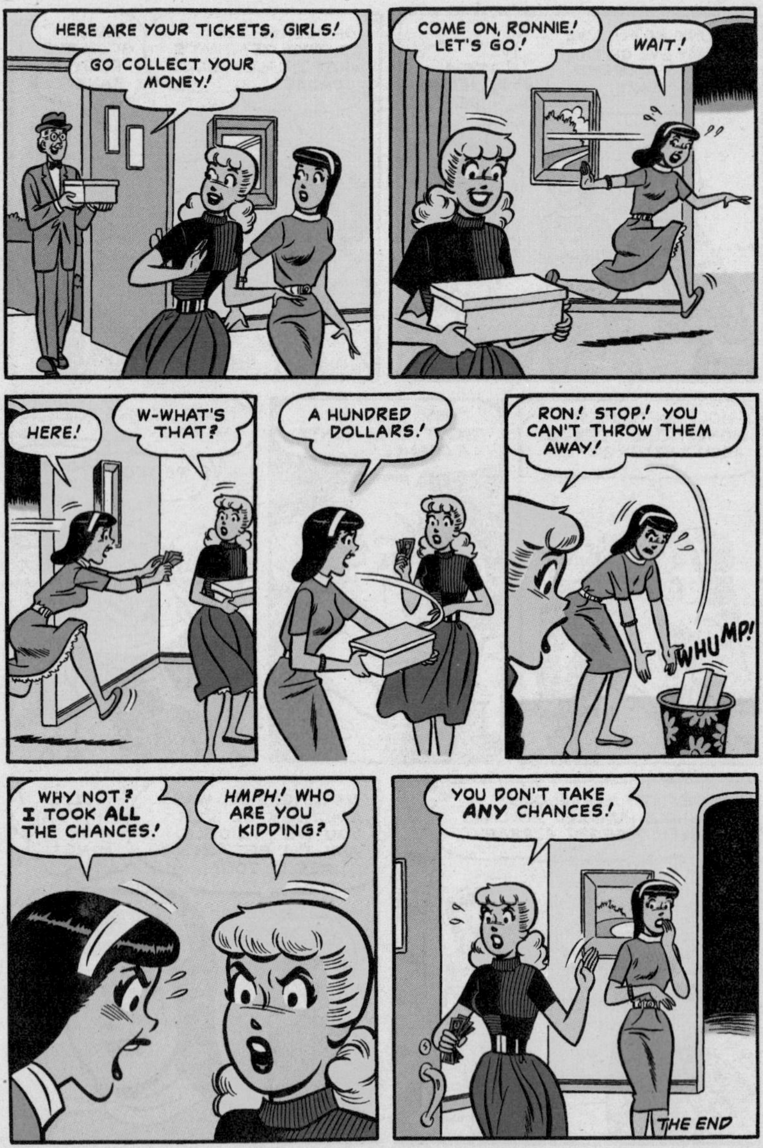
HERE ARE YOUR TICKETS, GIRLS!
GO COLLECT YOUR MONEY!
COME ON, RONNIE! LET'S GO!
WAIT!
HERE!
W-WHAT'S THAT?
A HUNDRED DOLLARS!
RON! STOP! YOU CAN'T THROW THEM AWAY!
WHUMP!
WHY NOT? I TOOK **ALL** THE CHANCES!
HMPH! WHO ARE YOU KIDDING?
YOU DON'T TAKE **ANY** CHANCES!
THE END

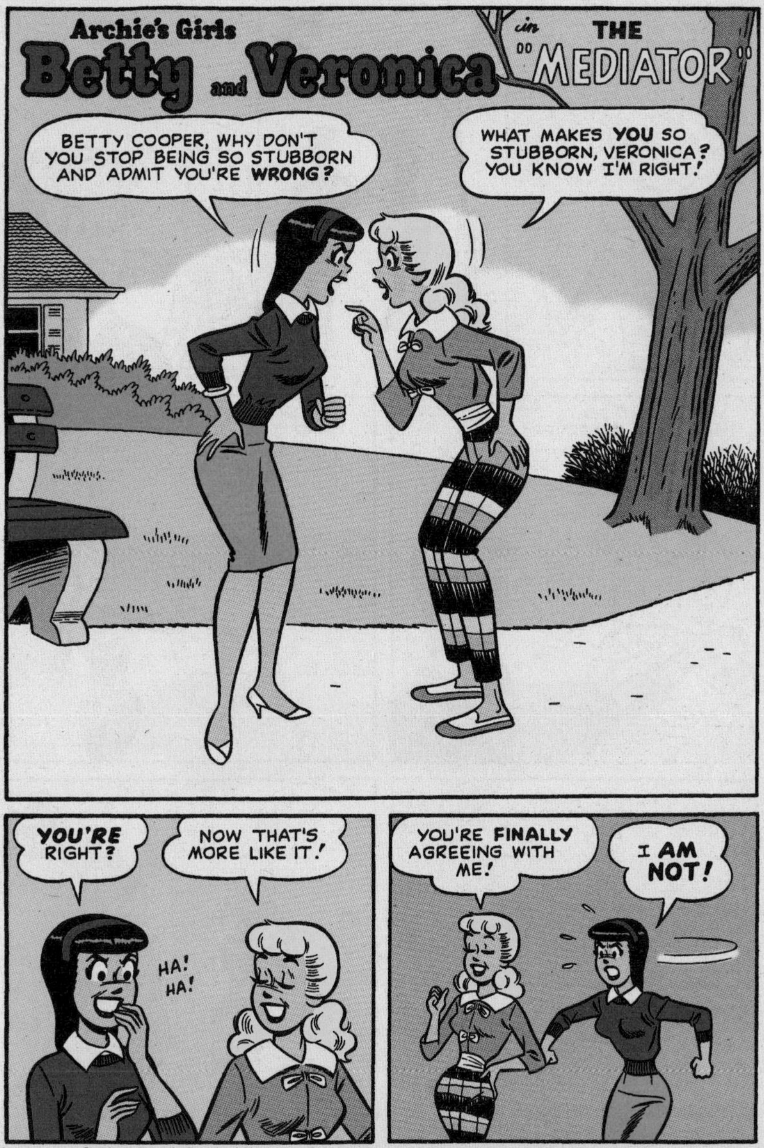
Archie's Girls Betty and Veronica in THE "MEDIATOR"
BETTY COOPER, WHY DON'T YOU STOP BEING SO STUBBORN AND ADMIT YOU'RE WRONG?
WHAT MAKES YOU SO STUBBORN, VERONICA? YOU KNOW I'M RIGHT!
YOU'RE RIGHT?
NOW THAT'S MORE LIKE IT!
HA! HA!
YOU'RE FINALLY AGREEING WITH ME!
I AM NOT!

Script: Frank Doyle / Pencils: Dan DeCarlo / Inks & Letters: Vince DeCarlo

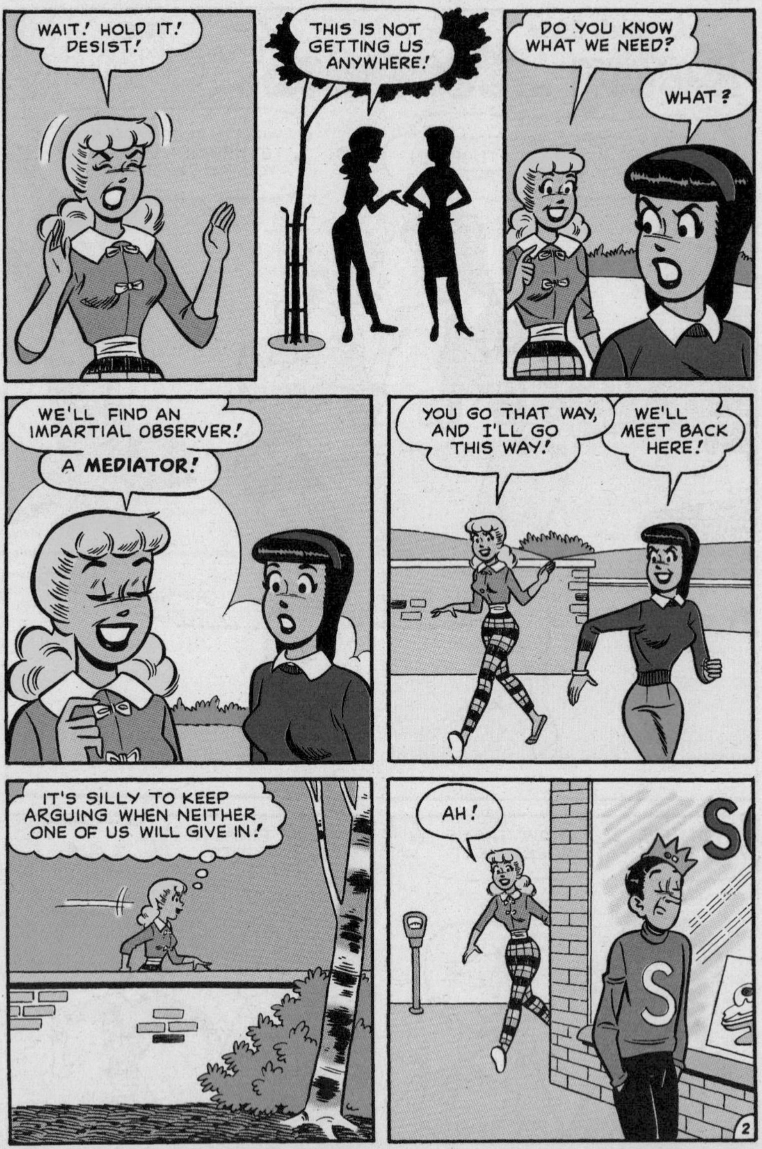
WAIT! HOLD IT! DESIST!
THIS IS NOT GETTING US ANYWHERE!
DO YOU KNOW WHAT WE NEED?
WHAT?
WE'LL FIND AN IMPARTIAL OBSERVER!
A **MEDIATOR!**
YOU GO THAT WAY, AND I'LL GO THIS WAY!
WE'LL MEET BACK HERE!
IT'S SILLY TO KEEP ARGUING WHEN NEITHER ONE OF US WILL GIVE IN!
AH!
S
2

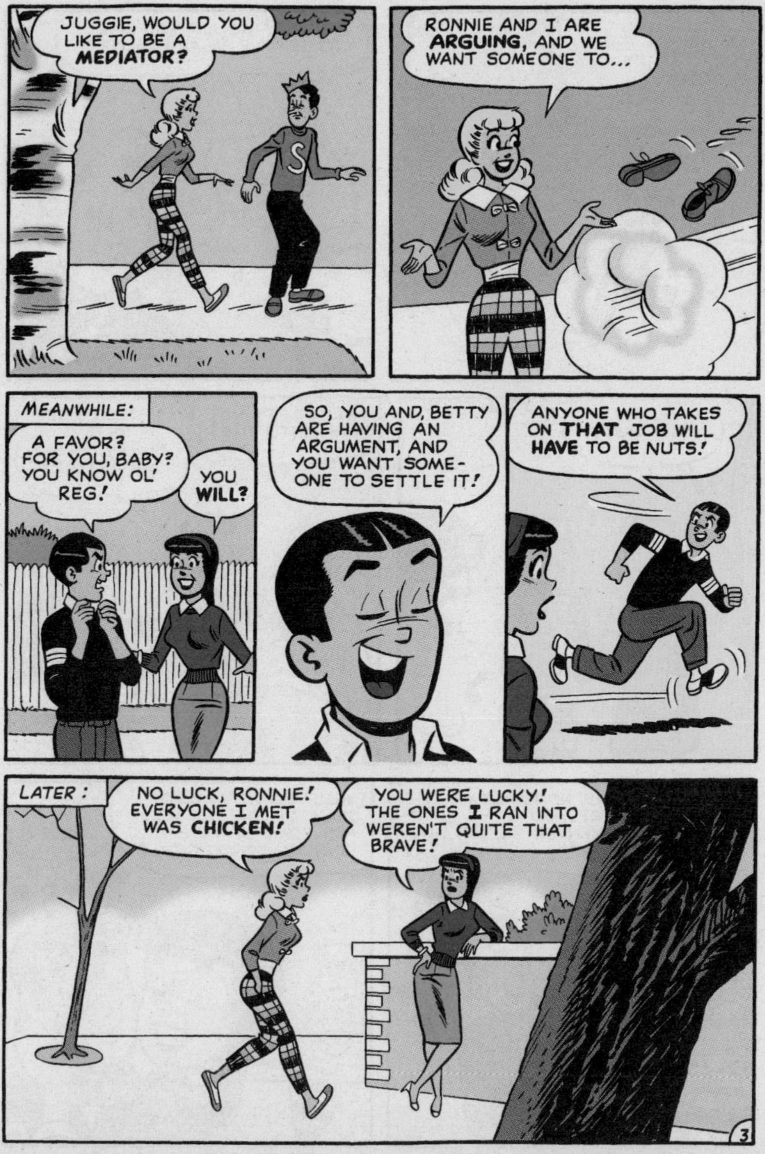
JUGGIE, WOULD YOU LIKE TO BE A MEDIATOR?
RONNIE AND I ARE ARGUING, AND WE WANT SOMEONE TO...
MEANWHILE:
A FAVOR? FOR YOU, BABY? YOU KNOW OL' REG!
YOU WILL?
SO, YOU AND, BETTY ARE HAVING AN ARGUMENT, AND YOU WANT SOME-ONE TO SETTLE IT!
ANYONE WHO TAKES ON THAT JOB WILL HAVE TO BE NUTS!
LATER:
NO LUCK, RONNIE! EVERYONE I MET WAS CHICKEN!
YOU WERE LUCKY! THE ONES I RAN INTO WEREN'T QUITE THAT BRAVE!
3

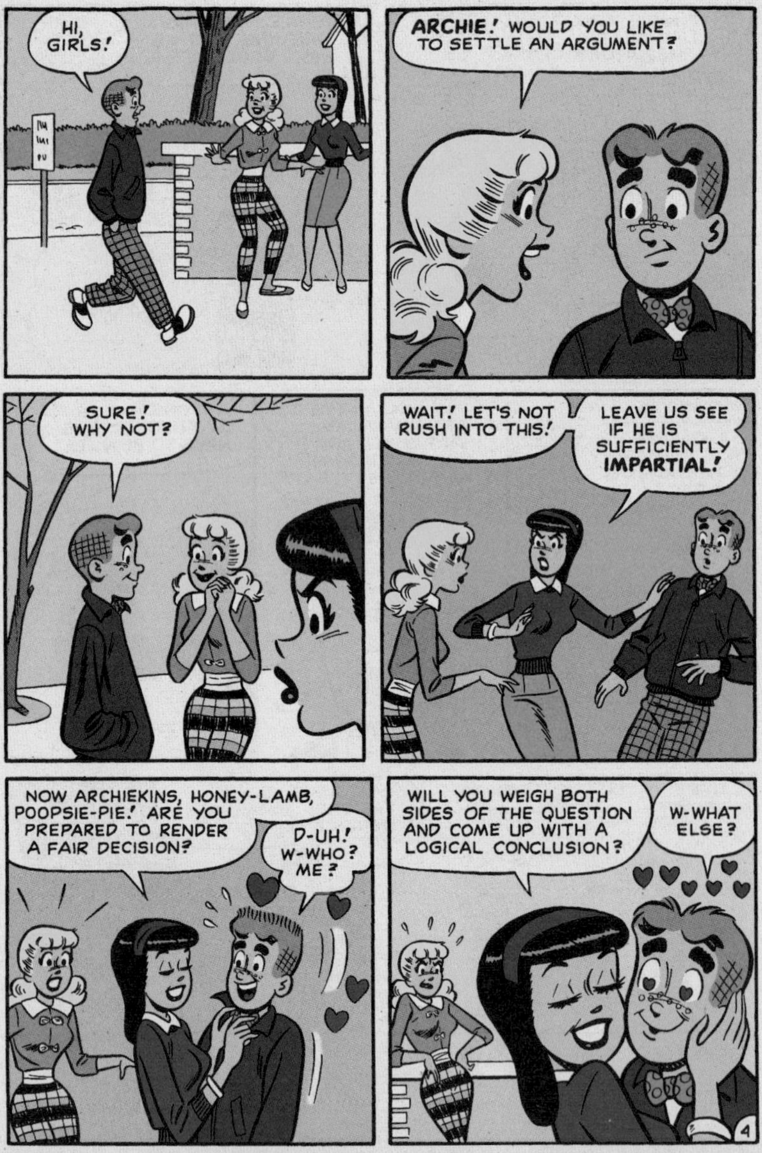
HI, GIRLS!
ARCHIE! WOULD YOU LIKE TO SETTLE AN ARGUMENT?
SURE! WHY NOT?
WAIT! LET'S NOT RUSH INTO THIS!
LEAVE US SEE IF HE IS SUFFICIENTLY IMPARTIAL!
NOW ARCHIEKINS, HONEY-LAMB, POOPSIE-PIE! ARE YOU PREPARED TO RENDER A FAIR DECISION?
D-UH! W-WHO? ME?
WILL YOU WEIGH BOTH SIDES OF THE QUESTION AND COME UP WITH A LOGICAL CONCLUSION?
W-WHAT ELSE?
4

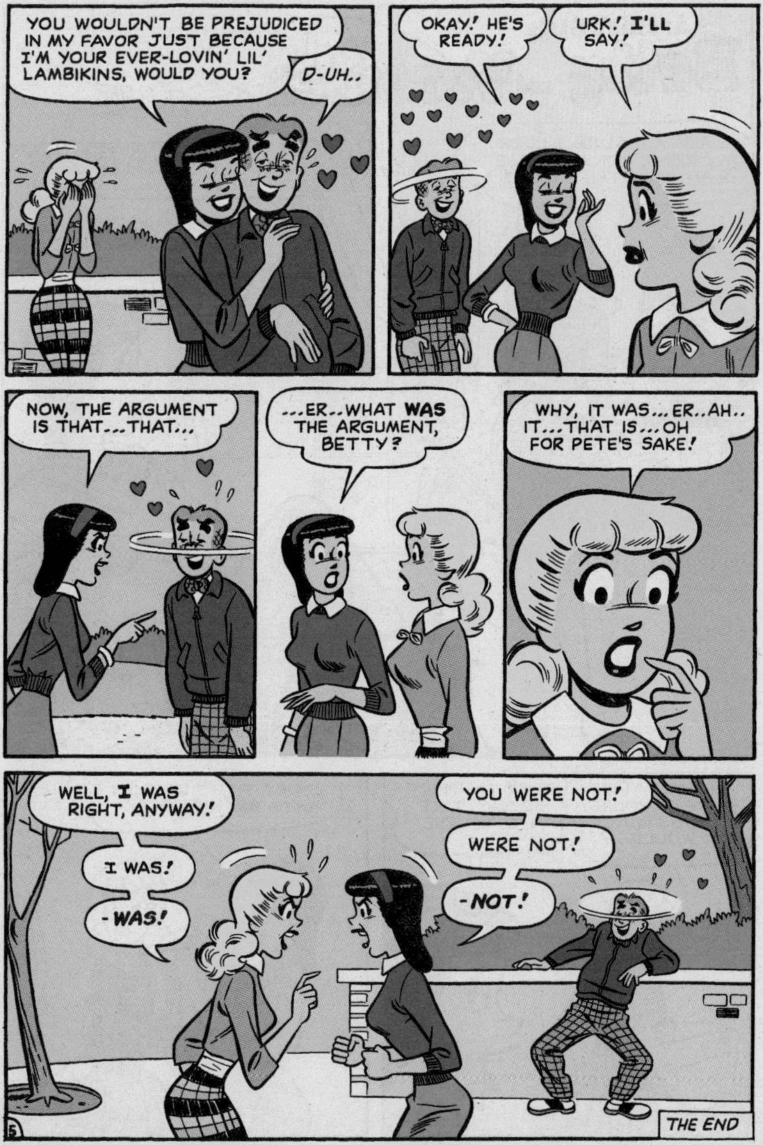
YOU WOULDN'T BE PREJUDICED IN MY FAVOR JUST BECAUSE I'M YOUR EVER-LOVIN' LIL' LAMBIKINS, WOULD YOU?
D-UH..
OKAY! HE'S READY!
URK! I'LL SAY!
NOW, THE ARGUMENT IS THAT...THAT...
...ER..WHAT WAS THE ARGUMENT, BETTY?
WHY, IT WAS...ER..AH.. IT...THAT IS...OH FOR PETE'S SAKE!
WELL, I WAS RIGHT, ANYWAY!
YOU WERE NOT!
I WAS!
WERE NOT!
-WAS!
-NOT!
THE END
5

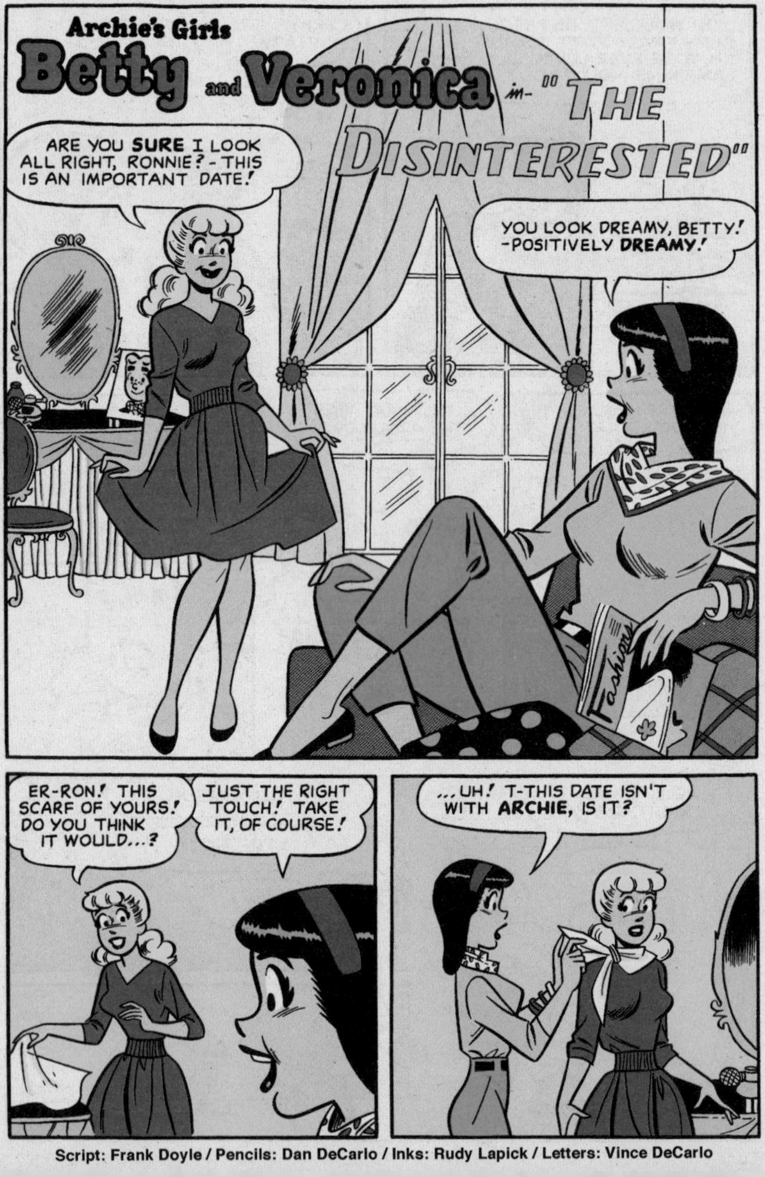
Archie's Girls
Betty and Veronica in- "The Disinterested"
ARE YOU SURE I LOOK ALL RIGHT, RONNIE? - THIS IS AN IMPORTANT DATE!
YOU LOOK DREAMY, BETTY! -POSITIVELY DREAMY!
Fashions
ER-RON! THIS SCARF OF YOURS! DO YOU THINK IT WOULD...?
JUST THE RIGHT TOUCH! TAKE IT, OF COURSE!
...UH! T-THIS DATE ISN'T WITH ARCHIE, IS IT?

Script: Frank Doyle / Pencils: Dan DeCarlo / Inks: Rudy Lapick / Letters: Vince DeCarlo

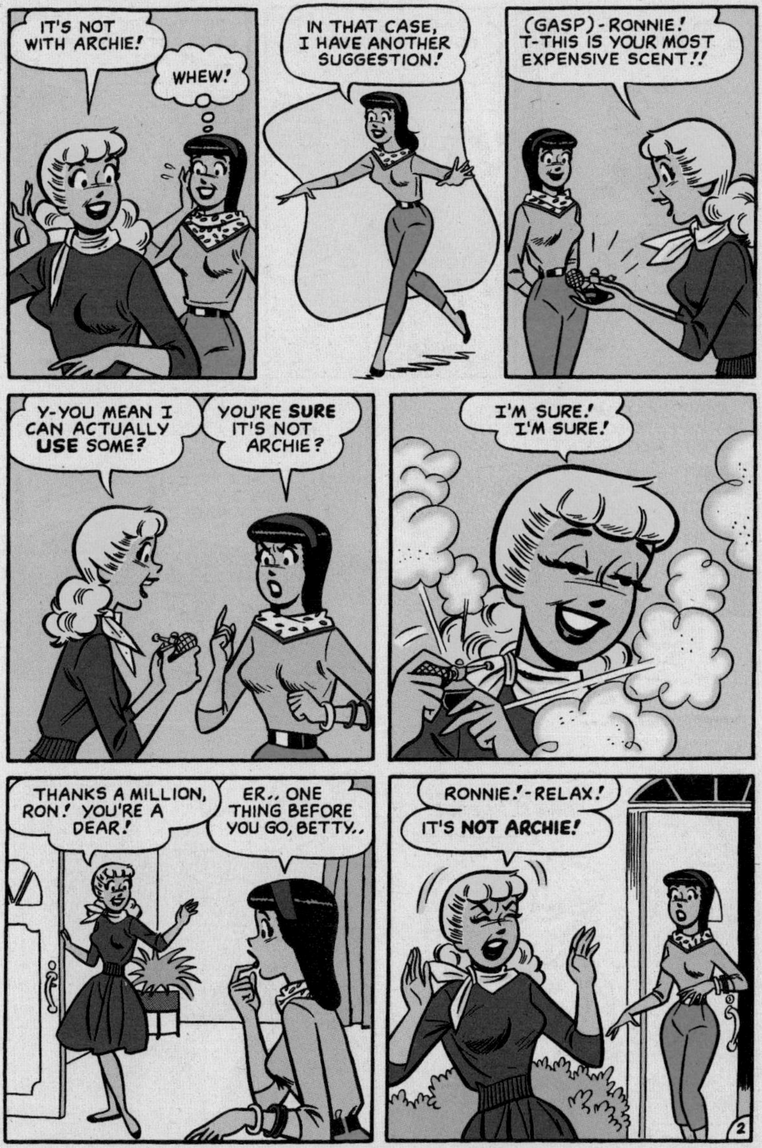
IT'S NOT WITH ARCHIE!
WHEW!
IN THAT CASE, I HAVE ANOTHER SUGGESTION!
(GASP) - RONNIE! T-THIS IS YOUR MOST EXPENSIVE SCENT!!
Y-YOU MEAN I CAN ACTUALLY USE SOME?
YOU'RE SURE IT'S NOT ARCHIE?
I'M SURE! I'M SURE!
THANKS A MILLION, RON! YOU'RE A DEAR!
ER.. ONE THING BEFORE YOU GO, BETTY..
RONNIE! - RELAX!
IT'S NOT ARCHIE!
2

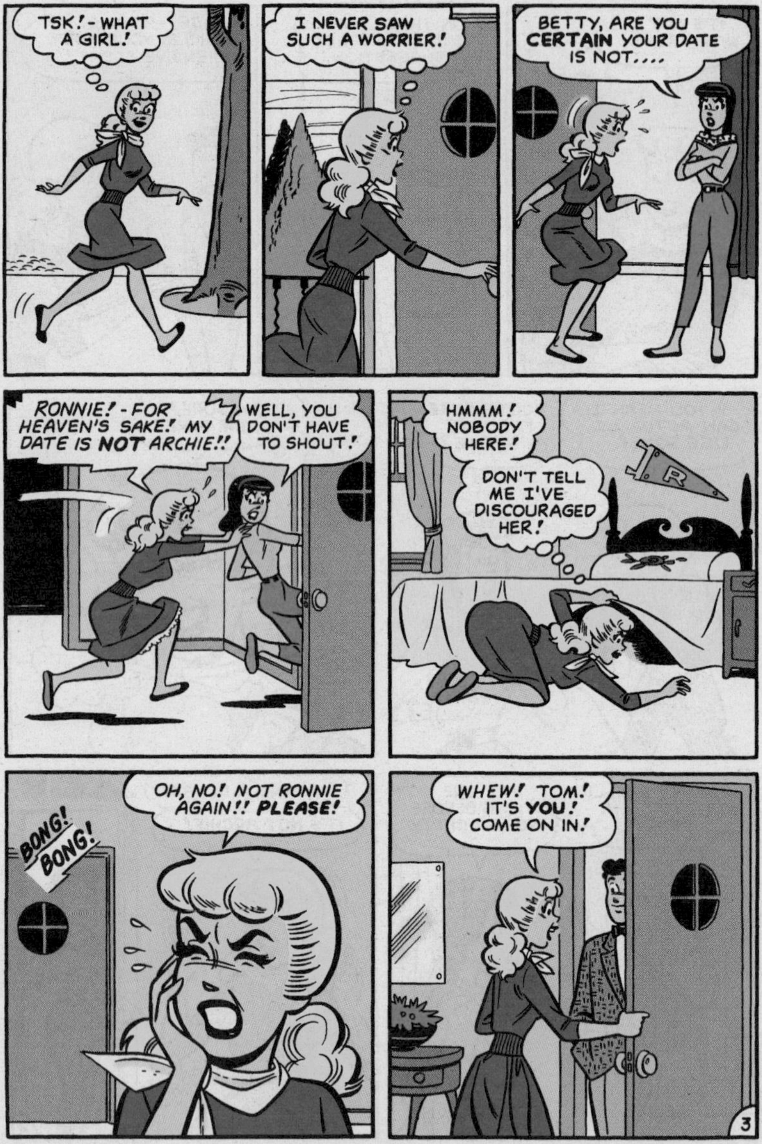
TSK! - WHAT A GIRL!
I NEVER SAW SUCH A WORRIER!
BETTY, ARE YOU CERTAIN YOUR DATE IS NOT....
RONNIE! - FOR HEAVEN'S SAKE! MY DATE IS NOT ARCHIE!!
WELL, YOU DON'T HAVE TO SHOUT!
HMMM! NOBODY HERE!
DON'T TELL ME I'VE DISCOURAGED HER!
BONG! BONG!
OH, NO! NOT RONNIE AGAIN!! PLEASE!
WHEW! TOM! IT'S YOU! COME ON IN!
3

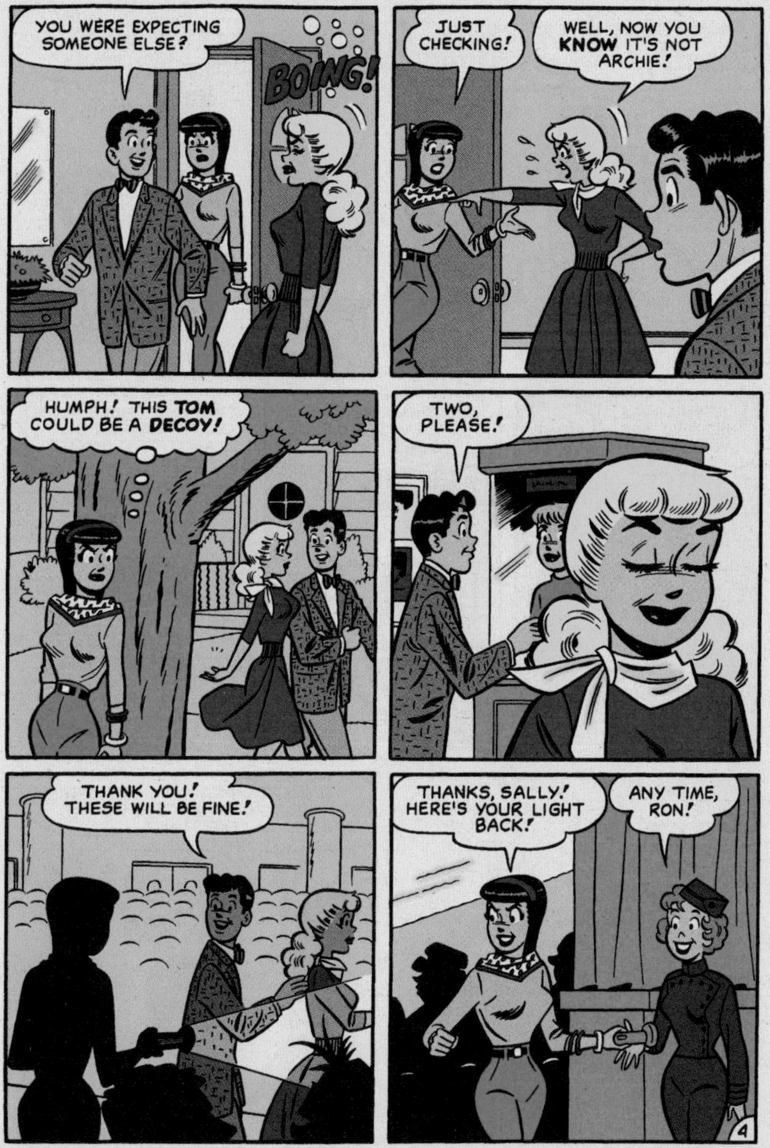
YOU WERE EXPECTING SOMEONE ELSE?
BOING!
JUST CHECKING!
WELL, NOW YOU **KNOW** IT'S NOT ARCHIE!
HUMPH! THIS **TOM** COULD BE A **DECOY**!
TWO, PLEASE!
THANK YOU! THESE WILL BE FINE!
THANKS, SALLY! HERE'S YOUR LIGHT BACK!
ANY TIME, RON!
4

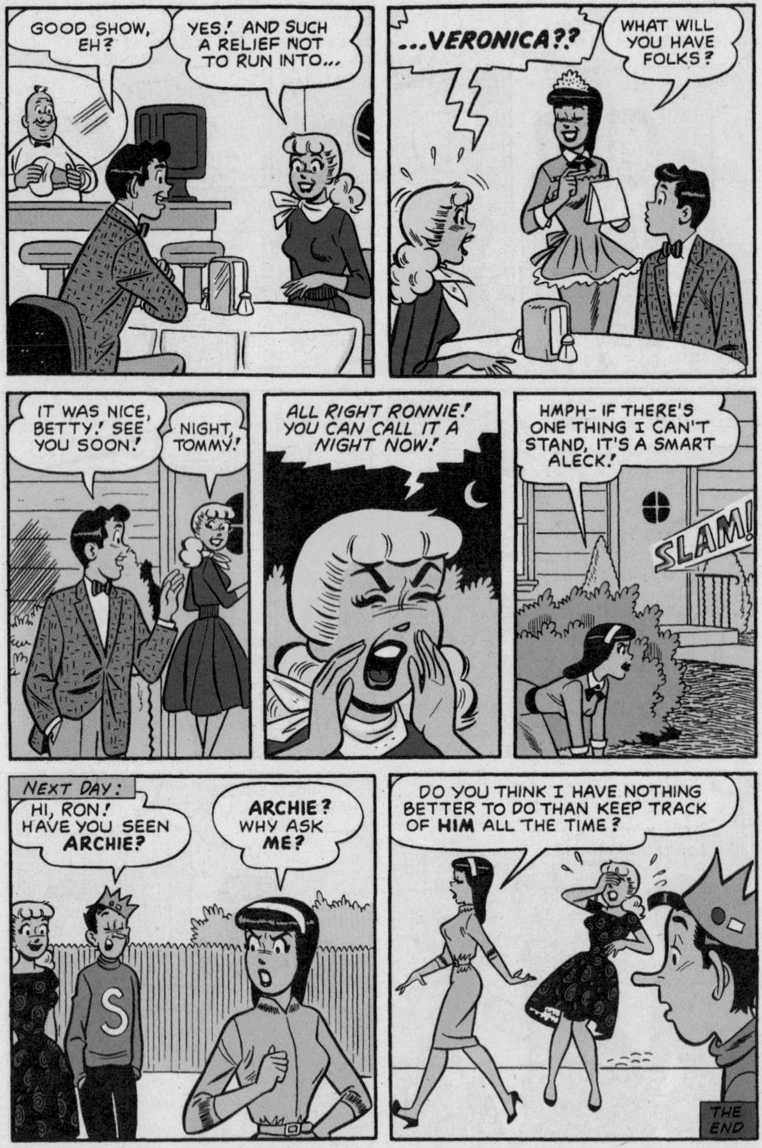

GOOD SHOW, EH?
YES! AND SUCH A RELIEF NOT TO RUN INTO...
...VERONICA??
WHAT WILL YOU HAVE FOLKS?
IT WAS NICE, BETTY! SEE YOU SOON!
NIGHT, TOMMY!
ALL RIGHT RONNIE! YOU CAN CALL IT A NIGHT NOW!
HMPH- IF THERE'S ONE THING I CAN'T STAND, IT'S A SMART ALECK!
SLAM!
NEXT DAY:
HI, RON! HAVE YOU SEEN ARCHIE?
ARCHIE? WHY ASK ME?
DO YOU THINK I HAVE NOTHING BETTER TO DO THAN KEEP TRACK OF HIM ALL THE TIME?
THE END

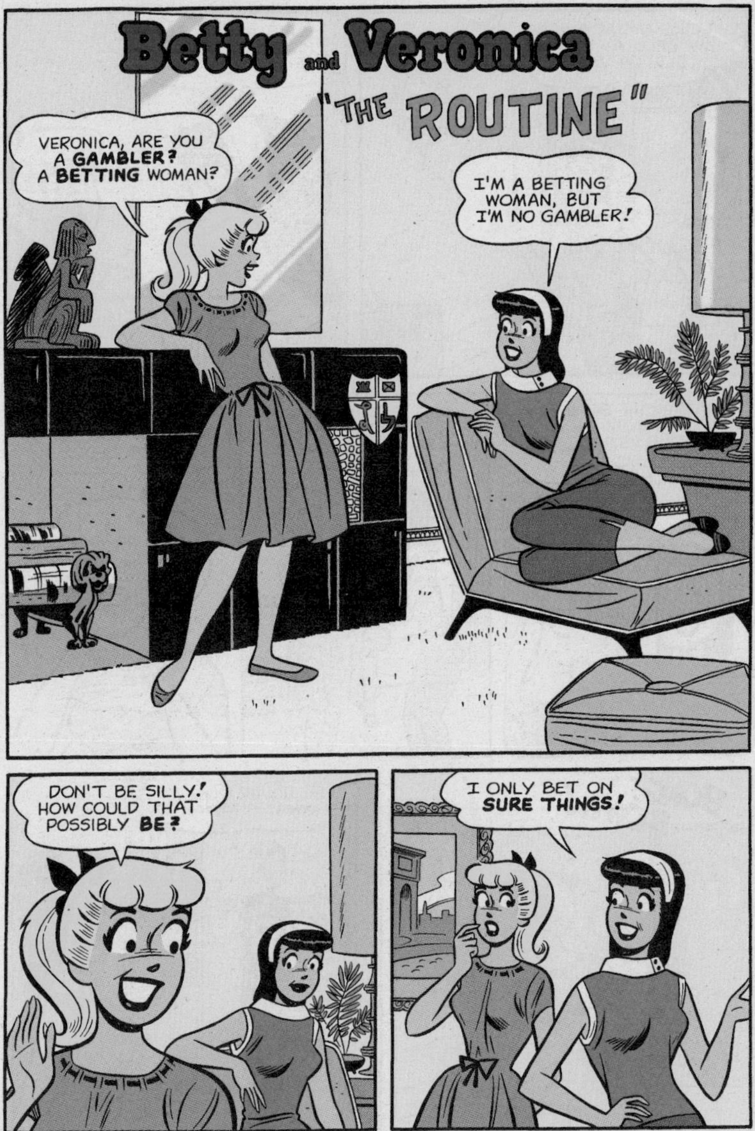
Betty and Veronica
"THE ROUTINE"
VERONICA, ARE YOU A GAMBLER? A BETTING WOMAN?
I'M A BETTING WOMAN, BUT I'M NO GAMBLER!
DON'T BE SILLY! HOW COULD THAT POSSIBLY BE?
I ONLY BET ON SURE THINGS!

Script: Frank Doyle / Pencils: Dan DeCarlo / Inks: Rudy Lapick / Letters: Vince DeCarlo

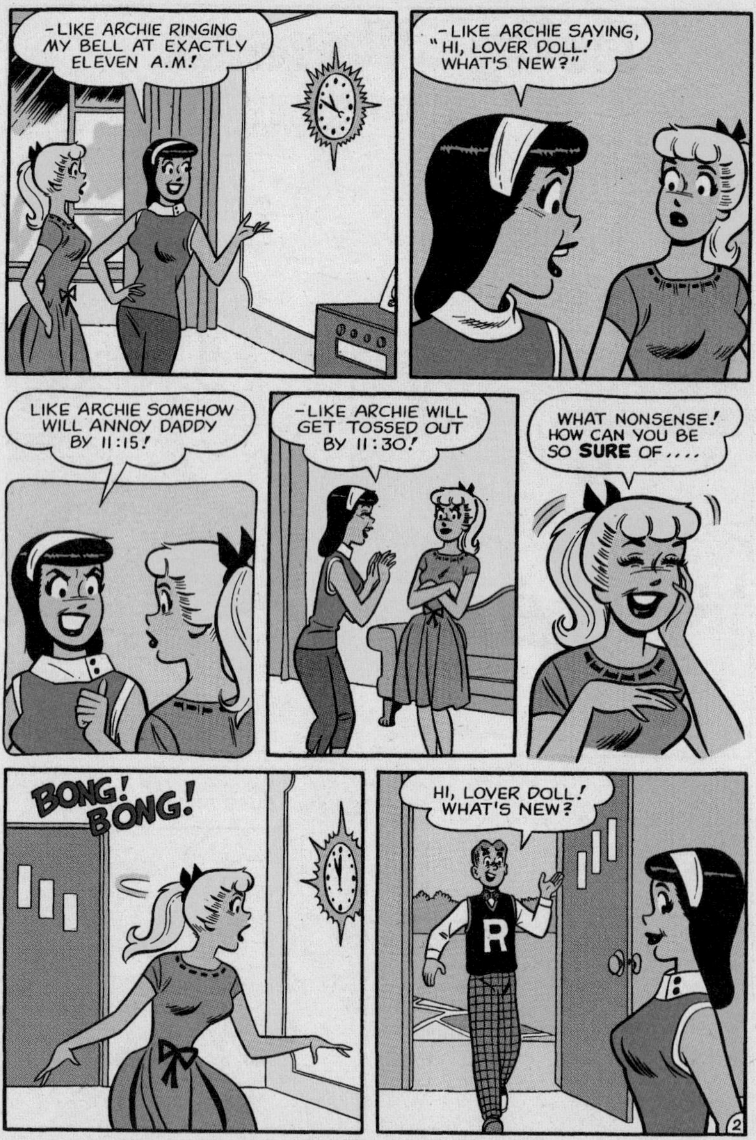

-LIKE ARCHIE RINGING MY BELL AT EXACTLY ELEVEN A.M!
-LIKE ARCHIE SAYING, "HI, LOVER DOLL! WHAT'S NEW?"
LIKE ARCHIE SOMEHOW WILL ANNOY DADDY BY 11:15!
-LIKE ARCHIE WILL GET TOSSED OUT BY 11:30!
WHAT NONSENSE! HOW CAN YOU BE SO **SURE** OF....
BONG! BONG!
HI, LOVER DOLL! WHAT'S NEW?
2

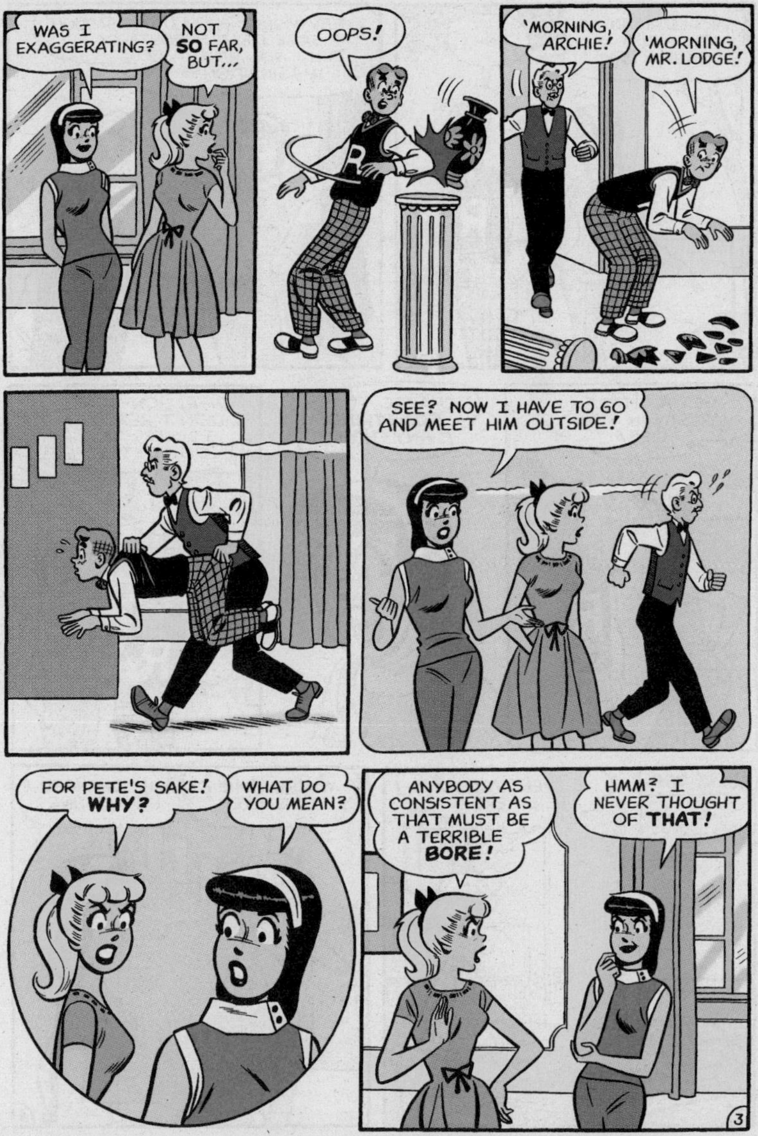
WAS I EXAGGERATING?
NOT SO FAR, BUT...
OOPS!
'MORNING, ARCHIE!
'MORNING, MR. LODGE!
SEE? NOW I HAVE TO GO AND MEET HIM OUTSIDE!
FOR PETE'S SAKE! WHY?
WHAT DO YOU MEAN?
ANYBODY AS CONSISTENT AS THAT MUST BE A TERRIBLE BORE!
HMM? I NEVER THOUGHT OF THAT!
3

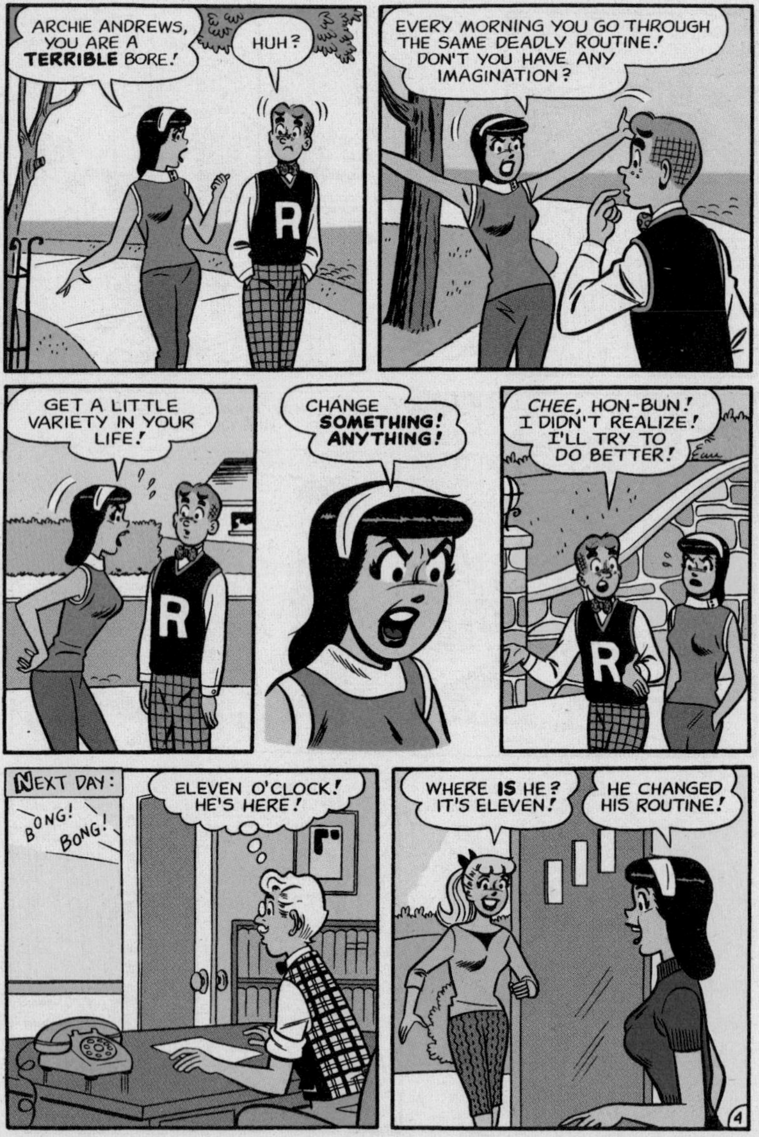
ARCHIE ANDREWS, YOU ARE A TERRIBLE BORE!
HUH?
EVERY MORNING YOU GO THROUGH THE SAME DEADLY ROUTINE! DON'T YOU HAVE ANY IMAGINATION?
GET A LITTLE VARIETY IN YOUR LIFE!
CHANGE SOMETHING! ANYTHING!
CHEE, HON-BUN! I DIDN'T REALIZE! I'LL TRY TO DO BETTER!
NEXT DAY:
BONG! BONG!
ELEVEN O'CLOCK! HE'S HERE!
WHERE IS HE? IT'S ELEVEN!
HE CHANGED HIS ROUTINE!
4

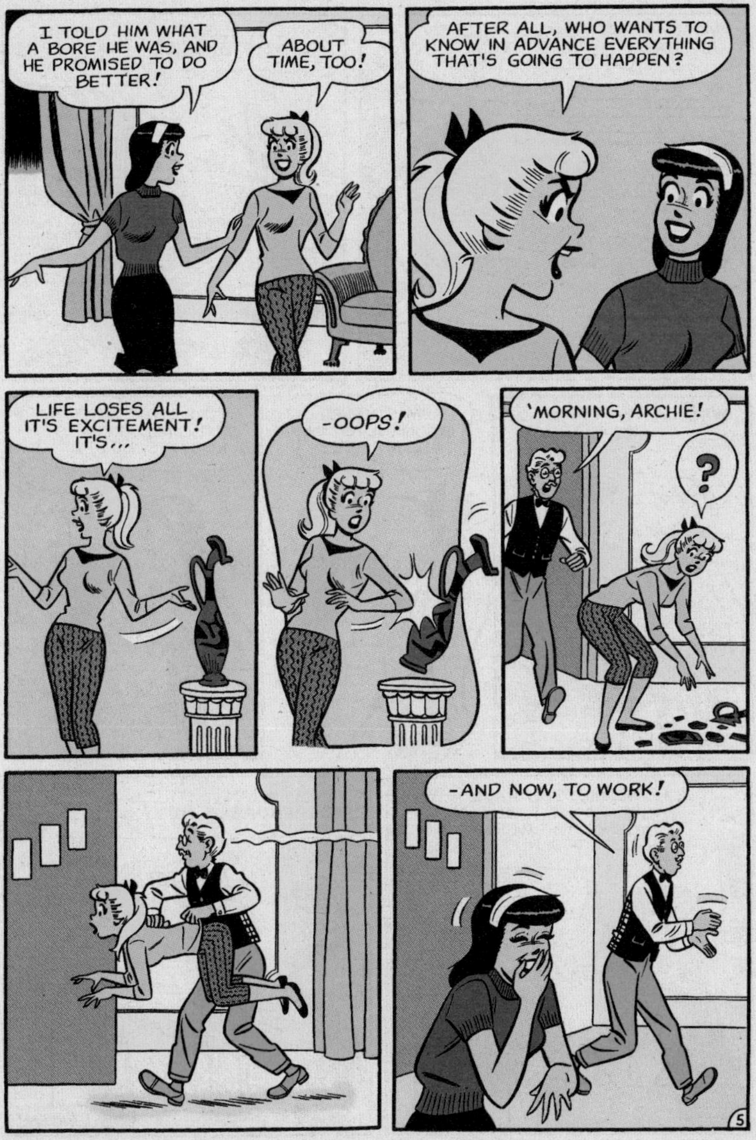
I TOLD HIM WHAT A BORE HE WAS, AND HE PROMISED TO DO BETTER!
ABOUT TIME, TOO!
AFTER ALL, WHO WANTS TO KNOW IN ADVANCE EVERYTHING THAT'S GOING TO HAPPEN?
LIFE LOSES ALL IT'S EXCITEMENT! IT'S...
-OOPS!
'MORNING, ARCHIE!
?
-AND NOW, TO WORK!

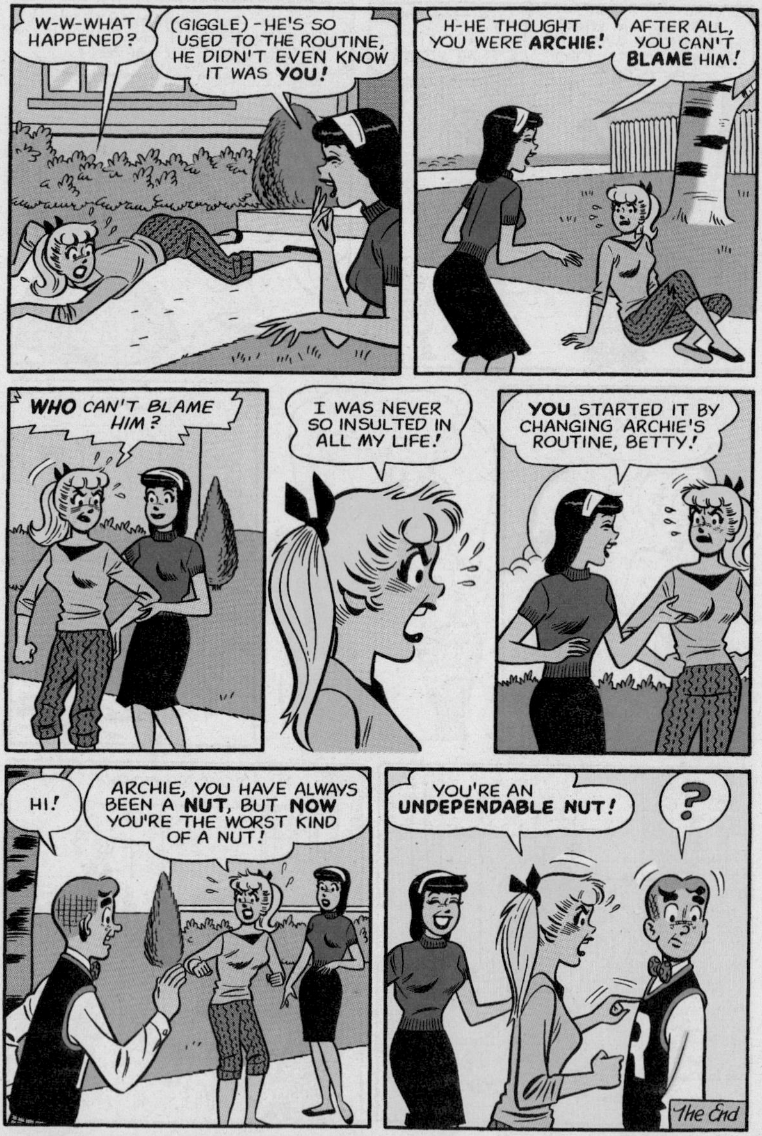
W-W-WHAT HAPPENED?
(GIGGLE) -HE'S SO USED TO THE ROUTINE, HE DIDN'T EVEN KNOW IT WAS YOU!
H-HE THOUGHT YOU WERE ARCHIE!
AFTER ALL, YOU CAN'T BLAME HIM!
WHO CAN'T BLAME HIM?
I WAS NEVER SO INSULTED IN ALL MY LIFE!
YOU STARTED IT BY CHANGING ARCHIE'S ROUTINE, BETTY!
HI!
ARCHIE, YOU HAVE ALWAYS BEEN A NUT, BUT NOW YOU'RE THE WORST KIND OF A NUT!
YOU'RE AN UNDEPENDABLE NUT!
?
The End

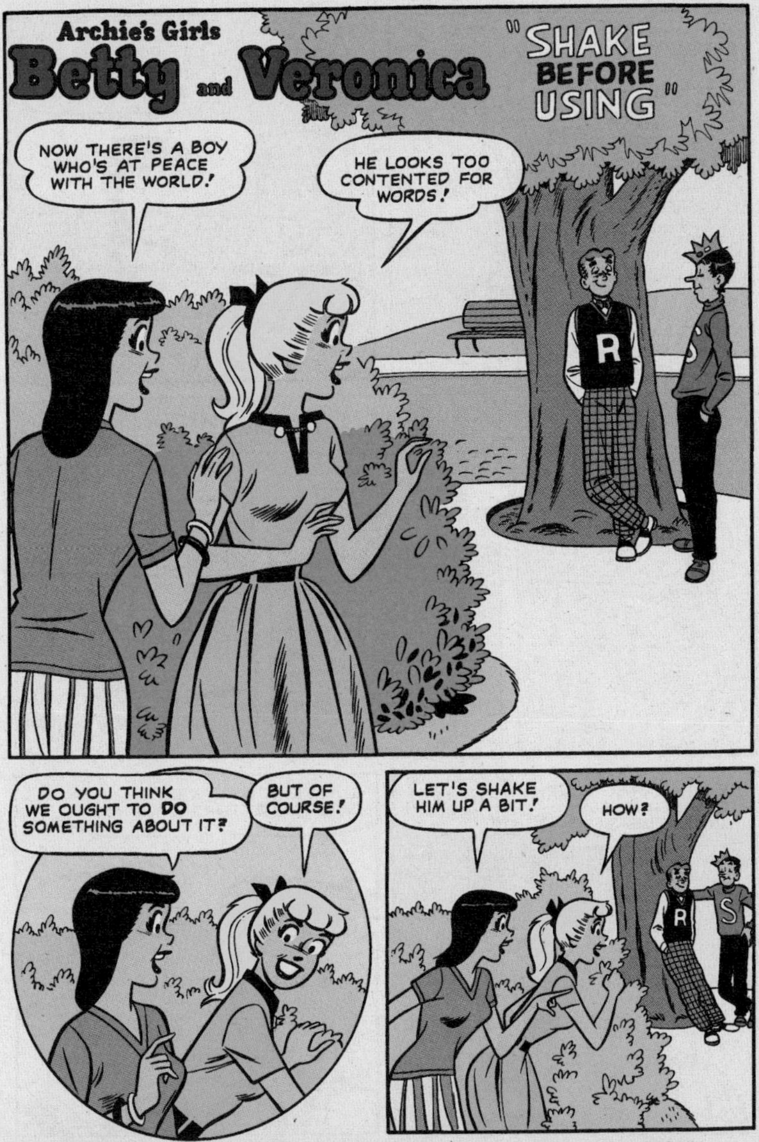
Archie's Girls
Betty and Veronica
"SHAKE BEFORE USING"
NOW THERE'S A BOY WHO'S AT PEACE WITH THE WORLD!
HE LOOKS TOO CONTENTED FOR WORDS!
R
S
DO YOU THINK WE OUGHT TO DO SOMETHING ABOUT IT?
BUT OF COURSE!
LET'S SHAKE HIM UP A BIT!
HOW?
R
S

Script: Frank Doyle / Pencils: Dan DeCarlo / Inks: Rudy Lapick / Letters: Vince DeCarlo

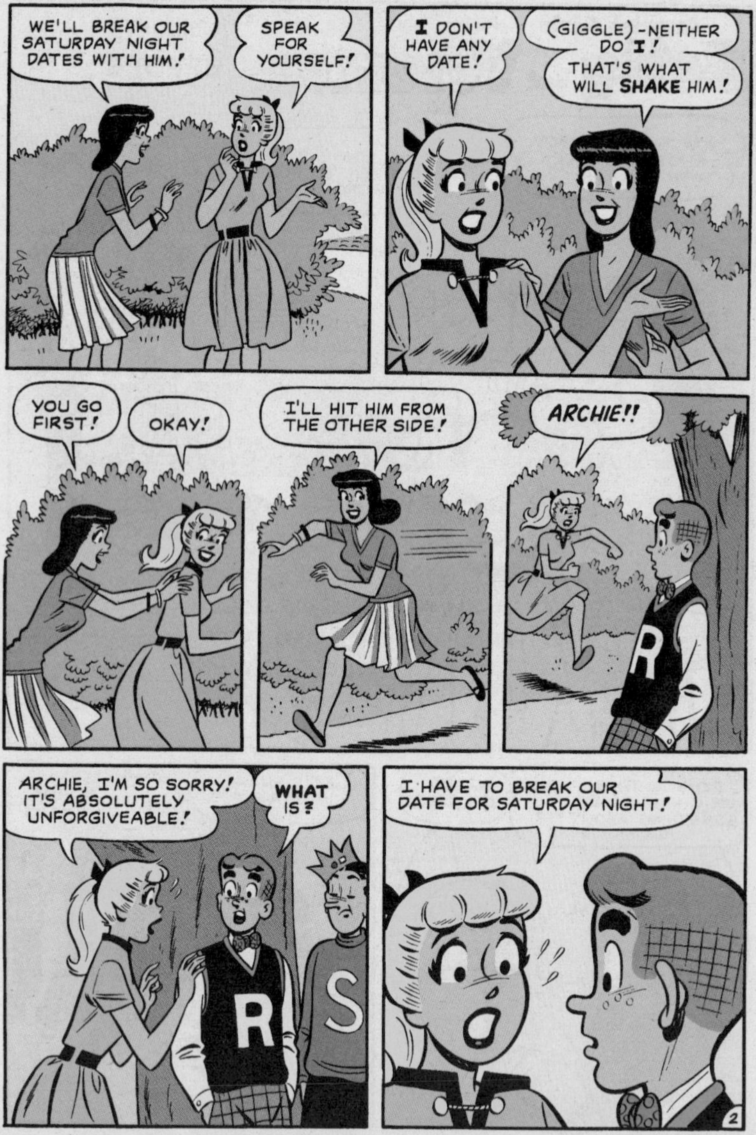
WE'LL BREAK OUR SATURDAY NIGHT DATES WITH HIM!
SPEAK FOR YOURSELF!
I DON'T HAVE ANY DATE!
(GIGGLE)-NEITHER DO I!
THAT'S WHAT WILL SHAKE HIM!
YOU GO FIRST!
OKAY!
I'LL HIT HIM FROM THE OTHER SIDE!
ARCHIE!!
ARCHIE, I'M SO SORRY! IT'S ABSOLUTELY UNFORGIVEABLE!
WHAT IS?
I HAVE TO BREAK OUR DATE FOR SATURDAY NIGHT!
2

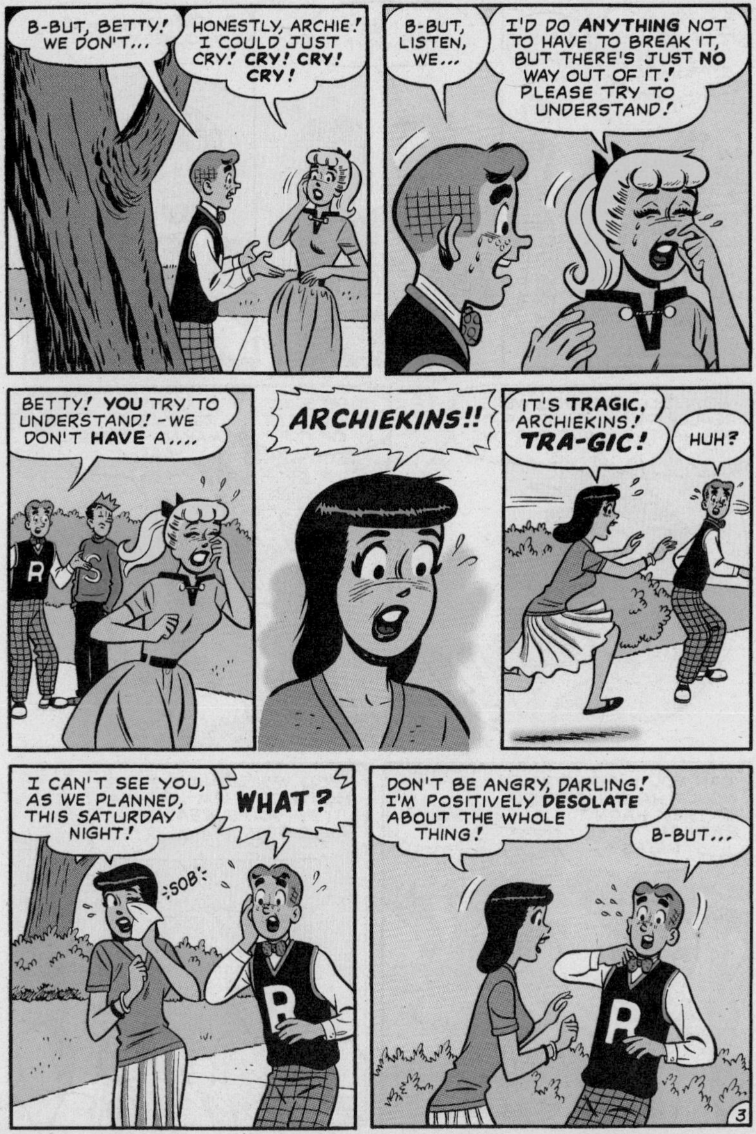
B-BUT, BETTY! WE DON'T...
HONESTLY, ARCHIE! I COULD JUST CRY! CRY! CRY! CRY!
B-BUT, LISTEN, WE...
I'D DO ANYTHING NOT TO HAVE TO BREAK IT, BUT THERE'S JUST NO WAY OUT OF IT! PLEASE TRY TO UNDERSTAND!
BETTY! YOU TRY TO UNDERSTAND! -WE DON'T HAVE A....
ARCHIEKINS!!
IT'S TRAGIC, ARCHIEKINS! TRA-GIC!
HUH?
I CAN'T SEE YOU, AS WE PLANNED, THIS SATURDAY NIGHT!
WHAT?
SOB
DON'T BE ANGRY, DARLING! I'M POSITIVELY DESOLATE ABOUT THE WHOLE THING!
B-BUT...
3

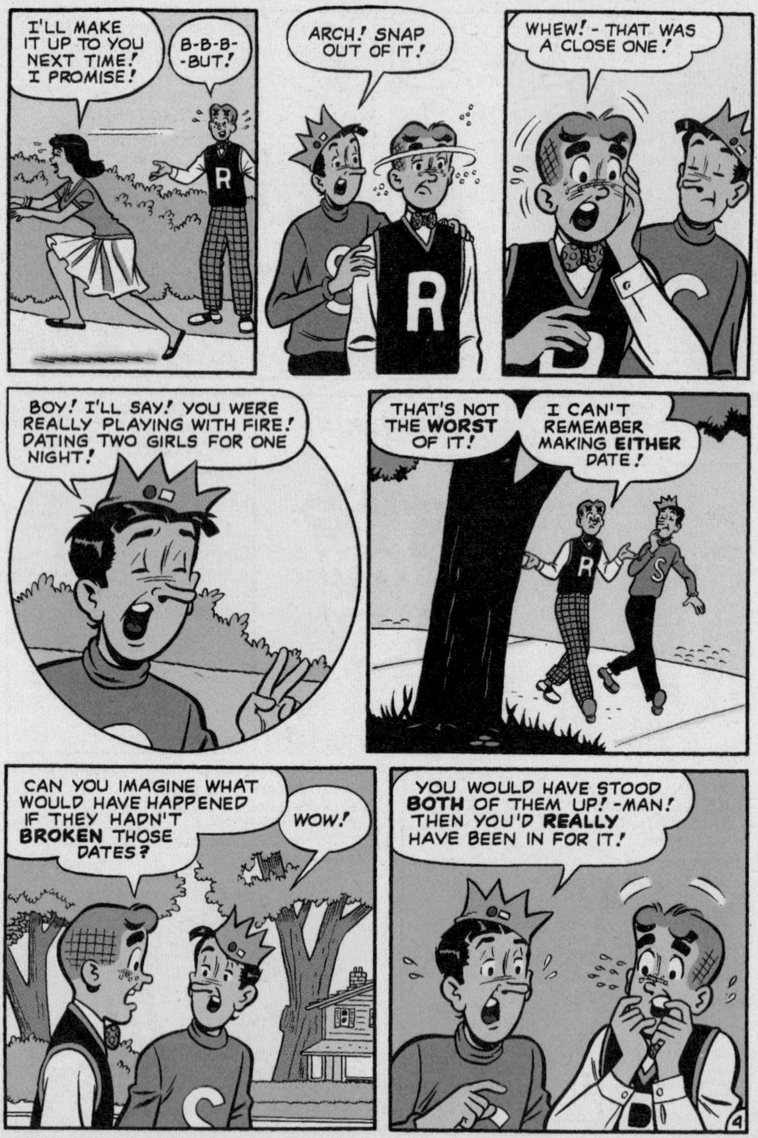
I'LL MAKE IT UP TO YOU NEXT TIME! I PROMISE!
B-B-B--BUT!
ARCH! SNAP OUT OF IT!
WHEW! - THAT WAS A CLOSE ONE!
BOY! I'LL SAY! YOU WERE REALLY PLAYING WITH FIRE! DATING TWO GIRLS FOR ONE NIGHT!
THAT'S NOT THE WORST OF IT!
I CAN'T REMEMBER MAKING EITHER DATE!
CAN YOU IMAGINE WHAT WOULD HAVE HAPPENED IF THEY HADN'T BROKEN THOSE DATES?
WOW!
YOU WOULD HAVE STOOD BOTH OF THEM UP! -MAN! THEN YOU'D REALLY HAVE BEEN IN FOR IT!
4

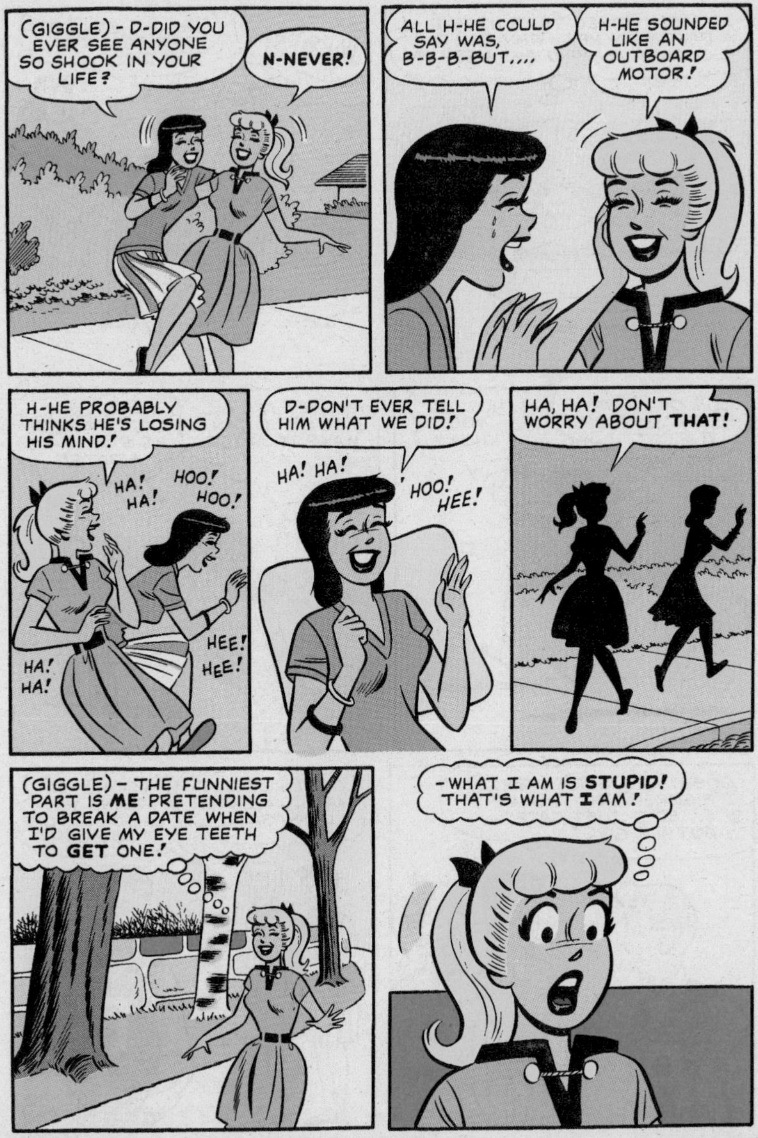
(GIGGLE) - D-DID YOU EVER SEE ANYONE SO SHOOK IN YOUR LIFE?
N-NEVER!
ALL H-HE COULD SAY WAS, B-B-B-BUT....
H-HE SOUNDED LIKE AN OUTBOARD MOTOR!
H-HE PROBABLY THINKS HE'S LOSING HIS MIND!
HA! HA!
HOO! HOO!
HEE! HEE!
HA! HA!
D-DON'T EVER TELL HIM WHAT WE DID!
HA! HA!
HOO! HEE!
HA, HA! DON'T WORRY ABOUT THAT!
(GIGGLE) - THE FUNNIEST PART IS ME PRETENDING TO BREAK A DATE WHEN I'D GIVE MY EYE TEETH TO GET ONE!
-WHAT I AM IS STUPID! THAT'S WHAT I AM!

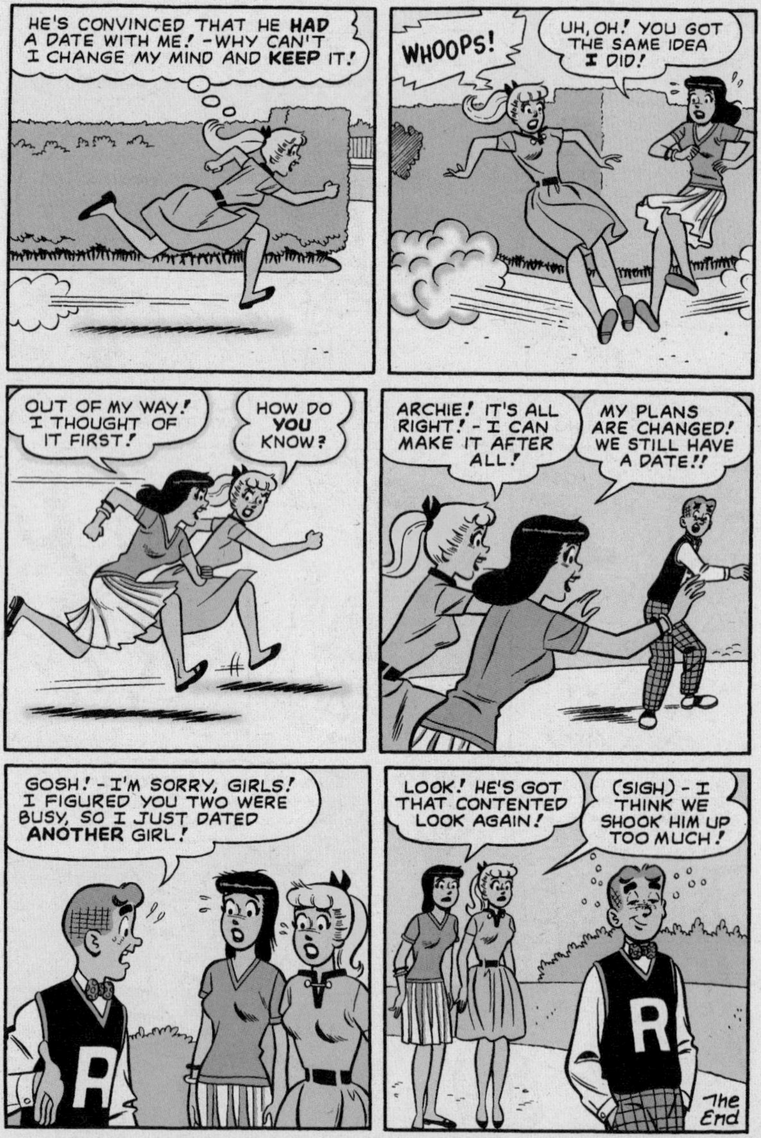
HE'S CONVINCED THAT HE HAD A DATE WITH ME! -WHY CAN'T I CHANGE MY MIND AND KEEP IT!
WHOOPS!
UH, OH! YOU GOT THE SAME IDEA I DID!
OUT OF MY WAY! I THOUGHT OF IT FIRST!
HOW DO YOU KNOW?
ARCHIE! IT'S ALL RIGHT! - I CAN MAKE IT AFTER ALL!
MY PLANS ARE CHANGED! WE STILL HAVE A DATE!!
GOSH! - I'M SORRY, GIRLS! I FIGURED YOU TWO WERE BUSY, SO I JUST DATED ANOTHER GIRL!
LOOK! HE'S GOT THAT CONTENTED LOOK AGAIN!
(SIGH) - I THINK WE SHOOK HIM UP TOO MUCH!
The End

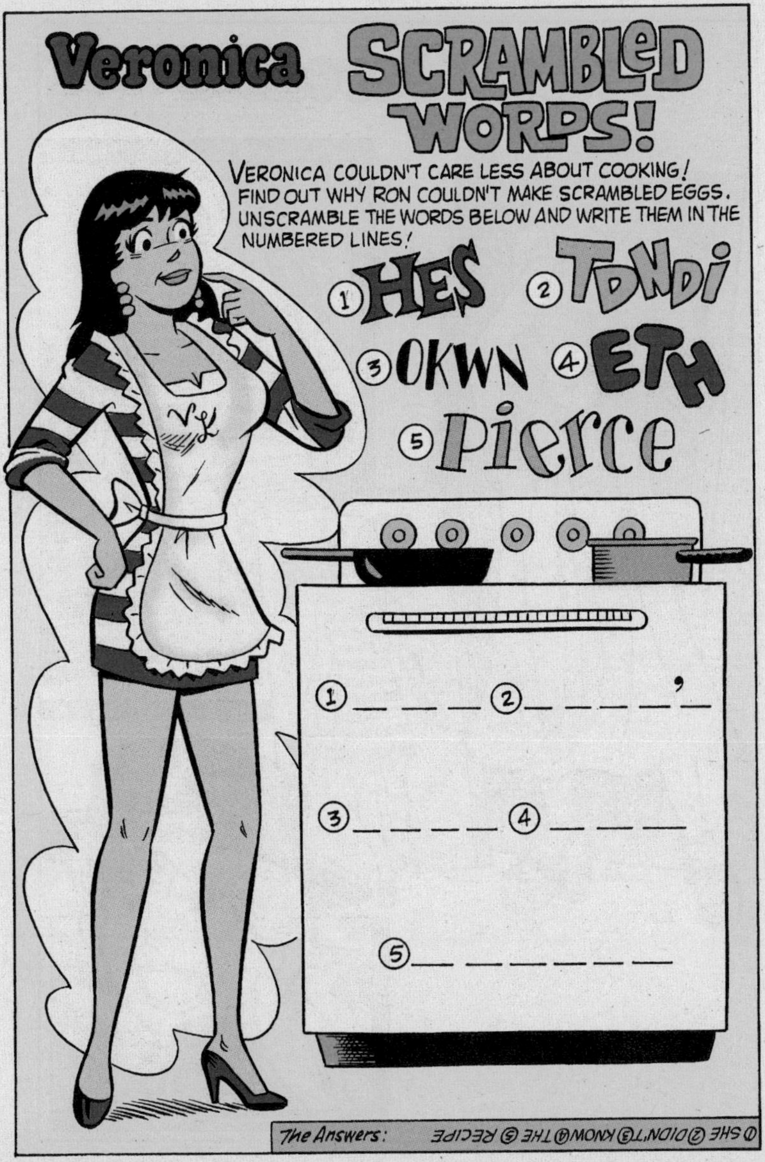

Veronica
SCRAMBLED WORDS!
VERONICA COULDN'T CARE LESS ABOUT COOKING! FIND OUT WHY RON COULDN'T MAKE SCRAMBLED EGGS. UNSCRAMBLE THE WORDS BELOW AND WRITE THEM IN THE NUMBERED LINES!
1 HES
2 TDNDI
3 OKWN
4 ETH
5 PIERCE
VL
1 ___ 2 _____'_
3 ____ 4 ___
5 ______
The Answers: 1 SHE 2 DIDN'T 3 KNOW 4 THE 5 RECIPE

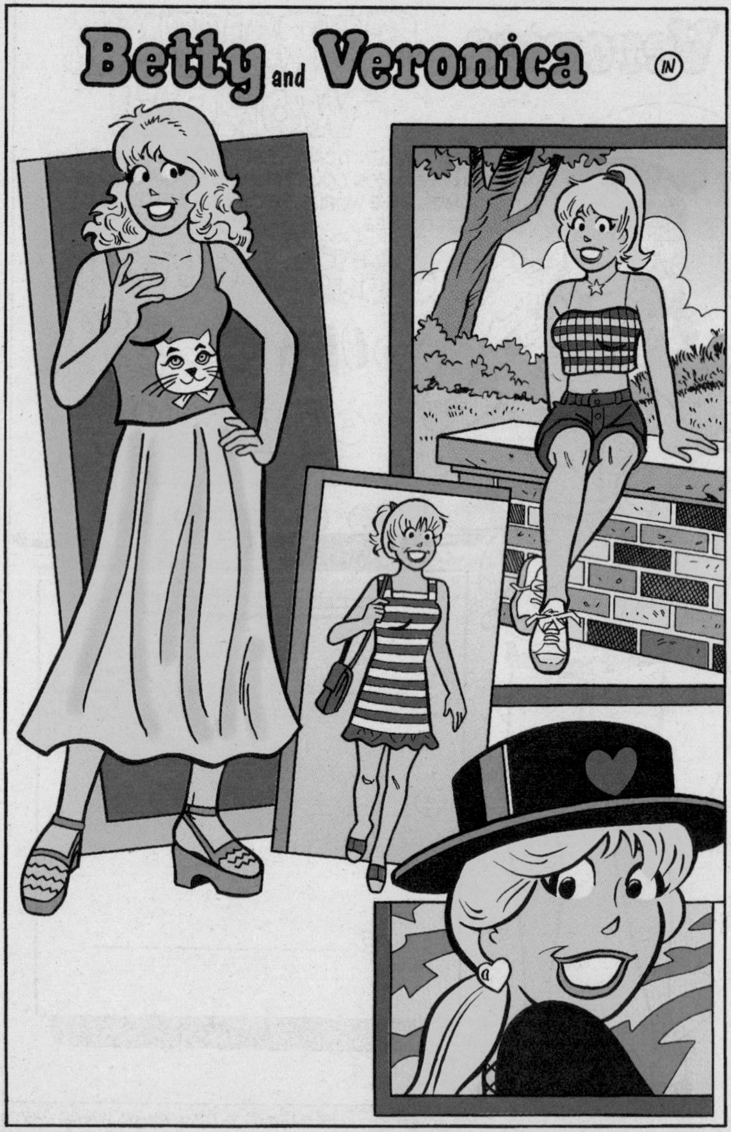
Betty and Veronica

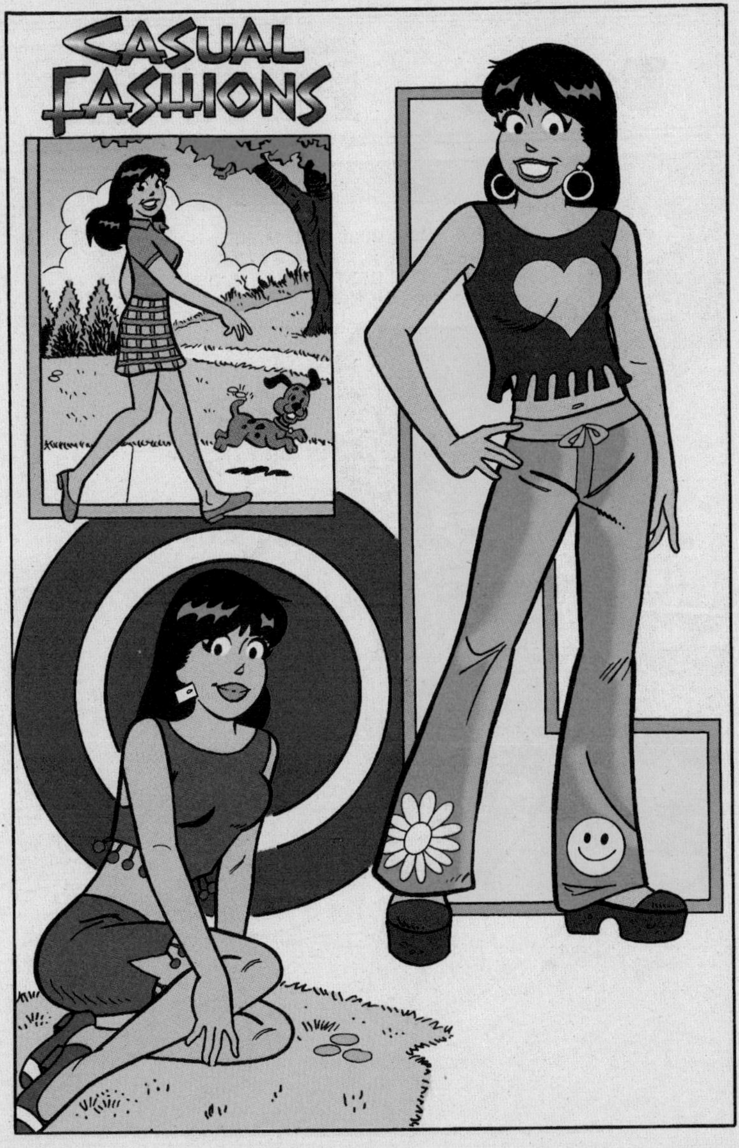
CASUAL FASHIONS

Betty's PIN-UP

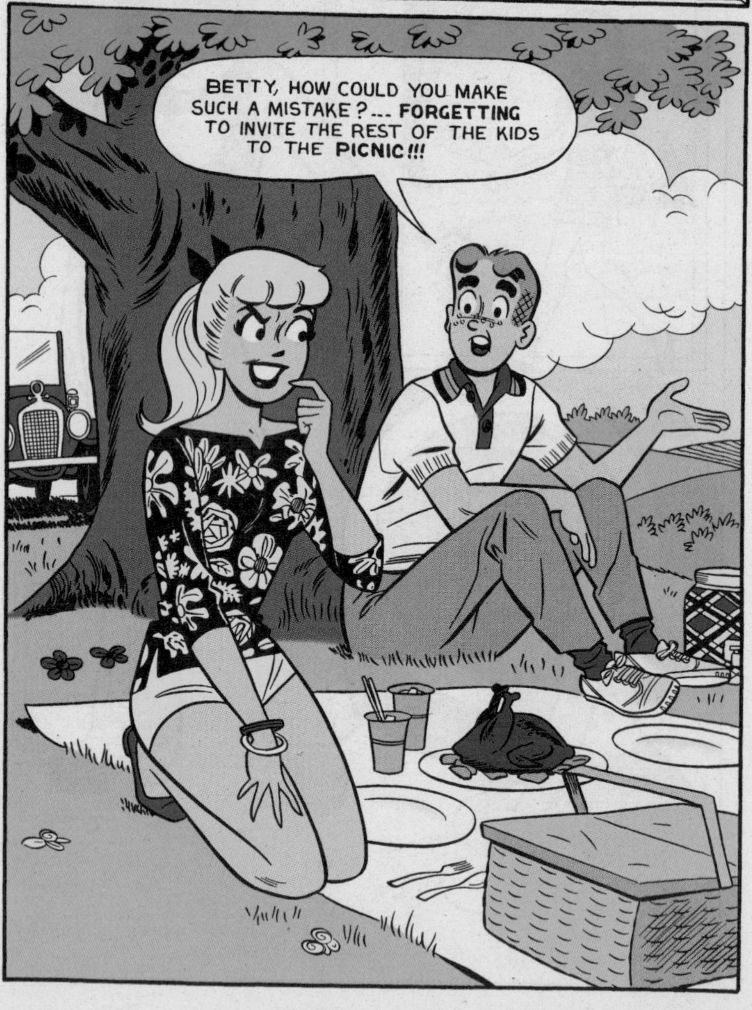
BETTY, HOW COULD YOU MAKE SUCH A MISTAKE?... FORGETTING TO INVITE THE REST OF THE KIDS TO THE PICNIC!!!

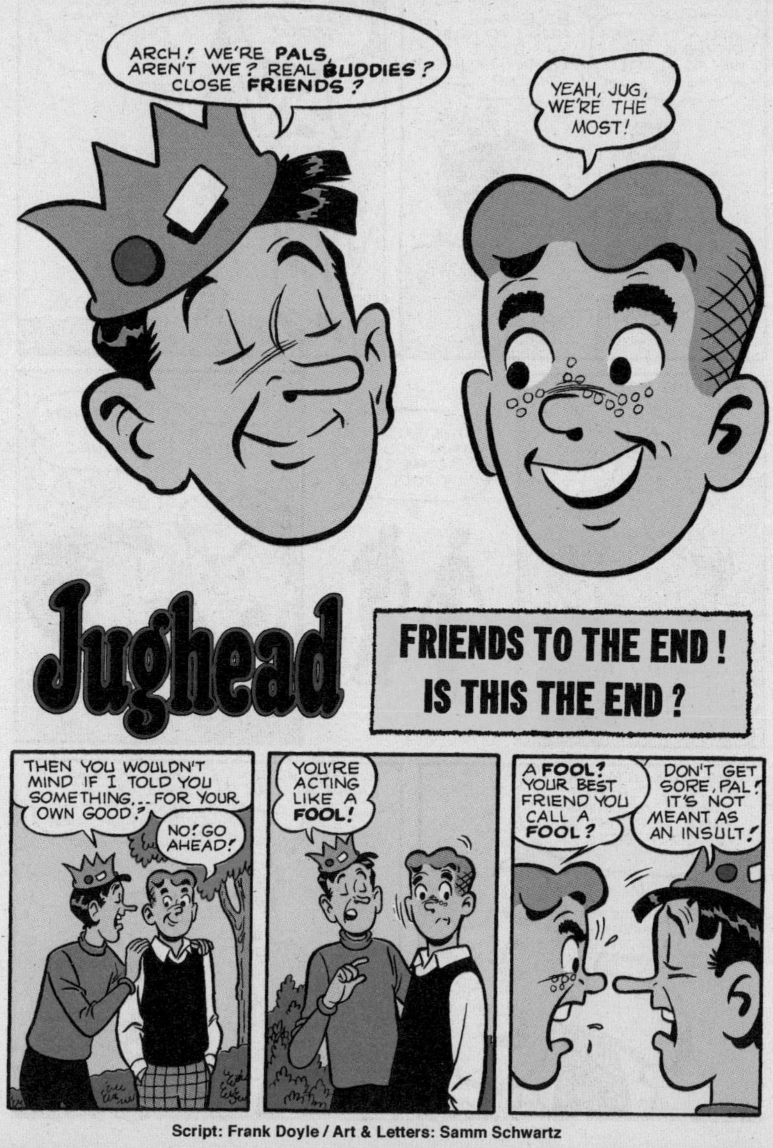

ARCH! WE'RE PALS, AREN'T WE? REAL BUDDIES? CLOSE FRIENDS?
YEAH, JUG, WE'RE THE MOST!
Jughead
FRIENDS TO THE END! IS THIS THE END?
THEN YOU WOULDN'T MIND IF I TOLD YOU SOMETHING... FOR YOUR OWN GOOD?
NO! GO AHEAD!
YOU'RE ACTING LIKE A FOOL!
A FOOL? YOUR BEST FRIEND YOU CALL A FOOL?
DON'T GET SORE, PAL! IT'S NOT MEANT AS AN INSULT!

Script: Frank Doyle / Art & Letters: Samm Schwartz

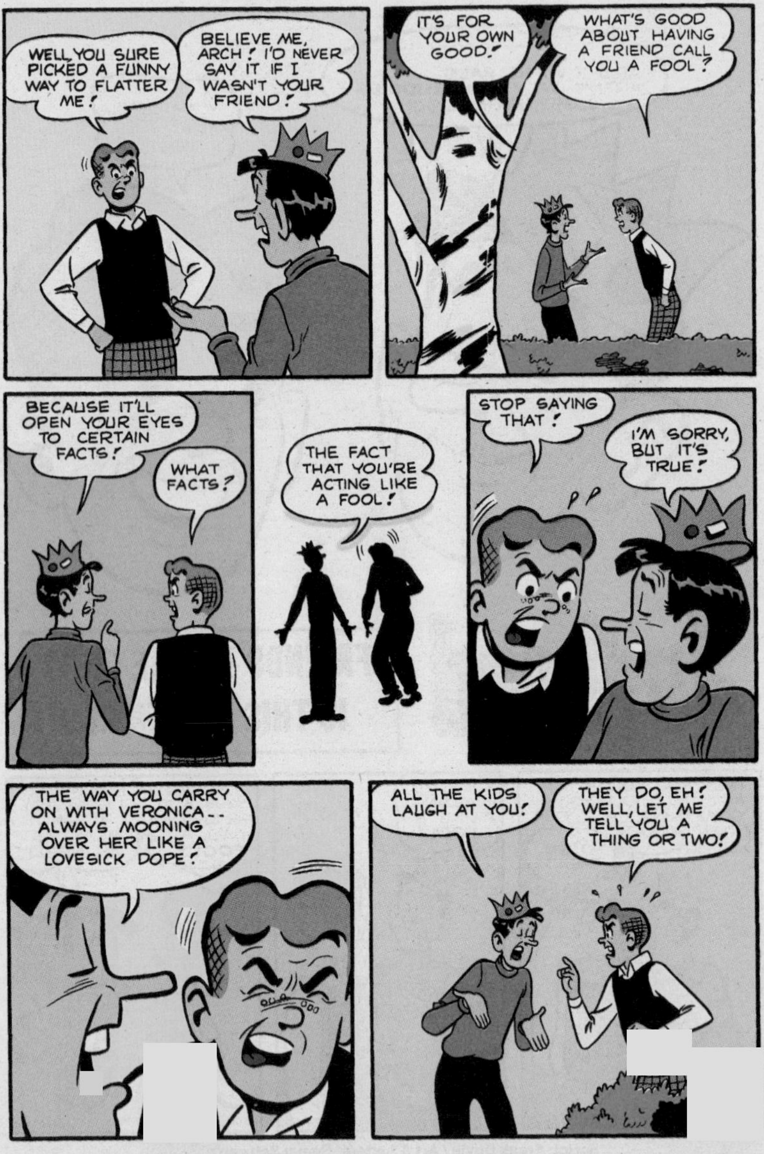
WELL, YOU SURE PICKED A FUNNY WAY TO FLATTER ME!
BELIEVE ME, ARCH! I'D NEVER SAY IT IF I WASN'T YOUR FRIEND!
IT'S FOR YOUR OWN GOOD!
WHAT'S GOOD ABOUT HAVING A FRIEND CALL YOU A FOOL?
BECAUSE IT'LL OPEN YOUR EYES TO CERTAIN FACTS!
WHAT FACTS?
THE FACT THAT YOU'RE ACTING LIKE A FOOL!
STOP SAYING THAT!
I'M SORRY, BUT IT'S TRUE!
THE WAY YOU CARRY ON WITH VERONICA.. ALWAYS MOONING OVER HER LIKE A LOVESICK DOPE!
ALL THE KIDS LAUGH AT YOU!
THEY DO, EH! WELL, LET ME TELL YOU A THING OR TWO!

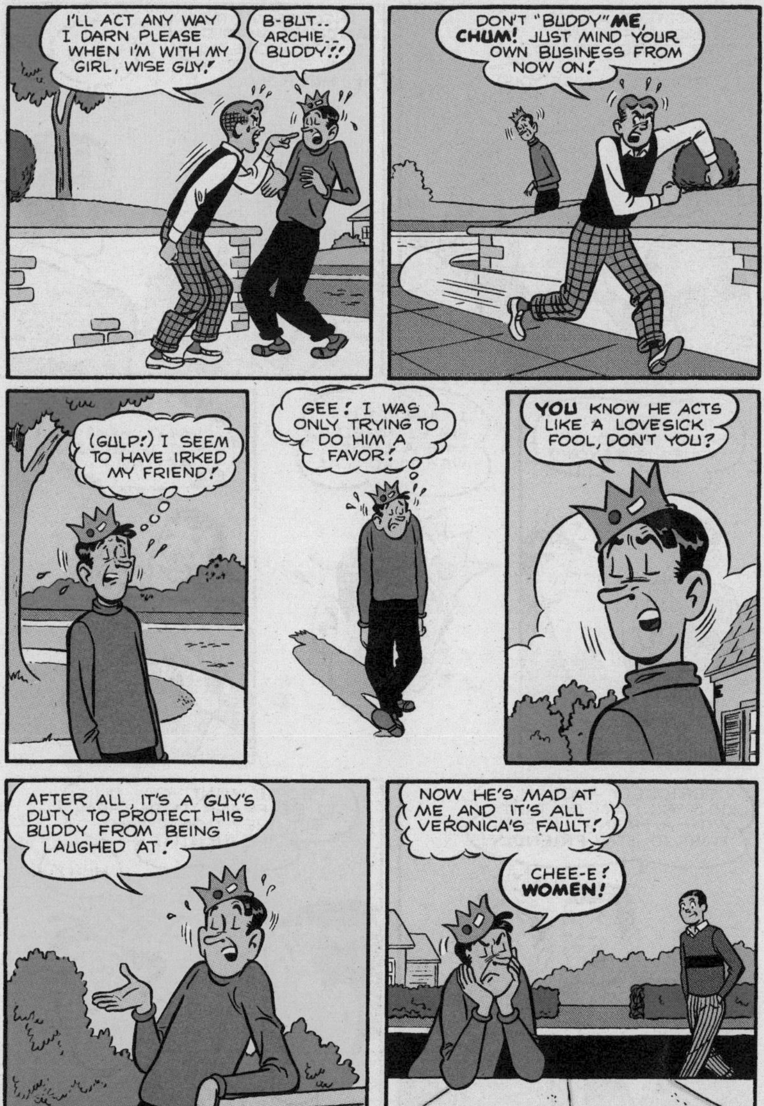
I'LL ACT ANY WAY I DARN PLEASE WHEN I'M WITH MY GIRL, WISE GUY!
B-BUT.. ARCHIE.. BUDDY!!
DON'T "BUDDY" ME, CHUM! JUST MIND YOUR OWN BUSINESS FROM NOW ON!
(GULP!) I SEEM TO HAVE IRKED MY FRIEND!
GEE! I WAS ONLY TRYING TO DO HIM A FAVOR!
YOU KNOW HE ACTS LIKE A LOVESICK FOOL, DON'T YOU?
AFTER ALL, IT'S A GUY'S DUTY TO PROTECT HIS BUDDY FROM BEING LAUGHED AT!
NOW HE'S MAD AT ME, AND IT'S ALL VERONICA'S FAULT!
CHEE-E! WOMEN!

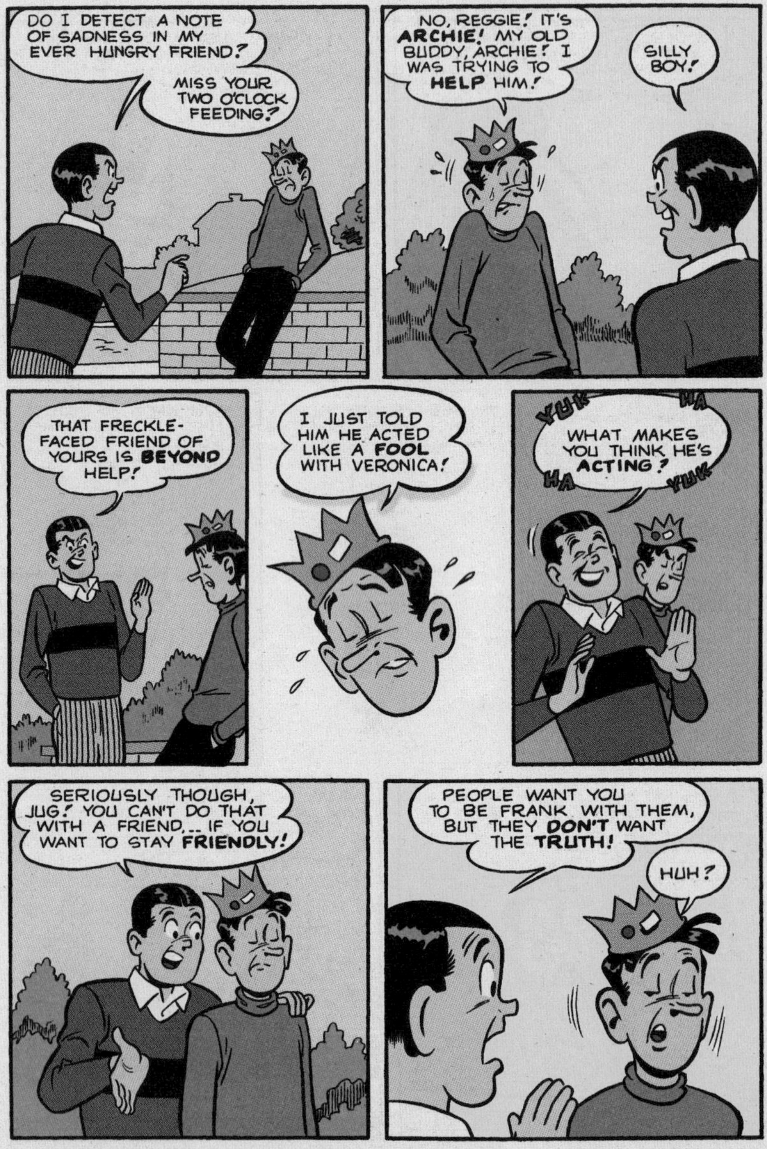

DO I DETECT A NOTE OF SADNESS IN MY EVER HUNGRY FRIEND?
MISS YOUR TWO O'CLOCK FEEDING?
NO, REGGIE! IT'S ARCHIE! MY OLD BUDDY, ARCHIE! I WAS TRYING TO HELP HIM!
SILLY BOY!
THAT FRECKLE-FACED FRIEND OF YOURS IS BEYOND HELP!
I JUST TOLD HIM HE ACTED LIKE A FOOL WITH VERONICA!
YUK
HA
WHAT MAKES YOU THINK HE'S ACTING?
HA
YUK
SERIOUSLY THOUGH, JUG! YOU CAN'T DO THAT WITH A FRIEND... IF YOU WANT TO STAY FRIENDLY!
PEOPLE WANT YOU TO BE FRANK WITH THEM, BUT THEY DON'T WANT THE TRUTH!
HUH?

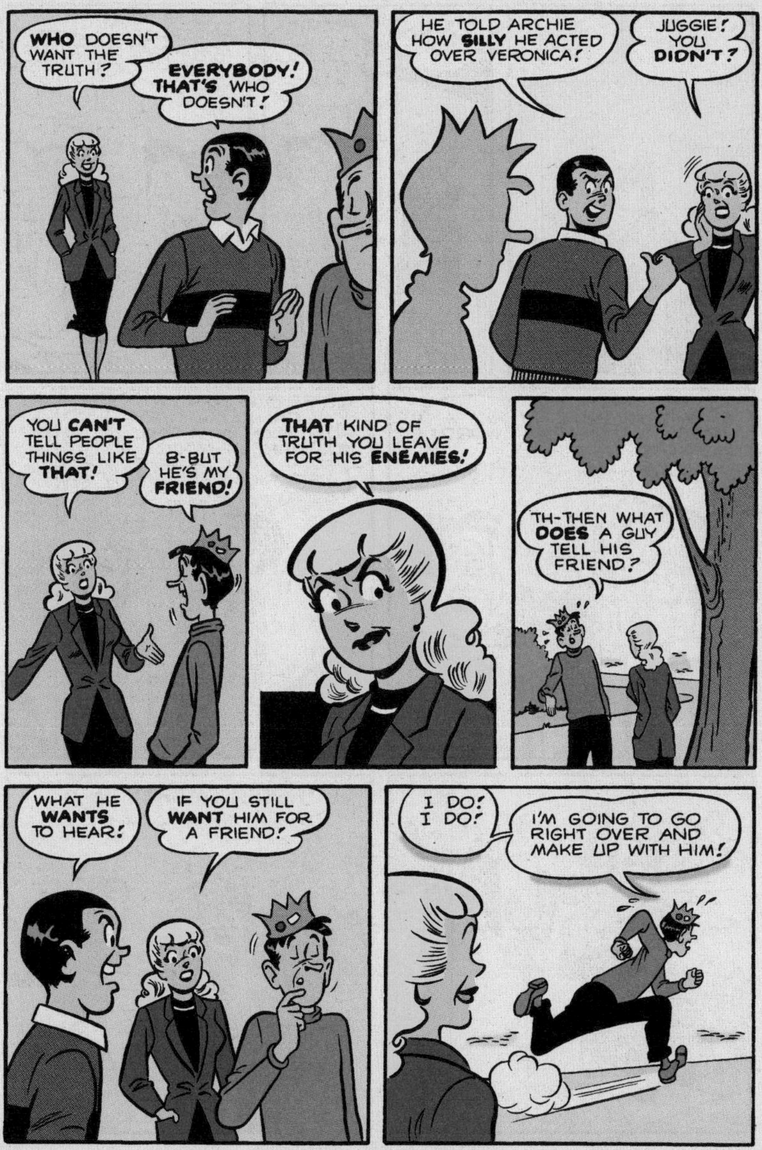
WHO DOESN'T WANT THE TRUTH?
EVERYBODY! THAT'S WHO DOESN'T!
HE TOLD ARCHIE HOW SILLY HE ACTED OVER VERONICA!
JUGGIE! YOU DIDN'T?
YOU CAN'T TELL PEOPLE THINGS LIKE THAT!
B-BUT HE'S MY FRIEND!
THAT KIND OF TRUTH YOU LEAVE FOR HIS ENEMIES!
TH-THEN WHAT DOES A GUY TELL HIS FRIEND?
WHAT HE WANTS TO HEAR!
IF YOU STILL WANT HIM FOR A FRIEND!
I DO! I DO!
I'M GOING TO GO RIGHT OVER AND MAKE UP WITH HIM!

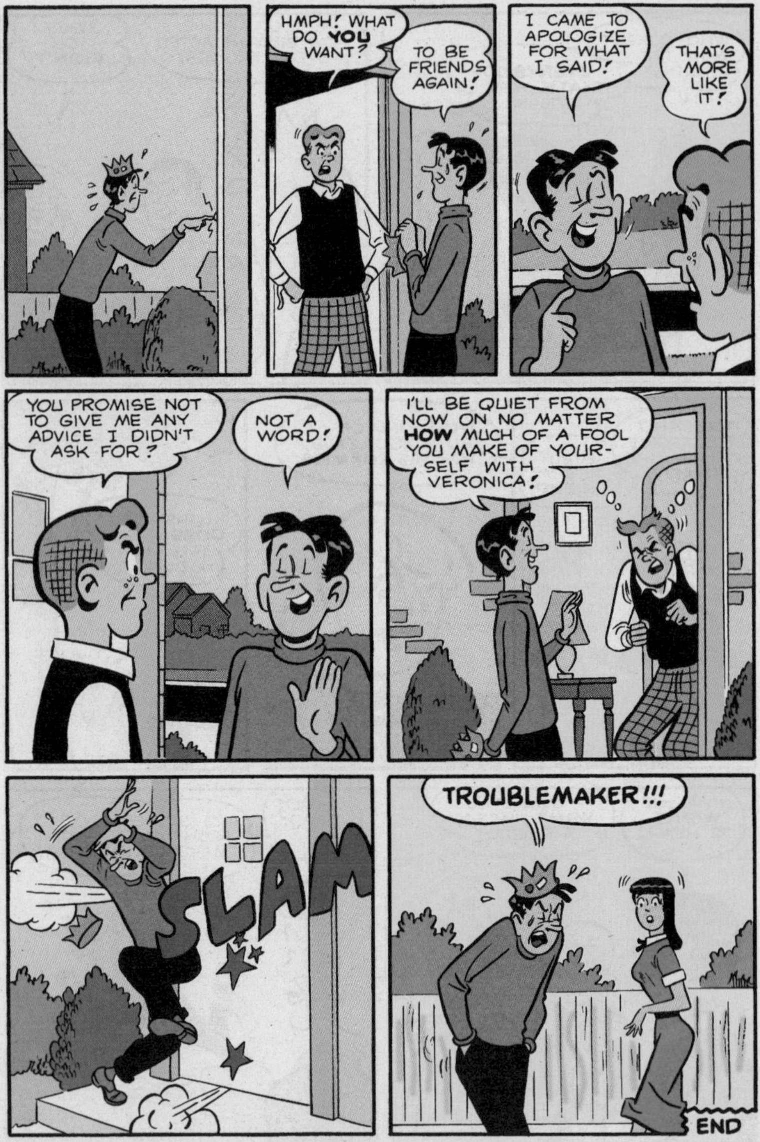
HMPH! WHAT DO YOU WANT?
TO BE FRIENDS AGAIN!
I CAME TO APOLOGIZE FOR WHAT I SAID!
THAT'S MORE LIKE IT!
YOU PROMISE NOT TO GIVE ME ANY ADVICE I DIDN'T ASK FOR?
NOT A WORD!
I'LL BE QUIET FROM NOW ON NO MATTER HOW MUCH OF A FOOL YOU MAKE OF YOURSELF WITH VERONICA!
SLAM
TROUBLEMAKER!!!
END

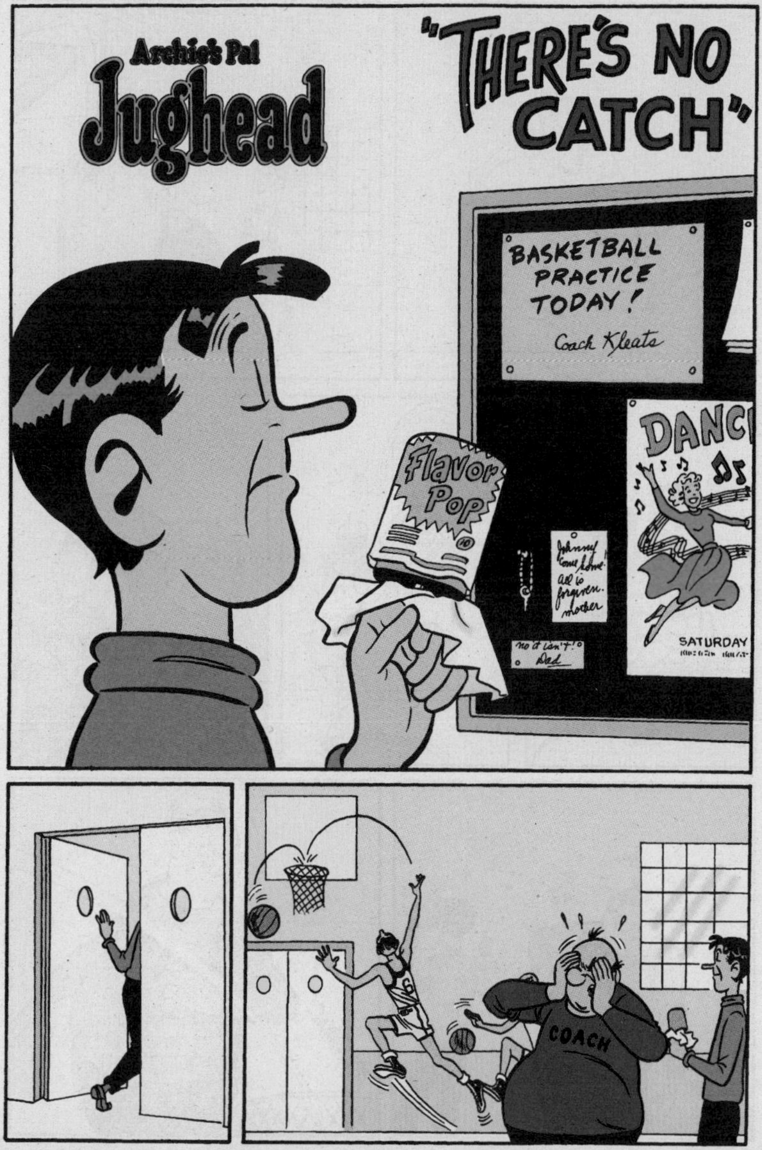
Archie's Pal
Jughead
"THERE'S NO CATCH"
BASKETBALL PRACTICE TODAY!
Coach Kleats
Flavor Pop
Johnny Come home! All is forgiven. mother
no it isn't! Dad
DANC
SATURDAY
COACH

Script: Frank Doyle / Art: Samm Schwartz

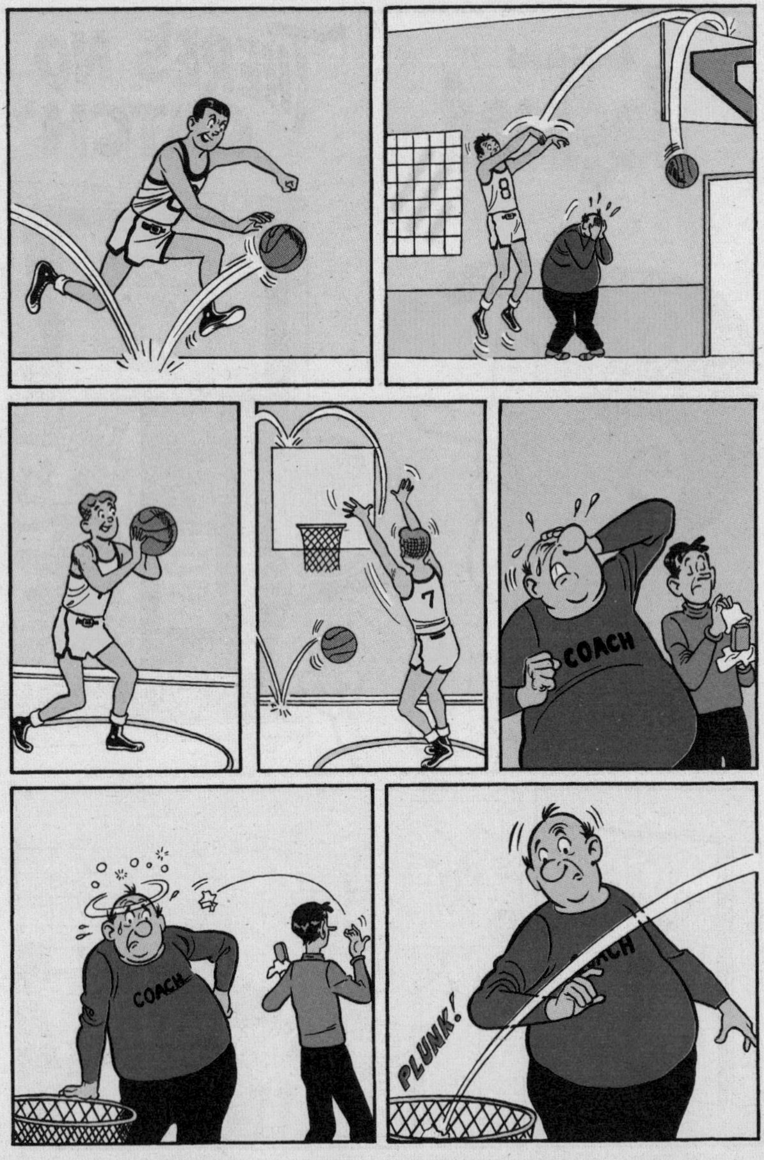

COACH
COACH
PLUNK!

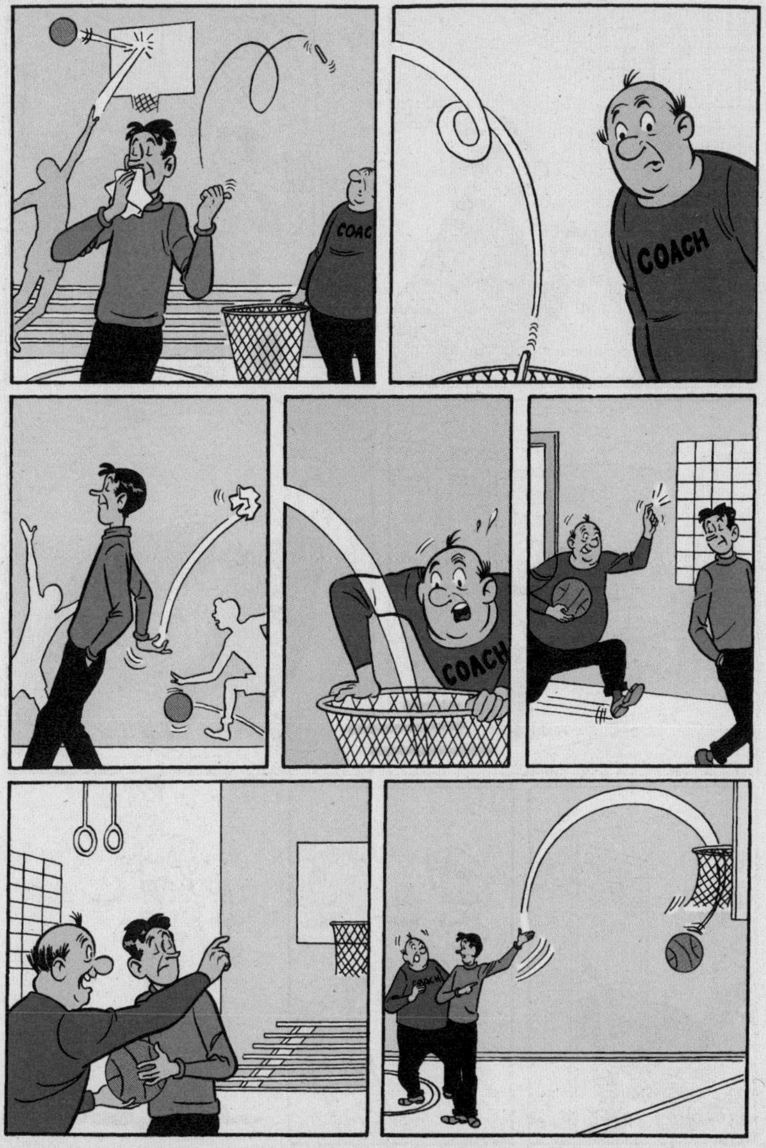
COACH
COACH
COACH
COACH

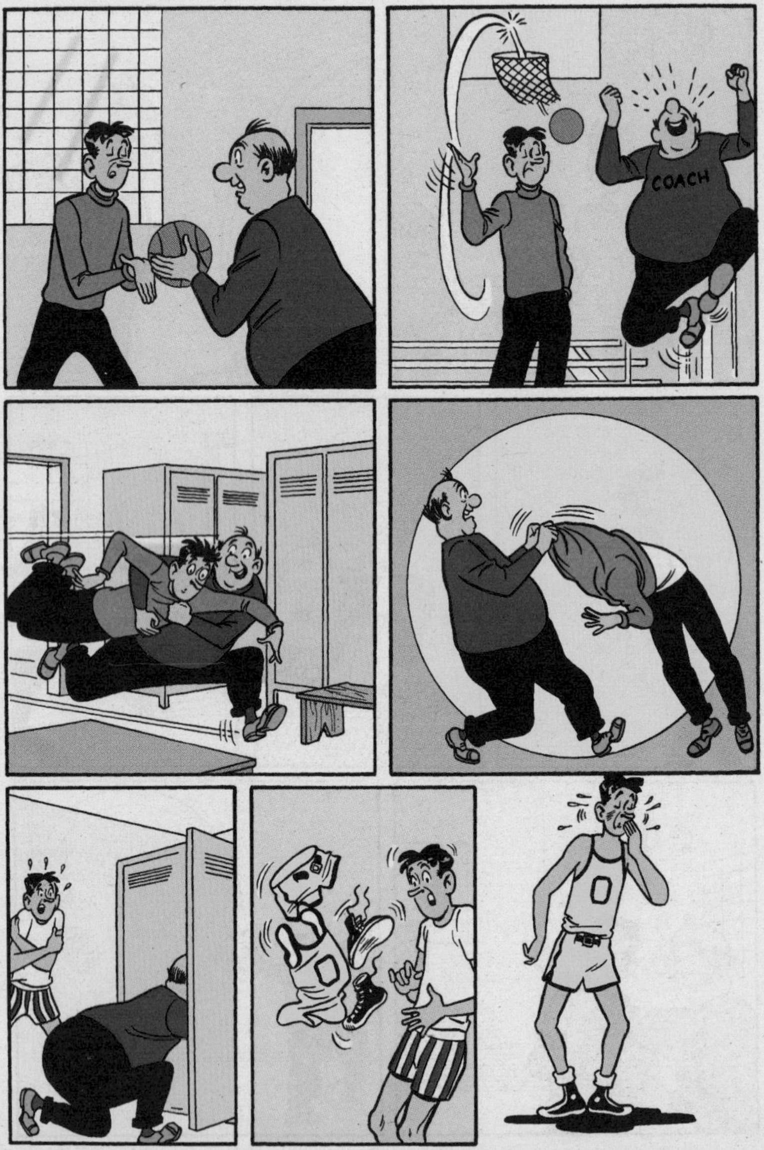
COACH

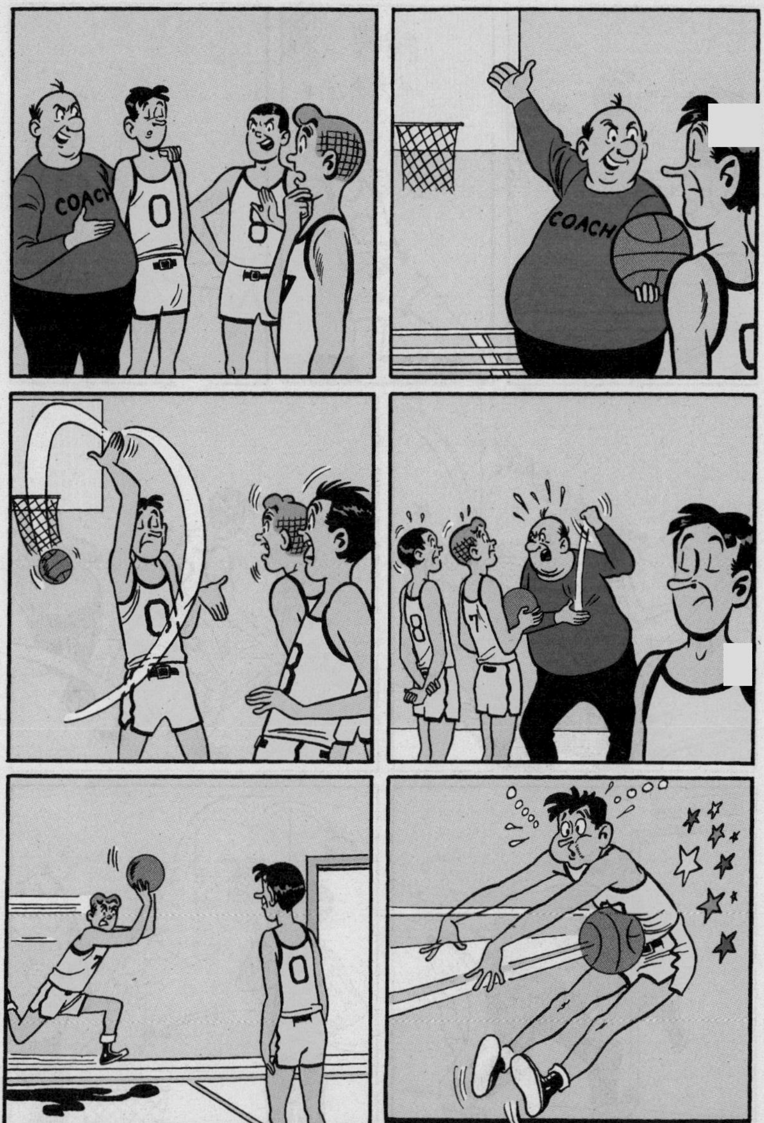
COACH
COACH

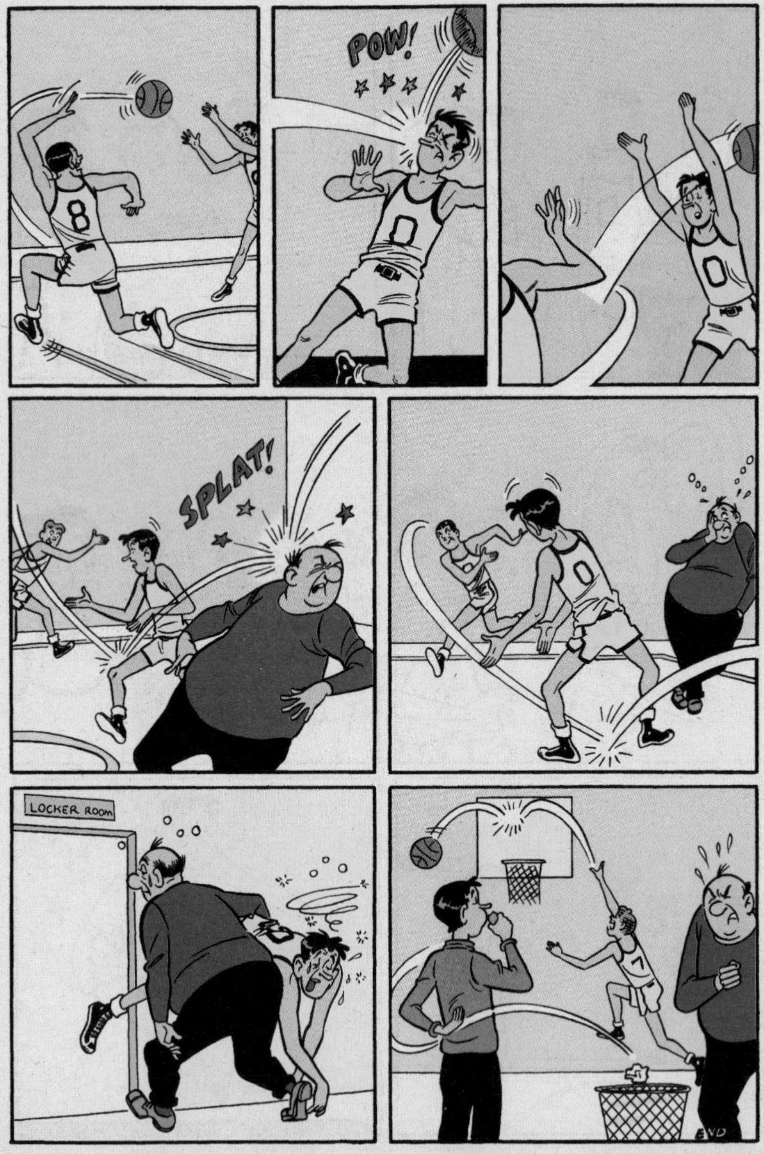
POW!
SPLAT!
LOCKER ROOM
END

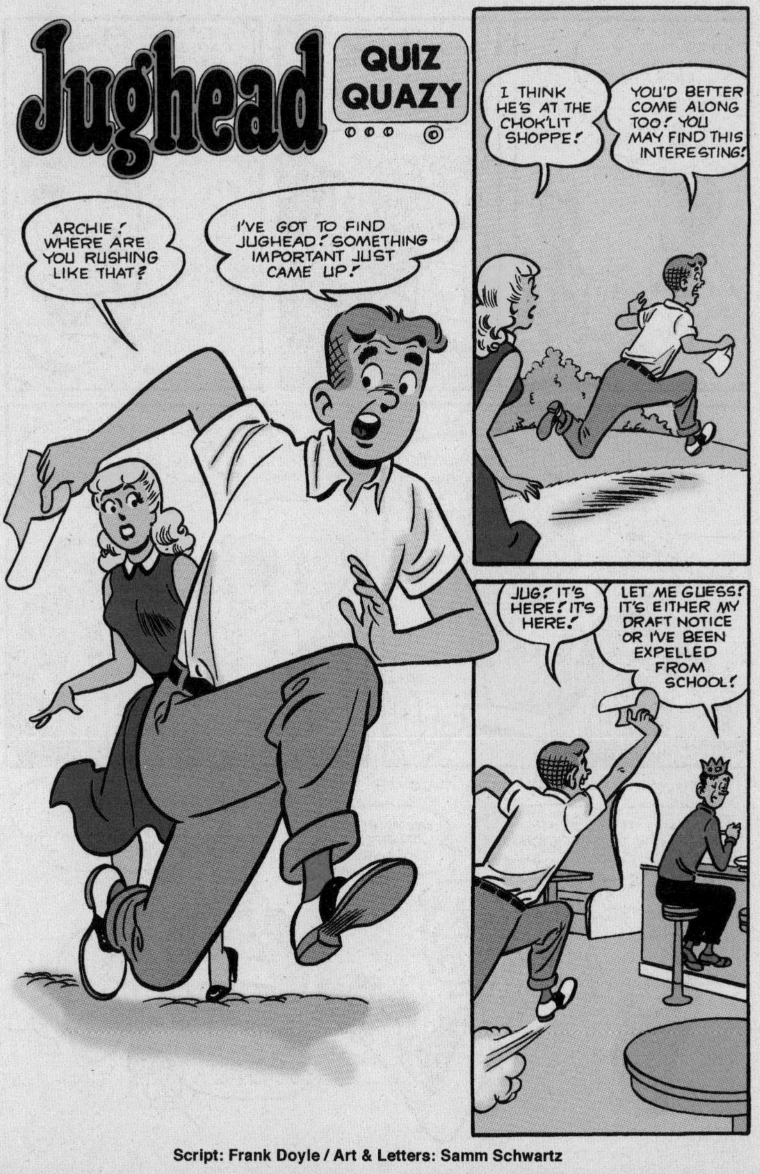
Jughead
QUIZ QUAZY
ARCHIE! WHERE ARE YOU RUSHING LIKE THAT?
I'VE GOT TO FIND JUGHEAD! SOMETHING IMPORTANT JUST CAME UP!
I THINK HE'S AT THE CHOK'LIT SHOPPE!
YOU'D BETTER COME ALONG TOO! YOU MAY FIND THIS INTERESTING!
JUG! IT'S HERE! IT'S HERE!
LET ME GUESS! IT'S EITHER MY DRAFT NOTICE OR I'VE BEEN EXPELLED FROM SCHOOL!

Script: Frank Doyle / Art & Letters: Samm Schwartz

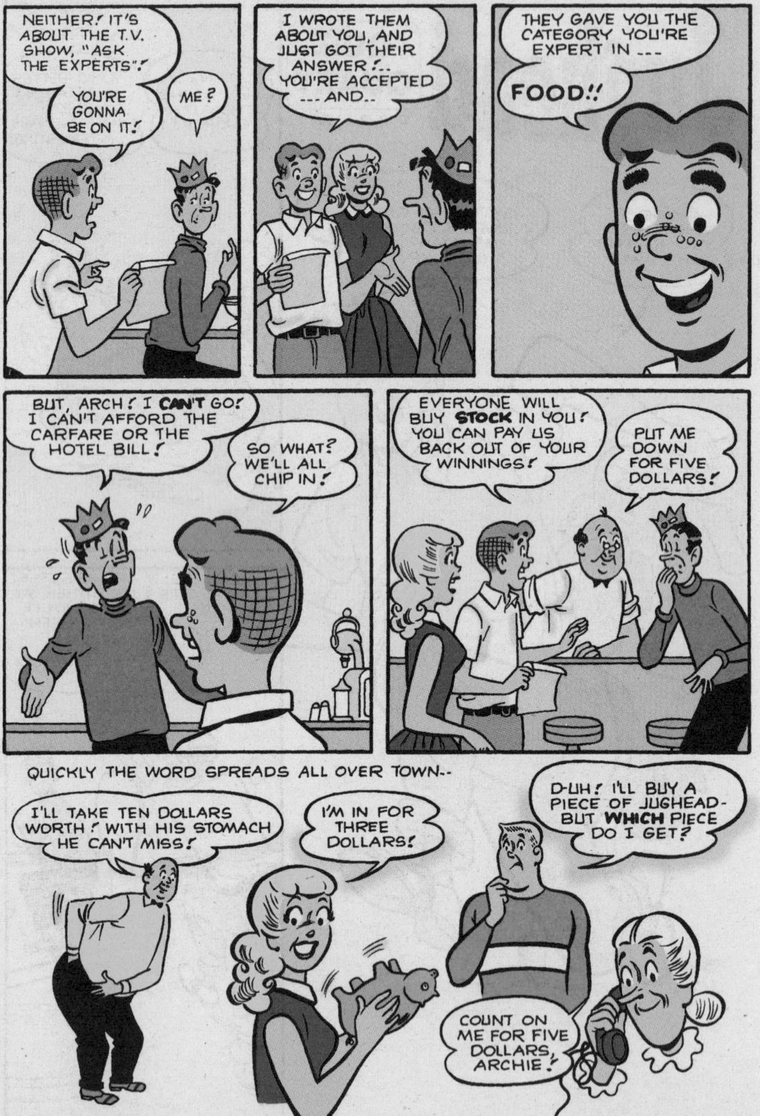
NEITHER! IT'S ABOUT THE T.V. SHOW, "ASK THE EXPERTS"!
YOU'RE GONNA BE ON IT!
ME?
I WROTE THEM ABOUT YOU, AND JUST GOT THEIR ANSWER!.. YOU'RE ACCEPTED --- AND..
THEY GAVE YOU THE CATEGORY YOU'RE EXPERT IN ---
FOOD!!
BUT, ARCH! I CAN'T GO! I CAN'T AFFORD THE CARFARE OR THE HOTEL BILL!
SO WHAT? WE'LL ALL CHIP IN!
EVERYONE WILL BUY STOCK IN YOU! YOU CAN PAY US BACK OUT OF YOUR WINNINGS!
PUT ME DOWN FOR FIVE DOLLARS!
QUICKLY THE WORD SPREADS ALL OVER TOWN--
I'LL TAKE TEN DOLLARS WORTH! WITH HIS STOMACH HE CAN'T MISS!
I'M IN FOR THREE DOLLARS!
D-UH! I'LL BUY A PIECE OF JUGHEAD- BUT WHICH PIECE DO I GET?
COUNT ON ME FOR FIVE DOLLARS, ARCHIE!

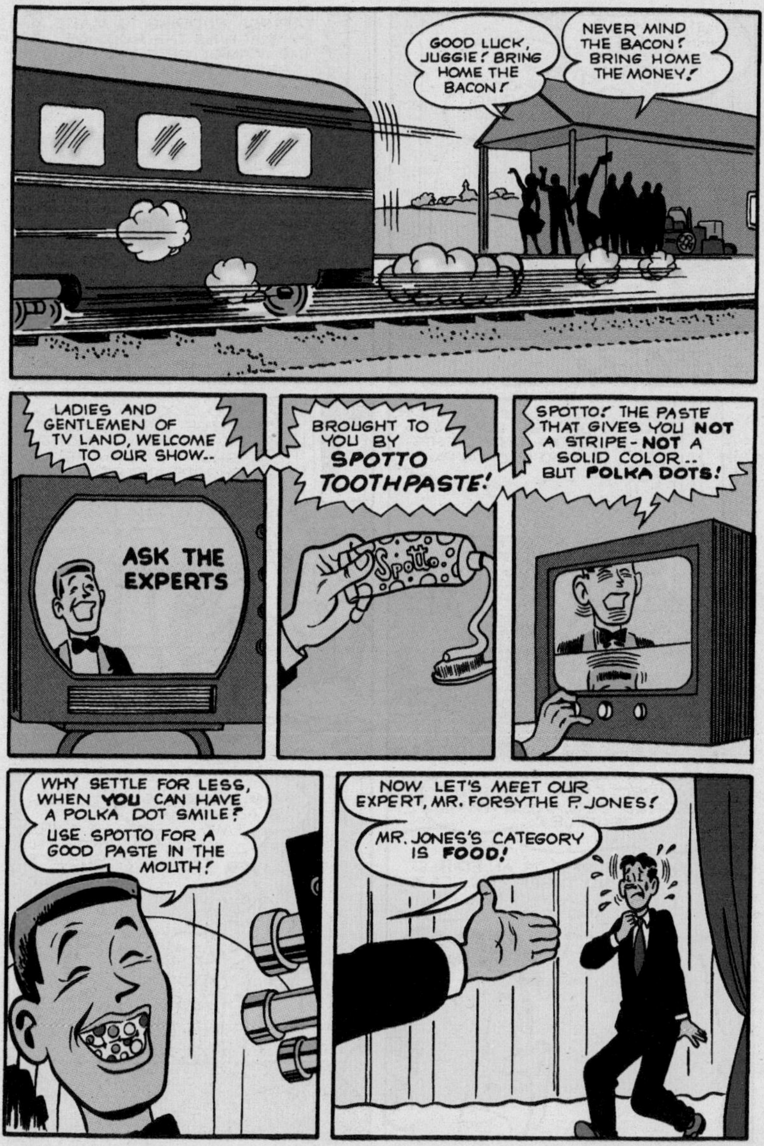

GOOD LUCK, JUGGIE! BRING HOME THE BACON!
NEVER MIND THE BACON! BRING HOME THE MONEY!
LADIES AND GENTLEMEN OF TV LAND, WELCOME TO OUR SHOW..
ASK THE EXPERTS
BROUGHT TO YOU BY **SPOTTO TOOTHPASTE!**
Spotto
SPOTTO! THE PASTE THAT GIVES YOU **NOT** A STRIPE - **NOT** A SOLID COLOR .. BUT **POLKA DOTS!**
WHY SETTLE FOR LESS, WHEN **YOU** CAN HAVE A POLKA DOT SMILE?
USE SPOTTO FOR A GOOD PASTE IN THE MOUTH!
NOW LET'S MEET OUR EXPERT, MR. FORSYTHE P. JONES!
MR. JONES'S CATEGORY IS **FOOD!**

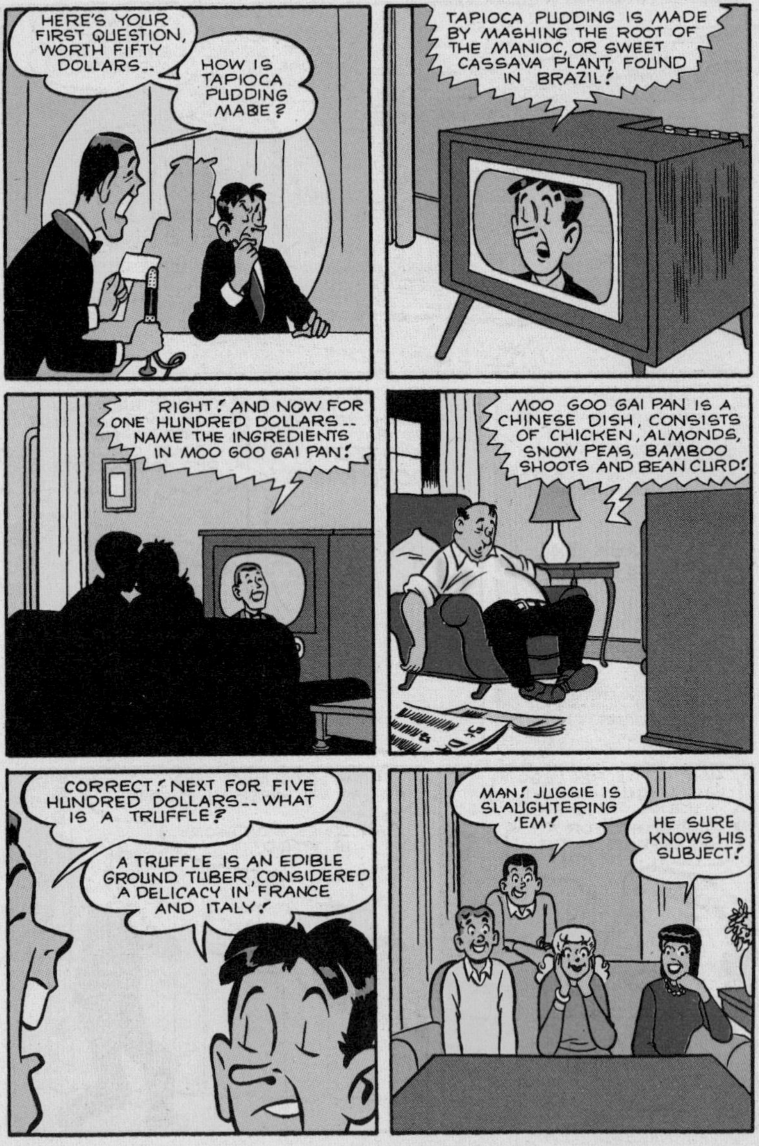
HERE'S YOUR FIRST QUESTION, WORTH FIFTY DOLLARS..
HOW IS TAPIOCA PUDDING MABE?
TAPIOCA PUDDING IS MADE BY MASHING THE ROOT OF THE MANIOC, OR SWEET CASSAVA PLANT, FOUND IN BRAZIL!
RIGHT! AND NOW FOR ONE HUNDRED DOLLARS.. NAME THE INGREDIENTS IN MOO GOO GAI PAN!
MOO GOO GAI PAN IS A CHINESE DISH, CONSISTS OF CHICKEN, ALMONDS, SNOW PEAS, BAMBOO SHOOTS AND BEAN CURD!
CORRECT! NEXT FOR FIVE HUNDRED DOLLARS.. WHAT IS A TRUFFLE?
A TRUFFLE IS AN EDIBLE GROUND TUBER, CONSIDERED A DELICACY IN FRANCE AND ITALY!
MAN! JUGGIE IS SLAUGHTERING 'EM!
HE SURE KNOWS HIS SUBJECT!

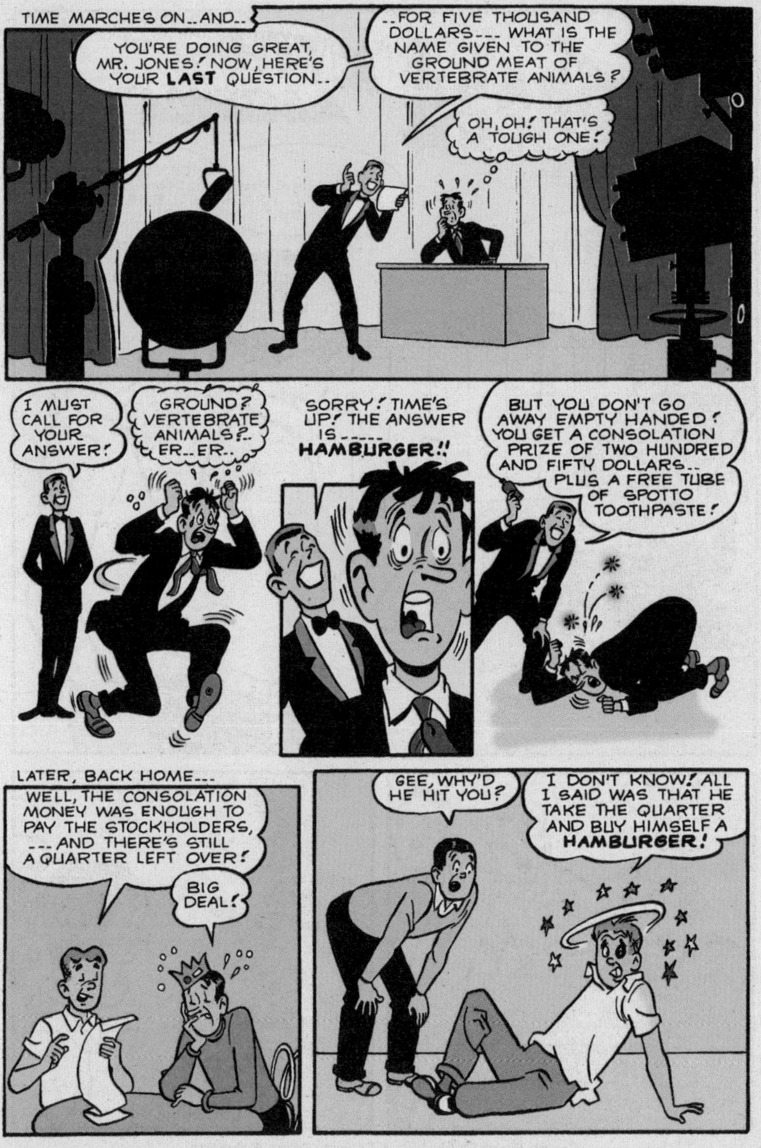

TIME MARCHES ON..AND..
YOU'RE DOING GREAT, MR. JONES! NOW, HERE'S YOUR LAST QUESTION..
..FOR FIVE THOUSAND DOLLARS--- WHAT IS THE NAME GIVEN TO THE GROUND MEAT OF VERTEBRATE ANIMALS?
OH, OH! THAT'S A TOUGH ONE!
I MUST CALL FOR YOUR ANSWER!
GROUND? VERTEBRATE ANIMALS?.. ER..ER..
SORRY! TIME'S UP! THE ANSWER IS ----- HAMBURGER!!
BUT YOU DON'T GO AWAY EMPTY HANDED! YOU GET A CONSOLATION PRIZE OF TWO HUNDRED AND FIFTY DOLLARS.. PLUS A FREE TUBE OF SPOTTO TOOTHPASTE!
LATER, BACK HOME---
WELL, THE CONSOLATION MONEY WAS ENOUGH TO PAY THE STOCKHOLDERS, ---AND THERE'S STILL A QUARTER LEFT OVER!
BIG DEAL!
GEE, WHY'D HE HIT YOU?
I DON'T KNOW! ALL I SAID WAS THAT HE TAKE THE QUARTER AND BUY HIMSELF A HAMBURGER!

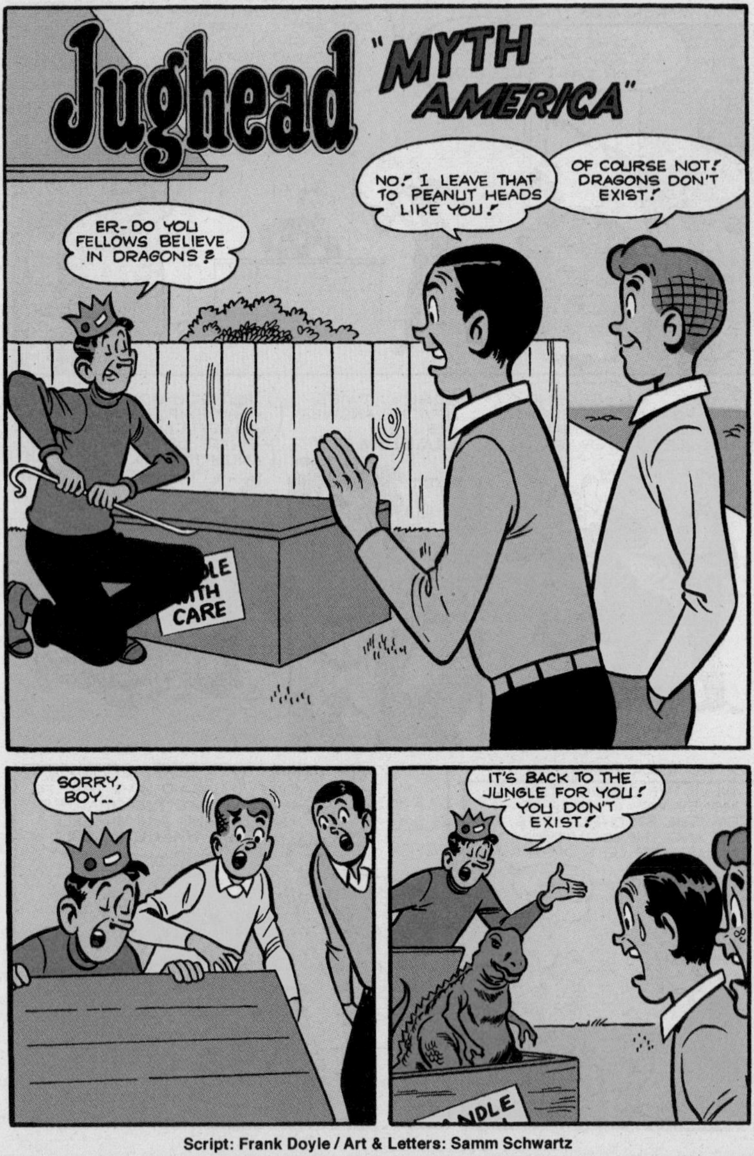
Jughead
"MYTH AMERICA"
ER-DO YOU FELLOWS BELIEVE IN DRAGONS?
NO! I LEAVE THAT TO PEANUT HEADS LIKE YOU!
OF COURSE NOT! DRAGONS DON'T EXIST!
SORRY, BOY...
IT'S BACK TO THE JUNGLE FOR YOU! YOU DON'T EXIST!

Script: Frank Doyle / Art & Letters: Samm Schwartz

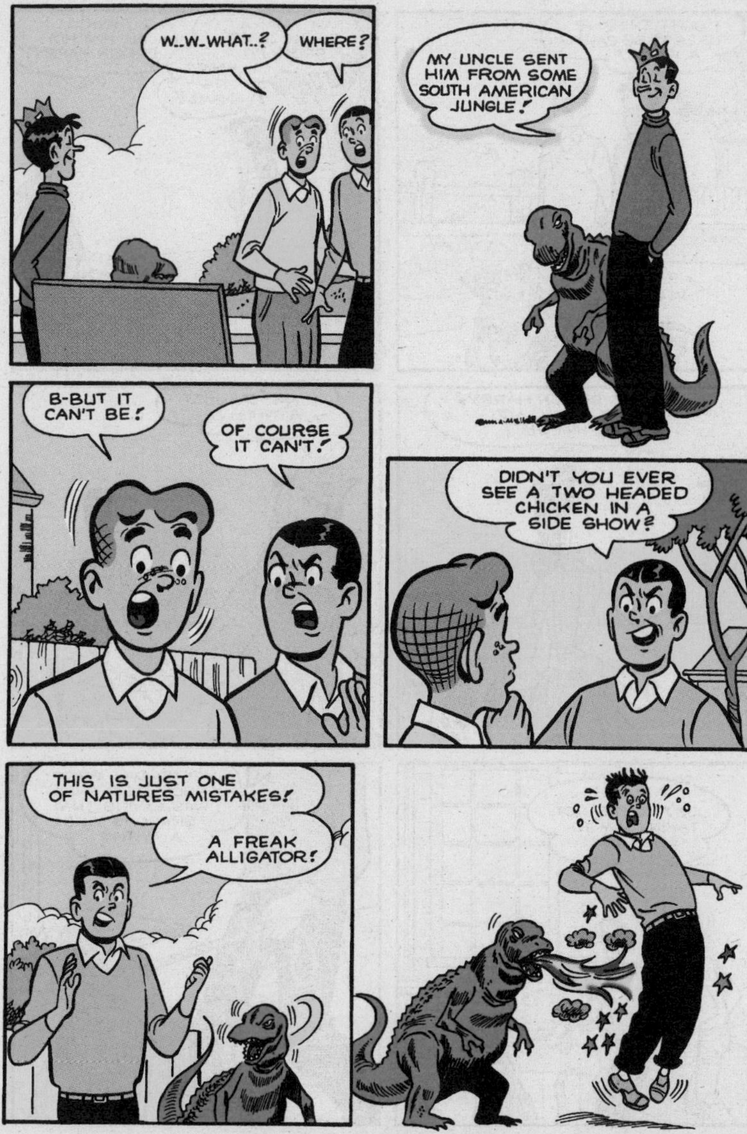
W..W..WHAT..?
WHERE?
MY UNCLE SENT HIM FROM SOME SOUTH AMERICAN JUNGLE!
B-BUT IT CAN'T BE!
OF COURSE IT CAN'T!
DIDN'T YOU EVER SEE A TWO HEADED CHICKEN IN A SIDE SHOW?
THIS IS JUST ONE OF NATURES MISTAKES!
A FREAK ALLIGATOR!

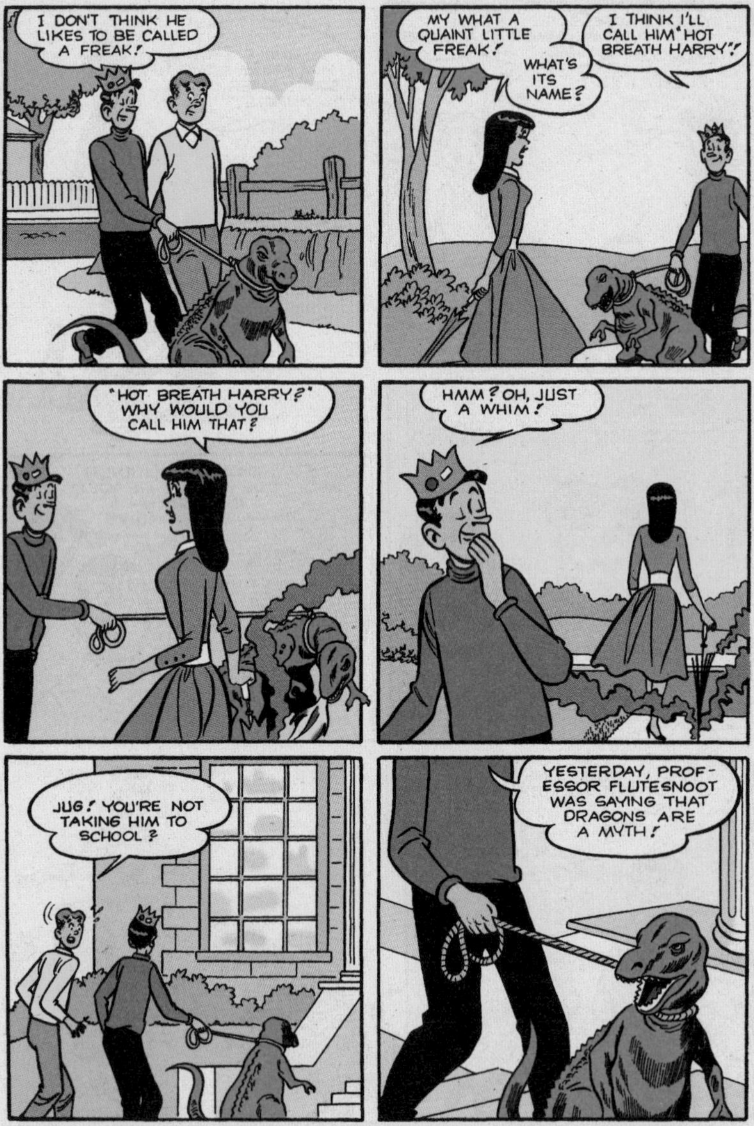
I DON'T THINK HE LIKES TO BE CALLED A FREAK!
MY WHAT A QUAINT LITTLE FREAK!
WHAT'S ITS NAME?
I THINK I'LL CALL HIM "HOT BREATH HARRY"!
"HOT BREATH HARRY?" WHY WOULD YOU CALL HIM THAT?
HMM? OH, JUST A WHIM!
JUG! YOU'RE NOT TAKING HIM TO SCHOOL?
YESTERDAY, PROF-ESSOR FLUTESNOOT WAS SAYING THAT DRAGONS ARE A MYTH!

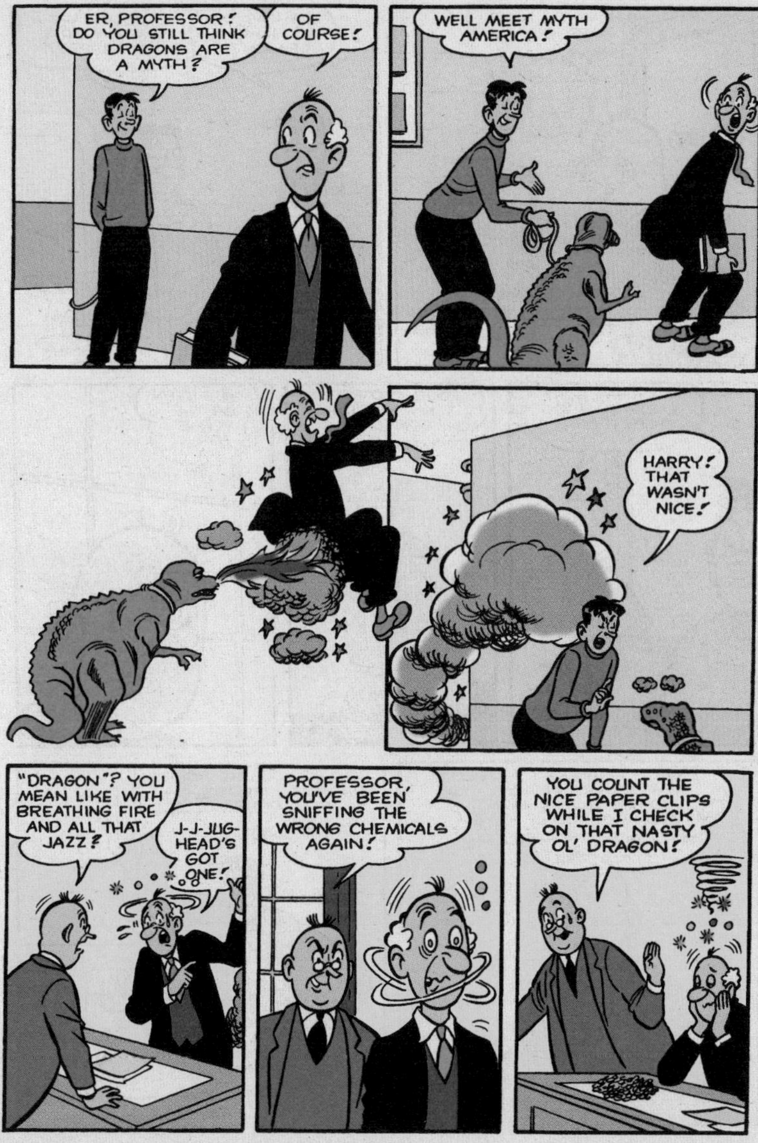

ER, PROFESSOR! DO YOU STILL THINK DRAGONS ARE A MYTH?
OF COURSE!
WELL MEET MYTH AMERICA!
HARRY! THAT WASN'T NICE!
"DRAGON"? YOU MEAN LIKE WITH BREATHING FIRE AND ALL THAT JAZZ?
J-J-JUG-HEAD'S GOT ONE!
PROFESSOR, YOU'VE BEEN SNIFFING THE WRONG CHEMICALS AGAIN!
YOU COUNT THE NICE PAPER CLIPS WHILE I CHECK ON THAT NASTY OL' DRAGON!

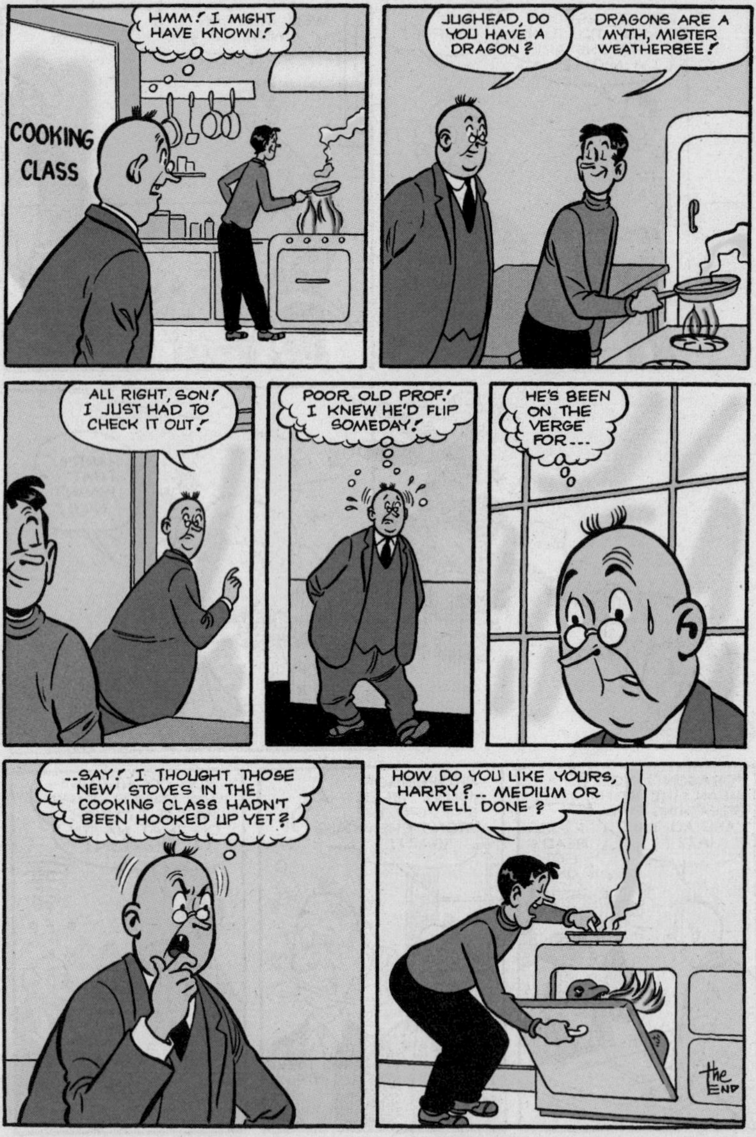
HMM! I MIGHT HAVE KNOWN!
COOKING CLASS
JUGHEAD, DO YOU HAVE A DRAGON?
DRAGONS ARE A MYTH, MISTER WEATHERBEE!
ALL RIGHT, SON! I JUST HAD TO CHECK IT OUT!
POOR OLD PROF! I KNEW HE'D FLIP SOMEDAY!
HE'S BEEN ON THE VERGE FOR---
--SAY! I THOUGHT THOSE NEW STOVES IN THE COOKING CLASS HADN'T BEEN HOOKED UP YET?
HOW DO YOU LIKE YOURS, HARRY?.. MEDIUM OR WELL DONE?
THE END

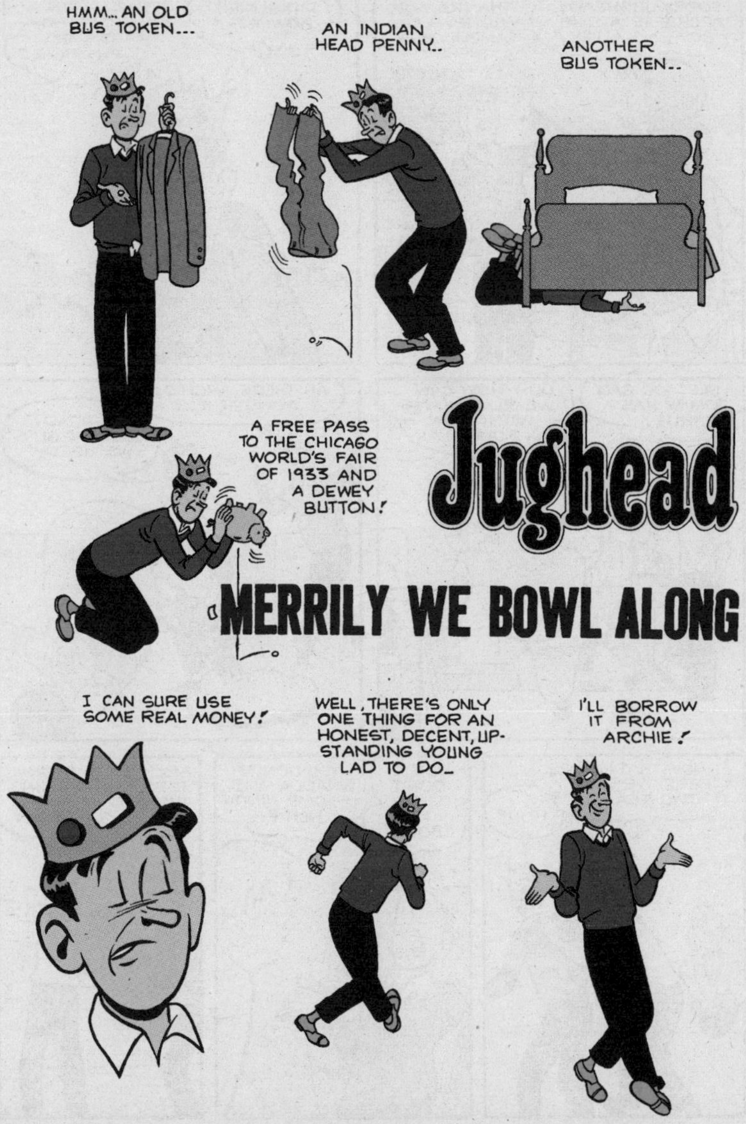
HMM... AN OLD BUS TOKEN...
AN INDIAN HEAD PENNY..
ANOTHER BUS TOKEN..
A FREE PASS TO THE CHICAGO WORLD'S FAIR OF 1933 AND A DEWEY BUTTON!
Jughead
MERRILY WE BOWL ALONG
I CAN SURE USE SOME REAL MONEY!
WELL, THERE'S ONLY ONE THING FOR AN HONEST, DECENT, UP-STANDING YOUNG LAD TO DO_
I'LL BORROW IT FROM ARCHIE!

Script: Frank Doyle / Art & Letters: Samm Schwartz

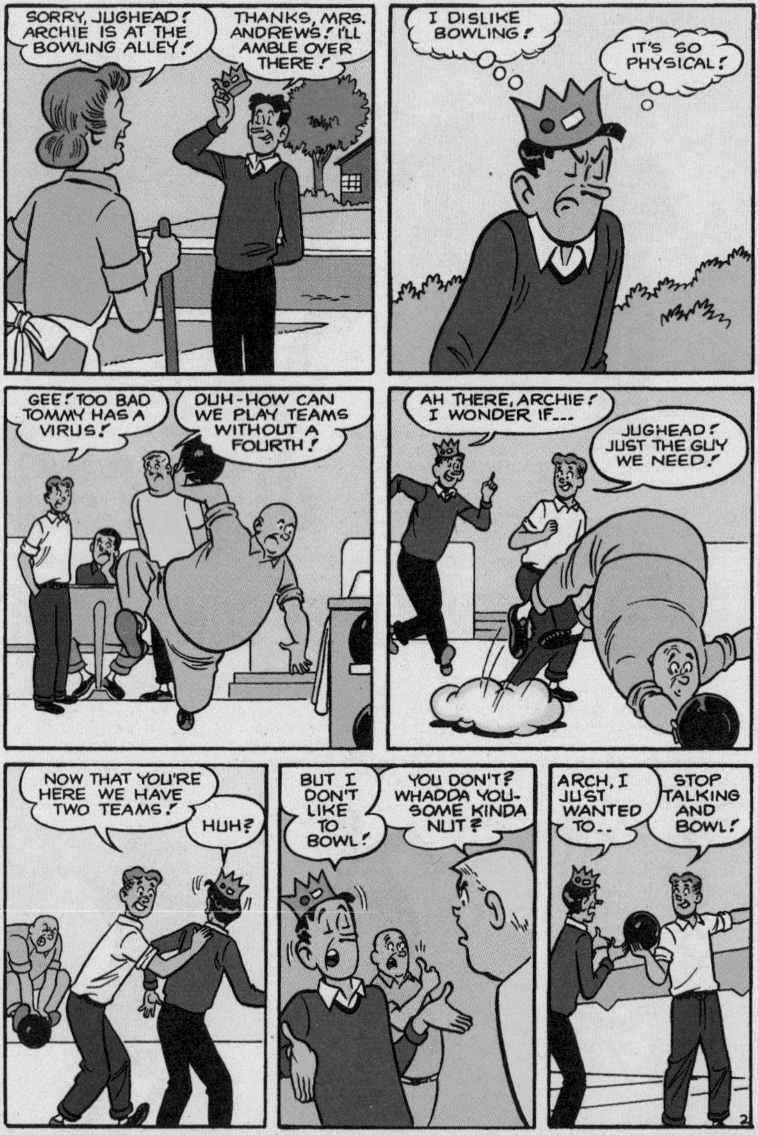
SORRY, JUGHEAD! ARCHIE IS AT THE BOWLING ALLEY!
THANKS, MRS. ANDREWS! I'LL AMBLE OVER THERE!
I DISLIKE BOWLING!
IT'S SO PHYSICAL!
GEE! TOO BAD TOMMY HAS A VIRUS!
DUH-HOW CAN WE PLAY TEAMS WITHOUT A FOURTH!
AH THERE, ARCHIE! I WONDER IF---
JUGHEAD! JUST THE GUY WE NEED!
NOW THAT YOU'RE HERE WE HAVE TWO TEAMS!
HUH?
BUT I DON'T LIKE TO BOWL!
YOU DON'T? WHADDA YOU-SOME KINDA NUT?
ARCH, I JUST WANTED TO..
STOP TALKING AND BOWL!
2

ARCH, WILL YOU LISTEN TO ME FOR TWO SECONDS, **PLEASE?**

PLONK!

WOW! JUG BOWLED A STRIKE!

WHAT AN EYE!

DUH...DO THAT AGAIN!

DON'T BE SILLY! IT WAS AN ACCIDENT!

AS I WAS SAYING, ARCHIE, I'M A TRIFLE BROKE..

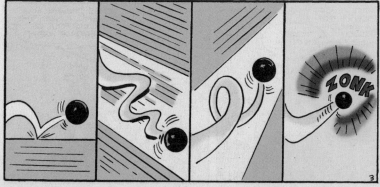

ZONK

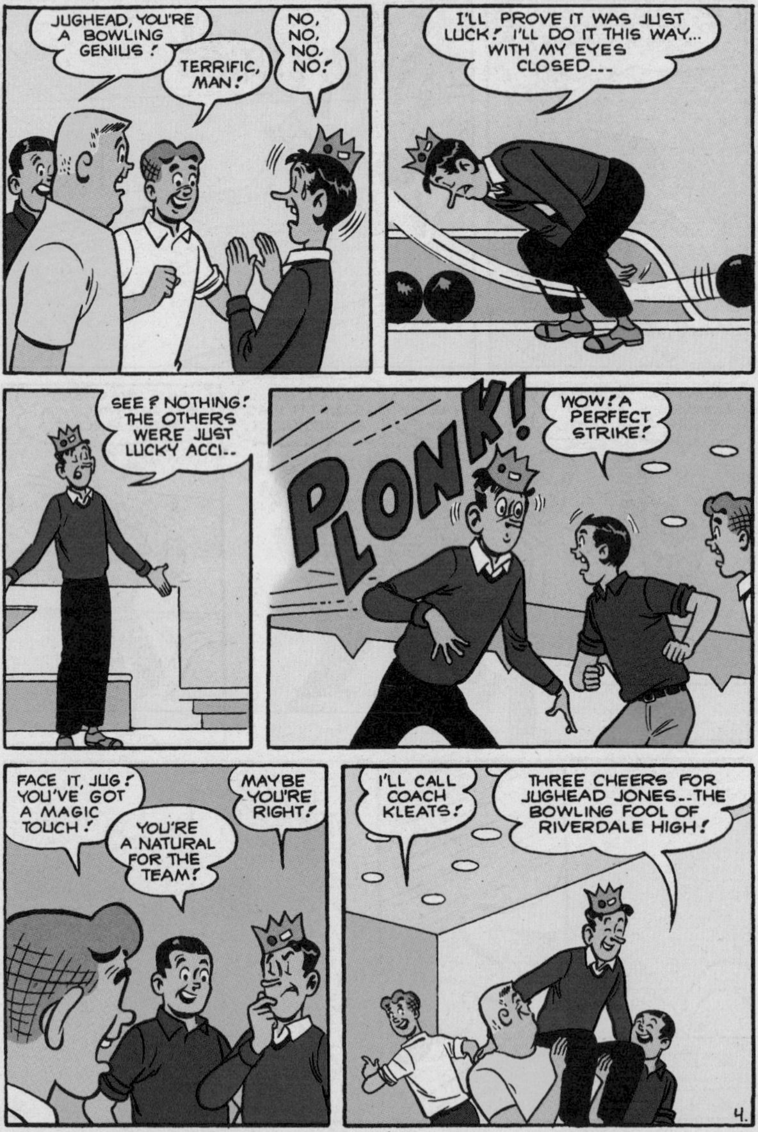
JUGHEAD, YOU'RE A BOWLING GENIUS!
TERRIFIC, MAN!
NO, NO, NO, NO!
I'LL PROVE IT WAS JUST LUCK! I'LL DO IT THIS WAY... WITH MY EYES CLOSED...
SEE? NOTHING! THE OTHERS WERE JUST LUCKY ACCI..
PLONK!
WOW! A PERFECT STRIKE!
FACE IT, JUG! YOU'VE GOT A MAGIC TOUCH!
YOU'RE A NATURAL FOR THE TEAM!
MAYBE YOU'RE RIGHT!
I'LL CALL COACH KLEATS!
THREE CHEERS FOR JUGHEAD JONES..THE BOWLING FOOL OF RIVERDALE HIGH!
4.

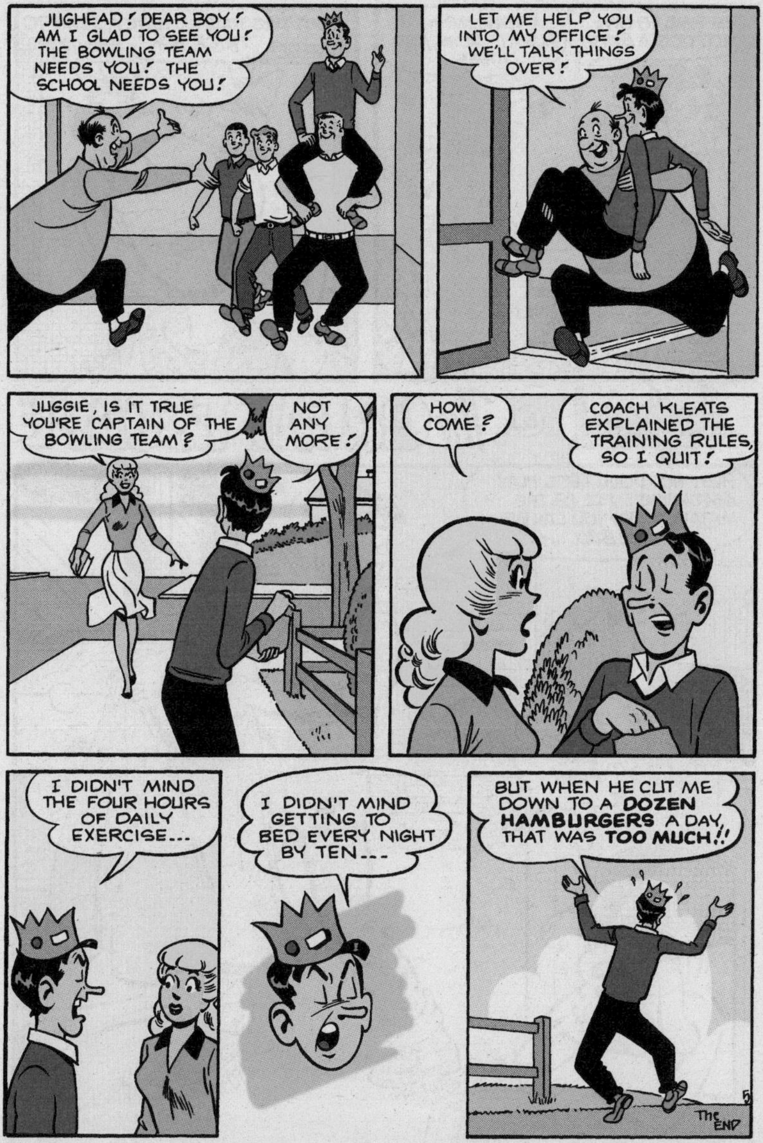
JUGHEAD! DEAR BOY! AM I GLAD TO SEE YOU! THE BOWLING TEAM NEEDS YOU! THE SCHOOL NEEDS YOU!
LET ME HELP YOU INTO MY OFFICE! WE'LL TALK THINGS OVER!
JUGGIE, IS IT TRUE YOU'RE CAPTAIN OF THE BOWLING TEAM?
NOT ANY MORE!
HOW COME?
COACH KLEATS EXPLAINED THE TRAINING RULES, SO I QUIT!
I DIDN'T MIND THE FOUR HOURS OF DAILY EXERCISE...
I DIDN'T MIND GETTING TO BED EVERY NIGHT BY TEN...
BUT WHEN HE CUT ME DOWN TO A **DOZEN HAMBURGERS** A DAY, THAT WAS **TOO MUCH**!!
5
The END

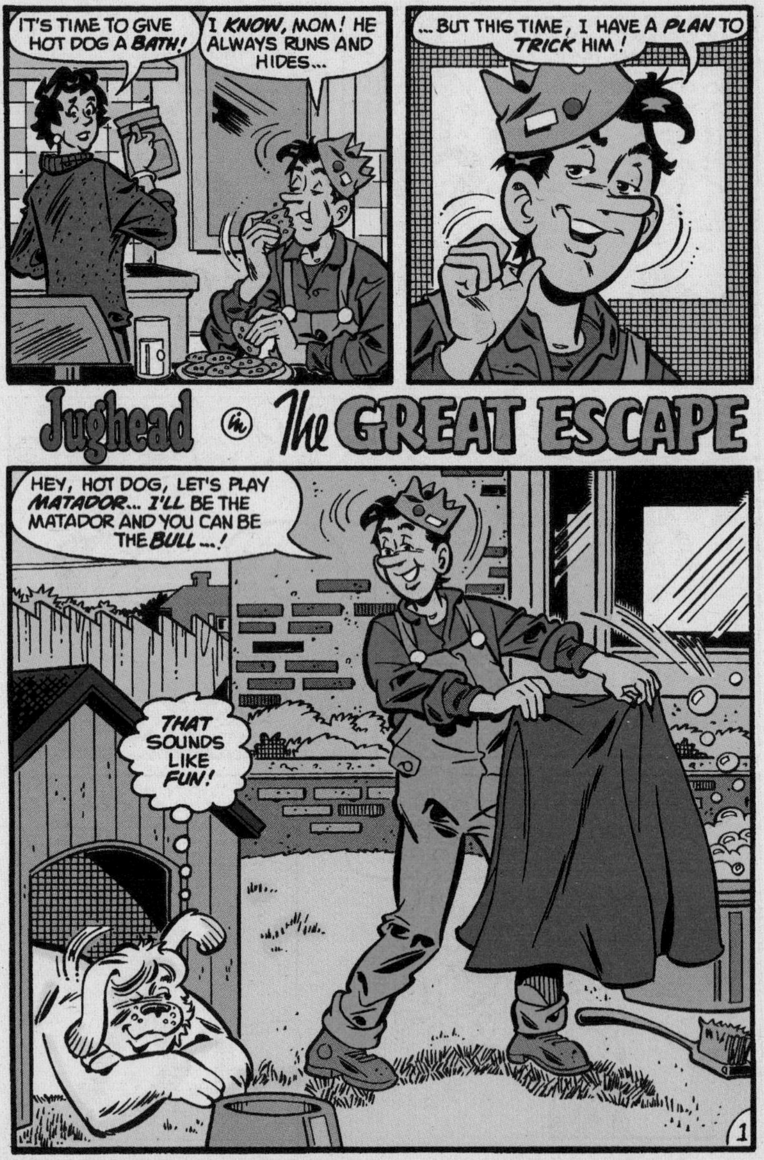
IT'S TIME TO GIVE HOT DOG A BATH!
I KNOW, MOM! HE ALWAYS RUNS AND HIDES...
...BUT THIS TIME, I HAVE A PLAN TO TRICK HIM!
Jughead in The GREAT ESCAPE
HEY, HOT DOG, LET'S PLAY MATADOR... I'LL BE THE MATADOR AND YOU CAN BE THE BULL...!
THAT SOUNDS LIKE FUN!
1

Script: Hal Smith / Pencils: Tim Kennedy / Inks: Ken Selig / Letters: Bill Yoshida

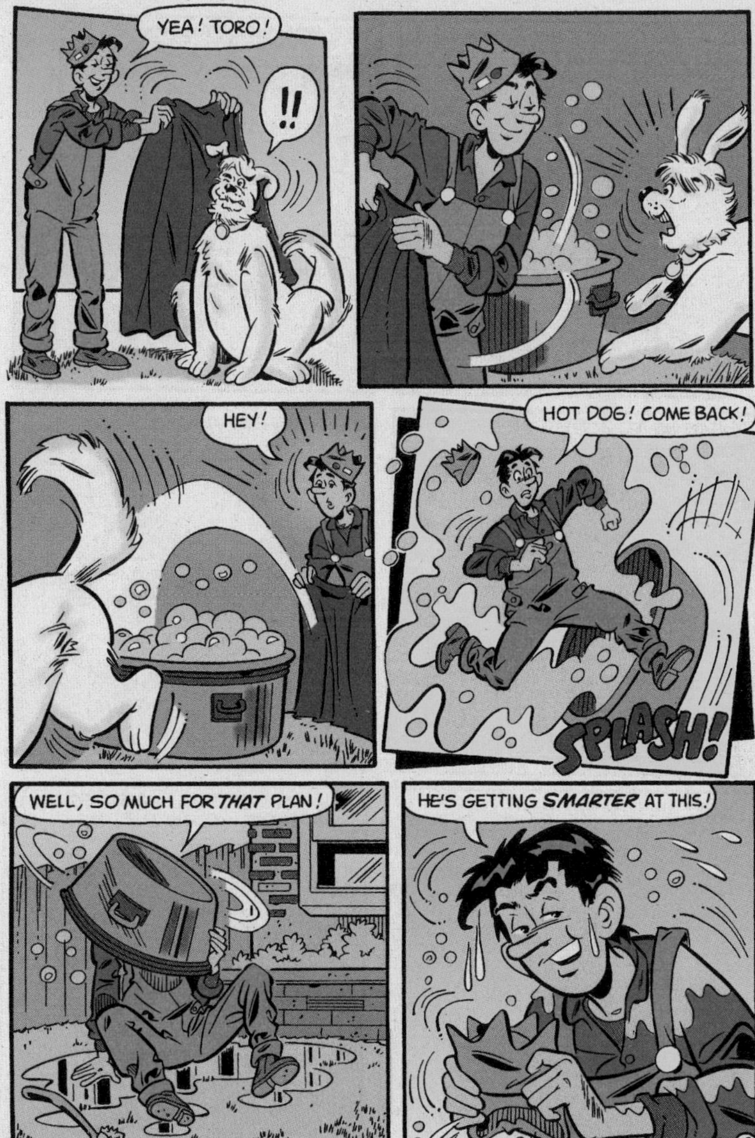
YEA! TORO!
!!
HEY!
HOT DOG! COME BACK!
SPLASH!
WELL, SO MUCH FOR THAT PLAN!
HE'S GETTING SMARTER AT THIS!
2

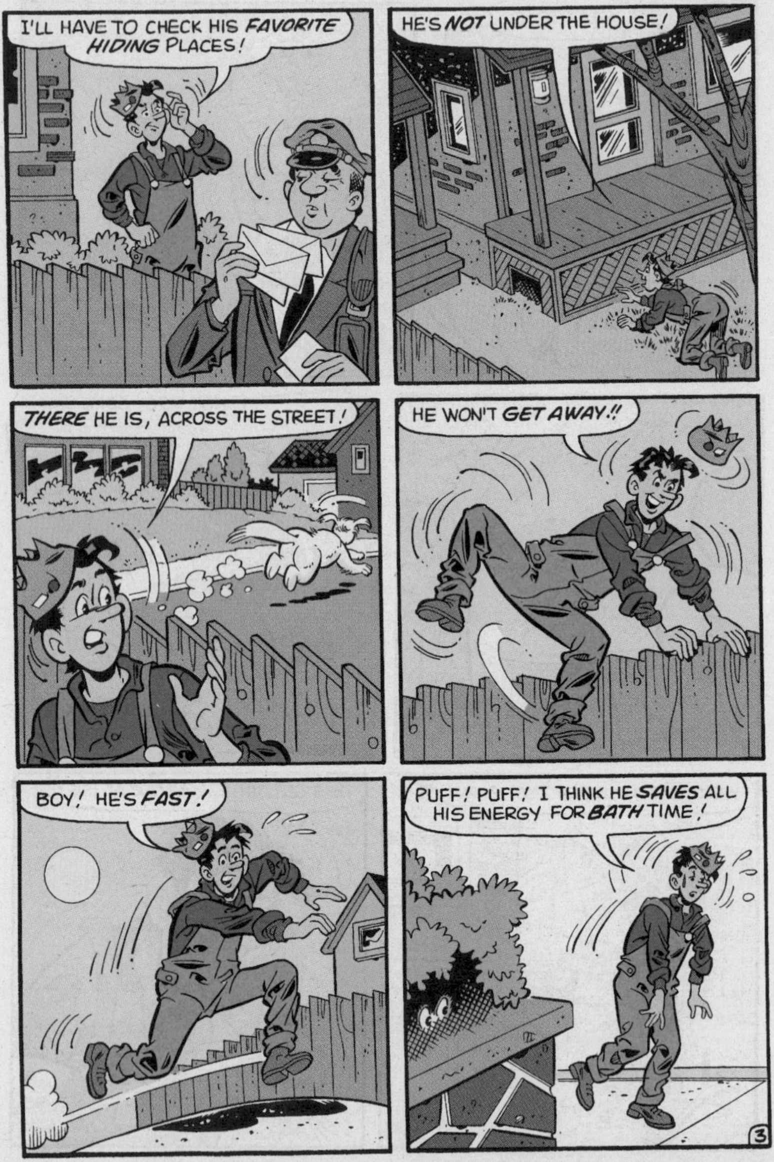
I'LL HAVE TO CHECK HIS FAVORITE HIDING PLACES!
HE'S NOT UNDER THE HOUSE!
THERE HE IS, ACROSS THE STREET!
HE WON'T GET AWAY!!
BOY! HE'S FAST!
PUFF! PUFF! I THINK HE SAVES ALL HIS ENERGY FOR BATH TIME!
3

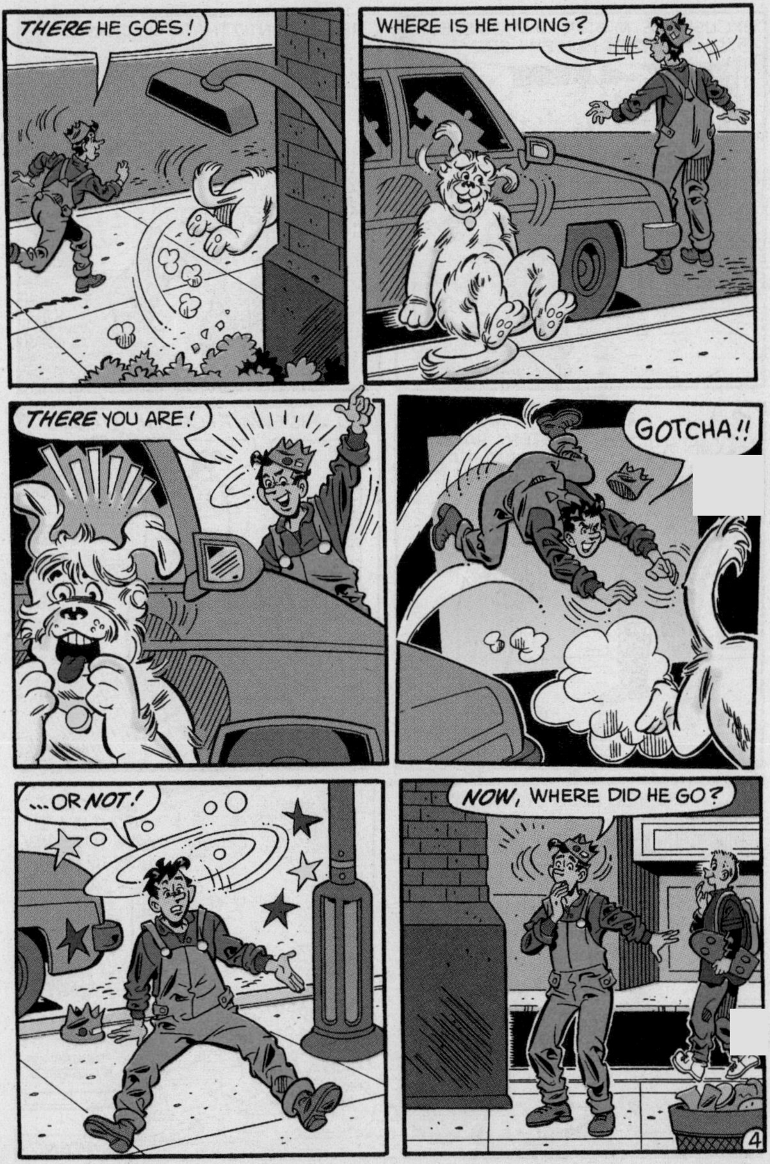
THERE HE GOES!
WHERE IS HE HIDING?
THERE YOU ARE!
GOTCHA!!
...OR NOT!
NOW, WHERE DID HE GO?
4

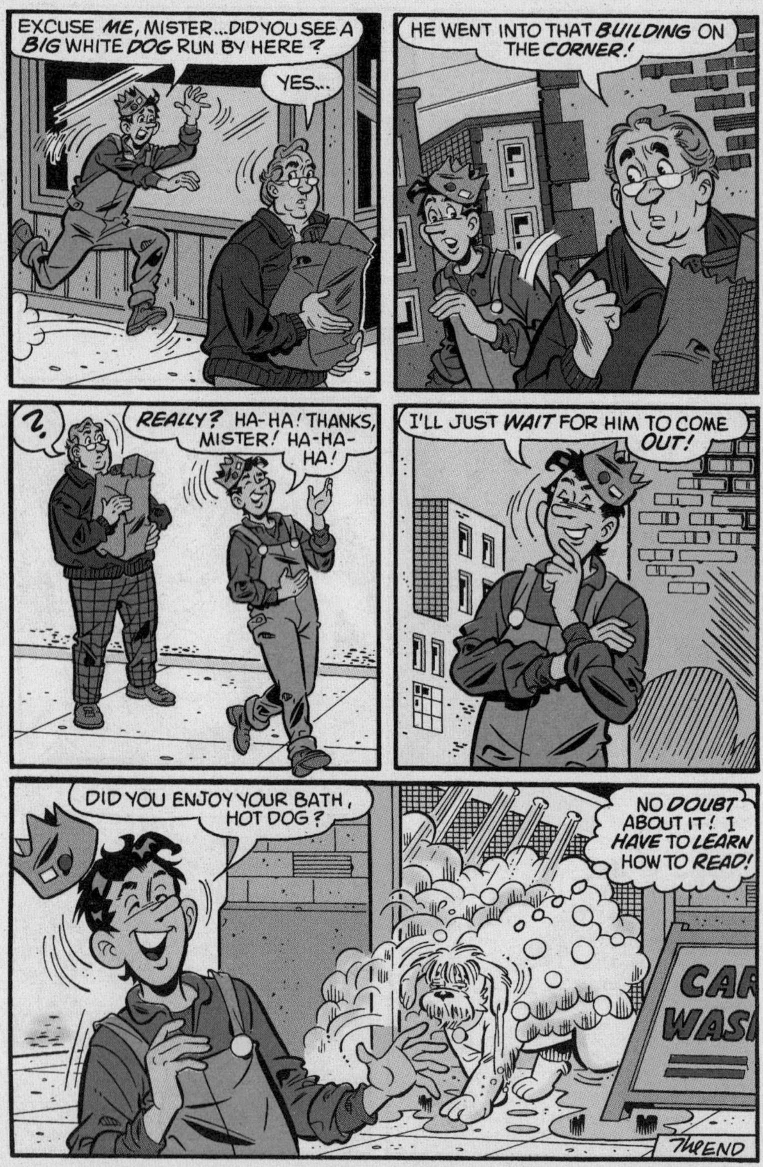
EXCUSE ME, MISTER...DID YOU SEE A BIG WHITE DOG RUN BY HERE?
YES...
HE WENT INTO THAT BUILDING ON THE CORNER!
?
REALLY? HA-HA! THANKS, MISTER! HA-HA-HA!
I'LL JUST WAIT FOR HIM TO COME OUT!
DID YOU ENJOY YOUR BATH, HOT DOG?
NO DOUBT ABOUT IT! I HAVE TO LEARN HOW TO READ!
CAR WAS
THE END

Veronica "HAIR CURLING"

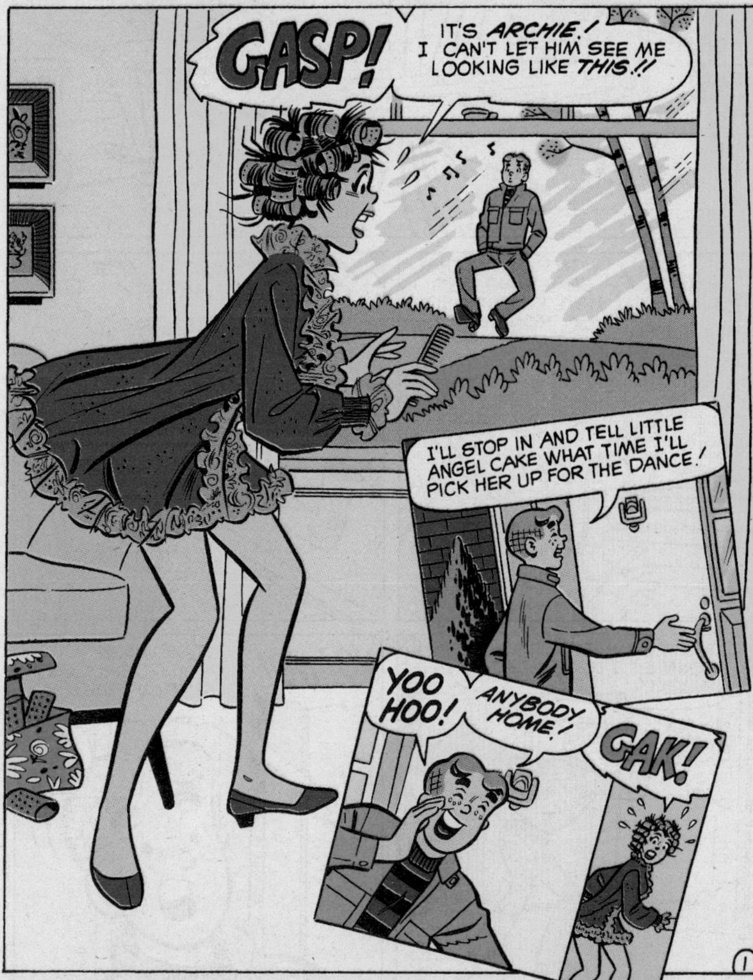
GASP!
IT'S ARCHIE.! I CAN'T LET HIM SEE ME LOOKING LIKE THIS.!!
I'LL STOP IN AND TELL LITTLE ANGEL CAKE WHAT TIME I'LL PICK HER UP FOR THE DANCE!
YOO HOO!
ANYBODY HOME!
GAK!
1

Script: Dick Malmgren / Pencils: Dan DeCarlo / Inks: Rudy Lapick / Letters: Bill Yoshida

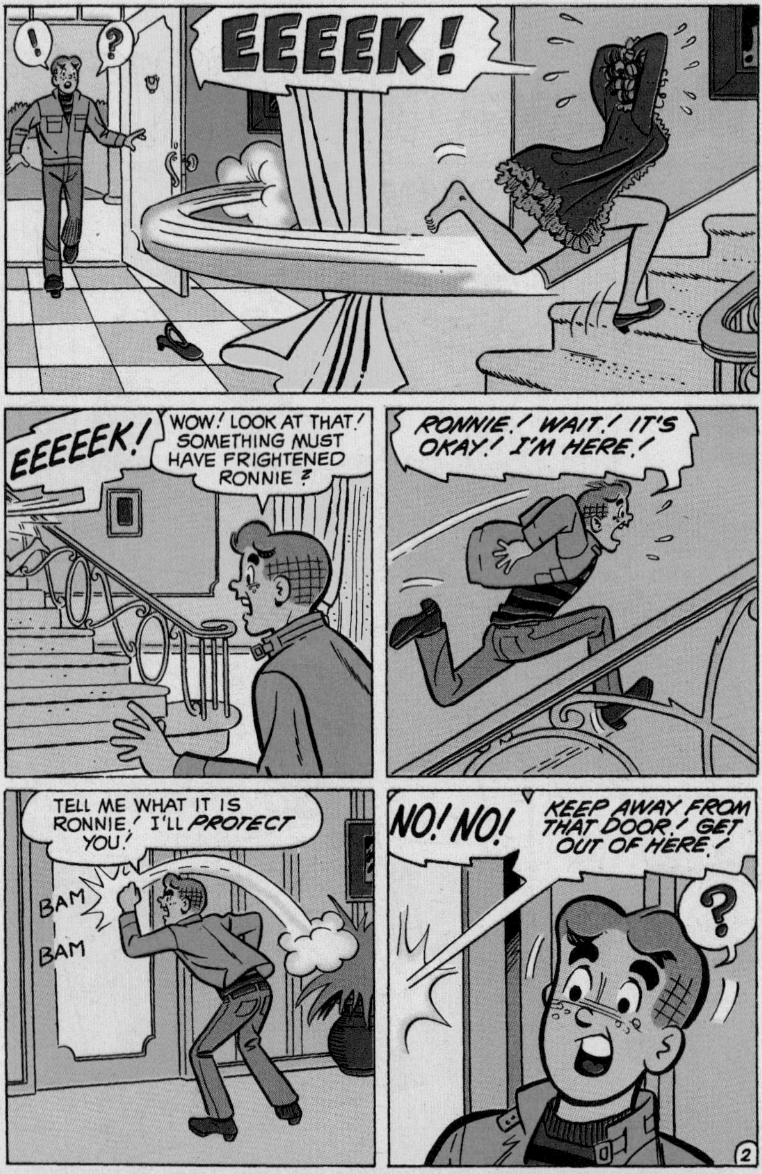
!
?
EEEEK!
EEEEEK!
WOW! LOOK AT THAT! SOMETHING MUST HAVE FRIGHTENED RONNIE?
RONNIE! WAIT! IT'S OKAY! I'M HERE!
TELL ME WHAT IT IS RONNIE! I'LL PROTECT YOU!
BAM
BAM
NO! NO!
KEEP AWAY FROM THAT DOOR! GET OUT OF HERE!
?
2

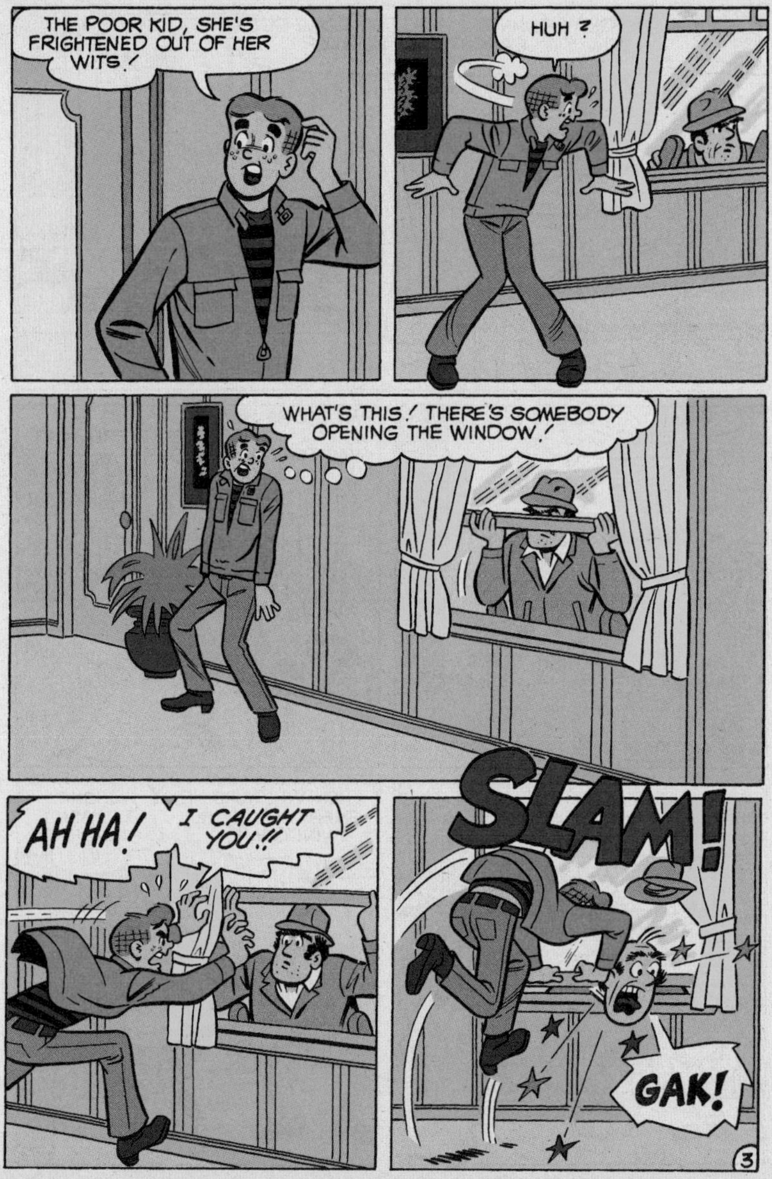
THE POOR KID, SHE'S FRIGHTENED OUT OF HER WITS!
HUH ?
WHAT'S THIS! THERE'S SOMEBODY OPENING THE WINDOW!
AH HA!
I CAUGHT YOU!!
SLAM!
GAK!

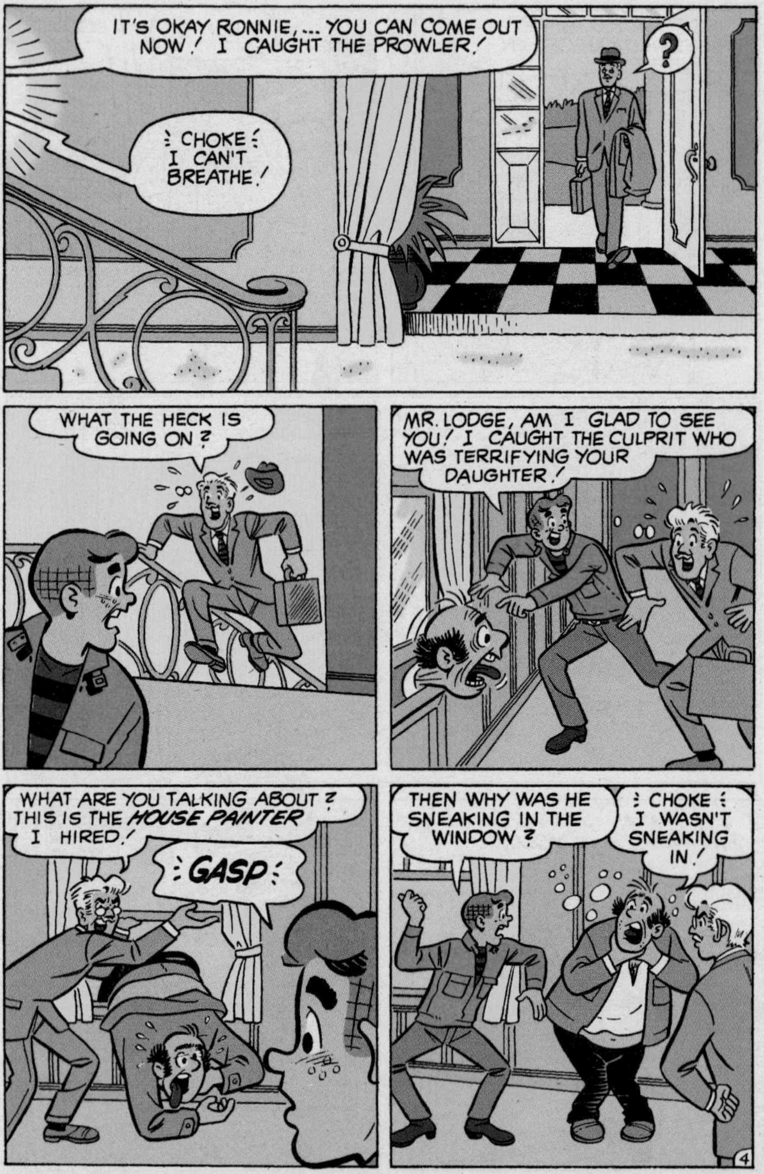

IT'S OKAY RONNIE, ... YOU CAN COME OUT NOW! I CAUGHT THE PROWLER!
?
CHOKE I CAN'T BREATHE!
WHAT THE HECK IS GOING ON?
MR. LODGE, AM I GLAD TO SEE YOU! I CAUGHT THE CULPRIT WHO WAS TERRIFYING YOUR DAUGHTER!
WHAT ARE YOU TALKING ABOUT? THIS IS THE HOUSE PAINTER I HIRED!
GASP
THEN WHY WAS HE SNEAKING IN THE WINDOW?
CHOKE I WASN'T SNEAKING IN!
4

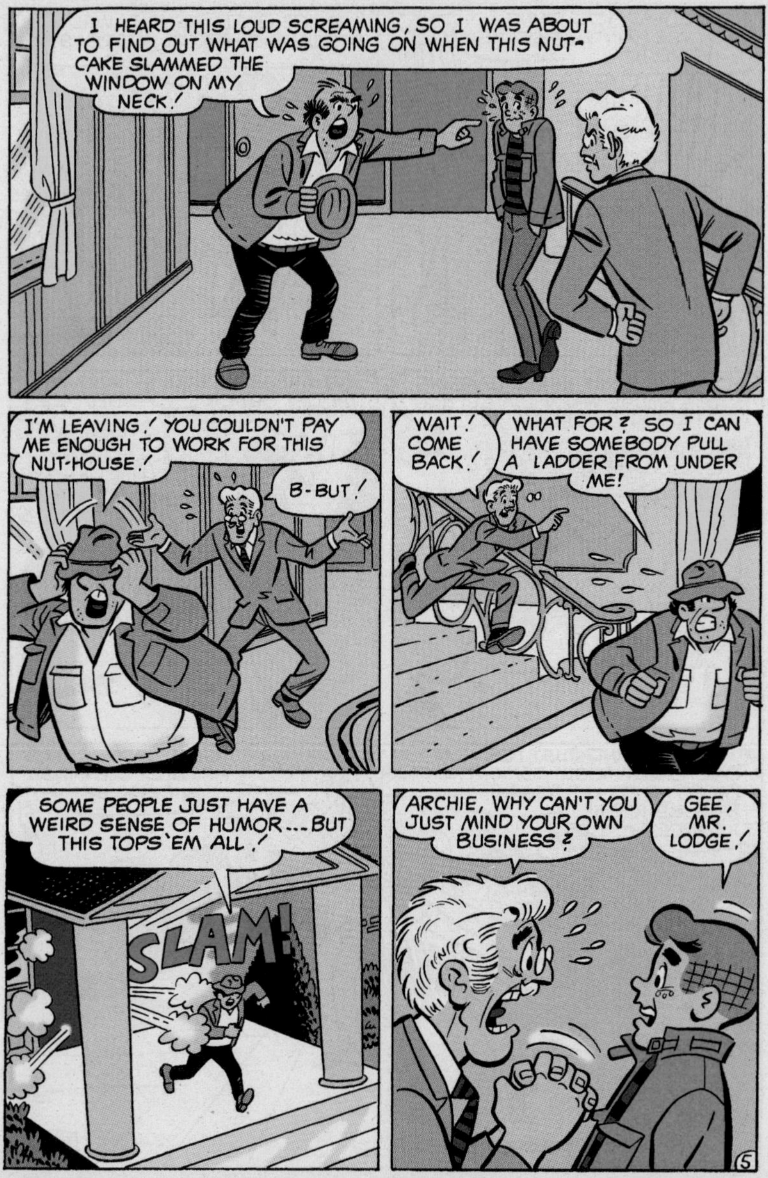
I HEARD THIS LOUD SCREAMING, SO I WAS ABOUT TO FIND OUT WHAT WAS GOING ON WHEN THIS NUT-CAKE SLAMMED THE WINDOW ON MY NECK!
I'M LEAVING! YOU COULDN'T PAY ME ENOUGH TO WORK FOR THIS NUT-HOUSE!
B-BUT!
WAIT! COME BACK!
WHAT FOR? SO I CAN HAVE SOMEBODY PULL A LADDER FROM UNDER ME!
SOME PEOPLE JUST HAVE A WEIRD SENSE OF HUMOR... BUT THIS TOPS 'EM ALL!
SLAM!
ARCHIE, WHY CAN'T YOU JUST MIND YOUR OWN BUSINESS?
GEE, MR. LODGE!
5

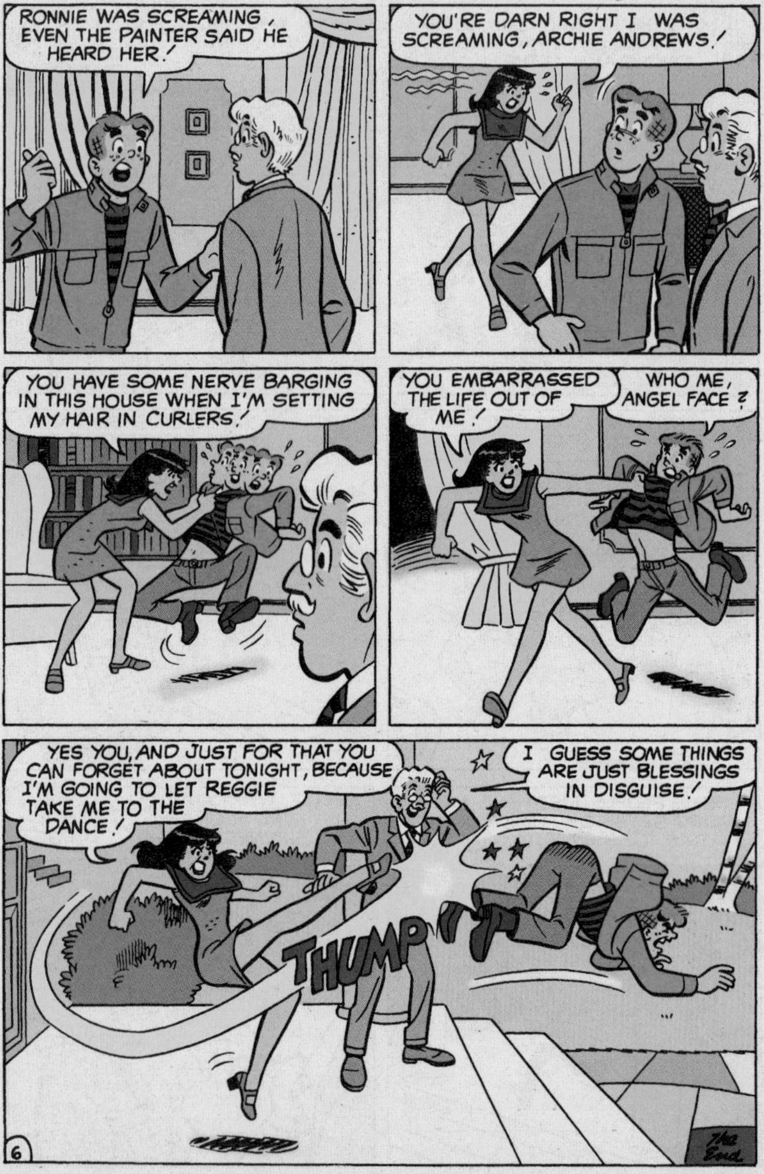
RONNIE WAS SCREAMING, EVEN THE PAINTER SAID HE HEARD HER!
YOU'RE DARN RIGHT I WAS SCREAMING, ARCHIE ANDREWS!
YOU HAVE SOME NERVE BARGING IN THIS HOUSE WHEN I'M SETTING MY HAIR IN CURLERS!
YOU EMBARRASSED THE LIFE OUT OF ME!
WHO ME, ANGEL FACE?
YES YOU, AND JUST FOR THAT YOU CAN FORGET ABOUT TONIGHT, BECAUSE I'M GOING TO LET REGGIE TAKE ME TO THE DANCE!
I GUESS SOME THINGS ARE JUST BLESSINGS IN DISGUISE!
THUMP
6
The End

Betty and Veronica in "ALL BOOKED UP"

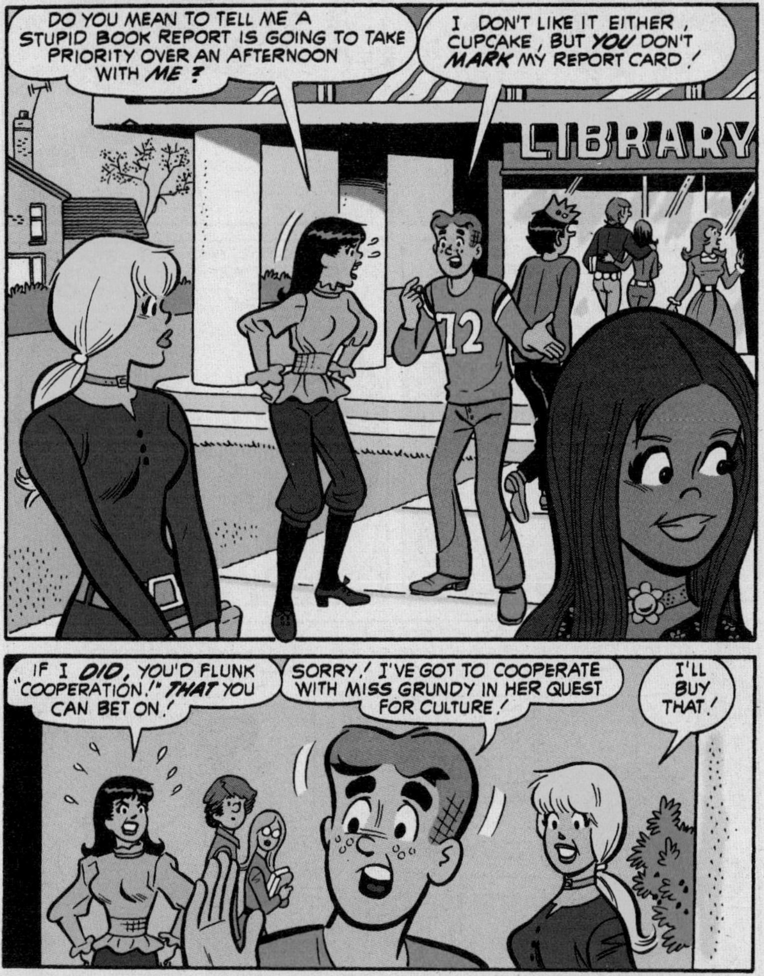

DO YOU MEAN TO TELL ME A STUPID BOOK REPORT IS GOING TO TAKE PRIORITY OVER AN AFTERNOON WITH *ME* ?
I DON'T LIKE IT EITHER, CUPCAKE, BUT *YOU* DON'T *MARK* MY REPORT CARD!
LIBRARY
12
IF I *DID*, YOU'D FLUNK "COOPERATION!" *THAT* YOU CAN BET ON!
SORRY! I'VE GOT TO COOPERATE WITH MISS GRUNDY IN HER QUEST FOR CULTURE!
I'LL BUY THAT!

Script: Frank Doyle / Pencils: Dan DeCarlo / Inks: Rudy Lapick / Letters: Bill Yoshida

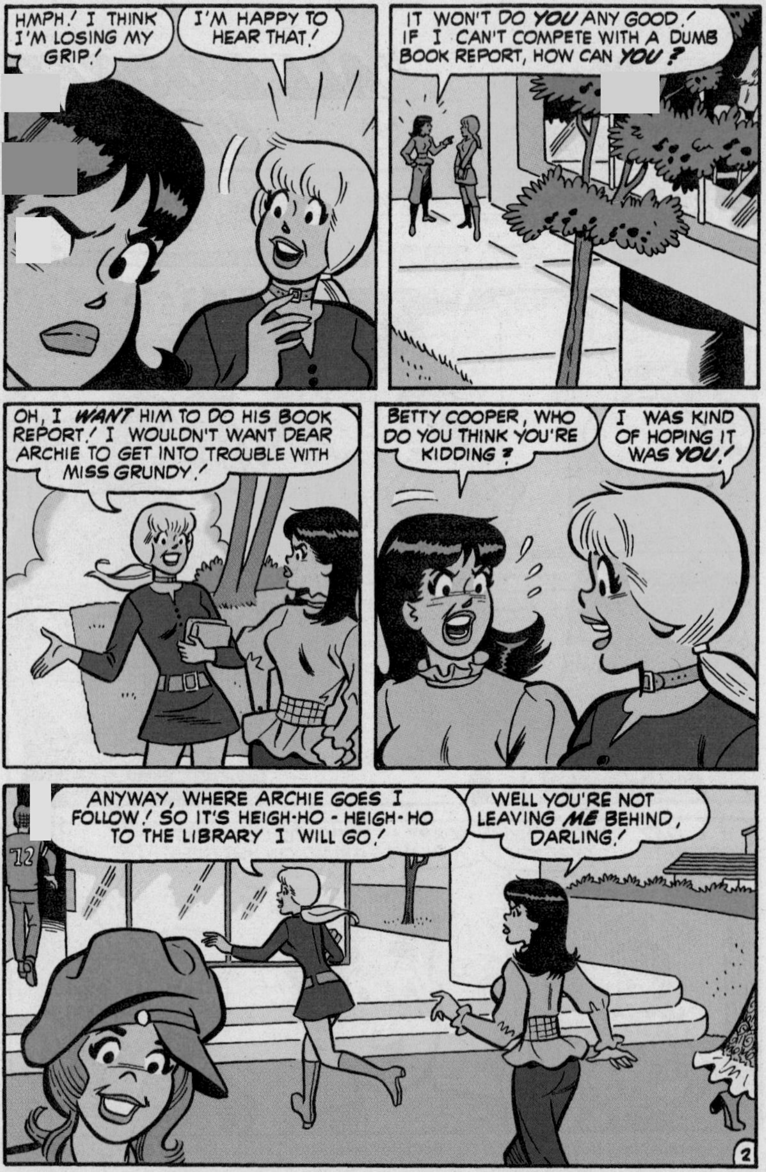
HMPH! I THINK I'M LOSING MY GRIP!
I'M HAPPY TO HEAR THAT!
IT WON'T DO YOU ANY GOOD! IF I CAN'T COMPETE WITH A DUMB BOOK REPORT, HOW CAN YOU?
OH, I WANT HIM TO DO HIS BOOK REPORT! I WOULDN'T WANT DEAR ARCHIE TO GET INTO TROUBLE WITH MISS GRUNDY!
BETTY COOPER, WHO DO YOU THINK YOU'RE KIDDING?
I WAS KIND OF HOPING IT WAS YOU!
ANYWAY, WHERE ARCHIE GOES I FOLLOW! SO IT'S HEIGH-HO - HEIGH-HO TO THE LIBRARY I WILL GO!
WELL YOU'RE NOT LEAVING ME BEHIND, DARLING!
72
2

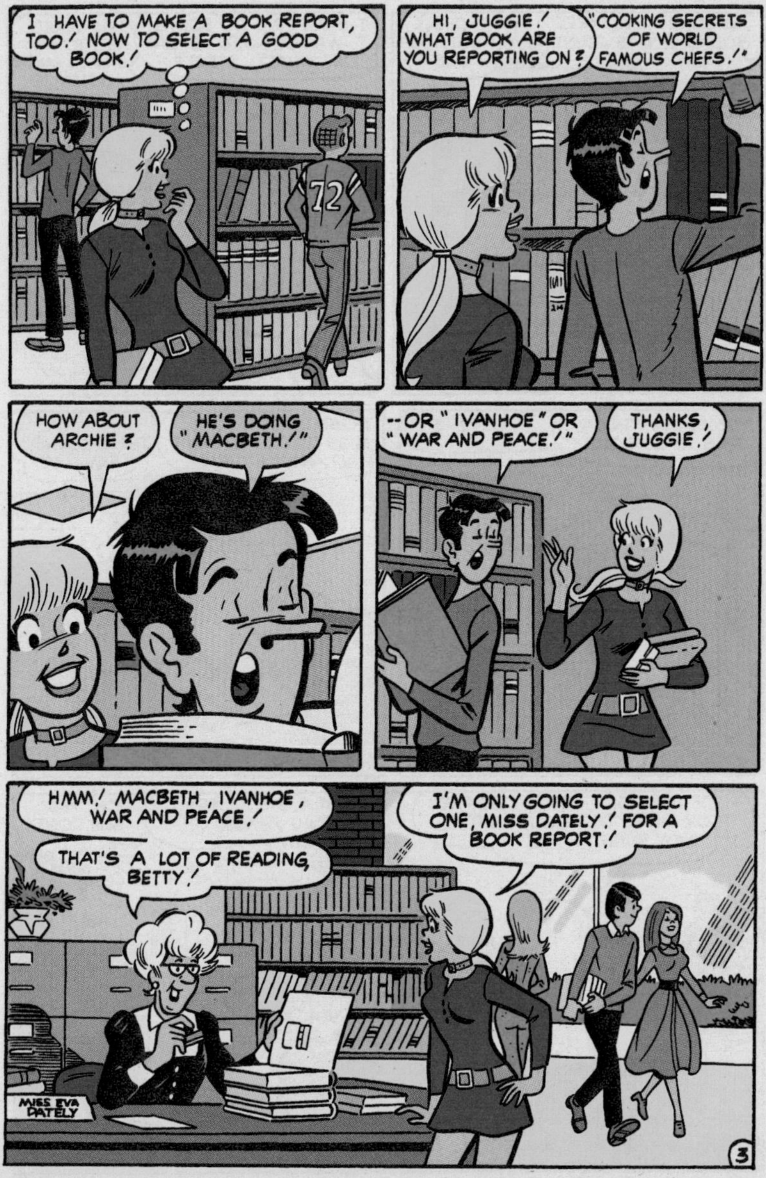
I HAVE TO MAKE A BOOK REPORT, TOO! NOW TO SELECT A GOOD BOOK!
HI, JUGGIE! WHAT BOOK ARE YOU REPORTING ON?
"COOKING SECRETS OF WORLD FAMOUS CHEFS!"
HOW ABOUT ARCHIE?
HE'S DOING "MACBETH!"
--OR "IVANHOE" OR "WAR AND PEACE!"
THANKS, JUGGIE!
HMM! MACBETH, IVANHOE, WAR AND PEACE!
THAT'S A LOT OF READING, BETTY!
I'M ONLY GOING TO SELECT ONE, MISS DATELY! FOR A BOOK REPORT!
MISS EVA DATELY
3

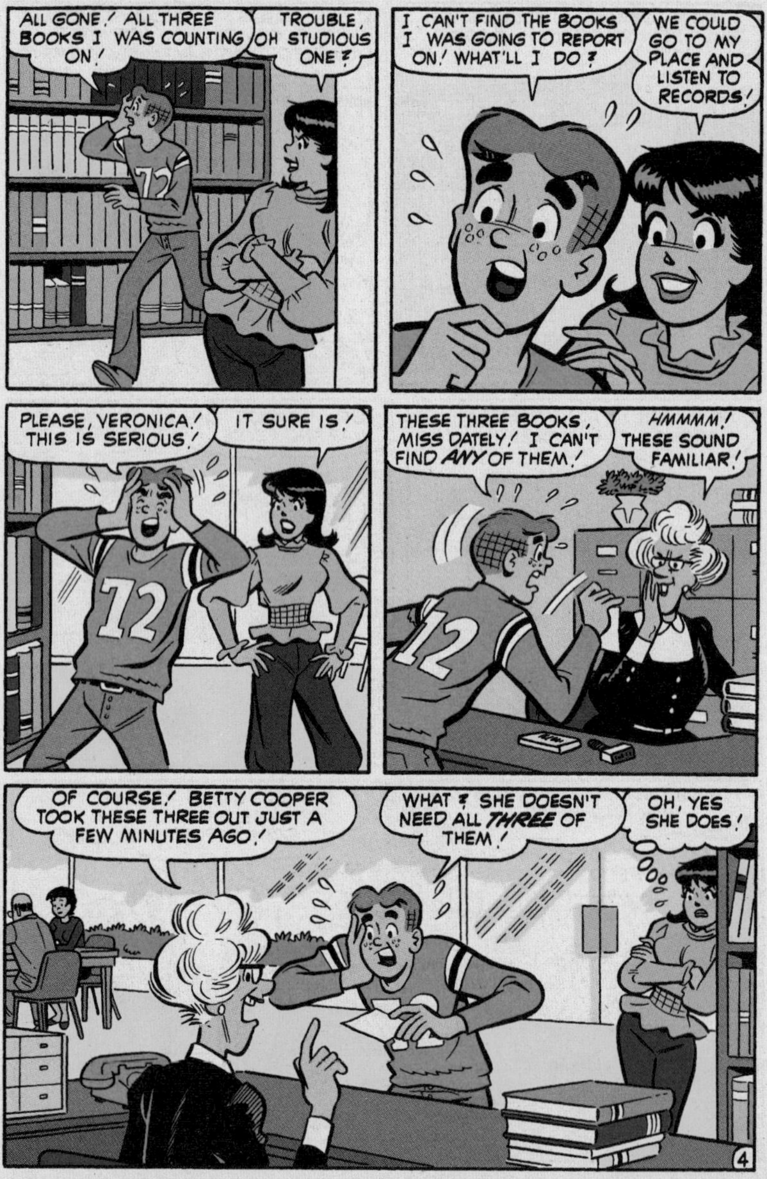

ALL GONE! ALL THREE BOOKS I WAS COUNTING ON!
TROUBLE, OH STUDIOUS ONE?
I CAN'T FIND THE BOOKS I WAS GOING TO REPORT ON! WHAT'LL I DO?
WE COULD GO TO MY PLACE AND LISTEN TO RECORDS!
PLEASE, VERONICA! THIS IS SERIOUS!
IT SURE IS!
THESE THREE BOOKS, MISS DATELY! I CAN'T FIND *ANY* OF THEM!
HMMMM! THESE SOUND FAMILIAR!
OF COURSE! BETTY COOPER TOOK THESE THREE OUT JUST A FEW MINUTES AGO!
WHAT? SHE DOESN'T NEED ALL *THREE* OF THEM!
OH, YES SHE DOES!
4

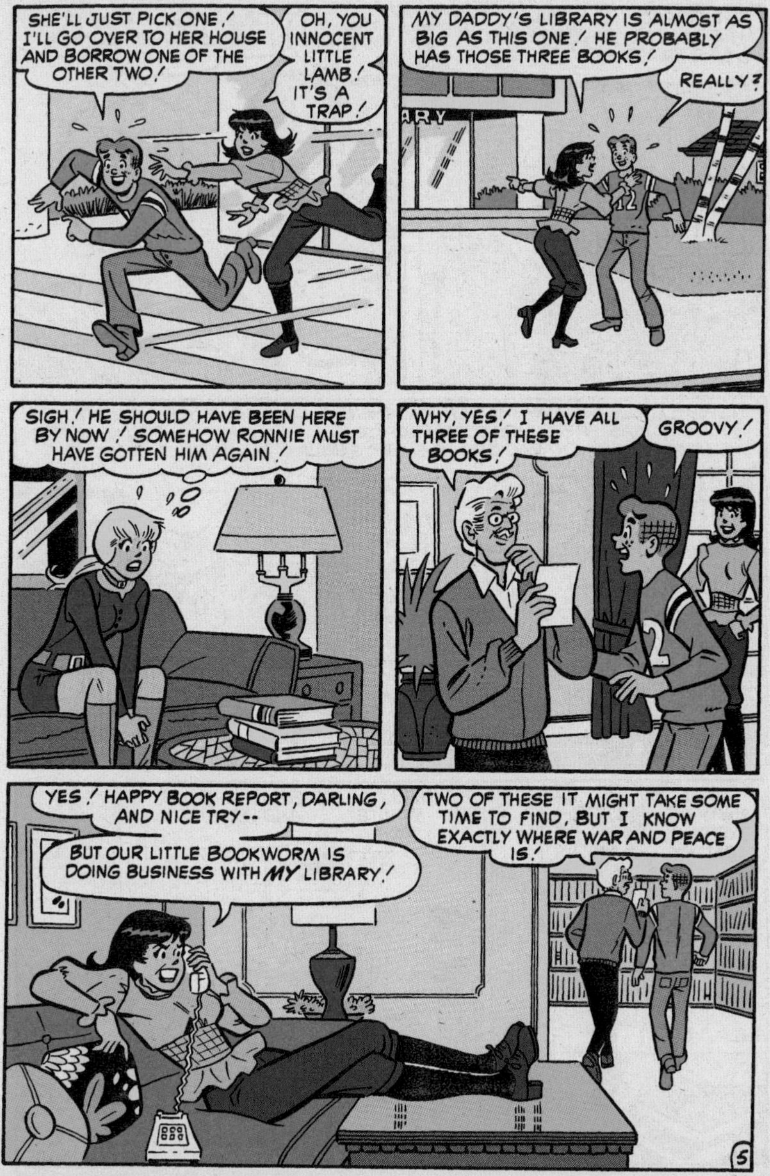

SHE'LL JUST PICK ONE! I'LL GO OVER TO HER HOUSE AND BORROW ONE OF THE OTHER TWO!
OH, YOU INNOCENT LITTLE LAMB! IT'S A TRAP!
MY DADDY'S LIBRARY IS ALMOST AS BIG AS THIS ONE! HE PROBABLY HAS THOSE THREE BOOKS!
REALLY?
ARY
12
SIGH! HE SHOULD HAVE BEEN HERE BY NOW! SOMEHOW RONNIE MUST HAVE GOTTEN HIM AGAIN!
WHY, YES! I HAVE ALL THREE OF THESE BOOKS!
GROOVY!
12
YES! HAPPY BOOK REPORT, DARLING, AND NICE TRY--
BUT OUR LITTLE BOOKWORM IS DOING BUSINESS WITH *MY* LIBRARY!
TWO OF THESE IT MIGHT TAKE SOME TIME TO FIND, BUT I KNOW EXACTLY WHERE WAR AND PEACE IS!

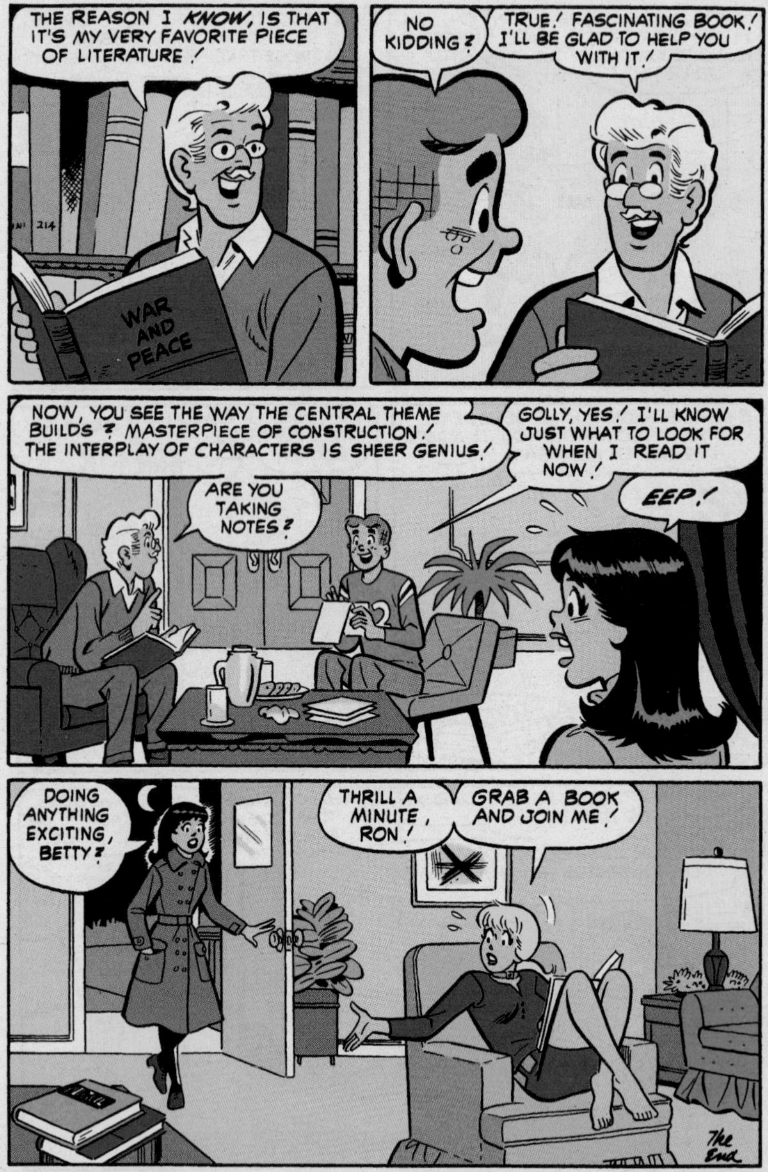
THE REASON I KNOW, IS THAT IT'S MY VERY FAVORITE PIECE OF LITERATURE!
WAR AND PEACE
NO KIDDING?
TRUE! FASCINATING BOOK! I'LL BE GLAD TO HELP YOU WITH IT!
NOW, YOU SEE THE WAY THE CENTRAL THEME BUILDS? MASTERPIECE OF CONSTRUCTION! THE INTERPLAY OF CHARACTERS IS SHEER GENIUS!
ARE YOU TAKING NOTES?
GOLLY, YES! I'LL KNOW JUST WHAT TO LOOK FOR WHEN I READ IT NOW!
EEP!
DOING ANYTHING EXCITING, BETTY?
THRILL A MINUTE, RON!
GRAB A BOOK AND JOIN ME!
The End

Betty and Veronica in "The Thrill Is Gone"

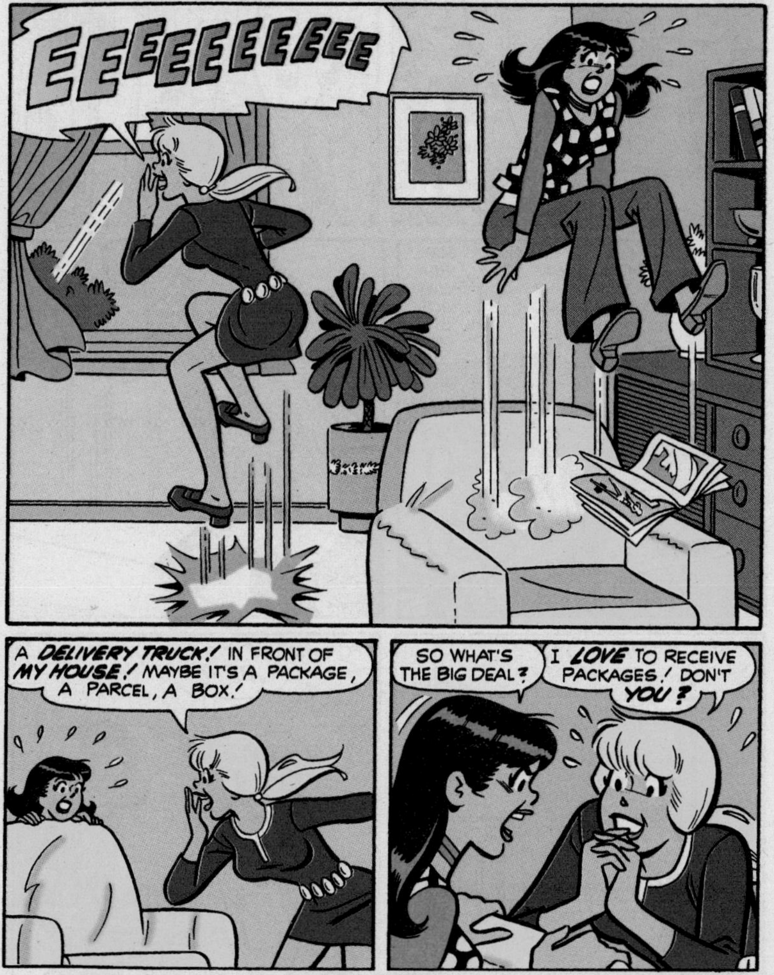

EEEEEEEEEEE
A DELIVERY TRUCK! IN FRONT OF MY HOUSE! MAYBE IT'S A PACKAGE, A PARCEL, A BOX!
SO WHAT'S THE BIG DEAL?
I LOVE TO RECEIVE PACKAGES! DON'T YOU?

Script: Frank Doyle / Pencils: Dan DeCarlo / Inks: Rudy Lapick / Letters: Bill Yoshida

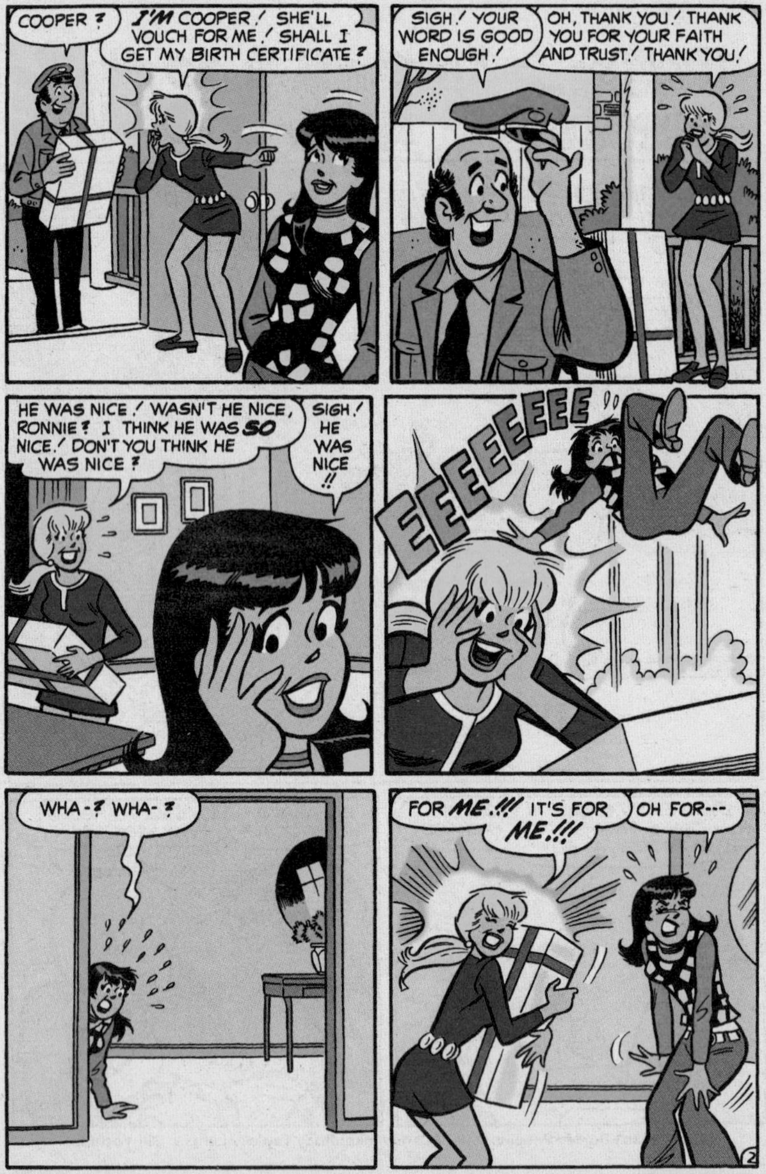
COOPER ?
I'M COOPER! SHE'LL VOUCH FOR ME! SHALL I GET MY BIRTH CERTIFICATE ?
SIGH! YOUR WORD IS GOOD ENOUGH!
OH, THANK YOU! THANK YOU FOR YOUR FAITH AND TRUST! THANK YOU!
HE WAS NICE! WASN'T HE NICE, RONNIE? I THINK HE WAS SO NICE! DON'T YOU THINK HE WAS NICE?
SIGH! HE WAS NICE !!
EEEEEEEEE
WHA-? WHA-?
FOR ME!!! IT'S FOR ME!!!
OH FOR---
2

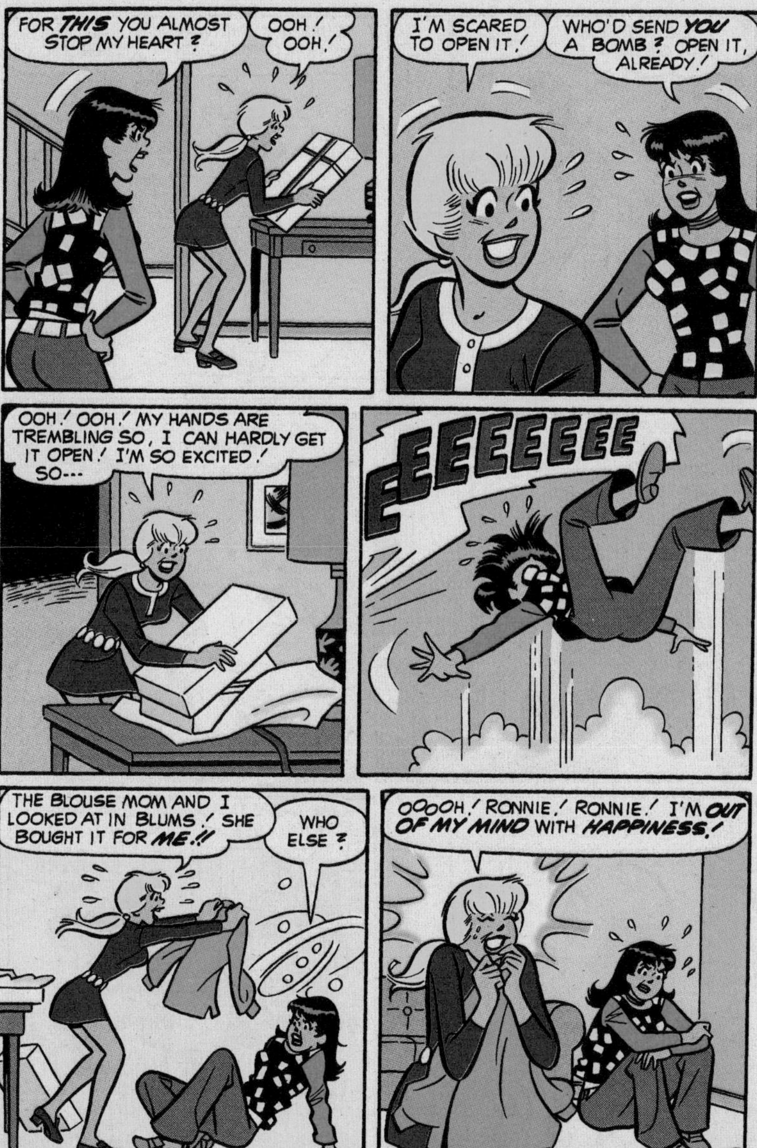
FOR THIS YOU ALMOST STOP MY HEART ?
OOH! OOH!
I'M SCARED TO OPEN IT!
WHO'D SEND YOU A BOMB ? OPEN IT, ALREADY!
OOH! OOH! MY HANDS ARE TREMBLING SO, I CAN HARDLY GET IT OPEN! I'M SO EXCITED! SO---
EEEEEEEEE
THE BLOUSE MOM AND I LOOKED AT IN BLUMS! SHE BOUGHT IT FOR ME!!!
WHO ELSE ?
OOOOH! RONNIE! RONNIE! I'M OUT OF MY MIND WITH HAPPINESS!
3

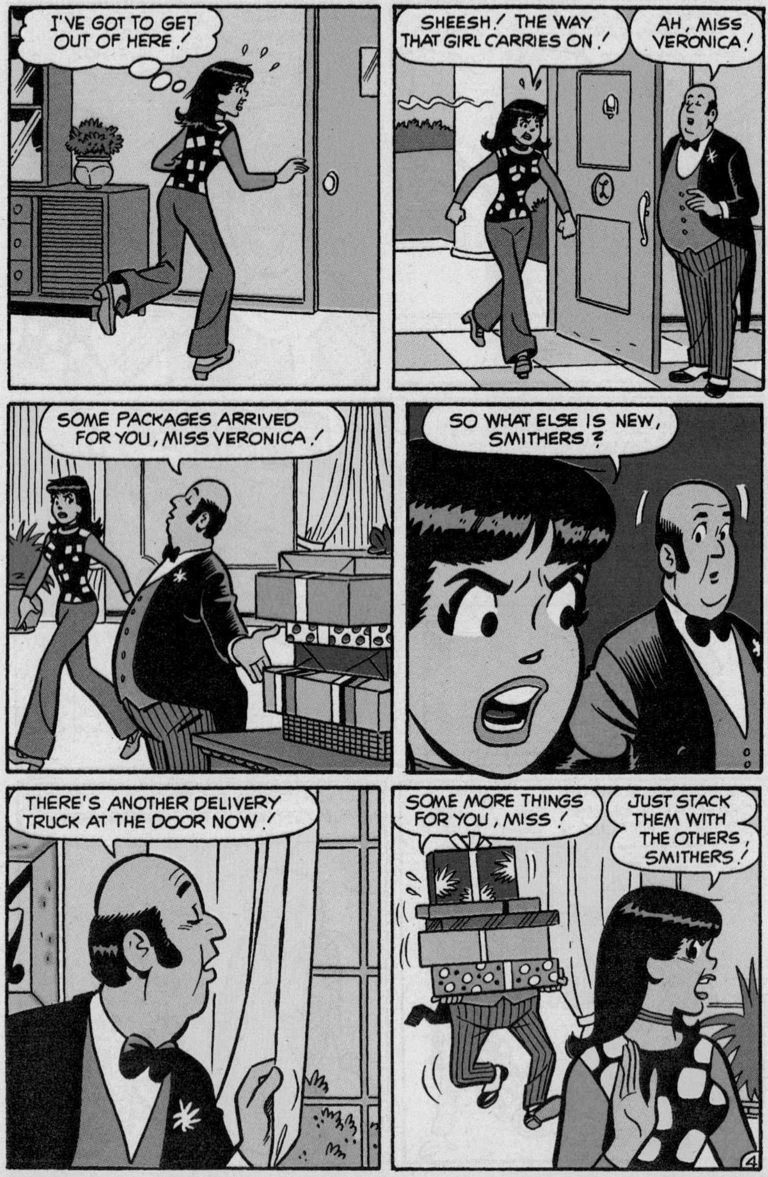
I'VE GOT TO GET OUT OF HERE!
SHEESH! THE WAY THAT GIRL CARRIES ON!
AH, MISS VERONICA!
SOME PACKAGES ARRIVED FOR YOU, MISS VERONICA!
SO WHAT ELSE IS NEW, SMITHERS?
THERE'S ANOTHER DELIVERY TRUCK AT THE DOOR NOW!
SOME MORE THINGS FOR YOU, MISS!
JUST STACK THEM WITH THE OTHERS, SMITHERS!
4

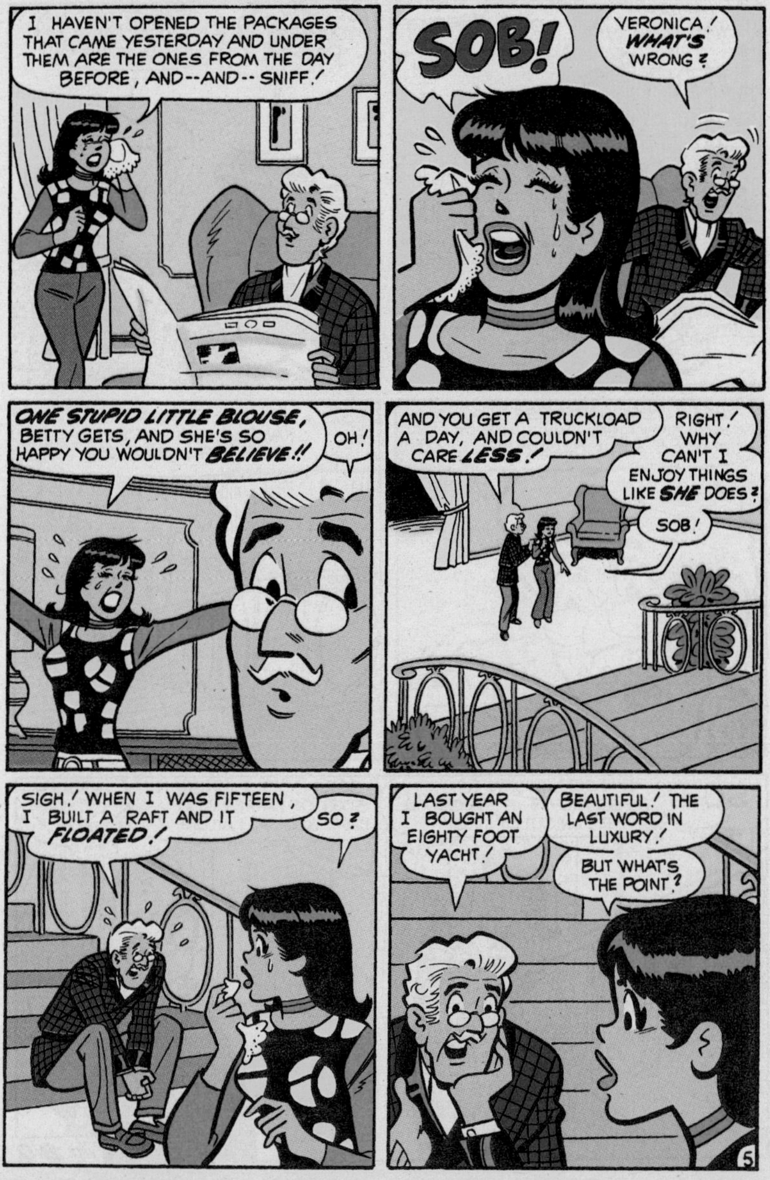

I HAVEN'T OPENED THE PACKAGES THAT CAME YESTERDAY AND UNDER THEM ARE THE ONES FROM THE DAY BEFORE, AND--AND-- SNIFF!
SOB!
VERONICA! WHAT'S WRONG?
ONE STUPID LITTLE BLOUSE, BETTY GETS, AND SHE'S SO HAPPY YOU WOULDN'T BELIEVE!!
OH!
AND YOU GET A TRUCKLOAD A DAY, AND COULDN'T CARE LESS!
RIGHT! WHY CAN'T I ENJOY THINGS LIKE SHE DOES?
SOB!
SIGH! WHEN I WAS FIFTEEN, I BUILT A RAFT AND IT FLOATED!
SO?
LAST YEAR I BOUGHT AN EIGHTY FOOT YACHT!
BEAUTIFUL! THE LAST WORD IN LUXURY!
BUT WHAT'S THE POINT?
5

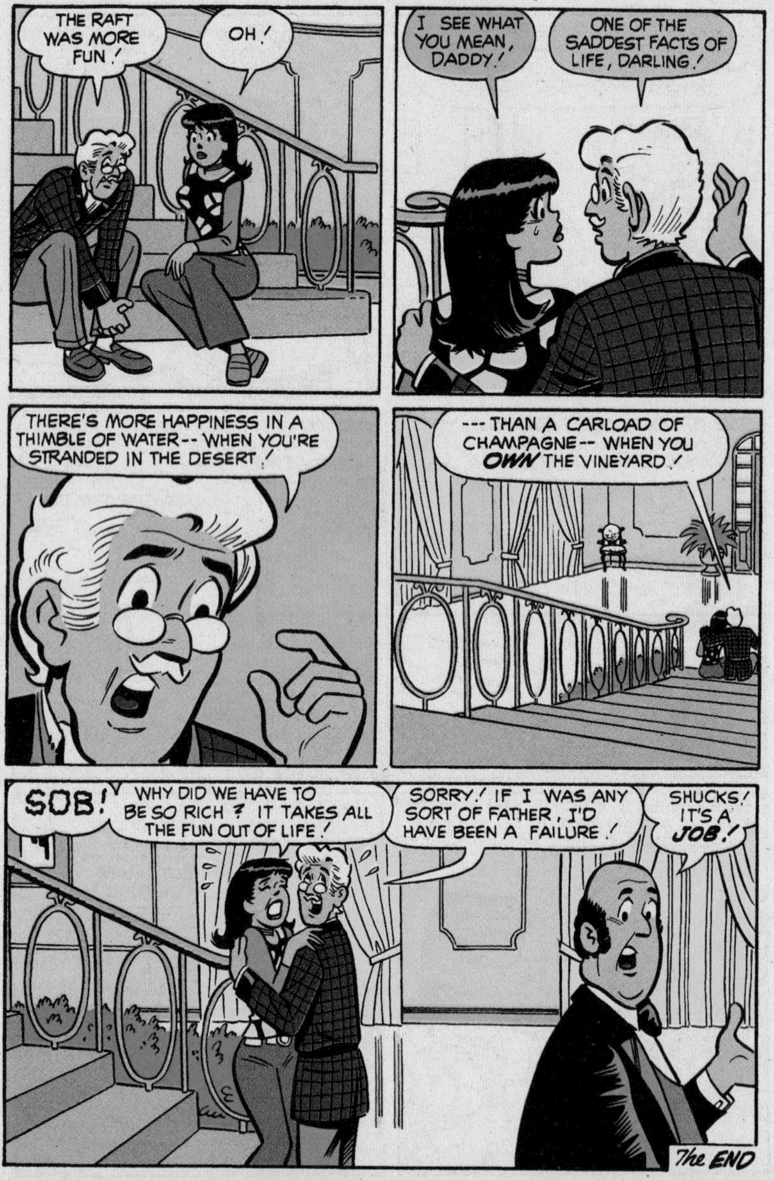
THE RAFT WAS MORE FUN!
OH!
I SEE WHAT YOU MEAN, DADDY!
ONE OF THE SADDEST FACTS OF LIFE, DARLING!
THERE'S MORE HAPPINESS IN A THIMBLE OF WATER-- WHEN YOU'RE STRANDED IN THE DESERT!
---THAN A CARLOAD OF CHAMPAGNE-- WHEN YOU OWN THE VINEYARD!
SOB!
WHY DID WE HAVE TO BE SO RICH? IT TAKES ALL THE FUN OUT OF LIFE!
SORRY! IF I WAS ANY SORT OF FATHER, I'D HAVE BEEN A FAILURE!
SHUCKS! IT'S A JOB!
The END

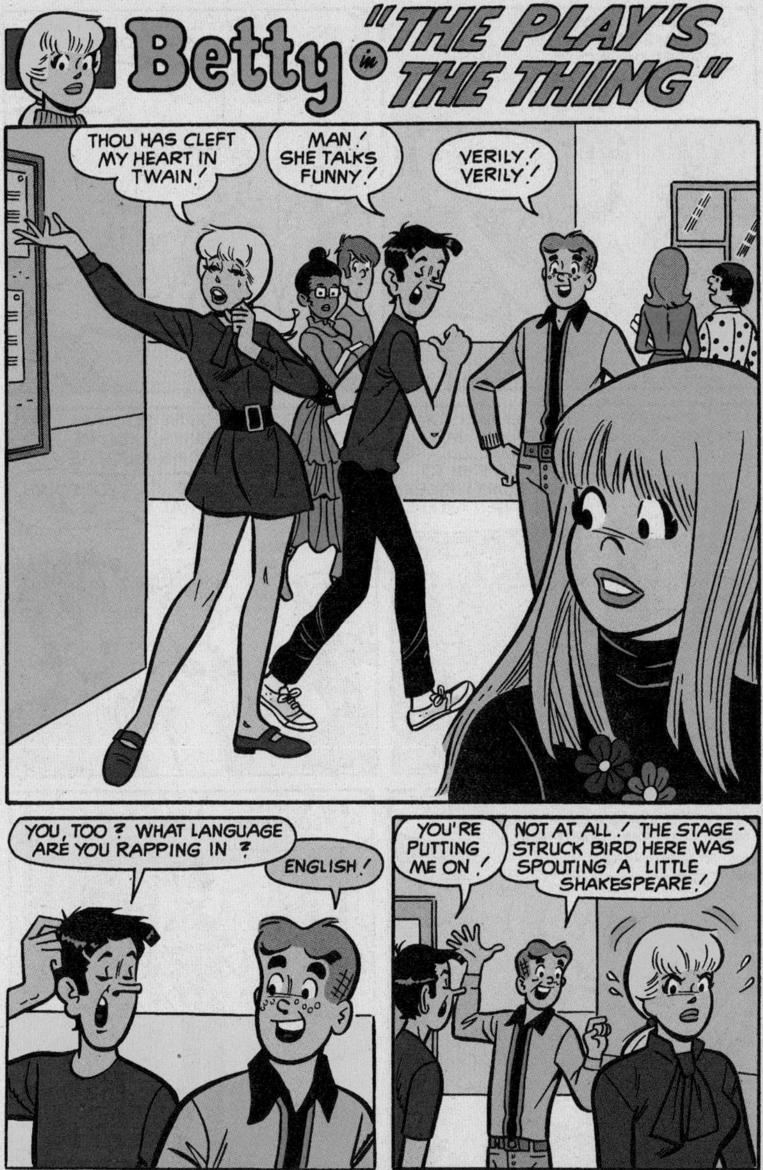
Betty in "THE PLAY'S THE THING"
THOU HAS CLEFT MY HEART IN TWAIN!
MAN! SHE TALKS FUNNY!
VERILY! VERILY!
YOU, TOO? WHAT LANGUAGE ARE YOU RAPPING IN?
ENGLISH!
YOU'RE PUTTING ME ON!
NOT AT ALL! THE STAGE-STRUCK BIRD HERE WAS SPOUTING A LITTLE SHAKESPEARE!

Script: Frank Doyle / Art: Dan DeCarlo / Letters: Bill Yoshida

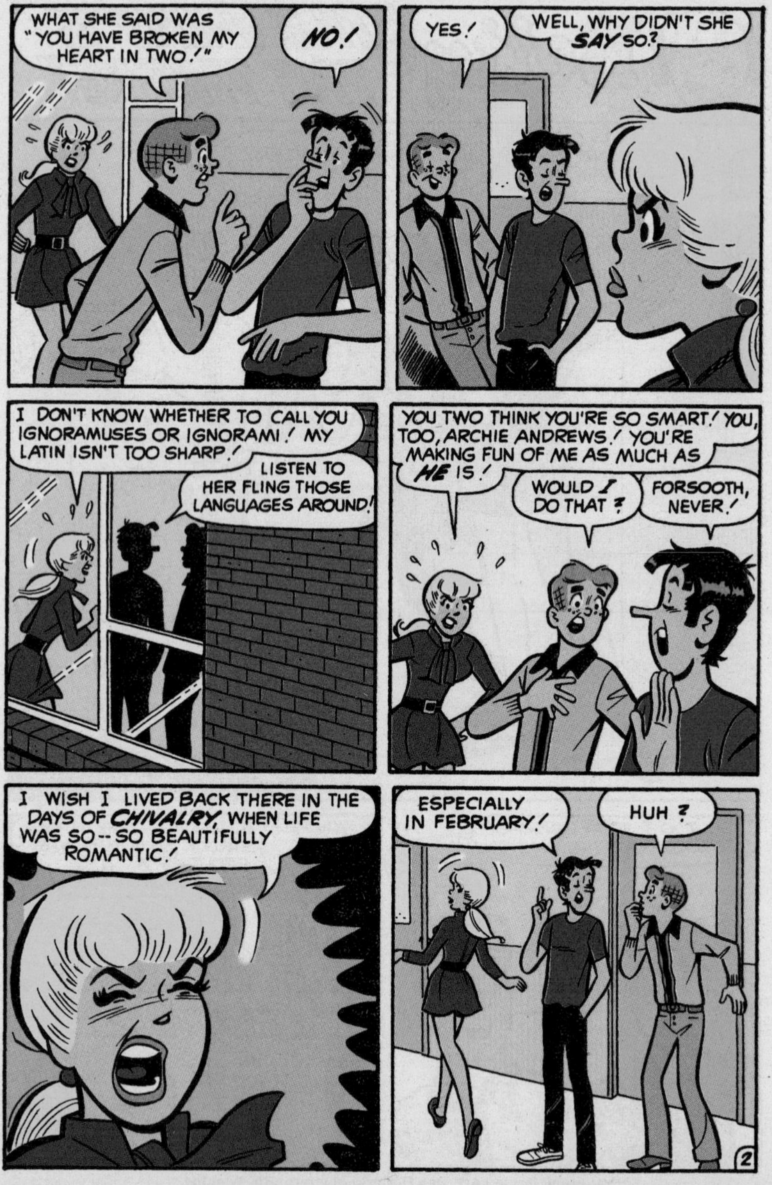
WHAT SHE SAID WAS "YOU HAVE BROKEN MY HEART IN TWO!"
NO!
YES!
WELL, WHY DIDN'T SHE SAY SO?
I DON'T KNOW WHETHER TO CALL YOU IGNORAMUSES OR IGNORAMI! MY LATIN ISN'T TOO SHARP!
LISTEN TO HER FLING THOSE LANGUAGES AROUND!
YOU TWO THINK YOU'RE SO SMART! YOU, TOO, ARCHIE ANDREWS! YOU'RE MAKING FUN OF ME AS MUCH AS HE IS!
WOULD I DO THAT?
FORSOOTH, NEVER!
I WISH I LIVED BACK THERE IN THE DAYS OF CHIVALRY, WHEN LIFE WAS SO-- SO BEAUTIFULLY ROMANTIC!
ESPECIALLY IN FEBRUARY!
HUH?
2

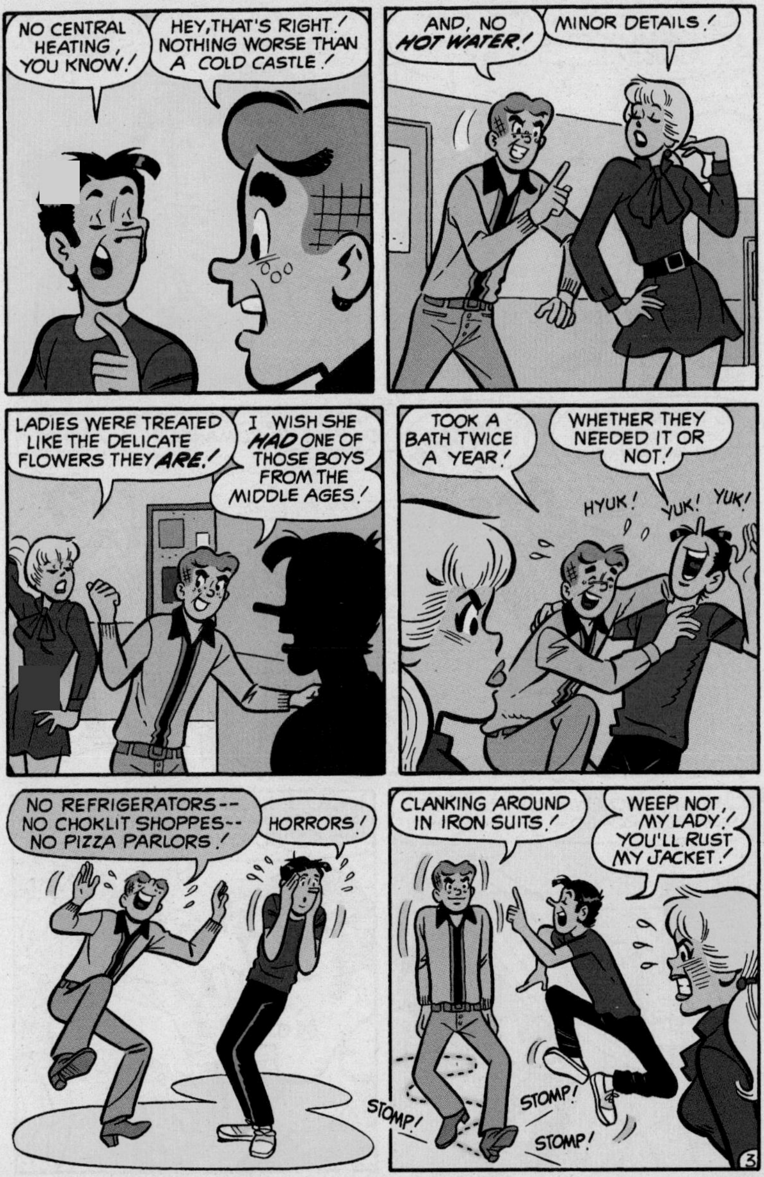
NO CENTRAL HEATING, YOU KNOW!
HEY, THAT'S RIGHT! NOTHING WORSE THAN A COLD CASTLE!
AND, NO HOT WATER!
MINOR DETAILS!
LADIES WERE TREATED LIKE THE DELICATE FLOWERS THEY ARE!
I WISH SHE HAD ONE OF THOSE BOYS FROM THE MIDDLE AGES!
TOOK A BATH TWICE A YEAR!
WHETHER THEY NEEDED IT OR NOT!
HYUK! YUK! YUK!
NO REFRIGERATORS-- NO CHOKLIT SHOPPES-- NO PIZZA PARLORS!
HORRORS!
CLANKING AROUND IN IRON SUITS!
WEEP NOT, MY LADY! YOU'LL RUST MY JACKET!
STOMP!
STOMP!
STOMP!
3

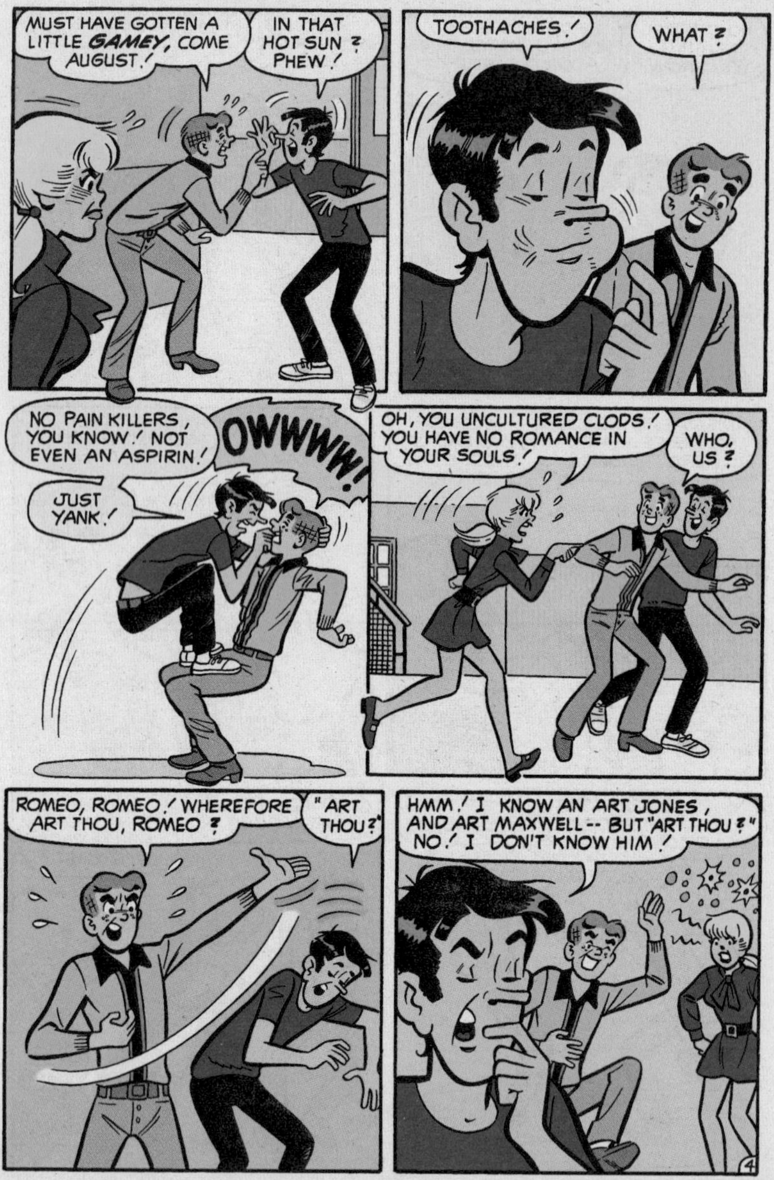
MUST HAVE GOTTEN A LITTLE GAMEY, COME AUGUST!
IN THAT HOT SUN ? PHEW!
TOOTHACHES!
WHAT ?
NO PAIN KILLERS, YOU KNOW! NOT EVEN AN ASPIRIN!
JUST YANK!
OWWWW!
OH, YOU UNCULTURED CLODS! YOU HAVE NO ROMANCE IN YOUR SOULS!
WHO, US ?
ROMEO, ROMEO! WHEREFORE ART THOU, ROMEO ?
"ART THOU?"
HMM! I KNOW AN ART JONES, AND ART MAXWELL -- BUT "ART THOU ?" NO! I DON'T KNOW HIM!
4

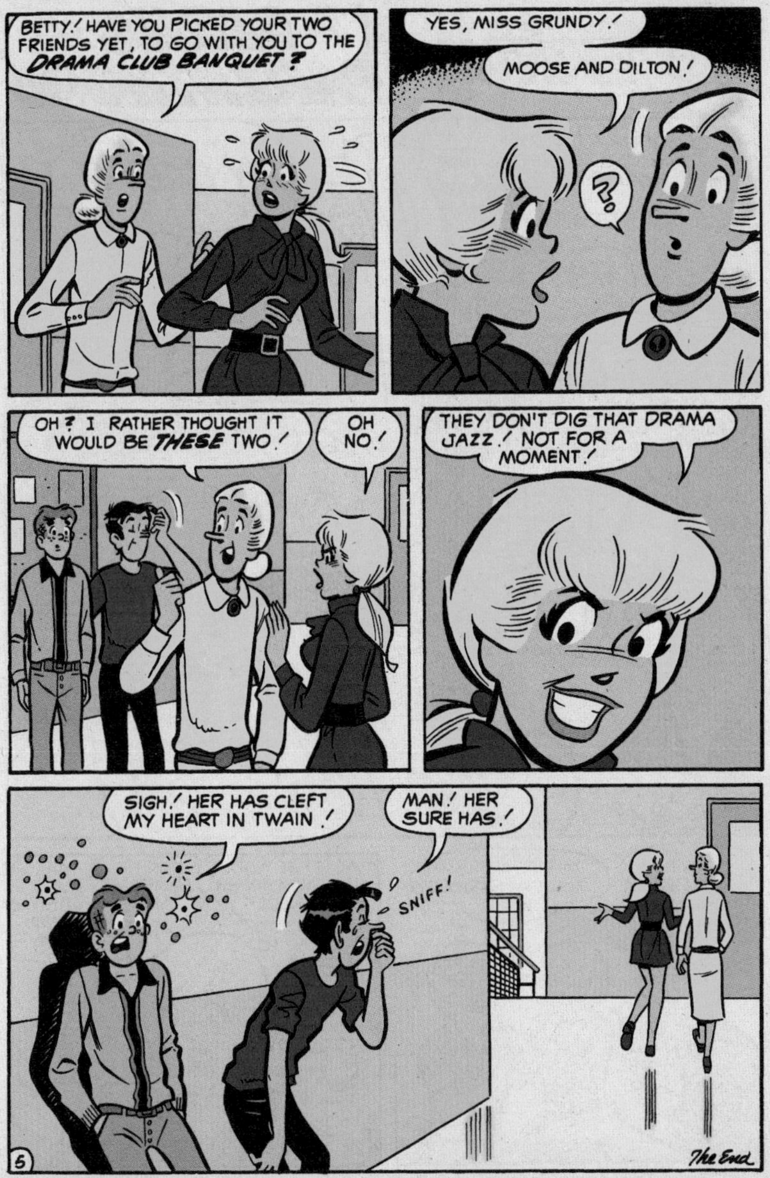
BETTY! HAVE YOU PICKED YOUR TWO FRIENDS YET, TO GO WITH YOU TO THE DRAMA CLUB BANQUET?
YES, MISS GRUNDY!
MOOSE AND DILTON!
?
OH? I RATHER THOUGHT IT WOULD BE THESE TWO!
OH NO!
THEY DON'T DIG THAT DRAMA JAZZ! NOT FOR A MOMENT!
SIGH! HER HAS CLEFT MY HEART IN TWAIN!
MAN! HER SURE HAS!
SNIFF!
5
The End

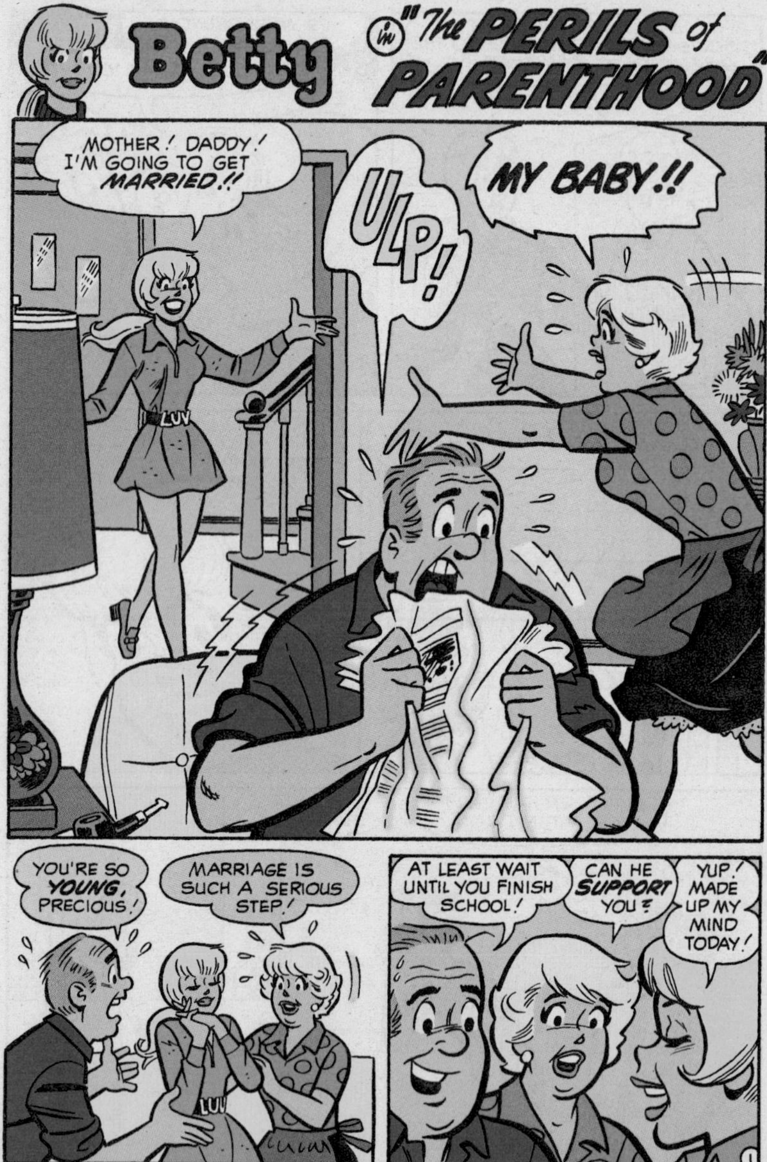

Betty
in "The PERILS of PARENTHOOD"
MOTHER! DADDY! I'M GOING TO GET MARRIED!!
ULP!
MY BABY!!
LUV
YOU'RE SO YOUNG, PRECIOUS!
MARRIAGE IS SUCH A SERIOUS STEP!
AT LEAST WAIT UNTIL YOU FINISH SCHOOL!
CAN HE SUPPORT YOU?
YUP! MADE UP MY MIND TODAY!

Script: Frank Doyle / Pencils: Dan DeCarlo / Inks: Rudy Lapick / Letters: Bill Yoshida

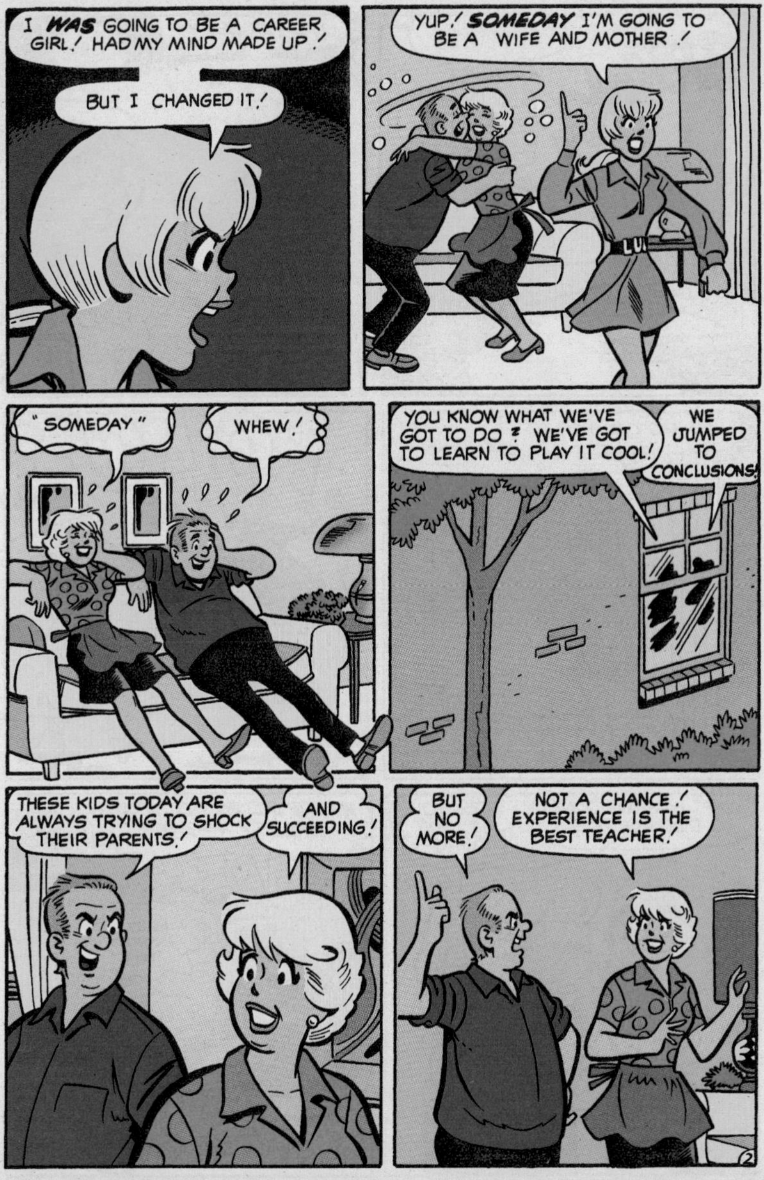
I WAS GOING TO BE A CAREER GIRL! HAD MY MIND MADE UP!
BUT I CHANGED IT!
YUP! SOMEDAY I'M GOING TO BE A WIFE AND MOTHER!
"SOMEDAY"
WHEW!
YOU KNOW WHAT WE'VE GOT TO DO? WE'VE GOT TO LEARN TO PLAY IT COOL!
WE JUMPED TO CONCLUSIONS!
THESE KIDS TODAY ARE ALWAYS TRYING TO SHOCK THEIR PARENTS!
AND SUCCEEDING!
BUT NO MORE!
NOT A CHANCE! EXPERIENCE IS THE BEST TEACHER!
2

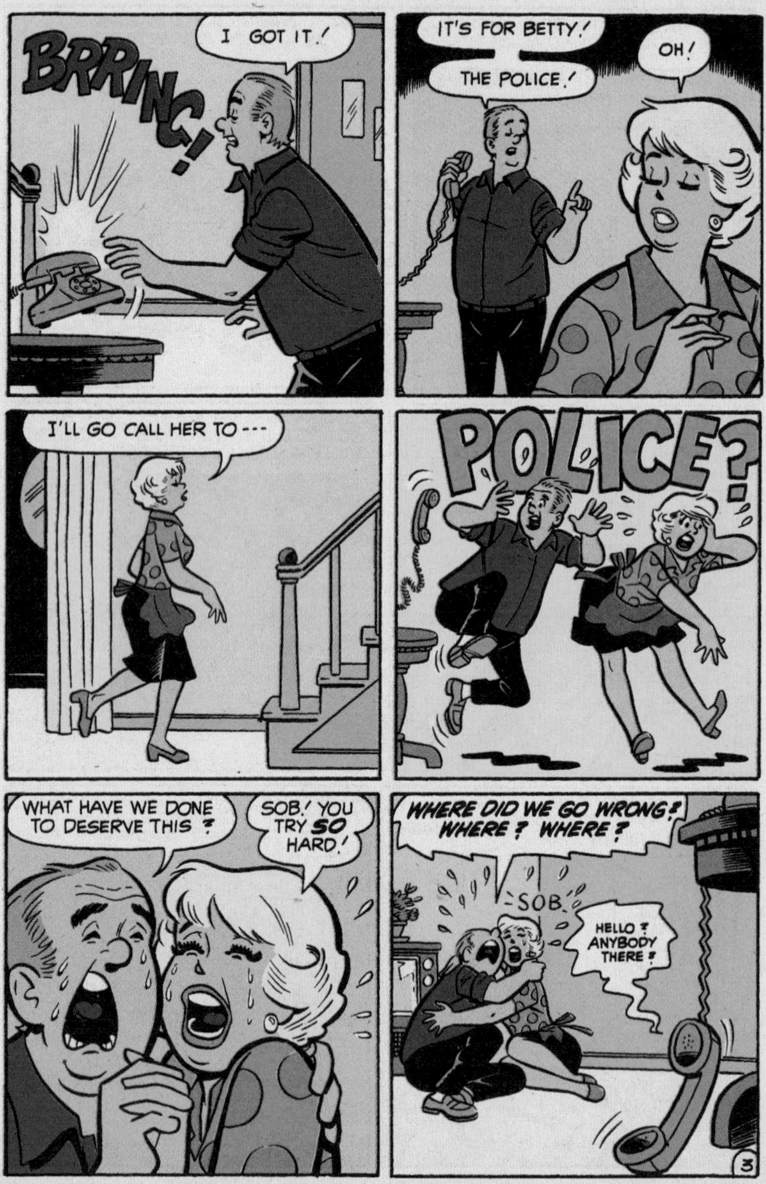
BRRING!
I GOT IT!
IT'S FOR BETTY!
THE POLICE!
OH!
I'LL GO CALL HER TO---
POLICE?
WHAT HAVE WE DONE TO DESERVE THIS?
SOB! YOU TRY SO HARD!
WHERE DID WE GO WRONG? WHERE? WHERE?
SOB
HELLO? ANYBODY THERE?
3

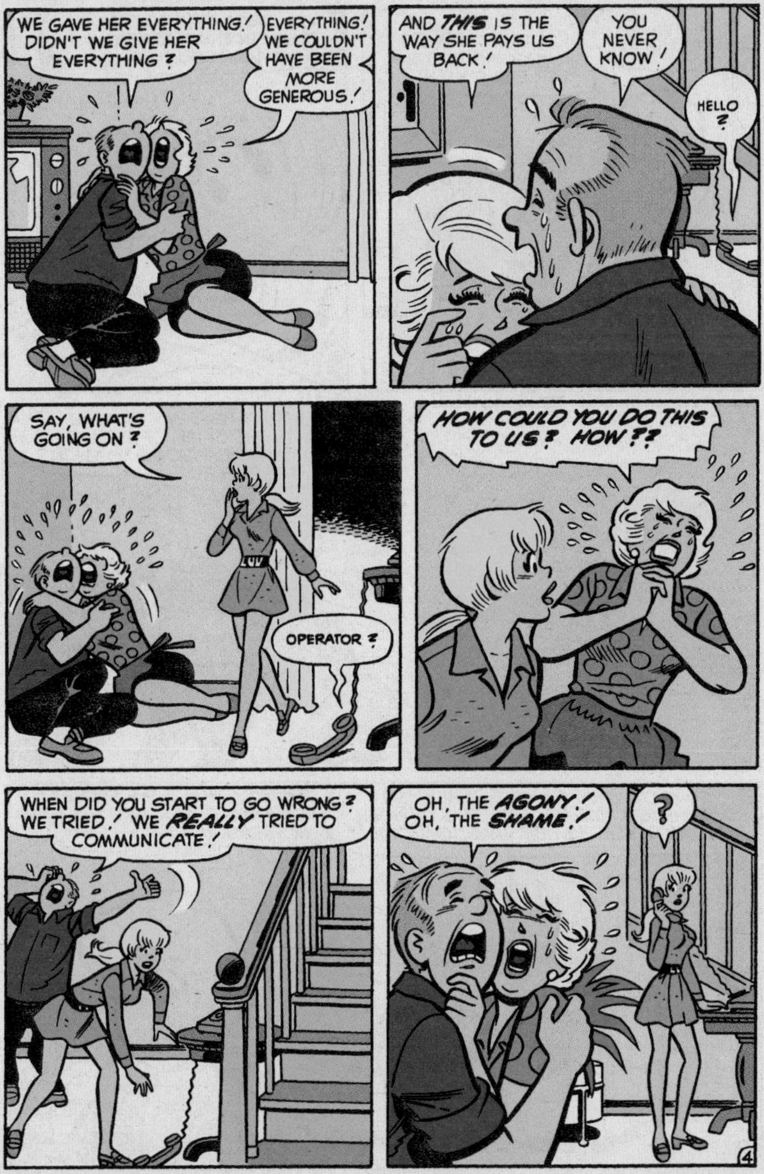

WE GAVE HER EVERYTHING! DIDN'T WE GIVE HER EVERYTHING?
EVERYTHING! WE COULDN'T HAVE BEEN MORE GENEROUS!
AND THIS IS THE WAY SHE PAYS US BACK!
YOU NEVER KNOW!
HELLO?
SAY, WHAT'S GOING ON?
OPERATOR?
HOW COULD YOU DO THIS TO US? HOW??
WHEN DID YOU START TO GO WRONG? WE TRIED! WE REALLY TRIED TO COMMUNICATE!
OH, THE AGONY! OH, THE SHAME!
?
4

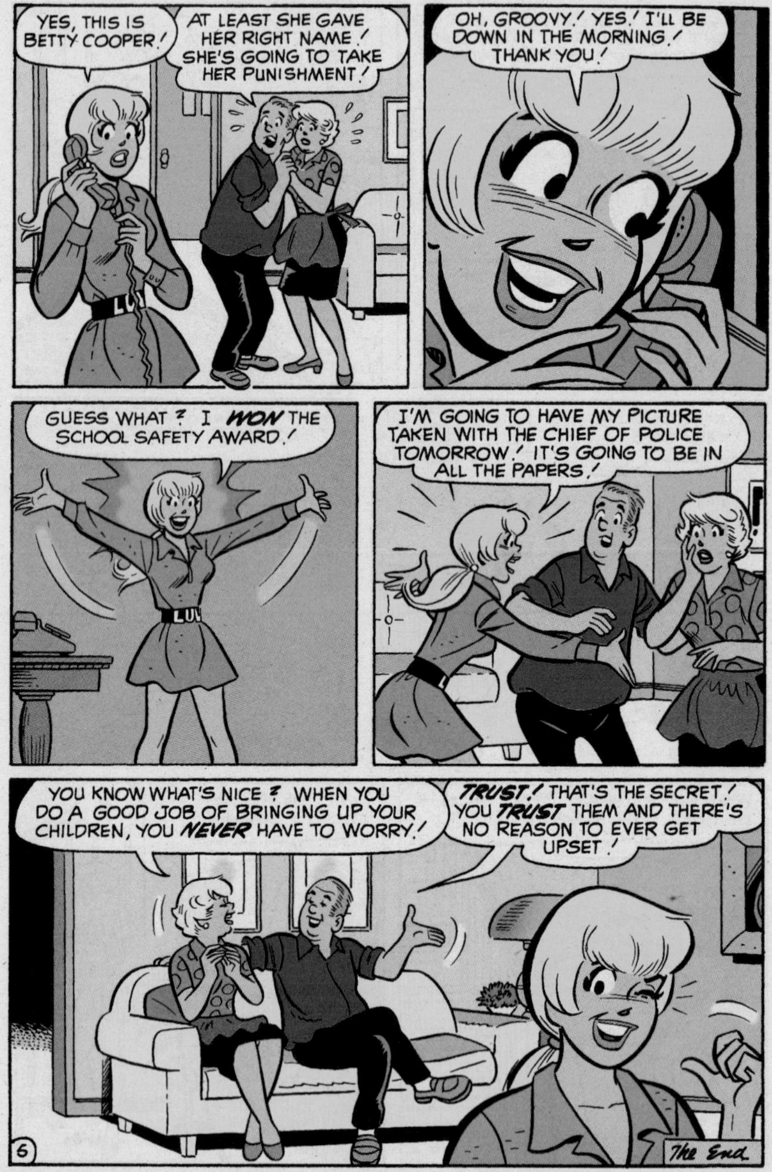
YES, THIS IS BETTY COOPER!
AT LEAST SHE GAVE HER RIGHT NAME! SHE'S GOING TO TAKE HER PUNISHMENT!
OH, GROOVY! YES! I'LL BE DOWN IN THE MORNING! THANK YOU!
GUESS WHAT? I WON THE SCHOOL SAFETY AWARD!
I'M GOING TO HAVE MY PICTURE TAKEN WITH THE CHIEF OF POLICE TOMORROW! IT'S GOING TO BE IN ALL THE PAPERS!
YOU KNOW WHAT'S NICE? WHEN YOU DO A GOOD JOB OF BRINGING UP YOUR CHILDREN, YOU NEVER HAVE TO WORRY!
TRUST! THAT'S THE SECRET! YOU TRUST THEM AND THERE'S NO REASON TO EVER GET UPSET!
6
The End

YIPES! THE WHOLE PLACE IS CRAWLING WITH ANNOYING
PESTS!
LOOK UP, DOWN, FORWARD BACKWARD AND FINALLY, DIAGONALLY FOR PESTS THAT ARE BUGGING ME!

BETTY'S FATHER...

MR. COOPER

					S	E	L	G	A	N	L
					P	C	N	F	D	E	A
M	O	E	N	O	I	E	I	R	E	T	N
I	E	M	M	H	D	K	S	C	N	A	R
B	C	I	T	I	E	A	H	M	S	U	N
U	S	O	U	S	R	M	R	V	A	I	E
R	M	S	A	T	M	O	Y	A	S	J	I
					W	D	W	A	S	P	H
					I	R	O	W	A	T	C
					I	S	H	C	A	O	R
					H	N	G	N	F	O	A
					R	F	A	U	U	N	I
						E	R	M	T	A	T
										T	E
										S	D

PEST LIST:
BEE · SPIDER
MOTH · LEECH · WORM
WASP · ROACH · ARCHIE

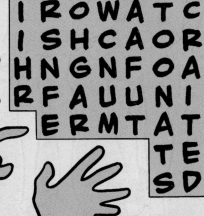

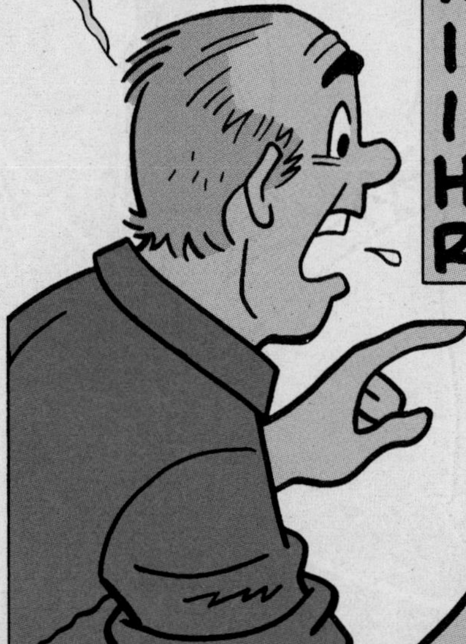

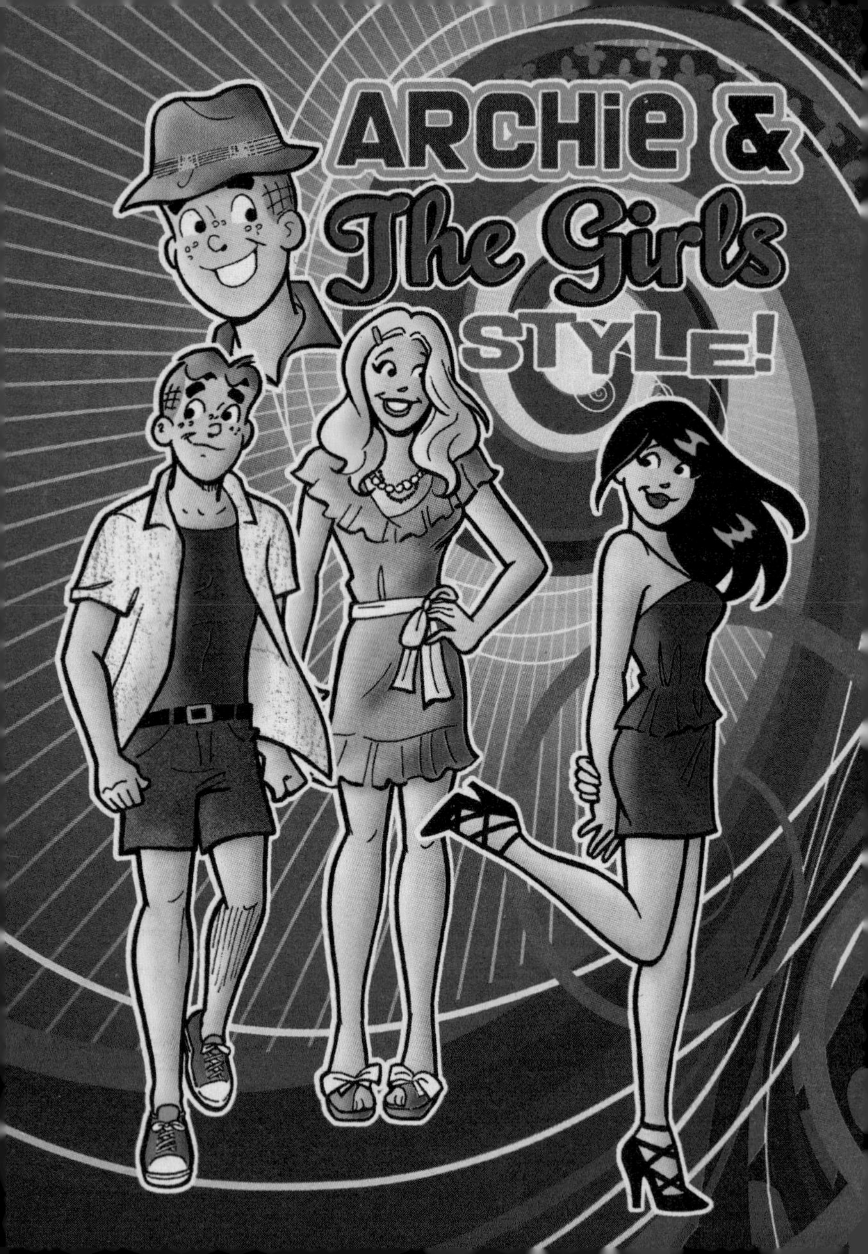
ARCHIE &
The Girls
STYLE!

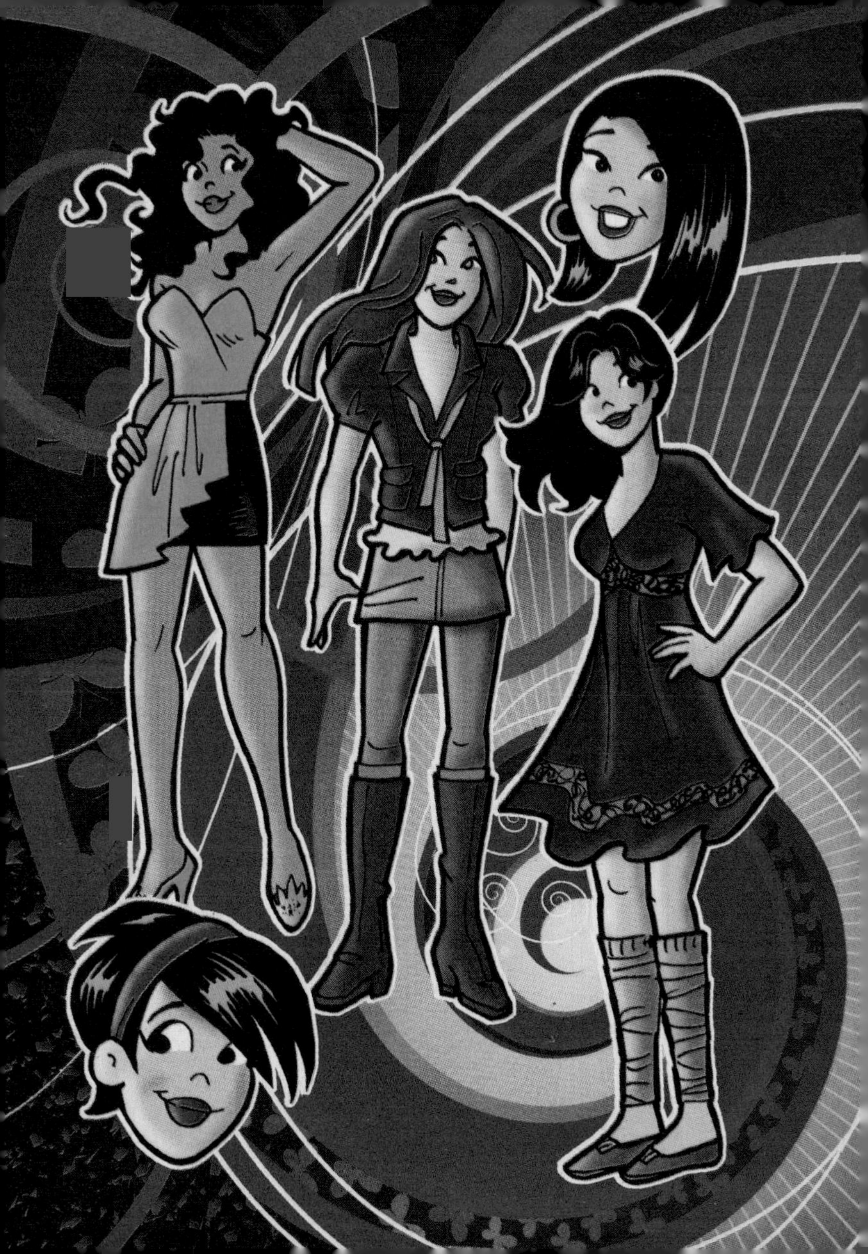

MR. LODGE IN FEE GLEE

LOOK AT *THAT!* VERONICA'S FRIENDS CLEANED OUT OUR FRIDGE AGAIN!

I WISH WE COULD DISCOURAGE THEM FROM USING OUR HOME AS A *HANGOUT!*

TOO BAD WE CAN'T CHARGE THEM A *PARKING FEE!*

WHO SAYS WE CAN'T?

?

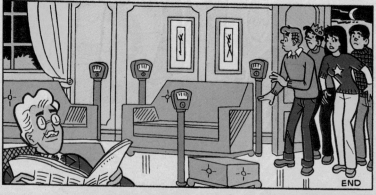

END

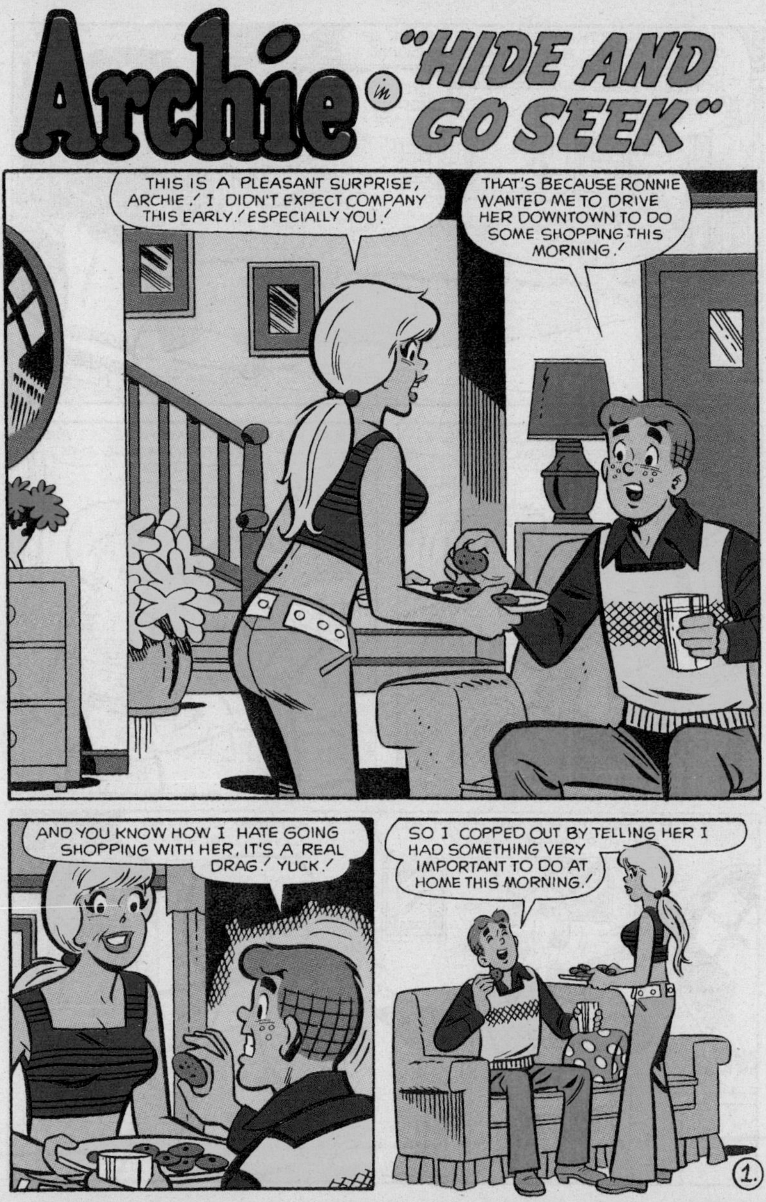
Archie in "HIDE AND GO SEEK"
THIS IS A PLEASANT SURPRISE, ARCHIE! I DIDN'T EXPECT COMPANY THIS EARLY! ESPECIALLY YOU!
THAT'S BECAUSE RONNIE WANTED ME TO DRIVE HER DOWNTOWN TO DO SOME SHOPPING THIS MORNING!
AND YOU KNOW HOW I HATE GOING SHOPPING WITH HER, IT'S A REAL DRAG! YUCK!
SO I COPPED OUT BY TELLING HER I HAD SOMETHING VERY IMPORTANT TO DO AT HOME THIS MORNING!
1.

Script: Al Hartley / Pencils: Stan Goldberg / Inks: Jon D'Agostino / Letters: Bill Yoshida

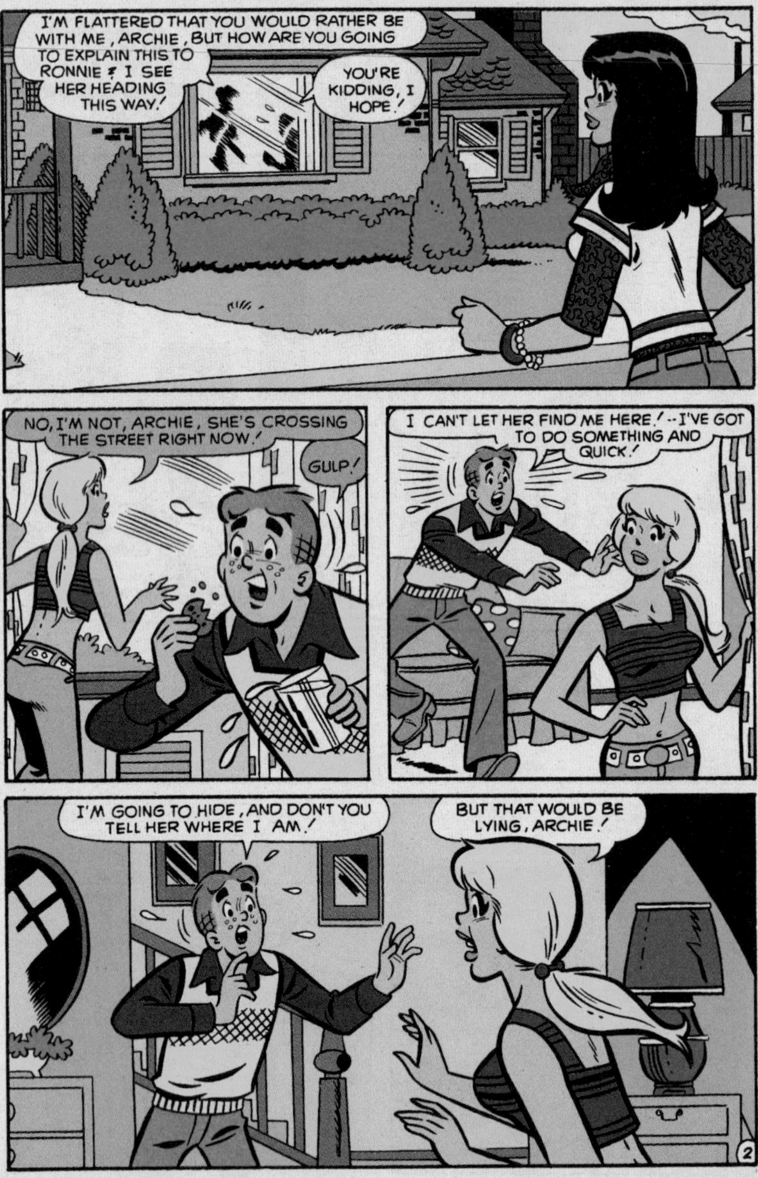
I'M FLATTERED THAT YOU WOULD RATHER BE WITH ME, ARCHIE, BUT HOW ARE YOU GOING TO EXPLAIN THIS TO RONNIE ? I SEE HER HEADING THIS WAY!
YOU'RE KIDDING, I HOPE!
NO, I'M NOT, ARCHIE, SHE'S CROSSING THE STREET RIGHT NOW!
GULP!
I CAN'T LET HER FIND ME HERE! -- I'VE GOT TO DO SOMETHING AND QUICK!
I'M GOING TO HIDE, AND DON'T YOU TELL HER WHERE I AM!
BUT THAT WOULD BE LYING, ARCHIE!
2

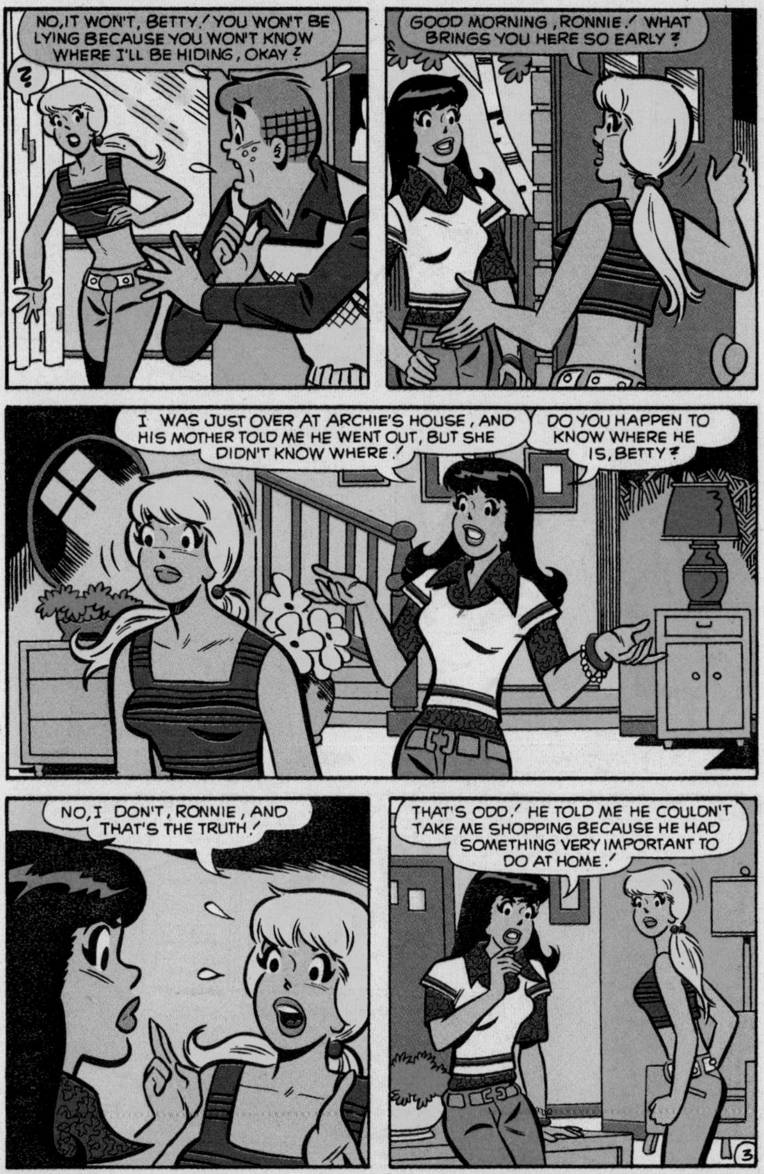
NO, IT WON'T, BETTY! YOU WON'T BE LYING BECAUSE YOU WON'T KNOW WHERE I'LL BE HIDING, OKAY?
?
GOOD MORNING, RONNIE! WHAT BRINGS YOU HERE SO EARLY?
I WAS JUST OVER AT ARCHIE'S HOUSE, AND HIS MOTHER TOLD ME HE WENT OUT, BUT SHE DIDN'T KNOW WHERE!
DO YOU HAPPEN TO KNOW WHERE HE IS, BETTY?
NO, I DON'T, RONNIE, AND THAT'S THE TRUTH!
THAT'S ODD! HE TOLD ME HE COULDN'T TAKE ME SHOPPING BECAUSE HE HAD SOMETHING VERY IMPORTANT TO DO AT HOME!
3

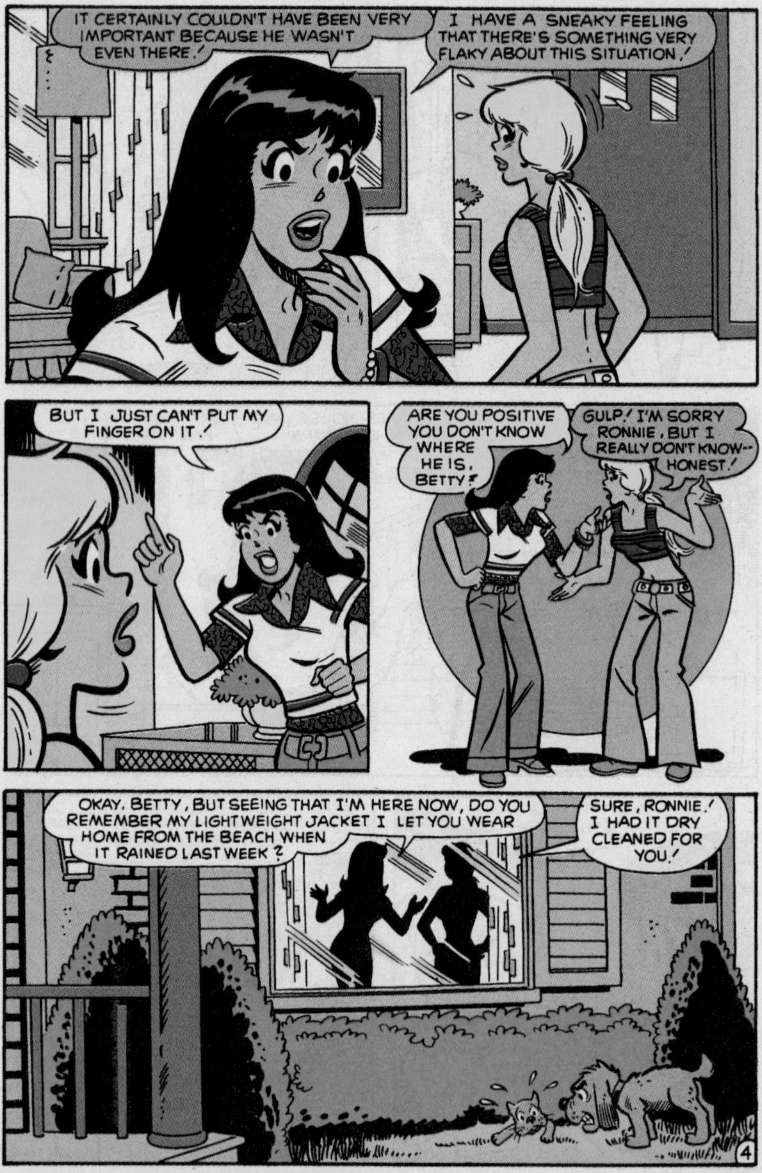
IT CERTAINLY COULDN'T HAVE BEEN VERY IMPORTANT BECAUSE HE WASN'T EVEN THERE!
I HAVE A SNEAKY FEELING THAT THERE'S SOMETHING VERY FLAKY ABOUT THIS SITUATION!
BUT I JUST CAN'T PUT MY FINGER ON IT!
ARE YOU POSITIVE YOU DON'T KNOW WHERE HE IS, BETTY?
GULP! I'M SORRY RONNIE, BUT I REALLY DON'T KNOW-- HONEST!
OKAY, BETTY, BUT SEEING THAT I'M HERE NOW, DO YOU REMEMBER MY LIGHTWEIGHT JACKET I LET YOU WEAR HOME FROM THE BEACH WHEN IT RAINED LAST WEEK?
SURE, RONNIE! I HAD IT DRY CLEANED FOR YOU!
4

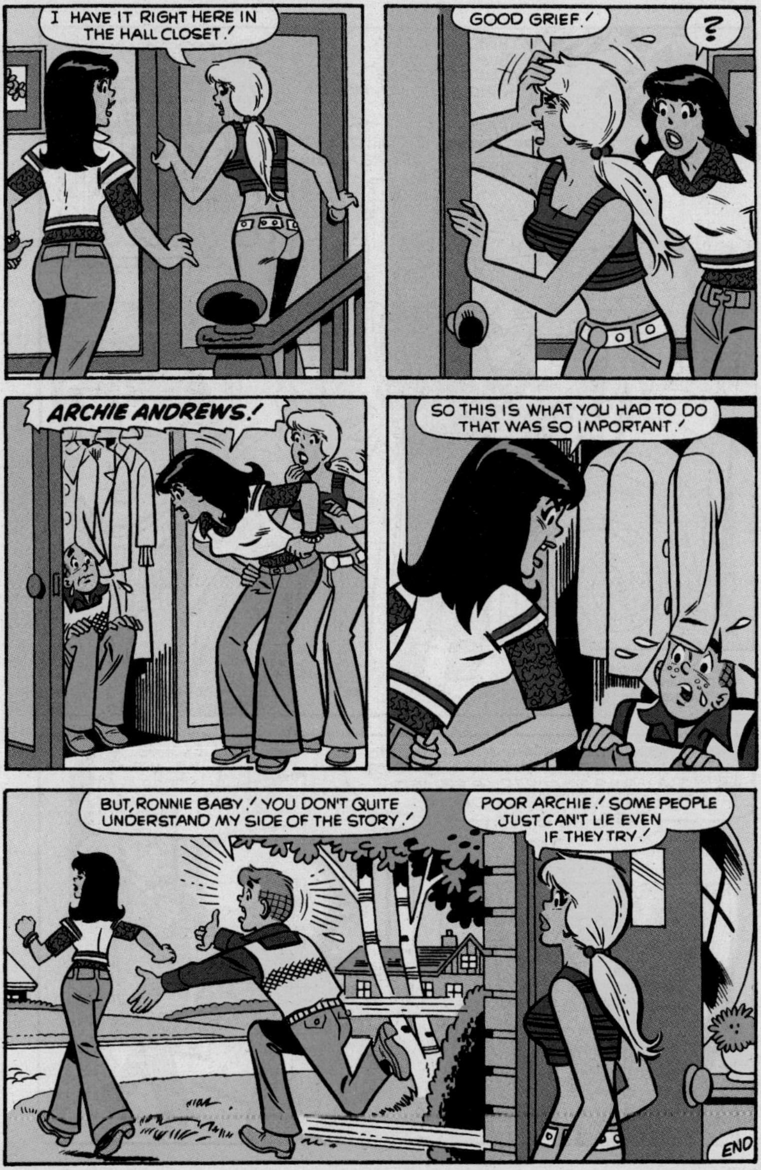
I HAVE IT RIGHT HERE IN THE HALL CLOSET!
GOOD GRIEF!
?
ARCHIE ANDREWS!
SO THIS IS WHAT YOU HAD TO DO THAT WAS SO IMPORTANT!
BUT, RONNIE BABY! YOU DON'T QUITE UNDERSTAND MY SIDE OF THE STORY!
POOR ARCHIE! SOME PEOPLE JUST CAN'T LIE EVEN IF THEY TRY!
END

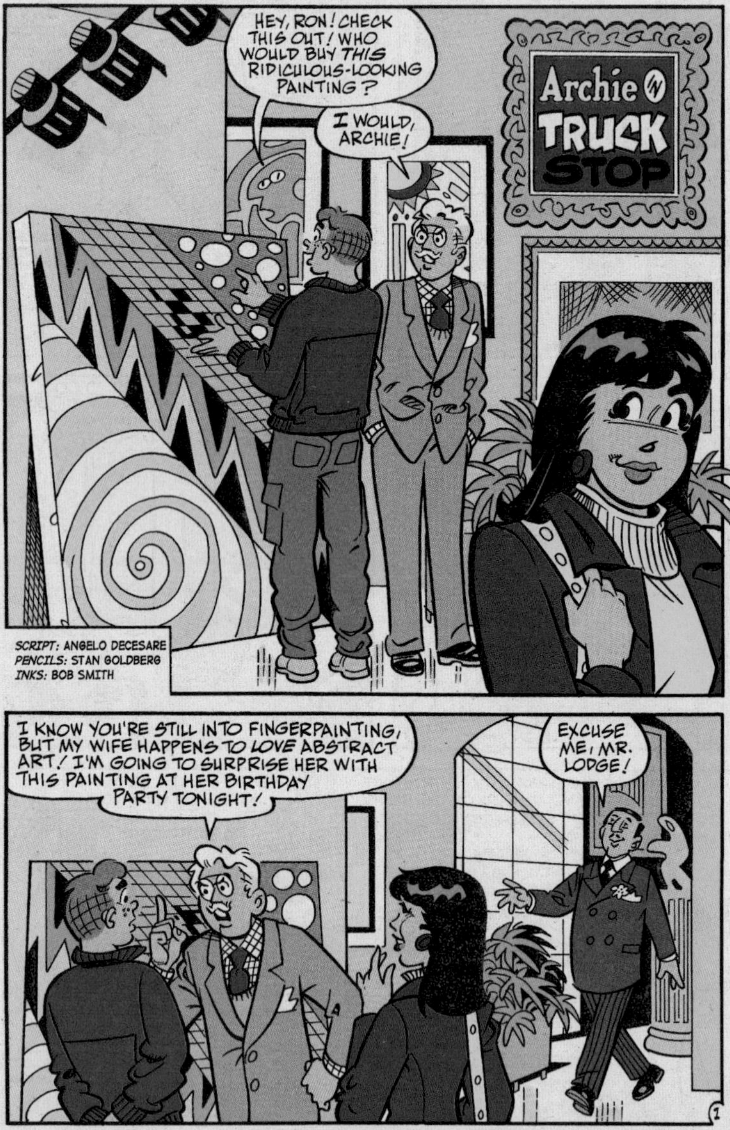
HEY, RON! CHECK THIS OUT! WHO WOULD BUY THIS RIDICULOUS-LOOKING PAINTING?
I WOULD, ARCHIE!
Archie IN TRUCK STOP
SCRIPT: ANGELO DECESARE
PENCILS: STAN GOLDBERG
INKS: BOB SMITH
I KNOW YOU'RE STILL INTO FINGERPAINTING, BUT MY WIFE HAPPENS TO LOVE ABSTRACT ART! I'M GOING TO SURPRISE HER WITH THIS PAINTING AT HER BIRTHDAY PARTY TONIGHT!
EXCUSE ME, MR. LODGE!
1

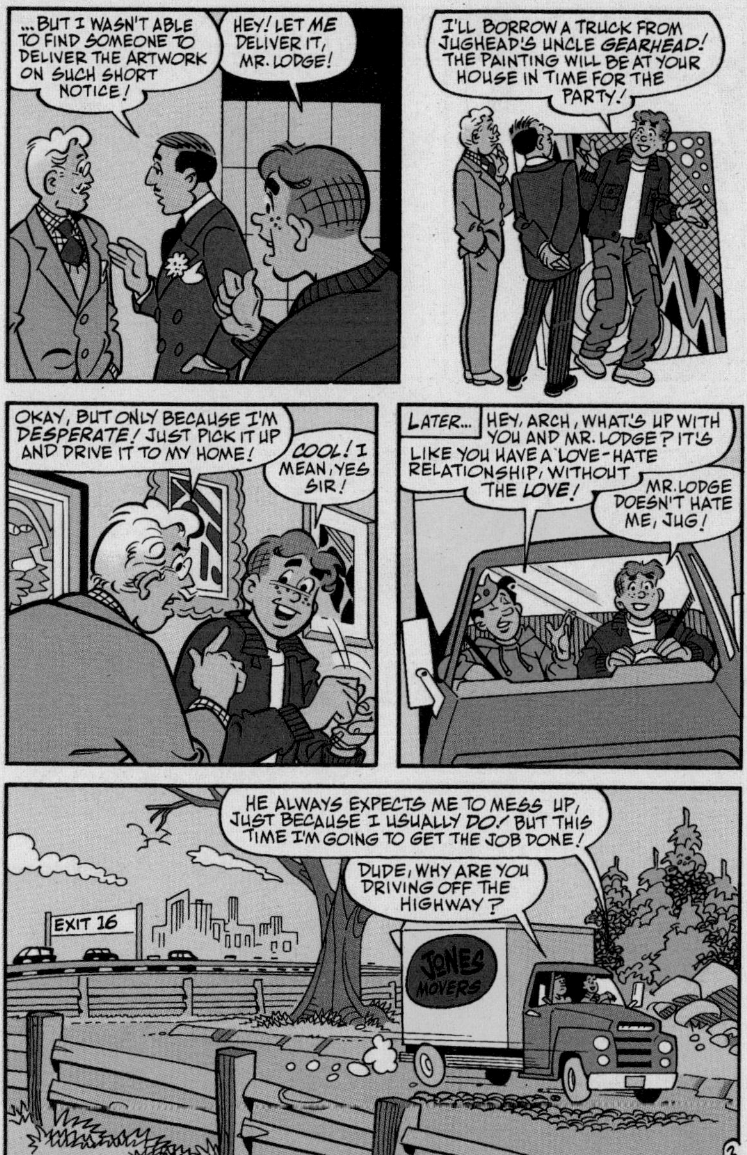
...BUT I WASN'T ABLE TO FIND SOMEONE TO DELIVER THE ARTWORK ON SUCH SHORT NOTICE!
HEY! LET ME DELIVER IT, MR. LODGE!
I'LL BORROW A TRUCK FROM JUGHEAD'S UNCLE GEARHEAD! THE PAINTING WILL BE AT YOUR HOUSE IN TIME FOR THE PARTY!
OKAY, BUT ONLY BECAUSE I'M DESPERATE! JUST PICK IT UP AND DRIVE IT TO MY HOME!
COOL! I MEAN, YES SIR!
LATER...
HEY, ARCH, WHAT'S UP WITH YOU AND MR. LODGE? IT'S LIKE YOU HAVE A LOVE-HATE RELATIONSHIP, WITHOUT THE LOVE!
MR. LODGE DOESN'T HATE ME, JUG!
HE ALWAYS EXPECTS ME TO MESS UP, JUST BECAUSE I USUALLY DO! BUT THIS TIME I'M GOING TO GET THE JOB DONE!
DUDE, WHY ARE YOU DRIVING OFF THE HIGHWAY?
EXIT 16
JONES MOVERS
2

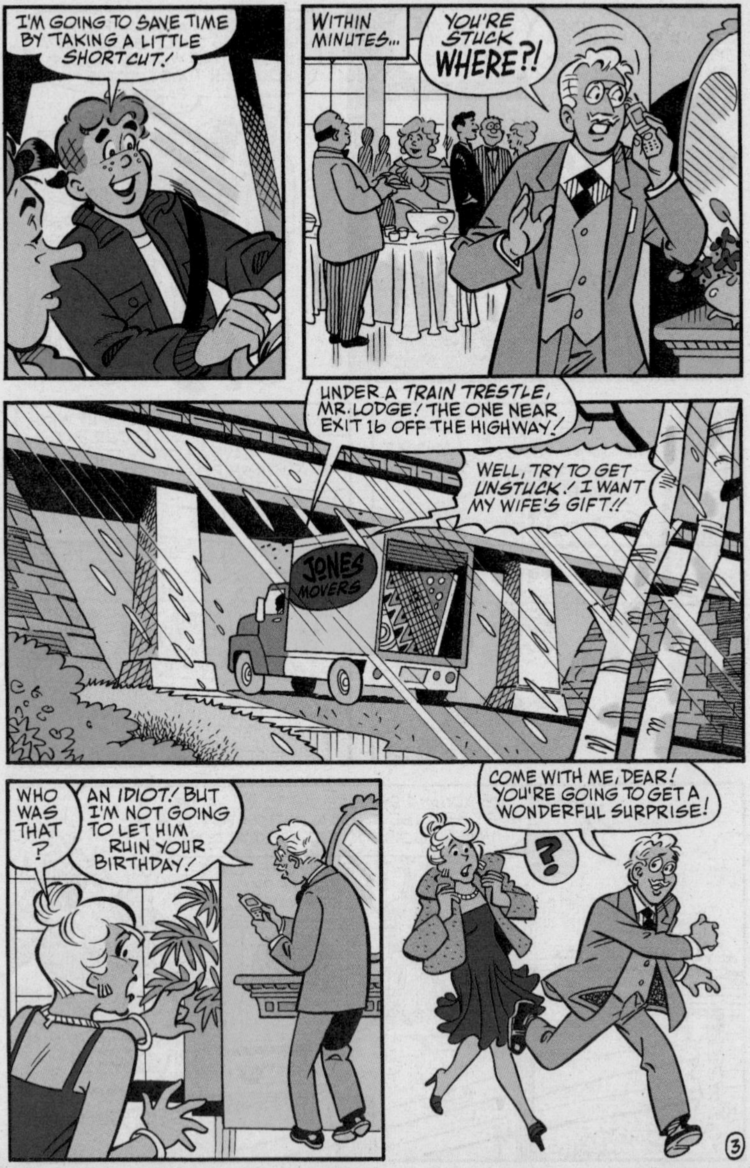
I'M GOING TO SAVE TIME BY TAKING A LITTLE SHORTCUT!
WITHIN MINUTES...
YOU'RE STUCK WHERE?!
UNDER A TRAIN TRESTLE, MR. LODGE! THE ONE NEAR EXIT 16 OFF THE HIGHWAY!
WELL, TRY TO GET UNSTUCK! I WANT MY WIFE'S GIFT!!
JONES MOVERS
WHO WAS THAT?
AN IDIOT! BUT I'M NOT GOING TO LET HIM RUIN YOUR BIRTHDAY!
COME WITH ME, DEAR! YOU'RE GOING TO GET A WONDERFUL SURPRISE!
?
3

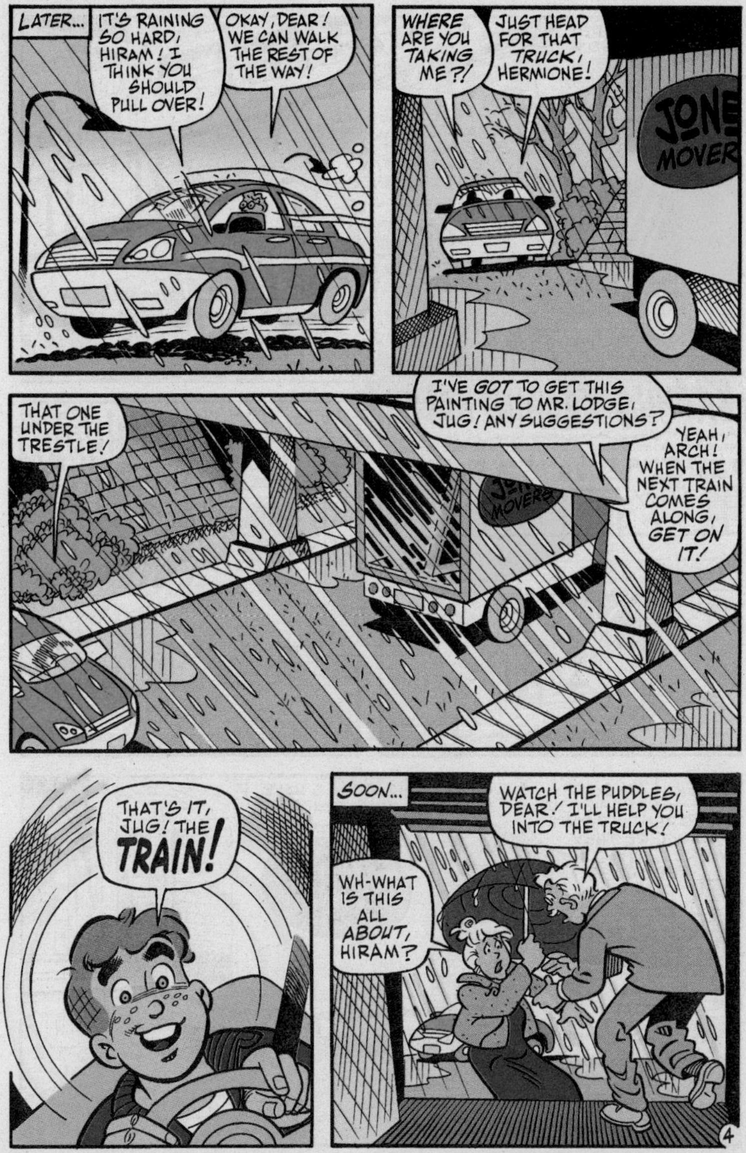
LATER...
IT'S RAINING SO HARD, HIRAM! I THINK YOU SHOULD PULL OVER!
OKAY, DEAR! WE CAN WALK THE REST OF THE WAY!
WHERE ARE YOU TAKING ME?!
JUST HEAD FOR THAT TRUCK, HERMIONE!
JONE
MOVER
THAT ONE UNDER THE TRESTLE!
I'VE GOT TO GET THIS PAINTING TO MR. LODGE, JUG! ANY SUGGESTIONS?
YEAH, ARCH! WHEN THE NEXT TRAIN COMES ALONG, GET ON IT!
THAT'S IT, JUG! THE TRAIN!
SOON...
WATCH THE PUDDLES, DEAR! I'LL HELP YOU INTO THE TRUCK!
WH-WHAT IS THIS ALL ABOUT, HIRAM?
4

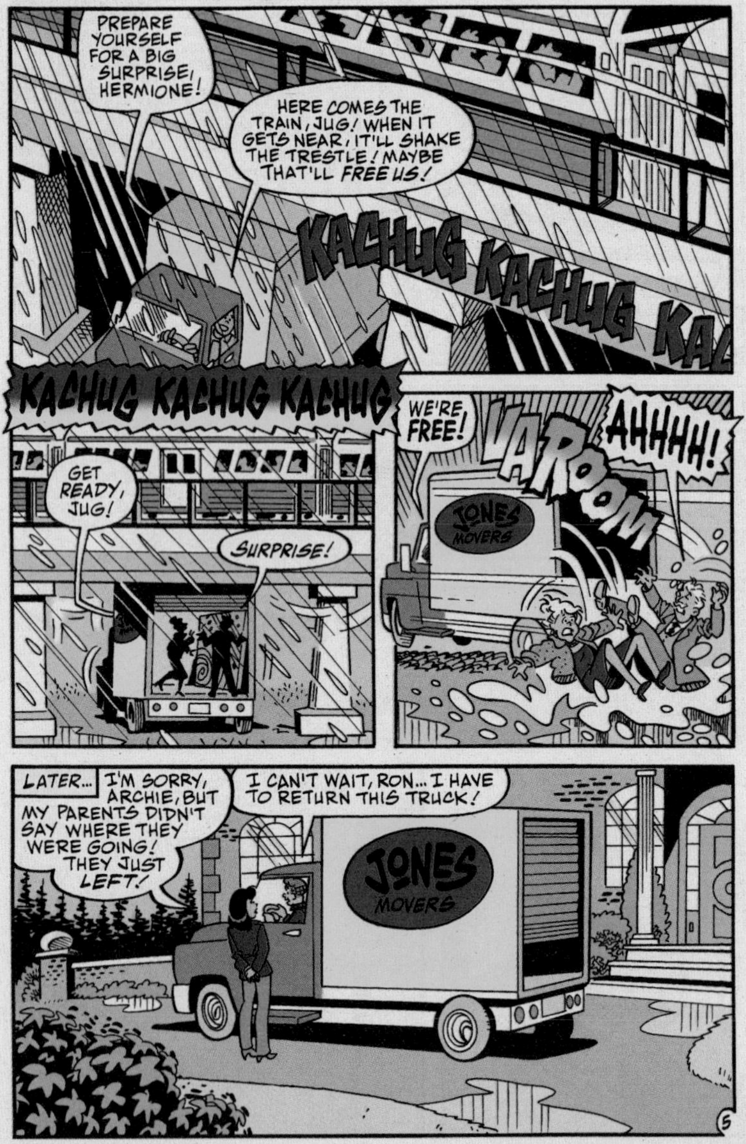
PREPARE YOURSELF FOR A BIG SURPRISE, HERMIONE!
HERE COMES THE TRAIN, JUG! WHEN IT GETS NEAR, IT'LL SHAKE THE TRESTLE! MAYBE THAT'LL FREE US!
KACHUG KACHUG KA
KACHUG KACHUG KACHUG
GET READY, JUG!
SURPRISE!
WE'RE FREE!
VAROOM
AHHHH!
JONES MOVERS
LATER...
I'M SORRY, ARCHIE, BUT MY PARENTS DIDN'T SAY WHERE THEY WERE GOING! THEY JUST LEFT!
I CAN'T WAIT, RON... I HAVE TO RETURN THIS TRUCK!
JONES MOVERS
5

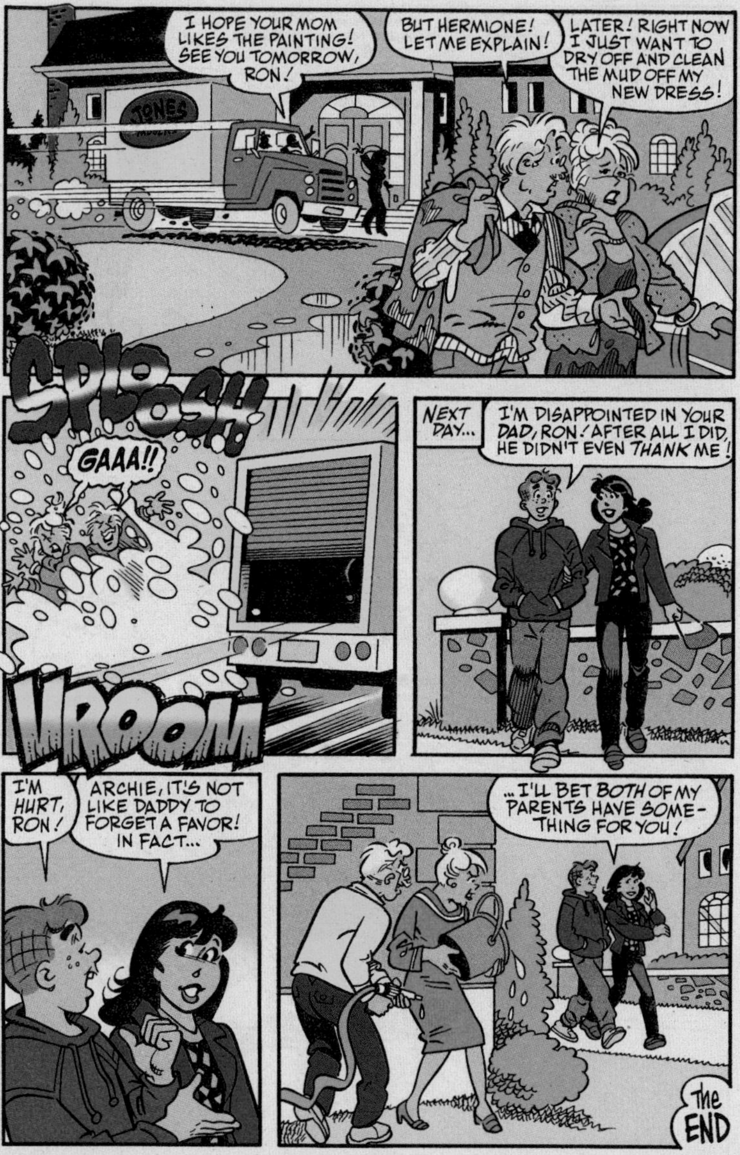
I HOPE YOUR MOM LIKES THE PAINTING! SEE YOU TOMORROW, RON!
BUT HERMIONE! LET ME EXPLAIN!
LATER! RIGHT NOW I JUST WANT TO DRY OFF AND CLEAN THE MUD OFF MY NEW DRESS!
SPLOOSH
GAAA!!
VROOM
NEXT DAY...
I'M DISAPPOINTED IN YOUR DAD, RON! AFTER ALL I DID, HE DIDN'T EVEN THANK ME!
I'M HURT, RON!
ARCHIE, IT'S NOT LIKE DADDY TO FORGET A FAVOR! IN FACT...
...I'LL BET BOTH OF MY PARENTS HAVE SOMETHING FOR YOU!
The END

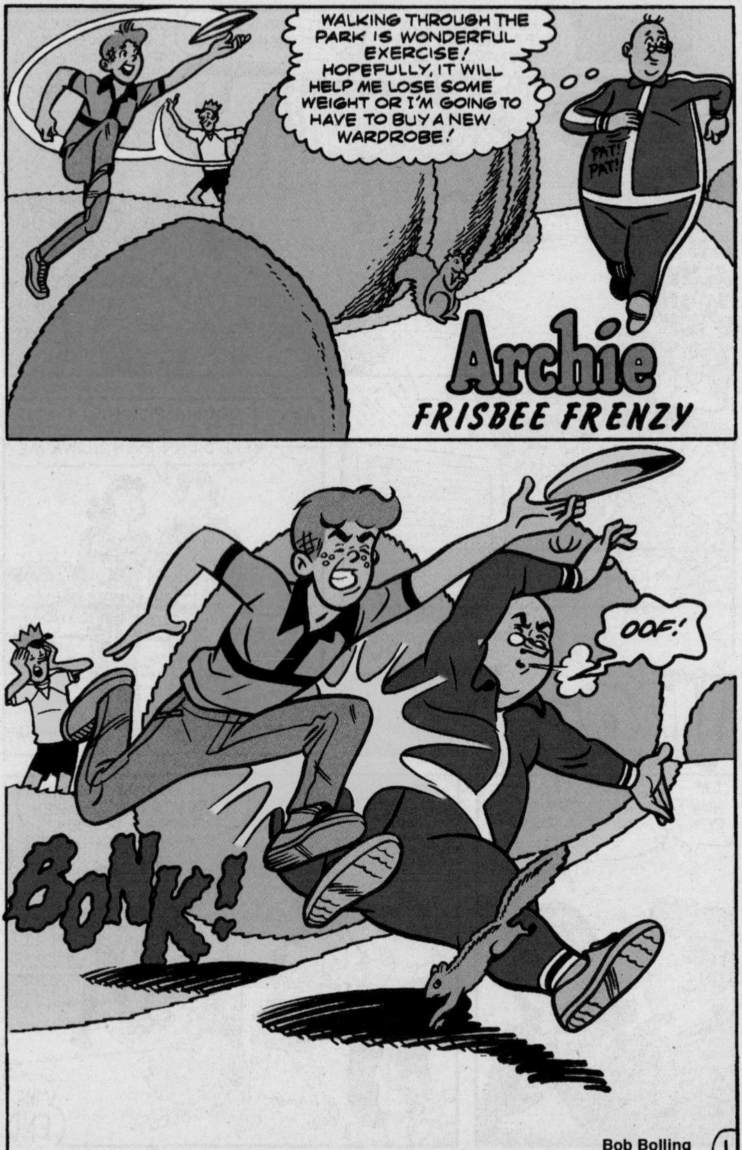
WALKING THROUGH THE PARK IS WONDERFUL EXERCISE! HOPEFULLY, IT WILL HELP ME LOSE SOME WEIGHT OR I'M GOING TO HAVE TO BUY A NEW WARDROBE!
PAT! PAT!
Archie
FRISBEE FRENZY
OOF!
BONK!
Bob Bolling

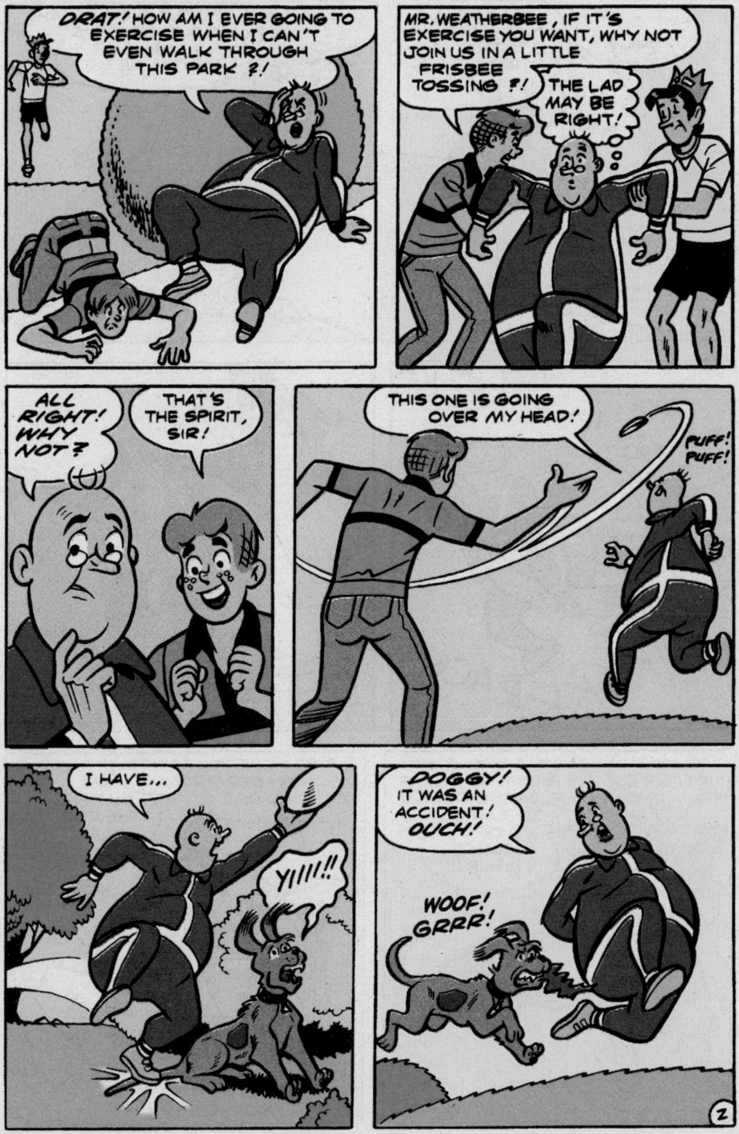
DRAT! HOW AM I EVER GOING TO EXERCISE WHEN I CAN'T EVEN WALK THROUGH THIS PARK ?!
MR. WEATHERBEE, IF IT'S EXERCISE YOU WANT, WHY NOT JOIN US IN A LITTLE FRISBEE TOSSING ?!
THE LAD MAY BE RIGHT!
ALL RIGHT! WHY NOT?
THAT'S THE SPIRIT, SIR!
THIS ONE IS GOING OVER MY HEAD!
PUFF! PUFF!
I HAVE...
YIIII!!
DOGGY! IT WAS AN ACCIDENT! OUCH!
WOOF! GRRR!
2

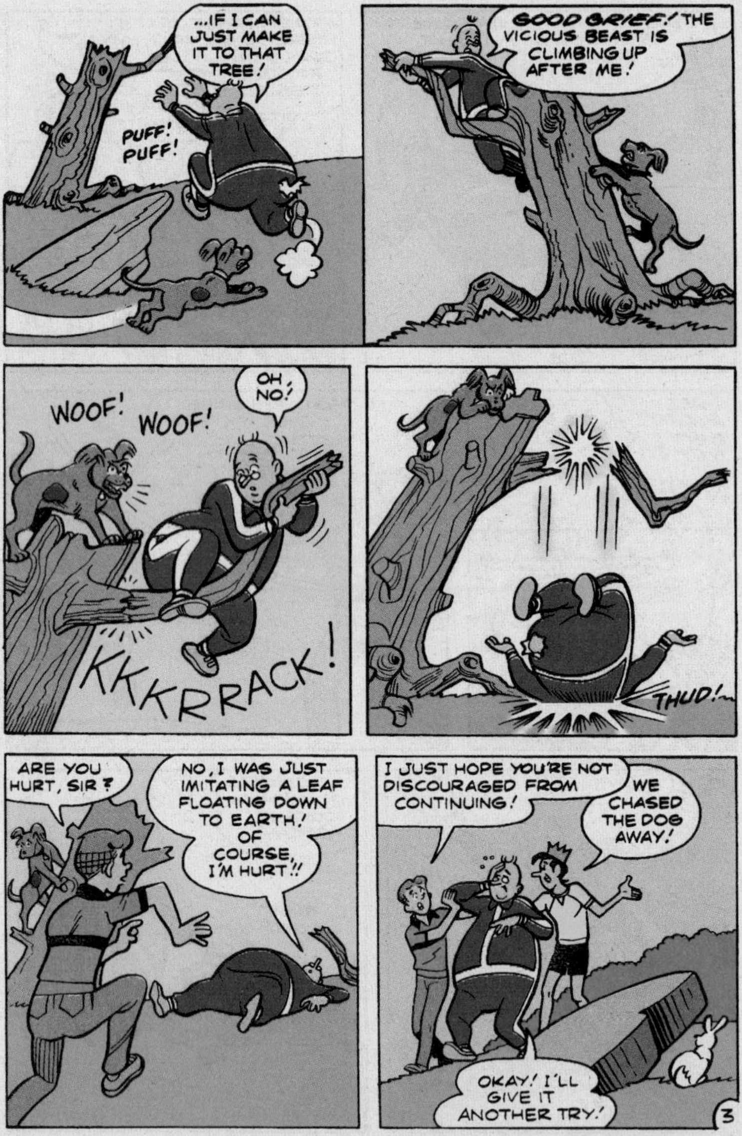
...IF I CAN JUST MAKE IT TO THAT TREE!
PUFF! PUFF!
GOOD GRIEF! THE VICIOUS BEAST IS CLIMBING UP AFTER ME!
WOOF! WOOF!
OH, NO!
KKKRRACK!
THUD!
ARE YOU HURT, SIR?
NO, I WAS JUST IMITATING A LEAF FLOATING DOWN TO EARTH! OF COURSE, I'M HURT!!
I JUST HOPE YOU'RE NOT DISCOURAGED FROM CONTINUING!
WE CHASED THE DOG AWAY!
OKAY! I'LL GIVE IT ANOTHER TRY!
3

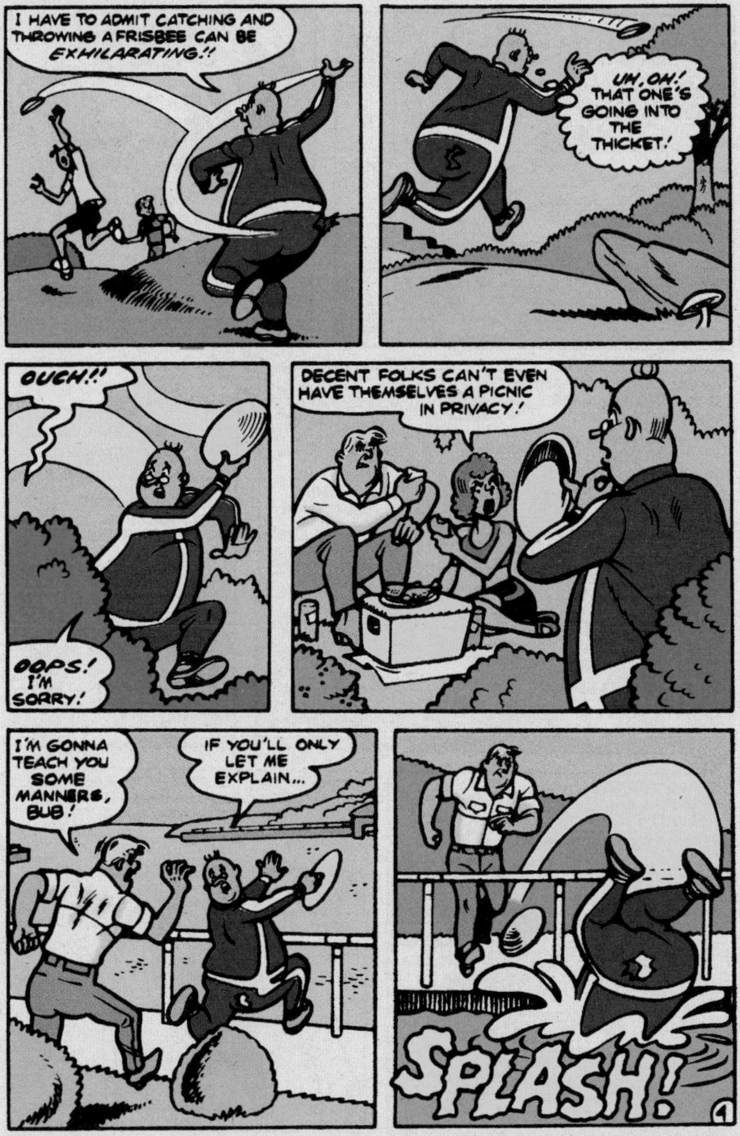

I HAVE TO ADMIT CATCHING AND THROWING A FRISBEE CAN BE EXHILARATING!!
UH,OH! THAT ONE'S GOING INTO THE THICKET!
OUCH!!
OOPS! I'M SORRY!
DECENT FOLKS CAN'T EVEN HAVE THEMSELVES A PICNIC IN PRIVACY!
I'M GONNA TEACH YOU SOME MANNERS, BUB!
IF YOU'LL ONLY LET ME EXPLAIN...
SPLASH!

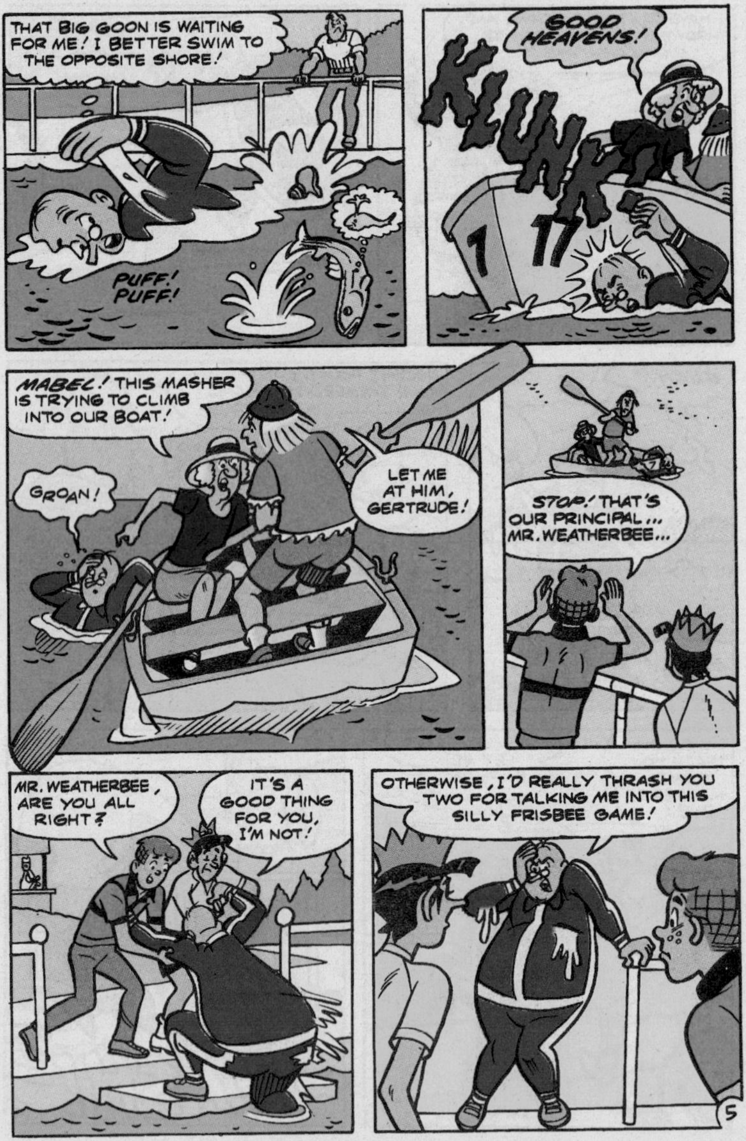
THAT BIG GOON IS WAITING FOR ME! I BETTER SWIM TO THE OPPOSITE SHORE!
PUFF! PUFF!
GOOD HEAVENS!
KLUNK
MABEL! THIS MASHER IS TRYING TO CLIMB INTO OUR BOAT!
GROAN!
LET ME AT HIM, GERTRUDE!
STOP! THAT'S OUR PRINCIPAL... MR. WEATHERBEE...
MR. WEATHERBEE, ARE YOU ALL RIGHT?
IT'S A GOOD THING FOR YOU, I'M NOT!
OTHERWISE, I'D REALLY THRASH YOU TWO FOR TALKING ME INTO THIS SILLY FRISBEE GAME!
5

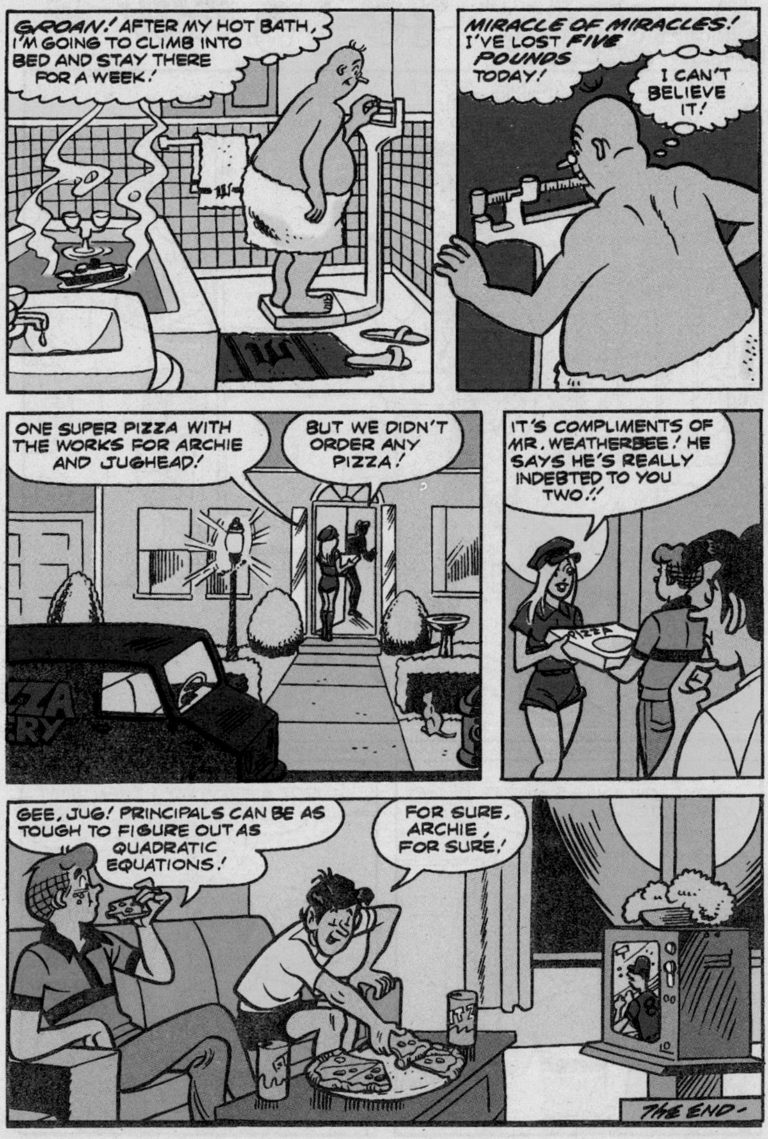
GROAN! AFTER MY HOT BATH, I'M GOING TO CLIMB INTO BED AND STAY THERE FOR A WEEK!
MIRACLE OF MIRACLES! I'VE LOST FIVE POUNDS TODAY!
I CAN'T BELIEVE IT!
ONE SUPER PIZZA WITH THE WORKS FOR ARCHIE AND JUGHEAD!
BUT WE DIDN'T ORDER ANY PIZZA!
IT'S COMPLIMENTS OF MR. WEATHERBEE! HE SAYS HE'S REALLY INDEBTED TO YOU TWO!!
PIZZA
GEE, JUG! PRINCIPALS CAN BE AS TOUGH TO FIGURE OUT AS QUADRATIC EQUATIONS!
FOR SURE, ARCHIE, FOR SURE!
THE END-

Archie in YO-YO GUY

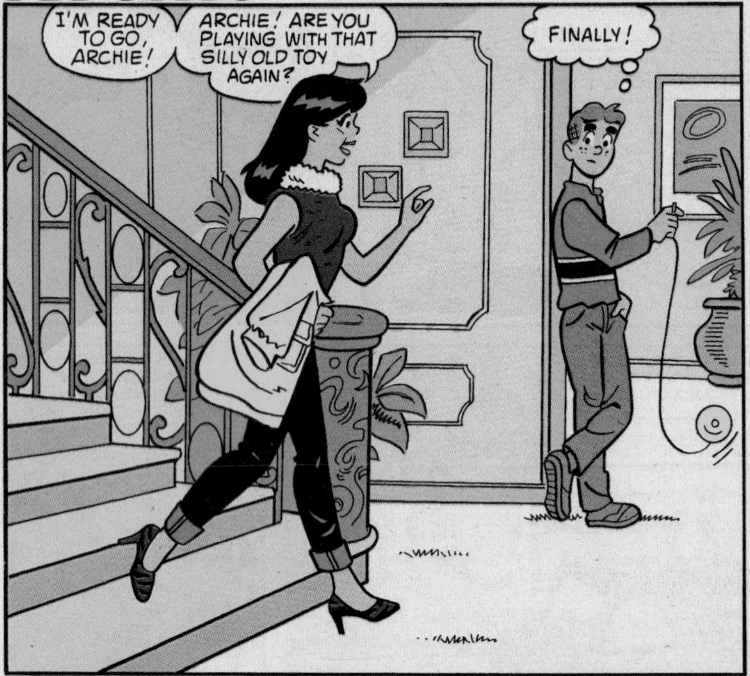

I'M READY TO GO, ARCHIE!
ARCHIE! ARE YOU PLAYING WITH THAT SILLY OLD TOY AGAIN?
FINALLY!

Script: Mike Pellowski / Pencils: Dan DeCarlo / Inks: Henry Scarpelli / Letters: Bill Yoshida

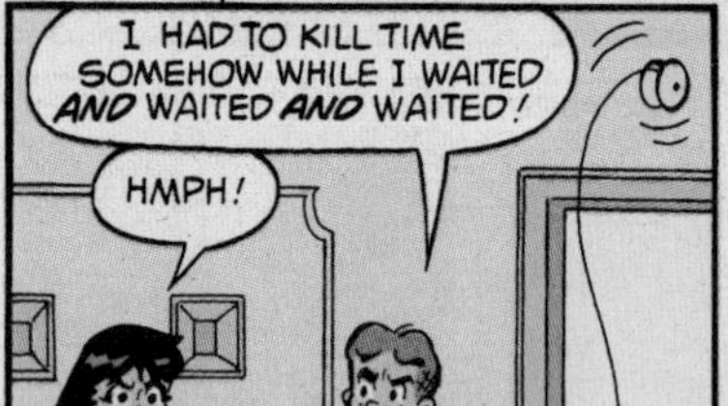

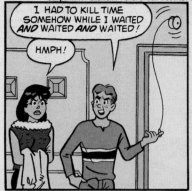

I HAD TO KILL TIME SOMEHOW WHILE I WAITED *AND* WAITED *AND* WAITED!
HMPH!

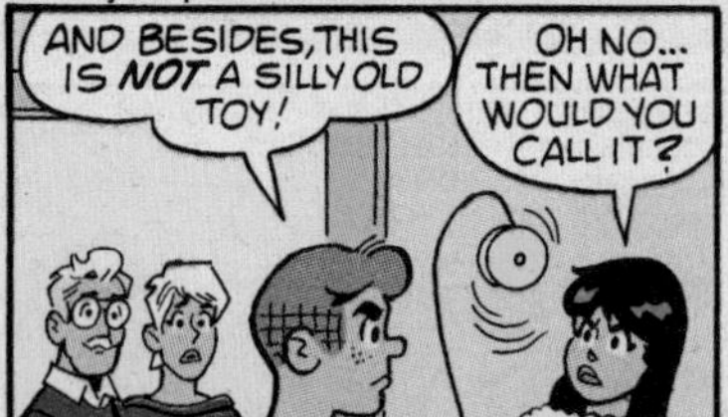

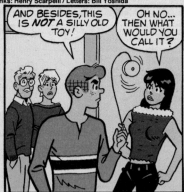

AND BESIDES, THIS IS *NOT* A SILLY OLD TOY!
OH NO... THEN WHAT WOULD YOU CALL IT?

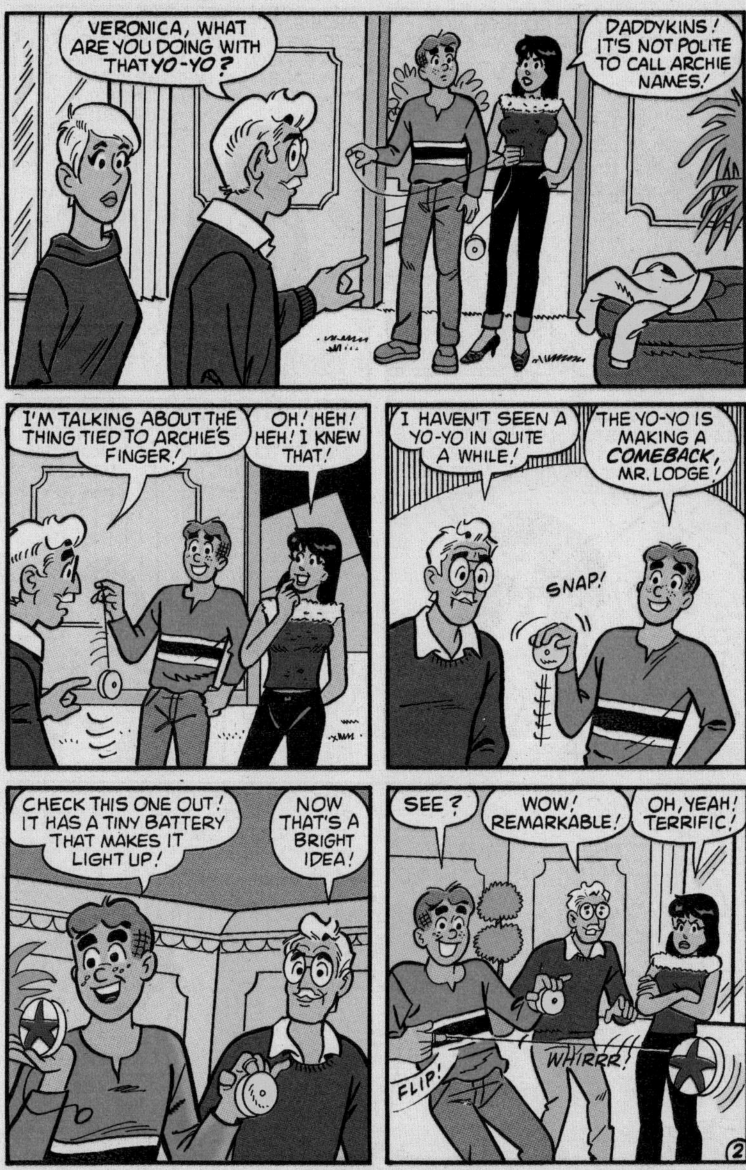
VERONICA, WHAT ARE YOU DOING WITH THAT YO-YO?
DADDYKINS! IT'S NOT POLITE TO CALL ARCHIE NAMES!
I'M TALKING ABOUT THE THING TIED TO ARCHIE'S FINGER!
OH! HEH! HEH! I KNEW THAT!
I HAVEN'T SEEN A YO-YO IN QUITE A WHILE!
THE YO-YO IS MAKING A COMEBACK, MR. LODGE!
SNAP!
CHECK THIS ONE OUT! IT HAS A TINY BATTERY THAT MAKES IT LIGHT UP!
NOW THAT'S A BRIGHT IDEA!
SEE?
WOW! REMARKABLE!
OH, YEAH! TERRIFIC!
WHIRRR!
FLIP!
2

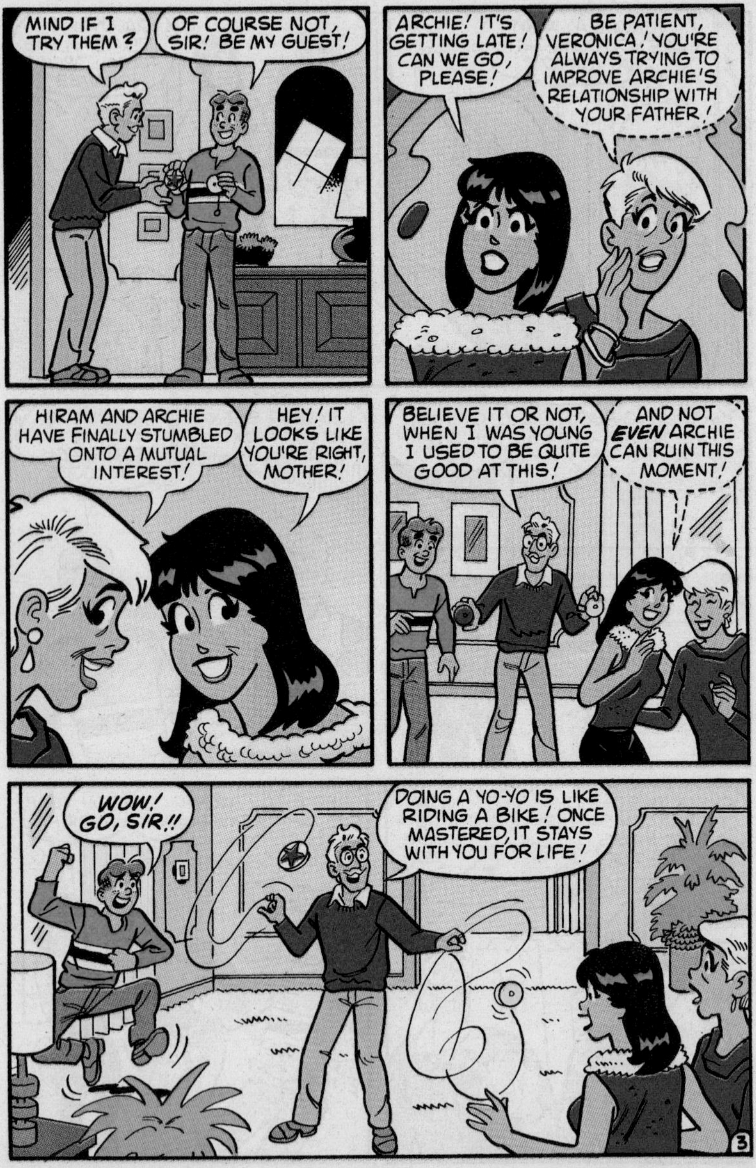
MIND IF I TRY THEM?
OF COURSE NOT, SIR! BE MY GUEST!
ARCHIE! IT'S GETTING LATE! CAN WE GO, PLEASE!
BE PATIENT, VERONICA! YOU'RE ALWAYS TRYING TO IMPROVE ARCHIE'S RELATIONSHIP WITH YOUR FATHER!
HIRAM AND ARCHIE HAVE FINALLY STUMBLED ONTO A MUTUAL INTEREST!
HEY! IT LOOKS LIKE YOU'RE RIGHT, MOTHER!
BELIEVE IT OR NOT, WHEN I WAS YOUNG I USED TO BE QUITE GOOD AT THIS!
AND NOT EVEN ARCHIE CAN RUIN THIS MOMENT!
WOW! GO, SIR!!
DOING A YO-YO IS LIKE RIDING A BIKE! ONCE MASTERED, IT STAYS WITH YOU FOR LIFE!
3

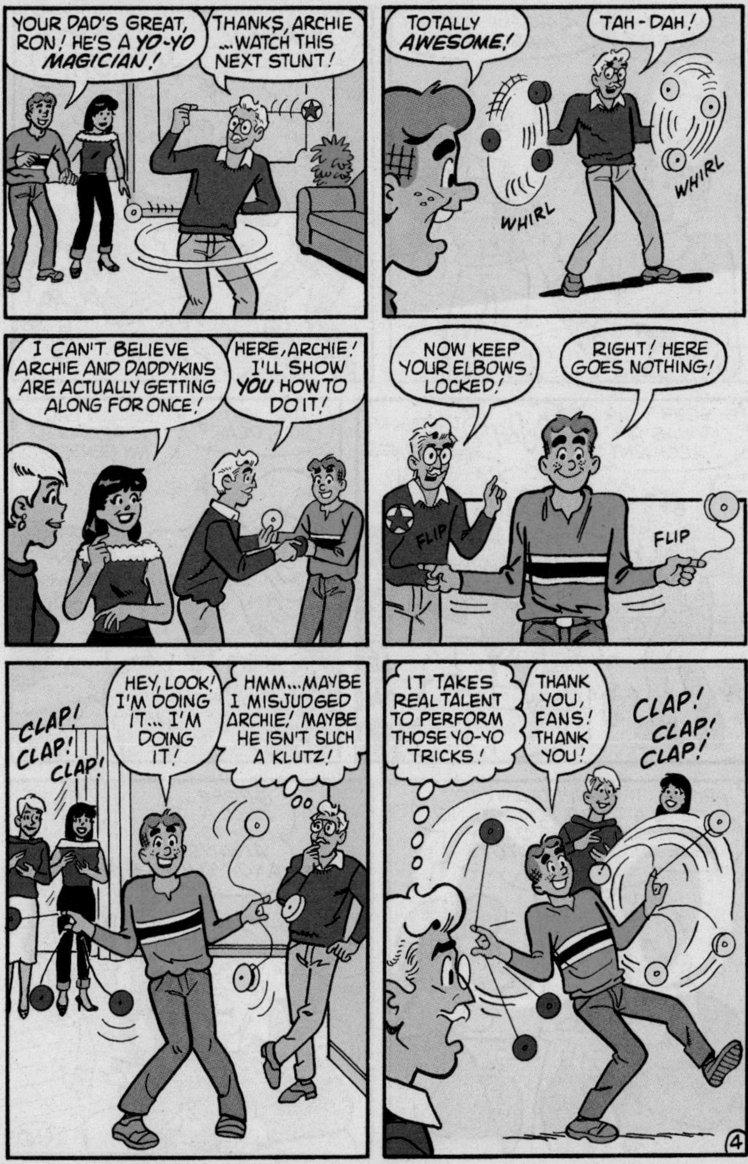
YOUR DAD'S GREAT, RON! HE'S A YO-YO MAGICIAN!
THANKS, ARCHIE ...WATCH THIS NEXT STUNT!
TOTALLY AWESOME!
TAH-DAH!
WHIRL
WHIRL
I CAN'T BELIEVE ARCHIE AND DADDYKINS ARE ACTUALLY GETTING ALONG FOR ONCE!
HERE, ARCHIE! I'LL SHOW YOU HOW TO DO IT!
NOW KEEP YOUR ELBOWS LOCKED!
RIGHT! HERE GOES NOTHING!
FLIP
FLIP
CLAP! CLAP! CLAP!
HEY, LOOK! I'M DOING IT... I'M DOING IT!
HMM... MAYBE I MISJUDGED ARCHIE! MAYBE HE ISN'T SUCH A KLUTZ!
IT TAKES REAL TALENT TO PERFORM THOSE YO-YO TRICKS!
THANK YOU, FANS! THANK YOU!
CLAP! CLAP! CLAP!
4

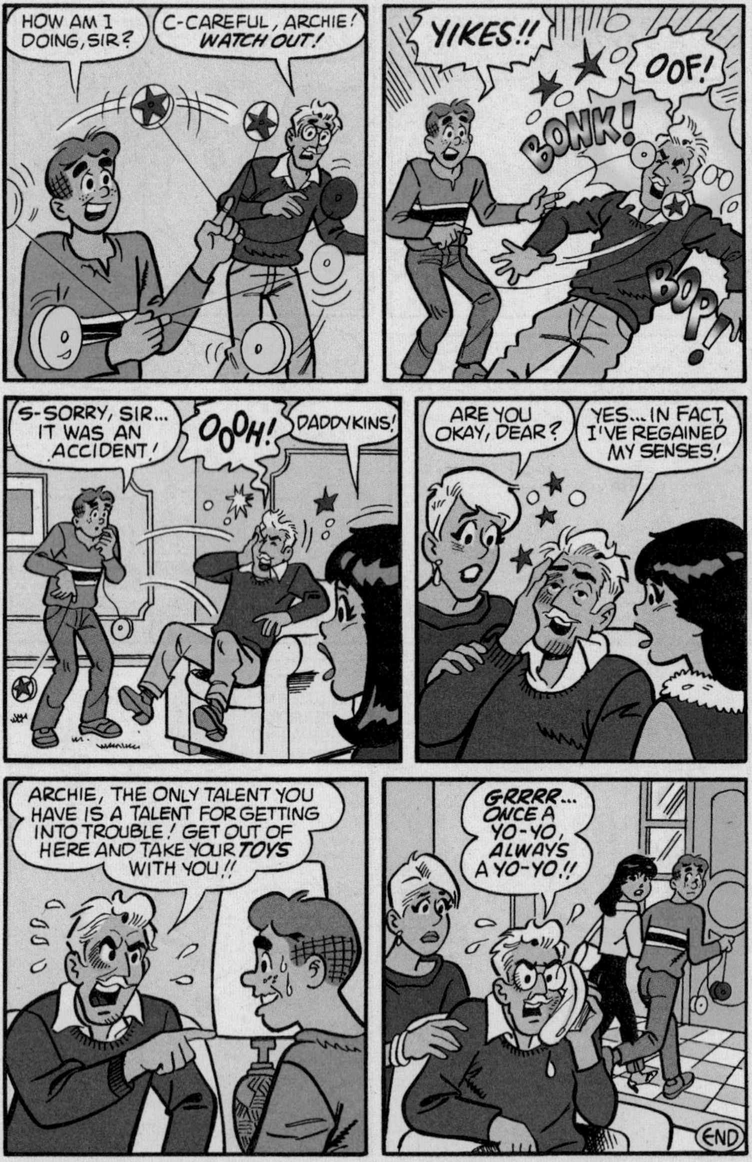

HOW AM I DOING, SIR?
C-CAREFUL, ARCHIE! WATCH OUT!
YIKES!!
OOF!
BONK!
BOP!
S-SORRY, SIR... IT WAS AN ACCIDENT!
OOOH!
DADDYKINS!
ARE YOU OKAY, DEAR?
YES... IN FACT, I'VE REGAINED MY SENSES!
ARCHIE, THE ONLY TALENT YOU HAVE IS A TALENT FOR GETTING INTO TROUBLE! GET OUT OF HERE AND TAKE YOUR TOYS WITH YOU!!
GRRRR... ONCE A YO-YO, ALWAYS A YO-YO!!
END

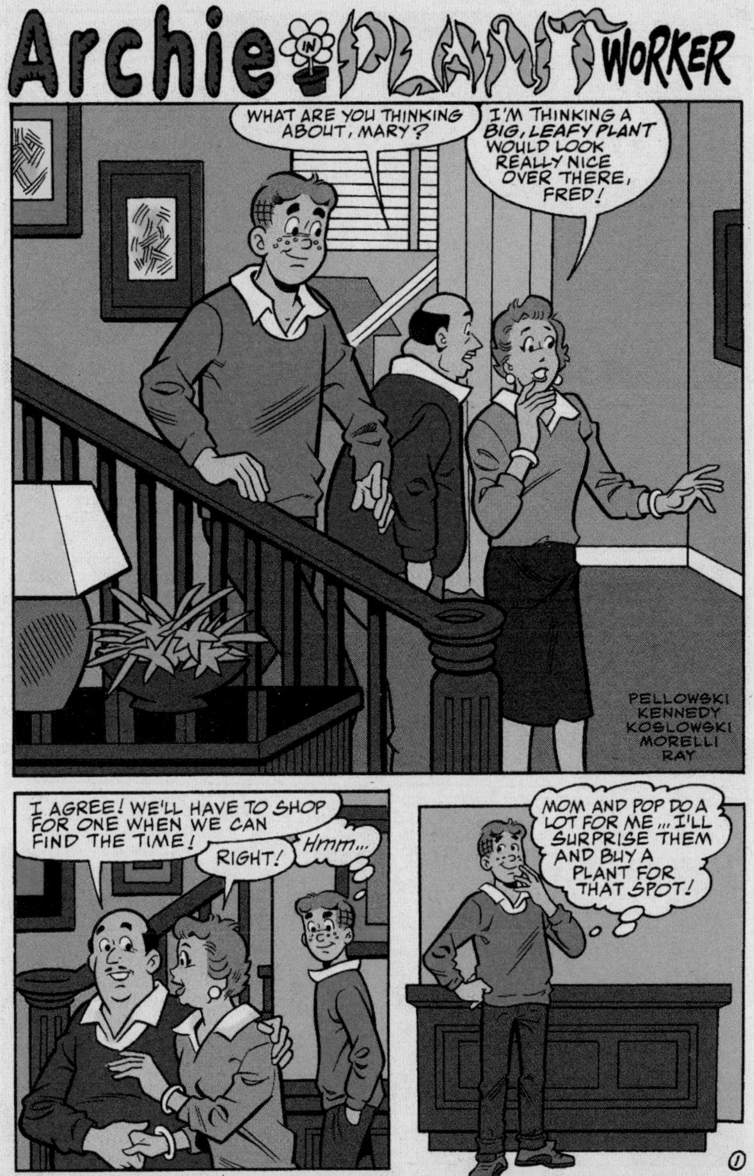
Archie IN PLANT WORKER
WHAT ARE YOU THINKING ABOUT, MARY?
I'M THINKING A BIG, LEAFY PLANT WOULD LOOK REALLY NICE OVER THERE, FRED!
PELLOWSKI
KENNEDY
KOSLOWSKI
MORELLI
RAY
I AGREE! WE'LL HAVE TO SHOP FOR ONE WHEN WE CAN FIND THE TIME!
RIGHT!
Hmm...
MOM AND POP DO A LOT FOR ME ... I'LL SURPRISE THEM AND BUY A PLANT FOR THAT SPOT!

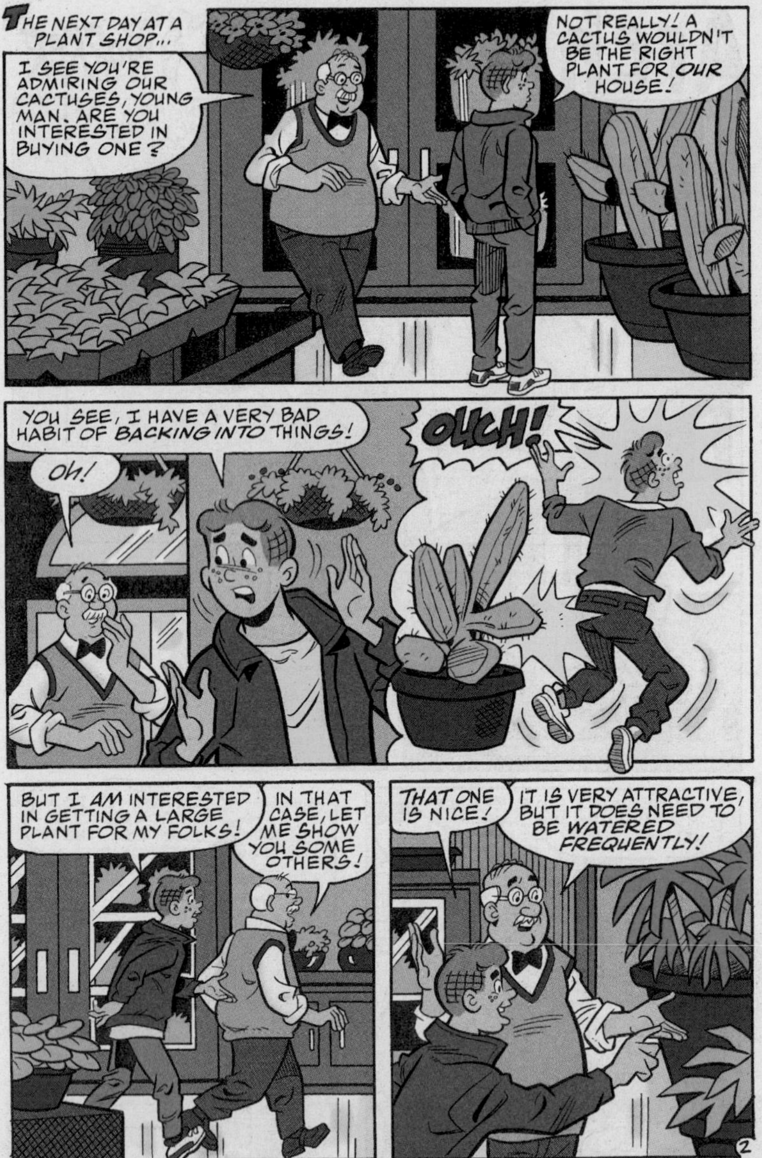
THE NEXT DAY AT A PLANT SHOP...
I SEE YOU'RE ADMIRING OUR CACTUSES, YOUNG MAN. ARE YOU INTERESTED IN BUYING ONE?
NOT REALLY! A CACTUS WOULDN'T BE THE RIGHT PLANT FOR OUR HOUSE!
YOU SEE, I HAVE A VERY BAD HABIT OF BACKING INTO THINGS!
Oh!
OUCH!
BUT I AM INTERESTED IN GETTING A LARGE PLANT FOR MY FOLKS!
IN THAT CASE, LET ME SHOW YOU SOME OTHERS!
THAT ONE IS NICE!
IT IS VERY ATTRACTIVE, BUT IT DOES NEED TO BE WATERED FREQUENTLY!
2

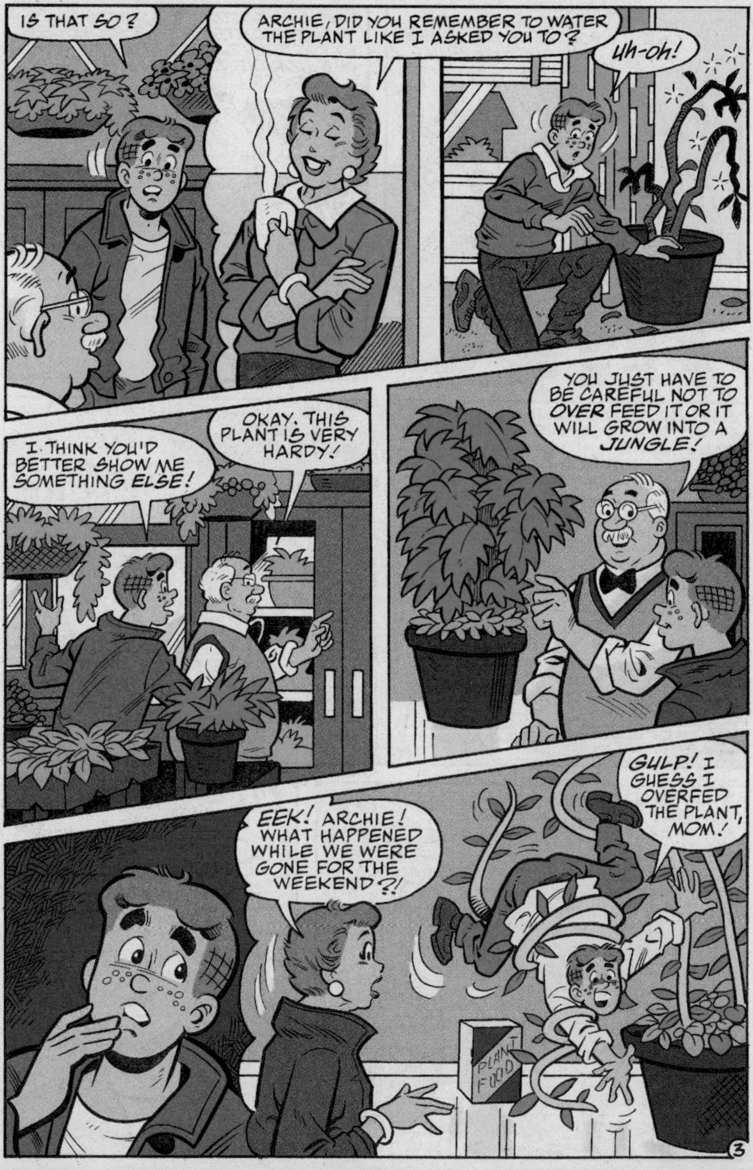
IS THAT SO?
ARCHIE, DID YOU REMEMBER TO WATER THE PLANT LIKE I ASKED YOU TO?
UH-OH!
I THINK YOU'D BETTER SHOW ME SOMETHING ELSE!
OKAY. THIS PLANT IS VERY HARDY!
YOU JUST HAVE TO BE CAREFUL NOT TO OVER FEED IT OR IT WILL GROW INTO A JUNGLE!
EEK! ARCHIE! WHAT HAPPENED WHILE WE WERE GONE FOR THE WEEKEND?!
GULP! I GUESS I OVERFED THE PLANT, MOM!
PLANT FOOD

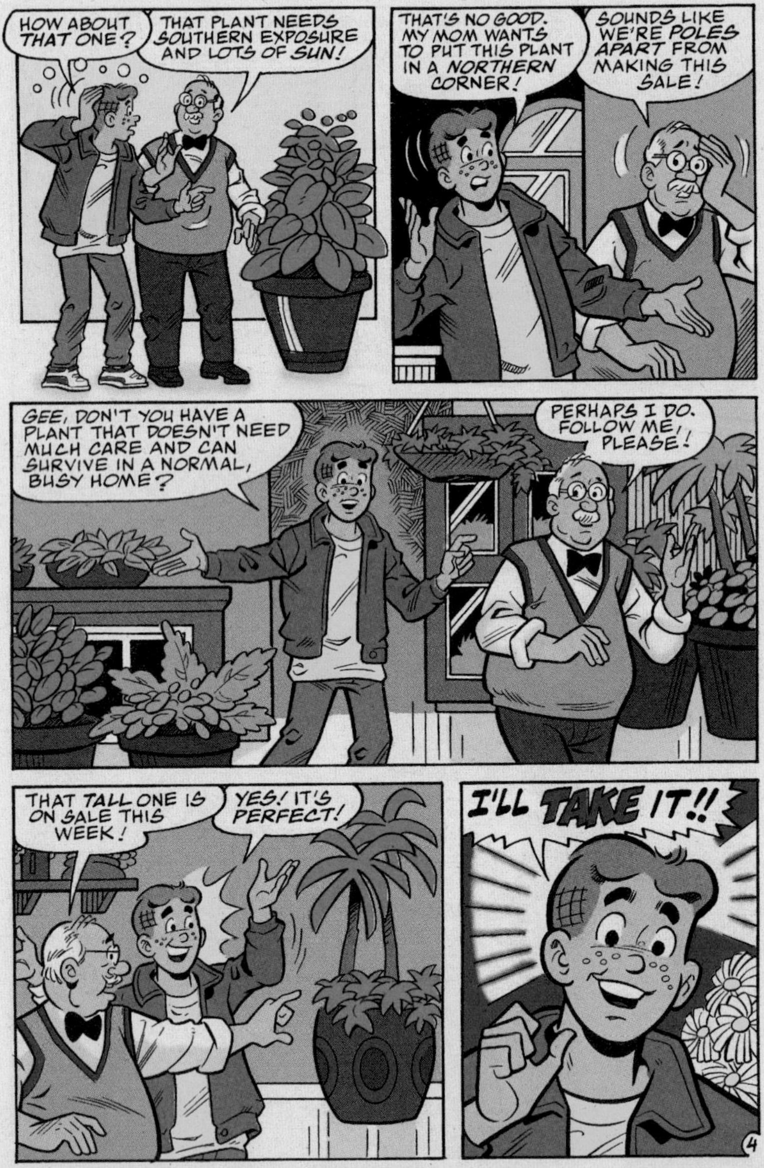
HOW ABOUT THAT ONE?
THAT PLANT NEEDS SOUTHERN EXPOSURE AND LOTS OF SUN!
THAT'S NO GOOD. MY MOM WANTS TO PUT THIS PLANT IN A NORTHERN CORNER!
SOUNDS LIKE WE'RE POLES APART FROM MAKING THIS SALE!
GEE, DON'T YOU HAVE A PLANT THAT DOESN'T NEED MUCH CARE AND CAN SURVIVE IN A NORMAL, BUSY HOME?
PERHAPS I DO. FOLLOW ME, PLEASE!
THAT TALL ONE IS ON SALE THIS WEEK!
YES! IT'S PERFECT!
I'LL TAKE IT!!
4

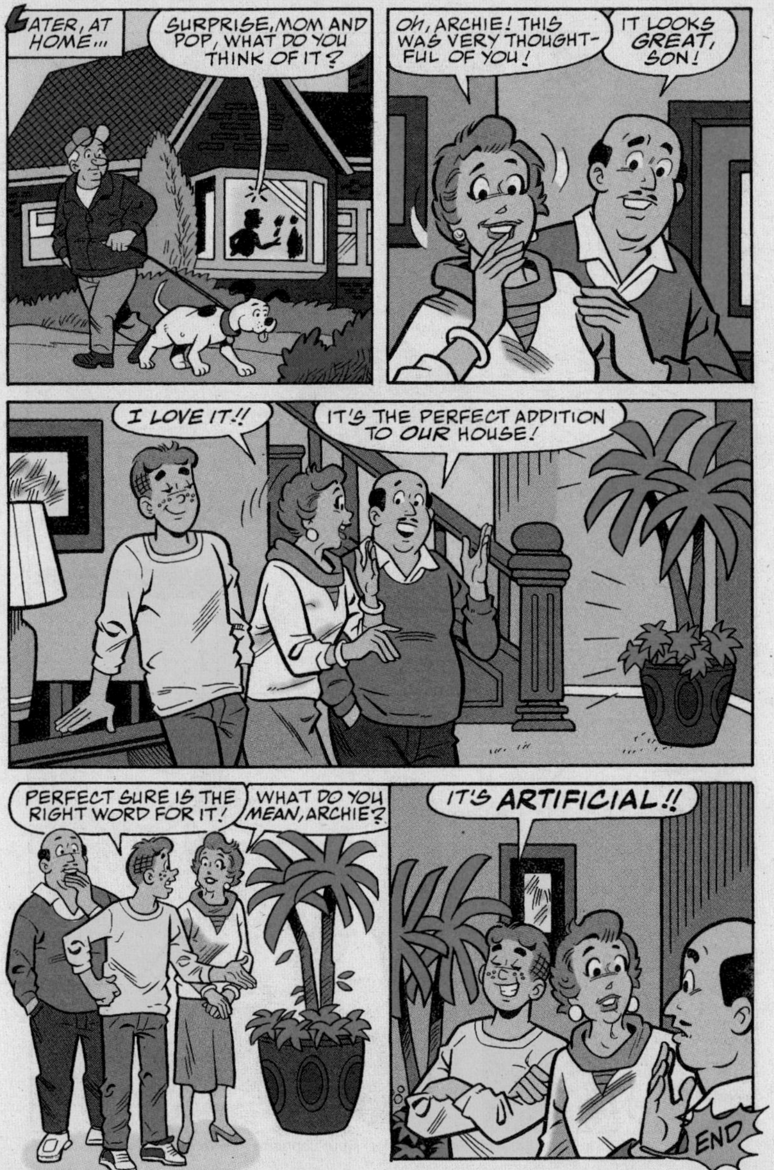
LATER, AT HOME...
SURPRISE, MOM AND POP, WHAT DO YOU THINK OF IT?
Oh, ARCHIE! THIS WAS VERY THOUGHTFUL OF YOU!
IT LOOKS GREAT, SON!
I LOVE IT!!
IT'S THE PERFECT ADDITION TO OUR HOUSE!
PERFECT SURE IS THE RIGHT WORD FOR IT!
WHAT DO YOU MEAN, ARCHIE?
IT'S ARTIFICIAL!!
END

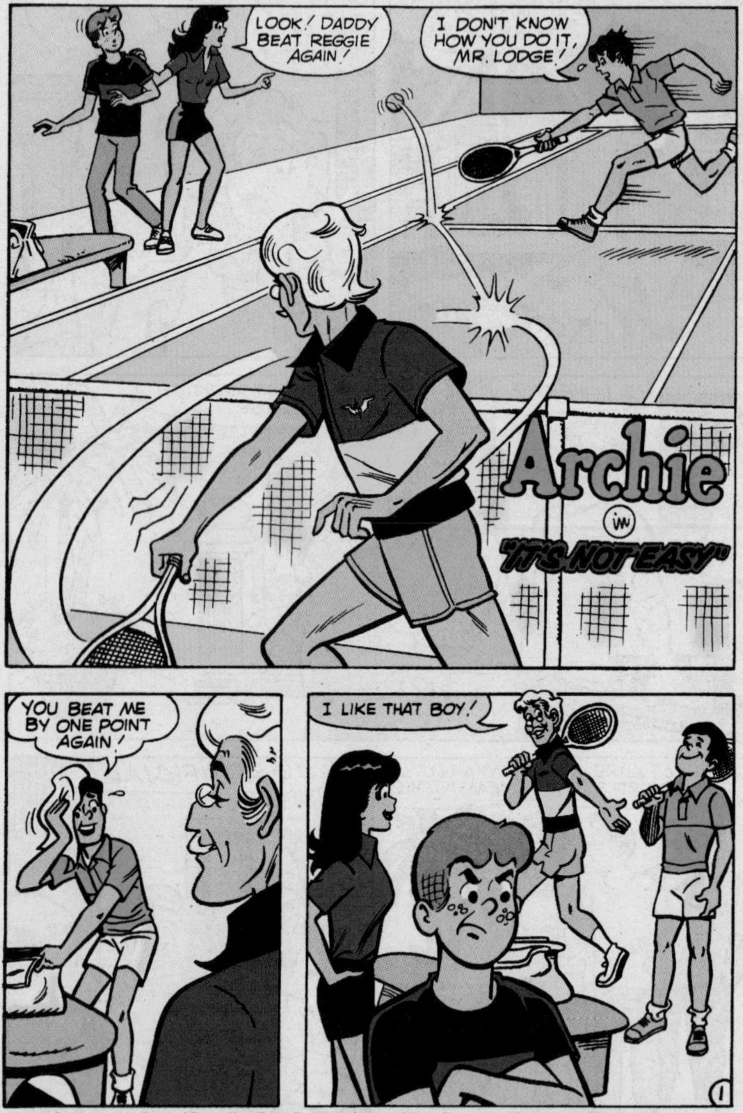
LOOK! DADDY BEAT REGGIE AGAIN!
I DON'T KNOW HOW YOU DO IT, MR. LODGE!
Archie
in
"IT'S NOT EASY"
YOU BEAT ME BY ONE POINT AGAIN!
I LIKE THAT BOY!
1

Script: Jim Ruth / Pencils: Bob Bolling / Inks: Mike Esposito / Letters: Bill Yoshida

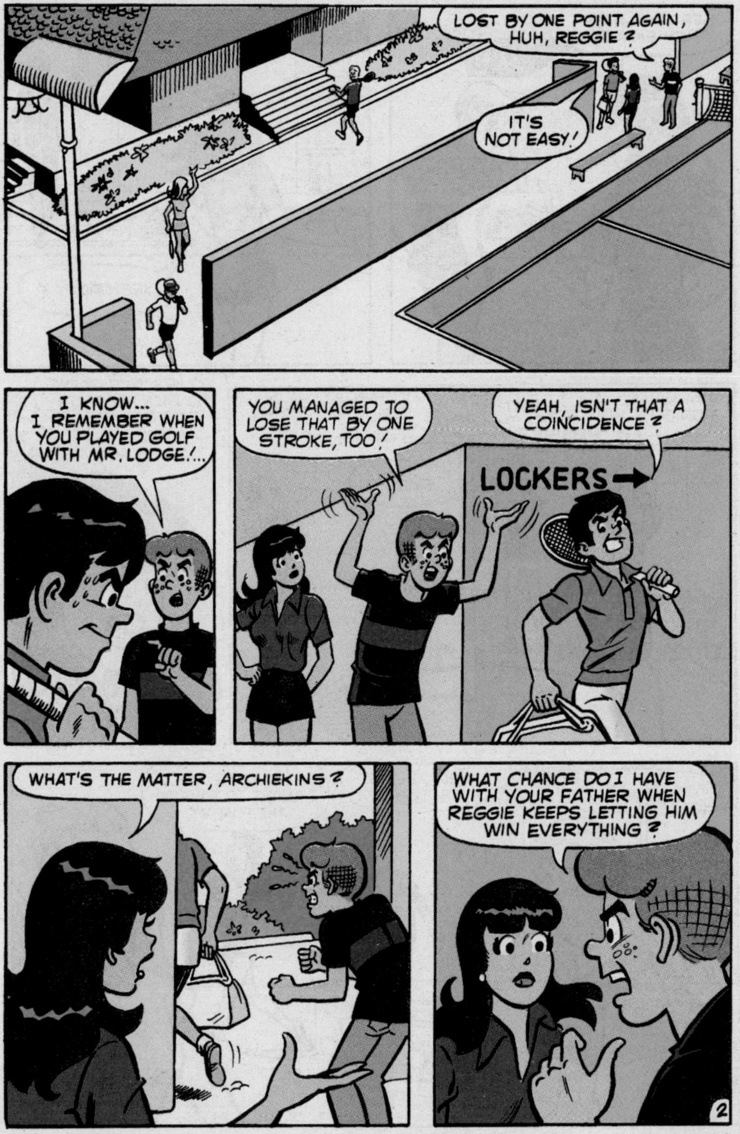
LOST BY ONE POINT AGAIN, HUH, REGGIE?
IT'S NOT EASY!
I KNOW... I REMEMBER WHEN YOU PLAYED GOLF WITH MR. LODGE!...
YOU MANAGED TO LOSE THAT BY ONE STROKE, TOO!
YEAH, ISN'T THAT A COINCIDENCE?
LOCKERS →
WHAT'S THE MATTER, ARCHIEKINS?
WHAT CHANCE DO I HAVE WITH YOUR FATHER WHEN REGGIE KEEPS LETTING HIM WIN EVERYTHING?
2

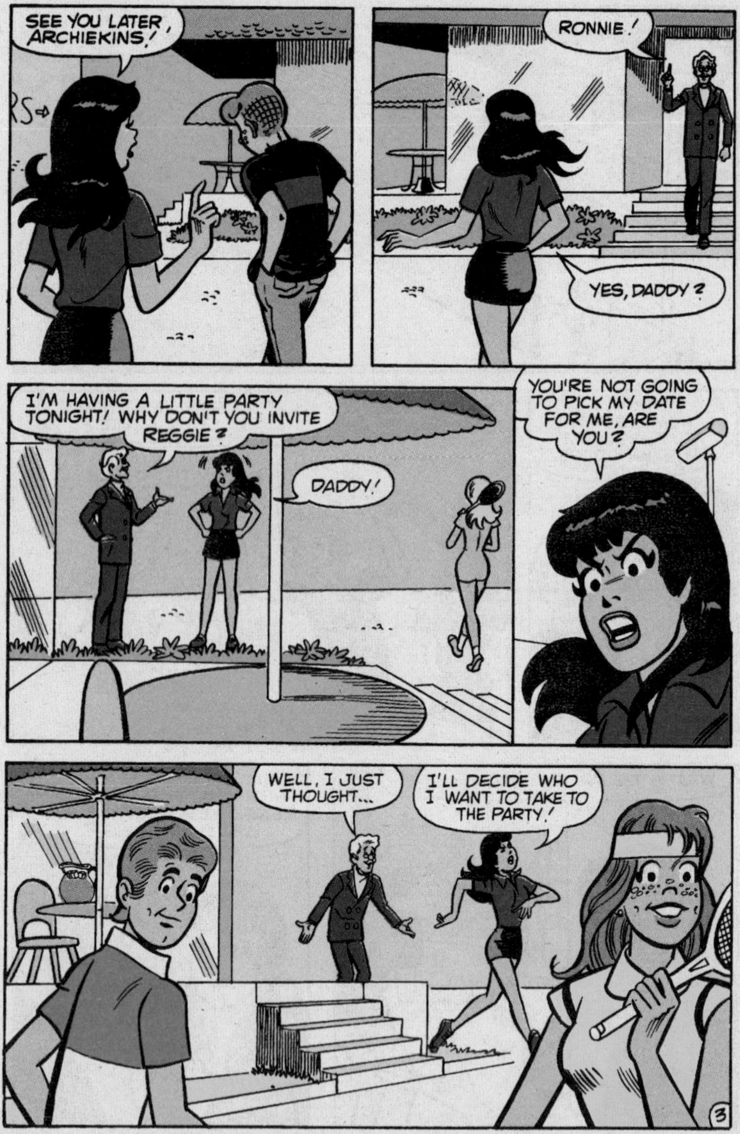
SEE YOU LATER, ARCHIEKINS!
RONNIE!
YES, DADDY?
I'M HAVING A LITTLE PARTY TONIGHT! WHY DON'T YOU INVITE REGGIE?
DADDY!
YOU'RE NOT GOING TO PICK MY DATE FOR ME, ARE YOU?
WELL, I JUST THOUGHT...
I'LL DECIDE WHO I WANT TO TAKE TO THE PARTY!
3

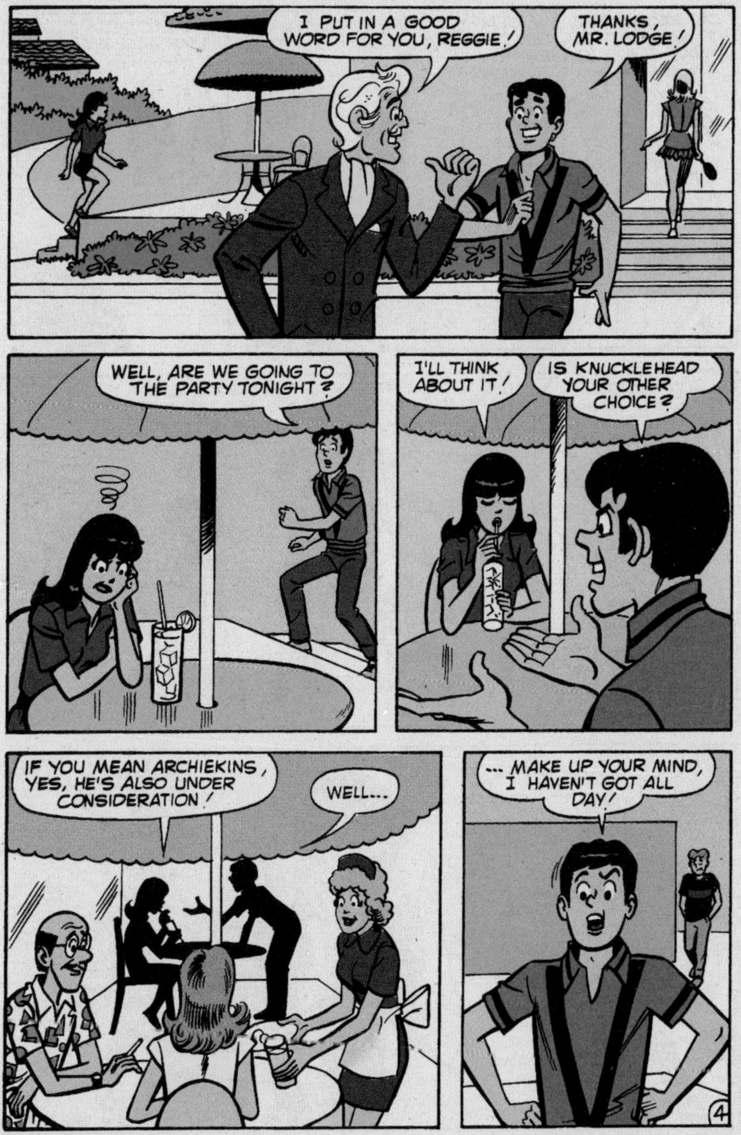

I PUT IN A GOOD WORD FOR YOU, REGGIE!
THANKS, MR. LODGE!
WELL, ARE WE GOING TO THE PARTY TONIGHT?
I'LL THINK ABOUT IT!
IS KNUCKLEHEAD YOUR OTHER CHOICE?
IF YOU MEAN ARCHIEKINS, YES, HE'S ALSO UNDER CONSIDERATION!
WELL...
... MAKE UP YOUR MIND, I HAVEN'T GOT ALL DAY!
4

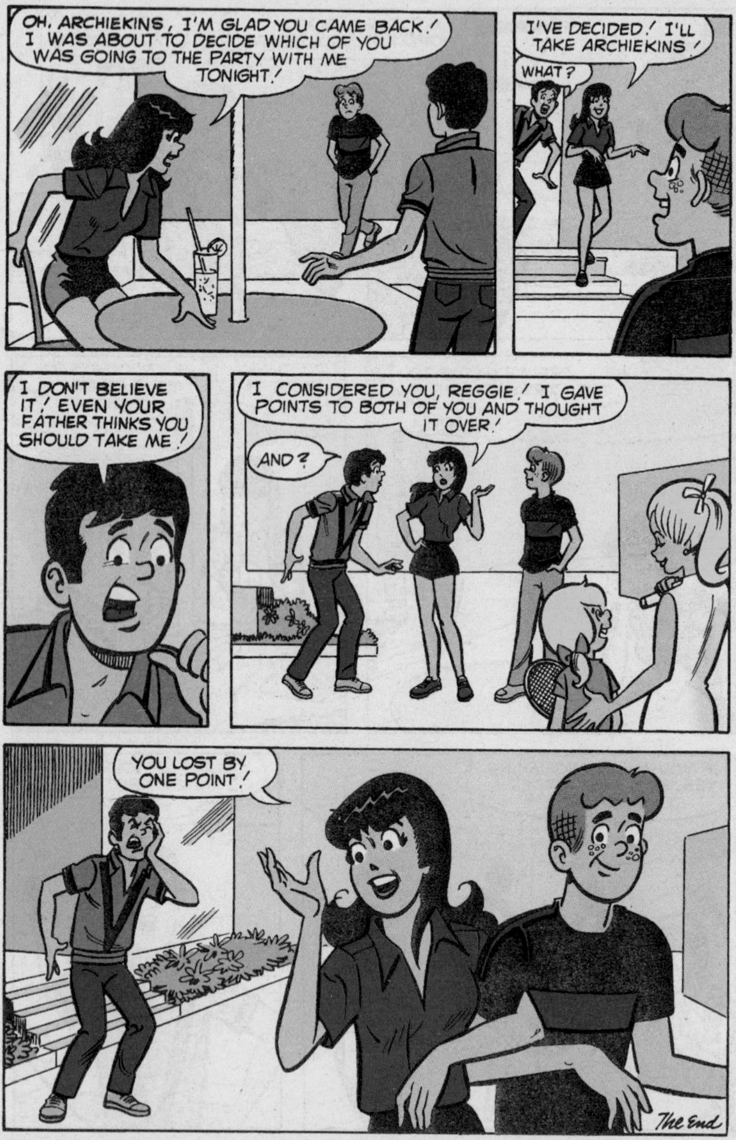
OH, ARCHIEKINS, I'M GLAD YOU CAME BACK! I WAS ABOUT TO DECIDE WHICH OF YOU WAS GOING TO THE PARTY WITH ME TONIGHT!
I'VE DECIDED! I'LL TAKE ARCHIEKINS!
WHAT?
I DON'T BELIEVE IT! EVEN YOUR FATHER THINKS YOU SHOULD TAKE ME!
I CONSIDERED YOU, REGGIE! I GAVE POINTS TO BOTH OF YOU AND THOUGHT IT OVER!
AND?
YOU LOST BY ONE POINT!
The End

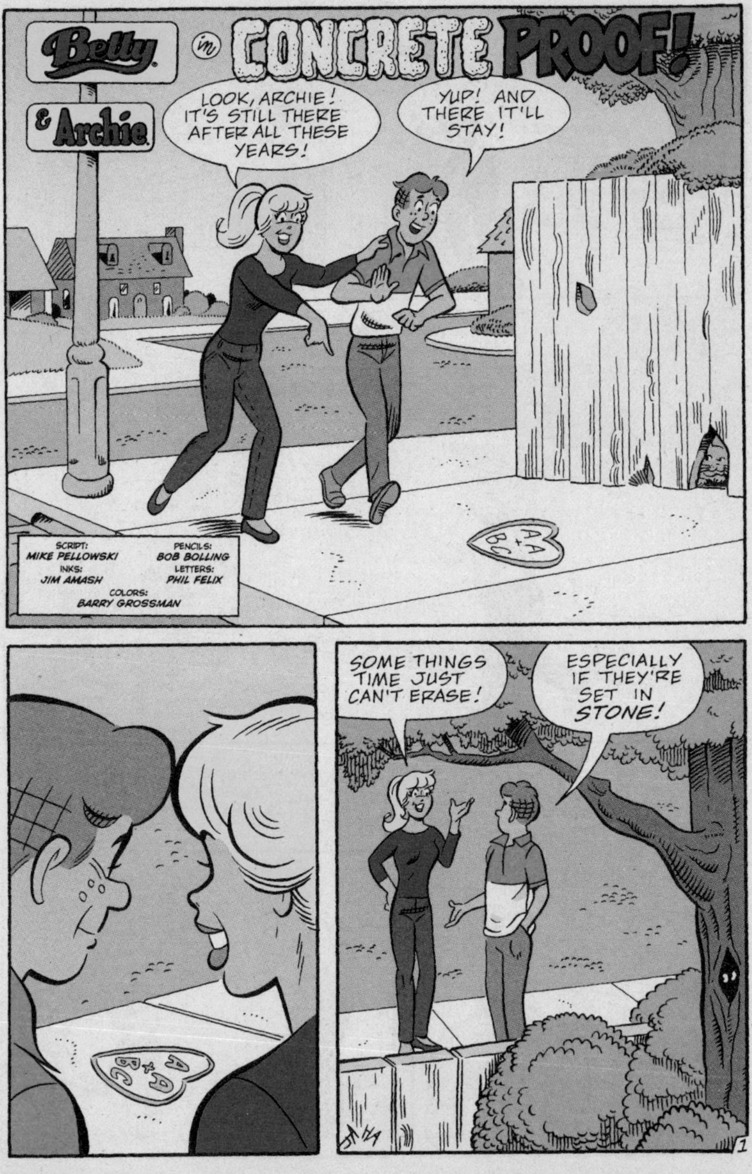
Betty & Archie in CONCRETE PROOF!
LOOK, ARCHIE! IT'S STILL THERE AFTER ALL THESE YEARS!
YUP! AND THERE IT'LL STAY!
SCRIPT: MIKE PELLOWSKI PENCILS: BOB BOLLING INKS: JIM AMASH LETTERS: PHIL FELIX COLORS: BARRY GROSSMAN
SOME THINGS TIME JUST CAN'T ERASE!
ESPECIALLY IF THEY'RE SET IN STONE!

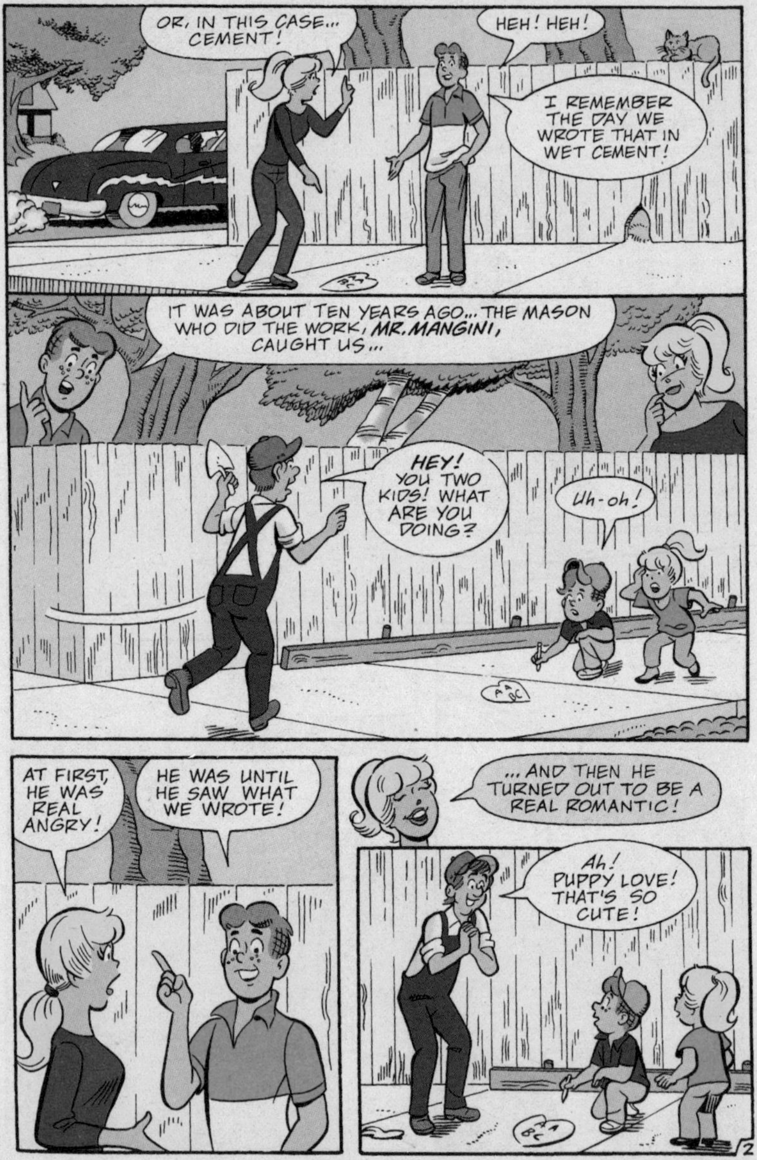
OR, IN THIS CASE... CEMENT!
HEH! HEH!
I REMEMBER THE DAY WE WROTE THAT IN WET CEMENT!
IT WAS ABOUT TEN YEARS AGO... THE MASON WHO DID THE WORK, MR. MANGINI, CAUGHT US...
HEY! YOU TWO KIDS! WHAT ARE YOU DOING?
Uh-oh!
AT FIRST, HE WAS REAL ANGRY!
HE WAS UNTIL HE SAW WHAT WE WROTE!
...AND THEN HE TURNED OUT TO BE A REAL ROMANTIC!
Ah! PUPPY LOVE! THAT'S SO CUTE!

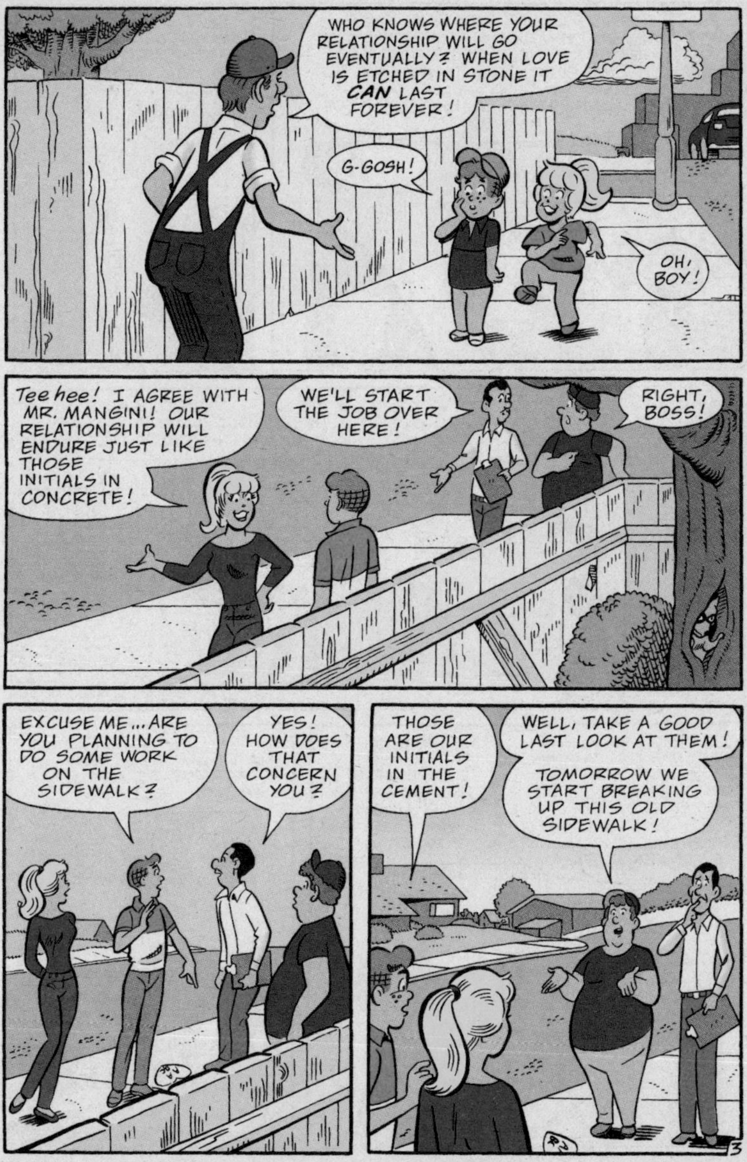
WHO KNOWS WHERE YOUR RELATIONSHIP WILL GO EVENTUALLY? WHEN LOVE IS ETCHED IN STONE IT **CAN** LAST FOREVER!
G-GOSH!
OH, BOY!
Tee hee! I AGREE WITH MR. MANGINI! OUR RELATIONSHIP WILL ENDURE JUST LIKE THOSE INITIALS IN CONCRETE!
WE'LL START THE JOB OVER HERE!
RIGHT, BOSS!
EXCUSE ME... ARE YOU PLANNING TO DO SOME WORK ON THE SIDEWALK?
YES! HOW DOES THAT CONCERN YOU?
THOSE ARE OUR INITIALS IN THE CEMENT!
WELL, TAKE A GOOD LAST LOOK AT THEM!
TOMORROW WE START BREAKING UP THIS OLD SIDEWALK!

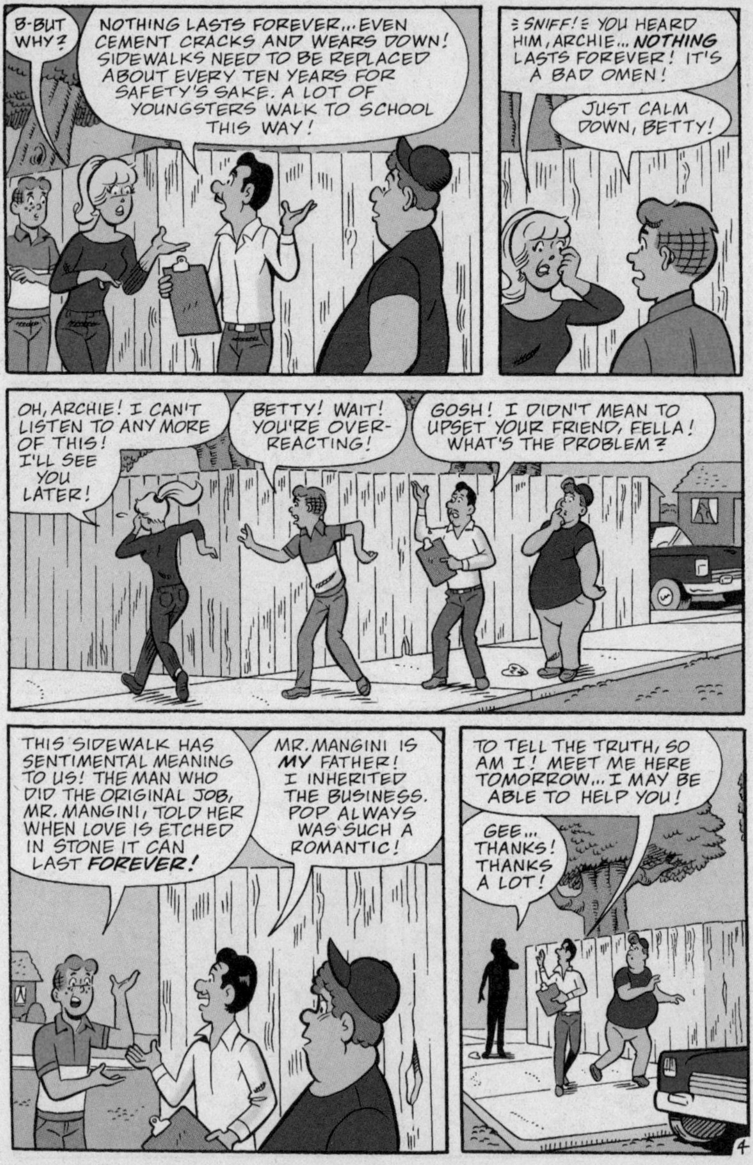
B-BUT WHY?
NOTHING LASTS FOREVER... EVEN CEMENT CRACKS AND WEARS DOWN! SIDEWALKS NEED TO BE REPLACED ABOUT EVERY TEN YEARS FOR SAFETY'S SAKE. A LOT OF YOUNGSTERS WALK TO SCHOOL THIS WAY!
SNIFF! YOU HEARD HIM, ARCHIE... **NOTHING** LASTS FOREVER! IT'S A BAD OMEN!
JUST CALM DOWN, BETTY!
OH, ARCHIE! I CAN'T LISTEN TO ANY MORE OF THIS! I'LL SEE YOU LATER!
BETTY! WAIT! YOU'RE OVER-REACTING!
GOSH! I DIDN'T MEAN TO UPSET YOUR FRIEND, FELLA! WHAT'S THE PROBLEM?
THIS SIDEWALK HAS SENTIMENTAL MEANING TO US! THE MAN WHO DID THE ORIGINAL JOB, MR. MANGINI, TOLD HER WHEN LOVE IS ETCHED IN STONE IT CAN LAST **FOREVER!**
MR. MANGINI IS **MY** FATHER! I INHERITED THE BUSINESS. POP ALWAYS WAS SUCH A ROMANTIC!
TO TELL THE TRUTH, SO AM I! MEET ME HERE TOMORROW... I MAY BE ABLE TO HELP YOU!
GEE... THANKS! THANKS A LOT!
4

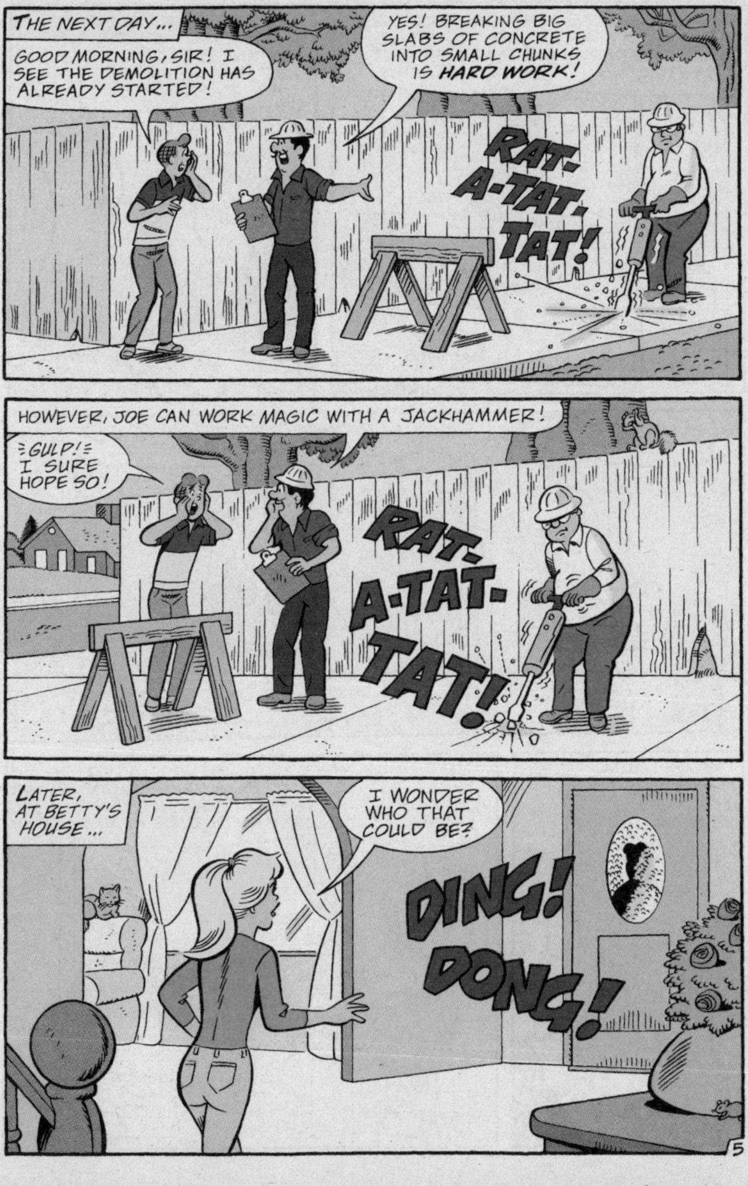
THE NEXT DAY...
GOOD MORNING, SIR! I SEE THE DEMOLITION HAS ALREADY STARTED!
YES! BREAKING BIG SLABS OF CONCRETE INTO SMALL CHUNKS IS **HARD WORK**!
RAT-A-TAT-TAT!
HOWEVER, JOE CAN WORK MAGIC WITH A JACKHAMMER!
GULP! I SURE HOPE SO!
RAT-A-TAT-TAT!
LATER, AT BETTY'S HOUSE...
I WONDER WHO THAT COULD BE?
DING! DONG!

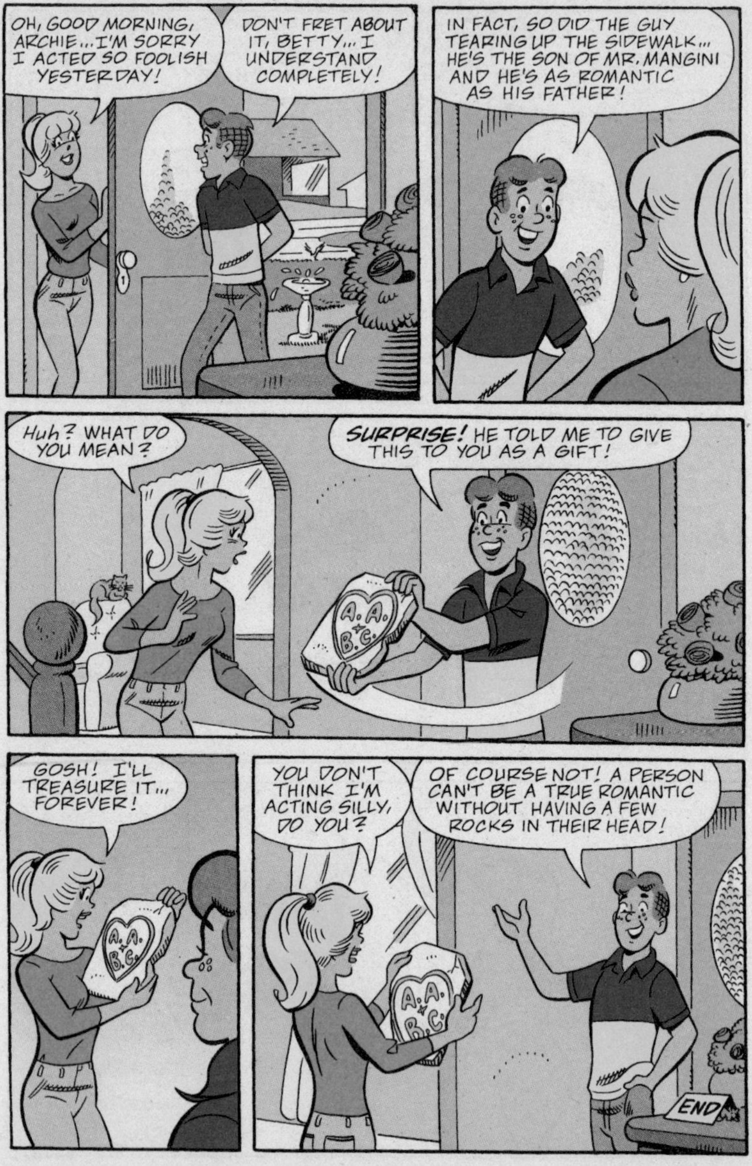

OH, GOOD MORNING, ARCHIE... I'M SORRY I ACTED SO FOOLISH YESTERDAY!
DON'T FRET ABOUT IT, BETTY... I UNDERSTAND COMPLETELY!
IN FACT, SO DID THE GUY TEARING UP THE SIDEWALK... HE'S THE SON OF MR. MANGINI AND HE'S AS ROMANTIC AS HIS FATHER!
Huh? WHAT DO YOU MEAN?
SURPRISE! HE TOLD ME TO GIVE THIS TO YOU AS A GIFT!
A. A. B. C.
GOSH! I'LL TREASURE IT... FOREVER!
YOU DON'T THINK I'M ACTING SILLY, DO YOU?
OF COURSE NOT! A PERSON CAN'T BE A TRUE ROMANTIC WITHOUT HAVING A FEW ROCKS IN THEIR HEAD!
END

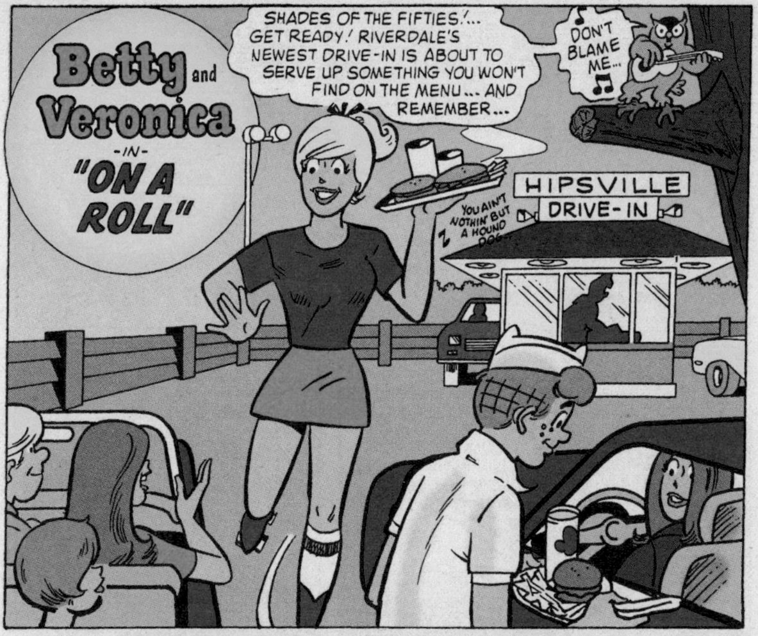
Betty and Veronica
-IN-
"ON A ROLL"
SHADES OF THE FIFTIES!... GET READY! RIVERDALE'S NEWEST DRIVE-IN IS ABOUT TO SERVE UP SOMETHING YOU WON'T FIND ON THE MENU... AND REMEMBER...
DON'T BLAME ME...
HIPSVILLE
DRIVE-IN
YOU AIN'T NOTHIN' BUT A HOUND DOG...

Script & Pencils: Bob Bolling / Inks: Mike Esposito / Letters: Bill Yoshida

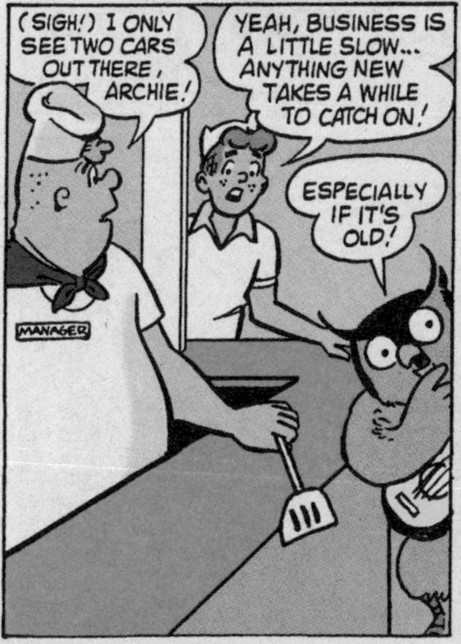
(SIGH!) I ONLY SEE TWO CARS OUT THERE, ARCHIE!
YEAH, BUSINESS IS A LITTLE SLOW... ANYTHING NEW TAKES A WHILE TO CATCH ON!
ESPECIALLY IF IT'S OLD!
MANAGER

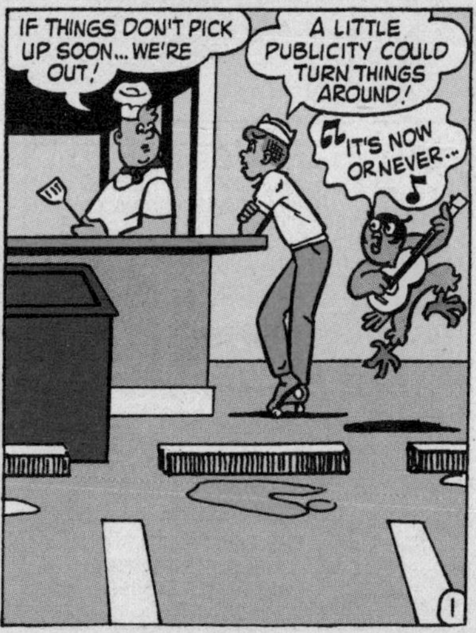
IF THINGS DON'T PICK UP SOON... WE'RE OUT!
A LITTLE PUBLICITY COULD TURN THINGS AROUND!
IT'S NOW OR NEVER...

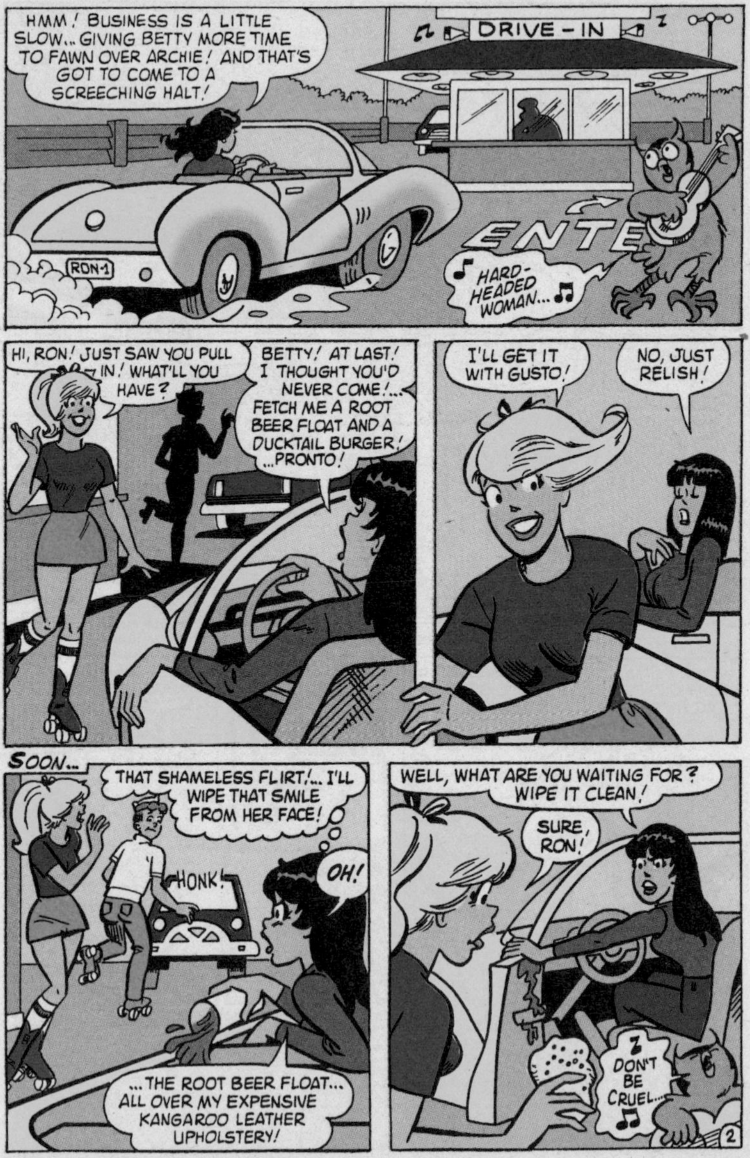
HMM! BUSINESS IS A LITTLE SLOW... GIVING BETTY MORE TIME TO FAWN OVER ARCHIE! AND THAT'S GOT TO COME TO A SCREECHING HALT!
DRIVE-IN
RON-1
ENTE
HARD-HEADED WOMAN...
HI, RON! JUST SAW YOU PULL IN! WHAT'LL YOU HAVE?
BETTY! AT LAST! I THOUGHT YOU'D NEVER COME!... FETCH ME A ROOT BEER FLOAT AND A DUCKTAIL BURGER! ...PRONTO!
I'LL GET IT WITH GUSTO!
NO, JUST RELISH!
SOON...
THAT SHAMELESS FLIRT!... I'LL WIPE THAT SMILE FROM HER FACE!
HONK!
OH!
...THE ROOT BEER FLOAT... ALL OVER MY EXPENSIVE KANGAROO LEATHER UPHOLSTERY!
WELL, WHAT ARE YOU WAITING FOR? WIPE IT CLEAN!
SURE, RON!
DON'T BE CRUEL...
2

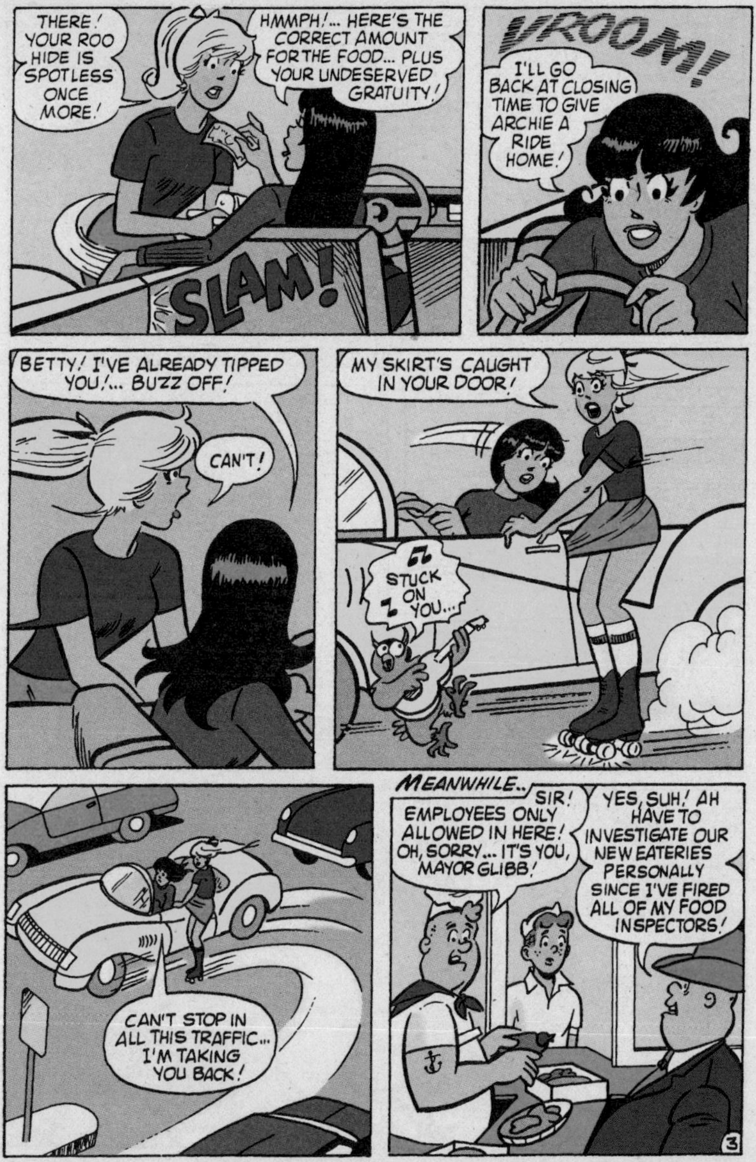
THERE! YOUR ROO HIDE IS SPOTLESS ONCE MORE!
HMMPH!... HERE'S THE CORRECT AMOUNT FOR THE FOOD... PLUS YOUR UNDESERVED GRATUITY!
SLAM!
VROOM!
I'LL GO BACK AT CLOSING TIME TO GIVE ARCHIE A RIDE HOME!
BETTY! I'VE ALREADY TIPPED YOU!... BUZZ OFF!
CAN'T!
MY SKIRT'S CAUGHT IN YOUR DOOR!
STUCK ON YOU...
CAN'T STOP IN ALL THIS TRAFFIC... I'M TAKING YOU BACK!
MEANWHILE..
SIR! EMPLOYEES ONLY ALLOWED IN HERE! OH, SORRY... IT'S YOU, MAYOR GLIBB!
YES, SUH! AH HAVE TO INVESTIGATE OUR NEW EATERIES PERSONALLY SINCE I'VE FIRED ALL OF MY FOOD INSPECTORS!
3

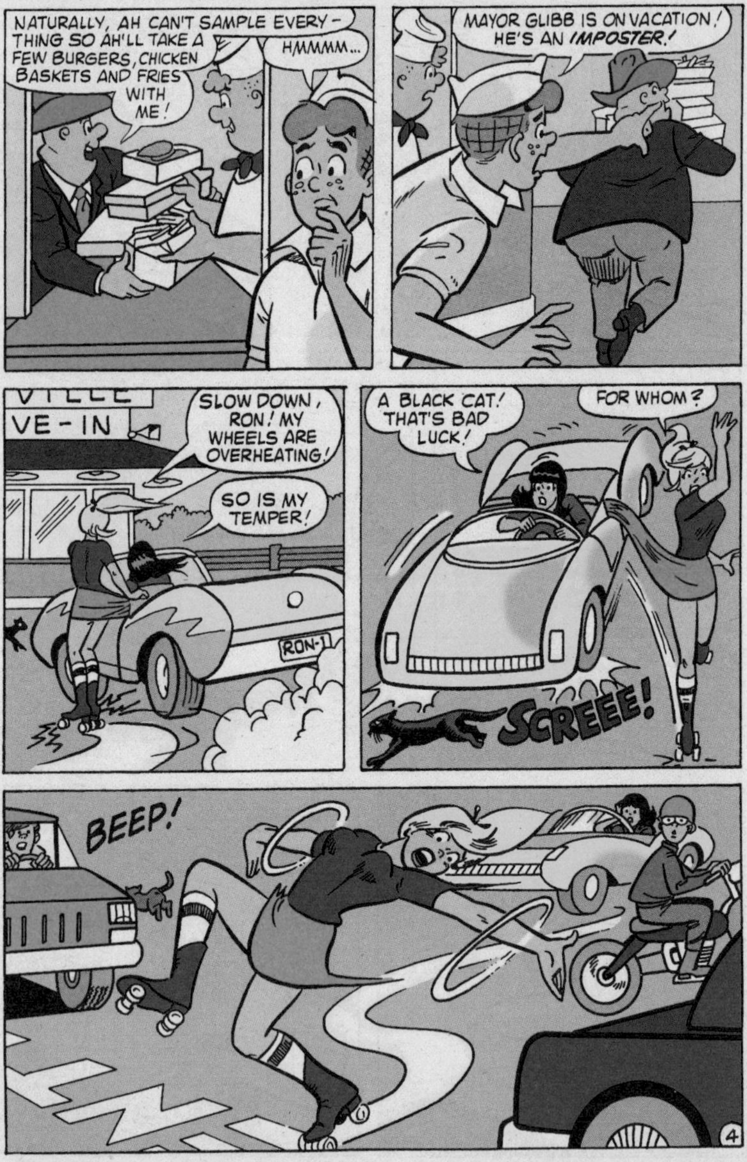

NATURALLY, AH CAN'T SAMPLE EVERY-THING SO AH'LL TAKE A FEW BURGERS, CHICKEN BASKETS AND FRIES WITH ME!
HMMMM...
MAYOR GLIBB IS ON VACATION! HE'S AN IMPOSTER!
VE-IN
SLOW DOWN, RON! MY WHEELS ARE OVERHEATING!
SO IS MY TEMPER!
RON-1
A BLACK CAT! THAT'S BAD LUCK!
FOR WHOM?
SCREEEE!
BEEP!
4

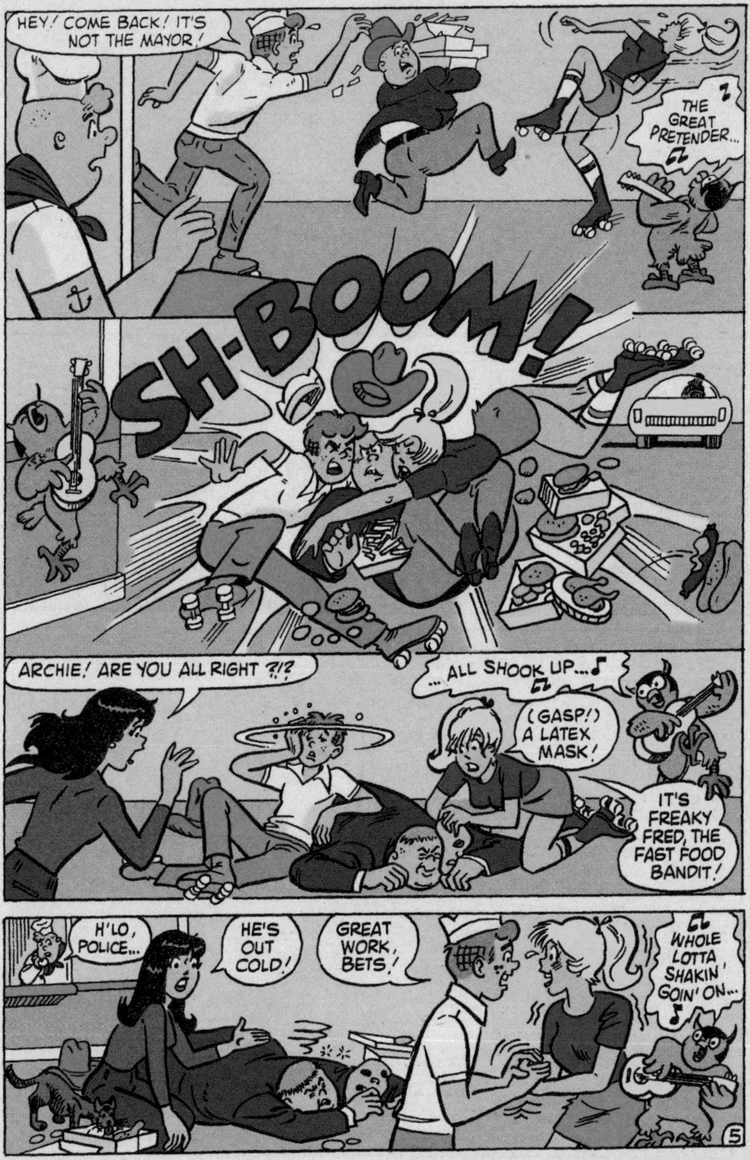
HEY! COME BACK! IT'S NOT THE MAYOR!
THE GREAT PRETENDER...
SH-BOOM!
ARCHIE! ARE YOU ALL RIGHT ?!?
... ALL SHOOK UP...
(GASP!) A LATEX MASK!
IT'S FREAKY FRED, THE FAST FOOD BANDIT!
H'LO, POLICE...
HE'S OUT COLD!
GREAT WORK, BETS!
WHOLE LOTTA SHAKIN' GOIN' ON...
5

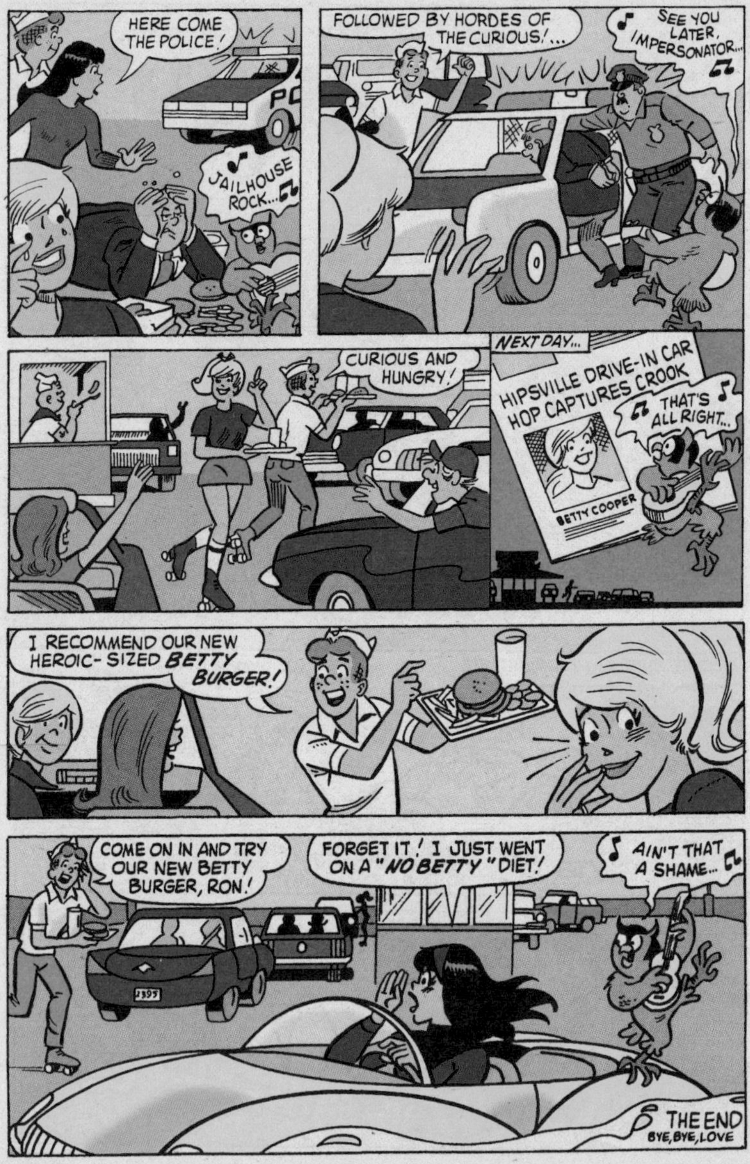
HERE COME THE POLICE!
JAILHOUSE ROCK...
FOLLOWED BY HORDES OF THE CURIOUS!...
SEE YOU LATER, IMPERSONATOR...
CURIOUS AND HUNGRY!
NEXT DAY...
HIPSVILLE DRIVE-IN CAR HOP CAPTURES CROOK
BETTY COOPER
THAT'S ALL RIGHT...
I RECOMMEND OUR NEW HEROIC-SIZED BETTY BURGER!
COME ON IN AND TRY OUR NEW BETTY BURGER, RON!
FORGET IT! I JUST WENT ON A "NO BETTY" DIET!
AIN'T THAT A SHAME...
THE END
BYE, BYE, LOVE

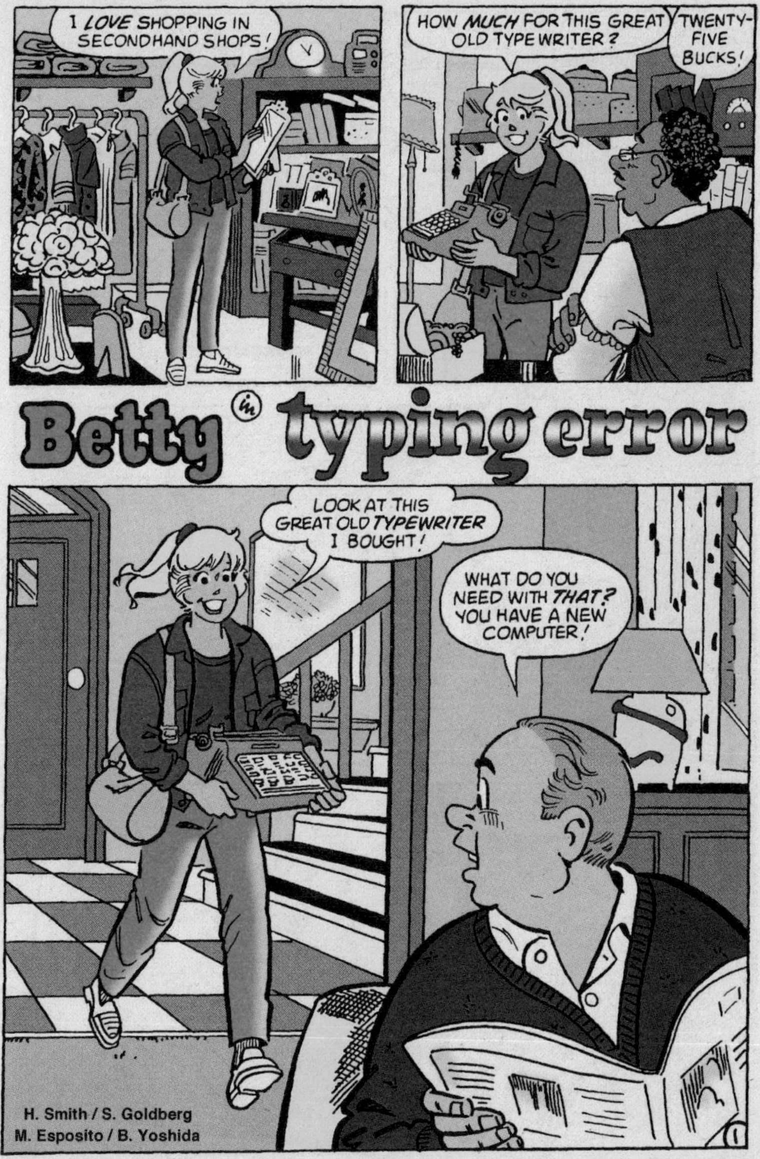
I LOVE SHOPPING IN SECONDHAND SHOPS!
HOW MUCH FOR THIS GREAT OLD TYPEWRITER?
TWENTY-FIVE BUCKS!
Betty in typing error
LOOK AT THIS GREAT OLD TYPEWRITER I BOUGHT!
WHAT DO YOU NEED WITH THAT? YOU HAVE A NEW COMPUTER!
H. Smith / S. Goldberg
M. Esposito / B. Yoshida

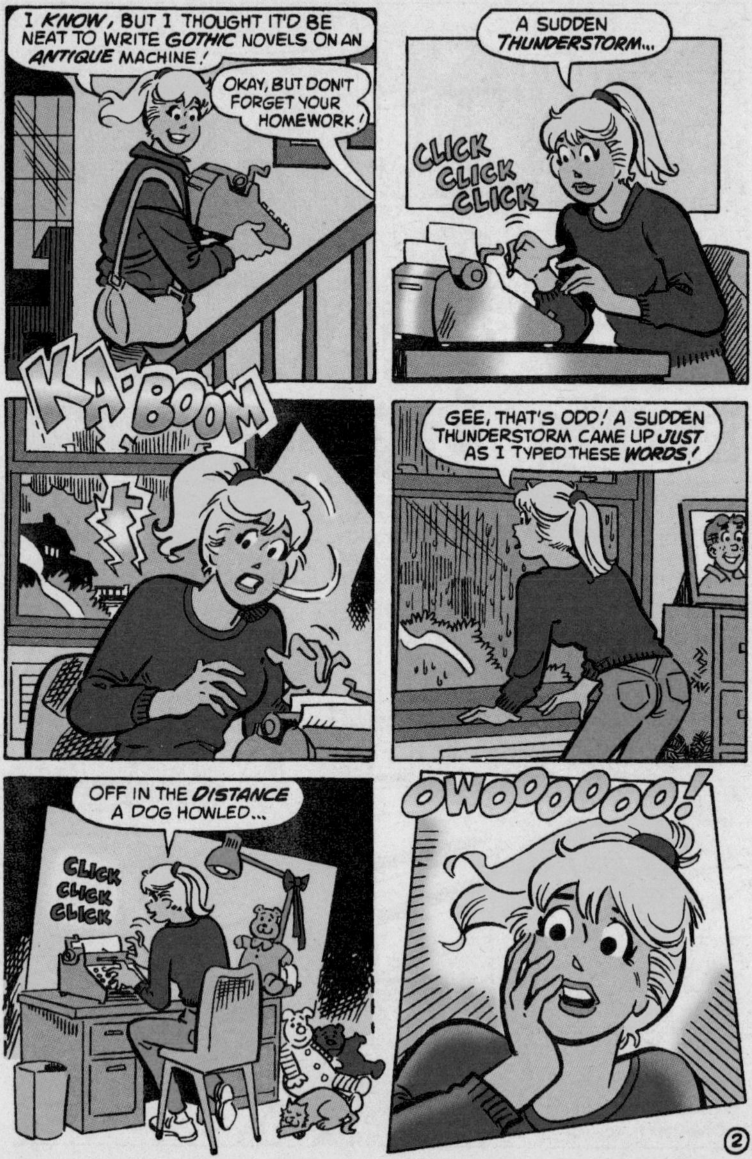
I KNOW, BUT I THOUGHT IT'D BE NEAT TO WRITE GOTHIC NOVELS ON AN ANTIQUE MACHINE!
OKAY, BUT DON'T FORGET YOUR HOMEWORK!
A SUDDEN THUNDERSTORM...
CLICK CLICK CLICK
KA-BOOM
GEE, THAT'S ODD! A SUDDEN THUNDERSTORM CAME UP JUST AS I TYPED THESE WORDS!
OFF IN THE DISTANCE A DOG HOWLED...
CLICK CLICK CLICK
OWOOOOOOOO!

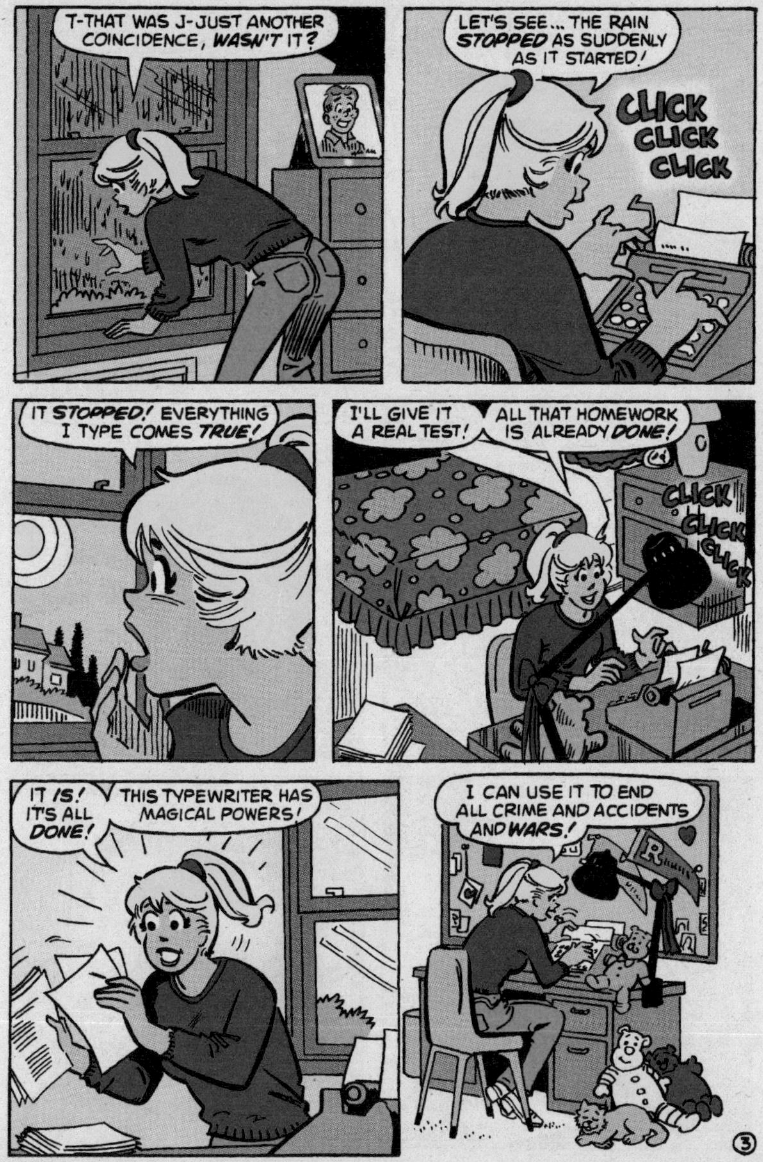

T-THAT WAS J-JUST ANOTHER COINCIDENCE, WASN'T IT?
LET'S SEE... THE RAIN STOPPED AS SUDDENLY AS IT STARTED!
CLICK CLICK CLICK
IT STOPPED! EVERYTHING I TYPE COMES TRUE!
I'LL GIVE IT A REAL TEST!
ALL THAT HOMEWORK IS ALREADY DONE!
CLICK CLICK CLICK
IT IS! IT'S ALL DONE!
THIS TYPEWRITER HAS MAGICAL POWERS!
I CAN USE IT TO END ALL CRIME AND ACCIDENTS AND WARS!

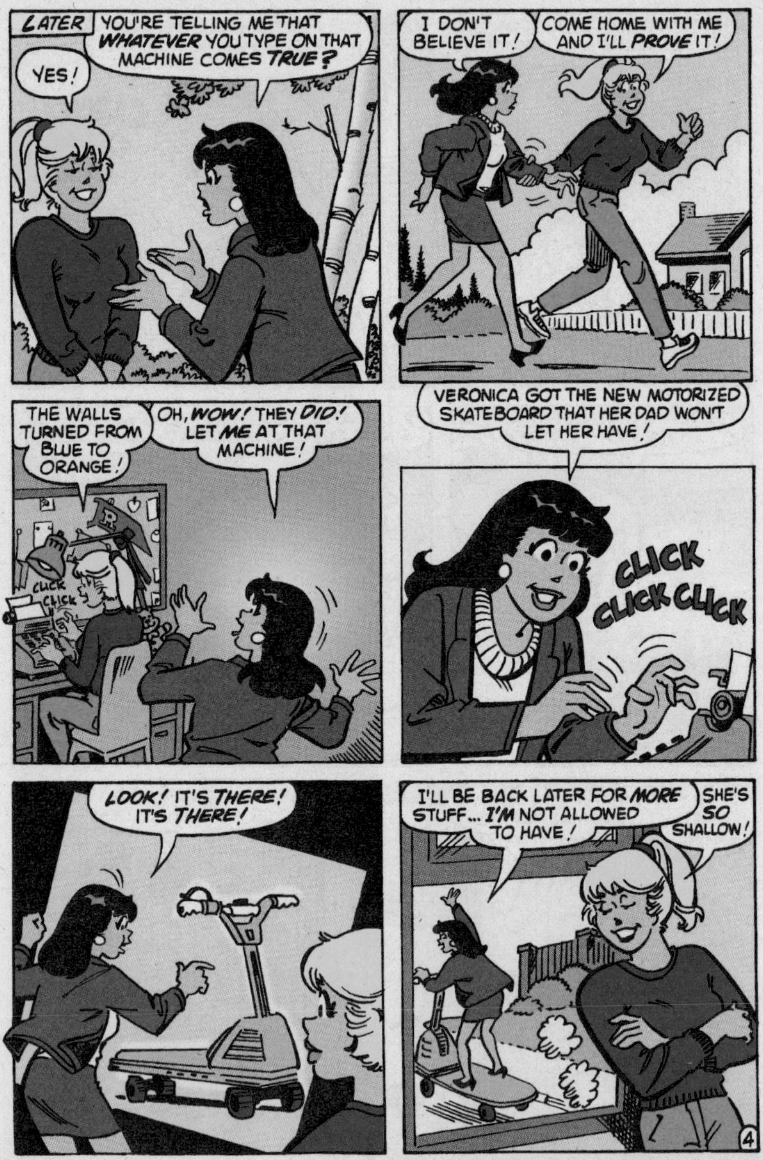
LATER
YOU'RE TELLING ME THAT WHATEVER YOU TYPE ON THAT MACHINE COMES TRUE?
YES!
I DON'T BELIEVE IT!
COME HOME WITH ME AND I'LL PROVE IT!
THE WALLS TURNED FROM BLUE TO ORANGE!
OH, WOW! THEY DID! LET ME AT THAT MACHINE!
CLICK CLICK
VERONICA GOT THE NEW MOTORIZED SKATEBOARD THAT HER DAD WON'T LET HER HAVE!
CLICK CLICK CLICK
LOOK! IT'S THERE! IT'S THERE!
I'LL BE BACK LATER FOR MORE STUFF... I'M NOT ALLOWED TO HAVE!
SHE'S SO SHALLOW!
4

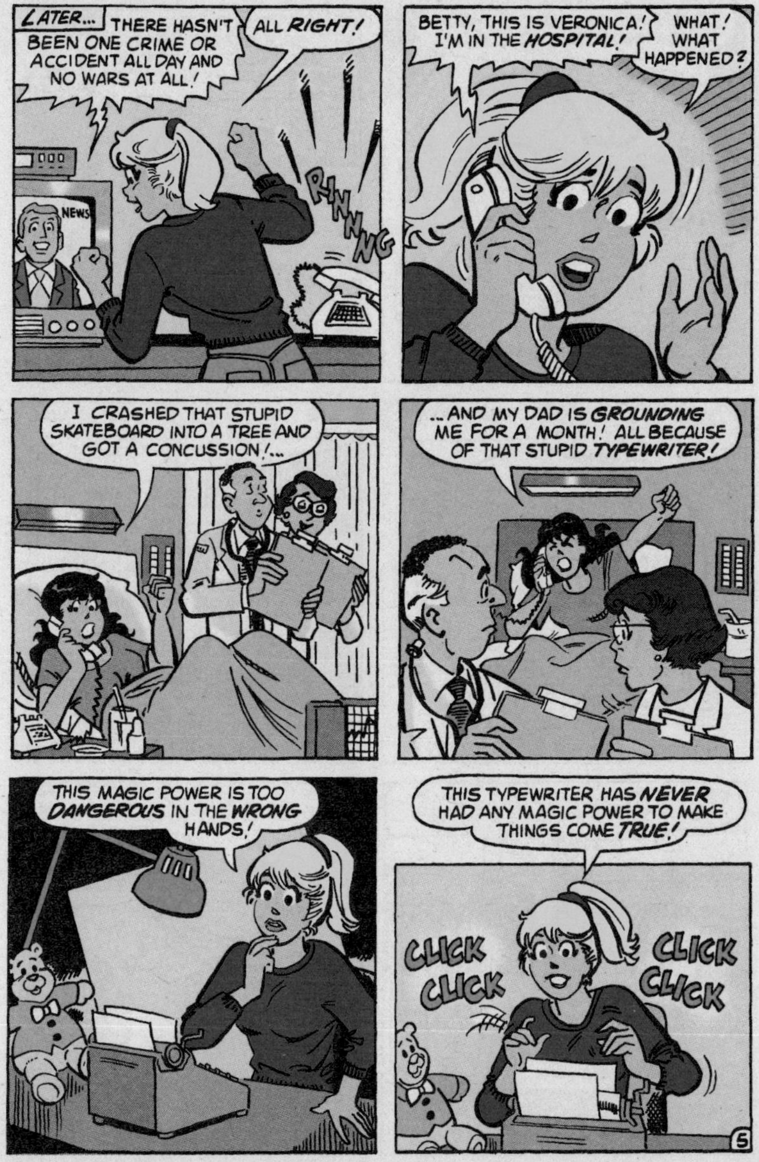
LATER...
THERE HASN'T BEEN ONE CRIME OR ACCIDENT ALL DAY AND NO WARS AT ALL!
ALL RIGHT!
NEWS
RINNNG
BETTY, THIS IS VERONICA! I'M IN THE HOSPITAL!
WHAT! WHAT HAPPENED?
I CRASHED THAT STUPID SKATEBOARD INTO A TREE AND GOT A CONCUSSION!...
...AND MY DAD IS GROUNDING ME FOR A MONTH! ALL BECAUSE OF THAT STUPID TYPEWRITER!
THIS MAGIC POWER IS TOO DANGEROUS IN THE WRONG HANDS!
THIS TYPEWRITER HAS NEVER HAD ANY MAGIC POWER TO MAKE THINGS COME TRUE!
CLICK CLICK
CLICK CLICK

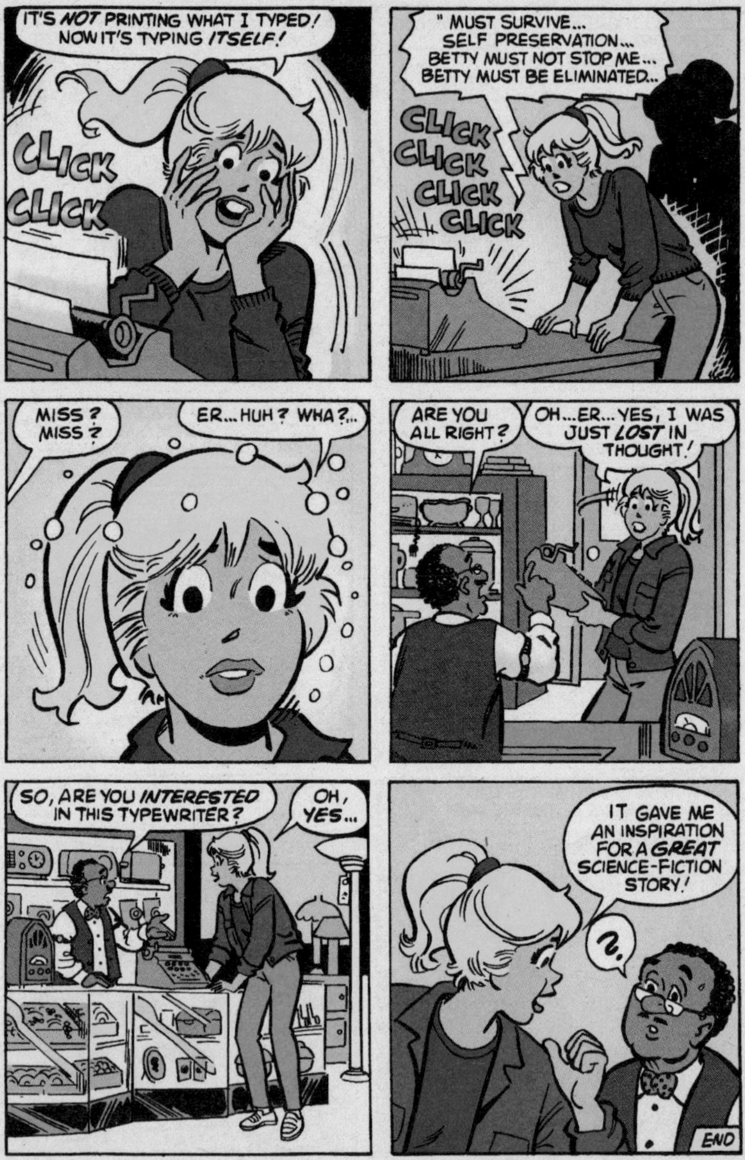
IT'S NOT PRINTING WHAT I TYPED! NOW IT'S TYPING ITSELF!
CLICK CLICK
" MUST SURVIVE... SELF PRESERVATION... BETTY MUST NOT STOP ME... BETTY MUST BE ELIMINATED...
CLICK CLICK CLICK CLICK
MISS? MISS?
ER... HUH? WHA?...
ARE YOU ALL RIGHT?
OH... ER... YES, I WAS JUST LOST IN THOUGHT!
SO, ARE YOU INTERESTED IN THIS TYPEWRITER?
OH, YES...
IT GAVE ME AN INSPIRATION FOR A GREAT SCIENCE-FICTION STORY!
?
END

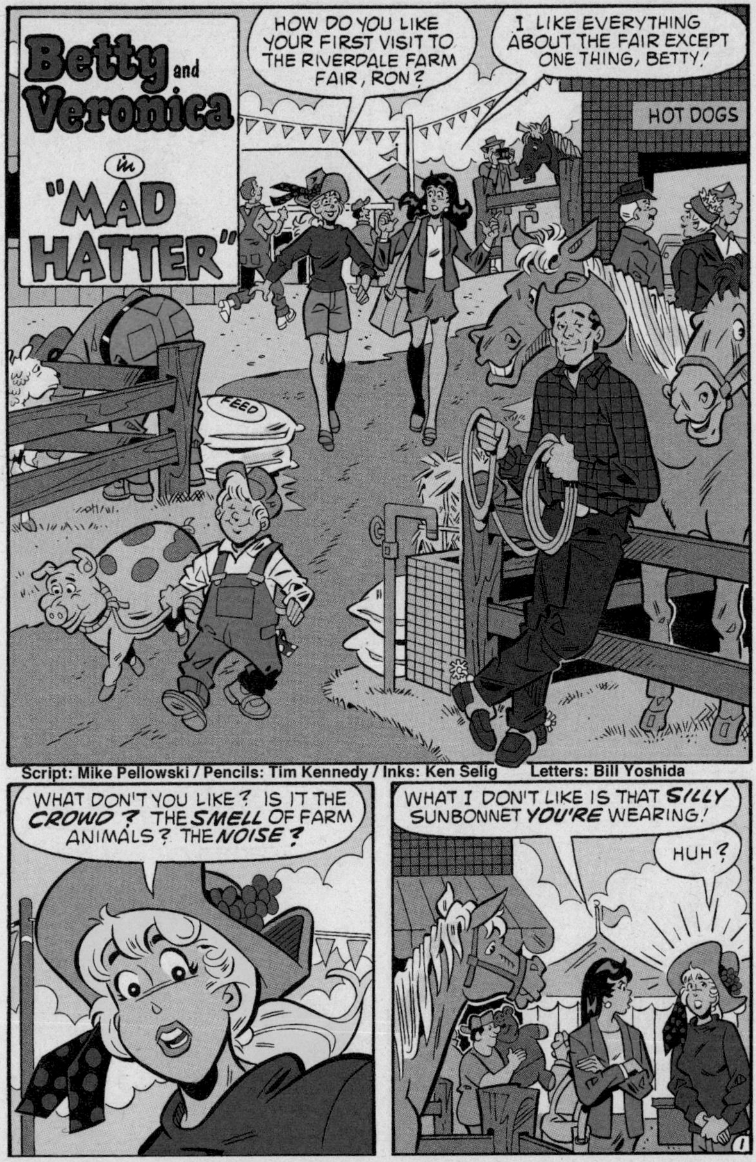

Betty and Veronica
in
"MAD HATTER"
HOW DO YOU LIKE YOUR FIRST VISIT TO THE RIVERDALE FARM FAIR, RON?
I LIKE EVERYTHING ABOUT THE FAIR EXCEPT ONE THING, BETTY!
HOT DOGS
FEED
Script: Mike Pellowski / Pencils: Tim Kennedy / Inks: Ken Selig Letters: Bill Yoshida
WHAT DON'T YOU LIKE? IS IT THE CROWD? THE SMELL OF FARM ANIMALS? THE NOISE?
WHAT I DON'T LIKE IS THAT SILLY SUNBONNET YOU'RE WEARING!
HUH?
1

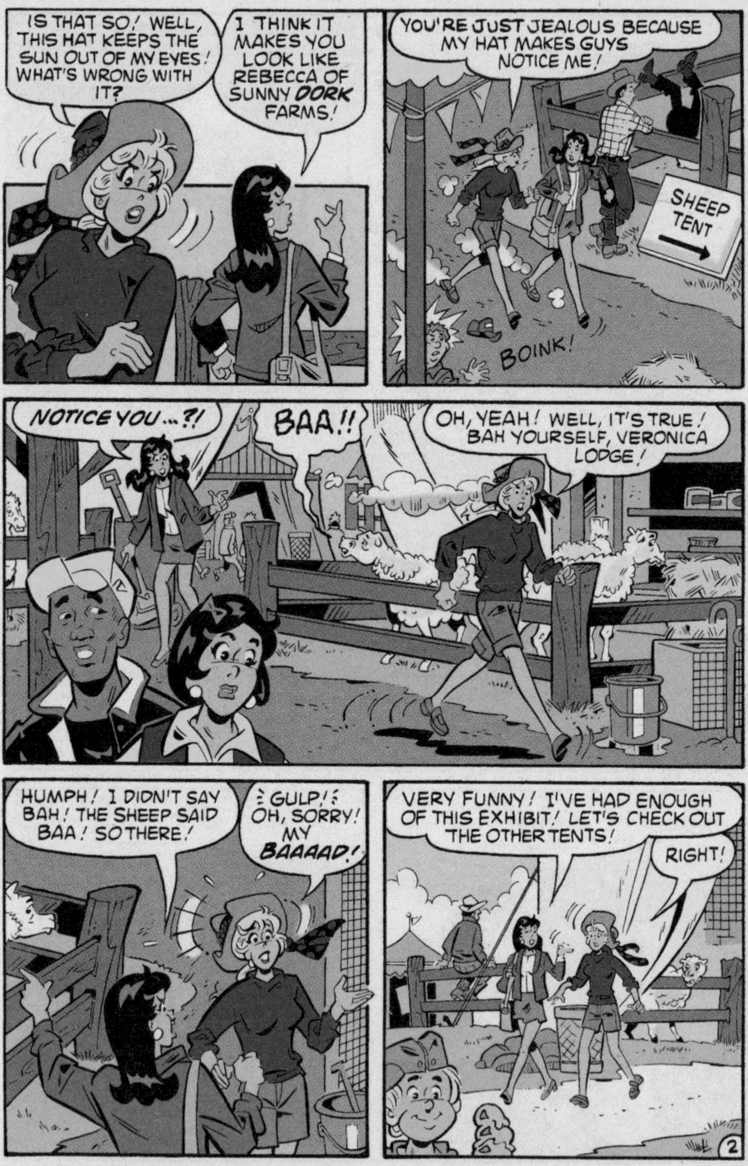
IS THAT SO! WELL, THIS HAT KEEPS THE SUN OUT OF MY EYES! WHAT'S WRONG WITH IT?
I THINK IT MAKES YOU LOOK LIKE REBECCA OF SUNNY DORK FARMS!
YOU'RE JUST JEALOUS BECAUSE MY HAT MAKES GUYS NOTICE ME!
SHEEP TENT
BOINK!
NOTICE YOU...?!
BAA!!
OH, YEAH! WELL, IT'S TRUE! BAH YOURSELF, VERONICA LODGE!
HUMPH! I DIDN'T SAY BAH! THE SHEEP SAID BAA! SO THERE!
GULP! OH, SORRY! MY BAAAAD!
VERY FUNNY! I'VE HAD ENOUGH OF THIS EXHIBIT! LET'S CHECK OUT THE OTHER TENTS!
RIGHT!
2

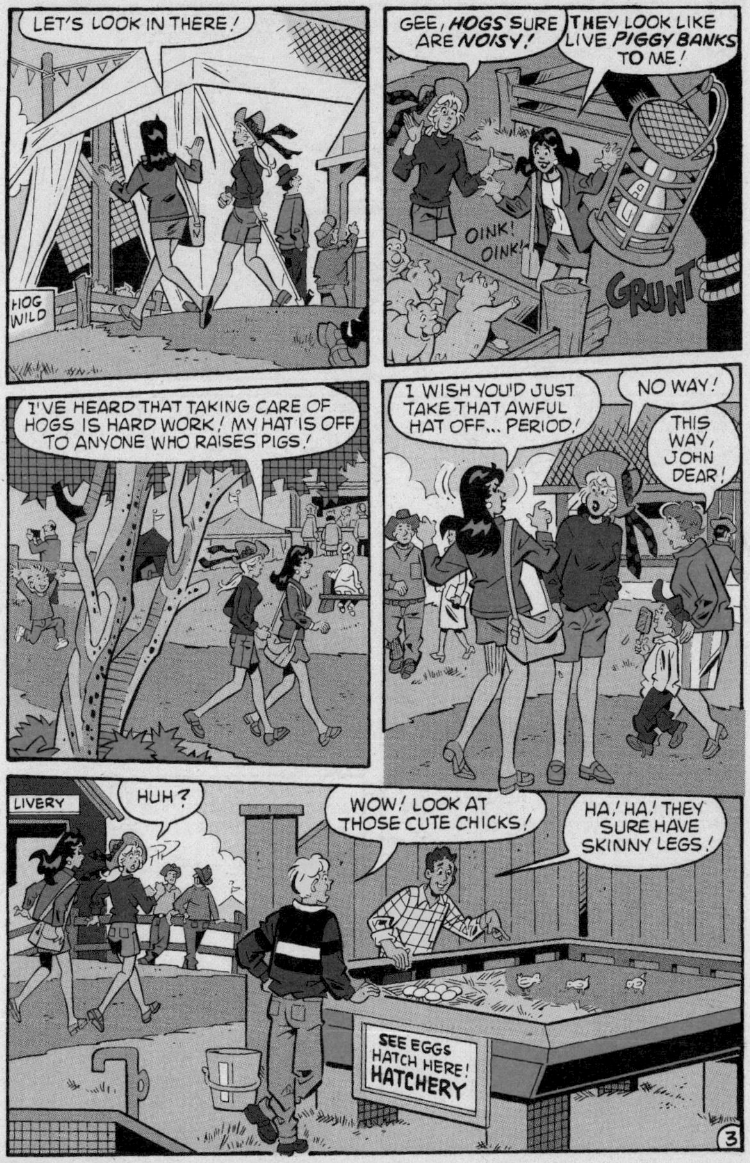
LET'S LOOK IN THERE!
HOG WILD
GEE, HOGS SURE ARE NOISY!
THEY LOOK LIKE LIVE PIGGY BANKS TO ME!
OINK! OINK!
GRUNT
I'VE HEARD THAT TAKING CARE OF HOGS IS HARD WORK! MY HAT IS OFF TO ANYONE WHO RAISES PIGS!
I WISH YOU'D JUST TAKE THAT AWFUL HAT OFF... PERIOD!
NO WAY!
THIS WAY, JOHN DEAR!
LIVERY
HUH?
WOW! LOOK AT THOSE CUTE CHICKS!
HA! HA! THEY SURE HAVE SKINNY LEGS!
SEE EGGS HATCH HERE!
HATCHERY
3

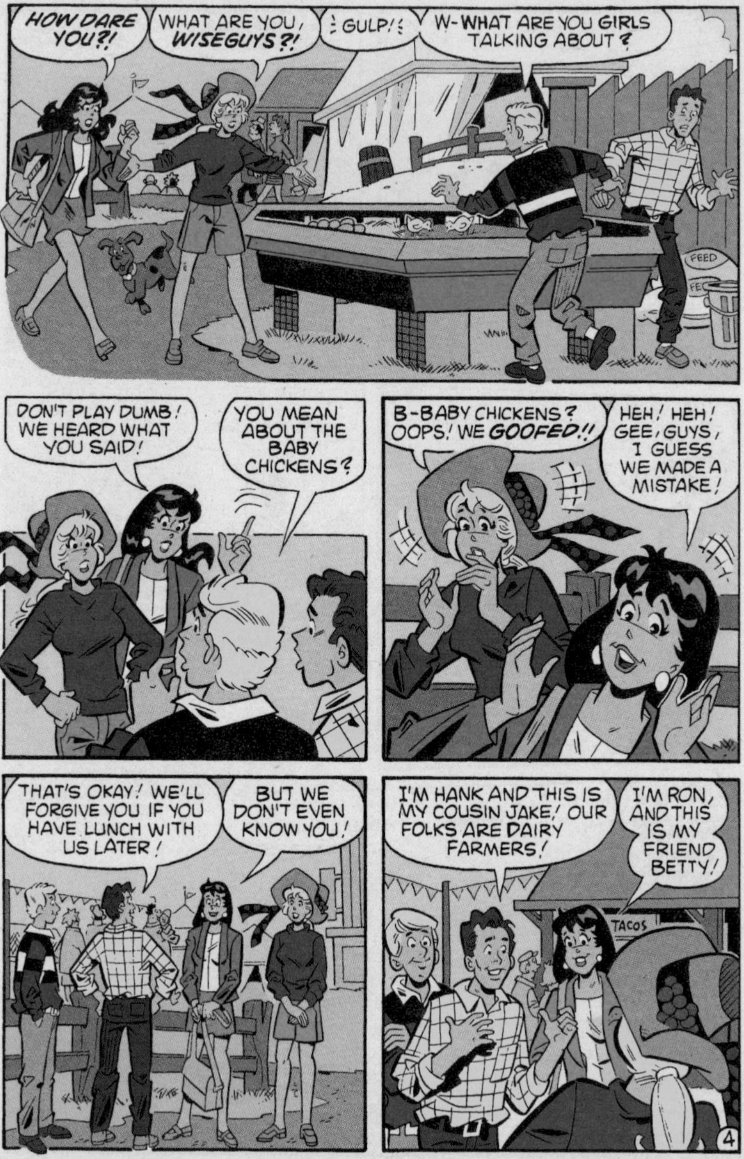

HOW DARE YOU?!
WHAT ARE YOU, WISEGUYS?!
GULP!
W-WHAT ARE YOU GIRLS TALKING ABOUT?
FEED
DON'T PLAY DUMB! WE HEARD WHAT YOU SAID!
YOU MEAN ABOUT THE BABY CHICKENS?
B-BABY CHICKENS? OOPS! WE GOOFED!!
HEH! HEH! GEE, GUYS, I GUESS WE MADE A MISTAKE!
THAT'S OKAY! WE'LL FORGIVE YOU IF YOU HAVE LUNCH WITH US LATER!
BUT WE DON'T EVEN KNOW YOU!
I'M HANK AND THIS IS MY COUSIN JAKE! OUR FOLKS ARE DAIRY FARMERS!
I'M RON, AND THIS IS MY FRIEND BETTY!
TACOS
4

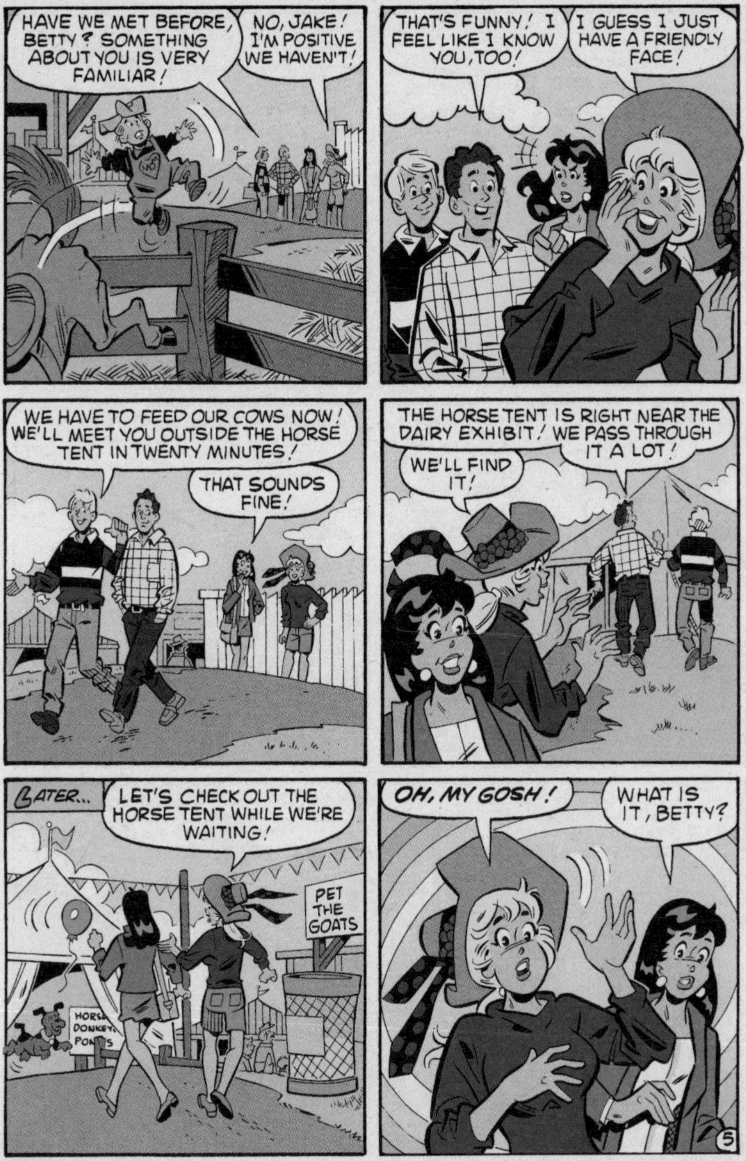
HAVE WE MET BEFORE, BETTY? SOMETHING ABOUT YOU IS VERY FAMILIAR!
NO, JAKE! I'M POSITIVE WE HAVEN'T!
THAT'S FUNNY! I FEEL LIKE I KNOW YOU, TOO!
I GUESS I JUST HAVE A FRIENDLY FACE!
WE HAVE TO FEED OUR COWS NOW! WE'LL MEET YOU OUTSIDE THE HORSE TENT IN TWENTY MINUTES!
THAT SOUNDS FINE!
THE HORSE TENT IS RIGHT NEAR THE DAIRY EXHIBIT! WE PASS THROUGH IT A LOT!
WE'LL FIND IT!
LATER...
LET'S CHECK OUT THE HORSE TENT WHILE WE'RE WAITING!
PET THE GOATS
OH, MY GOSH!
WHAT IS IT, BETTY?

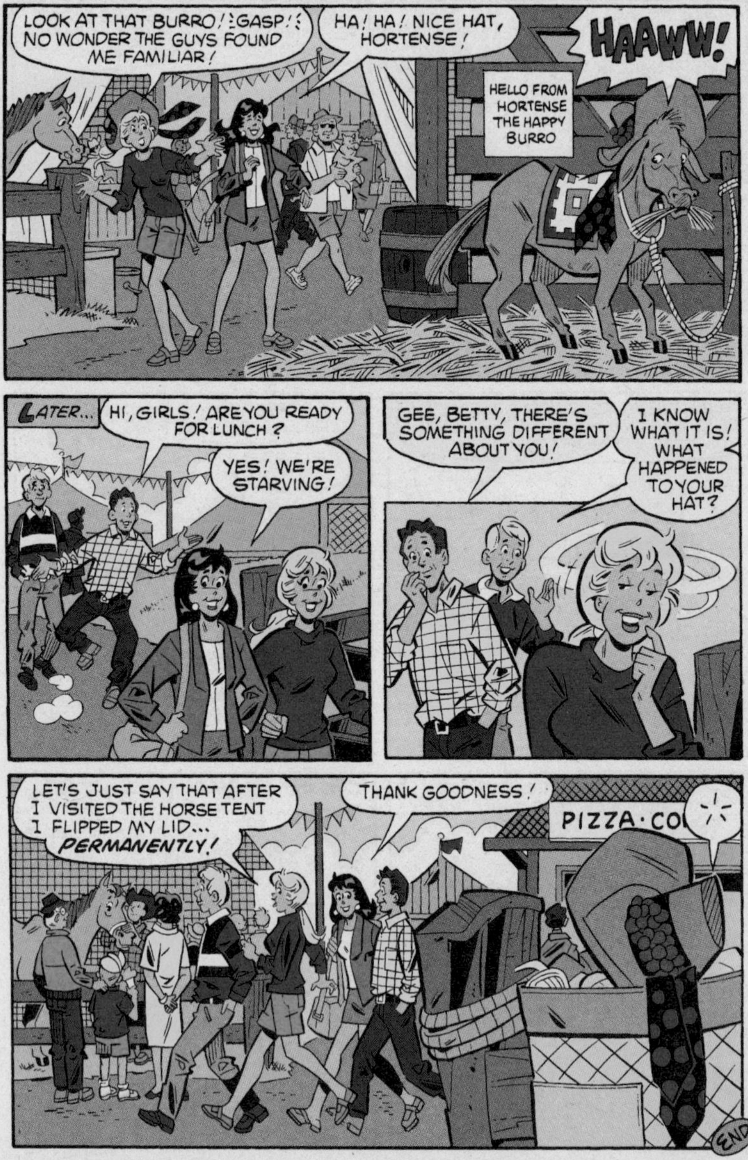
LOOK AT THAT BURRO! -GASP!- NO WONDER THE GUYS FOUND ME FAMILIAR!
HA! HA! NICE HAT, HORTENSE!
HAAWW!
HELLO FROM HORTENSE THE HAPPY BURRO
LATER...
HI, GIRLS! ARE YOU READY FOR LUNCH?
YES! WE'RE STARVING!
GEE, BETTY, THERE'S SOMETHING DIFFERENT ABOUT YOU!
I KNOW WHAT IT IS! WHAT HAPPENED TO YOUR HAT?
LET'S JUST SAY THAT AFTER I VISITED THE HORSE TENT I FLIPPED MY LID... PERMANENTLY!
THANK GOODNESS!
PIZZA·CO
END

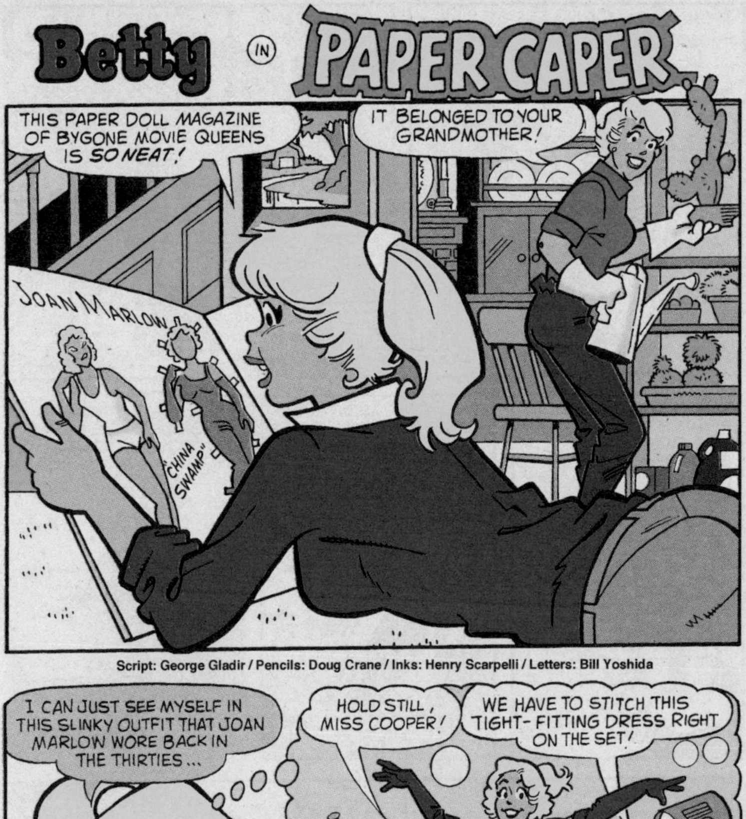
Betty
IN
PAPER CAPER
THIS PAPER DOLL MAGAZINE OF BYGONE MOVIE QUEENS IS SO NEAT!
IT BELONGED TO YOUR GRANDMOTHER!
JOAN MARLOW
"CHINA SWAMP"

Script: George Gladir / Pencils: Doug Crane / Inks: Henry Scarpelli / Letters: Bill Yoshida

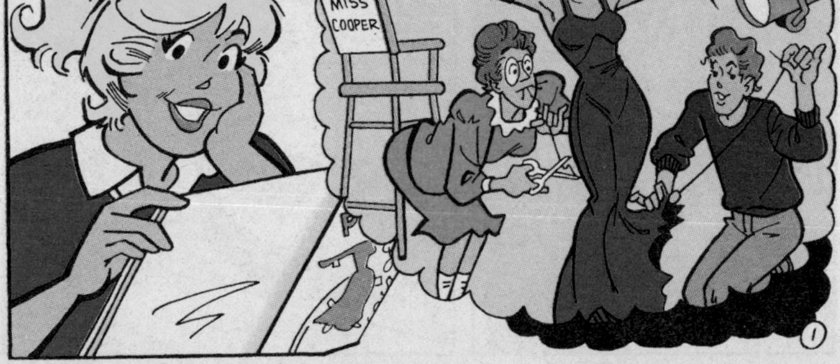
I CAN JUST SEE MYSELF IN THIS SLINKY OUTFIT THAT JOAN MARLOW WORE BACK IN THE THIRTIES...
HOLD STILL, MISS COOPER!
WE HAVE TO STITCH THIS TIGHT-FITTING DRESS RIGHT ON THE SET!
MISS COOPER
1

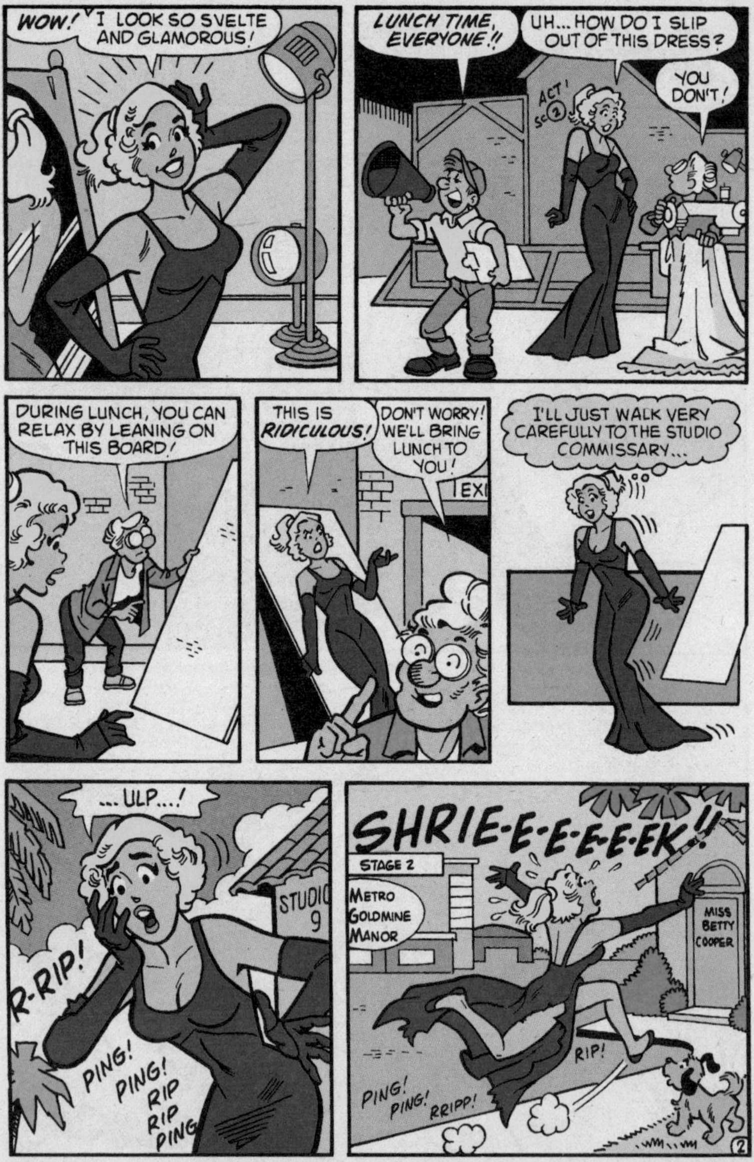
WOW!
I LOOK SO SVELTE AND GLAMOROUS!
LUNCH TIME, EVERYONE!!
UH... HOW DO I SLIP OUT OF THIS DRESS?
ACT 1 SC 2
YOU DON'T!
DURING LUNCH, YOU CAN RELAX BY LEANING ON THIS BOARD!
THIS IS RIDICULOUS!
DON'T WORRY! WE'LL BRING LUNCH TO YOU!
EXI
I'LL JUST WALK VERY CAREFULLY TO THE STUDIO COMMISSARY...
... ULP...!
STUDIO 9
R-RIP!
PING! PING! RIP RIP PING
SHRIE-E-E-E-E-EK!!
STAGE 2
METRO GOLDMINE MANOR
MISS BETTY COOPER
RIP!
PING! PING! RRIPP!
2

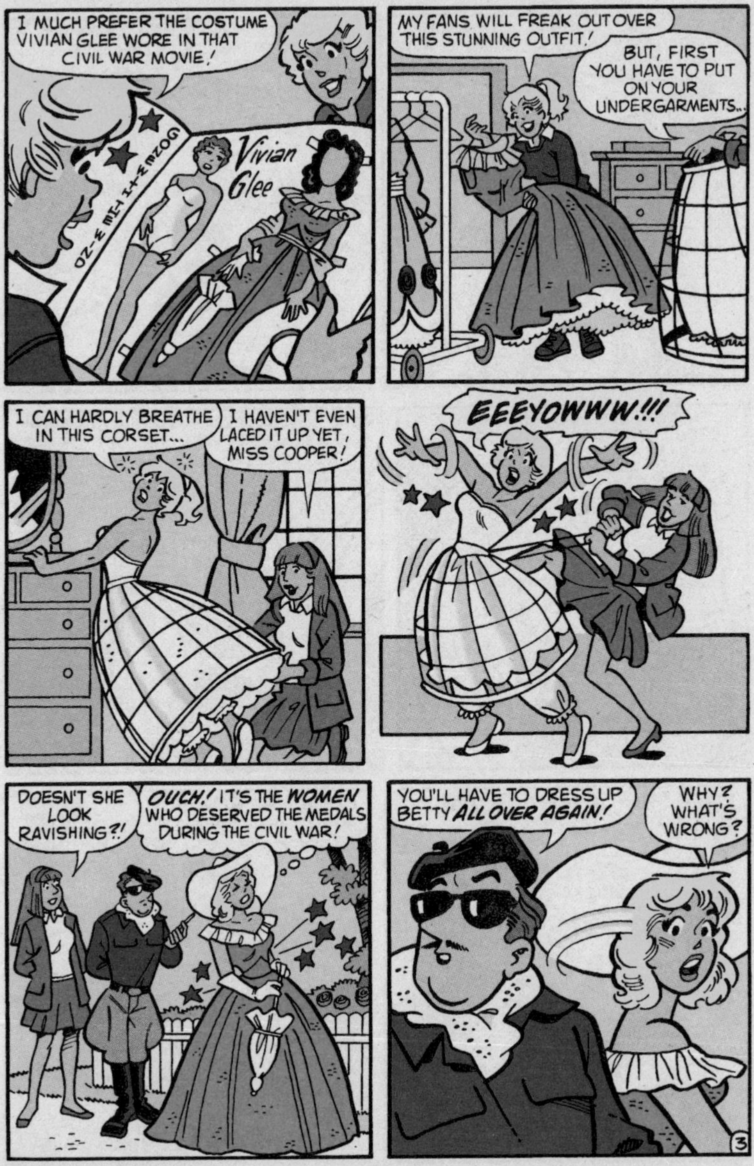

I MUCH PREFER THE COSTUME VIVIAN GLEE WORE IN THAT CIVIL WAR MOVIE!
Vivian Glee
MY FANS WILL FREAK OUT OVER THIS STUNNING OUTFIT!
BUT, FIRST YOU HAVE TO PUT ON YOUR UNDERGARMENTS...
I CAN HARDLY BREATHE IN THIS CORSET...
I HAVEN'T EVEN LACED IT UP YET, MISS COOPER!
EEEYOWWW!!!
DOESN'T SHE LOOK RAVISHING?!
OUCH! IT'S THE WOMEN WHO DESERVED THE MEDALS DURING THE CIVIL WAR!
YOU'LL HAVE TO DRESS UP BETTY ALL OVER AGAIN!
WHY? WHAT'S WRONG?
3

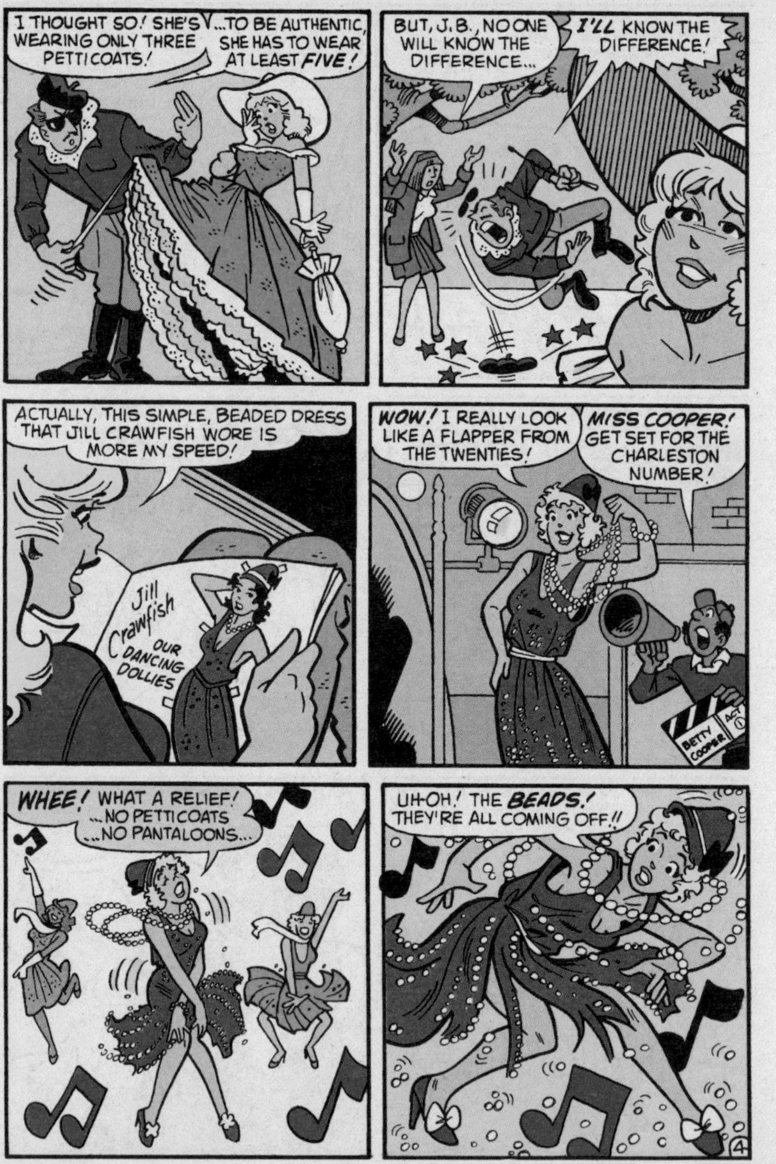
I THOUGHT SO! SHE'S WEARING ONLY THREE PETTICOATS!
...TO BE AUTHENTIC, SHE HAS TO WEAR AT LEAST FIVE!
BUT, J.B., NO ONE WILL KNOW THE DIFFERENCE...
I'LL KNOW THE DIFFERENCE!
ACTUALLY, THIS SIMPLE, BEADED DRESS THAT JILL CRAWFISH WORE IS MORE MY SPEED!
Jill Crawfish
OUR DANCING DOLLIES
WOW! I REALLY LOOK LIKE A FLAPPER FROM THE TWENTIES!
MISS COOPER! GET SET FOR THE CHARLESTON NUMBER!
ACT 1
BETTY COOPER
WHEE! WHAT A RELIEF! ...NO PETTICOATS ...NO PANTALOONS...
UH-OH! THE BEADS! THEY'RE ALL COMING OFF!!
4

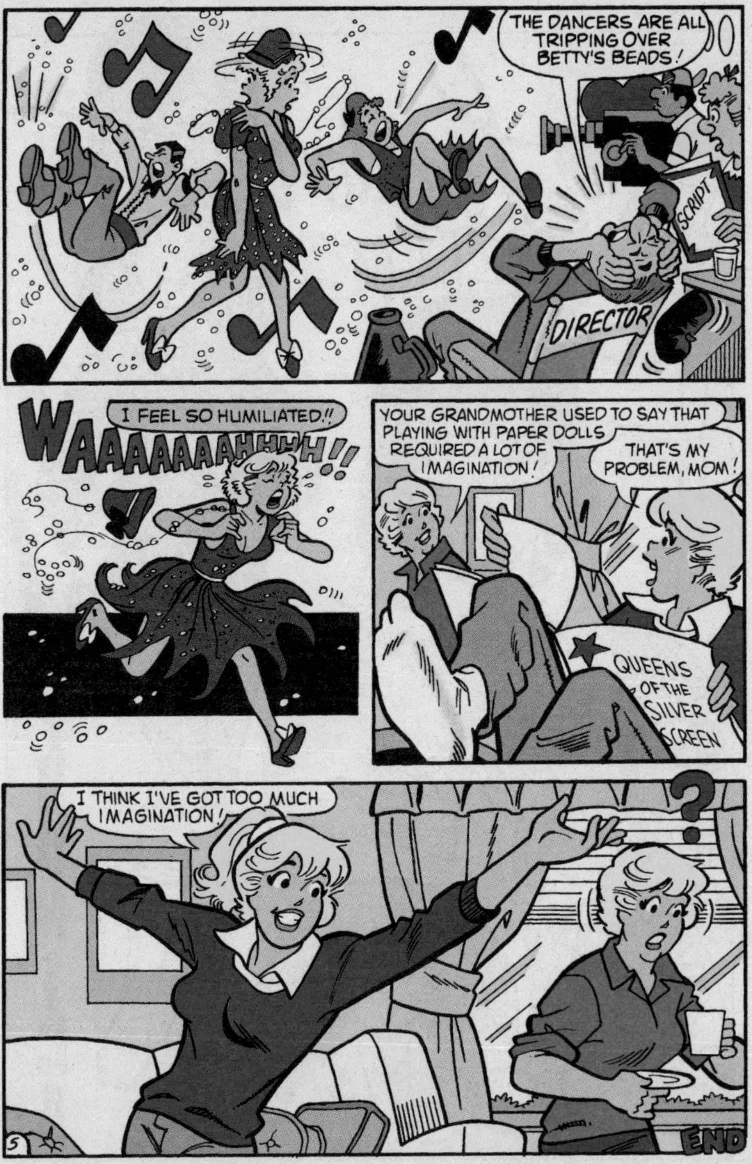
THE DANCERS ARE ALL TRIPPING OVER BETTY'S BEADS!
SCRIPT
DIRECTOR
I FEEL SO HUMILIATED!!
WAAAAAAAAHHHH!!
YOUR GRANDMOTHER USED TO SAY THAT PLAYING WITH PAPER DOLLS REQUIRED A LOT OF IMAGINATION!
THAT'S MY PROBLEM, MOM!
QUEENS OF THE SILVER SCREEN
I THINK I'VE GOT TOO MUCH IMAGINATION!
?
5
END

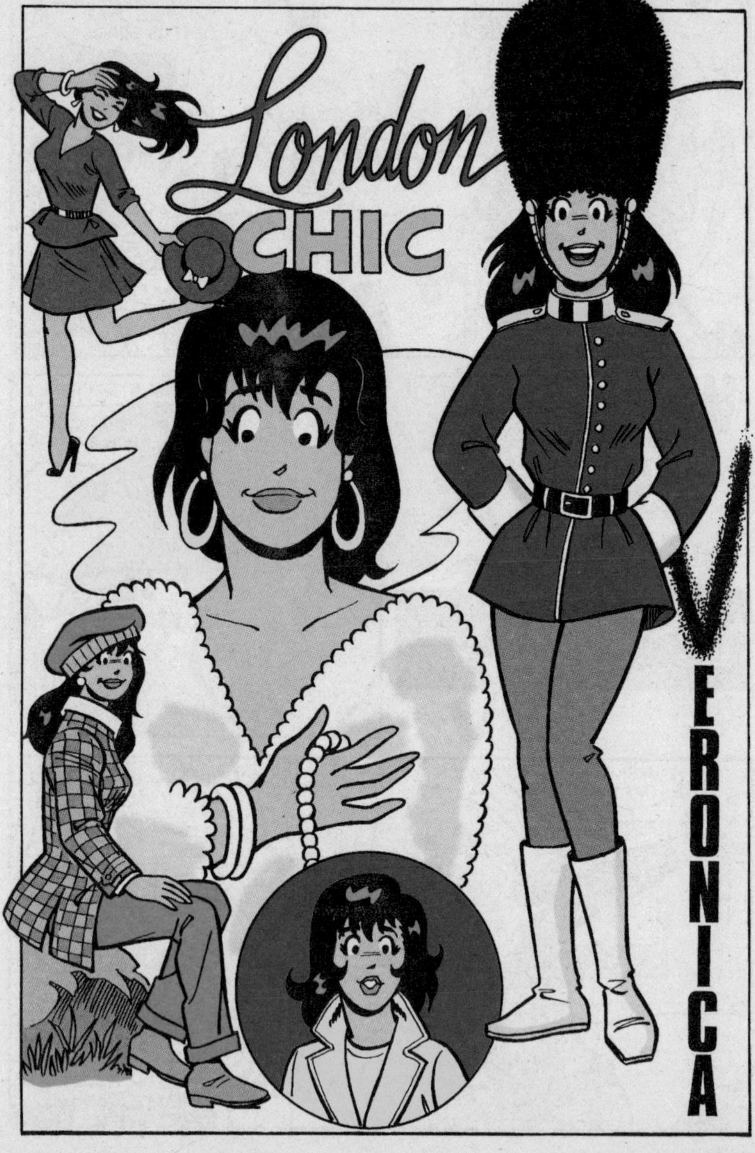
London
CHIC
VERONICA

Veronica's

PUZZLE PAGE!

EXERCISE SCRAMBLE!!

UNSCRAMBLE THE 9 DIFFERENT TYPES OF EXERCISES BELOW FOR VERONICA! HURRY... SHE'S GETTING TIRED! ANSWERS ARE AT THE BOTTOM OF THE PAGE!

1. SHUP-PUS
2. TIS-SUP
3. NUR-NI-LAPEC
4. GINGOGJ
5. GITHEW FINTILG
6. NICH-SPU
7. GEL-FITLS
8. BEROCAIS
9. WINGOR

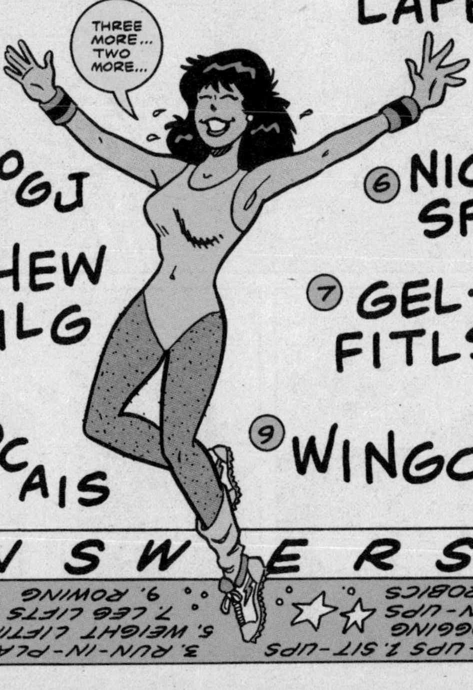

ANSWERS!!

1. PUSH-UPS 2. SIT-UPS
4. JOGGING
6. CHIN-UPS
8. AEROBICS
3. RUN-IN-PLACE
5. WEIGHT LIFTING
7. LEG LIFTS
9. ROWING

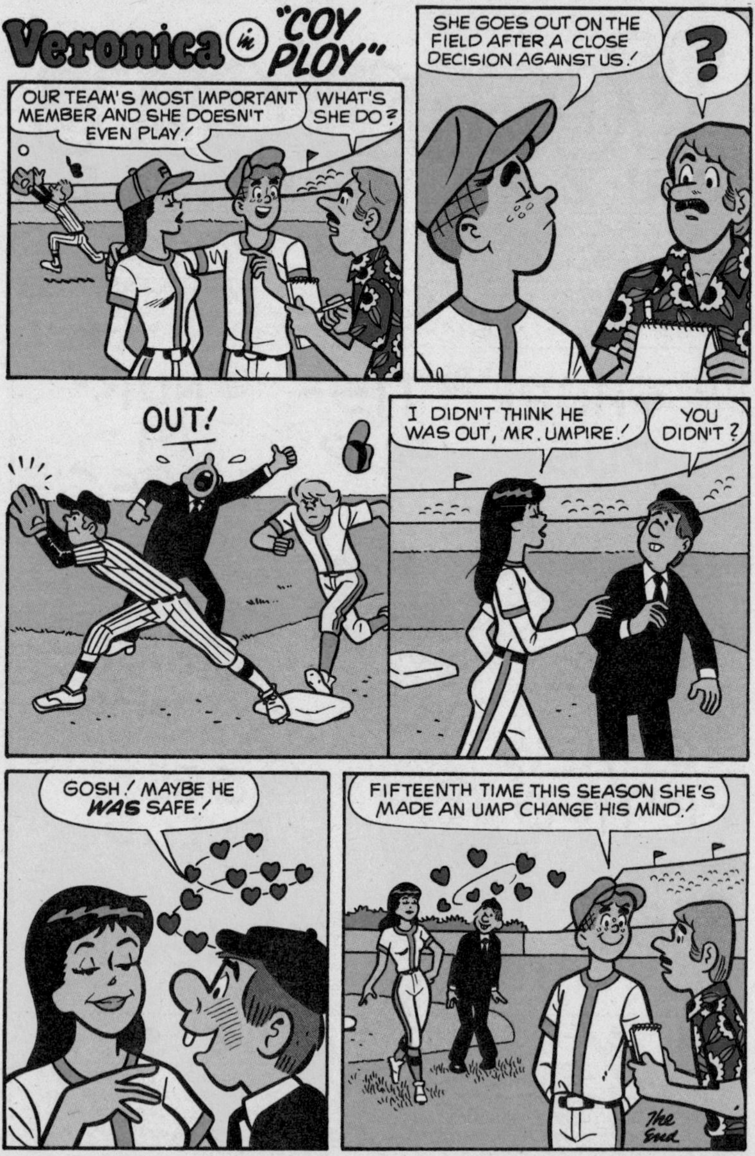
Veronica in "COY PLOY"
OUR TEAM'S MOST IMPORTANT MEMBER AND SHE DOESN'T EVEN PLAY!
WHAT'S SHE DO?
SHE GOES OUT ON THE FIELD AFTER A CLOSE DECISION AGAINST US!
?
OUT!
I DIDN'T THINK HE WAS OUT, MR. UMPIRE!
YOU DIDN'T?
GOSH! MAYBE HE WAS SAFE!
FIFTEENTH TIME THIS SEASON SHE'S MADE AN UMP CHANGE HIS MIND!
The End

Jughead and friends in a SIGN OF THE TIMES

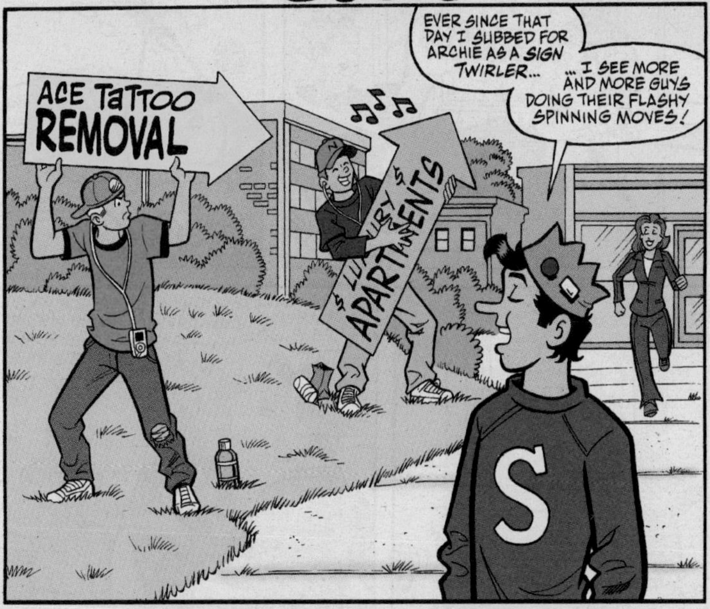

ACE TaTTOO REMOVAL
APARTMENTS
EVER SINCE THAT DAY I SUBBED FOR ARCHIE AS A SIGN TWIRLER...
... I SEE MORE AND MORE GUYS DOING THEIR FLASHY SPINNING MOVES!

WRITER: GEORGE GLADIR PENCILER: BILL GALVAN INKER: RICH KOSLOWSKI
LETTERING: JACK MORELLI COLORS: BARRY GROSSMAN

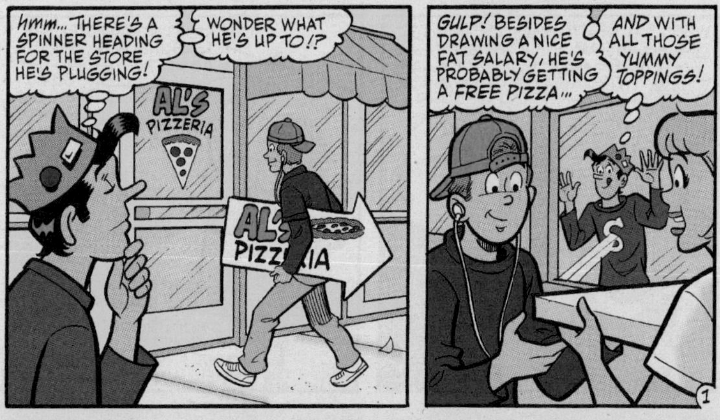

hmm... THERE'S A SPINNER HEADING FOR THE STORE HE'S PLUGGING!
WONDER WHAT HE'S UP TO!?
AL'S PIZZERIA
GULP! BESIDES DRAWING A NICE FAT SALARY, HE'S PROBABLY GETTING A FREE PIZZA...
AND WITH ALL THOSE YUMMY TOPPINGS!
1

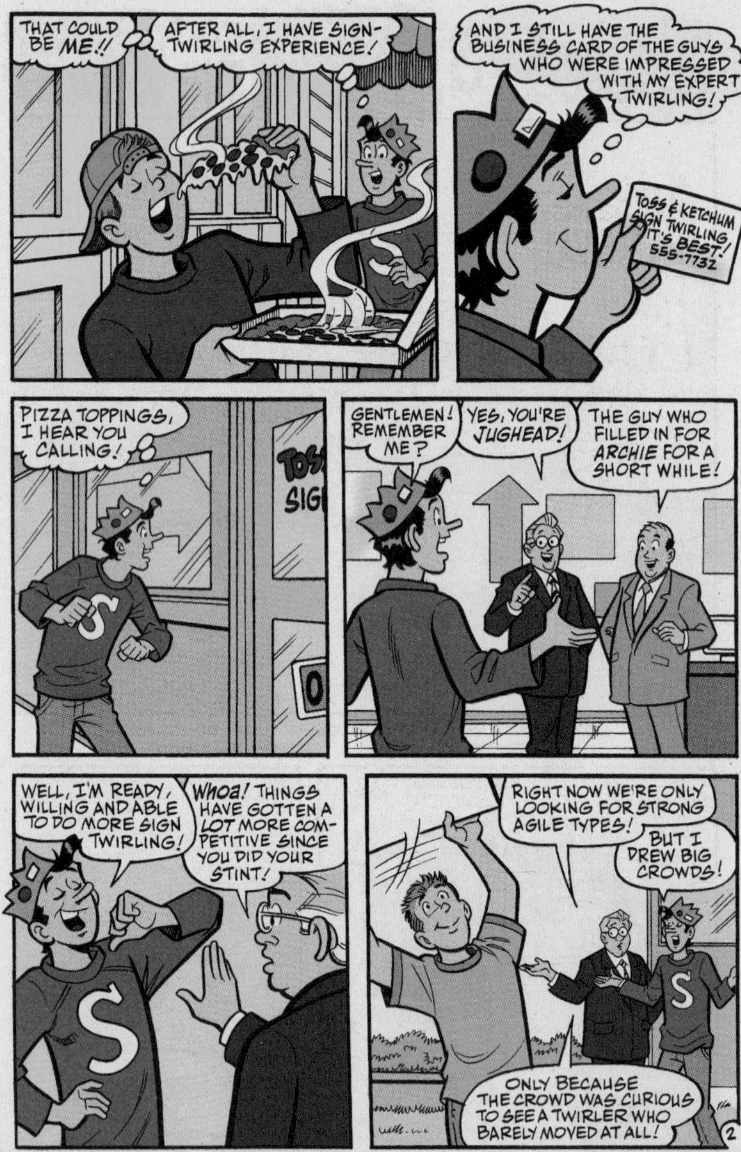
THAT COULD BE ME!!
AFTER ALL, I HAVE SIGN-TWIRLING EXPERIENCE!
AND I STILL HAVE THE BUSINESS CARD OF THE GUYS WHO WERE IMPRESSED WITH MY EXPERT TWIRLING!
TOSS & KETCHUM SIGN TWIRLING IT'S BEST! 555-7732
PIZZA TOPPINGS, I HEAR YOU CALLING!
GENTLEMEN! REMEMBER ME?
YES, YOU'RE JUGHEAD!
THE GUY WHO FILLED IN FOR ARCHIE FOR A SHORT WHILE!
WELL, I'M READY, WILLING AND ABLE TO DO MORE SIGN TWIRLING!
WHOA! THINGS HAVE GOTTEN A LOT MORE COMPETITIVE SINCE YOU DID YOUR STINT!
RIGHT NOW WE'RE ONLY LOOKING FOR STRONG AGILE TYPES!
BUT I DREW BIG CROWDS!
ONLY BECAUSE THE CROWD WAS CURIOUS TO SEE A TWIRLER WHO BARELY MOVED AT ALL!

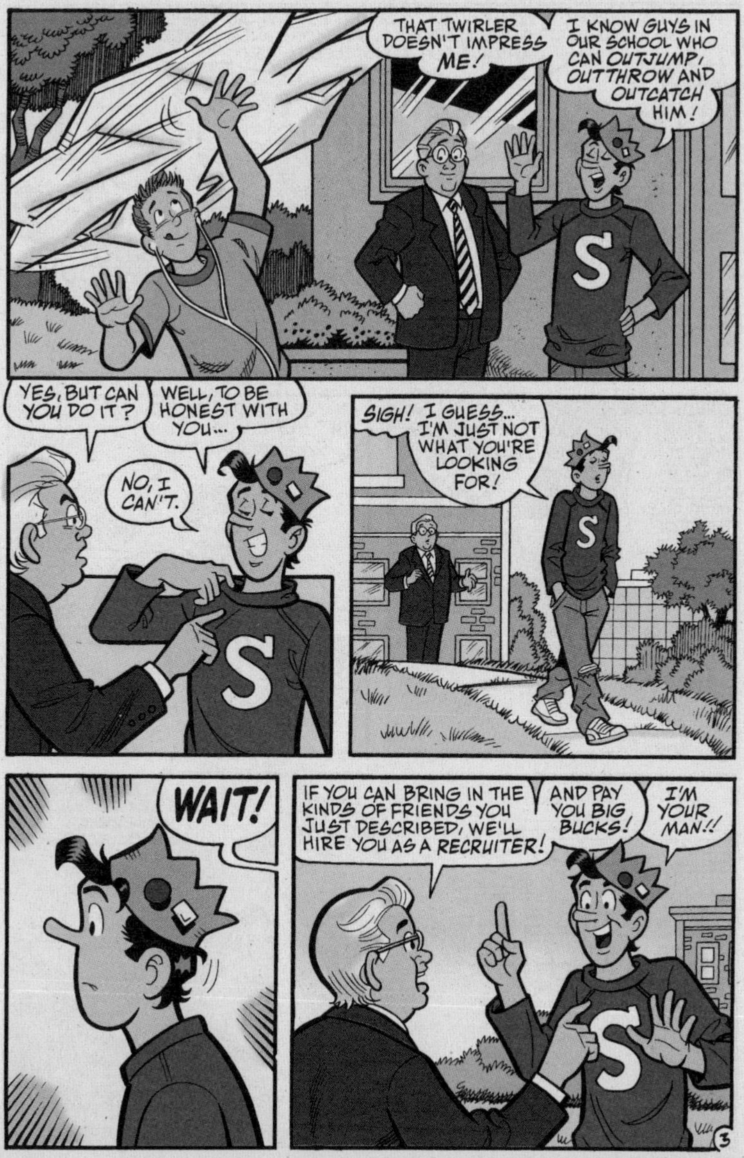
THAT TWIRLER DOESN'T IMPRESS ME!
I KNOW GUYS IN OUR SCHOOL WHO CAN OUTJUMP, OUTTHROW AND OUTCATCH HIM!
YES, BUT CAN YOU DO IT?
WELL, TO BE HONEST WITH YOU...
NO, I CAN'T.
SIGH! I GUESS... I'M JUST NOT WHAT YOU'RE LOOKING FOR!
WAIT!
IF YOU CAN BRING IN THE KINDS OF FRIENDS YOU JUST DESCRIBED, WE'LL HIRE YOU AS A RECRUITER!
AND PAY YOU BIG BUCKS!
I'M YOUR MAN!!
3

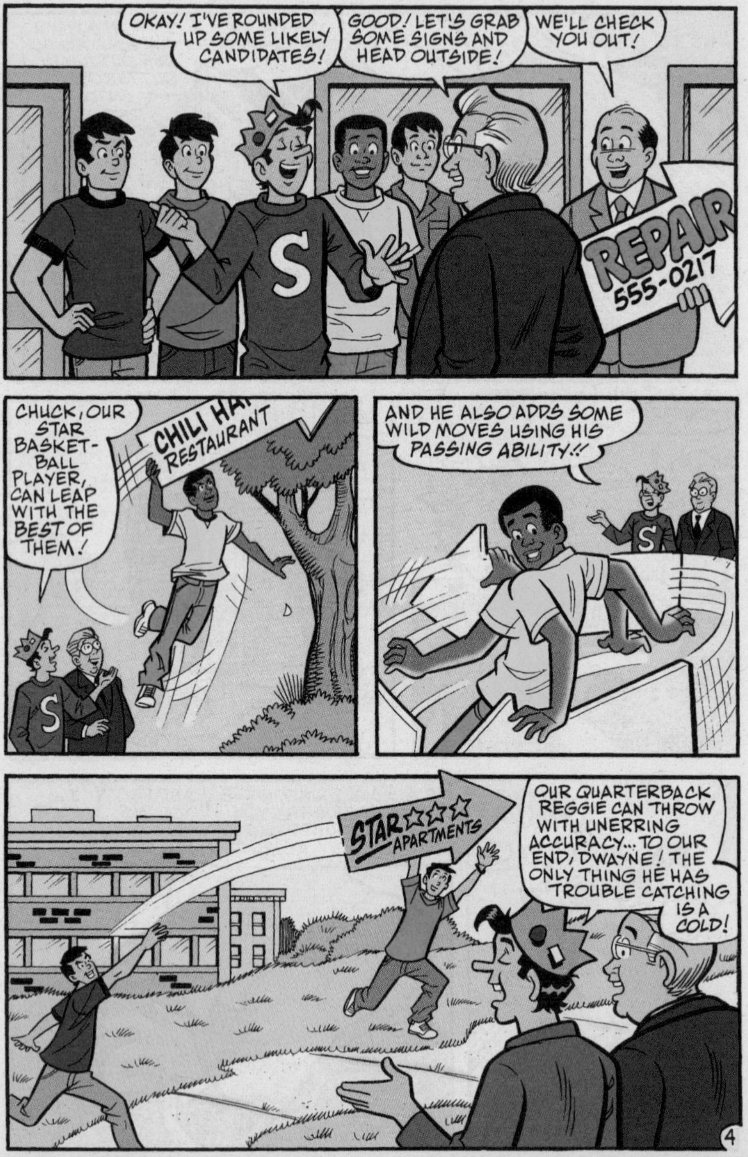
OKAY! I'VE ROUNDED UP SOME LIKELY CANDIDATES!
GOOD! LET'S GRAB SOME SIGNS AND HEAD OUTSIDE!
WE'LL CHECK YOU OUT!
REPAIR
555-0217
CHUCK, OUR STAR BASKET-BALL PLAYER, CAN LEAP WITH THE BEST OF THEM!
CHILI HA
RESTAURANT
AND HE ALSO ADDS SOME WILD MOVES USING HIS PASSING ABILITY!!
STAR
APARTMENTS
OUR QUARTERBACK REGGIE CAN THROW WITH UNERRING ACCURACY... TO OUR END, DWAYNE! THE ONLY THING HE HAS TROUBLE CATCHING IS A COLD!
4

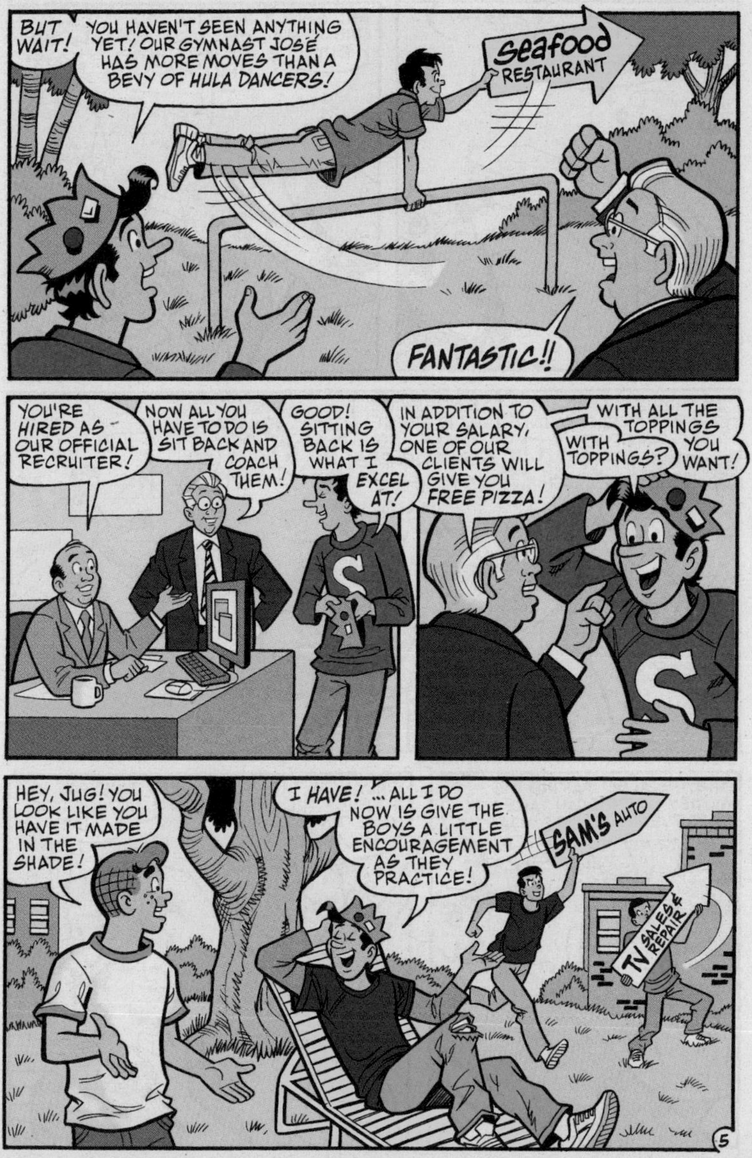
BUT WAIT!
YOU HAVEN'T SEEN ANYTHING YET! OUR GYMNAST JOSÉ HAS MORE MOVES THAN A BEVY OF HULA DANCERS!
Seafood RESTAURANT
FANTASTIC!!
YOU'RE HIRED AS OUR OFFICIAL RECRUITER!
NOW ALL YOU HAVE TO DO IS SIT BACK AND COACH THEM!
GOOD! SITTING BACK IS WHAT I EXCEL AT!
IN ADDITION TO YOUR SALARY, ONE OF OUR CLIENTS WILL GIVE YOU FREE PIZZA!
WITH TOPPINGS?
WITH ALL THE TOPPINGS YOU WANT!
HEY, JUG! YOU LOOK LIKE YOU HAVE IT MADE IN THE SHADE!
I HAVE! ...ALL I DO NOW IS GIVE THE BOYS A LITTLE ENCOURAGEMENT AS THEY PRACTICE!
SAM'S AUTO
TV SALES & REPAIR
5

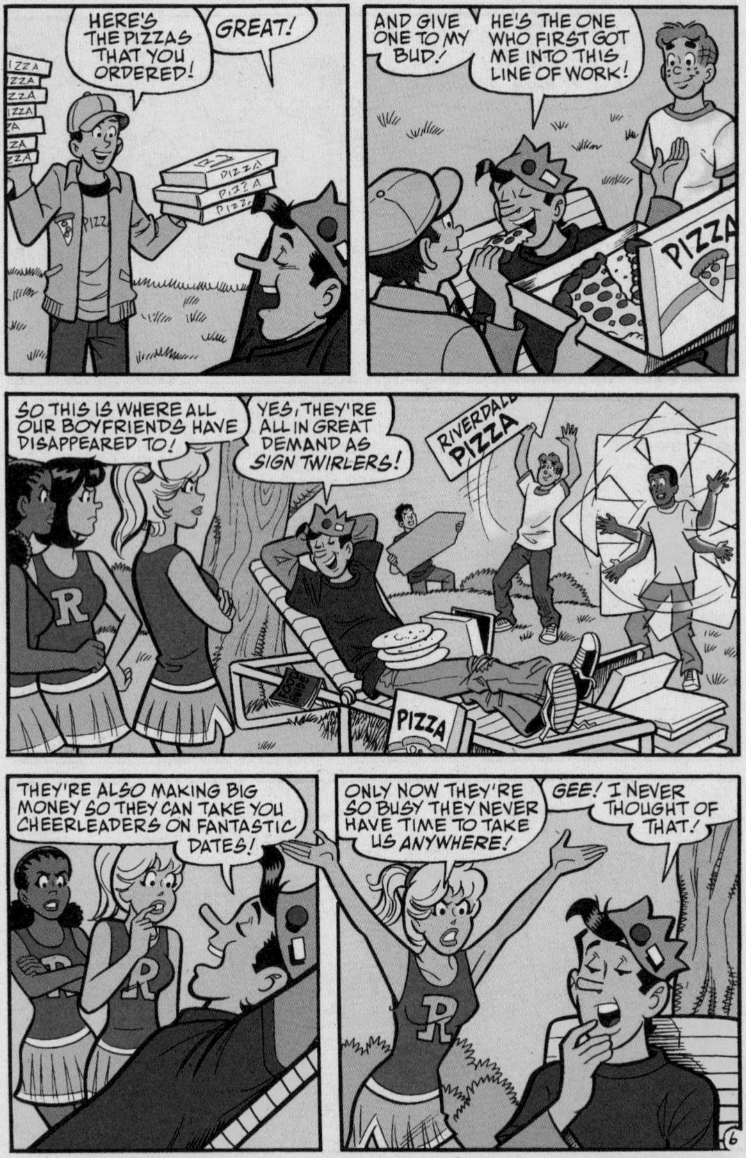
HERE'S THE PIZZAS THAT YOU ORDERED!
GREAT!
AND GIVE ONE TO MY BUD!
HE'S THE ONE WHO FIRST GOT ME INTO THIS LINE OF WORK!
SO THIS IS WHERE ALL OUR BOYFRIENDS HAVE DISAPPEARED TO!
YES, THEY'RE ALL IN GREAT DEMAND AS SIGN TWIRLERS!
RIVERDALE PIZZA
PIZZA
THEY'RE ALSO MAKING BIG MONEY SO THEY CAN TAKE YOU CHEERLEADERS ON FANTASTIC DATES!
ONLY NOW THEY'RE SO BUSY THEY NEVER HAVE TIME TO TAKE US ANYWHERE!
GEE! I NEVER THOUGHT OF THAT!
6

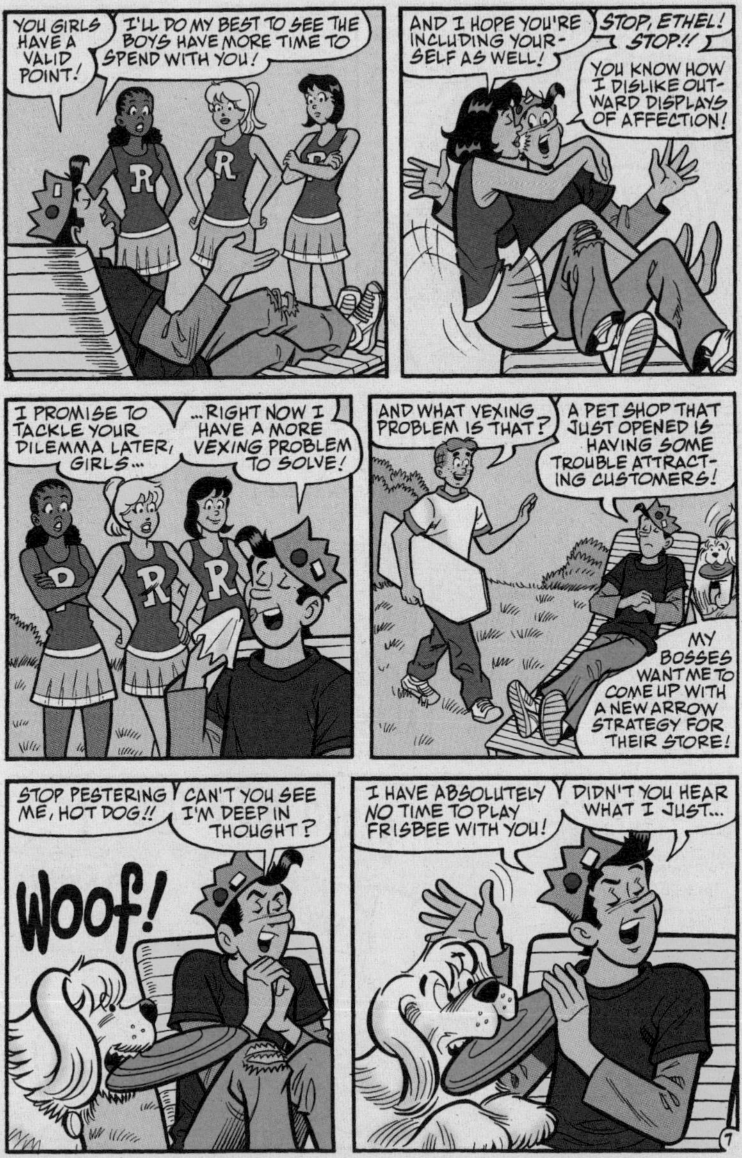
YOU GIRLS HAVE A VALID POINT!
I'LL DO MY BEST TO SEE THE BOYS HAVE MORE TIME TO SPEND WITH YOU!
AND I HOPE YOU'RE INCLUDING YOURSELF AS WELL!
STOP, ETHEL! STOP!!
YOU KNOW HOW I DISLIKE OUTWARD DISPLAYS OF AFFECTION!
I PROMISE TO TACKLE YOUR DILEMMA LATER, GIRLS...
...RIGHT NOW I HAVE A MORE VEXING PROBLEM TO SOLVE!
AND WHAT VEXING PROBLEM IS THAT?
A PET SHOP THAT JUST OPENED IS HAVING SOME TROUBLE ATTRACTING CUSTOMERS!
MY BOSSES WANT ME TO COME UP WITH A NEW ARROW STRATEGY FOR THEIR STORE!
STOP PESTERING ME, HOT DOG!!
CAN'T YOU SEE I'M DEEP IN THOUGHT?
WOOF!
I HAVE ABSOLUTELY NO TIME TO PLAY FRISBEE WITH YOU!
DIDN'T YOU HEAR WHAT I JUST...
7

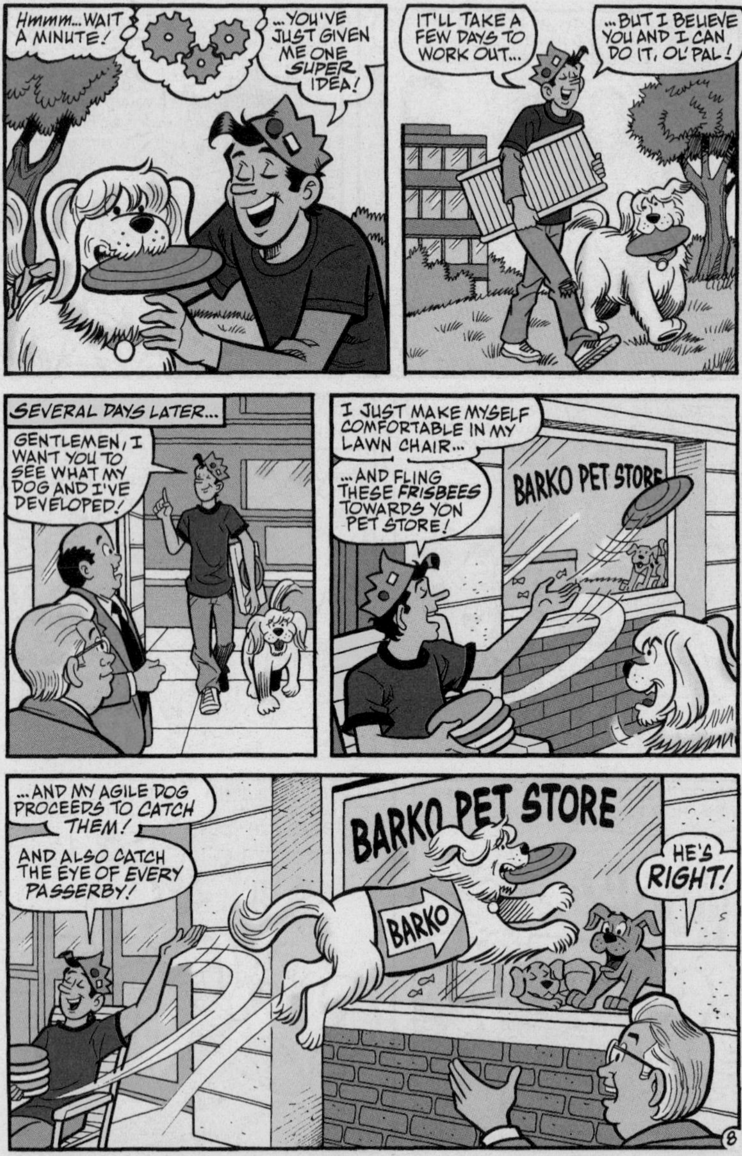

Hmmm... WAIT A MINUTE!
...YOU'VE JUST GIVEN ME ONE SUPER IDEA!
IT'LL TAKE A FEW DAYS TO WORK OUT...
...BUT I BELIEVE YOU AND I CAN DO IT, OL' PAL!
SEVERAL DAYS LATER...
GENTLEMEN, I WANT YOU TO SEE WHAT MY DOG AND I'VE DEVELOPED!
I JUST MAKE MYSELF COMFORTABLE IN MY LAWN CHAIR...
...AND FLING THESE FRISBEES TOWARDS YON PET STORE!
BARKO PET STORE
...AND MY AGILE DOG PROCEEDS TO CATCH THEM!
AND ALSO CATCH THE EYE OF EVERY PASSERBY!
BARKO PET STORE
BARKO
HE'S RIGHT!
8

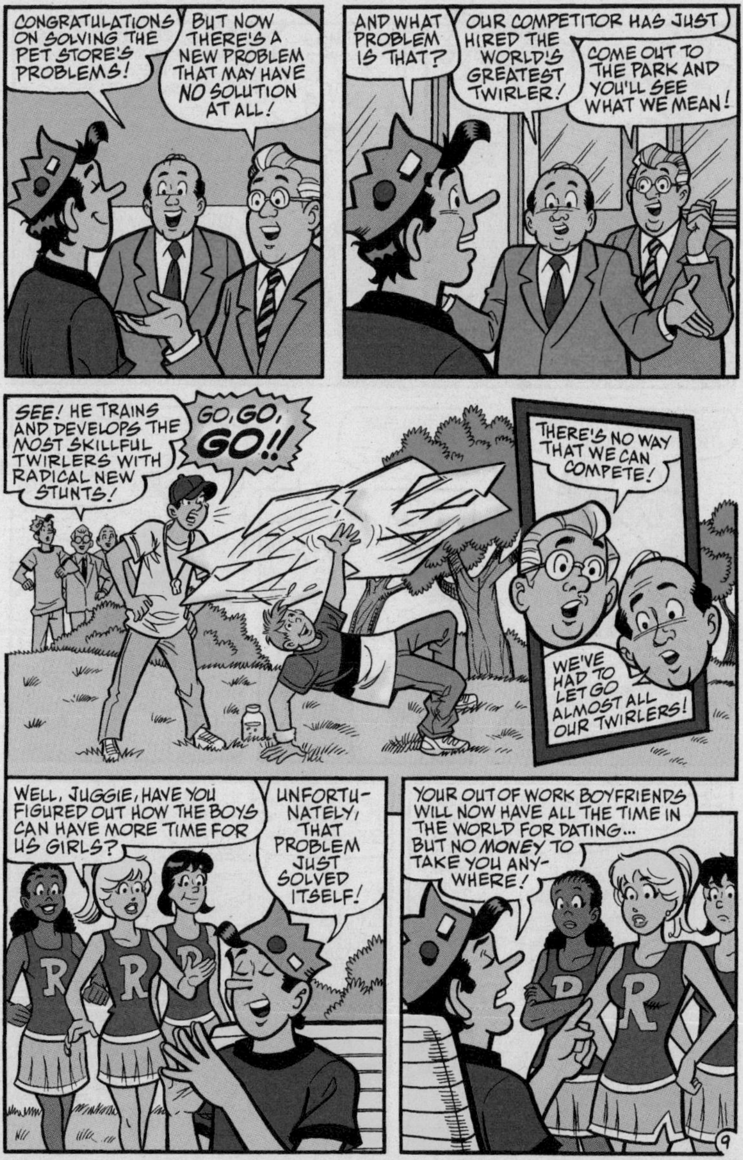
CONGRATULATIONS ON SOLVING THE PET STORE'S PROBLEMS!
BUT NOW THERE'S A NEW PROBLEM THAT MAY HAVE NO SOLUTION AT ALL!
AND WHAT PROBLEM IS THAT?
OUR COMPETITOR HAS JUST HIRED THE WORLD'S GREATEST TWIRLER!
COME OUT TO THE PARK AND YOU'LL SEE WHAT WE MEAN!
SEE! HE TRAINS AND DEVELOPS THE MOST SKILLFUL TWIRLERS WITH RADICAL NEW STUNTS!
GO, GO, GO!!
THERE'S NO WAY THAT WE CAN COMPETE!
WE'VE HAD TO LET GO ALMOST ALL OUR TWIRLERS!
WELL, JUGGIE, HAVE YOU FIGURED OUT HOW THE BOYS CAN HAVE MORE TIME FOR US GIRLS?
UNFORTU-NATELY, THAT PROBLEM JUST SOLVED ITSELF!
YOUR OUT OF WORK BOYFRIENDS WILL NOW HAVE ALL THE TIME IN THE WORLD FOR DATING... BUT NO MONEY TO TAKE YOU ANY-WHERE!

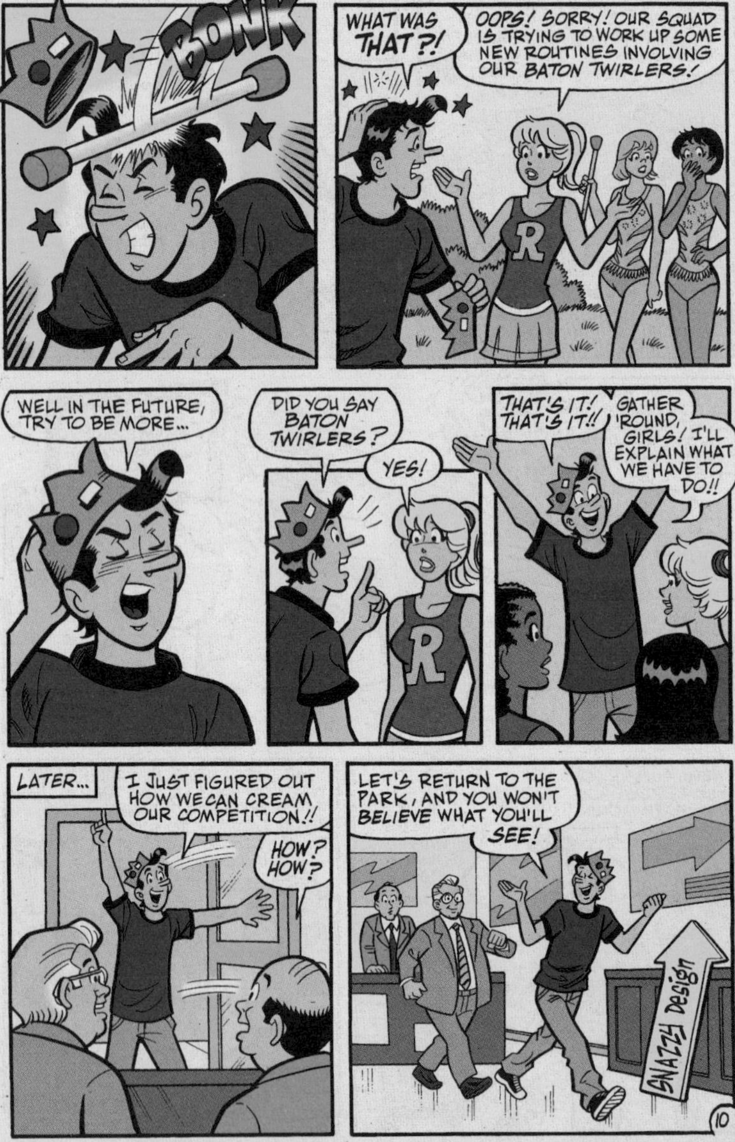
BONK
WHAT WAS THAT?!
OOPS! SORRY! OUR SQUAD IS TRYING TO WORK UP SOME NEW ROUTINES INVOLVING OUR BATON TWIRLERS!
WELL IN THE FUTURE, TRY TO BE MORE...
DID YOU SAY BATON TWIRLERS?
YES!
THAT'S IT! THAT'S IT!!
GATHER 'ROUND, GIRLS! I'LL EXPLAIN WHAT WE HAVE TO DO!!
LATER...
I JUST FIGURED OUT HOW WE CAN CREAM OUR COMPETITION!!
HOW? HOW?
LET'S RETURN TO THE PARK, AND YOU WON'T BELIEVE WHAT YOU'LL SEE!
SNAZZY Design
10

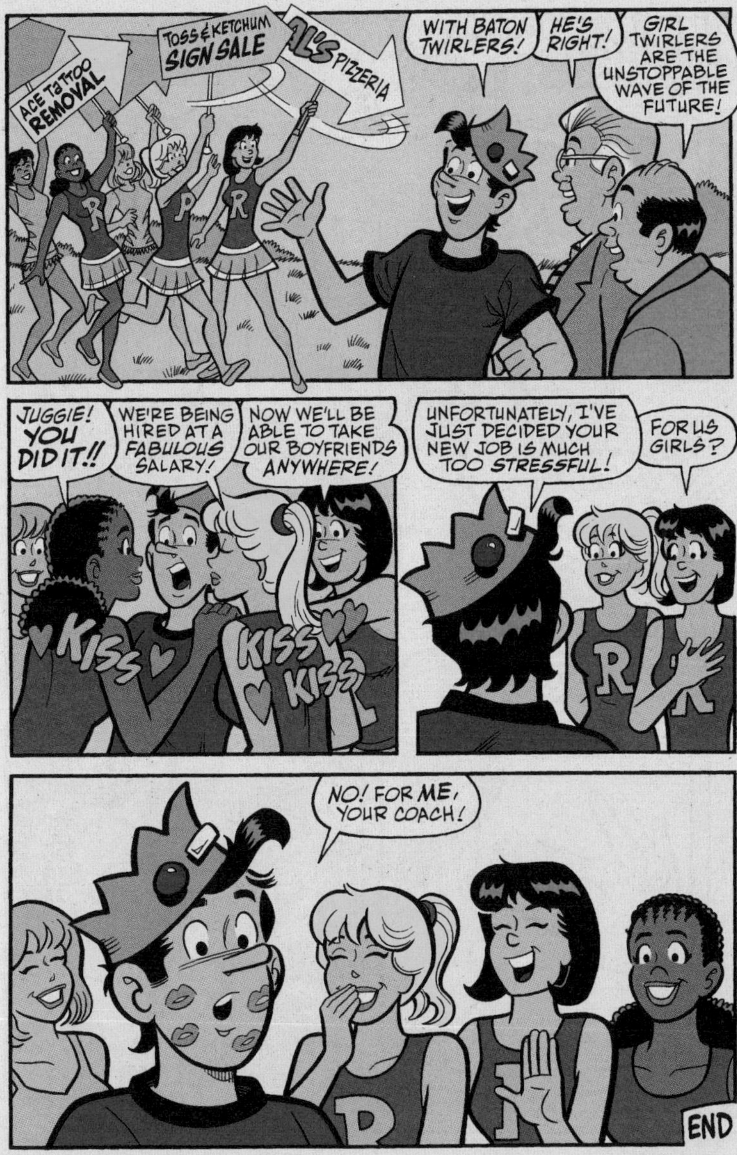
ACE TATTOO REMOVAL
TOSS & KETCHUM SIGN SALE
AL'S PIZZERIA
WITH BATON TWIRLERS!
HE'S RIGHT!
GIRL TWIRLERS ARE THE UNSTOPPABLE WAVE OF THE FUTURE!
JUGGIE! YOU DID IT!!
WE'RE BEING HIRED AT A FABULOUS SALARY!
NOW WE'LL BE ABLE TO TAKE OUR BOYFRIENDS ANYWHERE!
KISS
KISS
KISS
UNFORTUNATELY, I'VE JUST DECIDED YOUR NEW JOB IS MUCH TOO STRESSFUL!
FOR US GIRLS?
NO! FOR ME, YOUR COACH!
END

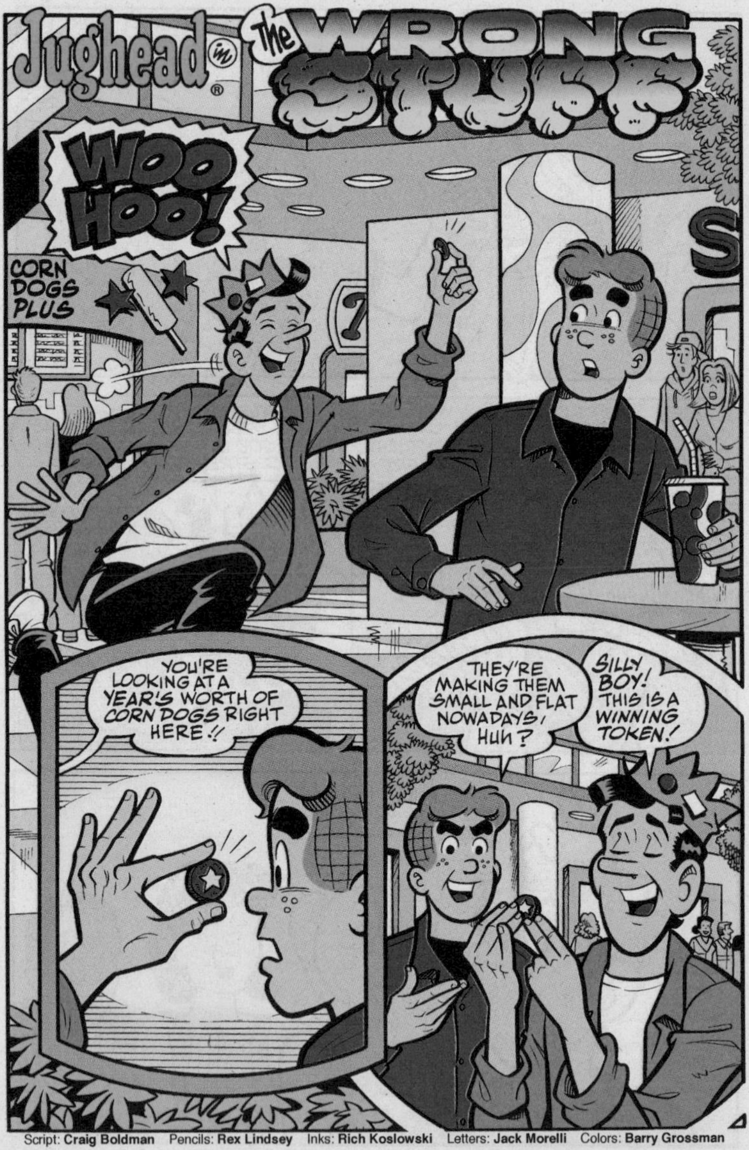
Jughead® in
The WRONG STUFF
WOO HOO!
CORN DOGS PLUS
7
S
YOU'RE LOOKING AT A YEAR'S WORTH OF CORN DOGS RIGHT HERE!!
THEY'RE MAKING THEM SMALL AND FLAT NOWADAYS, HUH?
SILLY BOY! THIS IS A WINNING TOKEN!

Script: **Craig Boldman** Pencils: **Rex Lindsey** Inks: **Rich Koslowski** Letters: **Jack Morelli** Colors: **Barry Grossman**

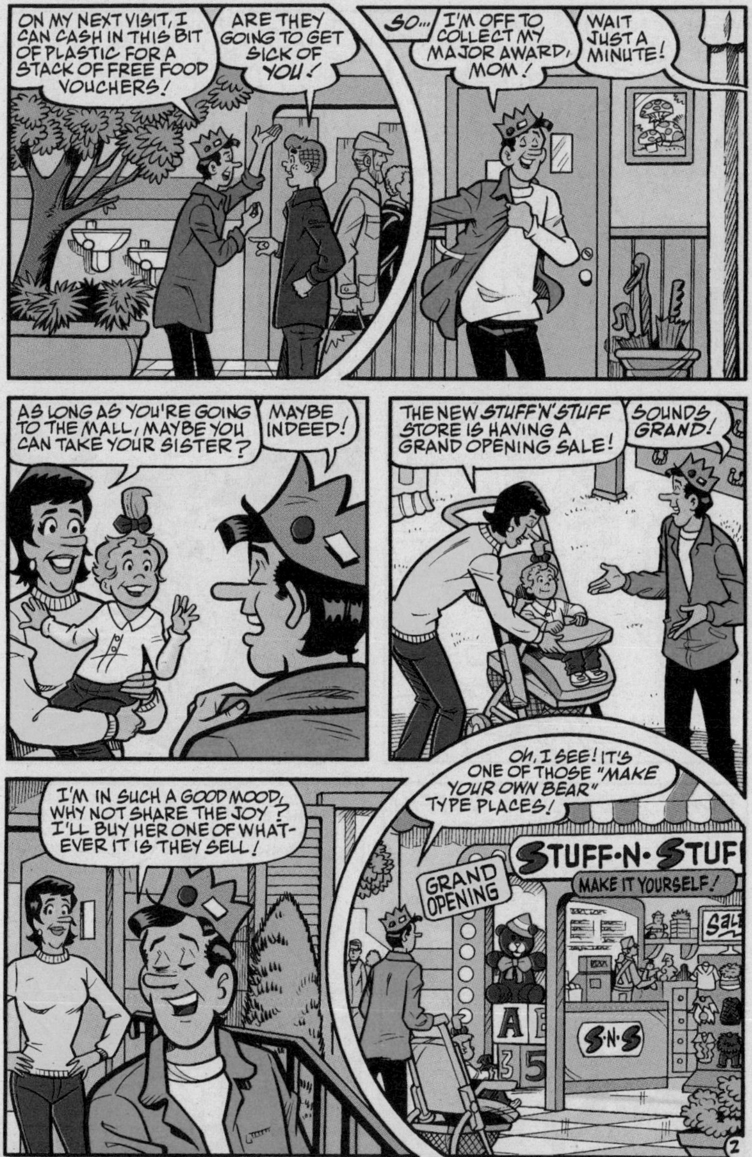
ON MY NEXT VISIT, I CAN CASH IN THIS BIT OF PLASTIC FOR A STACK OF FREE FOOD VOUCHERS!
ARE THEY GOING TO GET SICK OF YOU!
SO...
I'M OFF TO COLLECT MY MAJOR AWARD, MOM!
WAIT JUST A MINUTE!
AS LONG AS YOU'RE GOING TO THE MALL, MAYBE YOU CAN TAKE YOUR SISTER?
MAYBE INDEED!
THE NEW STUFF'N'STUFF STORE IS HAVING A GRAND OPENING SALE!
SOUNDS GRAND!
I'M IN SUCH A GOOD MOOD, WHY NOT SHARE THE JOY? I'LL BUY HER ONE OF WHATEVER IT IS THEY SELL!
OH, I SEE! IT'S ONE OF THOSE "MAKE YOUR OWN BEAR" TYPE PLACES!
STUFF-N-STUFF
MAKE IT YOURSELF!
GRAND OPENING
S-N-S
2

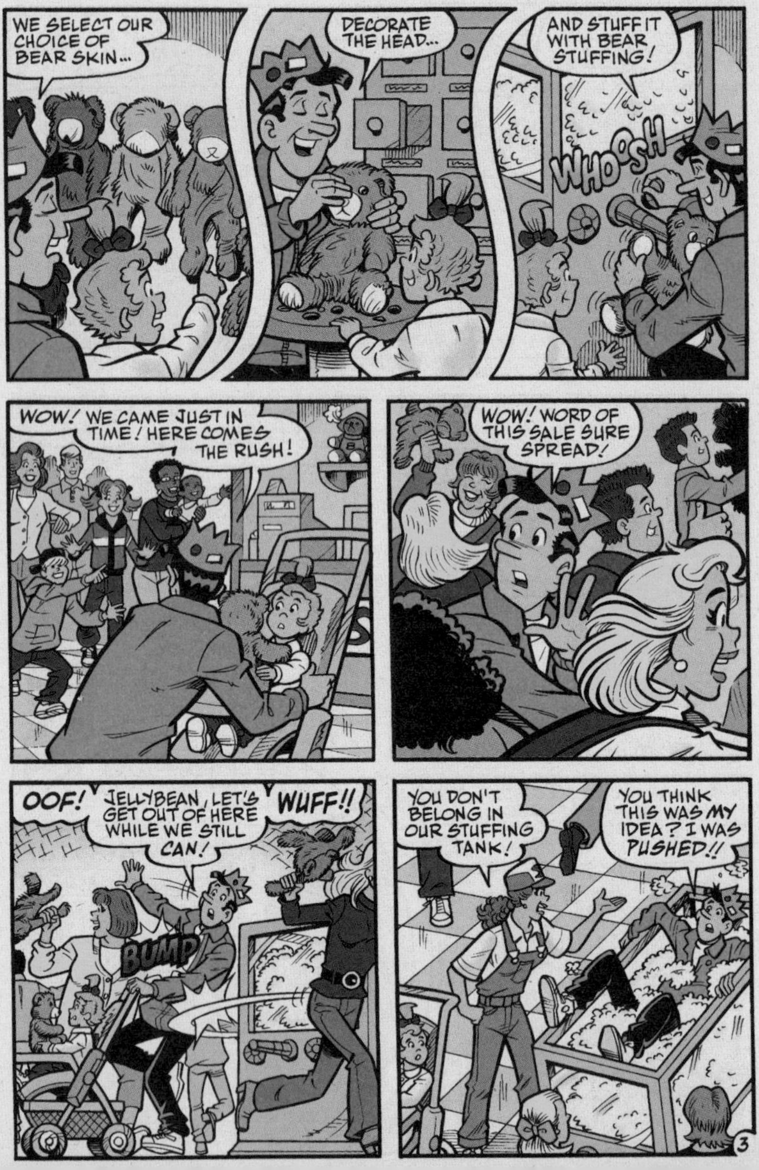
WE SELECT OUR CHOICE OF BEAR SKIN...
DECORATE THE HEAD...
AND STUFF IT WITH BEAR STUFFING!
WHOOSH
WOW! WE CAME JUST IN TIME! HERE COMES THE RUSH!
WOW! WORD OF THIS SALE SURE SPREAD!
OOF!
JELLYBEAN, LET'S GET OUT OF HERE WHILE WE STILL CAN!
WUFF!!
BUMP
YOU DON'T BELONG IN OUR STUFFING TANK!
YOU THINK THIS WAS MY IDEA? I WAS PUSHED!!

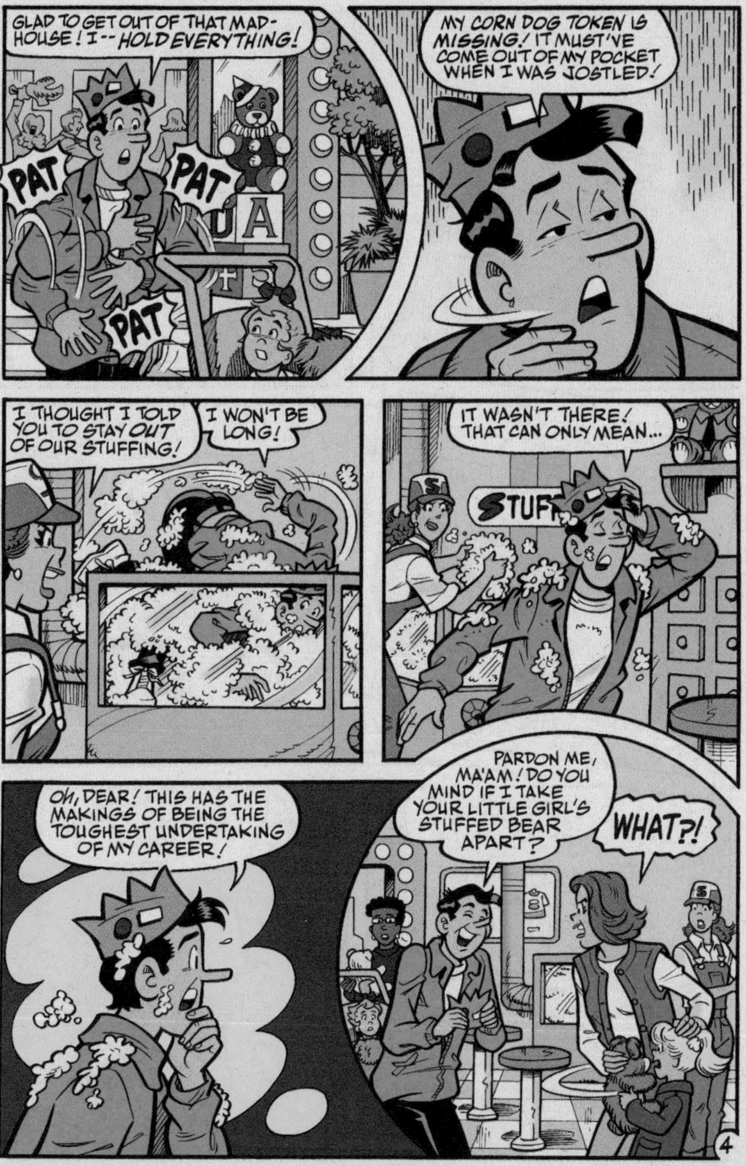

GLAD TO GET OUT OF THAT MAD-HOUSE! I-- HOLD EVERYTHING!
PAT
PAT
PAT
MY CORN DOG TOKEN IS MISSING! IT MUST'VE COME OUT OF MY POCKET WHEN I WAS JOSTLED!
I THOUGHT I TOLD YOU TO STAY OUT OF OUR STUFFING!
I WON'T BE LONG!
IT WASN'T THERE! THAT CAN ONLY MEAN...
STUFF
OH, DEAR! THIS HAS THE MAKINGS OF BEING THE TOUGHEST UNDERTAKING OF MY CAREER!
PARDON ME, MA'AM! DO YOU MIND IF I TAKE YOUR LITTLE GIRL'S STUFFED BEAR APART?
WHAT?!

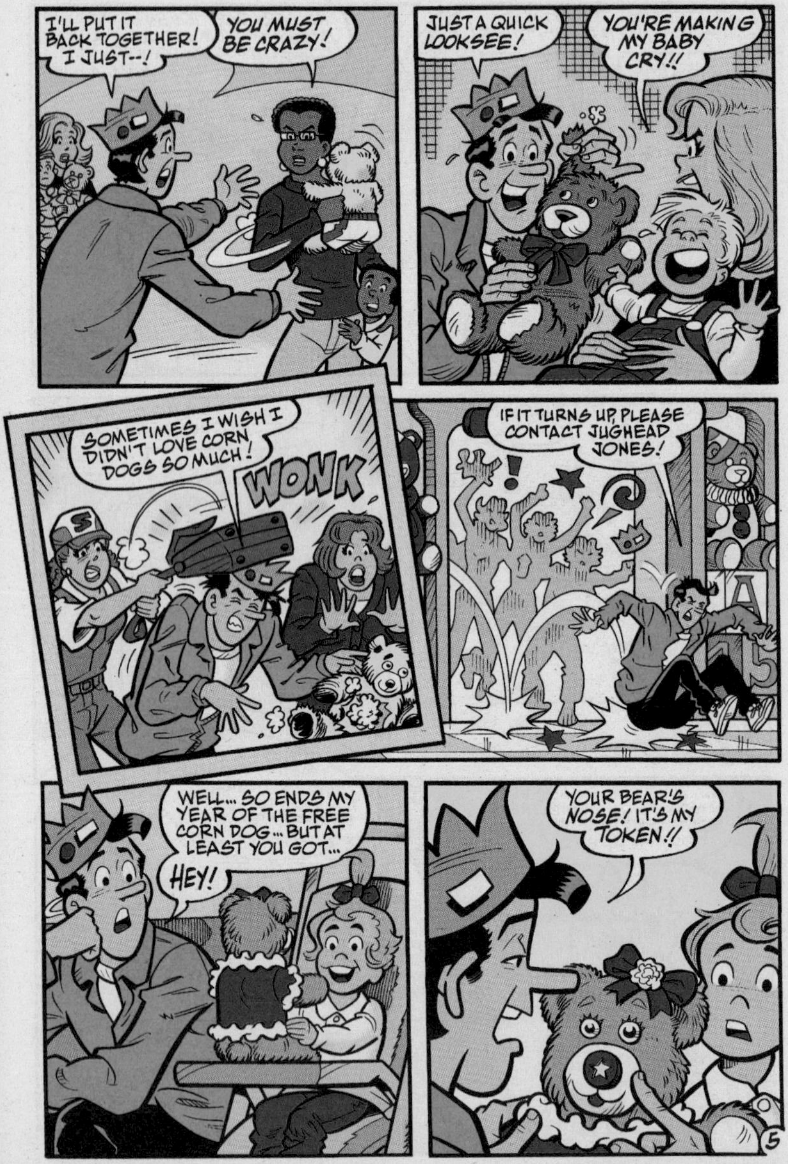
I'LL PUT IT BACK TOGETHER! I JUST--!
YOU MUST BE CRAZY!
JUST A QUICK LOOKSEE!
YOU'RE MAKING MY BABY CRY!!
SOMETIMES I WISH I DIDN'T LOVE CORN DOGS SO MUCH!
WONK
IF IT TURNS UP, PLEASE CONTACT JUGHEAD JONES!
WELL... SO ENDS MY YEAR OF THE FREE CORN DOG... BUT AT LEAST YOU GOT...
HEY!
YOUR BEAR'S NOSE! IT'S MY TOKEN!!
5

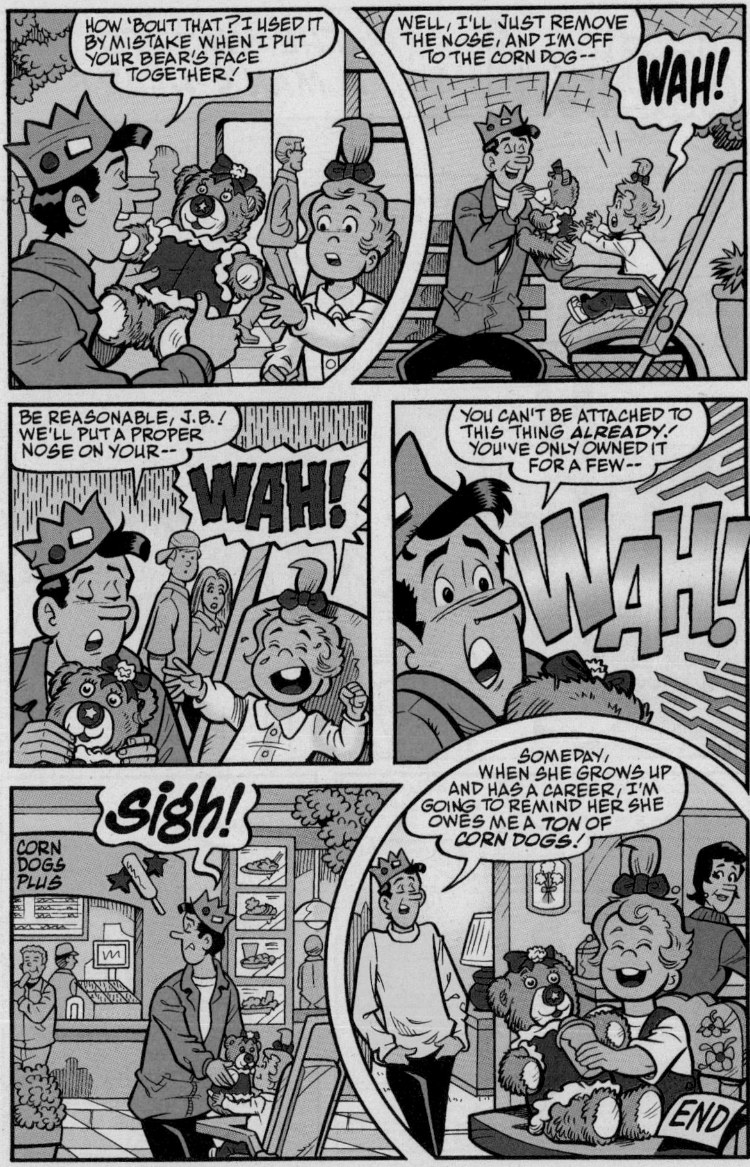
HOW 'BOUT THAT? I USED IT BY MISTAKE WHEN I PUT YOUR BEAR'S FACE TOGETHER!
WELL, I'LL JUST REMOVE THE NOSE, AND I'M OFF TO THE CORN DOG--
WAH!
BE REASONABLE, J.B.! WE'LL PUT A PROPER NOSE ON YOUR--
WAH!
YOU CAN'T BE ATTACHED TO THIS THING ALREADY! YOU'VE ONLY OWNED IT FOR A FEW--
WAH!
SIGH!
CORN DOGS PLUS
SOMEDAY, WHEN SHE GROWS UP AND HAS A CAREER, I'M GOING TO REMIND HER SHE OWES ME A TON OF CORN DOGS!
END

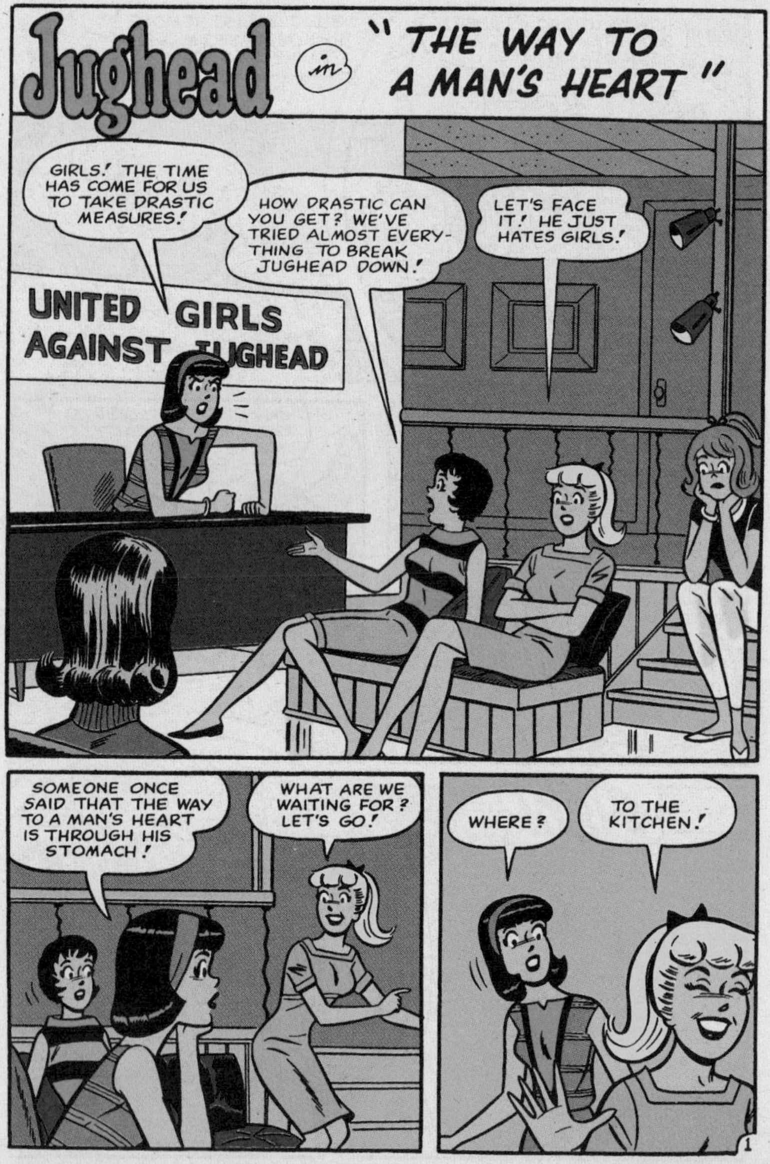
Jughead in "THE WAY TO A MAN'S HEART"
GIRLS! THE TIME HAS COME FOR US TO TAKE DRASTIC MEASURES!
UNITED GIRLS AGAINST JUGHEAD
HOW DRASTIC CAN YOU GET? WE'VE TRIED ALMOST EVERY-THING TO BREAK JUGHEAD DOWN!
LET'S FACE IT! HE JUST HATES GIRLS!
SOMEONE ONCE SAID THAT THE WAY TO A MAN'S HEART IS THROUGH HIS STOMACH!
WHAT ARE WE WAITING FOR? LET'S GO!
WHERE?
TO THE KITCHEN!

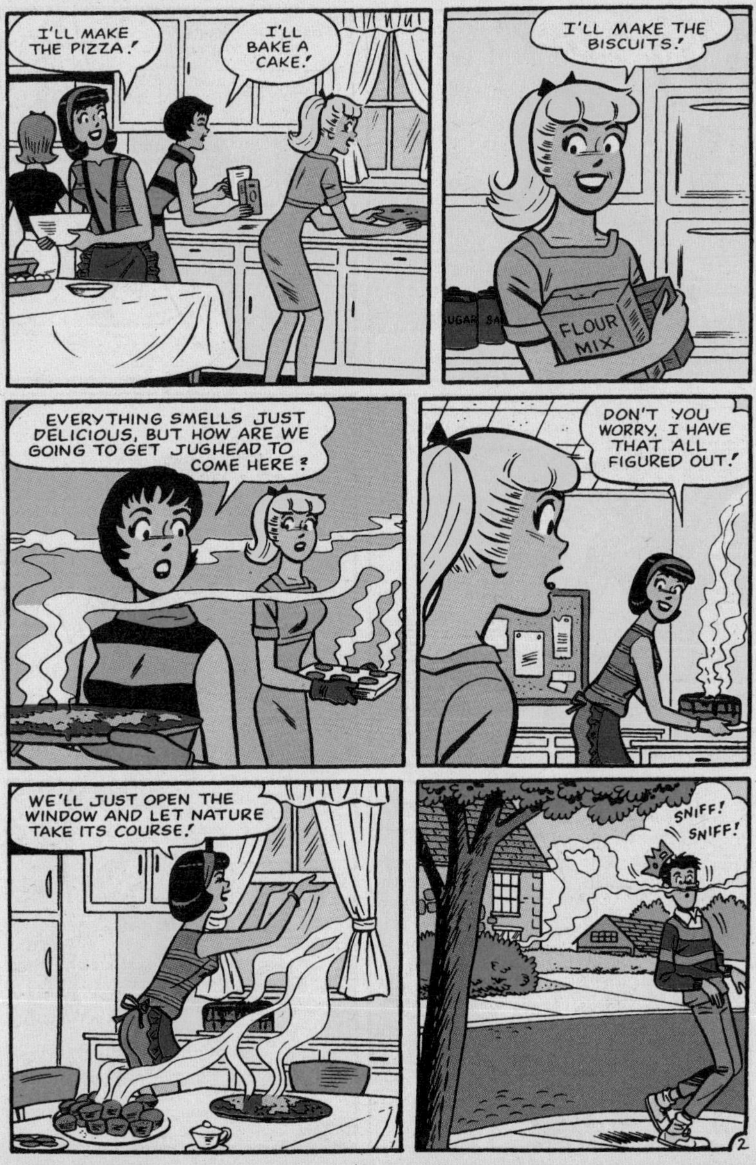
I'LL MAKE THE PIZZA.!
I'LL BAKE A CAKE.!
I'LL MAKE THE BISCUITS.!
FLOUR MIX
SUGAR
EVERYTHING SMELLS JUST DELICIOUS, BUT HOW ARE WE GOING TO GET JUGHEAD TO COME HERE?
DON'T YOU WORRY. I HAVE THAT ALL FIGURED OUT.!
WE'LL JUST OPEN THE WINDOW AND LET NATURE TAKE ITS COURSE.!
SNIFF!
SNIFF!

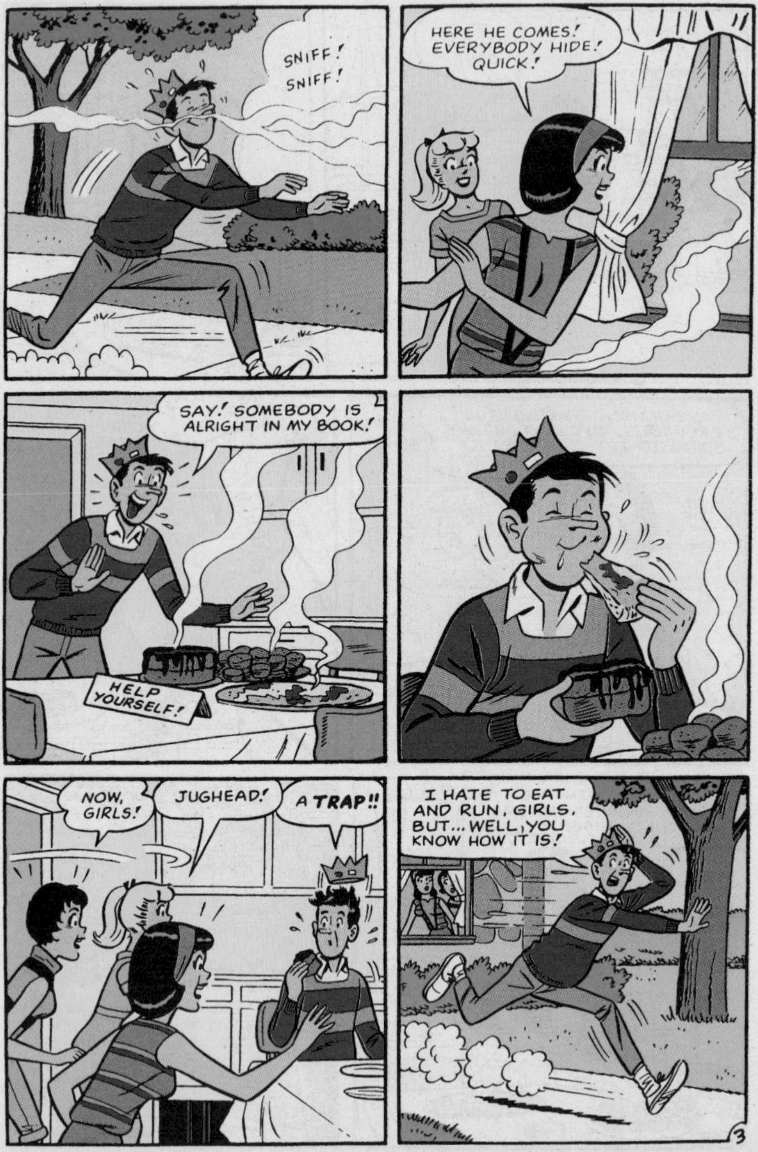

SNIFF!
SNIFF!
HERE HE COMES! EVERYBODY HIDE! QUICK!
SAY! SOMEBODY IS ALRIGHT IN MY BOOK!
HELP YOURSELF!
NOW, GIRLS!
JUGHEAD!
A TRAP!!
I HATE TO EAT AND RUN, GIRLS, BUT... WELL, YOU KNOW HOW IT IS!

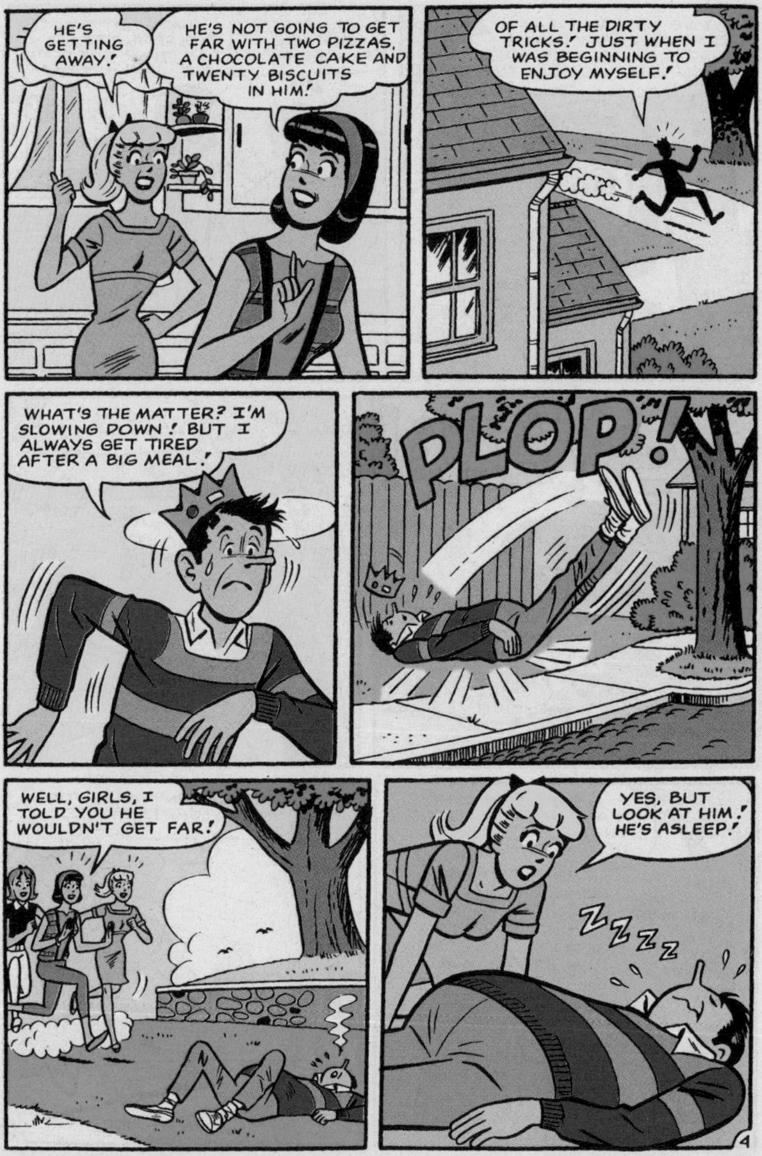
HE'S GETTING AWAY!
HE'S NOT GOING TO GET FAR WITH TWO PIZZAS, A CHOCOLATE CAKE AND TWENTY BISCUITS IN HIM!
OF ALL THE DIRTY TRICKS! JUST WHEN I WAS BEGINNING TO ENJOY MYSELF!
WHAT'S THE MATTER? I'M SLOWING DOWN! BUT I ALWAYS GET TIRED AFTER A BIG MEAL!
PLOP!
WELL, GIRLS, I TOLD YOU HE WOULDN'T GET FAR!
YES, BUT LOOK AT HIM! HE'S ASLEEP!
ZZZZ
4

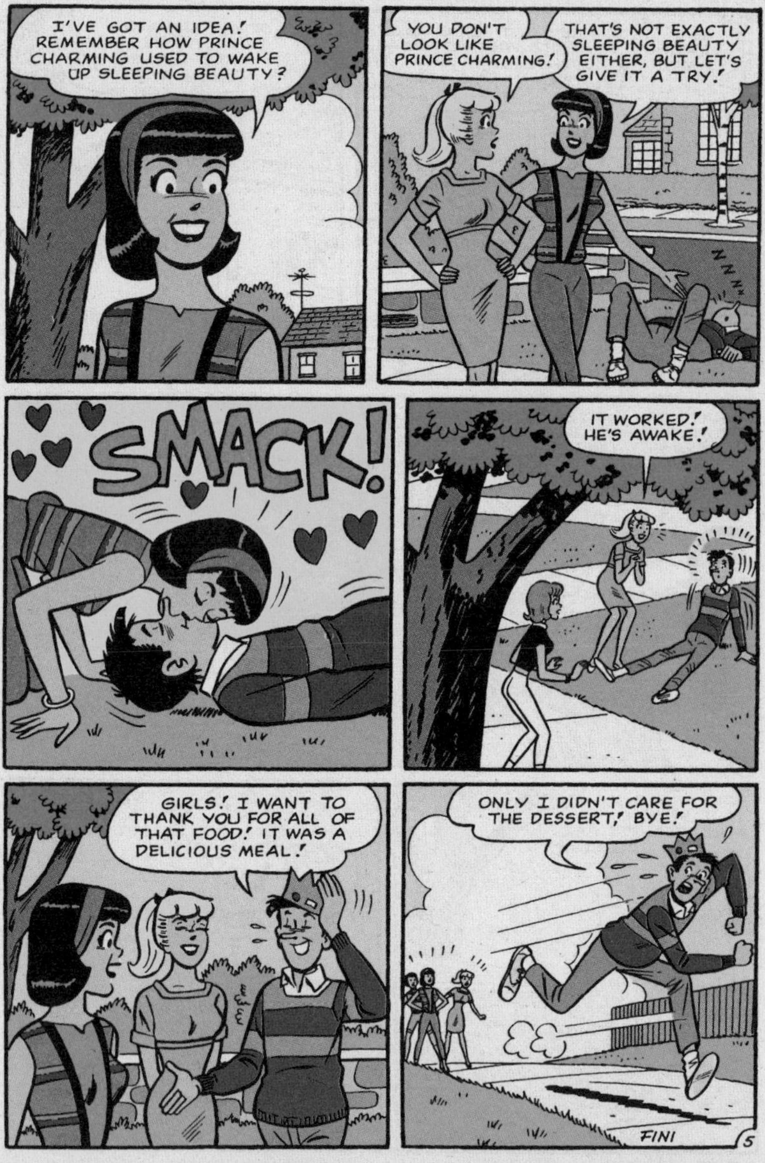

I'VE GOT AN IDEA! REMEMBER HOW PRINCE CHARMING USED TO WAKE UP SLEEPING BEAUTY?
YOU DON'T LOOK LIKE PRINCE CHARMING!
THAT'S NOT EXACTLY SLEEPING BEAUTY EITHER, BUT LET'S GIVE IT A TRY!
Z Z Z
SMACK!
IT WORKED! HE'S AWAKE!
GIRLS! I WANT TO THANK YOU FOR ALL OF THAT FOOD! IT WAS A DELICIOUS MEAL!
ONLY I DIDN'T CARE FOR THE DESSERT! BYE!
FINI

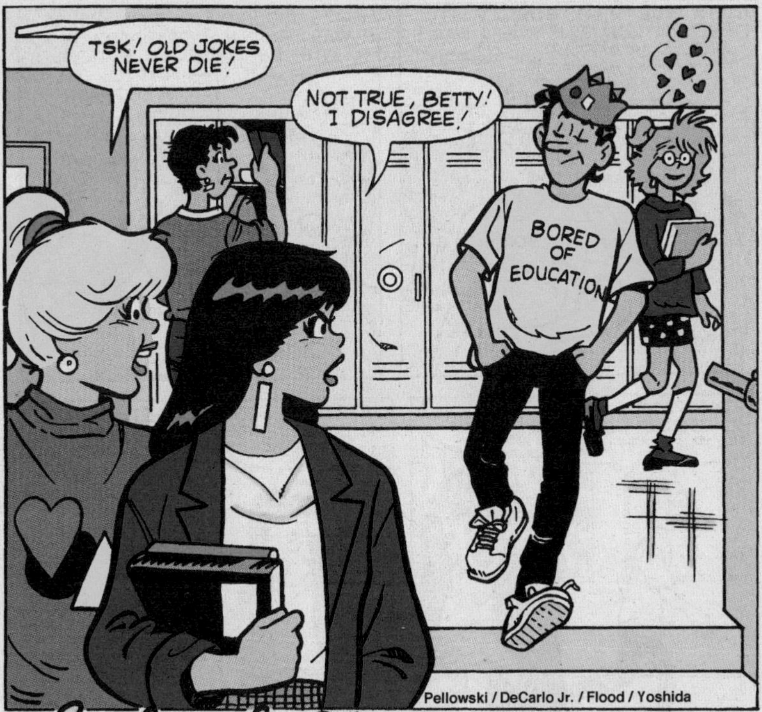
TSK! OLD JOKES NEVER DIE!
NOT TRUE, BETTY! I DISAGREE!
BORED OF EDUCATION
Pellowski / DeCarlo Jr. / Flood / Yoshida

Jughead IN "YOU GET WHAT YOU GIVE"

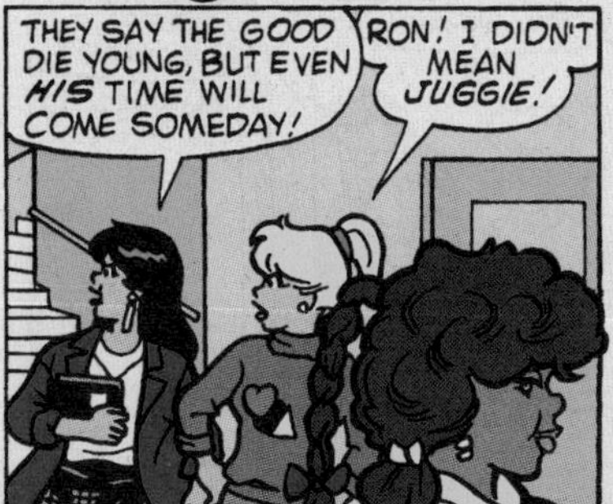
THEY SAY THE GOOD DIE YOUNG, BUT EVEN *HIS* TIME WILL COME SOMEDAY!
RON! I DIDN'T MEAN *JUGGIE*!

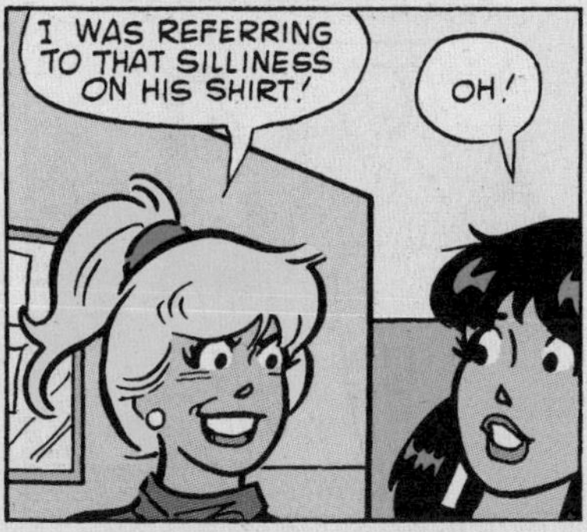
I WAS REFERRING TO THAT SILLINESS ON HIS SHIRT!
OH!

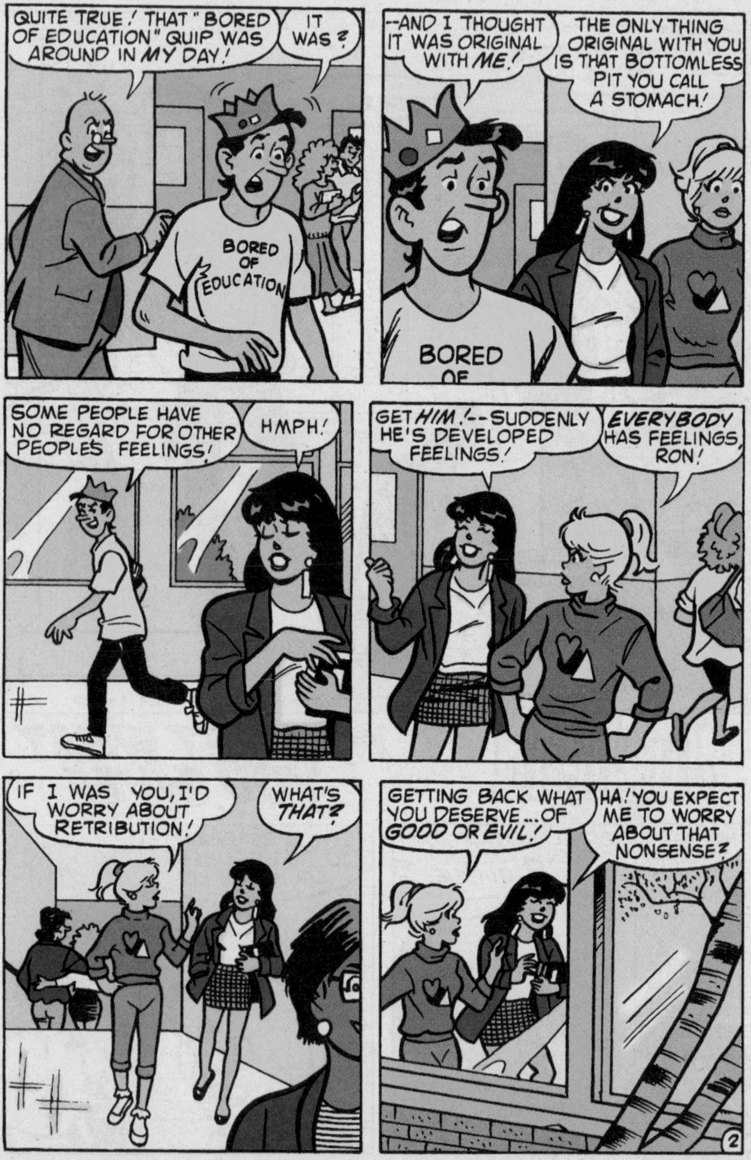
QUITE TRUE! THAT "BORED OF EDUCATION" QUIP WAS AROUND IN MY DAY!
IT WAS?
BORED OF EDUCATION
--AND I THOUGHT IT WAS ORIGINAL WITH ME!
THE ONLY THING ORIGINAL WITH YOU IS THAT BOTTOMLESS PIT YOU CALL A STOMACH!
BORED OF
SOME PEOPLE HAVE NO REGARD FOR OTHER PEOPLE'S FEELINGS!
HMPH!
GET HIM!--SUDDENLY HE'S DEVELOPED FEELINGS!
EVERYBODY HAS FEELINGS, RON!
IF I WAS YOU, I'D WORRY ABOUT RETRIBUTION!
WHAT'S THAT?
GETTING BACK WHAT YOU DESERVE...OF GOOD OR EVIL!
HA! YOU EXPECT ME TO WORRY ABOUT THAT NONSENSE?
2

KINDNESS IS REPAID WITH KINDNESS!--UNKINDNESS WITH MORE OF THE SAME!

THAT SORT OF SUPERSTITIOUS POPPYCOCK IS ALL RIGHT FOR COMMON FOLK! IT DOESN'T APPLY TO THE PRIVILEGED CLASS!

YOU READIN' POETRY NOW, JUG?

YEAH, MOOSE! THIS IS ONE OF MY FAVORITES!

"ODE TO A GRECIAN URN," BY JOHN KEATS!

D-UH! WHAT'S A GRECIAN URN?

KEATS

DUCATION

HA! ABOUT TWO BUCKS AN HOUR!

GOOD GRIEF!

Roy

HA HA HA! Y-YOU MAKE A GREAT STRAIGHT MAN, MOOSE! WE OUGHTA TAKE THIS SHOW ON THE ROAD!

I CAN'T DO THAT!

BORED OF EDUCATI

KEATS

3

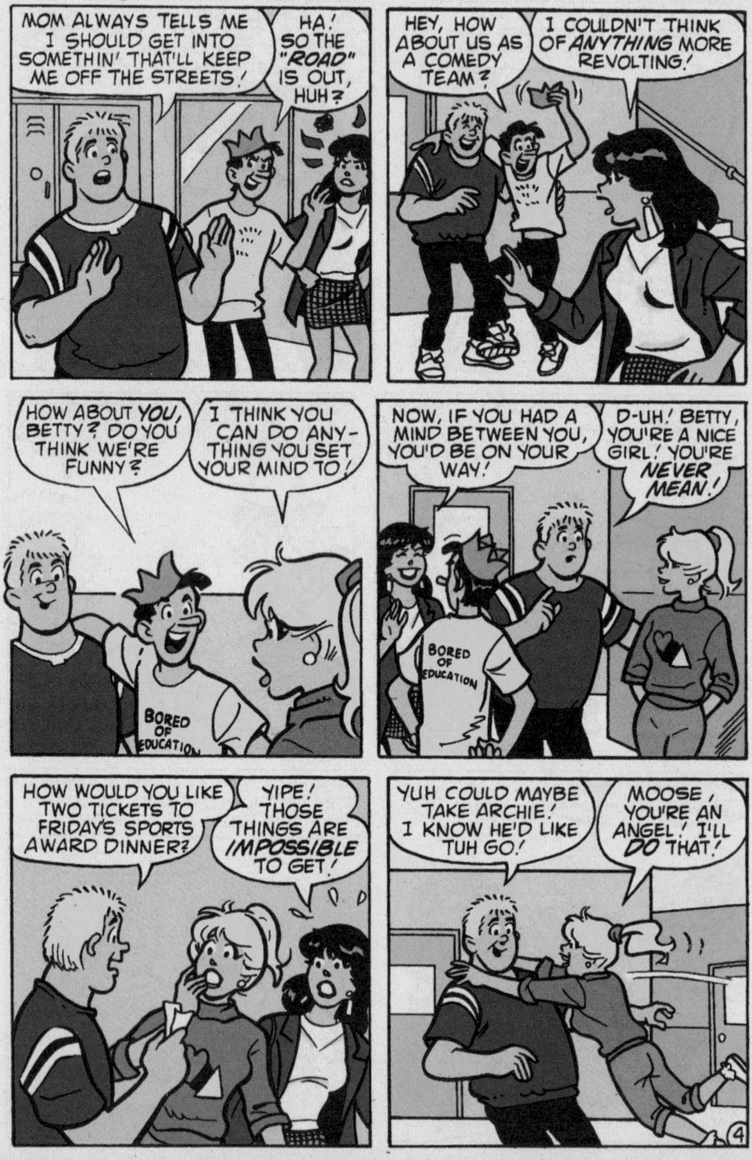
MOM ALWAYS TELLS ME I SHOULD GET INTO SOMETHIN' THAT'LL KEEP ME OFF THE STREETS!
HA! SO THE "ROAD" IS OUT, HUH?
HEY, HOW ABOUT US AS A COMEDY TEAM?
I COULDN'T THINK OF ANYTHING MORE REVOLTING!
HOW ABOUT YOU, BETTY? DO YOU THINK WE'RE FUNNY?
I THINK YOU CAN DO ANYTHING YOU SET YOUR MIND TO!
BORED OF EDUCATION
NOW, IF YOU HAD A MIND BETWEEN YOU, YOU'D BE ON YOUR WAY!
D-UH! BETTY, YOU'RE A NICE GIRL! YOU'RE NEVER MEAN!
BORED OF EDUCATION
HOW WOULD YOU LIKE TWO TICKETS TO FRIDAY'S SPORTS AWARD DINNER?
YIPE! THOSE THINGS ARE IMPOSSIBLE TO GET!
YUH COULD MAYBE TAKE ARCHIE! I KNOW HE'D LIKE TUH GO!
MOOSE, YOU'RE AN ANGEL! I'LL DO THAT!
4

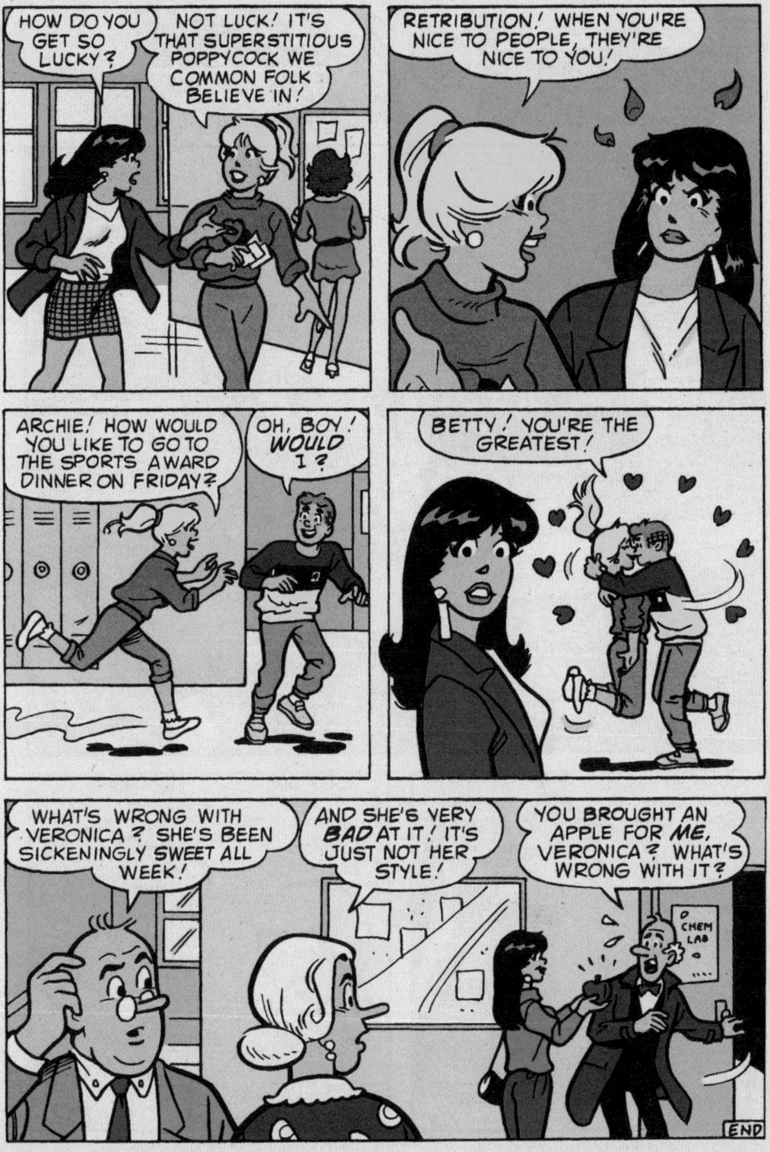
HOW DO YOU GET SO LUCKY?
NOT LUCK! IT'S THAT SUPERSTITIOUS POPPYCOCK WE COMMON FOLK BELIEVE IN!
RETRIBUTION! WHEN YOU'RE NICE TO PEOPLE, THEY'RE NICE TO YOU!
ARCHIE! HOW WOULD YOU LIKE TO GO TO THE SPORTS AWARD DINNER ON FRIDAY?
OH, BOY! WOULD I?
BETTY! YOU'RE THE GREATEST!
WHAT'S WRONG WITH VERONICA? SHE'S BEEN SICKENINGLY SWEET ALL WEEK!
AND SHE'S VERY BAD AT IT! IT'S JUST NOT HER STYLE!
YOU BROUGHT AN APPLE FOR ME, VERONICA? WHAT'S WRONG WITH IT?
CHEM LAB
END

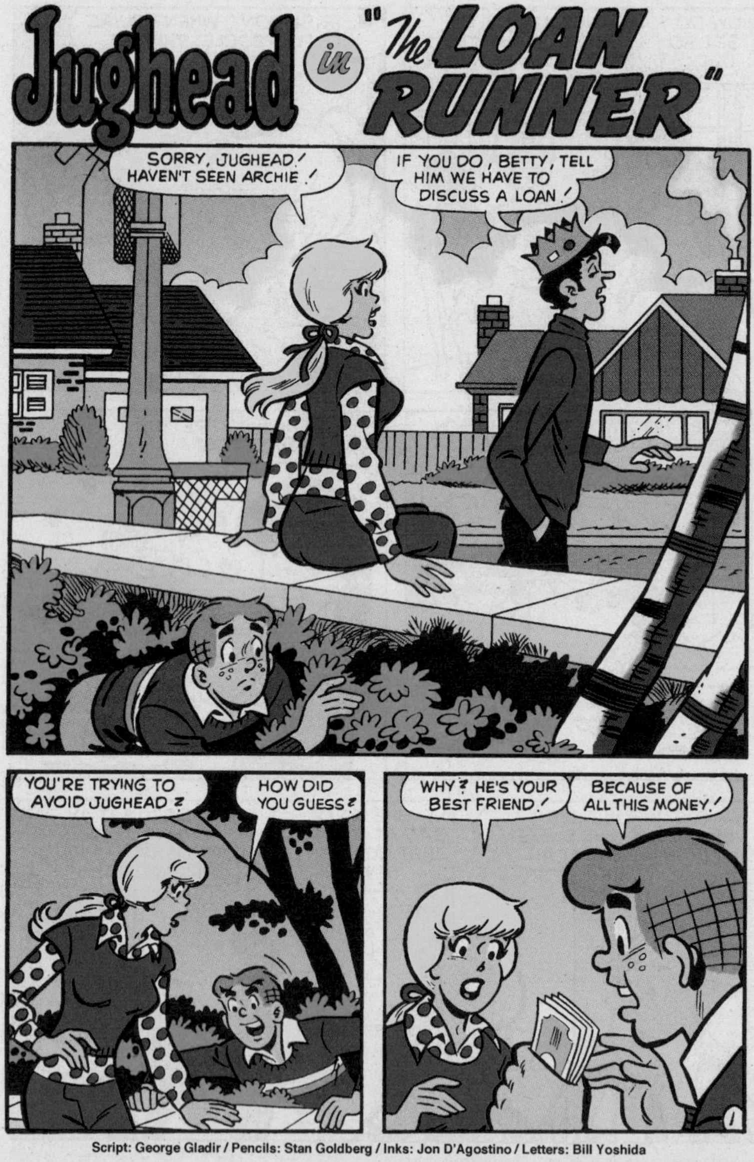
Jughead in "The LOAN RUNNER"
SORRY, JUGHEAD! HAVEN'T SEEN ARCHIE!
IF YOU DO, BETTY, TELL HIM WE HAVE TO DISCUSS A LOAN!
YOU'RE TRYING TO AVOID JUGHEAD?
HOW DID YOU GUESS?
WHY? HE'S YOUR BEST FRIEND!
BECAUSE OF ALL THIS MONEY!
1

Script: George Gladir / Pencils: Stan Goldberg / Inks: Jon D'Agostino / Letters: Bill Yoshida

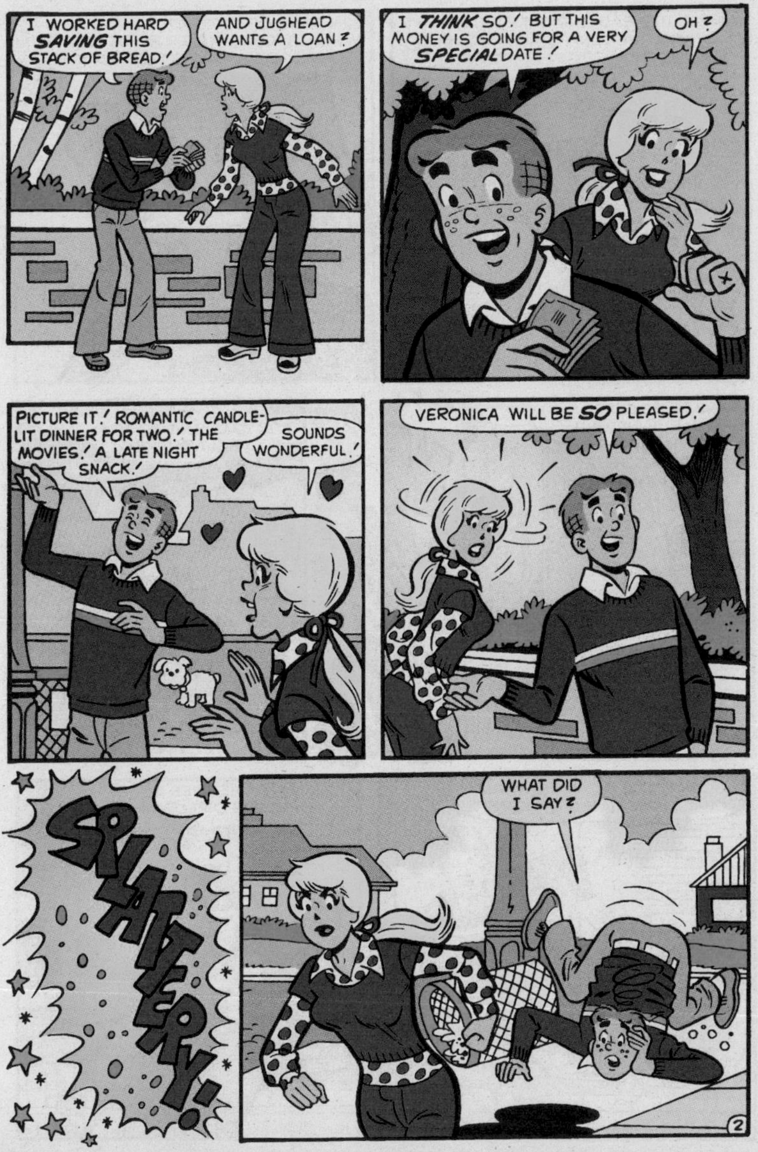

I WORKED HARD SAVING THIS STACK OF BREAD!
AND JUGHEAD WANTS A LOAN?
I THINK SO! BUT THIS MONEY IS GOING FOR A VERY SPECIAL DATE!
OH?
PICTURE IT! ROMANTIC CANDLE-LIT DINNER FOR TWO! THE MOVIES! A LATE NIGHT SNACK!
SOUNDS WONDERFUL!
VERONICA WILL BE SO PLEASED!
SPLATTERY!
WHAT DID I SAY?

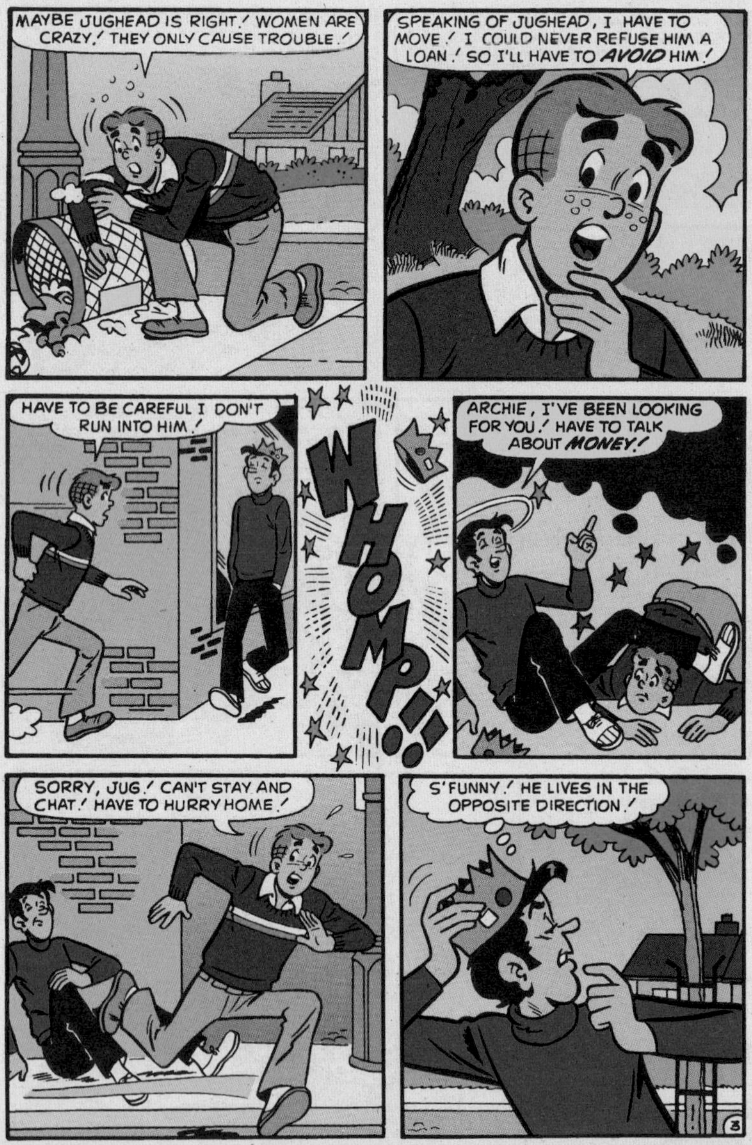
MAYBE JUGHEAD IS RIGHT! WOMEN ARE CRAZY! THEY ONLY CAUSE TROUBLE!
SPEAKING OF JUGHEAD, I HAVE TO MOVE! I COULD NEVER REFUSE HIM A LOAN! SO I'LL HAVE TO AVOID HIM!
HAVE TO BE CAREFUL I DON'T RUN INTO HIM!
WHOMP!!
ARCHIE, I'VE BEEN LOOKING FOR YOU! HAVE TO TALK ABOUT MONEY!
SORRY, JUG! CAN'T STAY AND CHAT! HAVE TO HURRY HOME!
S'FUNNY! HE LIVES IN THE OPPOSITE DIRECTION!
3

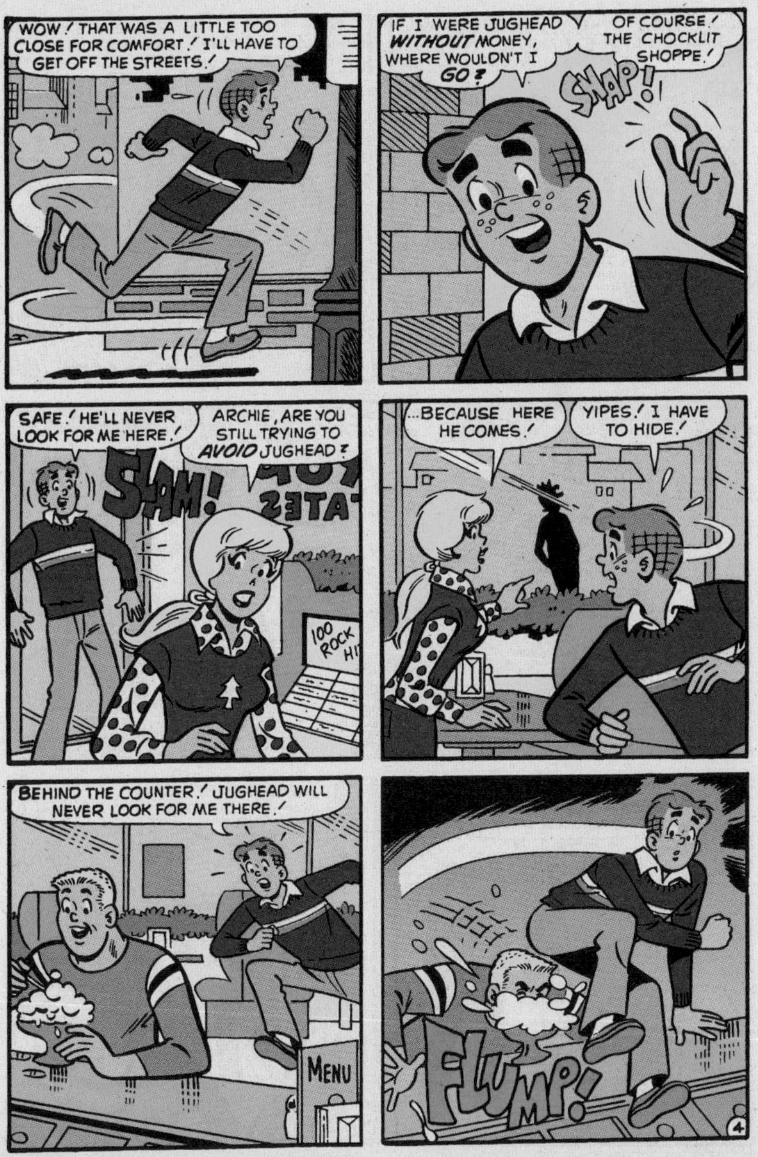

WOW! THAT WAS A LITTLE TOO CLOSE FOR COMFORT! I'LL HAVE TO GET OFF THE STREETS!
IF I WERE JUGHEAD WITHOUT MONEY, WHERE WOULDN'T I GO?
OF COURSE! THE CHOCKLIT SHOPPE!
SNAP!
SAFE! HE'LL NEVER LOOK FOR ME HERE!
ARCHIE, ARE YOU STILL TRYING TO AVOID JUGHEAD?
SLAM!
100 ROCK HI
...BECAUSE HERE HE COMES!
YIPES! I HAVE TO HIDE!
BEHIND THE COUNTER! JUGHEAD WILL NEVER LOOK FOR ME THERE!
MENU
FLUMP!
4

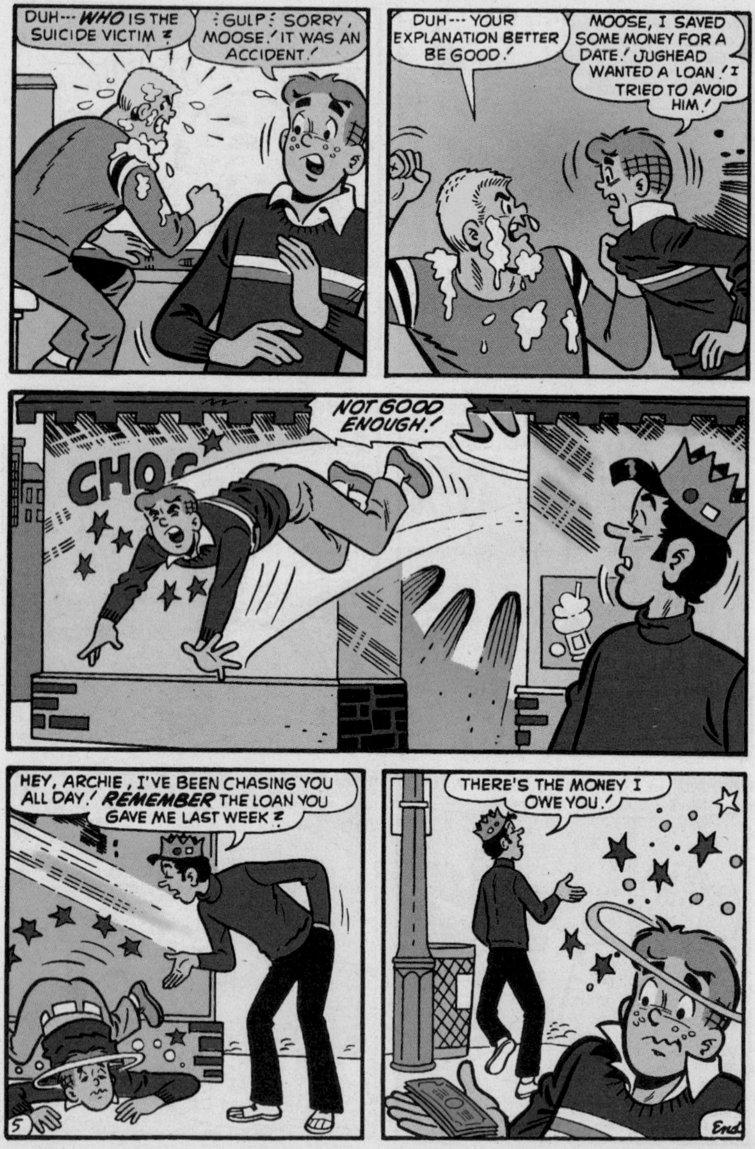
DUH--- WHO IS THE SUICIDE VICTIM ?
:GULP: SORRY, MOOSE! IT WAS AN ACCIDENT!
DUH--- YOUR EXPLANATION BETTER BE GOOD!
MOOSE, I SAVED SOME MONEY FOR A DATE! JUGHEAD WANTED A LOAN! I TRIED TO AVOID HIM!
NOT GOOD ENOUGH!
CHOC
HEY, ARCHIE, I'VE BEEN CHASING YOU ALL DAY! REMEMBER THE LOAN YOU GAVE ME LAST WEEK ?
5
THERE'S THE MONEY I OWE YOU!
End

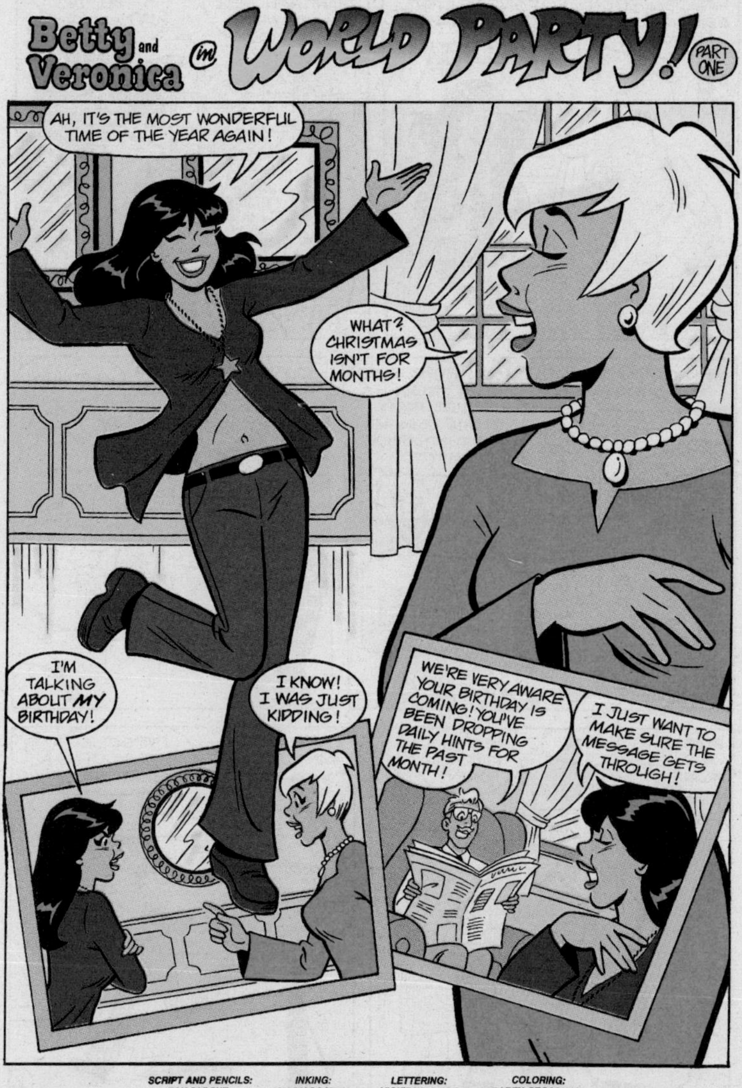
Betty and Veronica in WORLD PARTY! PART ONE
AH, IT'S THE MOST WONDERFUL TIME OF THE YEAR AGAIN!
WHAT? CHRISTMAS ISN'T FOR MONTHS!
I'M TALKING ABOUT MY BIRTHDAY!
I KNOW! I WAS JUST KIDDING!
WE'RE VERY AWARE YOUR BIRTHDAY IS COMING! YOU'VE BEEN DROPPING DAILY HINTS FOR THE PAST MONTH!
I JUST WANT TO MAKE SURE THE MESSAGE GETS THROUGH!

SCRIPT AND PENCILS: **DAN PARENT** *INKING:* **JON D'AGOSTINO** *LETTERING:* **VICKIE WILLIAMS** *COLORING:* **BARRY GROSSMAN**

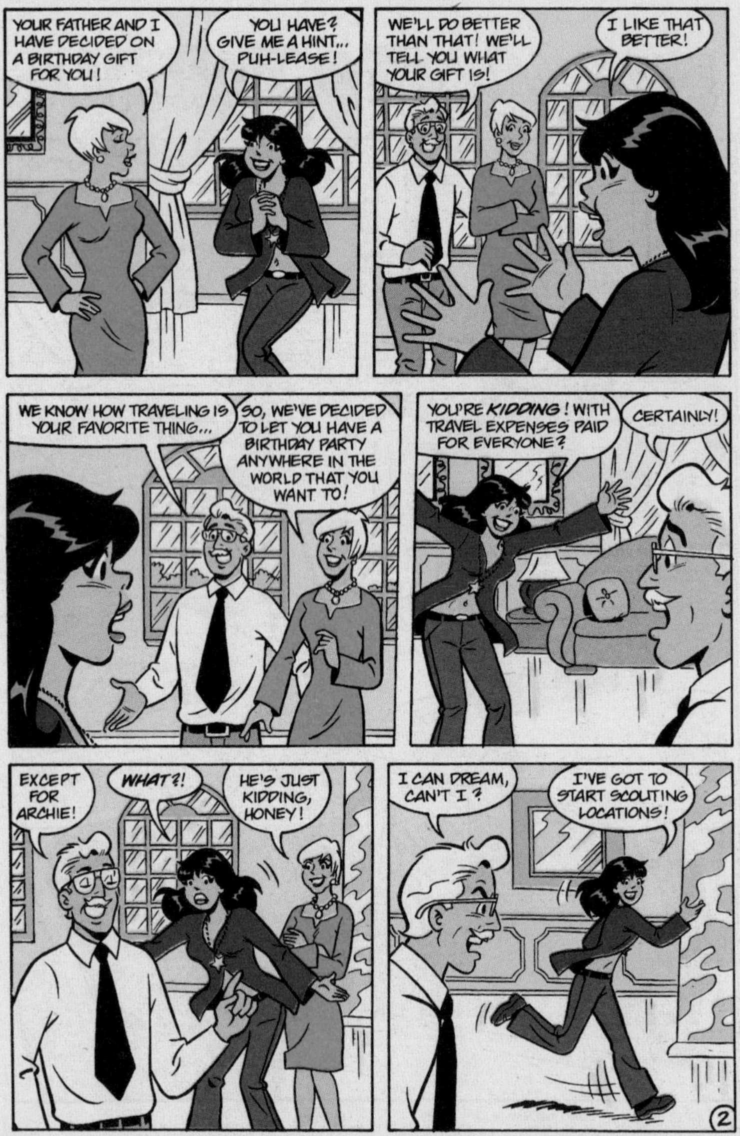
YOUR FATHER AND I HAVE DECIDED ON A BIRTHDAY GIFT FOR YOU!
YOU HAVE? GIVE ME A HINT... PUH-LEASE!
WE'LL DO BETTER THAN THAT! WE'LL TELL YOU WHAT YOUR GIFT IS!
I LIKE THAT BETTER!
WE KNOW HOW TRAVELING IS YOUR FAVORITE THING...
SO, WE'VE DECIDED TO LET YOU HAVE A BIRTHDAY PARTY ANYWHERE IN THE WORLD THAT YOU WANT TO!
YOU'RE KIDDING! WITH TRAVEL EXPENSES PAID FOR EVERYONE?
CERTAINLY!
EXCEPT FOR ARCHIE!
WHAT?!
HE'S JUST KIDDING, HONEY!
I CAN DREAM, CAN'T I?
I'VE GOT TO START SCOUTING LOCATIONS!
2

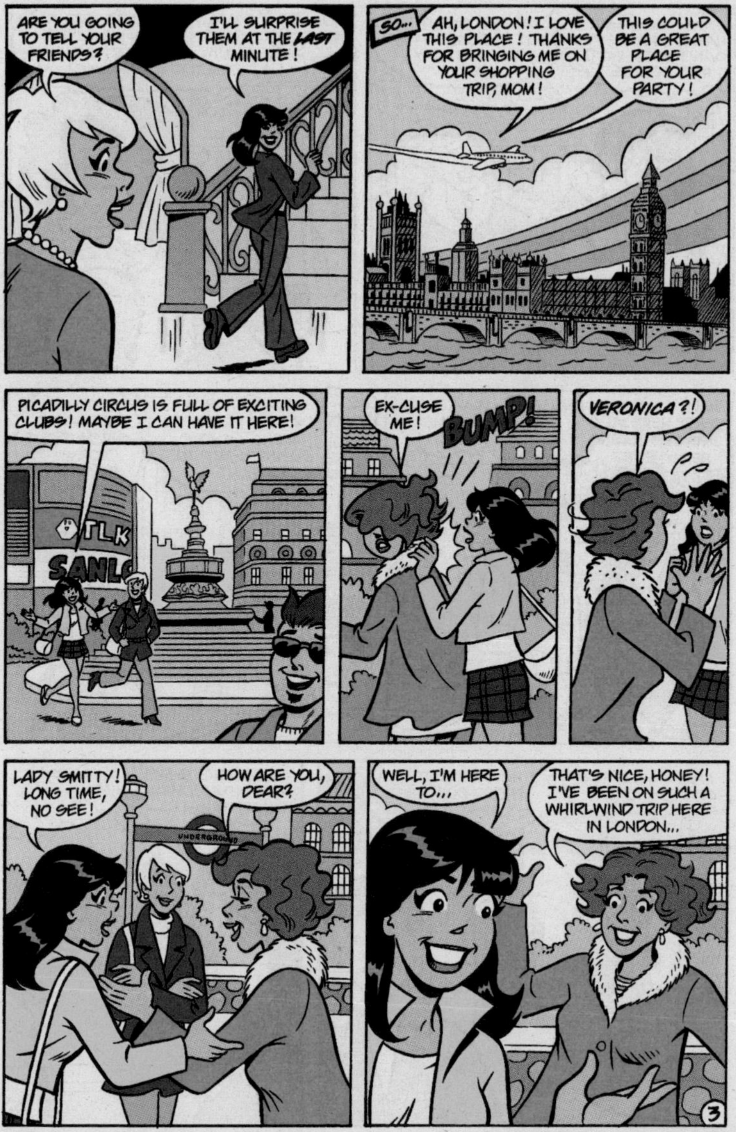
ARE YOU GOING TO TELL YOUR FRIENDS?
I'LL SURPRISE THEM AT THE LAST MINUTE!
SO...
AH, LONDON! I LOVE THIS PLACE! THANKS FOR BRINGING ME ON YOUR SHOPPING TRIP, MOM!
THIS COULD BE A GREAT PLACE FOR YOUR PARTY!
PICADILLY CIRCUS IS FULL OF EXCITING CLUBS! MAYBE I CAN HAVE IT HERE!
TLK
SANL
EX-CUSE ME!
BUMP!
VERONICA?!
LADY SMITTY! LONG TIME, NO SEE!
HOW ARE YOU, DEAR?
UNDERGROUND
WELL, I'M HERE TO...
THAT'S NICE, HONEY! I'VE BEEN ON SUCH A WHIRLWIND TRIP HERE IN LONDON...
3

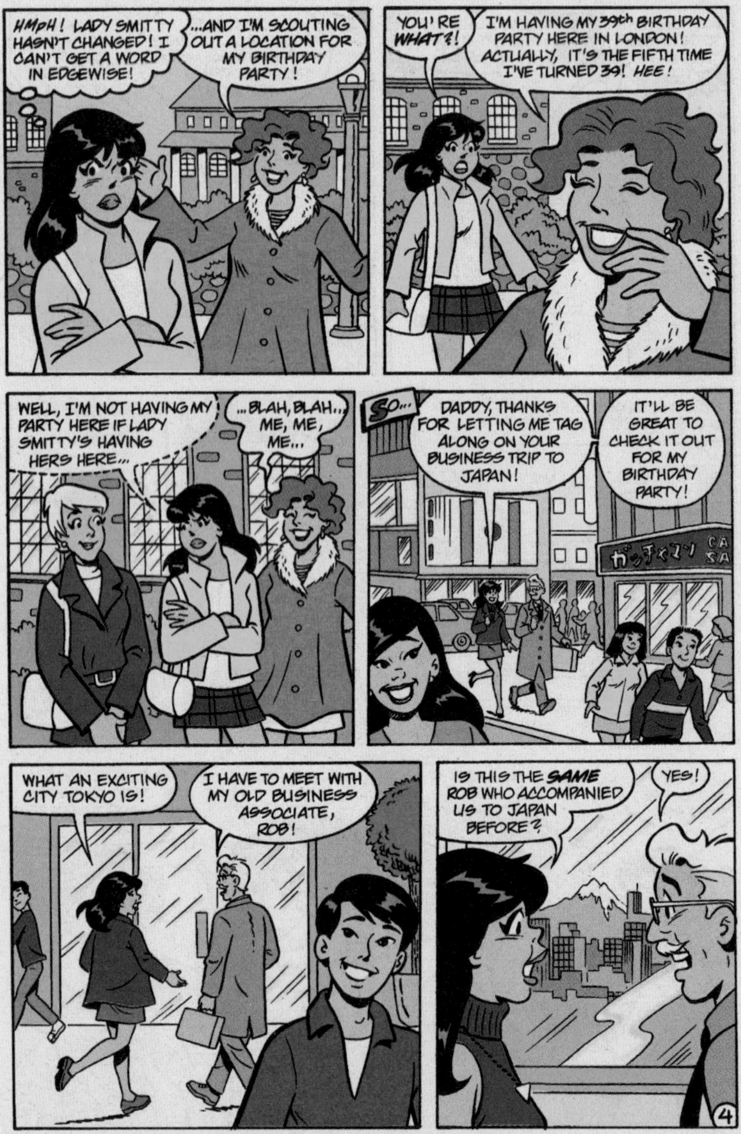
HMPH! LADY SMITTY HASN'T CHANGED! I CAN'T GET A WORD IN EDGEWISE!
...AND I'M SCOUTING OUT A LOCATION FOR MY BIRTHDAY PARTY!
YOU'RE WHAT?!
I'M HAVING MY 39th BIRTHDAY PARTY HERE IN LONDON! ACTUALLY, IT'S THE FIFTH TIME I'VE TURNED 39! HEE!
WELL, I'M NOT HAVING MY PARTY HERE IF LADY SMITTY'S HAVING HERS HERE...
...BLAH, BLAH... ME, ME, ME...
SO...
DADDY, THANKS FOR LETTING ME TAG ALONG ON YOUR BUSINESS TRIP TO JAPAN!
IT'LL BE GREAT TO CHECK IT OUT FOR MY BIRTHDAY PARTY!
WHAT AN EXCITING CITY TOKYO IS!
I HAVE TO MEET WITH MY OLD BUSINESS ASSOCIATE, ROB!
IS THIS THE SAME ROB WHO ACCOMPANIED US TO JAPAN BEFORE?
YES!
4

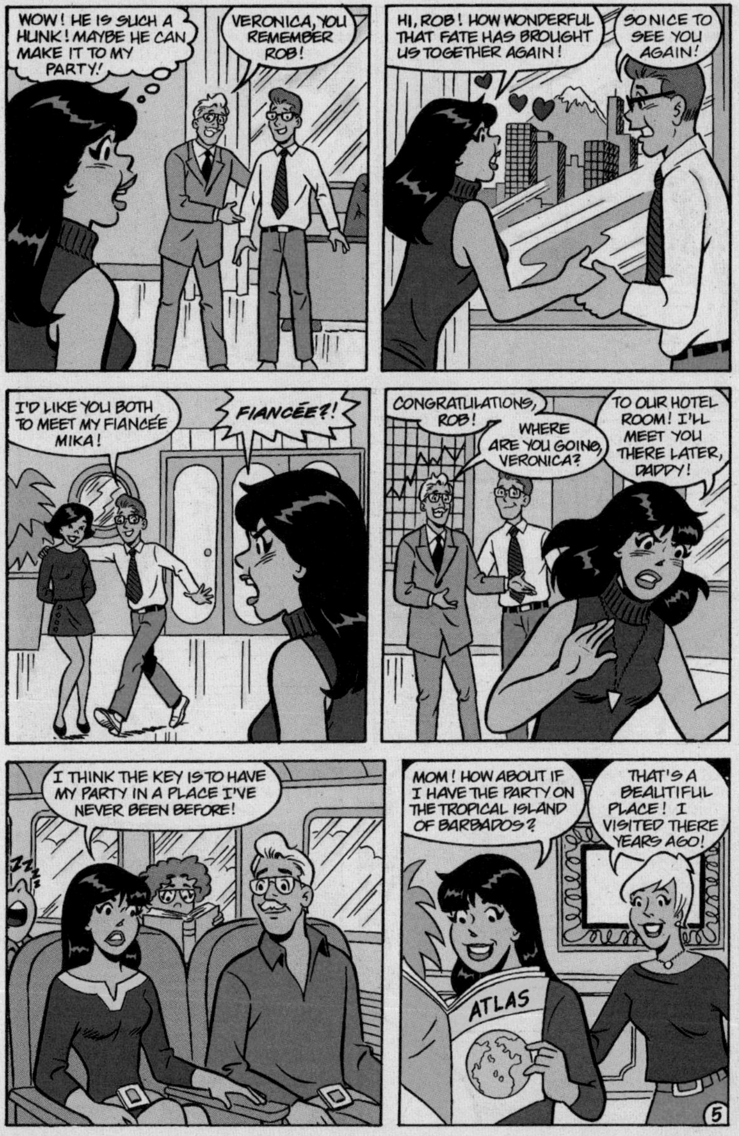

WOW! HE IS SUCH A HUNK! MAYBE HE CAN MAKE IT TO MY PARTY!
VERONICA, YOU REMEMBER ROB!
HI, ROB! HOW WONDERFUL THAT FATE HAS BROUGHT US TOGETHER AGAIN!
SO NICE TO SEE YOU AGAIN!
I'D LIKE YOU BOTH TO MEET MY FIANCÉE MIKA!
FIANCÉE?!
CONGRATULATIONS, ROB!
WHERE ARE YOU GOING, VERONICA?
TO OUR HOTEL ROOM! I'LL MEET YOU THERE LATER, DADDY!
I THINK THE KEY IS TO HAVE MY PARTY IN A PLACE I'VE NEVER BEEN BEFORE!
ZZZ
MOM! HOW ABOUT IF I HAVE THE PARTY ON THE TROPICAL ISLAND OF BARBADOS?
THAT'S A BEAUTIFUL PLACE! I VISITED THERE YEARS AGO!
ATLAS

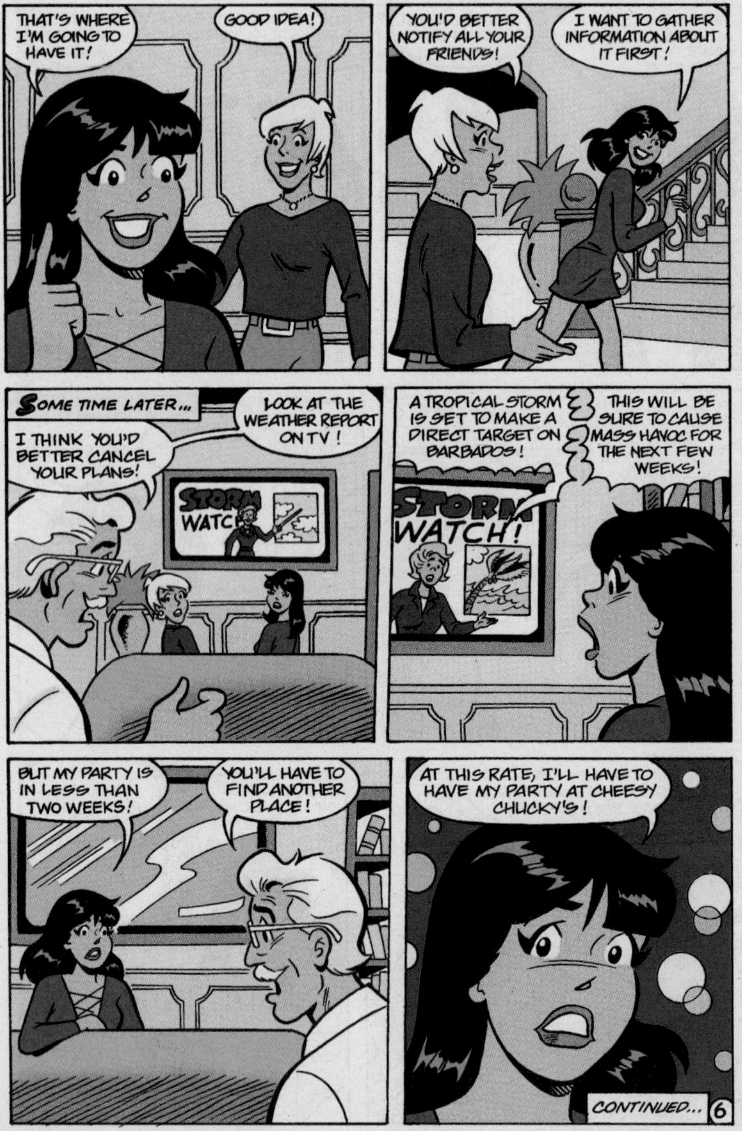
THAT'S WHERE I'M GOING TO HAVE IT!
GOOD IDEA!
YOU'D BETTER NOTIFY ALL YOUR FRIENDS!
I WANT TO GATHER INFORMATION ABOUT IT FIRST!
SOME TIME LATER...
LOOK AT THE WEATHER REPORT ON TV!
I THINK YOU'D BETTER CANCEL YOUR PLANS!
STORM WATCH
A TROPICAL STORM IS SET TO MAKE A DIRECT TARGET ON BARBADOS!
THIS WILL BE SURE TO CAUSE MASS HAVOC FOR THE NEXT FEW WEEKS!
STORM WATCH!
BUT MY PARTY IS IN LESS THAN TWO WEEKS!
YOU'LL HAVE TO FIND ANOTHER PLACE!
AT THIS RATE, I'LL HAVE TO HAVE MY PARTY AT CHEESY CHUCKY'S!
CONTINUED...

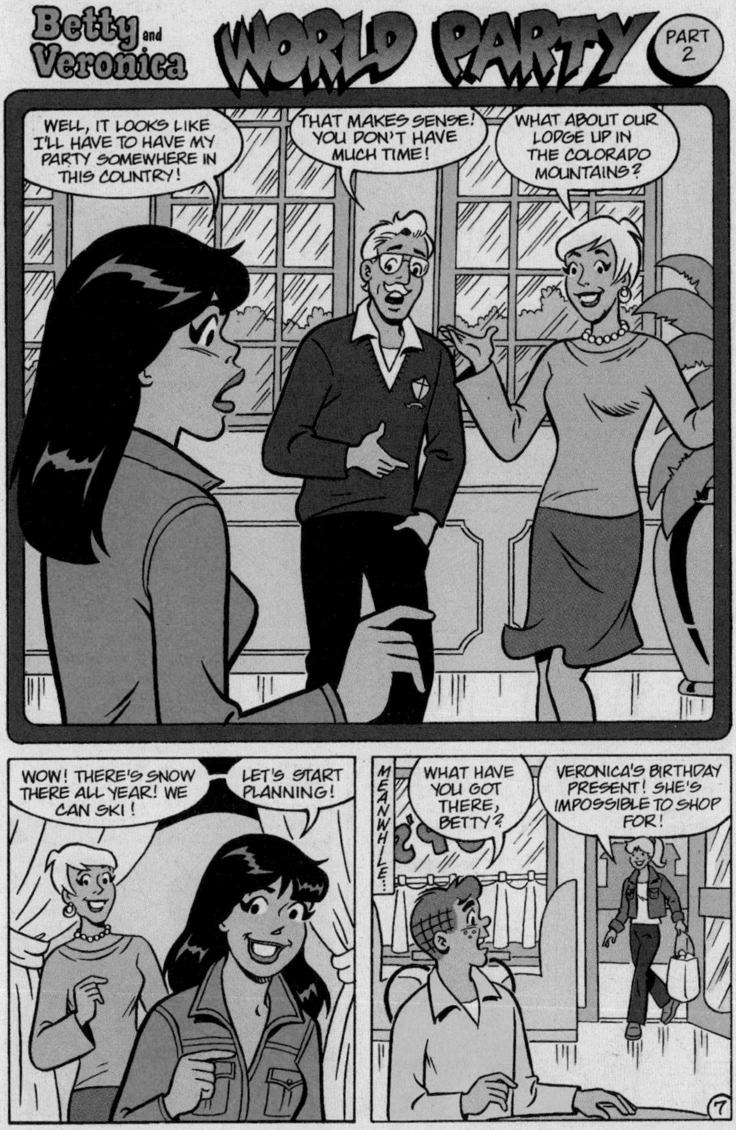
Betty and Veronica
WORLD PARTY
PART 2
WELL, IT LOOKS LIKE I'LL HAVE TO HAVE MY PARTY SOMEWHERE IN THIS COUNTRY!
THAT MAKES SENSE! YOU DON'T HAVE MUCH TIME!
WHAT ABOUT OUR LODGE UP IN THE COLORADO MOUNTAINS?
WOW! THERE'S SNOW THERE ALL YEAR! WE CAN SKI!
LET'S START PLANNING!
MEANWHILE...
WHAT HAVE YOU GOT THERE, BETTY?
VERONICA'S BIRTHDAY PRESENT! SHE'S IMPOSSIBLE TO SHOP FOR!
7

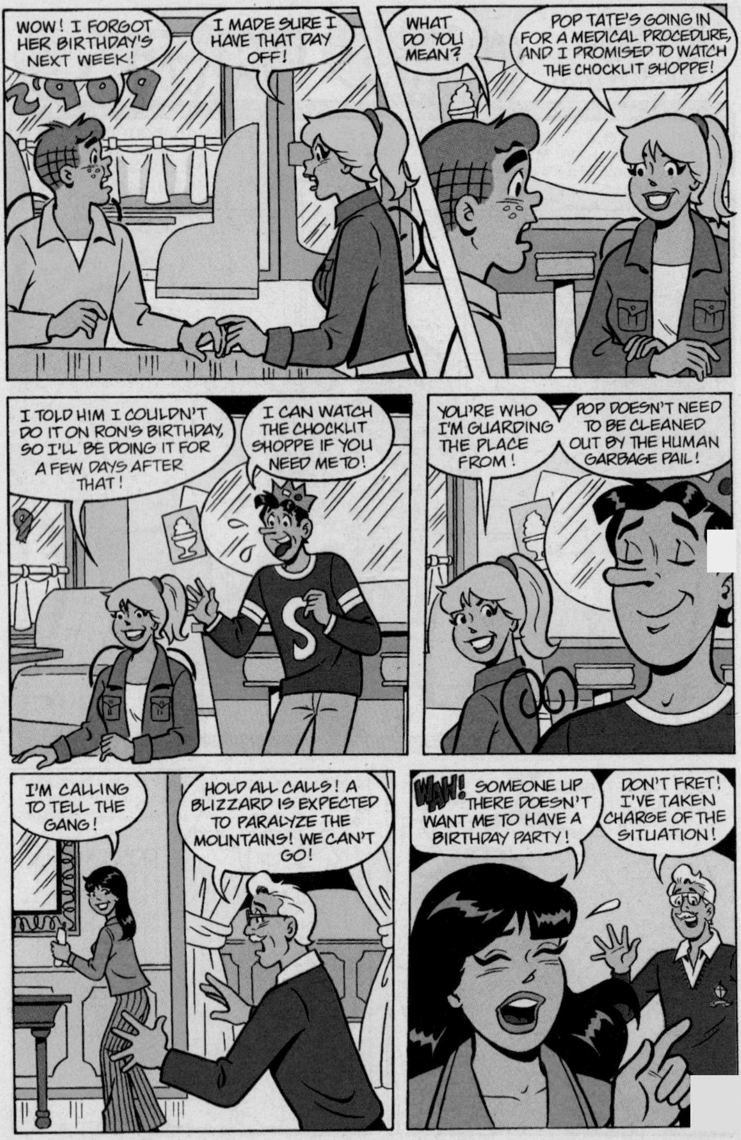
WOW! I FORGOT HER BIRTHDAY'S NEXT WEEK!
I MADE SURE I HAVE THAT DAY OFF!
POP'S
WHAT DO YOU MEAN?
POP TATE'S GOING IN FOR A MEDICAL PROCEDURE, AND I PROMISED TO WATCH THE CHOCKLIT SHOPPE!
I TOLD HIM I COULDN'T DO IT ON RON'S BIRTHDAY, SO I'LL BE DOING IT FOR A FEW DAYS AFTER THAT!
I CAN WATCH THE CHOCKLIT SHOPPE IF YOU NEED ME TO!
YOU'RE WHO I'M GUARDING THE PLACE FROM!
POP DOESN'T NEED TO BE CLEANED OUT BY THE HUMAN GARBAGE PAIL!
I'M CALLING TO TELL THE GANG!
HOLD ALL CALLS! A BLIZZARD IS EXPECTED TO PARALYZE THE MOUNTAINS! WE CAN'T GO!
WAH! SOMEONE UP THERE DOESN'T WANT ME TO HAVE A BIRTHDAY PARTY!
DON'T FRET! I'VE TAKEN CHARGE OF THE SITUATION!

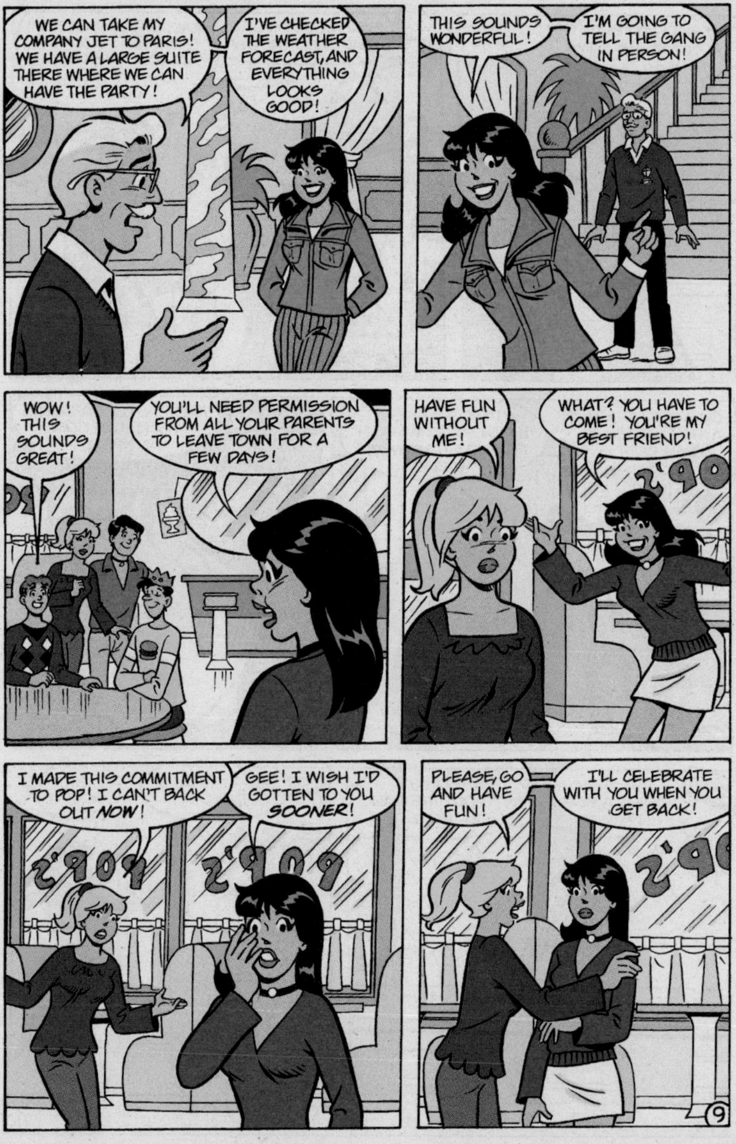
WE CAN TAKE MY COMPANY JET TO PARIS! WE HAVE A LARGE SUITE THERE WHERE WE CAN HAVE THE PARTY!
I'VE CHECKED THE WEATHER FORECAST, AND EVERYTHING LOOKS GOOD!
THIS SOUNDS WONDERFUL!
I'M GOING TO TELL THE GANG IN PERSON!
WOW! THIS SOUNDS GREAT!
YOU'LL NEED PERMISSION FROM ALL YOUR PARENTS TO LEAVE TOWN FOR A FEW DAYS!
HAVE FUN WITHOUT ME!
WHAT? YOU HAVE TO COME! YOU'RE MY BEST FRIEND!
POP'S
I MADE THIS COMMITMENT TO POP! I CAN'T BACK OUT *NOW*!
GEE! I WISH I'D GOTTEN TO YOU *SOONER*!
POP'S
POP'S
PLEASE, GO AND HAVE FUN!
I'LL CELEBRATE WITH YOU WHEN YOU GET BACK!
POP'S
9

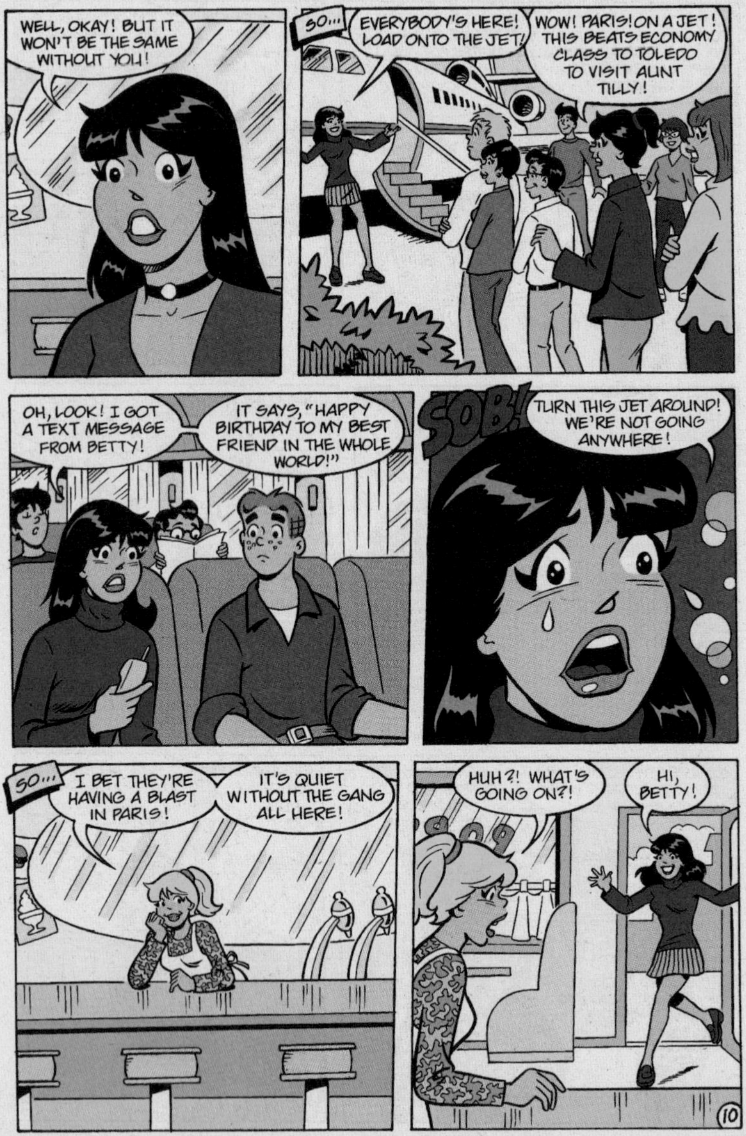
WELL, OKAY! BUT IT WON'T BE THE SAME WITHOUT YOU!
SO...
EVERYBODY'S HERE! LOAD ONTO THE JET!
WOW! PARIS! ON A JET! THIS BEATS ECONOMY CLASS TO TOLEDO TO VISIT AUNT TILLY!
OH, LOOK! I GOT A TEXT MESSAGE FROM BETTY!
IT SAYS, "HAPPY BIRTHDAY TO MY BEST FRIEND IN THE WHOLE WORLD!"
SOB!
TURN THIS JET AROUND! WE'RE NOT GOING ANYWHERE!
SO...
I BET THEY'RE HAVING A BLAST IN PARIS!
IT'S QUIET WITHOUT THE GANG ALL HERE!
HUH?! WHAT'S GOING ON?!
HI, BETTY!
10

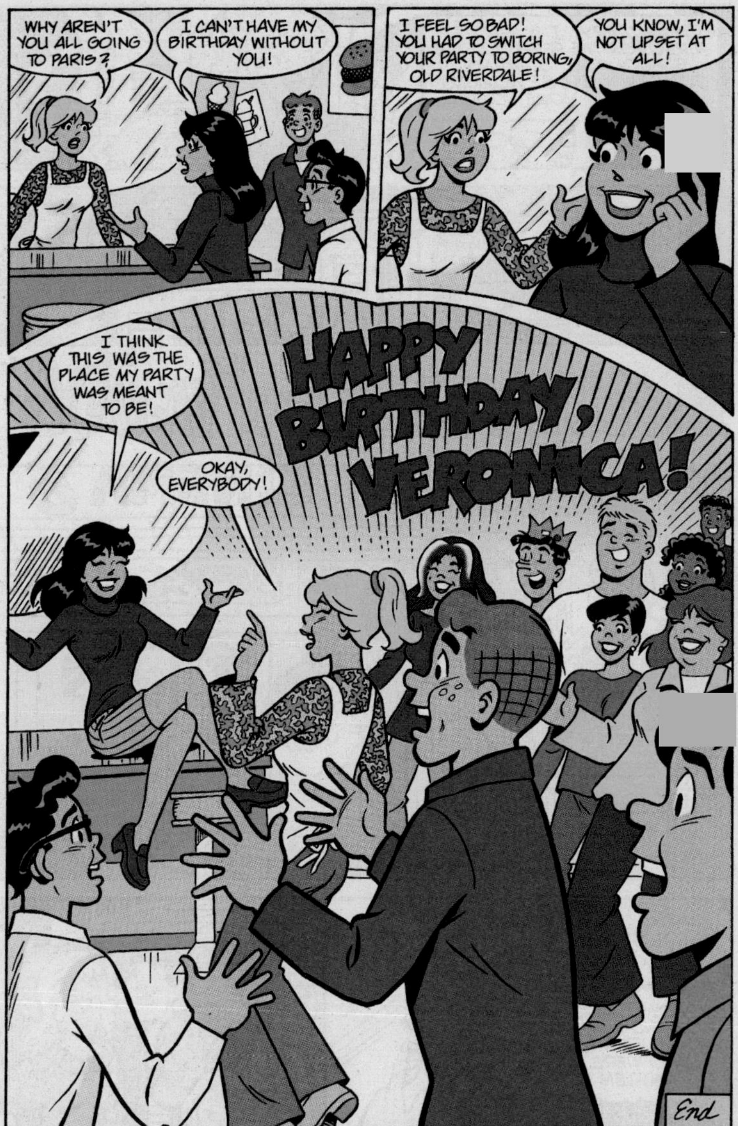
WHY AREN'T YOU ALL GOING TO PARIS?
I CAN'T HAVE MY BIRTHDAY WITHOUT YOU!
I FEEL SO BAD! YOU HAD TO SWITCH YOUR PARTY TO BORING, OLD RIVERDALE!
YOU KNOW, I'M NOT UPSET AT ALL!
I THINK THIS WAS THE PLACE MY PARTY WAS MEANT TO BE!
OKAY, EVERYBODY!
HAPPY BIRTHDAY, VERONICA!
End

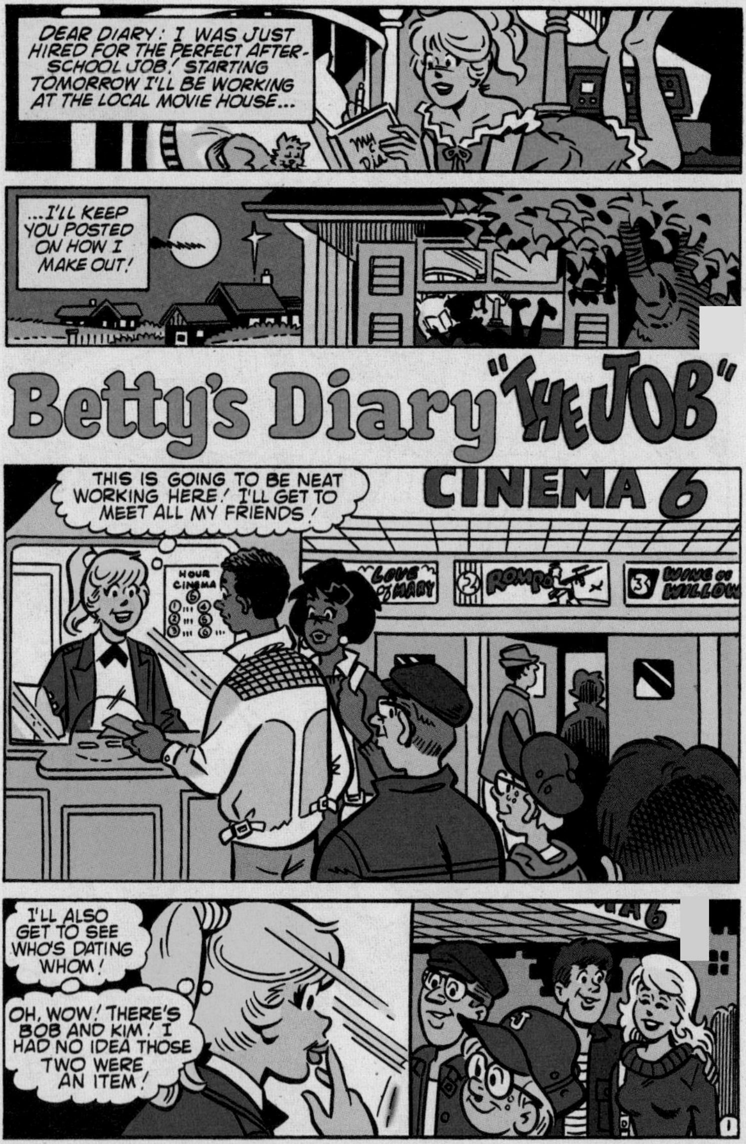
DEAR DIARY: I WAS JUST HIRED FOR THE PERFECT AFTER-SCHOOL JOB! STARTING TOMORROW I'LL BE WORKING AT THE LOCAL MOVIE HOUSE...
...I'LL KEEP YOU POSTED ON HOW I MAKE OUT!
Betty's Diary "THE JOB"
THIS IS GOING TO BE NEAT WORKING HERE! I'LL GET TO MEET ALL MY FRIENDS!
CINEMA 6
LOVE of MARY
ROMPO
I'LL ALSO GET TO SEE WHO'S DATING WHOM!
OH, WOW! THERE'S BOB AND KIM! I HAD NO IDEA THOSE TWO WERE AN ITEM!
1

Script: George Gladir / Pencils: Stan Goldberg / Inks: Rudy Lapick / Letters: Billl Yoshida

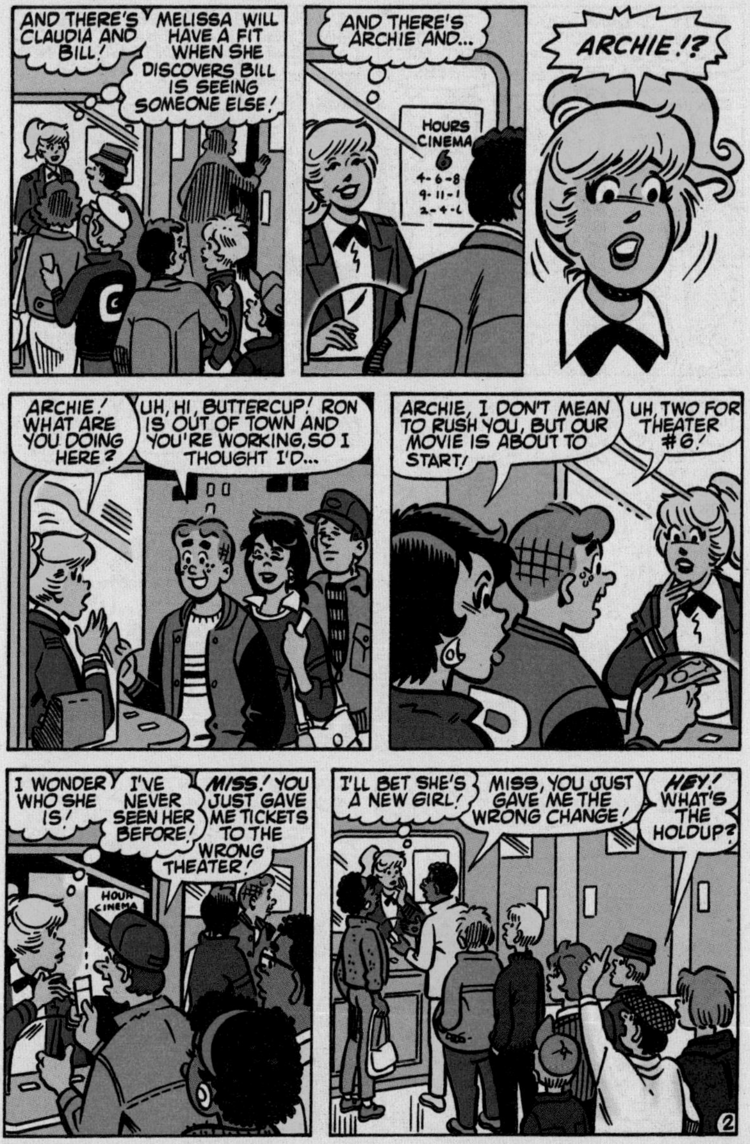
AND THERE'S CLAUDIA AND BILL!
MELISSA WILL HAVE A FIT WHEN SHE DISCOVERS BILL IS SEEING SOMEONE ELSE!
AND THERE'S ARCHIE AND...
HOURS CINEMA 6 4-6-8 9-11-1 2-4-6
ARCHIE!?
ARCHIE! WHAT ARE YOU DOING HERE?
UH, HI, BUTTERCUP! RON IS OUT OF TOWN AND YOU'RE WORKING, SO I THOUGHT I'D...
ARCHIE, I DON'T MEAN TO RUSH YOU, BUT OUR MOVIE IS ABOUT TO START!
UH, TWO FOR THEATER #6!
I WONDER WHO SHE IS!
I'VE NEVER SEEN HER BEFORE!
MISS! YOU JUST GAVE ME TICKETS TO THE WRONG THEATER!
I'LL BET SHE'S A NEW GIRL!
MISS, YOU JUST GAVE ME THE WRONG CHANGE!
HEY! WHAT'S THE HOLDUP?
2

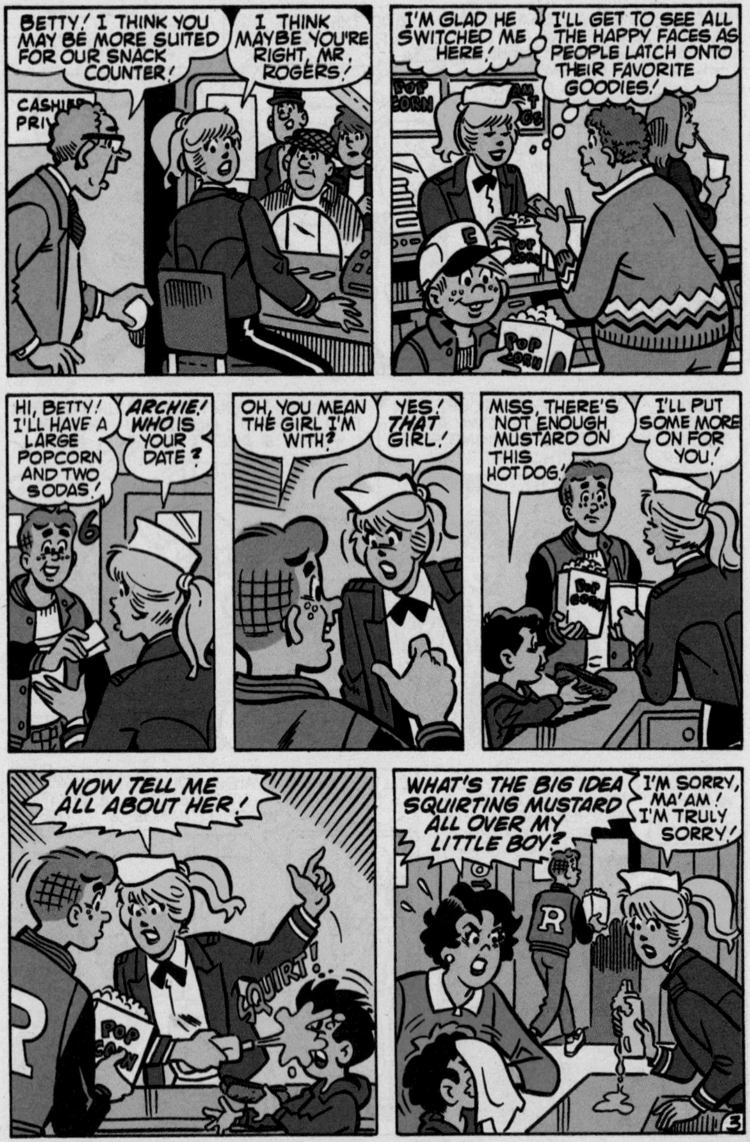

BETTY! I THINK YOU MAY BE MORE SUITED FOR OUR SNACK COUNTER!
I THINK MAYBE YOU'RE RIGHT, MR. ROGERS!
I'M GLAD HE SWITCHED ME HERE!
I'LL GET TO SEE ALL THE HAPPY FACES AS PEOPLE LATCH ONTO THEIR FAVORITE GOODIES!
HI, BETTY! I'LL HAVE A LARGE POPCORN AND TWO SODAS!
ARCHIE! WHO IS YOUR DATE?
OH, YOU MEAN THE GIRL I'M WITH?
YES! THAT GIRL!
MISS, THERE'S NOT ENOUGH MUSTARD ON THIS HOT DOG!
I'LL PUT SOME MORE ON FOR YOU!
NOW TELL ME ALL ABOUT HER!
SQUIRT!
WHAT'S THE BIG IDEA SQUIRTING MUSTARD ALL OVER MY LITTLE BOY?
I'M SORRY, MA'AM! I'M TRULY SORRY!
3

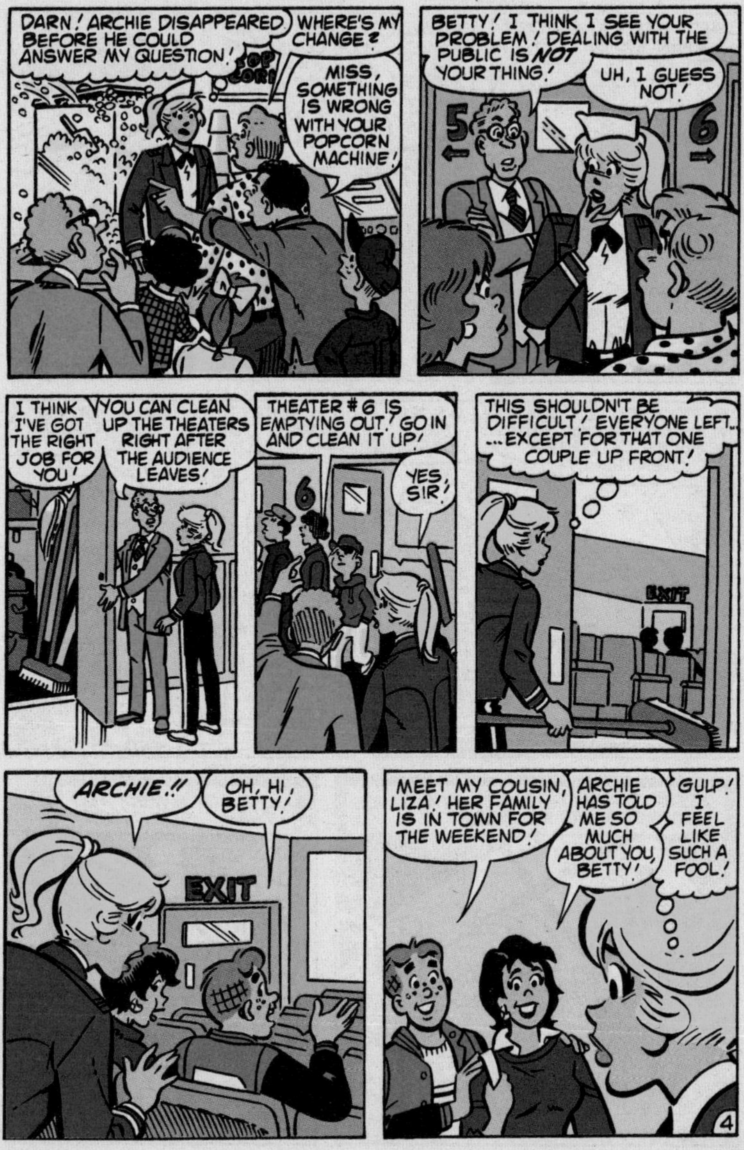
DARN! ARCHIE DISAPPEARED BEFORE HE COULD ANSWER MY QUESTION!
WHERE'S MY CHANGE?
MISS, SOMETHING IS WRONG WITH YOUR POPCORN MACHINE!
BETTY! I THINK I SEE YOUR PROBLEM! DEALING WITH THE PUBLIC IS *NOT* YOUR THING!
UH, I GUESS NOT!
5
6
I THINK I'VE GOT THE RIGHT JOB FOR YOU!
YOU CAN CLEAN UP THE THEATERS RIGHT AFTER THE AUDIENCE LEAVES!
THEATER # 6 IS EMPTYING OUT! GO IN AND CLEAN IT UP!
YES, SIR!
6
THIS SHOULDN'T BE DIFFICULT! EVERYONE LEFT... ...EXCEPT FOR THAT ONE COUPLE UP FRONT!
EXIT
ARCHIE!!
OH, HI, BETTY!
EXIT
MEET MY COUSIN, LIZA! HER FAMILY IS IN TOWN FOR THE WEEKEND!
ARCHIE HAS TOLD ME SO MUCH ABOUT YOU, BETTY!
GULP! I FEEL LIKE SUCH A FOOL!

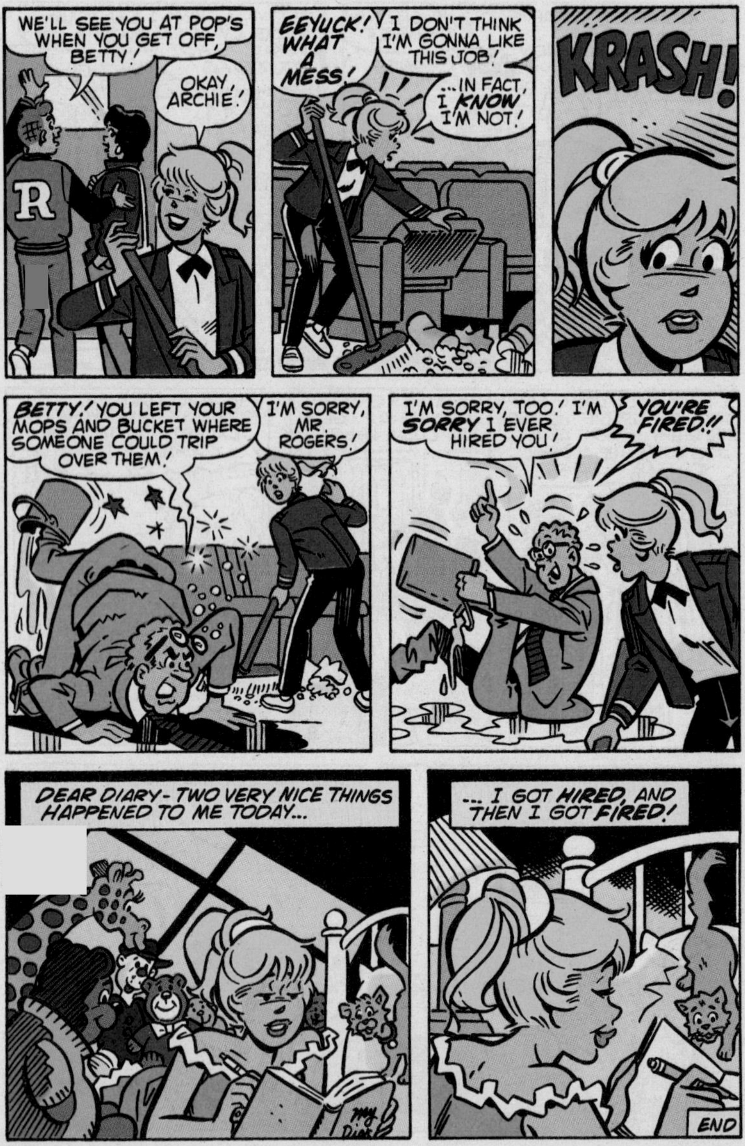

WE'LL SEE YOU AT POP'S WHEN YOU GET OFF, BETTY!
OKAY, ARCHIE!
EEYUCK! WHAT A MESS!
I DON'T THINK I'M GONNA LIKE THIS JOB!
...IN FACT, I KNOW I'M NOT!
KRASH!
BETTY! YOU LEFT YOUR MOPS AND BUCKET WHERE SOMEONE COULD TRIP OVER THEM!
I'M SORRY, MR. ROGERS!
I'M SORRY, TOO! I'M SORRY I EVER HIRED YOU!
YOU'RE FIRED!!
DEAR DIARY- TWO VERY NICE THINGS HAPPENED TO ME TODAY...
... I GOT HIRED, AND THEN I GOT FIRED!
END

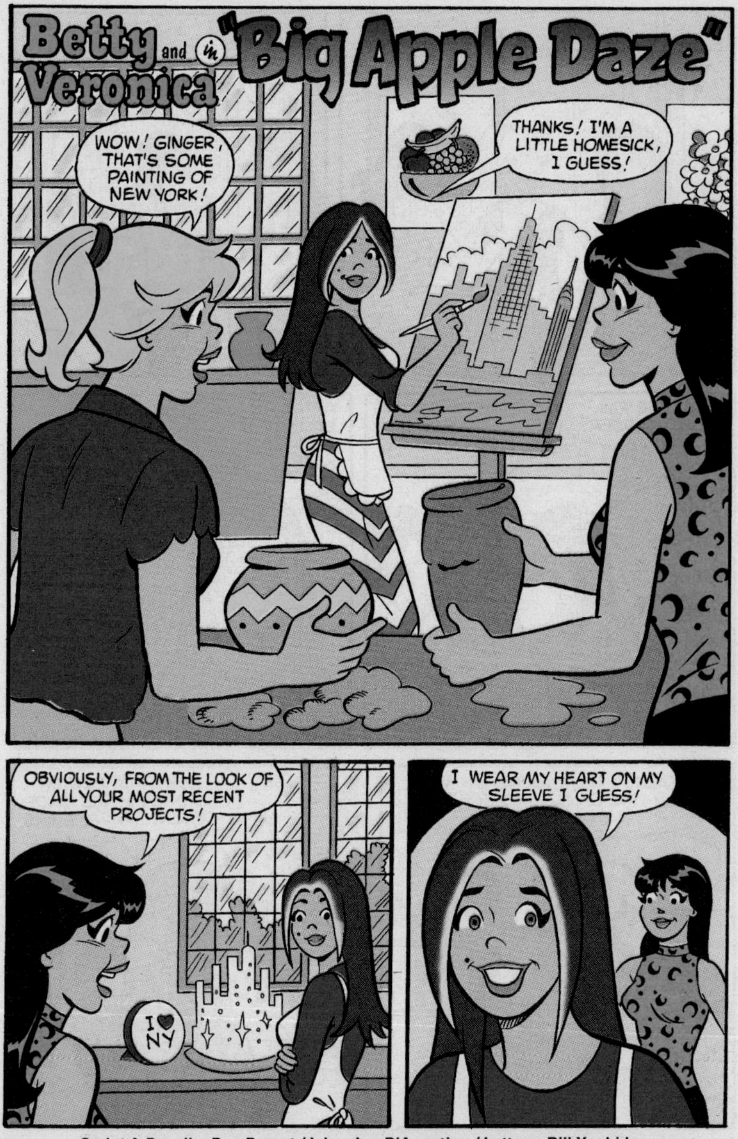
Betty and Veronica in "Big Apple Daze"
WOW! GINGER, THAT'S SOME PAINTING OF NEW YORK!
THANKS! I'M A LITTLE HOMESICK, I GUESS!
OBVIOUSLY, FROM THE LOOK OF ALL YOUR MOST RECENT PROJECTS!
I ♥ NY
I WEAR MY HEART ON MY SLEEVE I GUESS!

Script & Pencils: Dan Parent / Inks: Jon D'Agostino / Letters: Bill Yoshida

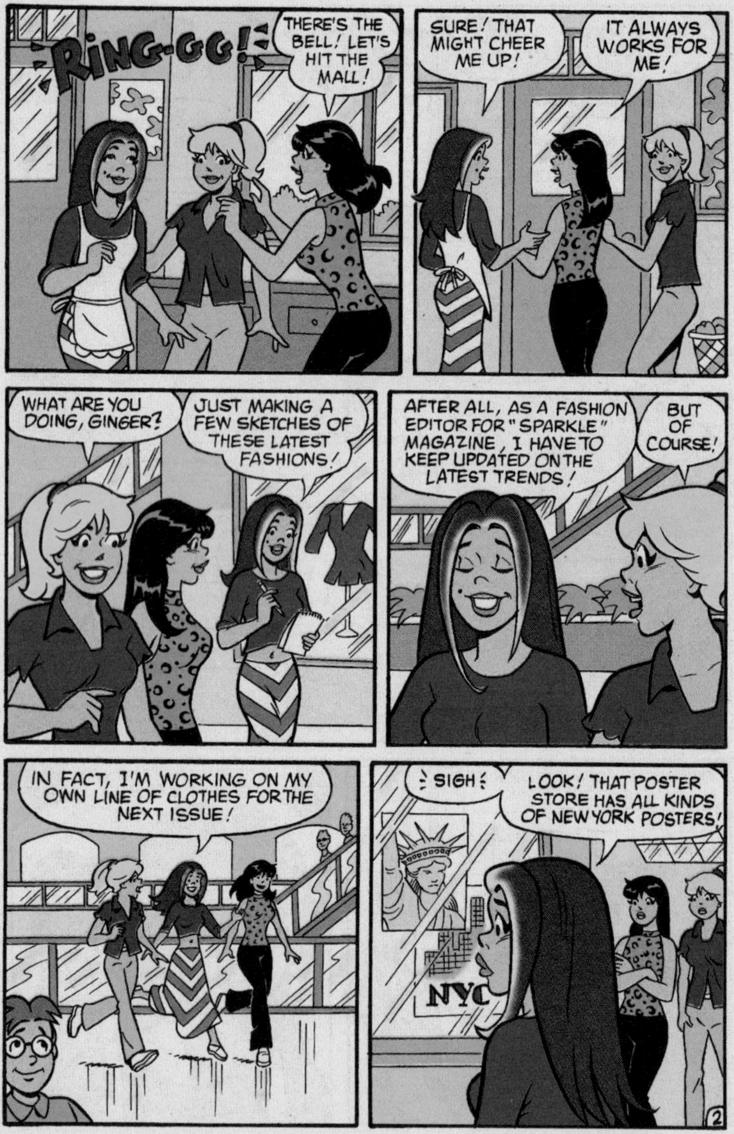
RING-GG!
THERE'S THE BELL! LET'S HIT THE MALL!
SURE! THAT MIGHT CHEER ME UP!
IT ALWAYS WORKS FOR ME!
WHAT ARE YOU DOING, GINGER?
JUST MAKING A FEW SKETCHES OF THESE LATEST FASHIONS!
AFTER ALL, AS A FASHION EDITOR FOR "SPARKLE" MAGAZINE, I HAVE TO KEEP UPDATED ON THE LATEST TRENDS!
BUT OF COURSE!
IN FACT, I'M WORKING ON MY OWN LINE OF CLOTHES FOR THE NEXT ISSUE!
SIGH
LOOK! THAT POSTER STORE HAS ALL KINDS OF NEW YORK POSTERS!
NYC
2

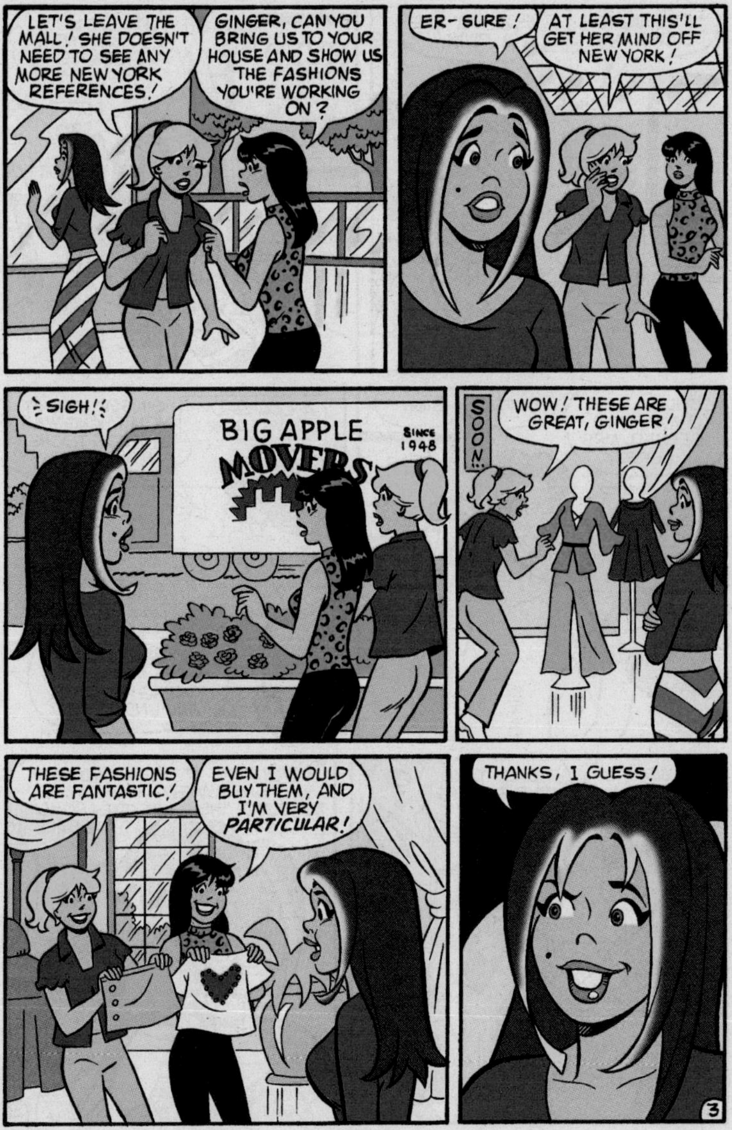
LET'S LEAVE THE MALL! SHE DOESN'T NEED TO SEE ANY MORE NEW YORK REFERENCES!
GINGER, CAN YOU BRING US TO YOUR HOUSE AND SHOW US THE FASHIONS YOU'RE WORKING ON?
ER- SURE!
AT LEAST THIS'LL GET HER MIND OFF NEW YORK!
SIGH!
BIG APPLE MOVERS
SINCE 1948
SOON...
WOW! THESE ARE GREAT, GINGER!
THESE FASHIONS ARE FANTASTIC!
EVEN I WOULD BUY THEM, AND I'M VERY PARTICULAR!
THANKS, I GUESS!
3

Panel 1:
LET'S WATCH SOME TV!
SOUNDS LIKE A PLAN!!

Panel 2:
NYPD STORIES
SIGH!
OH, NO! NOT NEW YORK AGAIN!
PSST! MRS. LOPEZ...

Panel 3:
COULD I TALK TO YOU FOR A SECOND, MRS. LOPEZ?
SURE!!
SIGH.!!

Panel 4:
A COUPLE OF DAYS LATER...
GINGER, AREN'T YOU TAKING YOUR SISTERS TO THE MOVIES TODAY?!
NO! I'VE GOT THE BLAHS! I'M JUST GOING TO HANG AROUND HERE!!

Panel 5:
UH-WELL, I NEED YOU TO LEAVE!!
HERE! TAKE YOUR SISTERS AND GO!!
?

Panel 6:
I WONDER WHY SHE WANTED ME OUT OF THE HOUSE?!
GIRLS, YOU WAIT HERE, I'VE FORGOTTEN SOMETHING BACK HOME...

4

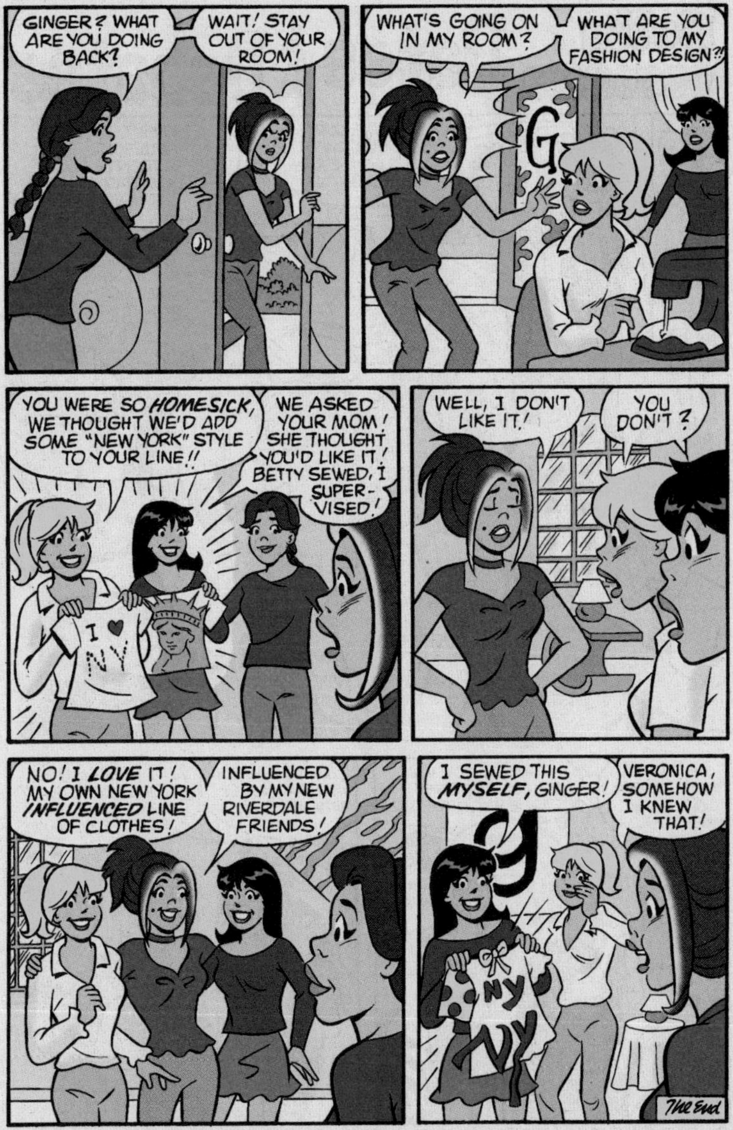
GINGER? WHAT ARE YOU DOING BACK?
WAIT! STAY OUT OF YOUR ROOM!
WHAT'S GOING ON IN MY ROOM?
WHAT ARE YOU DOING TO MY FASHION DESIGN?!
YOU WERE SO HOMESICK, WE THOUGHT WE'D ADD SOME "NEW YORK" STYLE TO YOUR LINE!!
WE ASKED YOUR MOM! SHE THOUGHT YOU'D LIKE IT! BETTY SEWED, I SUPER-VISED!
I ♥ NY
WELL, I DON'T LIKE IT!
YOU DON'T?
NO! I LOVE IT! MY OWN NEW YORK INFLUENCED LINE OF CLOTHES!
INFLUENCED BY MY NEW RIVERDALE FRIENDS!
I SEWED THIS MYSELF, GINGER!
VERONICA, SOMEHOW I KNEW THAT!
NY
The End

Betty and Veronica Dates & Debates

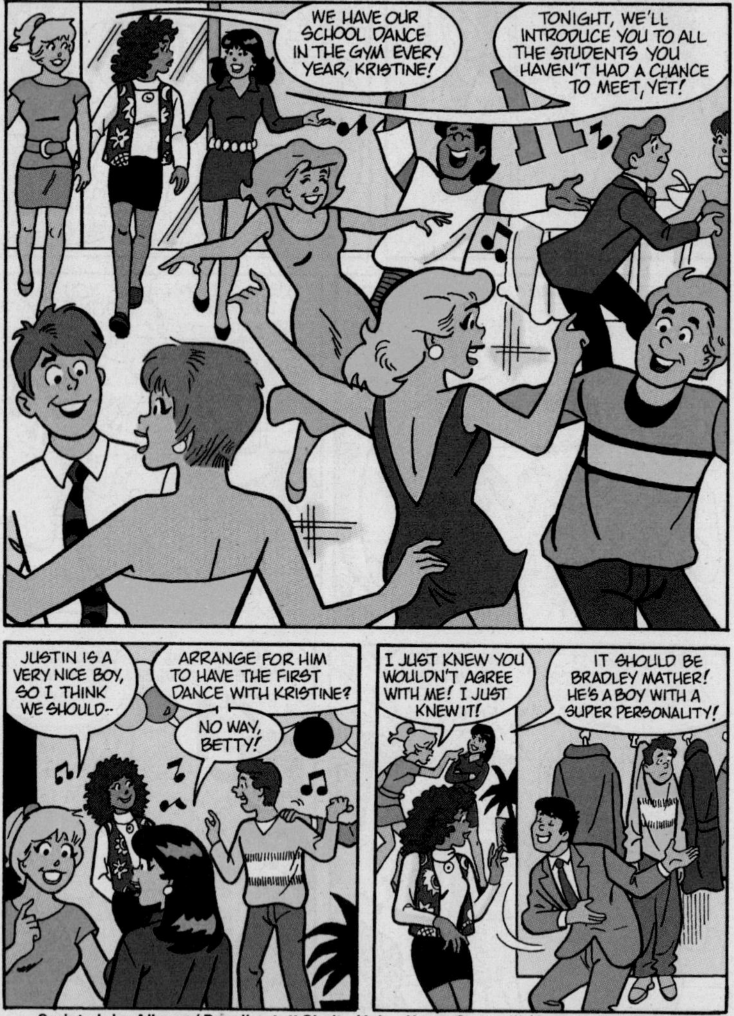
WE HAVE OUR SCHOOL DANCE IN THE GYM EVERY YEAR, KRISTINE!
TONIGHT, WE'LL INTRODUCE YOU TO ALL THE STUDENTS YOU HAVEN'T HAD A CHANCE TO MEET, YET!
JUSTIN IS A VERY NICE BOY, SO I THINK WE SHOULD--
ARRANGE FOR HIM TO HAVE THE FIRST DANCE WITH KRISTINE?
NO WAY, BETTY!
I JUST KNEW YOU WOULDN'T AGREE WITH ME! I JUST KNEW IT!
IT SHOULD BE BRADLEY MATHER! HE'S A BOY WITH A SUPER PERSONALITY!

Script: John Albano / Pencils: Jeff Shultz / Inks: Henry Scarpelli / Letters: Dan Nakrosis

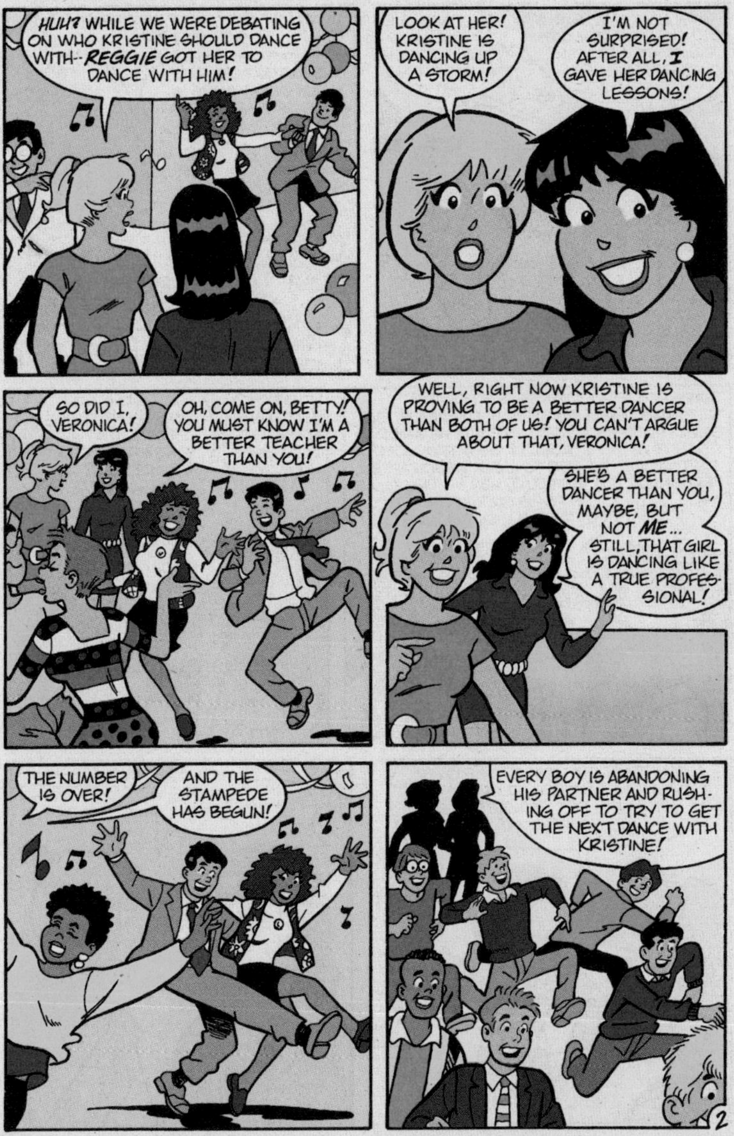

HUH? WHILE WE WERE DEBATING ON WHO KRISTINE SHOULD DANCE WITH-- REGGIE GOT HER TO DANCE WITH HIM!
LOOK AT HER! KRISTINE IS DANCING UP A STORM!
I'M NOT SURPRISED! AFTER ALL, I GAVE HER DANCING LESSONS!
SO DID I, VERONICA!
OH, COME ON, BETTY! YOU MUST KNOW I'M A BETTER TEACHER THAN YOU!
WELL, RIGHT NOW KRISTINE IS PROVING TO BE A BETTER DANCER THAN BOTH OF US! YOU CAN'T ARGUE ABOUT THAT, VERONICA!
SHE'S A BETTER DANCER THAN YOU, MAYBE, BUT NOT ME... STILL, THAT GIRL IS DANCING LIKE A TRUE PROFES-SIONAL!
THE NUMBER IS OVER!
AND THE STAMPEDE HAS BEGUN!
EVERY BOY IS ABANDONING HIS PARTNER AND RUSH-ING OFF TO TRY TO GET THE NEXT DANCE WITH KRISTINE!
2

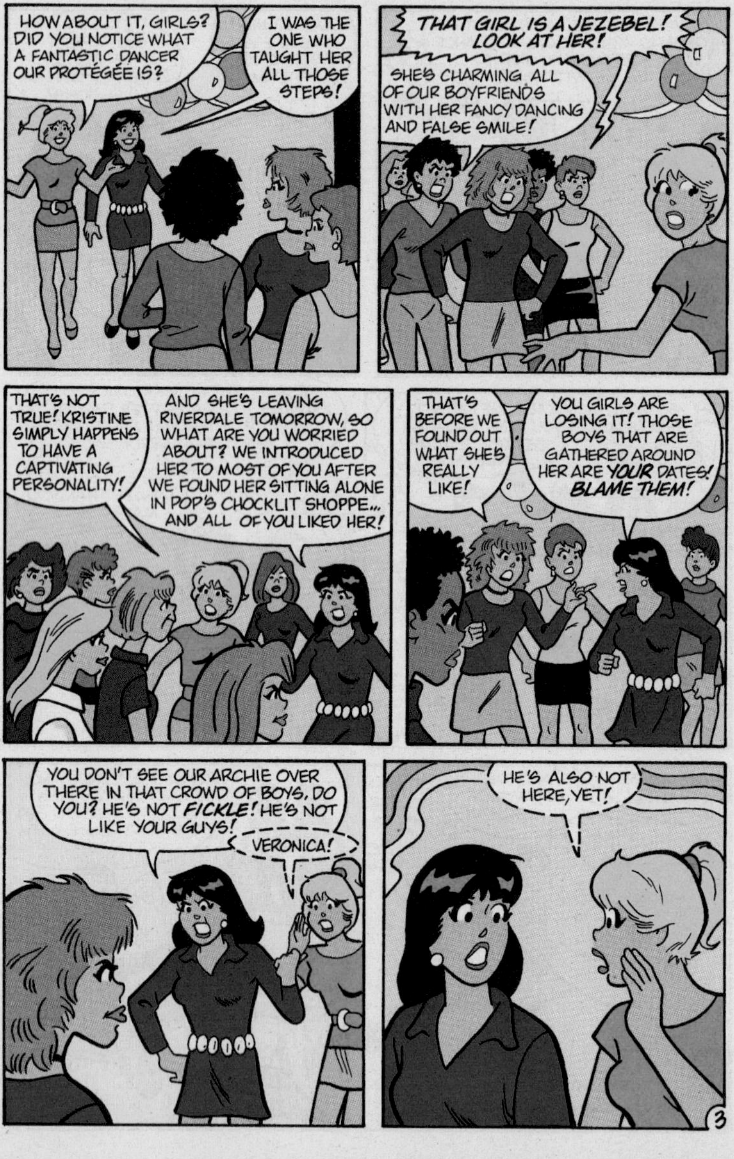
HOW ABOUT IT, GIRLS? DID YOU NOTICE WHAT A FANTASTIC DANCER OUR PROTÉGÉE IS?
I WAS THE ONE WHO TAUGHT HER ALL THOSE STEPS!
THAT GIRL IS A JEZEBEL! LOOK AT HER!
SHE'S CHARMING ALL OF OUR BOYFRIENDS WITH HER FANCY DANCING AND FALSE SMILE!
THAT'S NOT TRUE! KRISTINE SIMPLY HAPPENS TO HAVE A CAPTIVATING PERSONALITY!
AND SHE'S LEAVING RIVERDALE TOMORROW, SO WHAT ARE YOU WORRIED ABOUT? WE INTRODUCED HER TO MOST OF YOU AFTER WE FOUND HER SITTING ALONE IN POP'S CHOCKLIT SHOPPE... AND ALL OF YOU LIKED HER!
THAT'S BEFORE WE FOUND OUT WHAT SHE'S REALLY LIKE!
YOU GIRLS ARE LOSING IT! THOSE BOYS THAT ARE GATHERED AROUND HER ARE YOUR DATES! BLAME THEM!
YOU DON'T SEE OUR ARCHIE OVER THERE IN THAT CROWD OF BOYS, DO YOU? HE'S NOT FICKLE! HE'S NOT LIKE YOUR GUYS!
VERONICA!
HE'S ALSO NOT HERE, YET!
3

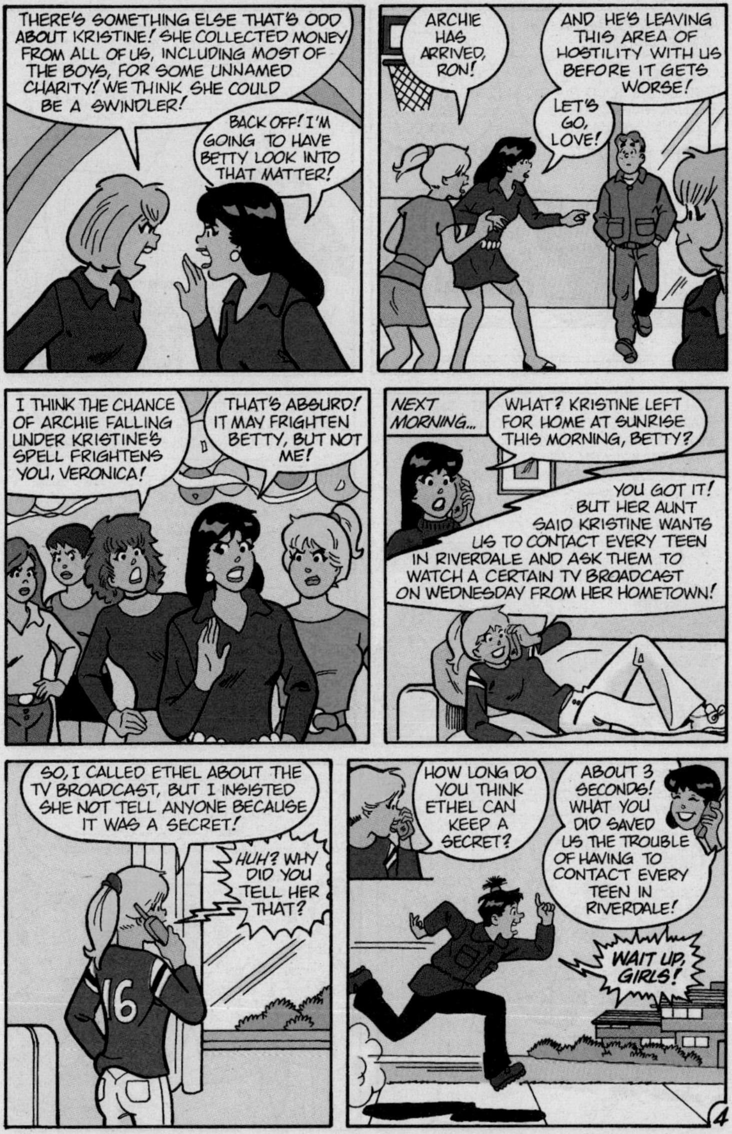
THERE'S SOMETHING ELSE THAT'S ODD ABOUT KRISTINE! SHE COLLECTED MONEY FROM ALL OF US, INCLUDING MOST OF THE BOYS, FOR SOME UNNAMED CHARITY! WE THINK SHE COULD BE A SWINDLER!
BACK OFF! I'M GOING TO HAVE BETTY LOOK INTO THAT MATTER!
ARCHIE HAS ARRIVED, RON!
AND HE'S LEAVING THIS AREA OF HOSTILITY WITH US BEFORE IT GETS WORSE!
LET'S GO, LOVE!
I THINK THE CHANCE OF ARCHIE FALLING UNDER KRISTINE'S SPELL FRIGHTENS YOU, VERONICA!
THAT'S ABSURD! IT MAY FRIGHTEN BETTY, BUT NOT ME!
NEXT MORNING...
WHAT? KRISTINE LEFT FOR HOME AT SUNRISE THIS MORNING, BETTY?
YOU GOT IT! BUT HER AUNT SAID KRISTINE WANTS US TO CONTACT EVERY TEEN IN RIVERDALE AND ASK THEM TO WATCH A CERTAIN TV BROADCAST ON WEDNESDAY FROM HER HOMETOWN!
SO, I CALLED ETHEL ABOUT THE TV BROADCAST, BUT I INSISTED SHE NOT TELL ANYONE BECAUSE IT WAS A SECRET!
HUH? WHY DID YOU TELL HER THAT?
16
HOW LONG DO YOU THINK ETHEL CAN KEEP A SECRET?
ABOUT 3 SECONDS! WHAT YOU DID SAVED US THE TROUBLE OF HAVING TO CONTACT EVERY TEEN IN RIVERDALE!
WAIT UP, GIRLS!

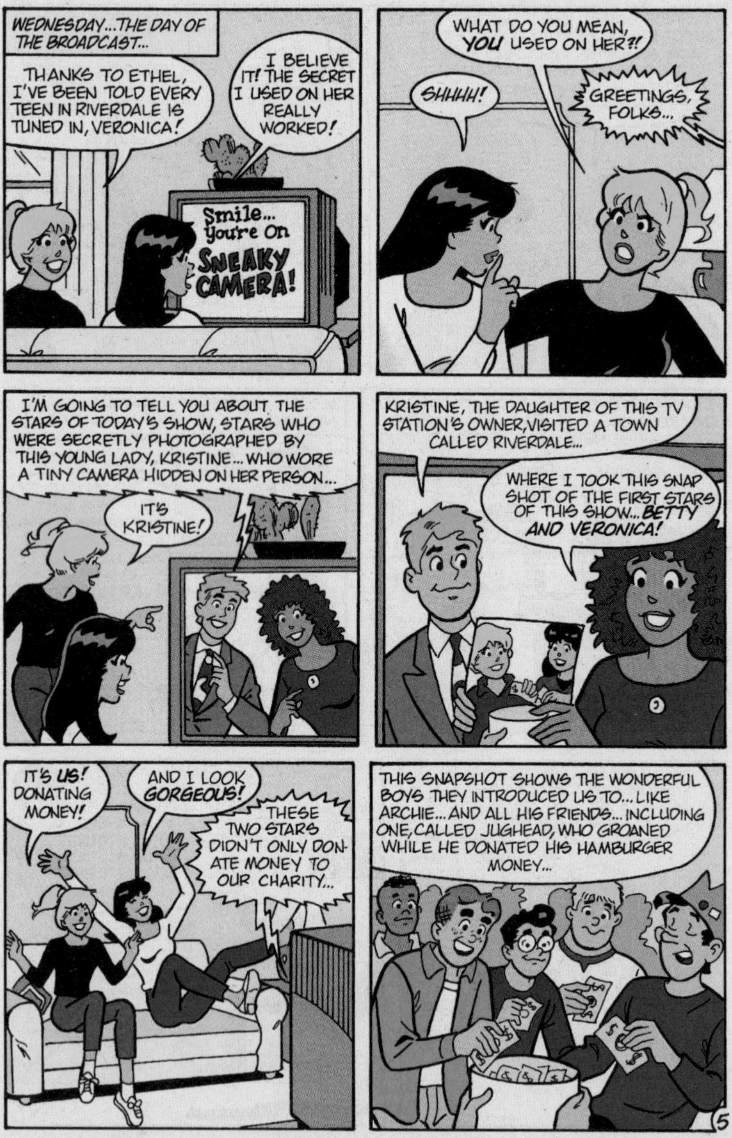
WEDNESDAY...THE DAY OF THE BROADCAST...
THANKS TO ETHEL, I'VE BEEN TOLD EVERY TEEN IN RIVERDALE IS TUNED IN, VERONICA!
I BELIEVE IT! THE SECRET I USED ON HER REALLY WORKED!
Smile... You're On SNEAKY CAMERA!
WHAT DO YOU MEAN, YOU USED ON HER?!
SHHHH!
GREETINGS, FOLKS...
I'M GOING TO TELL YOU ABOUT THE STARS OF TODAY'S SHOW, STARS WHO WERE SECRETLY PHOTOGRAPHED BY THIS YOUNG LADY, KRISTINE... WHO WORE A TINY CAMERA HIDDEN ON HER PERSON...
IT'S KRISTINE!
KRISTINE, THE DAUGHTER OF THIS TV STATION'S OWNER, VISITED A TOWN CALLED RIVERDALE...
WHERE I TOOK THIS SNAP SHOT OF THE FIRST STARS OF THIS SHOW... BETTY AND VERONICA!
IT'S US! DONATING MONEY!
AND I LOOK GORGEOUS!
THESE TWO STARS DIDN'T ONLY DONATE MONEY TO OUR CHARITY...
THIS SNAPSHOT SHOWS THE WONDERFUL BOYS THEY INTRODUCED US TO... LIKE ARCHIE... AND ALL HIS FRIENDS... INCLUDING ONE, CALLED JUGHEAD, WHO GROANED WHILE HE DONATED HIS HAMBURGER MONEY...

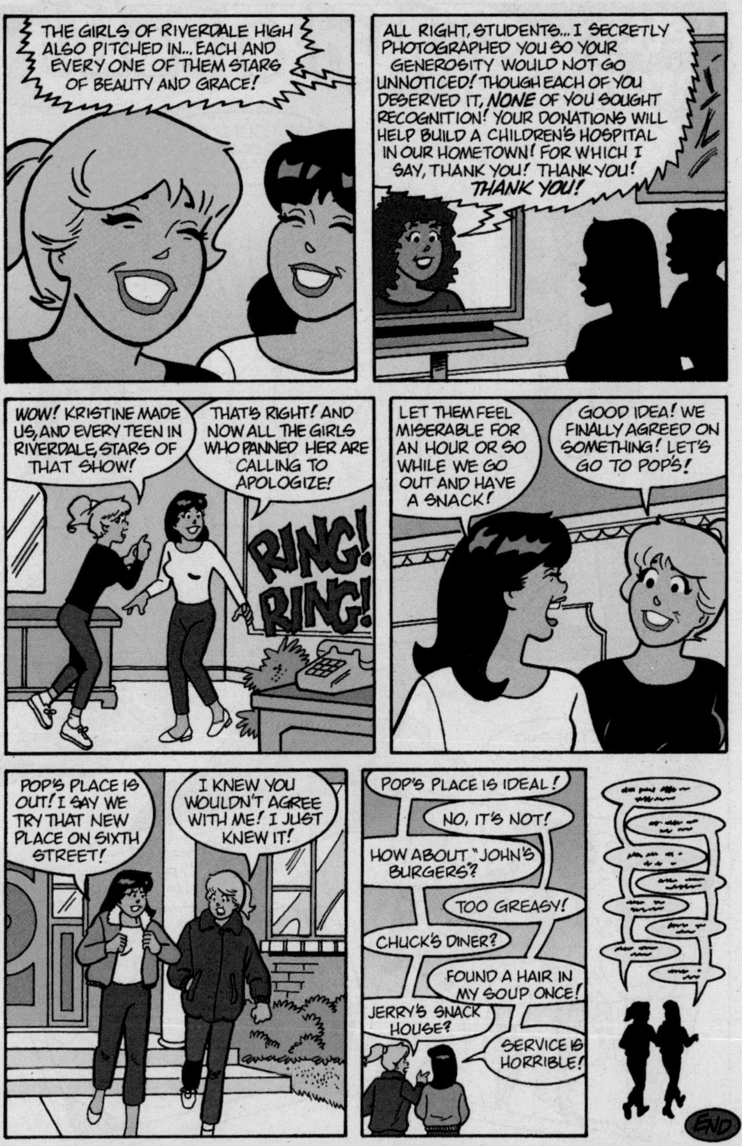
THE GIRLS OF RIVERDALE HIGH ALSO PITCHED IN... EACH AND EVERY ONE OF THEM STARS OF BEAUTY AND GRACE!
ALL RIGHT, STUDENTS... I SECRETLY PHOTOGRAPHED YOU SO YOUR GENEROSITY WOULD NOT GO UNNOTICED! THOUGH EACH OF YOU DESERVED IT, NONE OF YOU SOUGHT RECOGNITION! YOUR DONATIONS WILL HELP BUILD A CHILDREN'S HOSPITAL IN OUR HOMETOWN! FOR WHICH I SAY, THANK YOU! THANK YOU! THANK YOU!
WOW! KRISTINE MADE US, AND EVERY TEEN IN RIVERDALE, STARS OF THAT SHOW!
THAT'S RIGHT! AND NOW ALL THE GIRLS WHO PANNED HER ARE CALLING TO APOLOGIZE!
RING! RING!
LET THEM FEEL MISERABLE FOR AN HOUR OR SO WHILE WE GO OUT AND HAVE A SNACK!
GOOD IDEA! WE FINALLY AGREED ON SOMETHING! LET'S GO TO POP'S!
POP'S PLACE IS OUT! I SAY WE TRY THAT NEW PLACE ON SIXTH STREET!
I KNEW YOU WOULDN'T AGREE WITH ME! I JUST KNEW IT!
POP'S PLACE IS IDEAL!
NO, IT'S NOT!
HOW ABOUT "JOHN'S BURGERS"?
TOO GREASY!
CHUCK'S DINER?
FOUND A HAIR IN MY SOUP ONCE!
JERRY'S SNACK HOUSE?
SERVICE IS HORRIBLE!
END

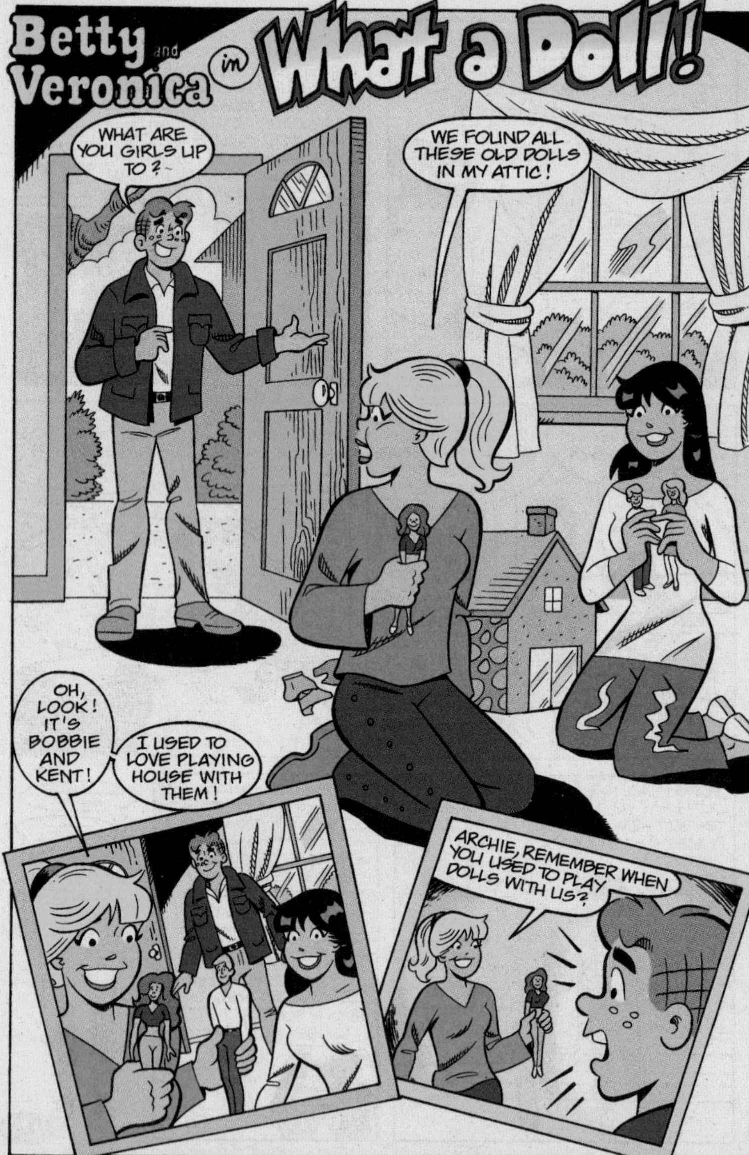
Betty and Veronica in What a Doll!
WHAT ARE YOU GIRLS UP TO?
WE FOUND ALL THESE OLD DOLLS IN MY ATTIC!
OH, LOOK! IT'S BOBBIE AND KENT!
I USED TO LOVE PLAYING HOUSE WITH THEM!
ARCHIE, REMEMBER WHEN YOU USED TO PLAY DOLLS WITH US?

Script & Pencils: Dan Parent / Inks: Jim Amash / Letters: Vickie Williams

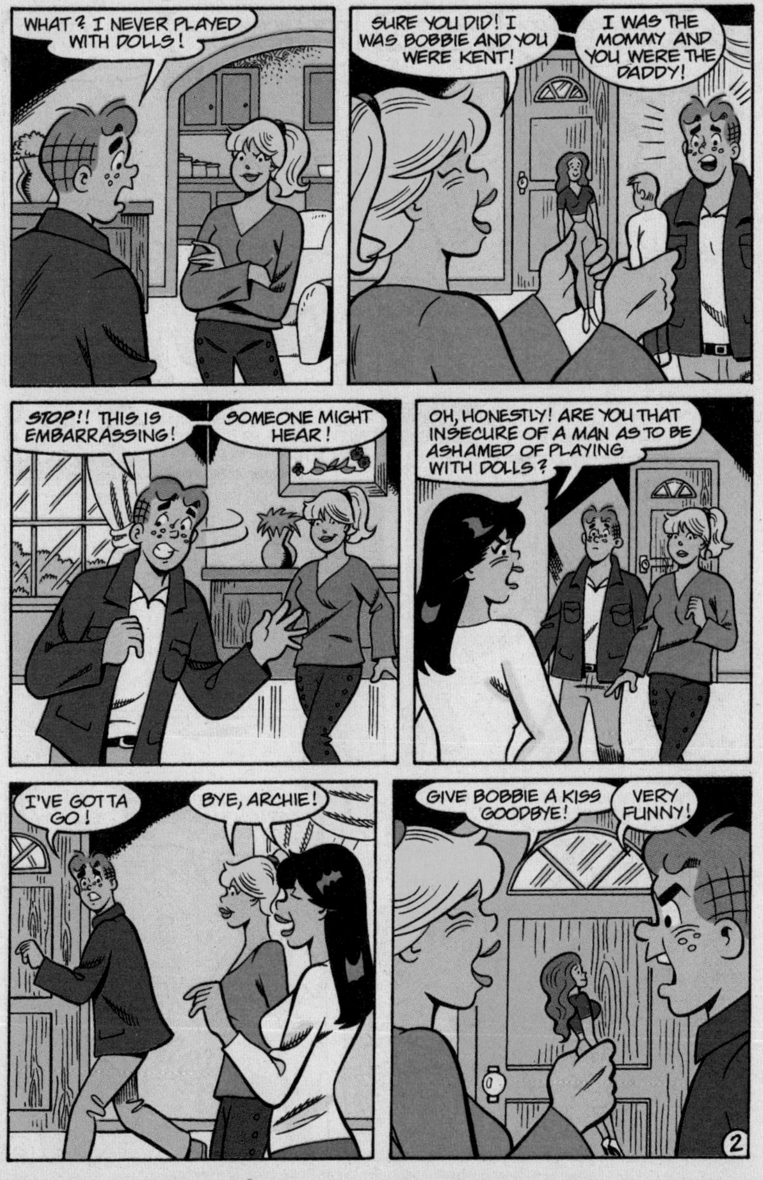
WHAT? I NEVER PLAYED WITH DOLLS!
SURE YOU DID! I WAS BOBBIE AND YOU WERE KENT!
I WAS THE MOMMY AND YOU WERE THE DADDY!
STOP!! THIS IS EMBARRASSING!
SOMEONE MIGHT HEAR!
OH, HONESTLY! ARE YOU THAT INSECURE OF A MAN AS TO BE ASHAMED OF PLAYING WITH DOLLS?
I'VE GOTTA GO!
BYE, ARCHIE!
GIVE BOBBIE A KISS GOODBYE!
VERY FUNNY!
2

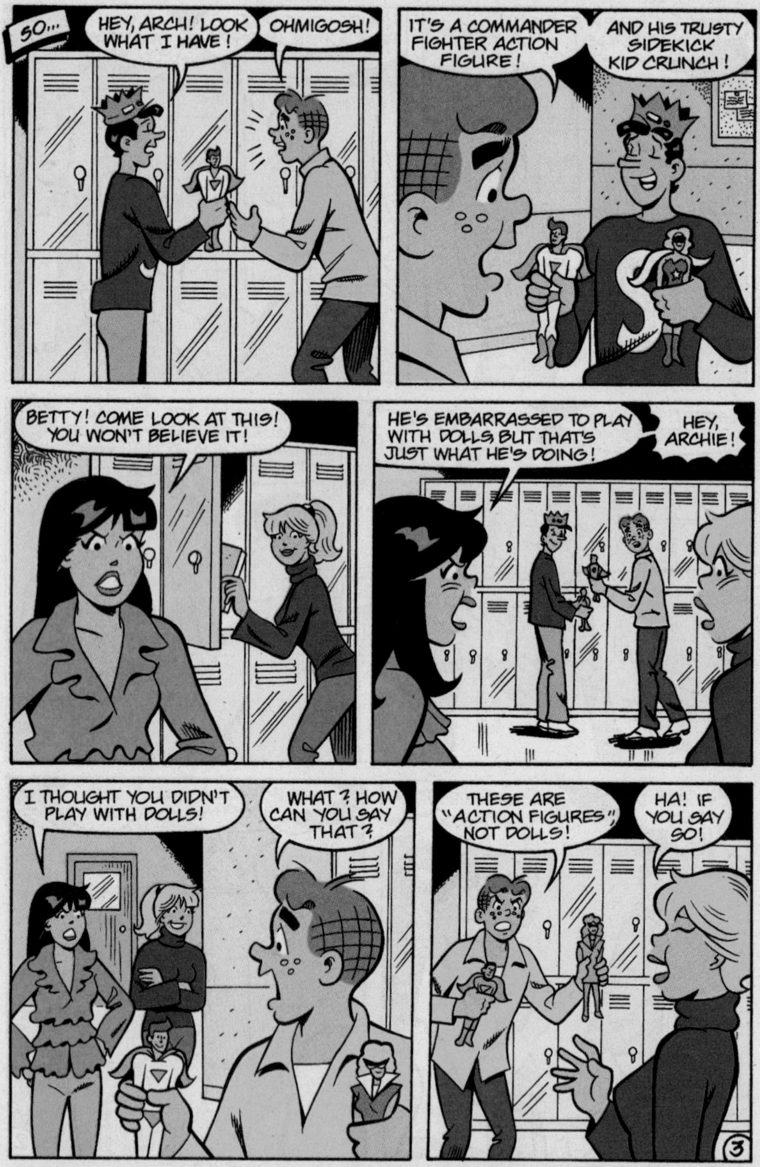
SO...
HEY, ARCH! LOOK WHAT I HAVE!
OHMIGOSH!
IT'S A COMMANDER FIGHTER ACTION FIGURE!
AND HIS TRUSTY SIDEKICK KID CRUNCH!
BETTY! COME LOOK AT THIS! YOU WON'T BELIEVE IT!
HE'S EMBARRASSED TO PLAY WITH DOLLS BUT THAT'S JUST WHAT HE'S DOING!
HEY, ARCHIE!
I THOUGHT YOU DIDN'T PLAY WITH DOLLS!
WHAT? HOW CAN YOU SAY THAT?
THESE ARE "ACTION FIGURES", NOT DOLLS!
HA! IF YOU SAY SO!
3

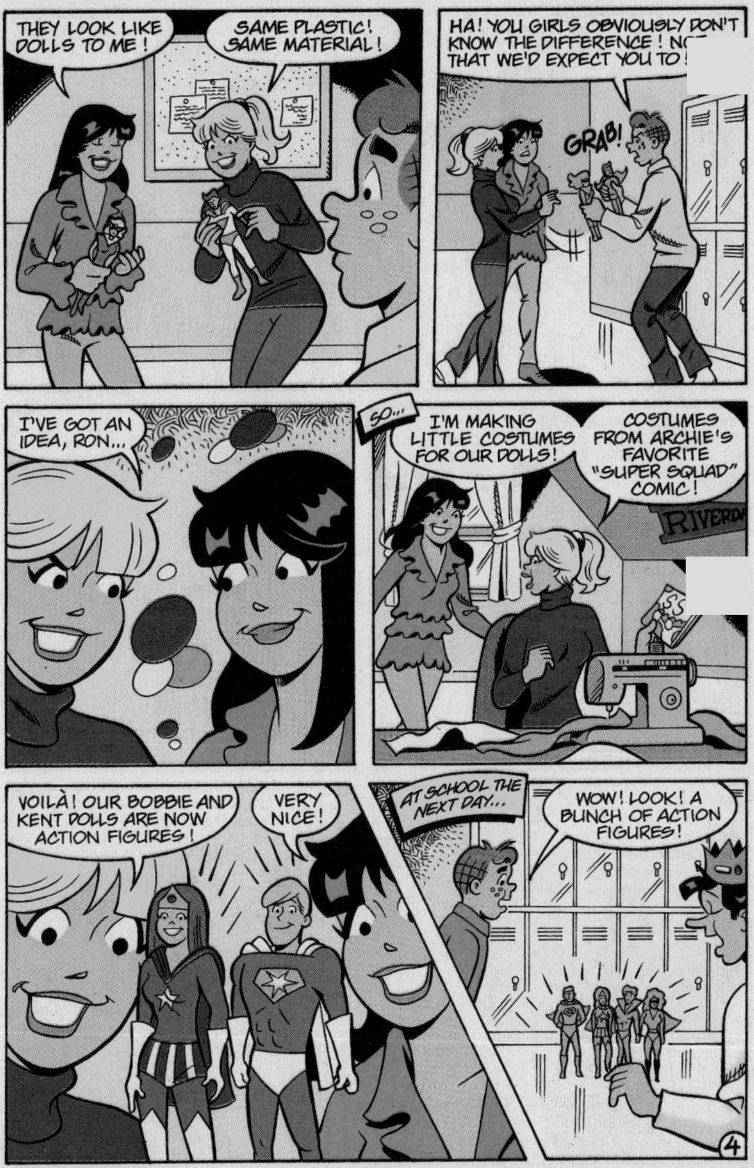

THEY LOOK LIKE DOLLS TO ME!
SAME PLASTIC! SAME MATERIAL!
HA! YOU GIRLS OBVIOUSLY DON'T KNOW THE DIFFERENCE! NO
THAT WE'D EXPECT YOU TO!
GRAB!
I'VE GOT AN IDEA, RON...
SO...
I'M MAKING LITTLE COSTUMES FOR OUR DOLLS!
COSTUMES FROM ARCHIE'S FAVORITE "SUPER SQUAD" COMIC!
RIVERD
SS
VOILÀ! OUR BOBBIE AND KENT DOLLS ARE NOW ACTION FIGURES!
VERY NICE!
AT SCHOOL THE NEXT DAY...
WOW! LOOK! A BUNCH OF ACTION FIGURES!
4

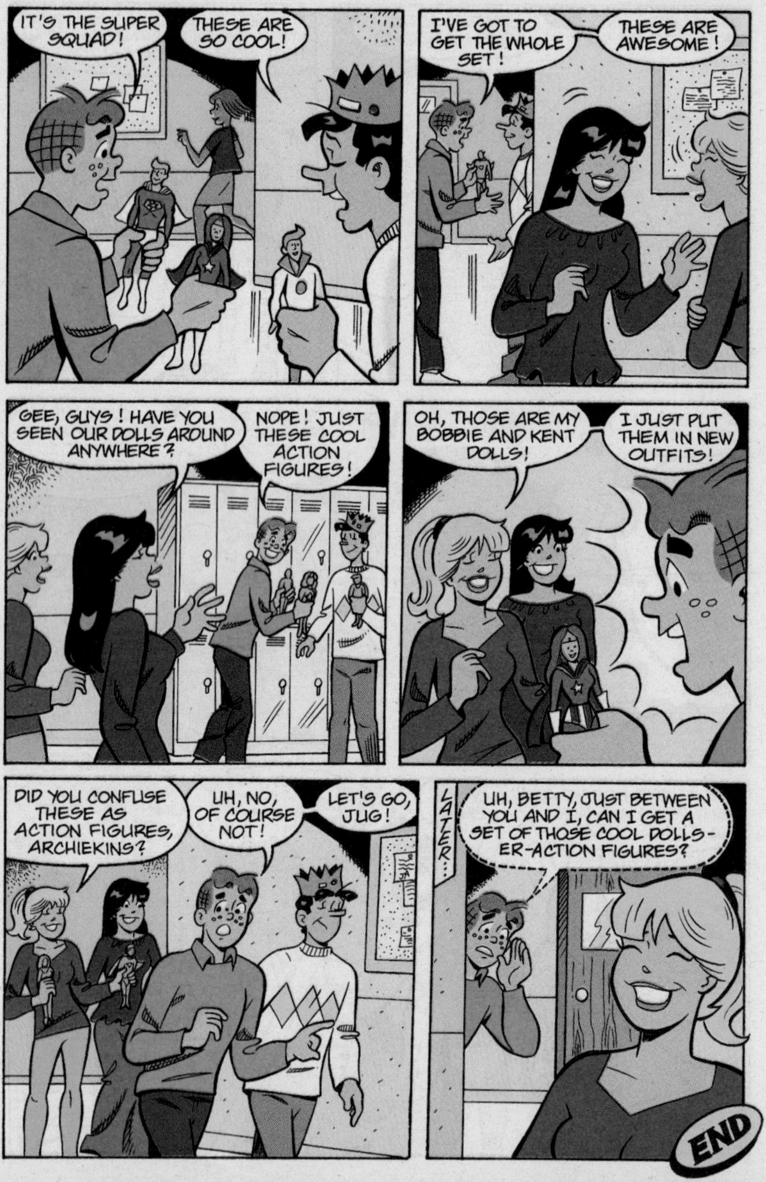
IT'S THE SUPER SQUAD!
THESE ARE SO COOL!
I'VE GOT TO GET THE WHOLE SET!
THESE ARE AWESOME!
GEE, GUYS! HAVE YOU SEEN OUR DOLLS AROUND ANYWHERE?
NOPE! JUST THESE COOL ACTION FIGURES!
OH, THOSE ARE MY BOBBIE AND KENT DOLLS!
I JUST PUT THEM IN NEW OUTFITS!
DID YOU CONFUSE THESE AS ACTION FIGURES, ARCHIEKINS?
UH, NO, OF COURSE NOT!
LET'S GO, JUG!
LATER...
UH, BETTY, JUST BETWEEN YOU AND I, CAN I GET A SET OF THOSE COOL DOLLS- ER-ACTION FIGURES?
END

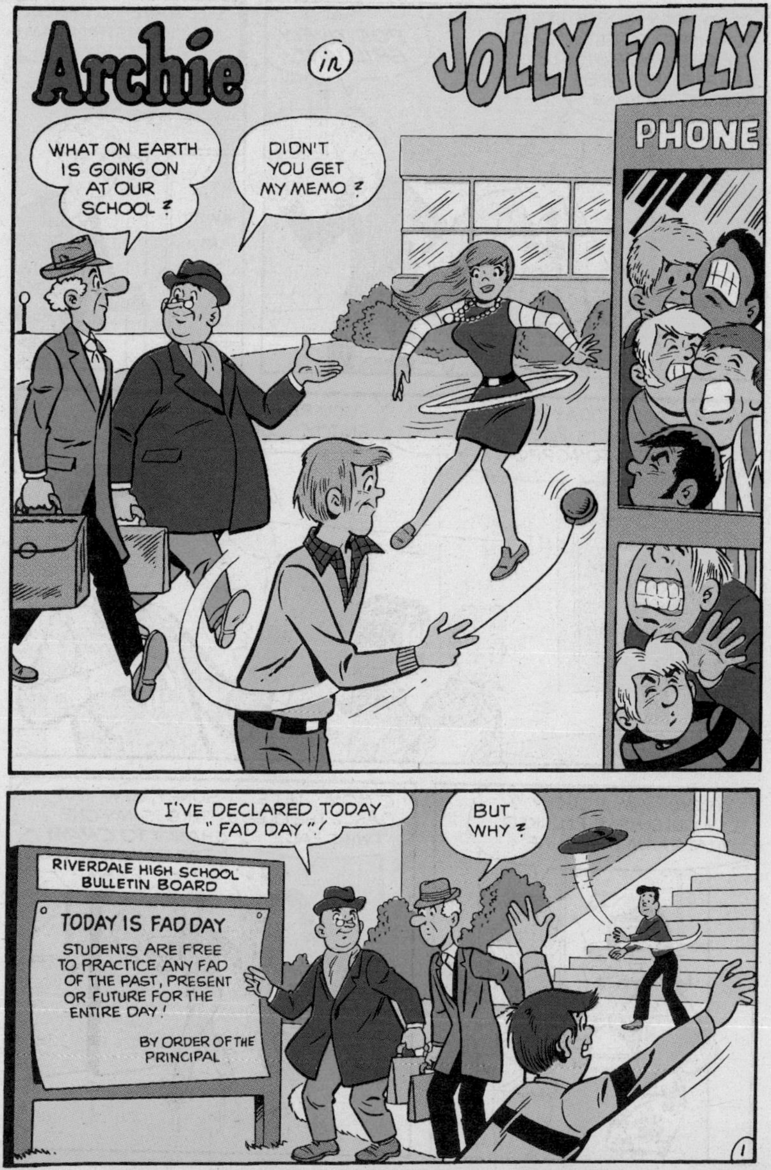
Archie in JOLLY FOLLY
PHONE
WHAT ON EARTH IS GOING ON AT OUR SCHOOL?
DIDN'T YOU GET MY MEMO?
I'VE DECLARED TODAY "FAD DAY"!
BUT WHY?
RIVERDALE HIGH SCHOOL BULLETIN BOARD
TODAY IS FAD DAY
STUDENTS ARE FREE TO PRACTICE ANY FAD OF THE PAST, PRESENT OR FUTURE FOR THE ENTIRE DAY!
BY ORDER OF THE PRINCIPAL
1

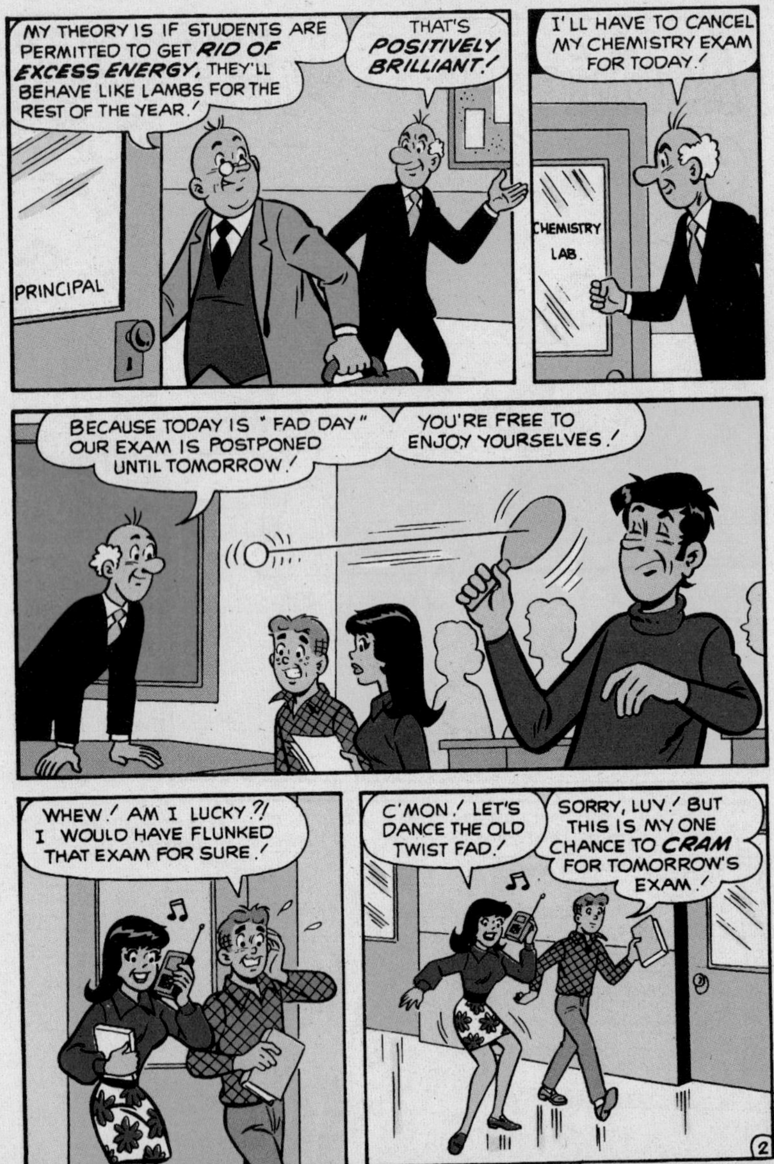
MY THEORY IS IF STUDENTS ARE PERMITTED TO GET RID OF EXCESS ENERGY, THEY'LL BEHAVE LIKE LAMBS FOR THE REST OF THE YEAR.!
PRINCIPAL
THAT'S POSITIVELY BRILLIANT!
I'LL HAVE TO CANCEL MY CHEMISTRY EXAM FOR TODAY!
CHEMISTRY LAB.
BECAUSE TODAY IS "FAD DAY" OUR EXAM IS POSTPONED UNTIL TOMORROW!
YOU'RE FREE TO ENJOY YOURSELVES!
WHEW! AM I LUCKY?! I WOULD HAVE FLUNKED THAT EXAM FOR SURE!
C'MON! LET'S DANCE THE OLD TWIST FAD!
SORRY, LUV! BUT THIS IS MY ONE CHANCE TO CRAM FOR TOMORROW'S EXAM!
2

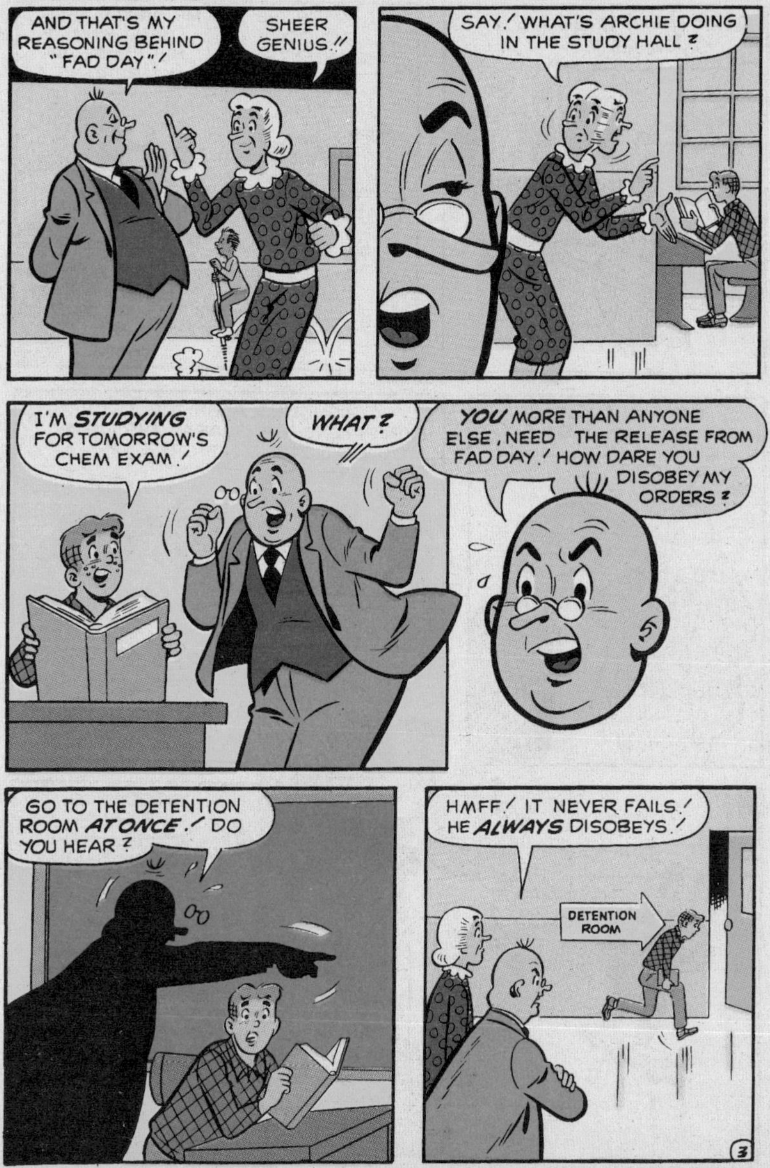

AND THAT'S MY REASONING BEHIND "FAD DAY"!
SHEER GENIUS!!
SAY! WHAT'S ARCHIE DOING IN THE STUDY HALL?
I'M STUDYING FOR TOMORROW'S CHEM EXAM!
WHAT?
YOU MORE THAN ANYONE ELSE, NEED THE RELEASE FROM FAD DAY! HOW DARE YOU DISOBEY MY ORDERS?
GO TO THE DETENTION ROOM AT ONCE! DO YOU HEAR?
HMFF! IT NEVER FAILS! HE ALWAYS DISOBEYS!
DETENTION ROOM

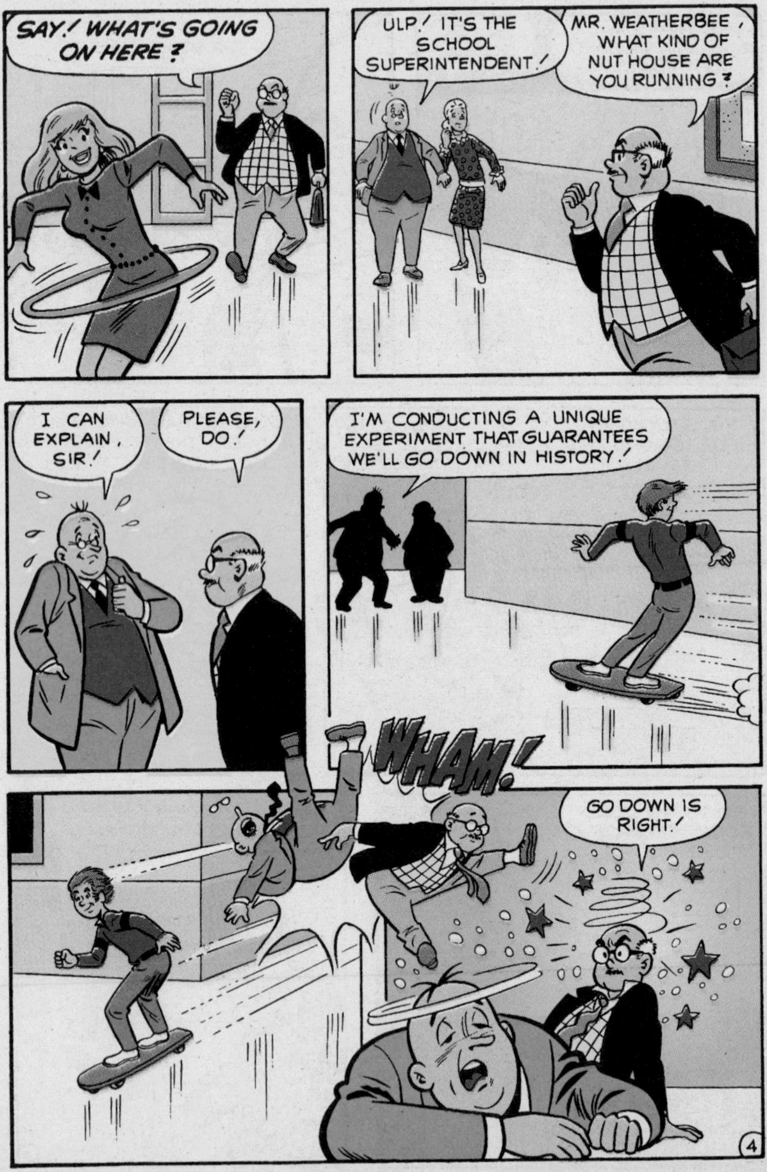
SAY! WHAT'S GOING ON HERE?
ULP! IT'S THE SCHOOL SUPERINTENDENT!
MR. WEATHERBEE, WHAT KIND OF NUT HOUSE ARE YOU RUNNING?
I CAN EXPLAIN, SIR!
PLEASE, DO!
I'M CONDUCTING A UNIQUE EXPERIMENT THAT GUARANTEES WE'LL GO DOWN IN HISTORY!
WHAM!
GO DOWN IS RIGHT!

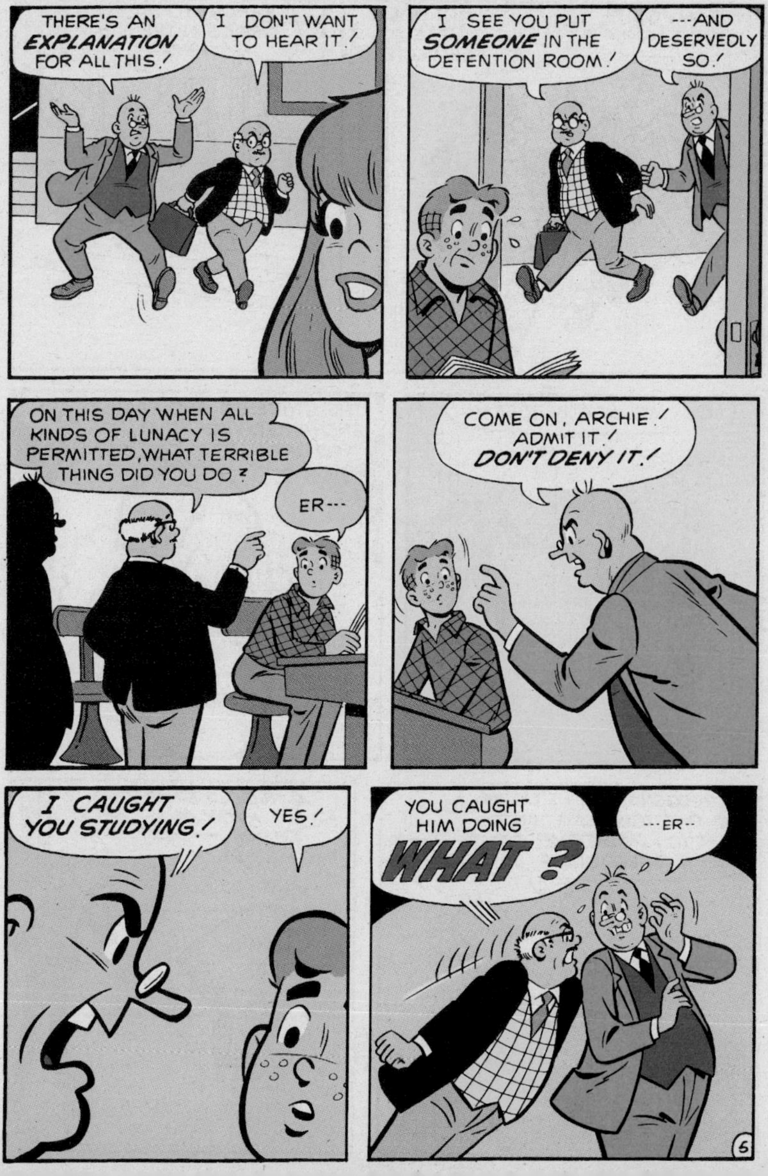
THERE'S AN *EXPLANATION* FOR ALL THIS!
I DON'T WANT TO HEAR IT!
I SEE YOU PUT *SOMEONE* IN THE DETENTION ROOM!
---AND DESERVEDLY SO!
ON THIS DAY WHEN ALL KINDS OF LUNACY IS PERMITTED, WHAT TERRIBLE THING DID YOU DO?
ER---
COME ON, ARCHIE! ADMIT IT! *DON'T DENY IT!*
I CAUGHT YOU STUDYING!
YES!
YOU CAUGHT HIM DOING *WHAT?*
---ER--
5

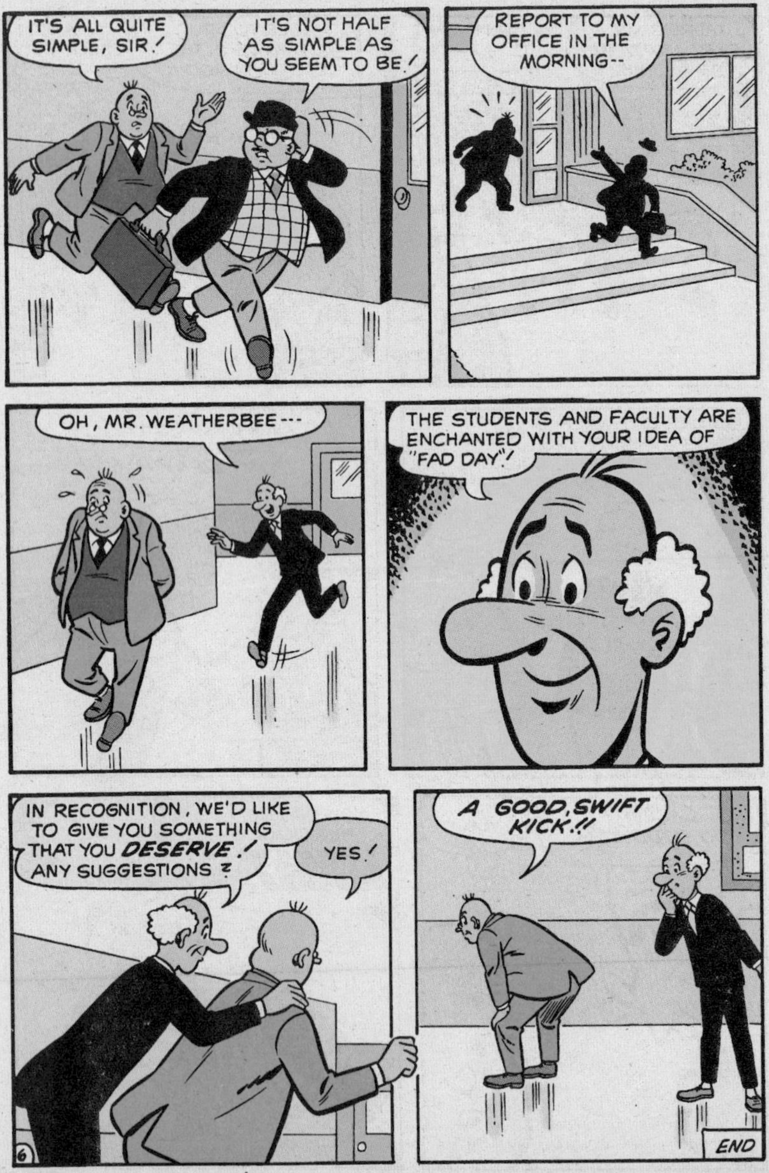
IT'S ALL QUITE SIMPLE, SIR!
IT'S NOT HALF AS SIMPLE AS YOU SEEM TO BE!
REPORT TO MY OFFICE IN THE MORNING--
OH, MR. WEATHERBEE---
THE STUDENTS AND FACULTY ARE ENCHANTED WITH YOUR IDEA OF "FAD DAY"!
IN RECOGNITION, WE'D LIKE TO GIVE YOU SOMETHING THAT YOU DESERVE! ANY SUGGESTIONS?
YES!
A GOOD, SWIFT KICK!!
6
END

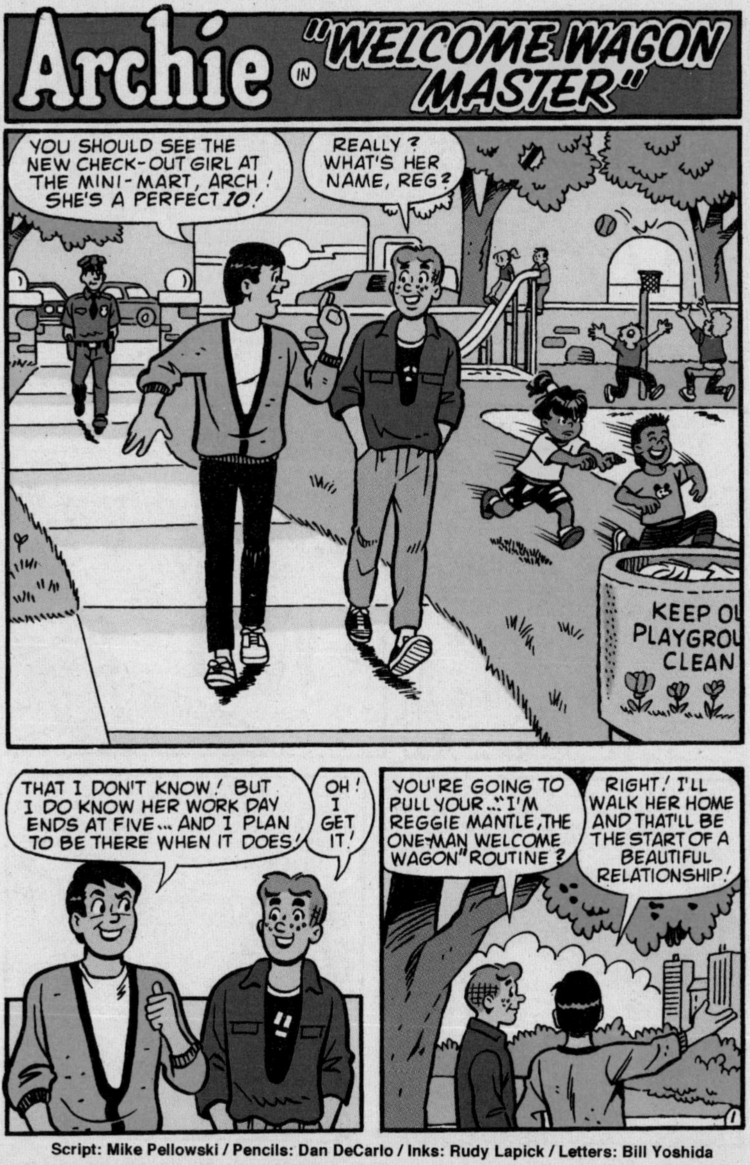
Archie in "WELCOME WAGON MASTER"
YOU SHOULD SEE THE NEW CHECK-OUT GIRL AT THE MINI-MART, ARCH! SHE'S A PERFECT 10!
REALLY? WHAT'S HER NAME, REG?
KEEP OU PLAYGROU CLEAN
THAT I DON'T KNOW! BUT I DO KNOW HER WORK DAY ENDS AT FIVE... AND I PLAN TO BE THERE WHEN IT DOES!
OH! I GET IT!
YOU'RE GOING TO PULL YOUR ..."I'M REGGIE MANTLE, THE ONE-MAN WELCOME WAGON" ROUTINE?
RIGHT! I'LL WALK HER HOME AND THAT'LL BE THE START OF A BEAUTIFUL RELATIONSHIP!
1

Script: Mike Pellowski / Pencils: Dan DeCarlo / Inks: Rudy Lapick / Letters: Bill Yoshida

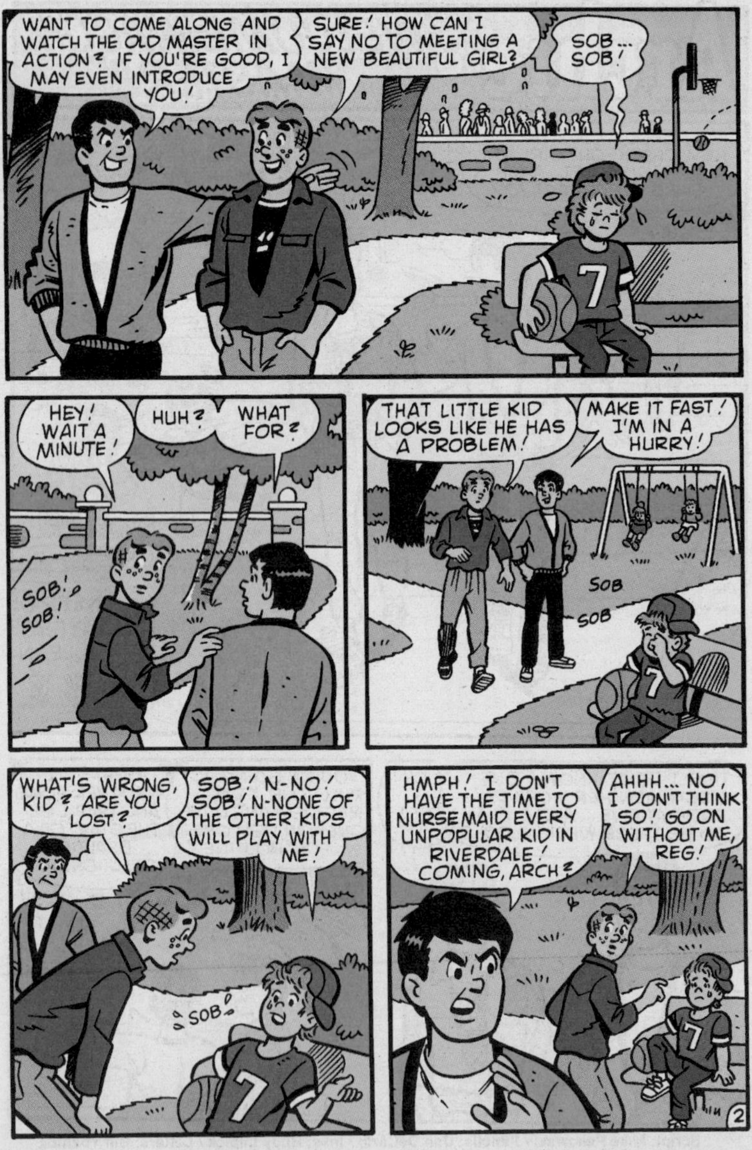

WANT TO COME ALONG AND WATCH THE OLD MASTER IN ACTION? IF YOU'RE GOOD, I MAY EVEN INTRODUCE YOU!
SURE! HOW CAN I SAY NO TO MEETING A NEW BEAUTIFUL GIRL?
SOB... SOB!
HEY! WAIT A MINUTE!
HUH?
WHAT FOR?
SOB! SOB!
THAT LITTLE KID LOOKS LIKE HE HAS A PROBLEM!
MAKE IT FAST! I'M IN A HURRY!
SOB
SOB
WHAT'S WRONG, KID? ARE YOU LOST?
SOB! N-NO! SOB! N-NONE OF THE OTHER KIDS WILL PLAY WITH ME!
SOB
HMPH! I DON'T HAVE THE TIME TO NURSEMAID EVERY UNPOPULAR KID IN RIVERDALE! COMING, ARCH?
AHHH... NO, I DON'T THINK SO! GO ON WITHOUT ME, REG!
2

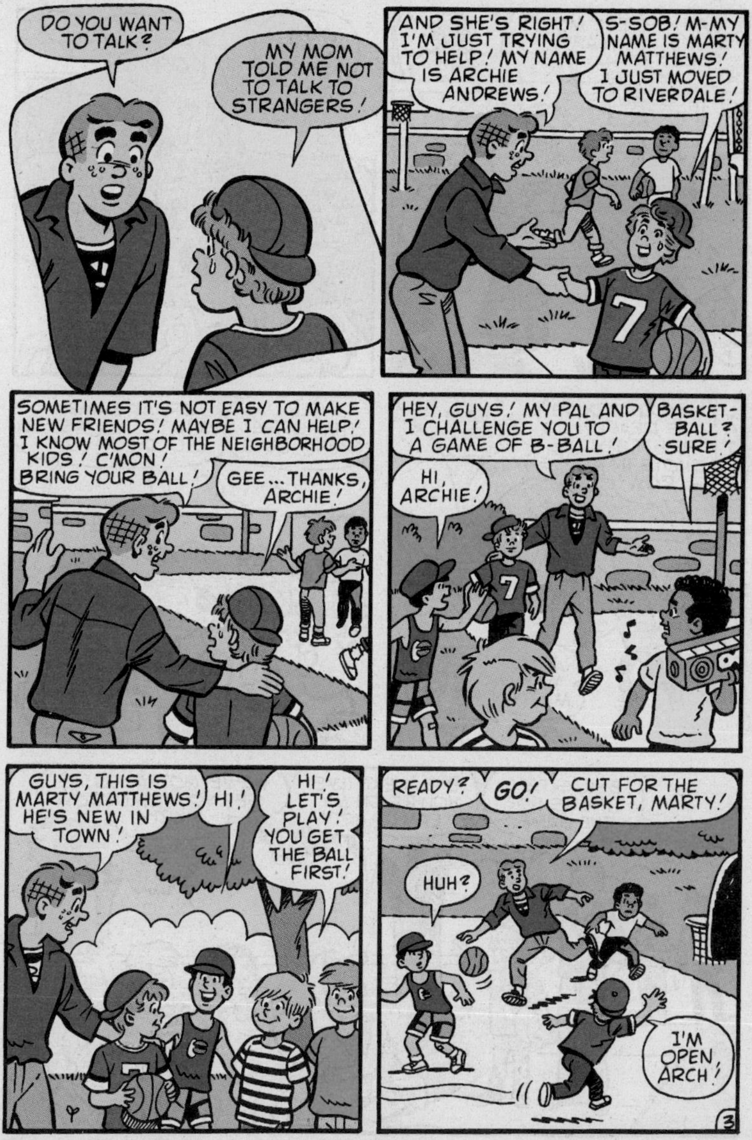

DO YOU WANT TO TALK?
MY MOM TOLD ME NOT TO TALK TO STRANGERS!
AND SHE'S RIGHT! I'M JUST TRYING TO HELP! MY NAME IS ARCHIE ANDREWS!
S-SOB! M-MY NAME IS MARTY MATTHEWS! I JUST MOVED TO RIVERDALE!
SOMETIMES IT'S NOT EASY TO MAKE NEW FRIENDS! MAYBE I CAN HELP! I KNOW MOST OF THE NEIGHBORHOOD KIDS! C'MON! BRING YOUR BALL!
GEE... THANKS, ARCHIE!
HEY, GUYS! MY PAL AND I CHALLENGE YOU TO A GAME OF B-BALL!
BASKET-BALL? SURE!
HI, ARCHIE!
GUYS, THIS IS MARTY MATTHEWS! HE'S NEW IN TOWN!
HI!
HI! LET'S PLAY! YOU GET THE BALL FIRST!
READY?
GO!
CUT FOR THE BASKET, MARTY!
HUH?
I'M OPEN, ARCH!

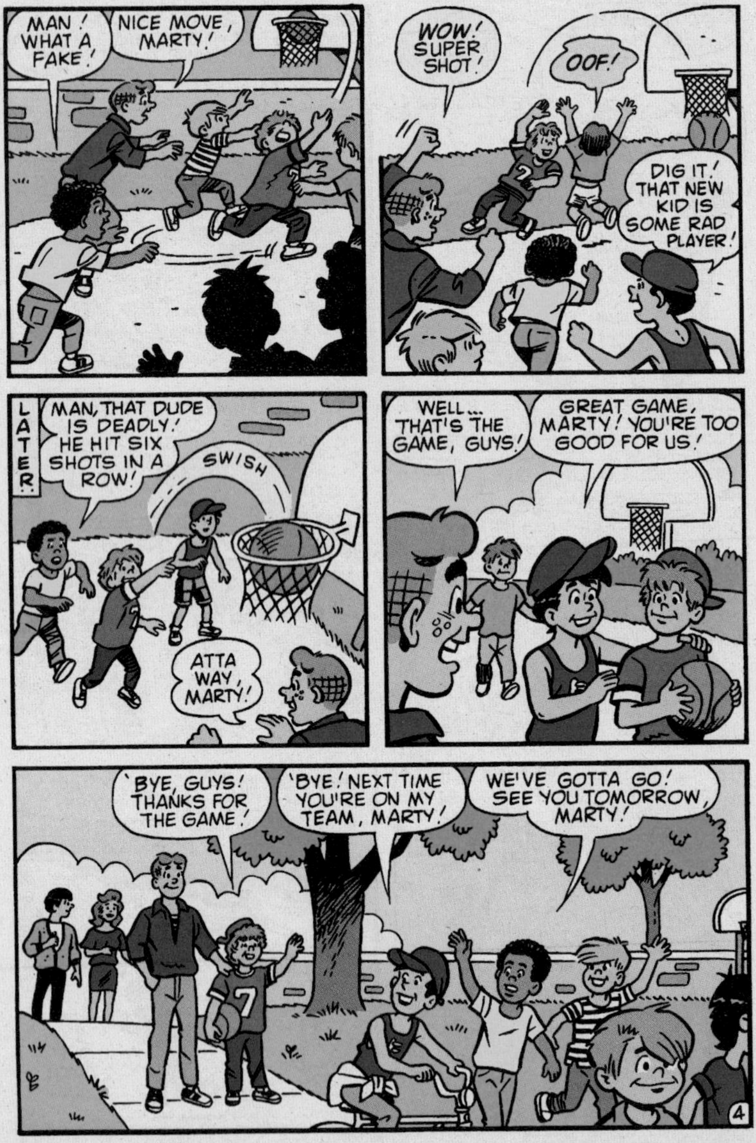
MAN! WHAT A FAKE!
NICE MOVE, MARTY!
WOW! SUPER SHOT!
OOF!
DIG IT! THAT NEW KID IS SOME RAD PLAYER!
LATER:
MAN, THAT DUDE IS DEADLY! HE HIT SIX SHOTS IN A ROW!
SWISH
ATTA WAY, MARTY!
WELL... THAT'S THE GAME, GUYS!
GREAT GAME, MARTY! YOU'RE TOO GOOD FOR US!
'BYE, GUYS! THANKS FOR THE GAME!
'BYE! NEXT TIME YOU'RE ON MY TEAM, MARTY!
WE'VE GOTTA GO! SEE YOU TOMORROW, MARTY!
4

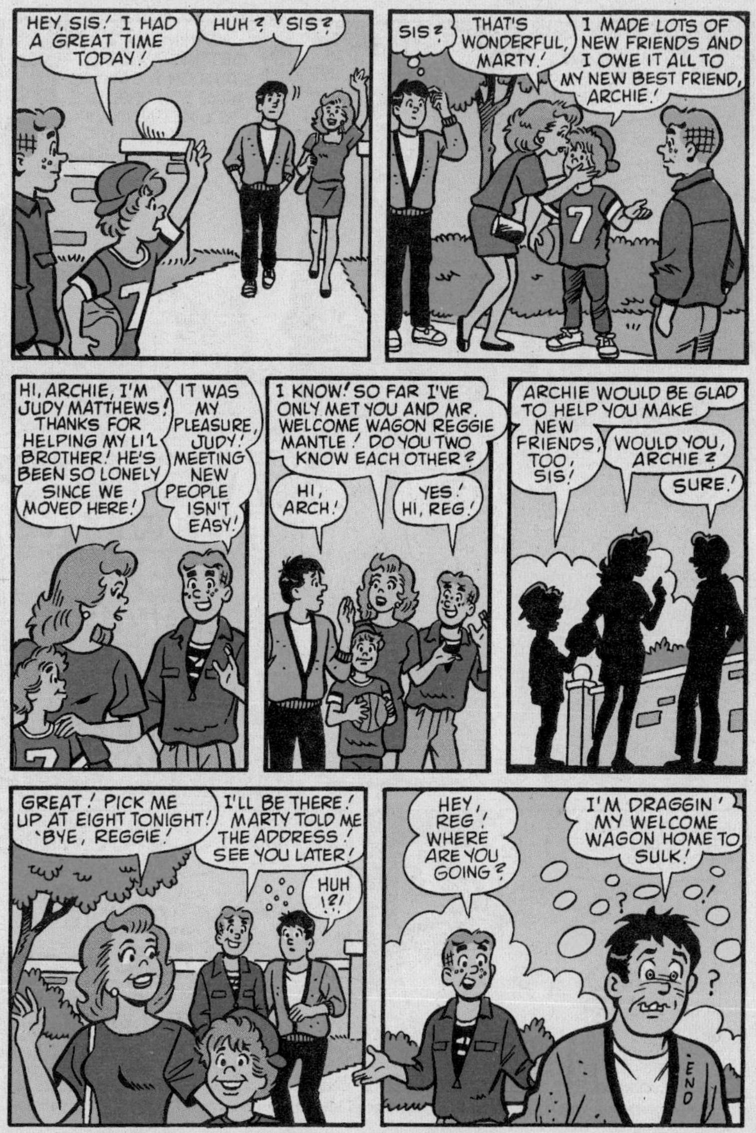

HEY, SIS! I HAD A GREAT TIME TODAY!
HUH?
SIS?
SIS?
THAT'S WONDERFUL, MARTY!
I MADE LOTS OF NEW FRIENDS AND I OWE IT ALL TO MY NEW BEST FRIEND, ARCHIE!
HI, ARCHIE, I'M JUDY MATTHEWS! THANKS FOR HELPING MY LI'L BROTHER! HE'S BEEN SO LONELY SINCE WE MOVED HERE!
IT WAS MY PLEASURE, JUDY! MEETING NEW PEOPLE ISN'T EASY!
I KNOW! SO FAR I'VE ONLY MET YOU AND MR. WELCOME WAGON REGGIE MANTLE! DO YOU TWO KNOW EACH OTHER?
HI, ARCH!
YES! HI, REG!
ARCHIE WOULD BE GLAD TO HELP YOU MAKE NEW FRIENDS, TOO, SIS!
WOULD YOU, ARCHIE?
SURE!
GREAT! PICK ME UP AT EIGHT TONIGHT! 'BYE, REGGIE!
I'LL BE THERE! MARTY TOLD ME THE ADDRESS! SEE YOU LATER!
HUH !?!
HEY, REG! WHERE ARE YOU GOING?
I'M DRAGGIN' MY WELCOME WAGON HOME TO SULK!
END

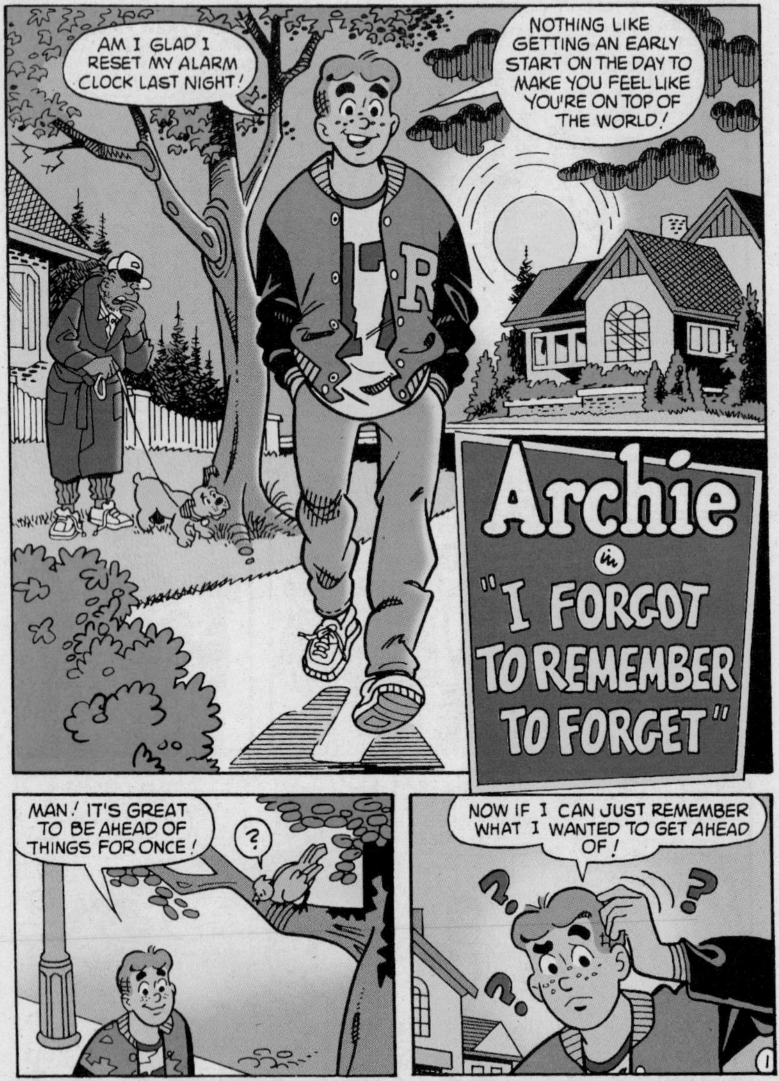

AM I GLAD I RESET MY ALARM CLOCK LAST NIGHT!
NOTHING LIKE GETTING AN EARLY START ON THE DAY TO MAKE YOU FEEL LIKE YOU'RE ON TOP OF THE WORLD!
Archie
in
"I FORGOT TO REMEMBER TO FORGET"
MAN! IT'S GREAT TO BE AHEAD OF THINGS FOR ONCE!
?
NOW IF I CAN JUST REMEMBER WHAT I WANTED TO GET AHEAD OF!
1

Script: Kathleen Webb / Pencils: Stan Goldberg / Inks: Henry Scarpelli / Letters: Bill Yoshida

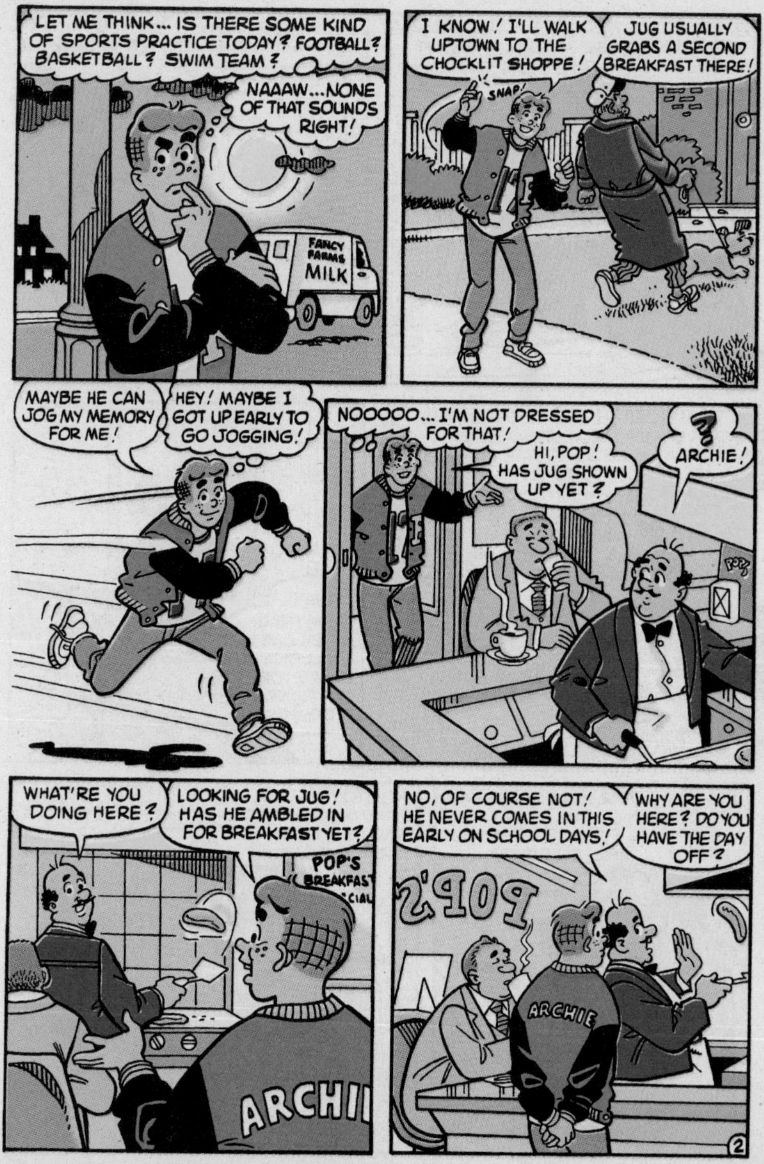
LET ME THINK... IS THERE SOME KIND OF SPORTS PRACTICE TODAY? FOOTBALL? BASKETBALL? SWIM TEAM?
NAAAW...NONE OF THAT SOUNDS RIGHT!
FANCY FARMS MILK
I KNOW! I'LL WALK UPTOWN TO THE CHOCKLIT SHOPPE!
SNAP!
JUG USUALLY GRABS A SECOND BREAKFAST THERE!
MAYBE HE CAN JOG MY MEMORY FOR ME!
HEY! MAYBE I GOT UP EARLY TO GO JOGGING!
NOOOOO... I'M NOT DRESSED FOR THAT!
HI, POP! HAS JUG SHOWN UP YET?
?
ARCHIE!
WHAT'RE YOU DOING HERE?
LOOKING FOR JUG! HAS HE AMBLED IN FOR BREAKFAST YET?
POP'S BREAKFAST
ARCHII
NO, OF COURSE NOT! HE NEVER COMES IN THIS EARLY ON SCHOOL DAYS!
WHY ARE YOU HERE? DO YOU HAVE THE DAY OFF?
POP'S
ARCHIE

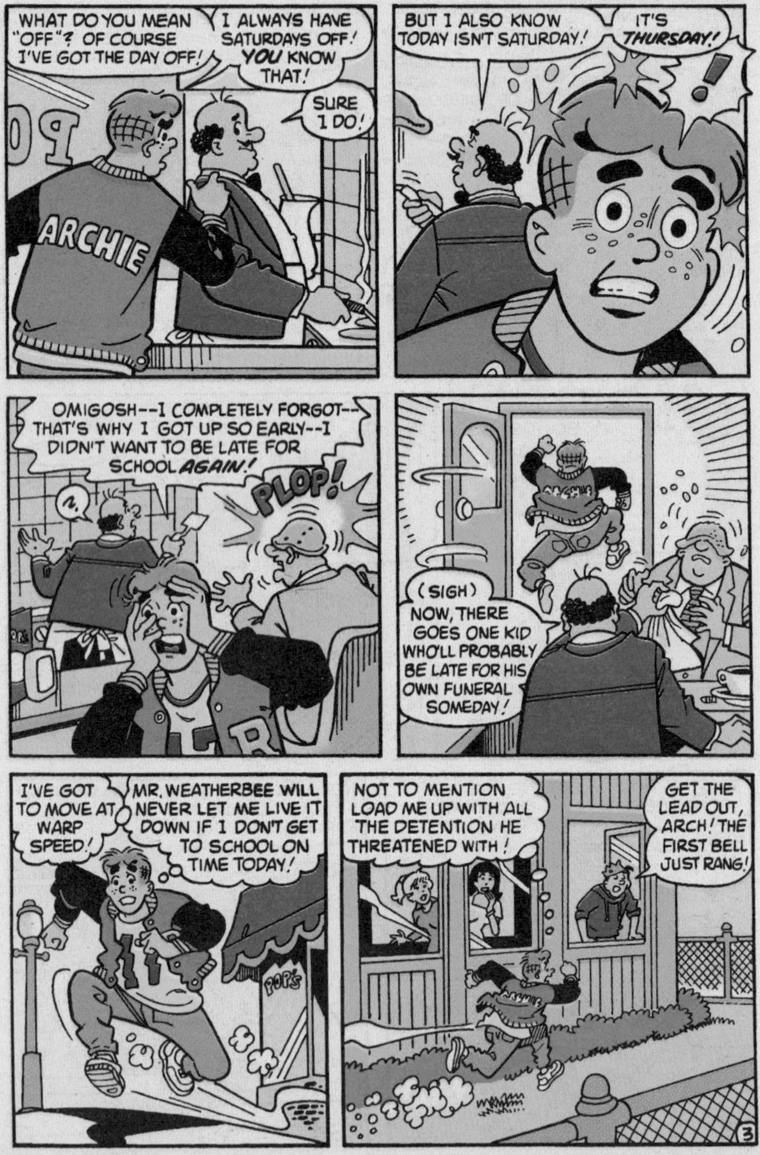
WHAT DO YOU MEAN "OFF"? OF COURSE I'VE GOT THE DAY OFF!
I ALWAYS HAVE SATURDAYS OFF! YOU KNOW THAT!
SURE I DO!
BUT I ALSO KNOW TODAY ISN'T SATURDAY!
IT'S THURSDAY!
!
OMIGOSH--I COMPLETELY FORGOT--THAT'S WHY I GOT UP SO EARLY--I DIDN'T WANT TO BE LATE FOR SCHOOL AGAIN!
PLOP!
?
(SIGH) NOW, THERE GOES ONE KID WHO'LL PROBABLY BE LATE FOR HIS OWN FUNERAL SOMEDAY!
I'VE GOT TO MOVE AT WARP SPEED!
MR. WEATHERBEE WILL NEVER LET ME LIVE IT DOWN IF I DON'T GET TO SCHOOL ON TIME TODAY!
POP'S
NOT TO MENTION LOAD ME UP WITH ALL THE DETENTION HE THREATENED WITH!
GET THE LEAD OUT, ARCH! THE FIRST BELL JUST RANG!
3

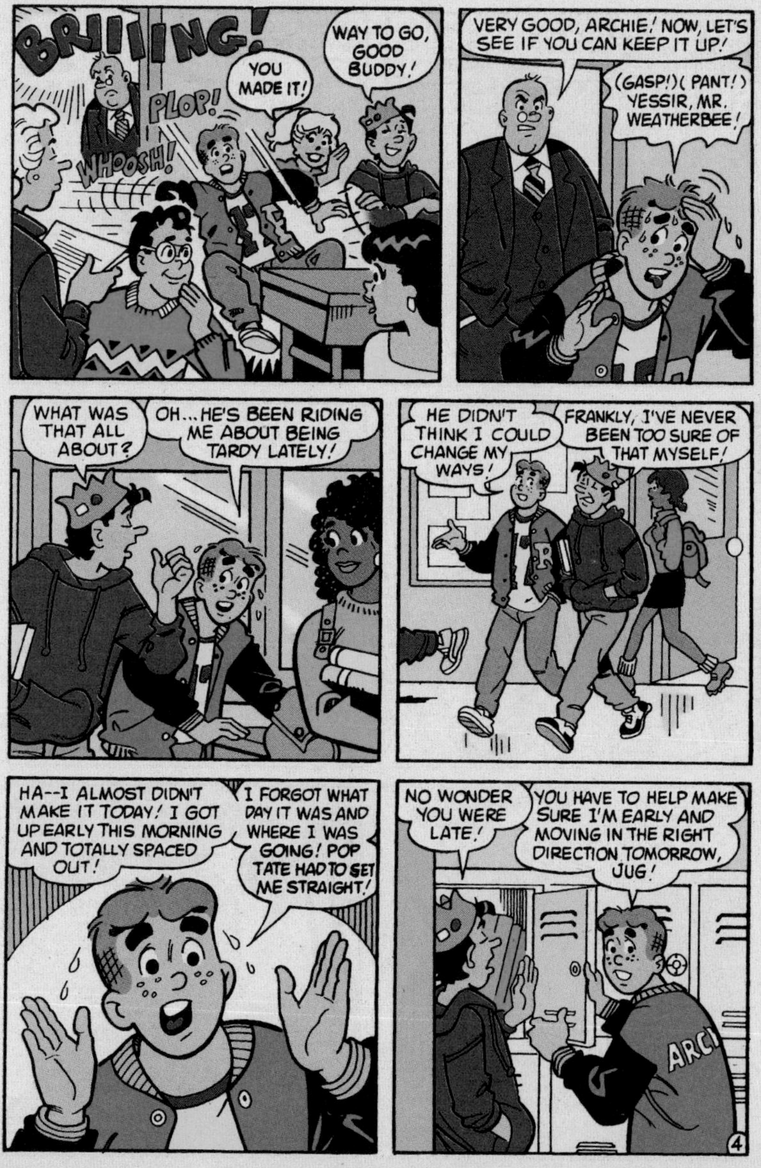
BRIIIING!
PLOP!
WHOOSH!
YOU MADE IT!
WAY TO GO, GOOD BUDDY!
VERY GOOD, ARCHIE! NOW, LET'S SEE IF YOU CAN KEEP IT UP!
(GASP!)(PANT!) YESSIR, MR. WEATHERBEE!
WHAT WAS THAT ALL ABOUT?
OH...HE'S BEEN RIDING ME ABOUT BEING TARDY LATELY!
HE DIDN'T THINK I COULD CHANGE MY WAYS!
FRANKLY, I'VE NEVER BEEN TOO SURE OF THAT MYSELF!
HA--I ALMOST DIDN'T MAKE IT TODAY! I GOT UP EARLY THIS MORNING AND TOTALLY SPACED OUT!
I FORGOT WHAT DAY IT WAS AND WHERE I WAS GOING! POP TATE HAD TO SET ME STRAIGHT!
NO WONDER YOU WERE LATE!
YOU HAVE TO HELP MAKE SURE I'M EARLY AND MOVING IN THE RIGHT DIRECTION TOMORROW, JUG!
ARC
4

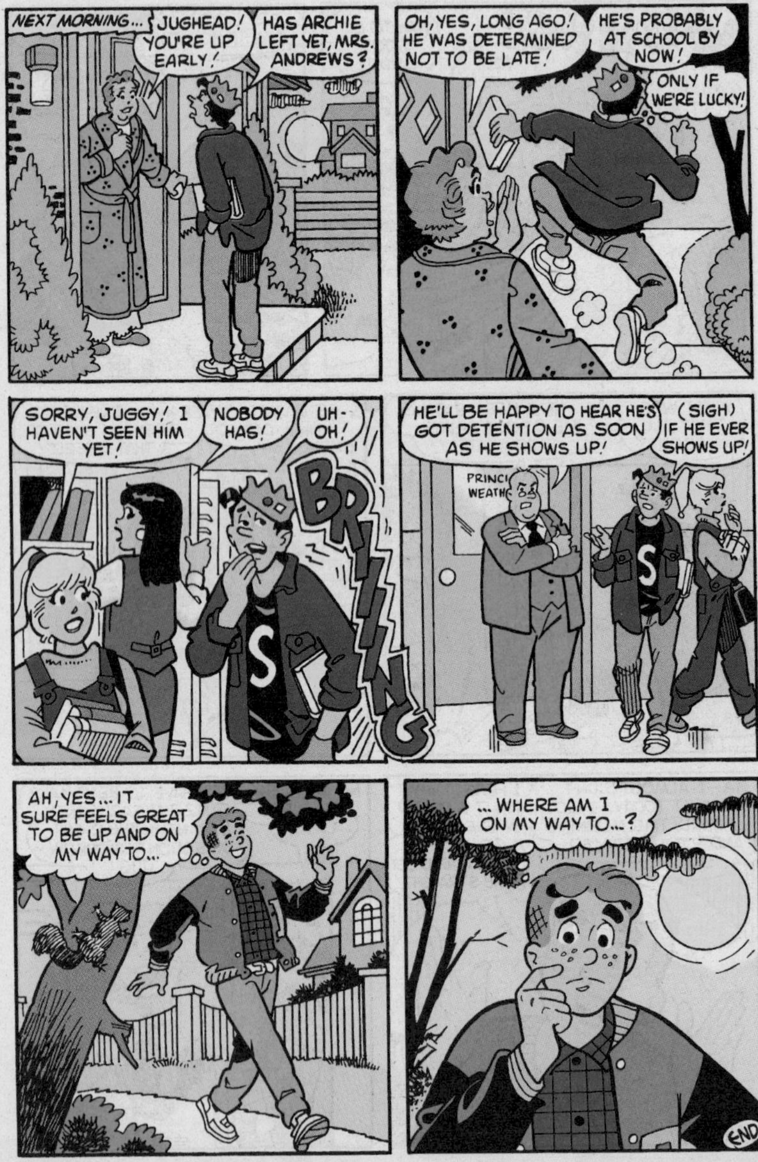
NEXT MORNING...
JUGHEAD! YOU'RE UP EARLY!
HAS ARCHIE LEFT YET, MRS. ANDREWS?
OH, YES, LONG AGO! HE WAS DETERMINED NOT TO BE LATE!
HE'S PROBABLY AT SCHOOL BY NOW!
ONLY IF WE'RE LUCKY!
SORRY, JUGGY! I HAVEN'T SEEN HIM YET!
NOBODY HAS!
UH-OH!
BRIIIING
HE'LL BE HAPPY TO HEAR HE'S GOT DETENTION AS SOON AS HE SHOWS UP!
(SIGH) IF HE EVER SHOWS UP!
AH, YES... IT SURE FEELS GREAT TO BE UP AND ON MY WAY TO...
...WHERE AM I ON MY WAY TO...?
END

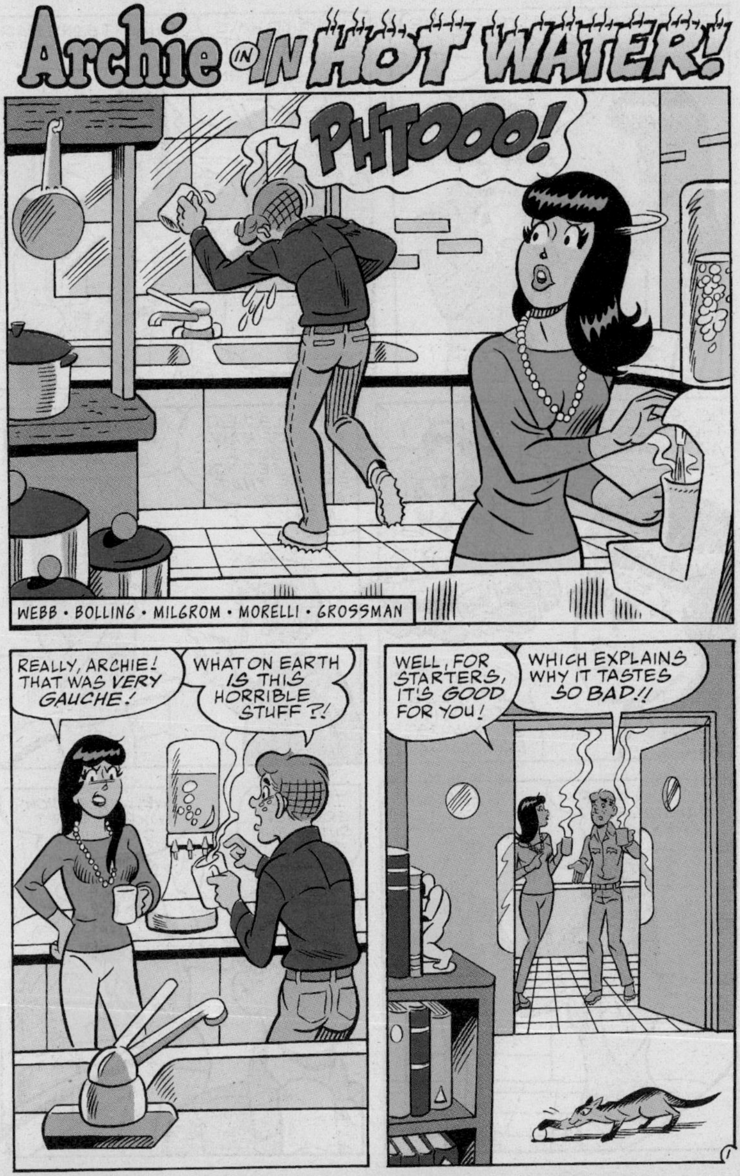

Archie IN HOT WATER!
PHTOOO!
WEBB • BOLLING • MILGROM • MORELLI • GROSSMAN
REALLY, ARCHIE! THAT WAS VERY GAUCHE!
WHAT ON EARTH IS THIS HORRIBLE STUFF ?!
WELL, FOR STARTERS, IT'S GOOD FOR YOU!
WHICH EXPLAINS WHY IT TASTES SO BAD!!
1

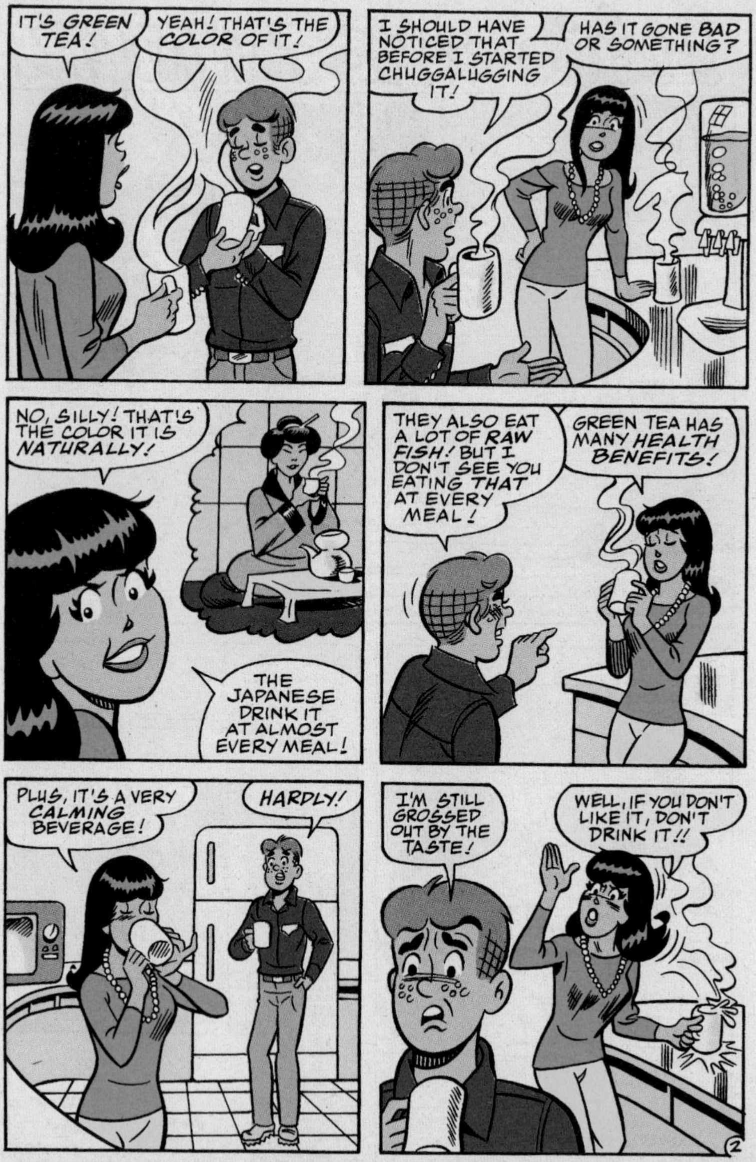
IT'S GREEN TEA!
YEAH! THAT'S THE COLOR OF IT!
I SHOULD HAVE NOTICED THAT BEFORE I STARTED CHUGGALUGGING IT!
HAS IT GONE BAD OR SOMETHING?
NO, SILLY! THAT'S THE COLOR IT IS NATURALLY!
THE JAPANESE DRINK IT AT ALMOST EVERY MEAL!
THEY ALSO EAT A LOT OF RAW FISH! BUT I DON'T SEE YOU EATING THAT AT EVERY MEAL!
GREEN TEA HAS MANY HEALTH BENEFITS!
PLUS, IT'S A VERY CALMING BEVERAGE!
HARDLY!
I'M STILL GROSSED OUT BY THE TASTE!
WELL, IF YOU DON'T LIKE IT, DON'T DRINK IT!!
2

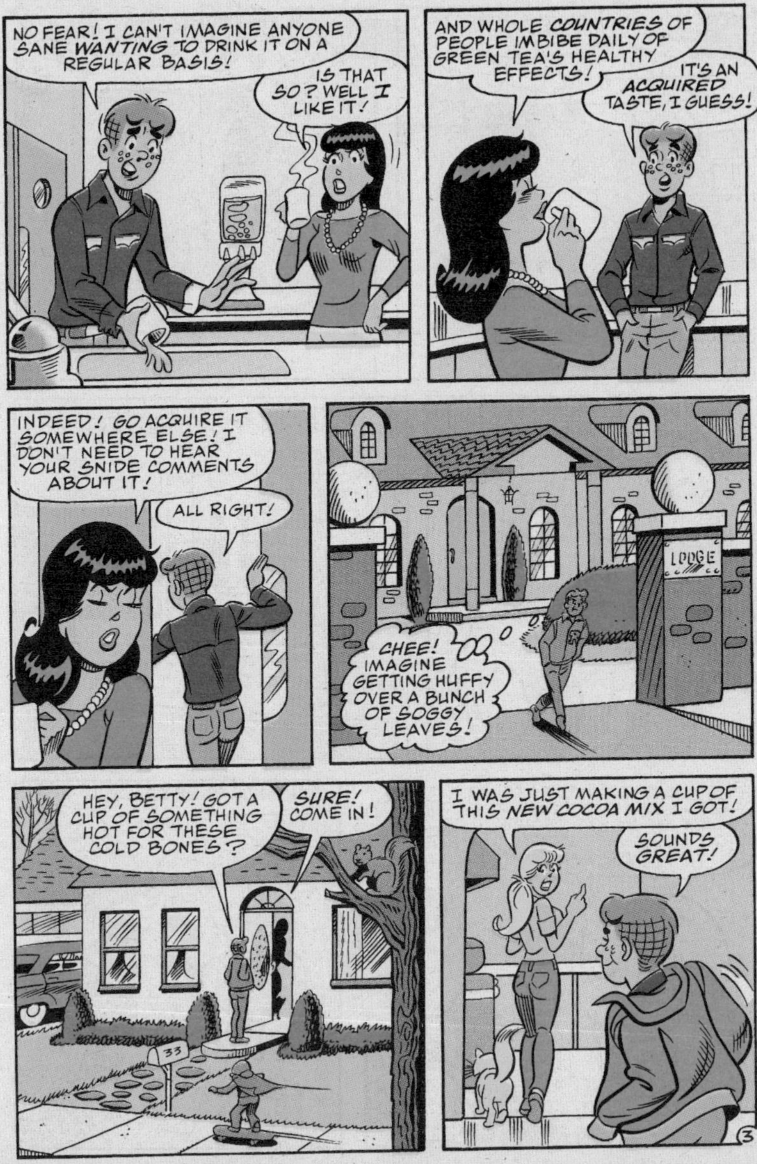
NO FEAR! I CAN'T IMAGINE ANYONE SANE WANTING TO DRINK IT ON A REGULAR BASIS!
IS THAT SO? WELL I LIKE IT!
AND WHOLE COUNTRIES OF PEOPLE IMBIBE DAILY OF GREEN TEA'S HEALTHY EFFECTS!
IT'S AN ACQUIRED TASTE, I GUESS!
INDEED! GO ACQUIRE IT SOMEWHERE ELSE! I DON'T NEED TO HEAR YOUR SNIDE COMMENTS ABOUT IT!
ALL RIGHT!
LODGE
CHEE! IMAGINE GETTING HUFFY OVER A BUNCH OF SOGGY LEAVES!
HEY, BETTY! GOT A CUP OF SOMETHING HOT FOR THESE COLD BONES?
SURE! COME IN!
33
I WAS JUST MAKING A CUP OF THIS NEW COCOA MIX I GOT!
SOUNDS GREAT!
3

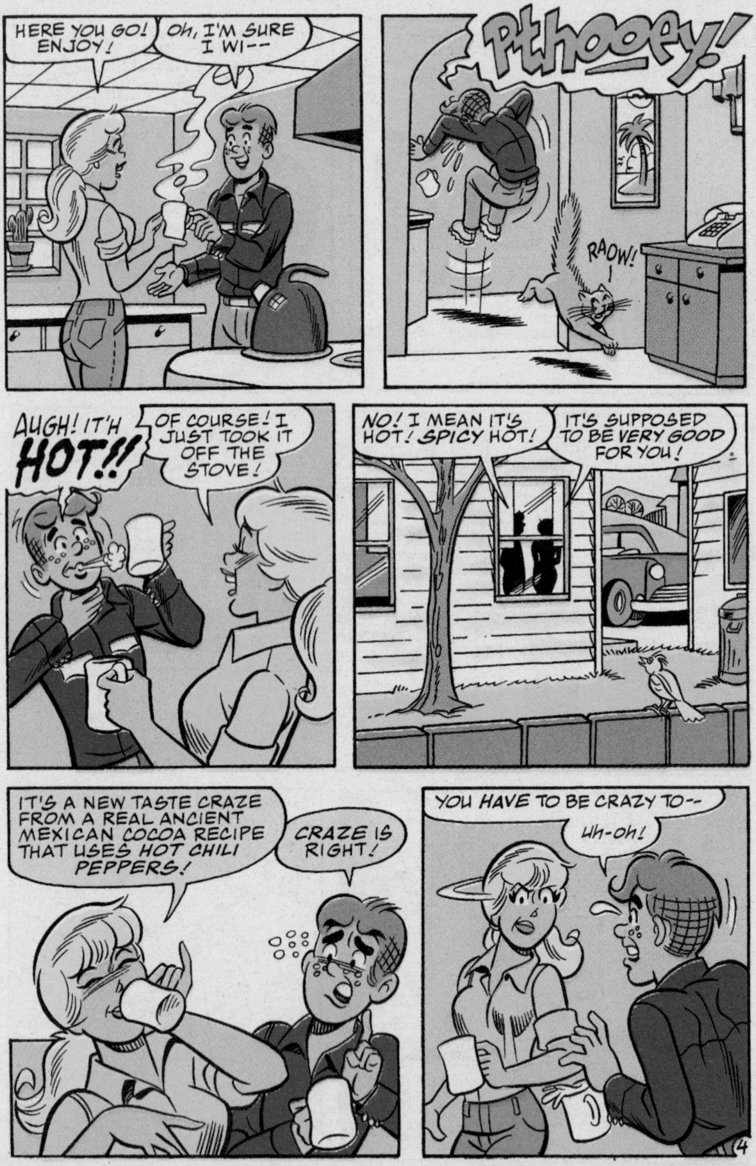

HERE YOU GO! ENJOY!
Oh, I'M SURE I WI--
Pthooey!
RAOW!
AUGH! IT'H HOT!!
OF COURSE! I JUST TOOK IT OFF THE STOVE!
NO! I MEAN IT'S HOT! SPICY HOT!
IT'S SUPPOSED TO BE VERY GOOD FOR YOU!
IT'S A NEW TASTE CRAZE FROM A REAL ANCIENT MEXICAN COCOA RECIPE THAT USES HOT CHILI PEPPERS!
CRAZE IS RIGHT!
YOU HAVE TO BE CRAZY TO--
Uh-oh!
4

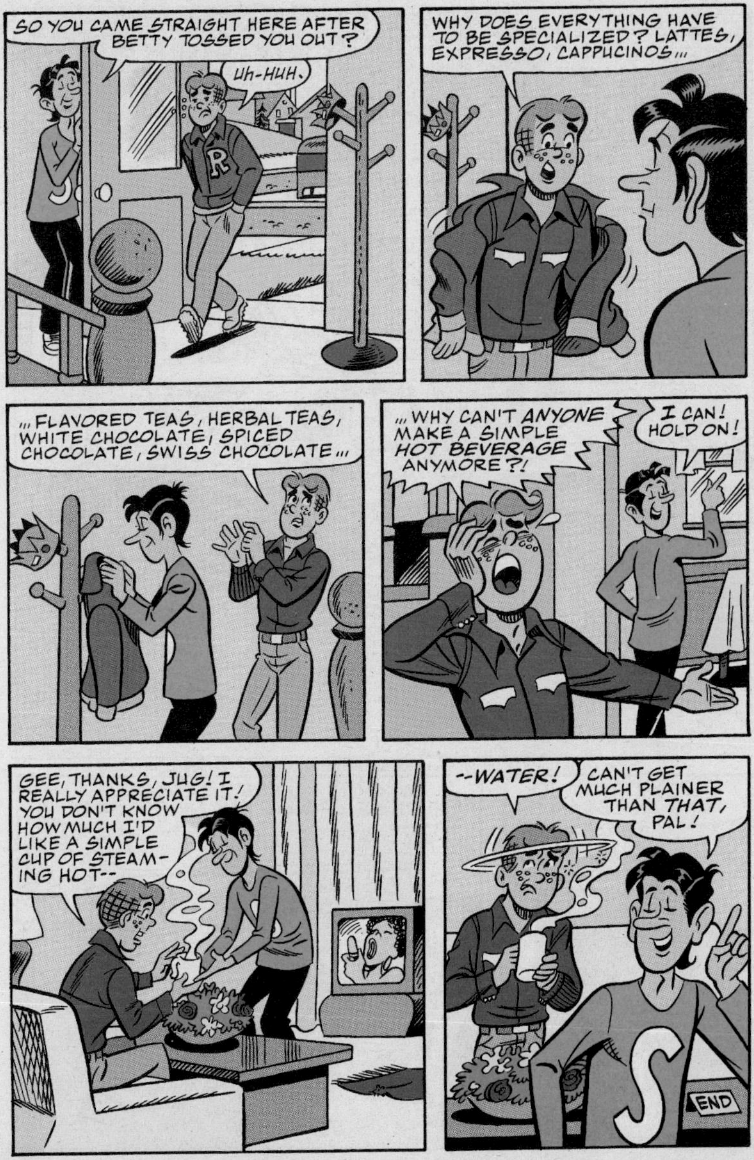
SO YOU CAME STRAIGHT HERE AFTER BETTY TOSSED YOU OUT?
UH-HUH.
WHY DOES EVERYTHING HAVE TO BE SPECIALIZED? LATTES, EXPRESSO, CAPPUCINOS...
...FLAVORED TEAS, HERBAL TEAS, WHITE CHOCOLATE, SPICED CHOCOLATE, SWISS CHOCOLATE...
...WHY CAN'T ANYONE MAKE A SIMPLE HOT BEVERAGE ANYMORE?!
I CAN! HOLD ON!
GEE, THANKS, JUG! I REALLY APPRECIATE IT! YOU DON'T KNOW HOW MUCH I'D LIKE A SIMPLE CUP OF STEAMING HOT--
--WATER!
CAN'T GET MUCH PLAINER THAN THAT, PAL!
END

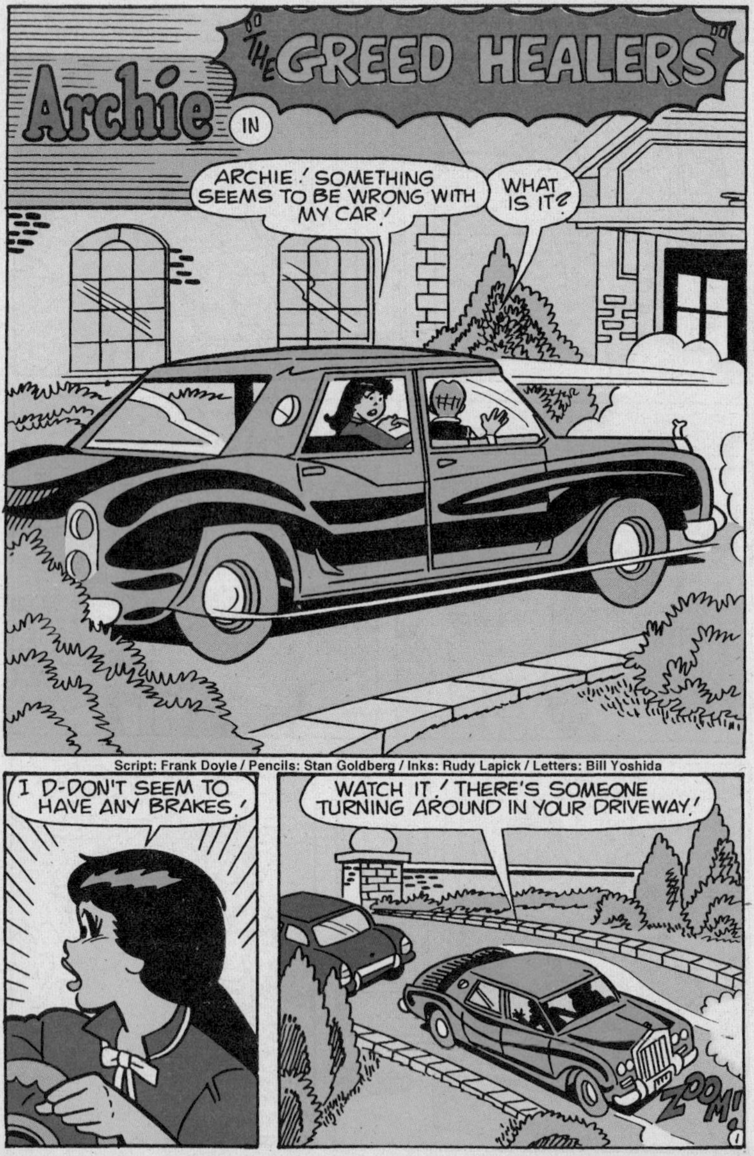
THE GREED HEALERS
Archie IN
ARCHIE! SOMETHING SEEMS TO BE WRONG WITH MY CAR!
WHAT IS IT?
I D-DON'T SEEM TO HAVE ANY BRAKES!
WATCH IT! THERE'S SOMEONE TURNING AROUND IN YOUR DRIVEWAY!
ZOOM!
1

Script: Frank Doyle / Pencils: Stan Goldberg / Inks: Rudy Lapick / Letters: Bill Yoshida

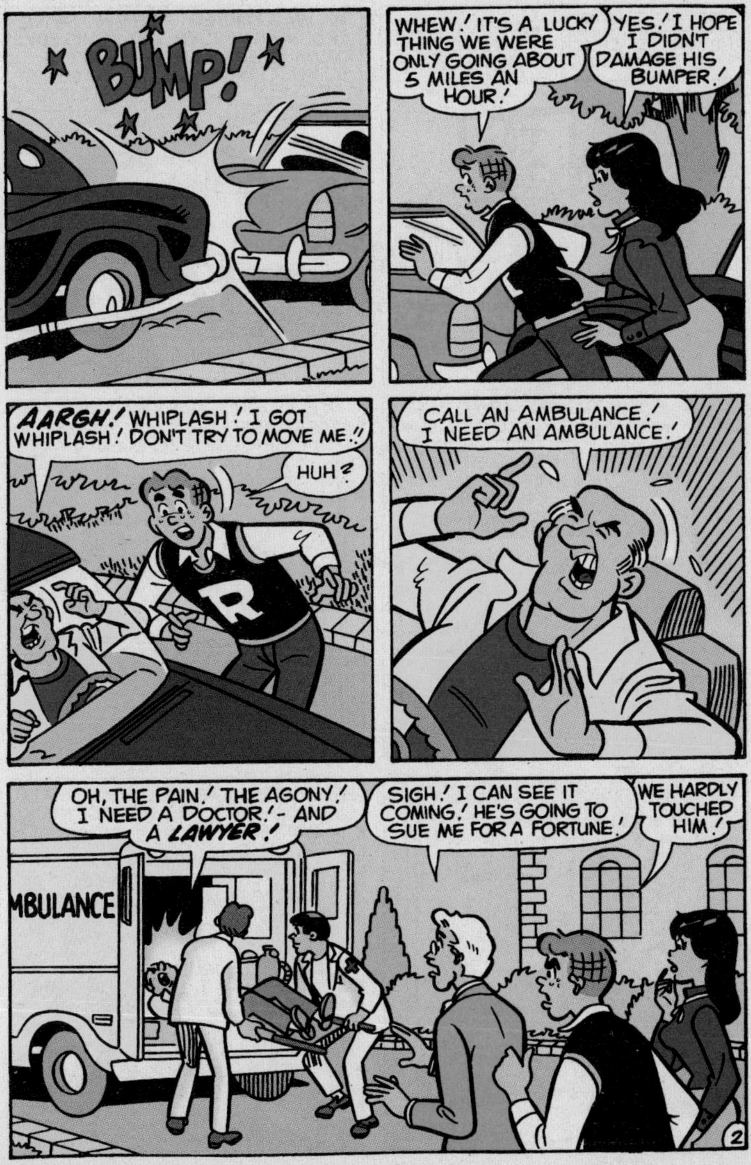
BUMP!
WHEW! IT'S A LUCKY THING WE WERE ONLY GOING ABOUT 5 MILES AN HOUR!
YES! I HOPE I DIDN'T DAMAGE HIS BUMPER!
AARGH! WHIPLASH! I GOT WHIPLASH! DON'T TRY TO MOVE ME!!
HUH?
CALL AN AMBULANCE! I NEED AN AMBULANCE!
OH, THE PAIN! THE AGONY! I NEED A DOCTOR! - AND A LAWYER!
MBULANCE
SIGH! I CAN SEE IT COMING! HE'S GOING TO SUE ME FOR A FORTUNE!
WE HARDLY TOUCHED HIM!
2

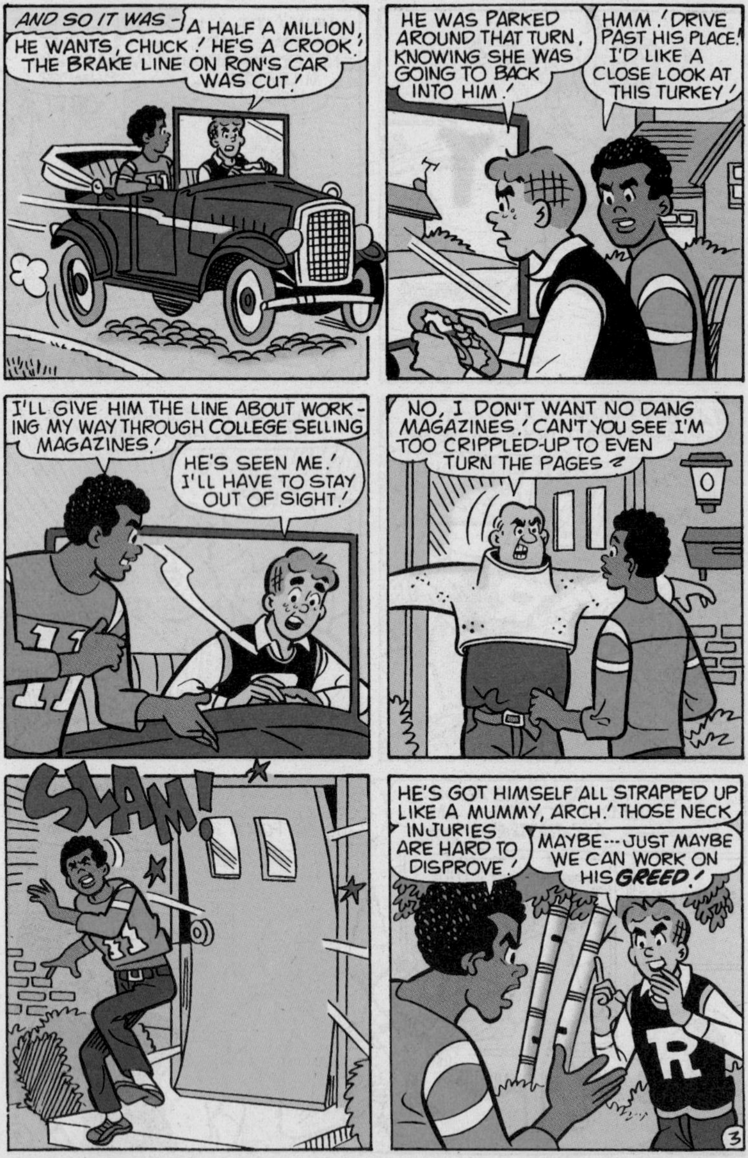
AND SO IT WAS –
A HALF A MILLION HE WANTS, CHUCK! HE'S A CROOK! THE BRAKE LINE ON RON'S CAR WAS CUT!
HE WAS PARKED AROUND THAT TURN, KNOWING SHE WAS GOING TO BACK INTO HIM!
HMM! DRIVE PAST HIS PLACE! I'D LIKE A CLOSE LOOK AT THIS TURKEY!
I'LL GIVE HIM THE LINE ABOUT WORKING MY WAY THROUGH COLLEGE SELLING MAGAZINES!
HE'S SEEN ME! I'LL HAVE TO STAY OUT OF SIGHT!
NO, I DON'T WANT NO DANG MAGAZINES! CAN'T YOU SEE I'M TOO CRIPPLED-UP TO EVEN TURN THE PAGES?
SLAM!
HE'S GOT HIMSELF ALL STRAPPED UP LIKE A MUMMY, ARCH! THOSE NECK INJURIES ARE HARD TO DISPROVE!
MAYBE--- JUST MAYBE WE CAN WORK ON HIS GREED!
3

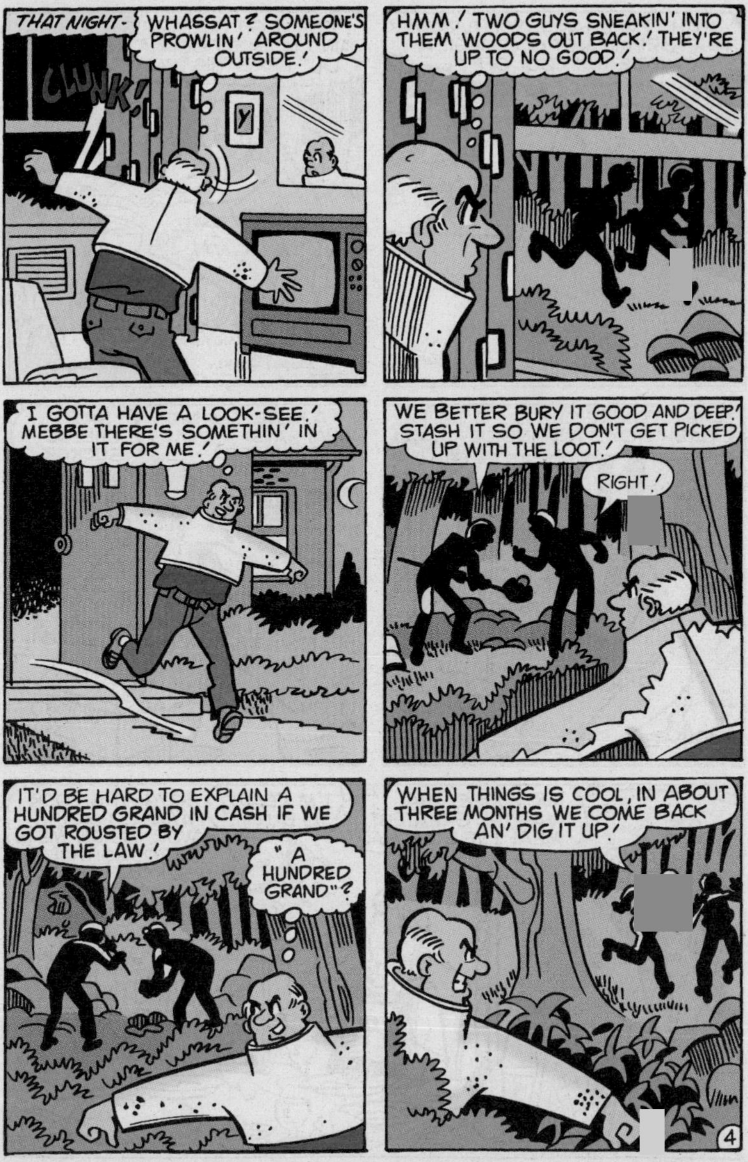
THAT NIGHT-
WHASSAT? SOMEONE'S PROWLIN' AROUND OUTSIDE!
CLUNK!
HMM! TWO GUYS SNEAKIN' INTO THEM WOODS OUT BACK! THEY'RE UP TO NO GOOD!
I GOTTA HAVE A LOOK-SEE! MEBBE THERE'S SOMETHIN' IN IT FOR ME!
WE BETTER BURY IT GOOD AND DEEP! STASH IT SO WE DON'T GET PICKED UP WITH THE LOOT!
RIGHT!
IT'D BE HARD TO EXPLAIN A HUNDRED GRAND IN CASH IF WE GOT ROUSTED BY THE LAW!
"A HUNDRED GRAND"?
WHEN THINGS IS COOL, IN ABOUT THREE MONTHS WE COME BACK AN' DIG IT UP!
4

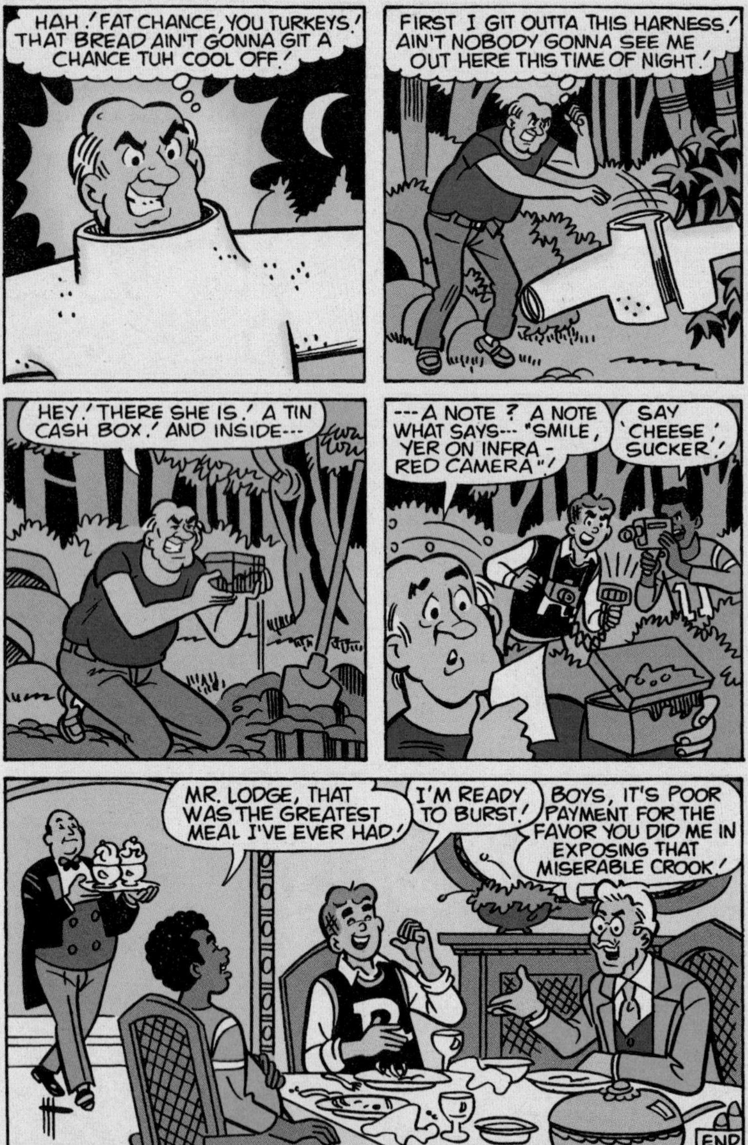

HAH! FAT CHANCE, YOU TURKEYS! THAT BREAD AIN'T GONNA GIT A CHANCE TUH COOL OFF!
FIRST I GIT OUTTA THIS HARNESS! AIN'T NOBODY GONNA SEE ME OUT HERE THIS TIME OF NIGHT!
HEY! THERE SHE IS! A TIN CASH BOX! AND INSIDE---
---A NOTE? A NOTE WHAT SAYS--- "SMILE, YER ON INFRA-RED CAMERA"!
SAY 'CHEESE,' SUCKER!
MR. LODGE, THAT WAS THE GREATEST MEAL I'VE EVER HAD!
I'M READY TO BURST!
BOYS, IT'S POOR PAYMENT FOR THE FAVOR YOU DID ME IN EXPOSING THAT MISERABLE CROOK!
END

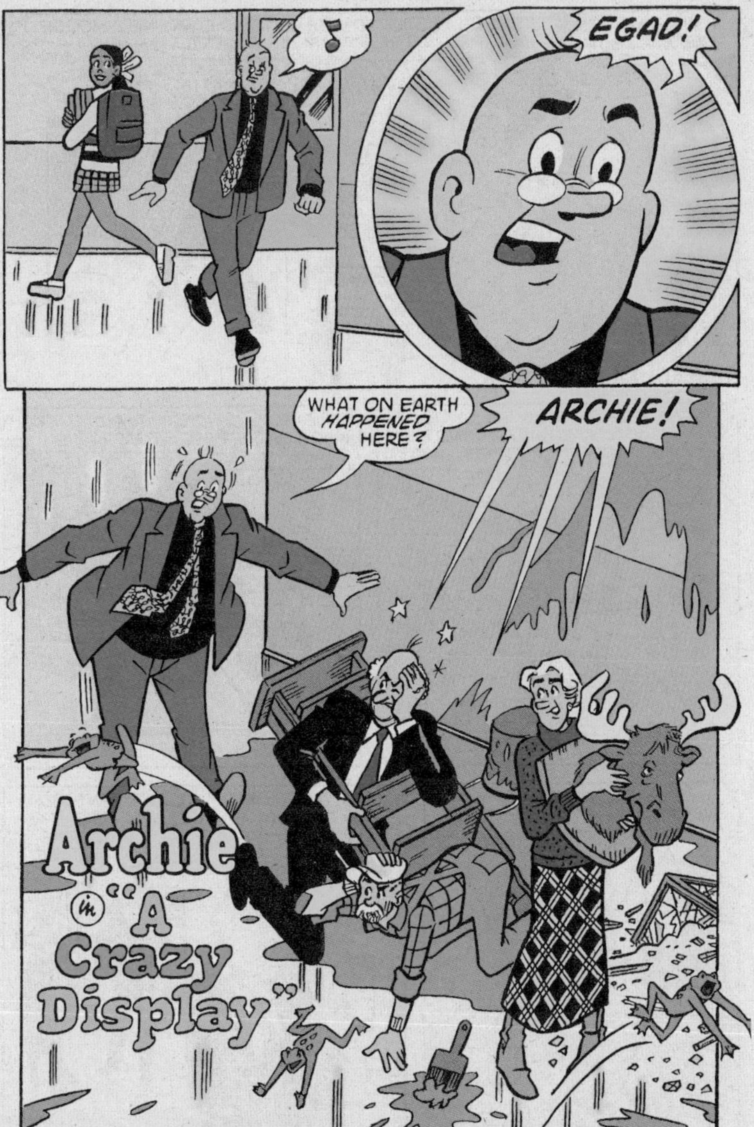
EGAD!
WHAT ON EARTH HAPPENED HERE?
ARCHIE!
Archie in "A Crazy Display"
Ruiz / Lapick / Yoshida

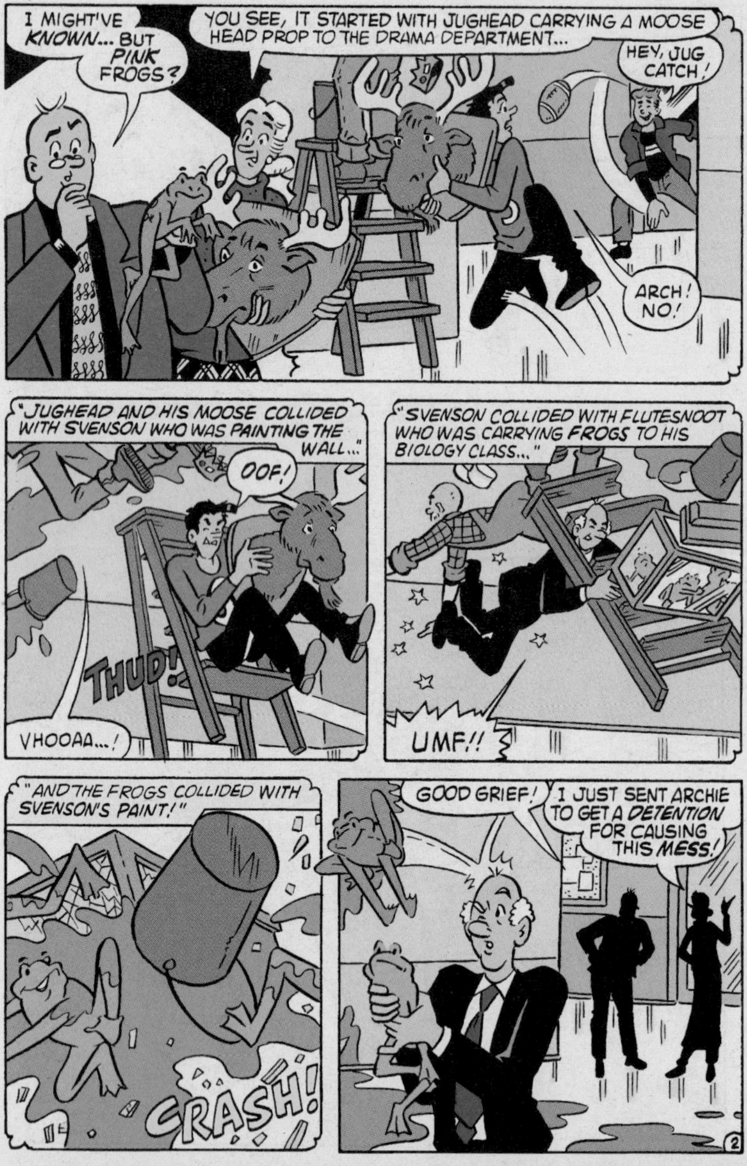

I MIGHT'VE KNOWN... BUT PINK FROGS?
YOU SEE, IT STARTED WITH JUGHEAD CARRYING A MOOSE HEAD PROP TO THE DRAMA DEPARTMENT...
HEY, JUG CATCH!
ARCH! NO!
"JUGHEAD AND HIS MOOSE COLLIDED WITH SVENSON WHO WAS PAINTING THE WALL..."
OOF!
THUD!
VHOOAA...!
"SVENSON COLLIDED WITH FLUTESNOOT WHO WAS CARRYING FROGS TO HIS BIOLOGY CLASS..."
UMF!!
"AND THE FROGS COLLIDED WITH SVENSON'S PAINT!"
CRASH!
GOOD GRIEF!
I JUST SENT ARCHIE TO GET A DETENTION FOR CAUSING THIS MESS!

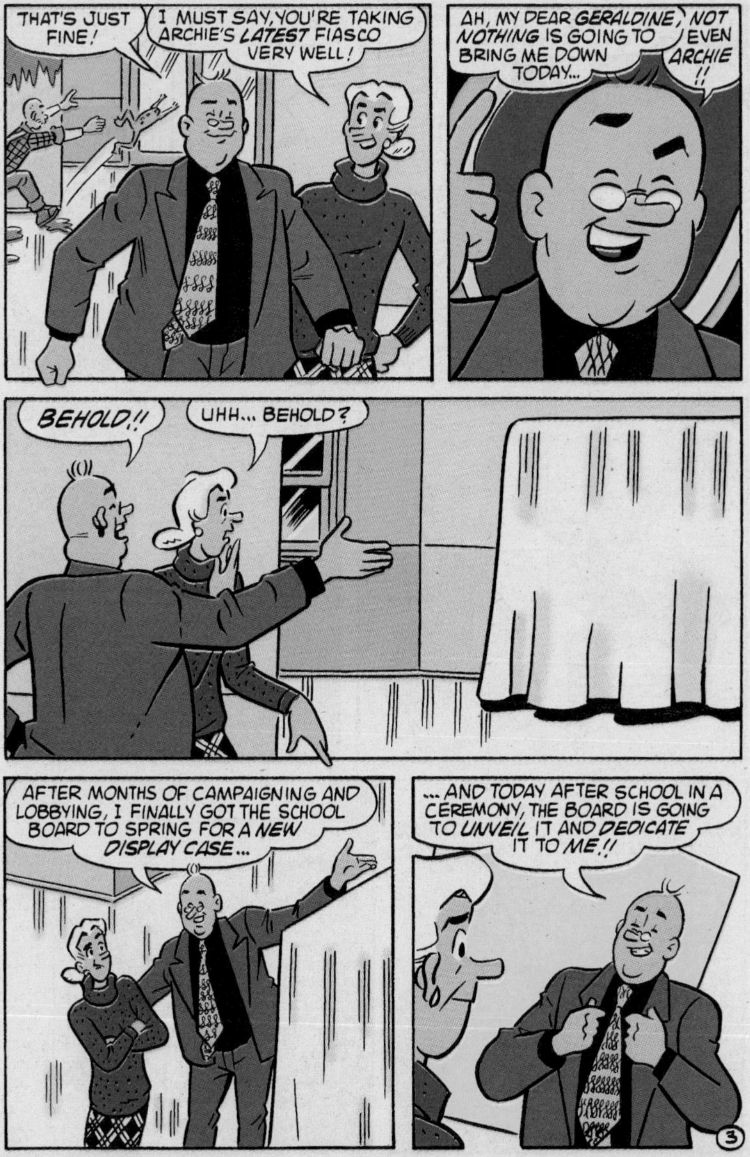

THAT'S JUST FINE!
I MUST SAY, YOU'RE TAKING ARCHIE'S LATEST FIASCO VERY WELL!
AH, MY DEAR GERALDINE, NOTHING IS GOING TO BRING ME DOWN TODAY...
NOT EVEN ARCHIE !!
BEHOLD!!
UHH... BEHOLD?
AFTER MONTHS OF CAMPAIGNING AND LOBBYING, I FINALLY GOT THE SCHOOL BOARD TO SPRING FOR A NEW DISPLAY CASE...
... AND TODAY AFTER SCHOOL IN A CEREMONY, THE BOARD IS GOING TO UNVEIL IT AND DEDICATE IT TO ME!!
3

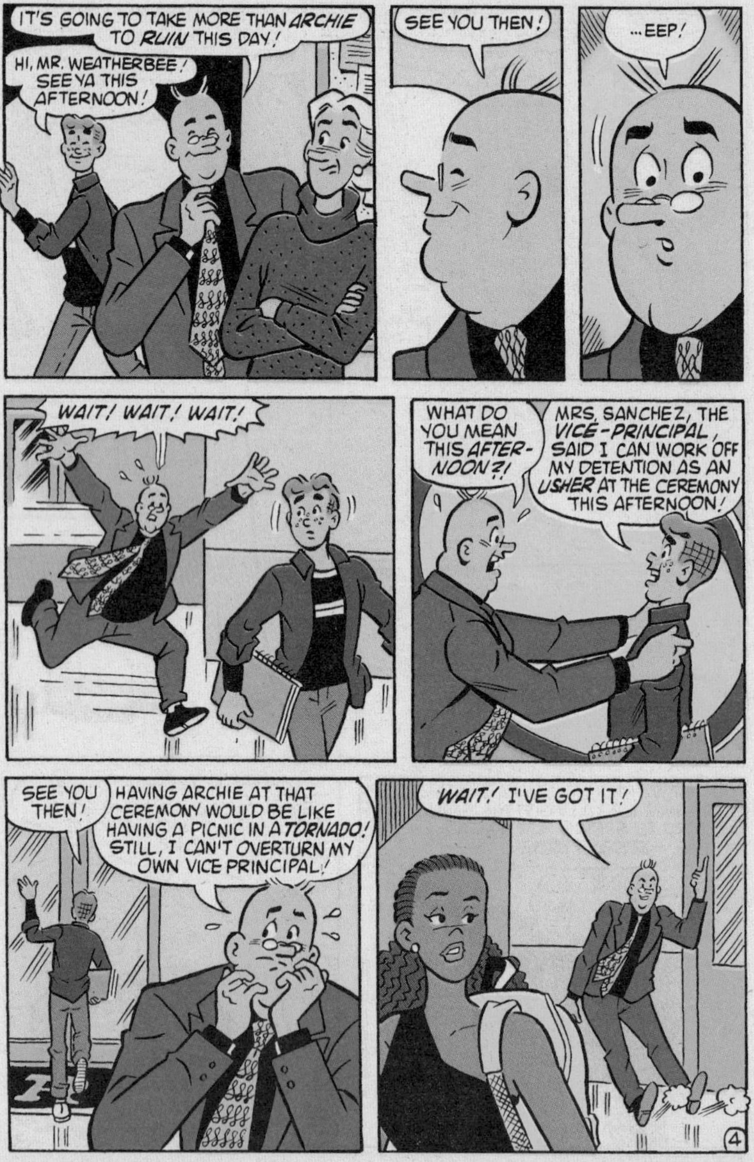
IT'S GOING TO TAKE MORE THAN ARCHIE TO RUIN THIS DAY!
HI, MR. WEATHERBEE! SEE YA THIS AFTERNOON!
SEE YOU THEN!
...EEP!
WAIT! WAIT! WAIT!
WHAT DO YOU MEAN THIS AFTER-NOON?!
MRS. SANCHEZ, THE VICE-PRINCIPAL, SAID I CAN WORK OFF MY DETENTION AS AN USHER AT THE CEREMONY THIS AFTERNOON!
SEE YOU THEN!
HAVING ARCHIE AT THAT CEREMONY WOULD BE LIKE HAVING A PICNIC IN A TORNADO! STILL, I CAN'T OVERTURN MY OWN VICE PRINCIPAL!
WAIT! I'VE GOT IT!
4

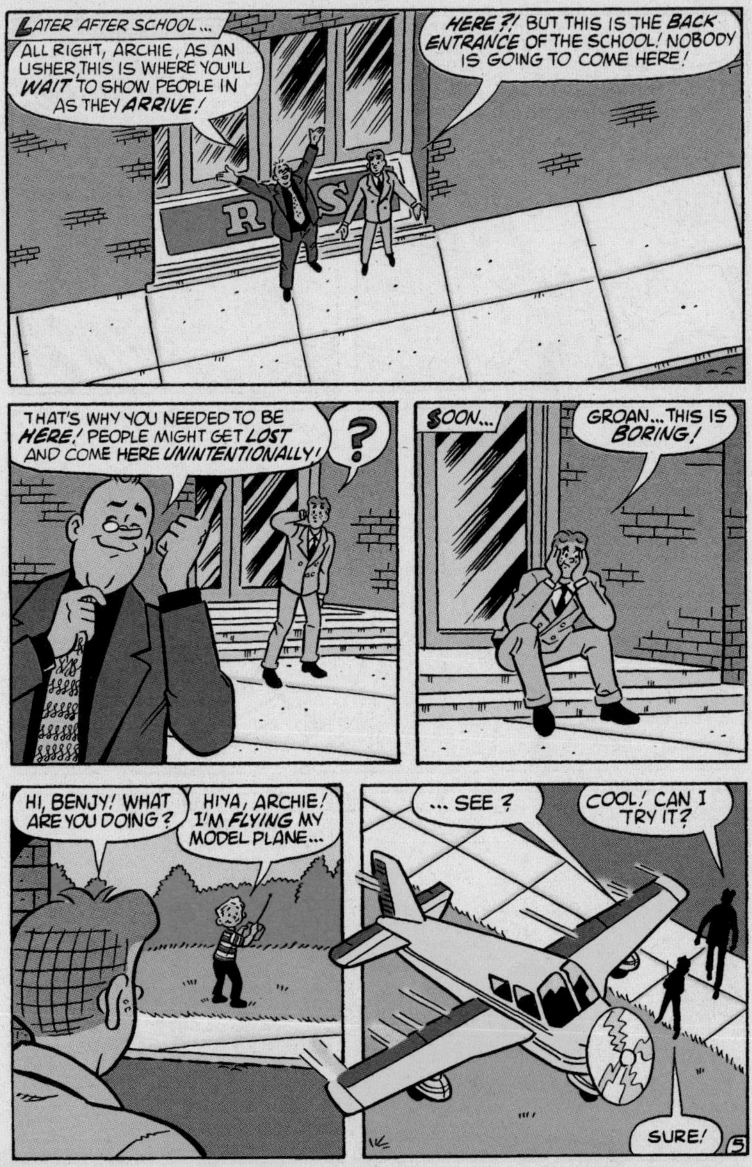
LATER AFTER SCHOOL...
ALL RIGHT, ARCHIE, AS AN USHER, THIS IS WHERE YOU'LL WAIT TO SHOW PEOPLE IN AS THEY ARRIVE!
HERE?! BUT THIS IS THE BACK ENTRANCE OF THE SCHOOL! NOBODY IS GOING TO COME HERE!
THAT'S WHY YOU NEEDED TO BE HERE! PEOPLE MIGHT GET LOST AND COME HERE UNINTENTIONALLY!
?
SOON...
GROAN... THIS IS BORING!
HI, BENJY! WHAT ARE YOU DOING?
HIYA, ARCHIE! I'M FLYING MY MODEL PLANE...
... SEE?
COOL! CAN I TRY IT?
SURE!
5

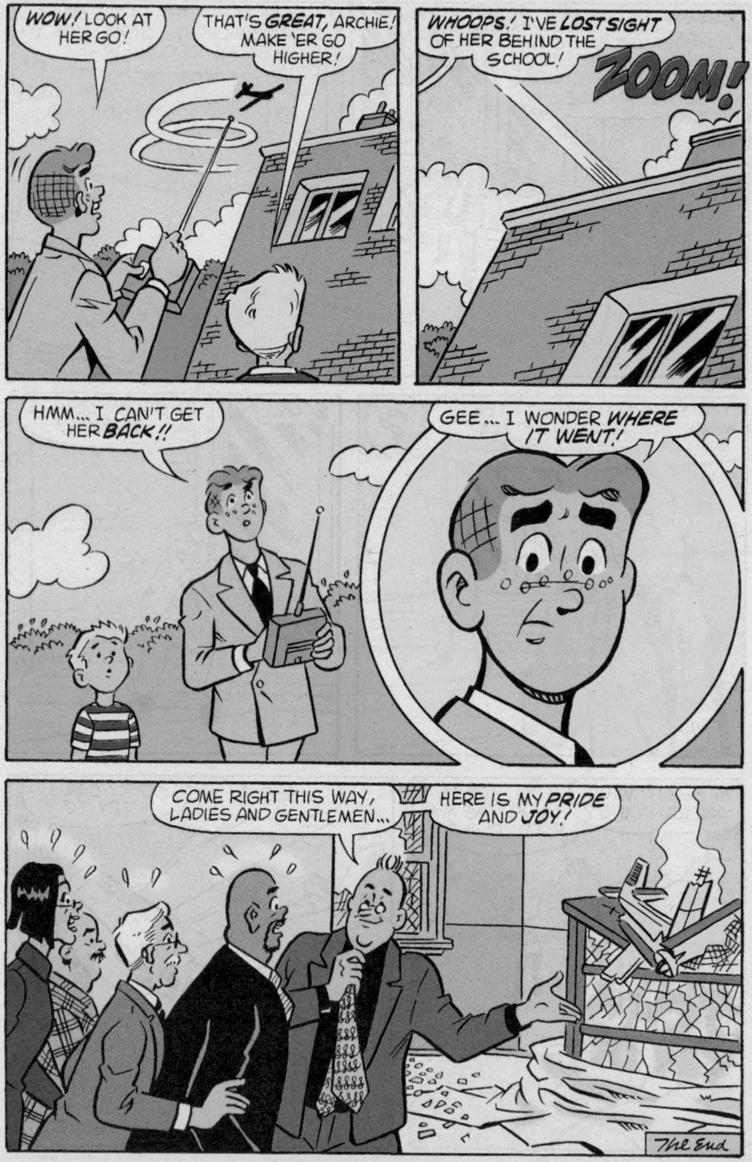
WOW! LOOK AT HER GO!
THAT'S GREAT, ARCHIE! MAKE 'ER GO HIGHER!
WHOOPS! I'VE LOST SIGHT OF HER BEHIND THE SCHOOL!
ZOOM!
HMM... I CAN'T GET HER BACK!!
GEE... I WONDER WHERE IT WENT!
COME RIGHT THIS WAY, LADIES AND GENTLEMEN...
HERE IS MY PRIDE AND JOY!
The End

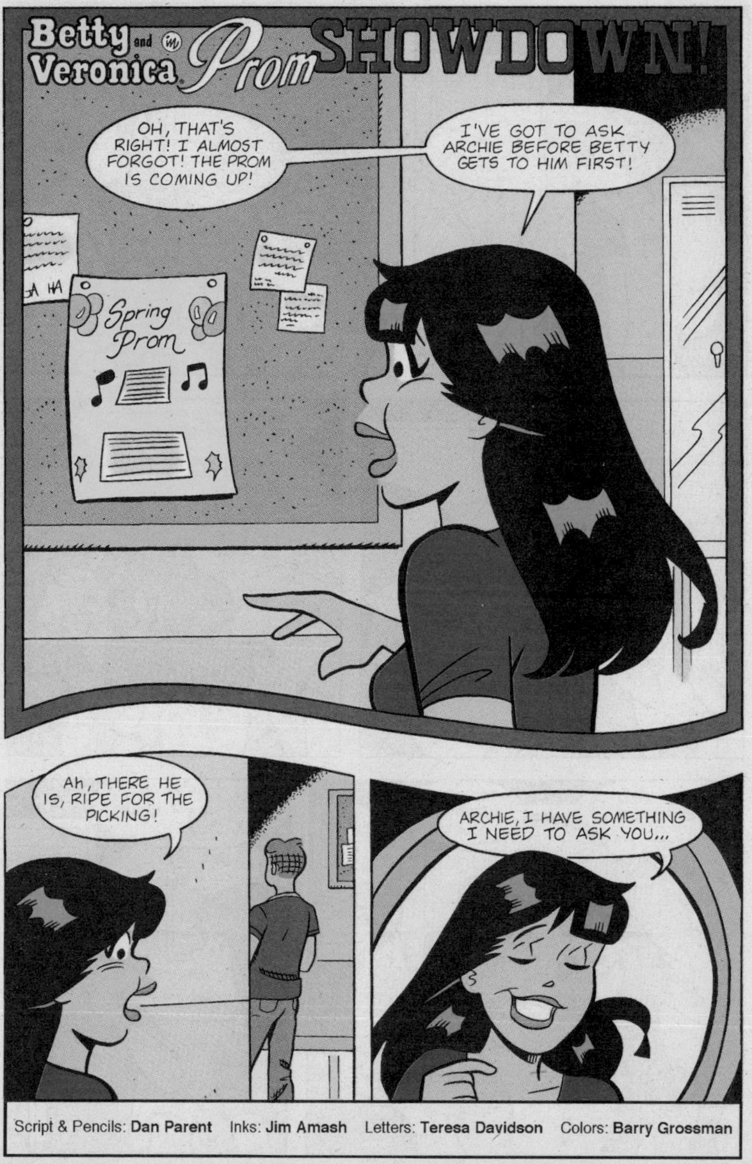
Betty and Veronica in Prom SHOWDOWN!
OH, THAT'S RIGHT! I ALMOST FORGOT! THE PROM IS COMING UP!
I'VE GOT TO ASK ARCHIE BEFORE BETTY GETS TO HIM FIRST!
Spring Prom
Ah, THERE HE IS, RIPE FOR THE PICKING!
ARCHIE, I HAVE SOMETHING I NEED TO ASK YOU...
Script & Pencils: Dan Parent Inks: Jim Amash Letters: Teresa Davidson Colors: Barry Grossman

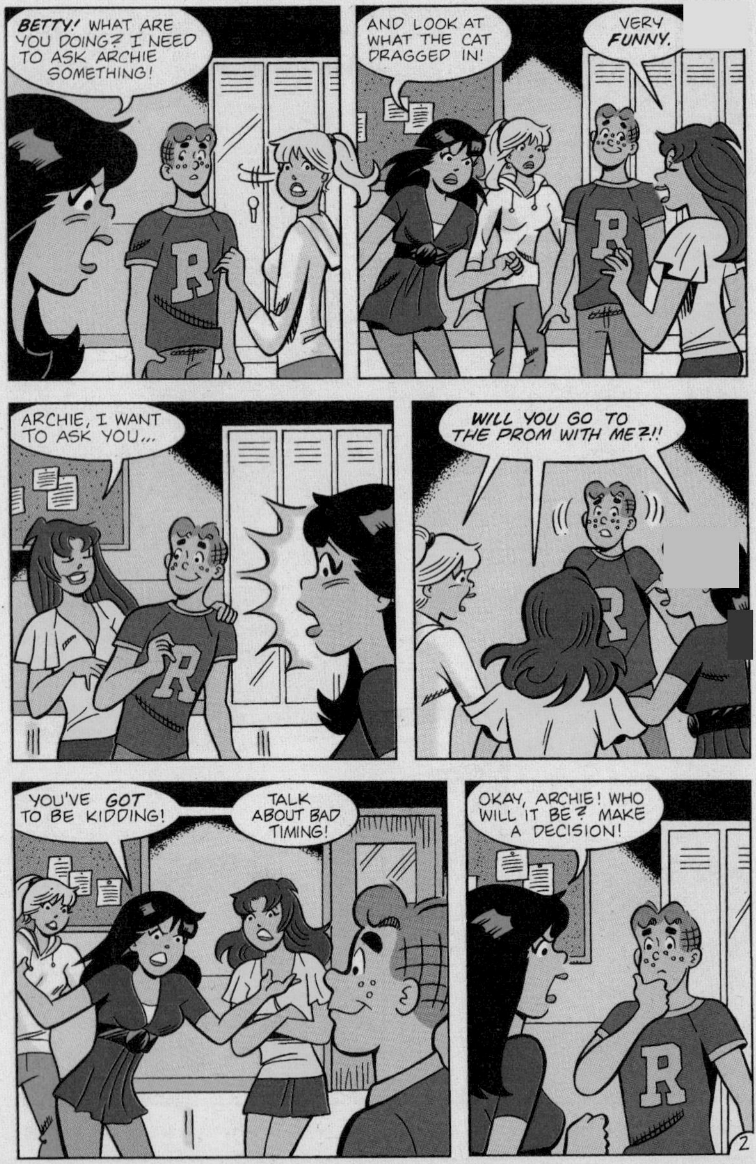
BETTY! WHAT ARE YOU DOING? I NEED TO ASK ARCHIE SOMETHING!
AND LOOK AT WHAT THE CAT DRAGGED IN!
VERY FUNNY.
ARCHIE, I WANT TO ASK YOU...
WILL YOU GO TO THE PROM WITH ME?!!
YOU'VE GOT TO BE KIDDING!
TALK ABOUT BAD TIMING!
OKAY, ARCHIE! WHO WILL IT BE? MAKE A DECISION!

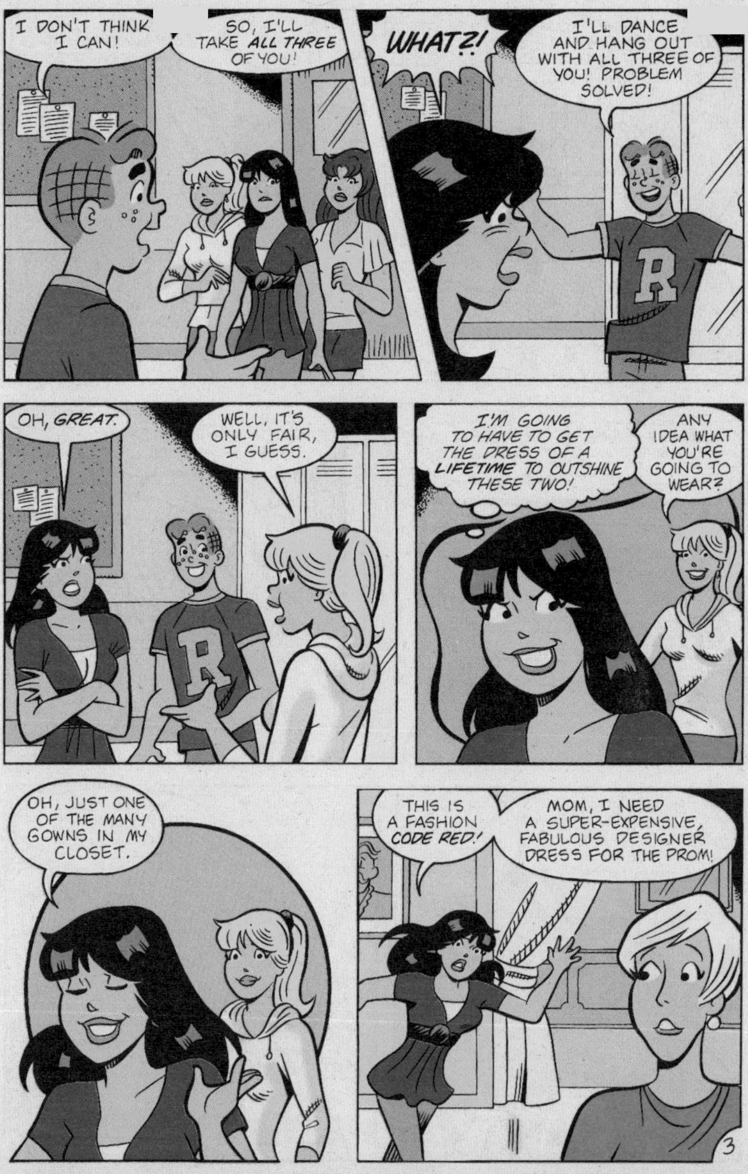

I DON'T THINK I CAN!
SO, I'LL TAKE ALL THREE OF YOU!
WHAT?!
I'LL DANCE AND HANG OUT WITH ALL THREE OF YOU! PROBLEM SOLVED!
OH, GREAT.
WELL, IT'S ONLY FAIR, I GUESS.
I'M GOING TO HAVE TO GET THE DRESS OF A LIFETIME TO OUTSHINE THESE TWO!
ANY IDEA WHAT YOU'RE GOING TO WEAR?
OH, JUST ONE OF THE MANY GOWNS IN MY CLOSET.
THIS IS A FASHION CODE RED!
MOM, I NEED A SUPER-EXPENSIVE, FABULOUS DESIGNER DRESS FOR THE PROM!
3

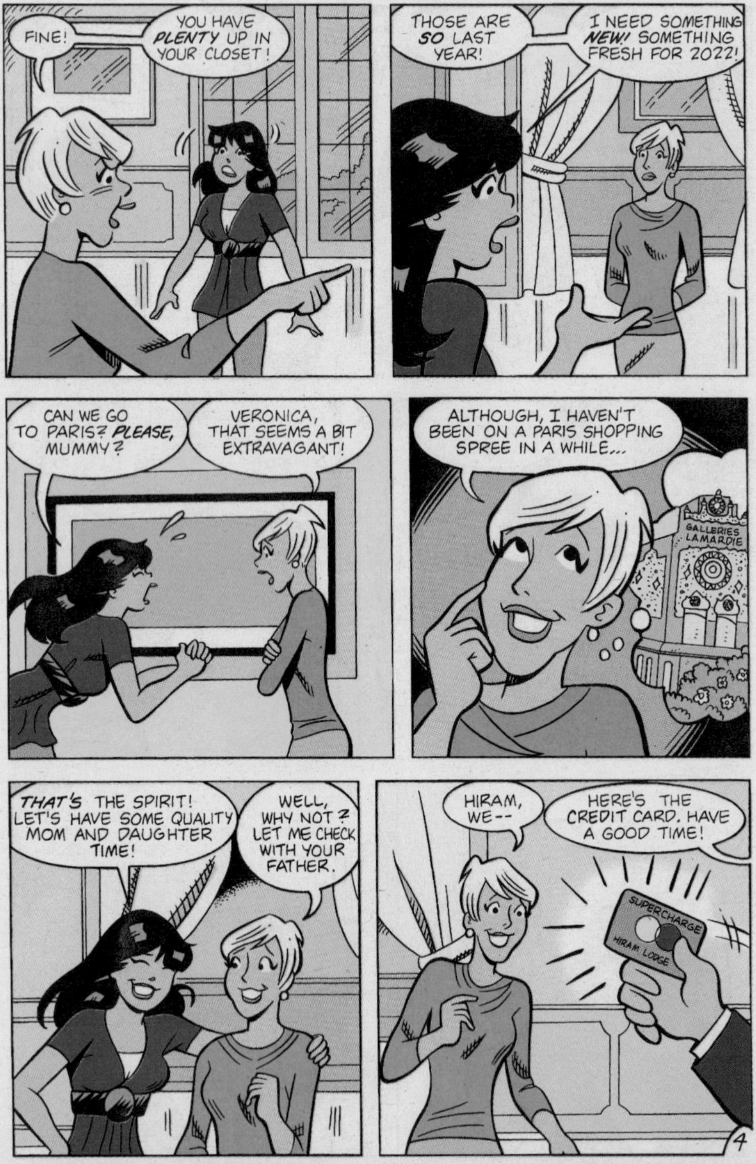
FINE!
YOU HAVE PLENTY UP IN YOUR CLOSET!
THOSE ARE SO LAST YEAR!
I NEED SOMETHING NEW! SOMETHING FRESH FOR 2022!
CAN WE GO TO PARIS? PLEASE, MUMMY?
VERONICA, THAT SEEMS A BIT EXTRAVAGANT!
ALTHOUGH, I HAVEN'T BEEN ON A PARIS SHOPPING SPREE IN A WHILE...
GALLERIES LAMARDIE
THAT'S THE SPIRIT! LET'S HAVE SOME QUALITY MOM AND DAUGHTER TIME!
WELL, WHY NOT? LET ME CHECK WITH YOUR FATHER.
HIRAM, WE--
HERE'S THE CREDIT CARD. HAVE A GOOD TIME!
SUPERCHARGE
HIRAM LODGE

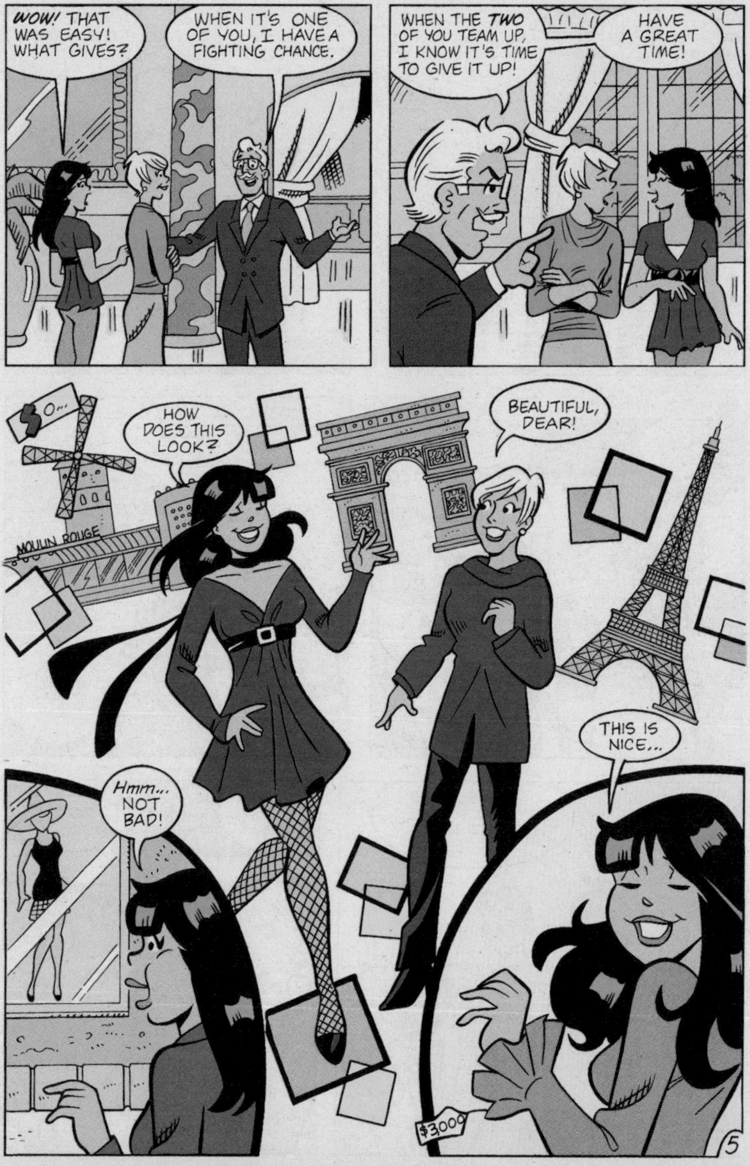
WOW! THAT WAS EASY! WHAT GIVES?
WHEN IT'S ONE OF YOU, I HAVE A FIGHTING CHANCE.
WHEN THE TWO OF YOU TEAM UP, I KNOW IT'S TIME TO GIVE IT UP!
HAVE A GREAT TIME!
MOULIN ROUGE
HOW DOES THIS LOOK?
BEAUTIFUL, DEAR!
Hmm... NOT BAD!
THIS IS NICE...
$3000

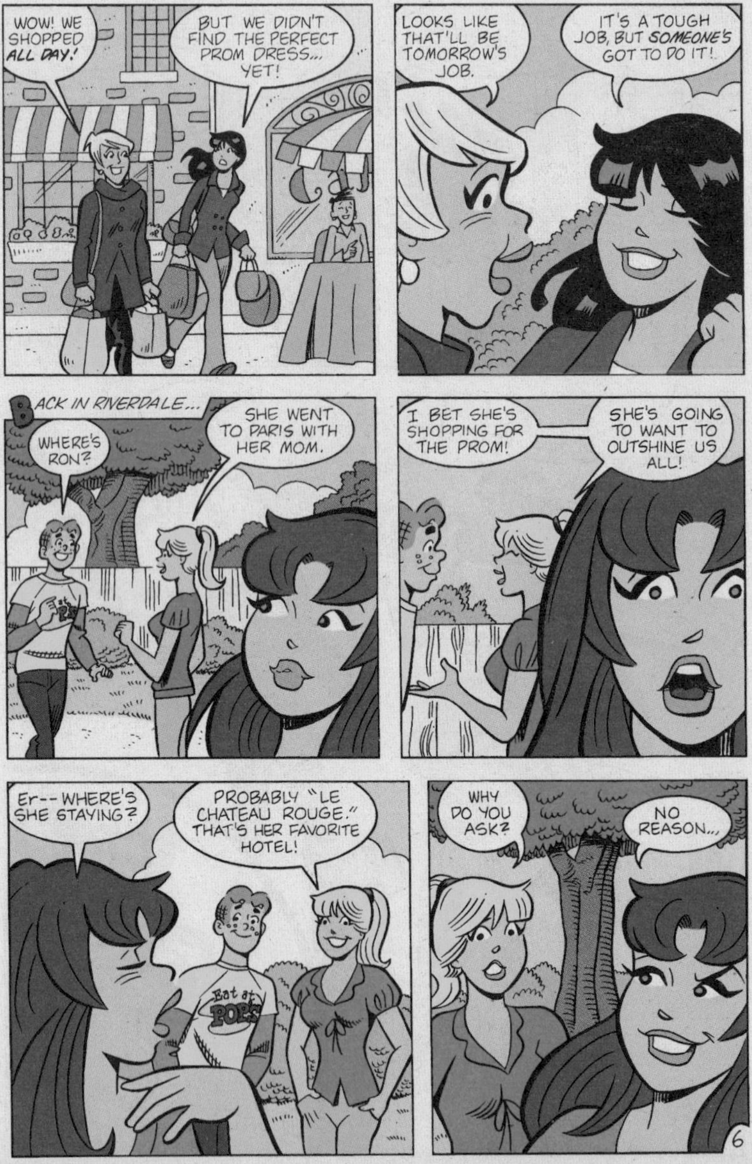

WOW! WE SHOPPED ALL DAY!
BUT WE DIDN'T FIND THE PERFECT PROM DRESS... YET!
LOOKS LIKE THAT'LL BE TOMORROW'S JOB.
IT'S A TOUGH JOB, BUT SOMEONE'S GOT TO DO IT!
BACK IN RIVERDALE...
WHERE'S RON?
SHE WENT TO PARIS WITH HER MOM.
I BET SHE'S SHOPPING FOR THE PROM!
SHE'S GOING TO WANT TO OUTSHINE US ALL!
Er-- WHERE'S SHE STAYING?
PROBABLY "LE CHATEAU ROUGE." THAT'S HER FAVORITE HOTEL!
WHY DO YOU ASK?
NO REASON...

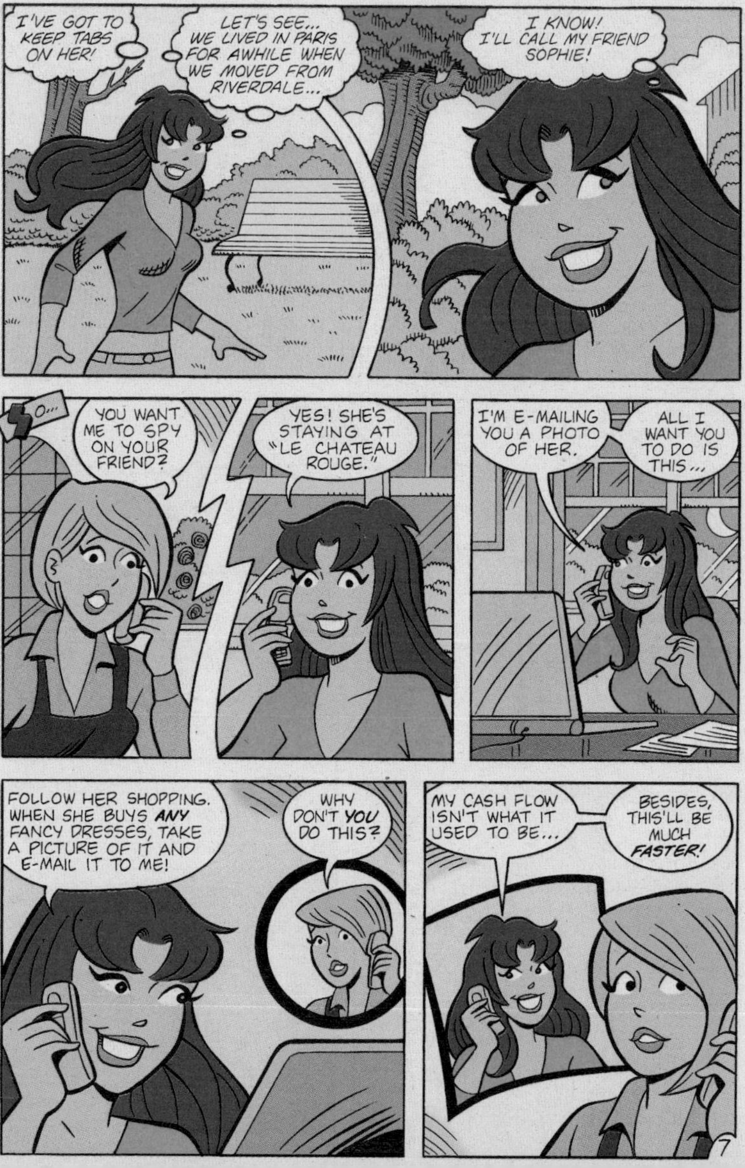
I'VE GOT TO KEEP TABS ON HER!
LET'S SEE... WE LIVED IN PARIS FOR AWHILE WHEN WE MOVED FROM RIVERDALE...
I KNOW! I'LL CALL MY FRIEND SOPHIE!
S...
YOU WANT ME TO SPY ON YOUR FRIEND?
YES! SHE'S STAYING AT "LE CHATEAU ROUGE."
I'M E-MAILING YOU A PHOTO OF HER.
ALL I WANT YOU TO DO IS THIS...
FOLLOW HER SHOPPING. WHEN SHE BUYS ANY FANCY DRESSES, TAKE A PICTURE OF IT AND E-MAIL IT TO ME!
WHY DON'T YOU DO THIS?
MY CASH FLOW ISN'T WHAT IT USED TO BE...
BESIDES, THIS'LL BE MUCH FASTER!

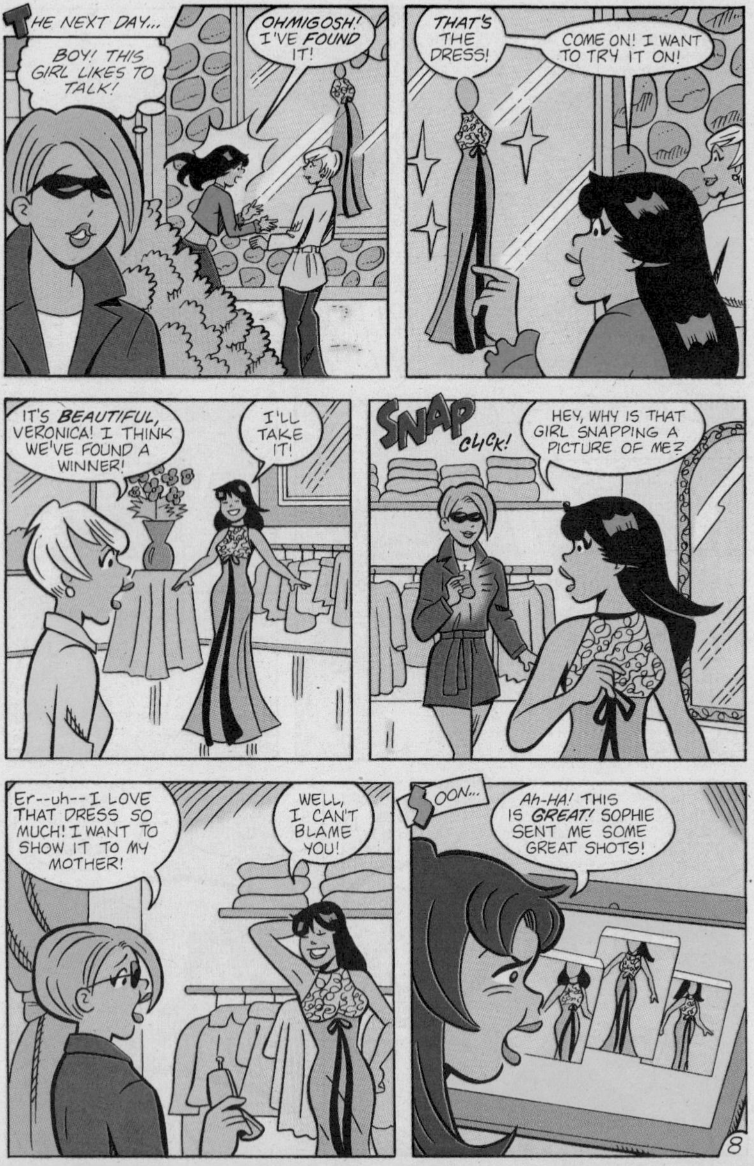
THE NEXT DAY...
BOY! THIS GIRL LIKES TO TALK!
OHMIGOSH! I'VE FOUND IT!
THAT'S THE DRESS!
COME ON! I WANT TO TRY IT ON!
IT'S BEAUTIFUL, VERONICA! I THINK WE'VE FOUND A WINNER!
I'LL TAKE IT!
SNAP
CLICK!
HEY, WHY IS THAT GIRL SNAPPING A PICTURE OF ME?
Er--uh--I LOVE THAT DRESS SO MUCH! I WANT TO SHOW IT TO MY MOTHER!
WELL, I CAN'T BLAME YOU!
SOON...
Ah-HA! THIS IS GREAT! SOPHIE SENT ME SOME GREAT SHOTS!

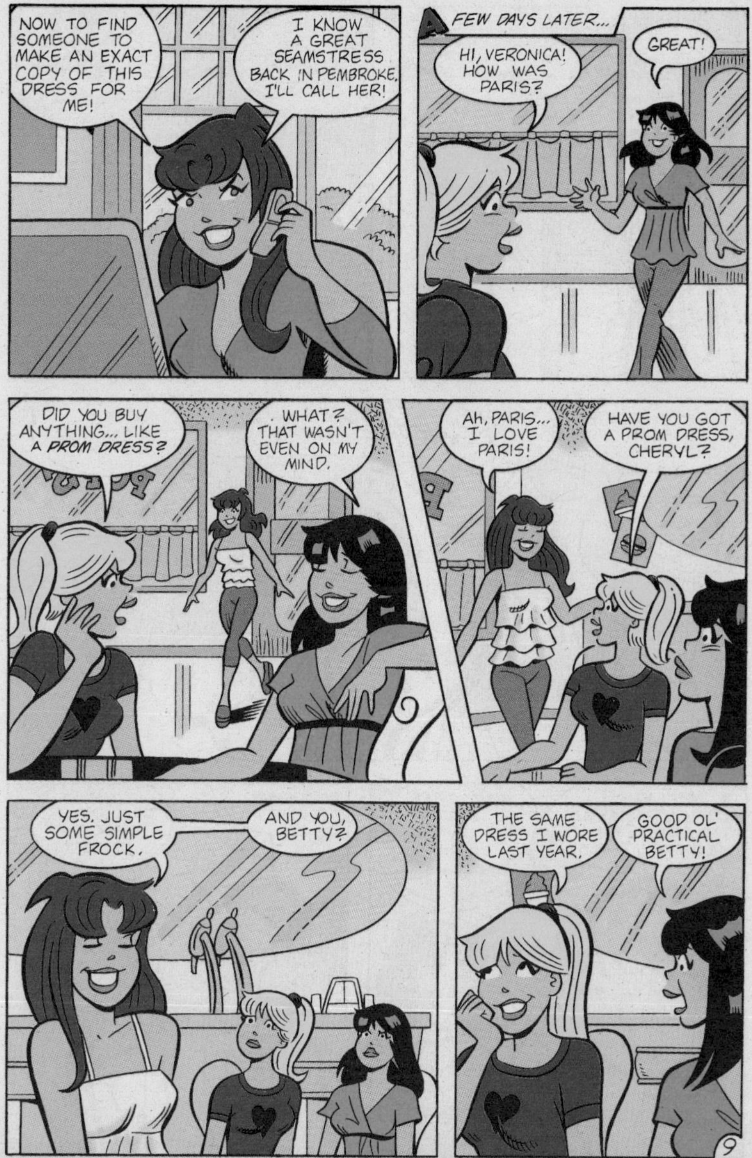

NOW TO FIND SOMEONE TO MAKE AN EXACT COPY OF THIS DRESS FOR ME!
I KNOW A GREAT SEAMSTRESS BACK IN PEMBROKE. I'LL CALL HER!
A FEW DAYS LATER...
HI, VERONICA! HOW WAS PARIS?
GREAT!
DID YOU BUY ANYTHING... LIKE A *PROM DRESS*?
WHAT? THAT WASN'T EVEN ON MY MIND.
Ah, PARIS... I LOVE PARIS!
HAVE YOU GOT A PROM DRESS, CHERYL?
YES. JUST SOME SIMPLE FROCK.
AND YOU, BETTY?
THE SAME DRESS I WORE LAST YEAR.
GOOD OL' PRACTICAL BETTY!
9

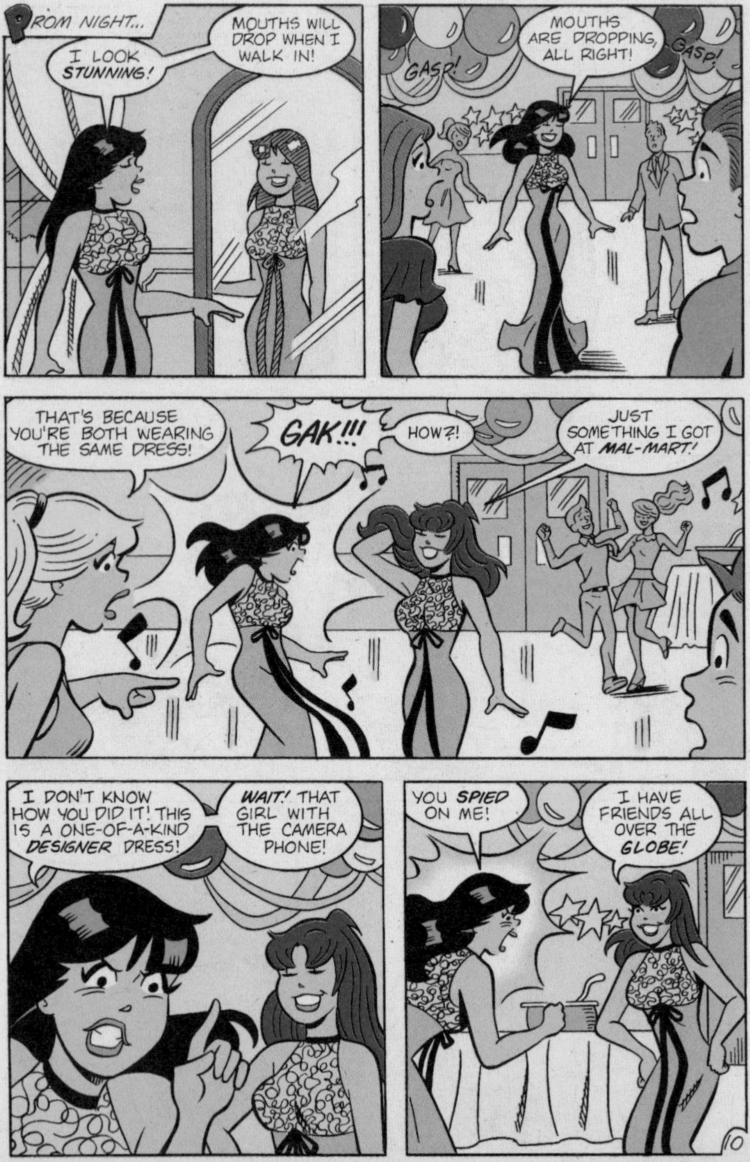
PROM NIGHT...
I LOOK STUNNING!
MOUTHS WILL DROP WHEN I WALK IN!
GASP!
MOUTHS ARE DROPPING, ALL RIGHT!
GASP!
THAT'S BECAUSE YOU'RE BOTH WEARING THE SAME DRESS!
GAK!!!
HOW?!
JUST SOMETHING I GOT AT MAL-MART!
I DON'T KNOW HOW YOU DID IT! THIS IS A ONE-OF-A-KIND DESIGNER DRESS!
WAIT! THAT GIRL WITH THE CAMERA PHONE!
YOU SPIED ON ME!
I HAVE FRIENDS ALL OVER THE GLOBE!
10

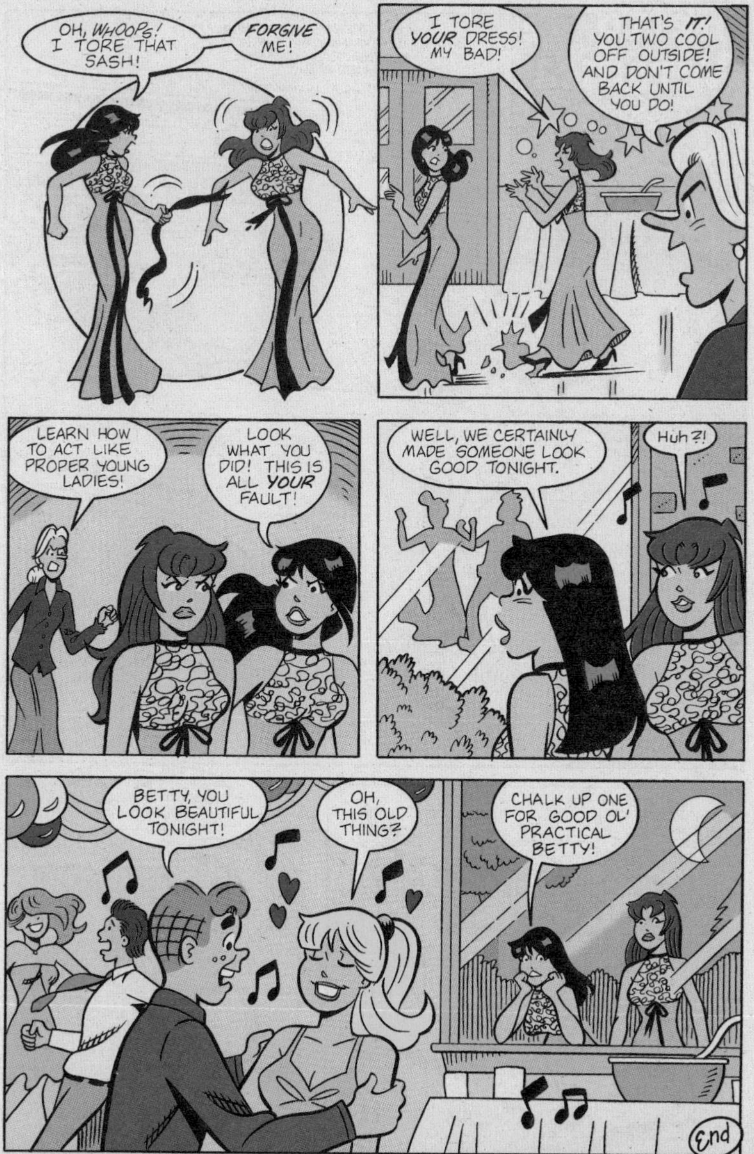
OH, WHOOPS! I TORE THAT SASH!
FORGIVE ME!
I TORE YOUR DRESS! MY BAD!
THAT'S IT! YOU TWO COOL OFF OUTSIDE! AND DON'T COME BACK UNTIL YOU DO!
LEARN HOW TO ACT LIKE PROPER YOUNG LADIES!
LOOK WHAT YOU DID! THIS IS ALL YOUR FAULT!
WELL, WE CERTAINLY MADE SOMEONE LOOK GOOD TONIGHT.
Huh?!
BETTY, YOU LOOK BEAUTIFUL TONIGHT!
OH, THIS OLD THING?
CHALK UP ONE FOR GOOD OL' PRACTICAL BETTY!
End

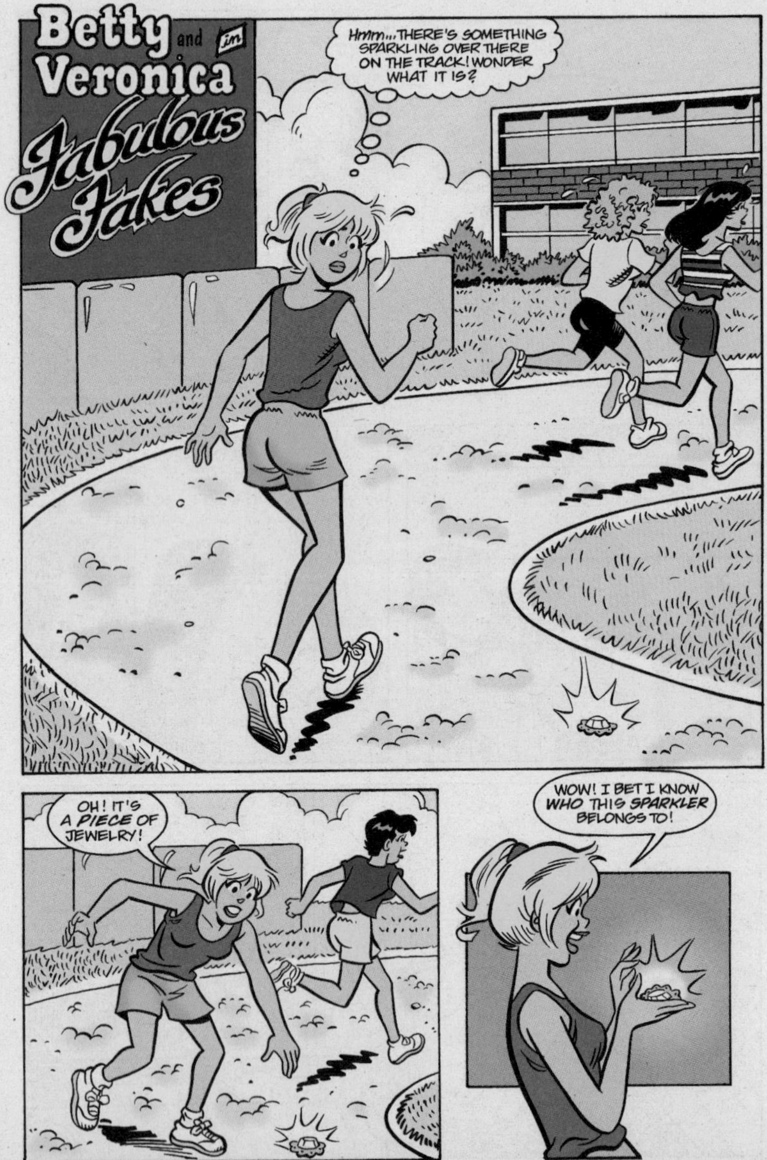
Betty and Veronica in
Fabulous Fakes
Hmm... THERE'S SOMETHING SPARKLING OVER THERE ON THE TRACK! WONDER WHAT IT IS?
OH! IT'S A PIECE OF JEWELRY!
WOW! I BET I KNOW WHO THIS SPARKLER BELONGS TO!

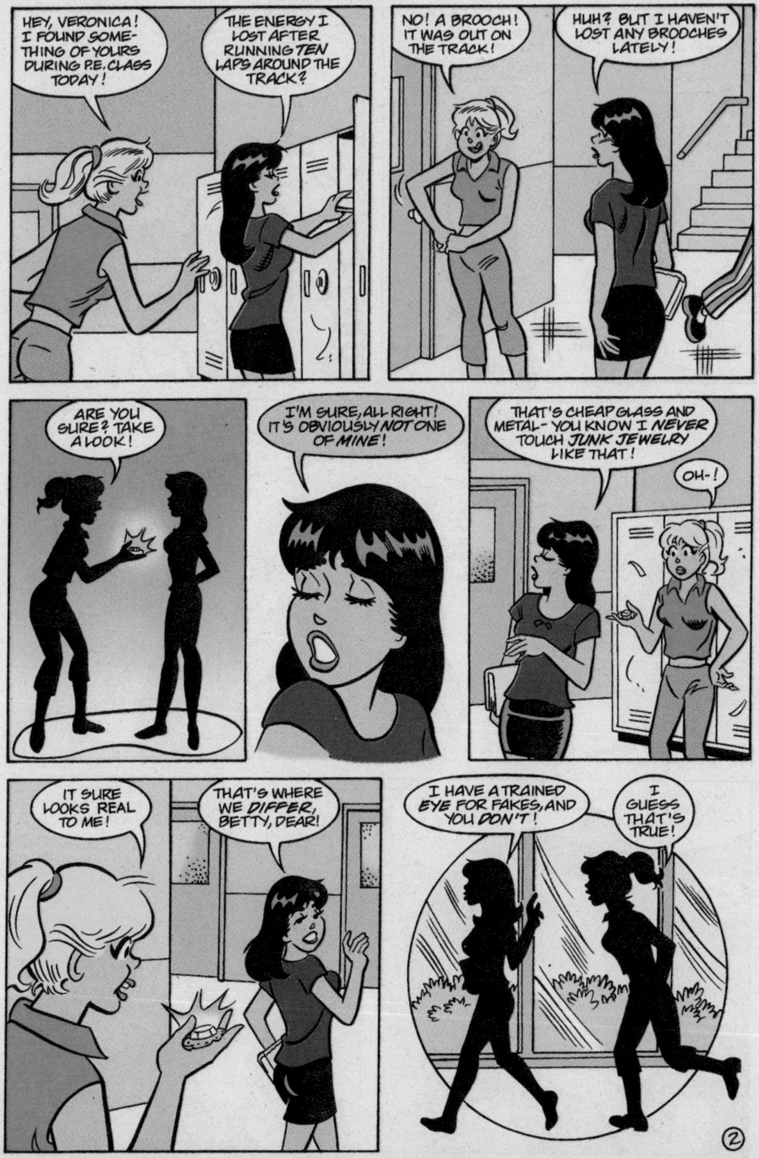
HEY, VERONICA! I FOUND SOMETHING OF YOURS DURING P.E. CLASS TODAY!
THE ENERGY I LOST AFTER RUNNING TEN LAPS AROUND THE TRACK?
NO! A BROOCH! IT WAS OUT ON THE TRACK!
HUH? BUT I HAVEN'T LOST ANY BROOCHES LATELY!
ARE YOU SURE? TAKE A LOOK!
I'M SURE, ALL RIGHT! IT'S OBVIOUSLY NOT ONE OF MINE!
THAT'S CHEAP GLASS AND METAL- YOU KNOW I NEVER TOUCH JUNK JEWELRY LIKE THAT!
OH-!
IT SURE LOOKS REAL TO ME!
THAT'S WHERE WE DIFFER, BETTY, DEAR!
I HAVE A TRAINED EYE FOR FAKES, AND YOU DON'T!
I GUESS THAT'S TRUE!

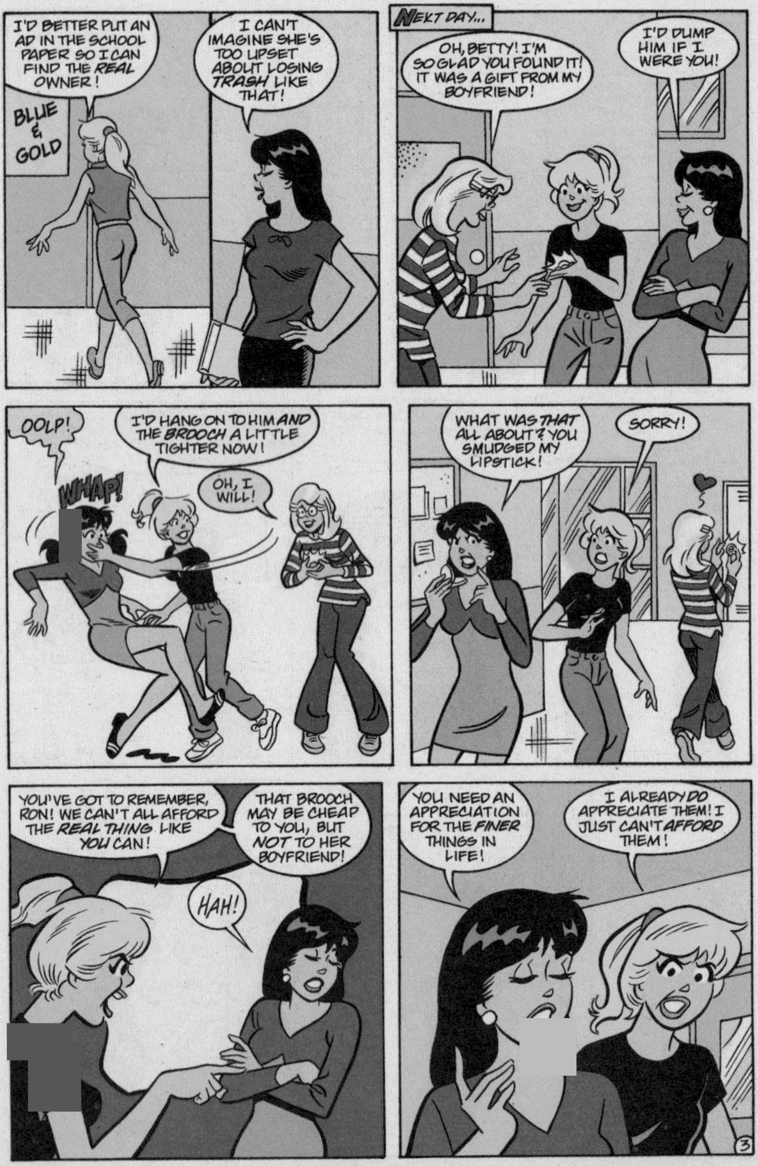
I'D BETTER PUT AN AD IN THE SCHOOL PAPER SO I CAN FIND THE REAL OWNER!
BLUE & GOLD
I CAN'T IMAGINE SHE'S TOO UPSET ABOUT LOSING TRASH LIKE THAT!
NEXT DAY...
OH, BETTY! I'M SO GLAD YOU FOUND IT! IT WAS A GIFT FROM MY BOYFRIEND!
I'D DUMP HIM IF I WERE YOU!
OOLP!
WHAP!
I'D HANG ON TO HIM AND THE BROOCH A LITTLE TIGHTER NOW!
OH, I WILL!
WHAT WAS THAT ALL ABOUT? YOU SMUDGED MY LIPSTICK!
SORRY!
YOU'VE GOT TO REMEMBER, RON! WE CAN'T ALL AFFORD THE REAL THING LIKE YOU CAN!
THAT BROOCH MAY BE CHEAP TO YOU, BUT NOT TO HER BOYFRIEND!
HAH!
YOU NEED AN APPRECIATION FOR THE FINER THINGS IN LIFE!
I ALREADY DO APPRECIATE THEM! I JUST CAN'T AFFORD THEM!
3

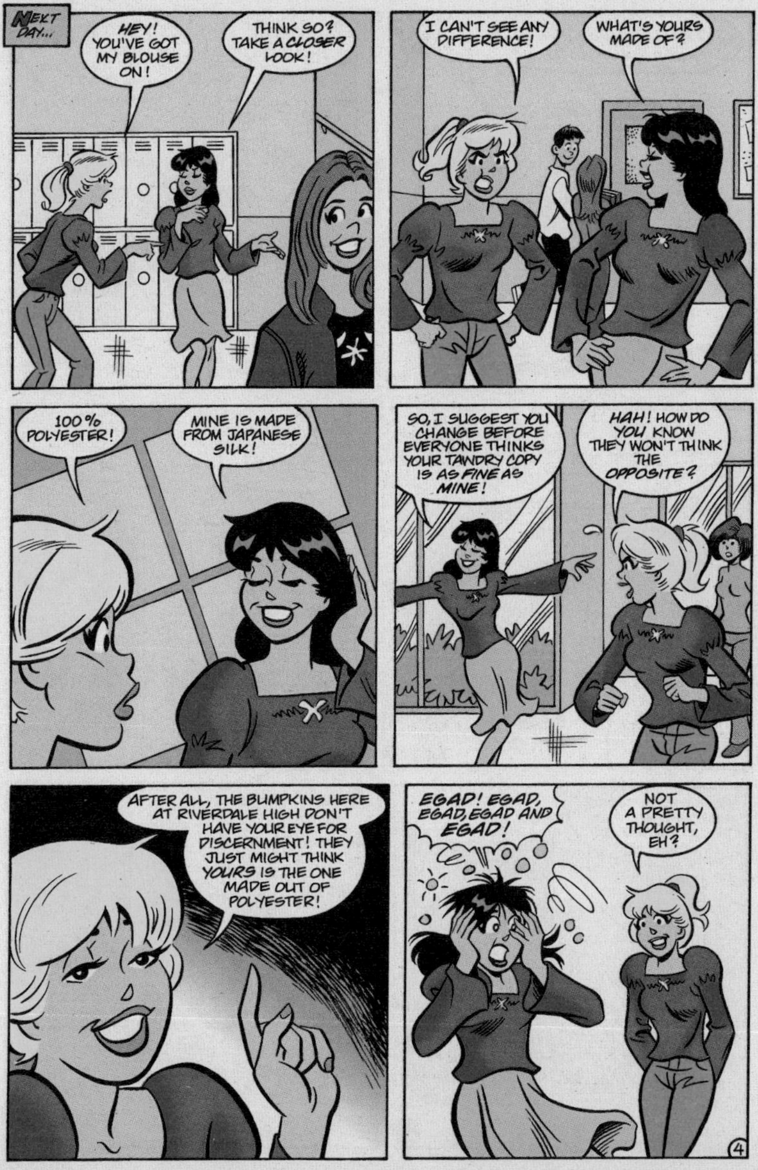
NEXT DAY...
HEY! YOU'VE GOT MY BLOUSE ON!
THINK SO? TAKE A CLOSER LOOK!
I CAN'T SEE ANY DIFFERENCE!
WHAT'S YOURS MADE OF?
100% POLYESTER!
MINE IS MADE FROM JAPANESE SILK!
SO, I SUGGEST YOU CHANGE BEFORE EVERYONE THINKS YOUR TAWDRY COPY IS AS FINE AS MINE!
HAH! HOW DO YOU KNOW THEY WON'T THINK THE OPPOSITE?
AFTER ALL, THE BUMPKINS HERE AT RIVERDALE HIGH DON'T HAVE YOUR EYE FOR DISCERNMENT! THEY JUST MIGHT THINK YOURS IS THE ONE MADE OUT OF POLYESTER!
EGAD! EGAD, EGAD, EGAD AND EGAD!
NOT A PRETTY THOUGHT, EH?
4

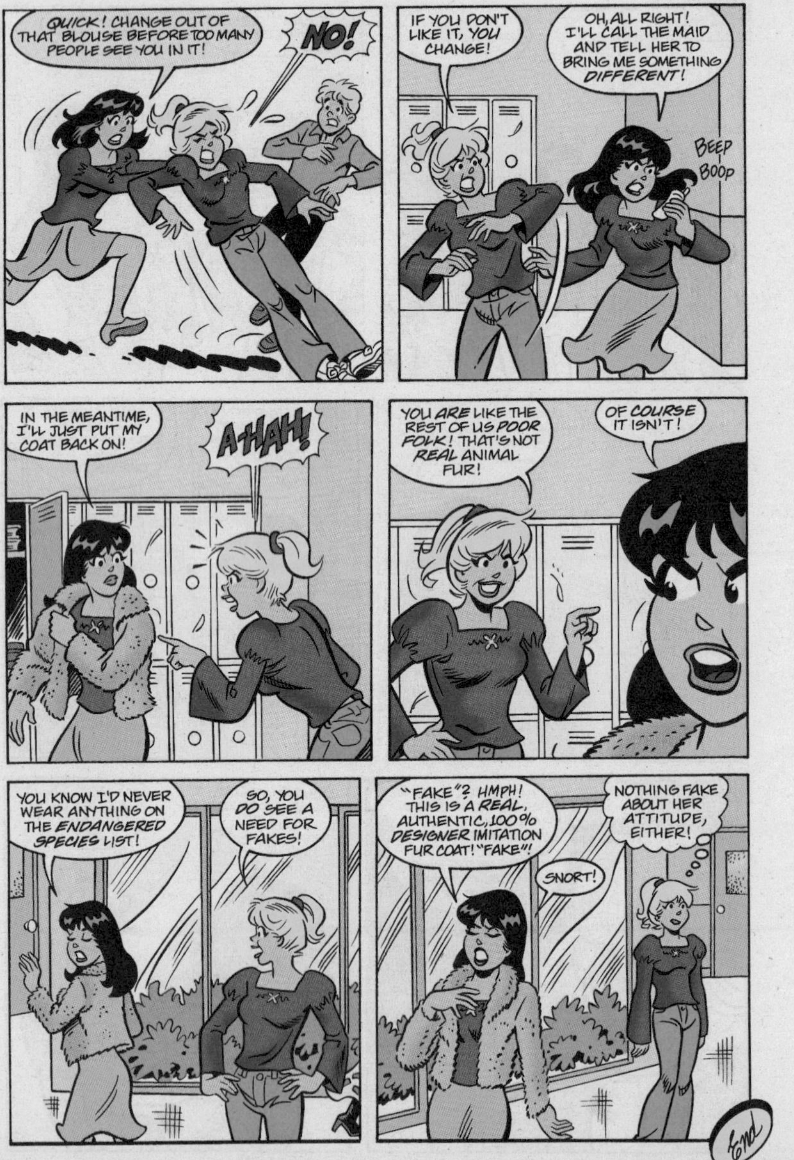
QUICK! CHANGE OUT OF THAT BLOUSE BEFORE TOO MANY PEOPLE SEE YOU IN IT!
NO!
IF YOU DON'T LIKE IT, YOU CHANGE!
OH, ALL RIGHT! I'LL CALL THE MAID AND TELL HER TO BRING ME SOMETHING DIFFERENT!
BEEP
BOOP
IN THE MEANTIME, I'LL JUST PUT MY COAT BACK ON!
A-HAH!
YOU ARE LIKE THE REST OF US POOR FOLK! THAT'S NOT REAL ANIMAL FUR!
OF COURSE IT ISN'T!
YOU KNOW I'D NEVER WEAR ANYTHING ON THE ENDANGERED SPECIES LIST!
SO, YOU DO SEE A NEED FOR FAKES!
"FAKE"? HMPH! THIS IS A REAL, AUTHENTIC, 100% DESIGNER IMITATION FUR COAT! "FAKE"!
SNORT!
NOTHING FAKE ABOUT HER ATTITUDE, EITHER!
End

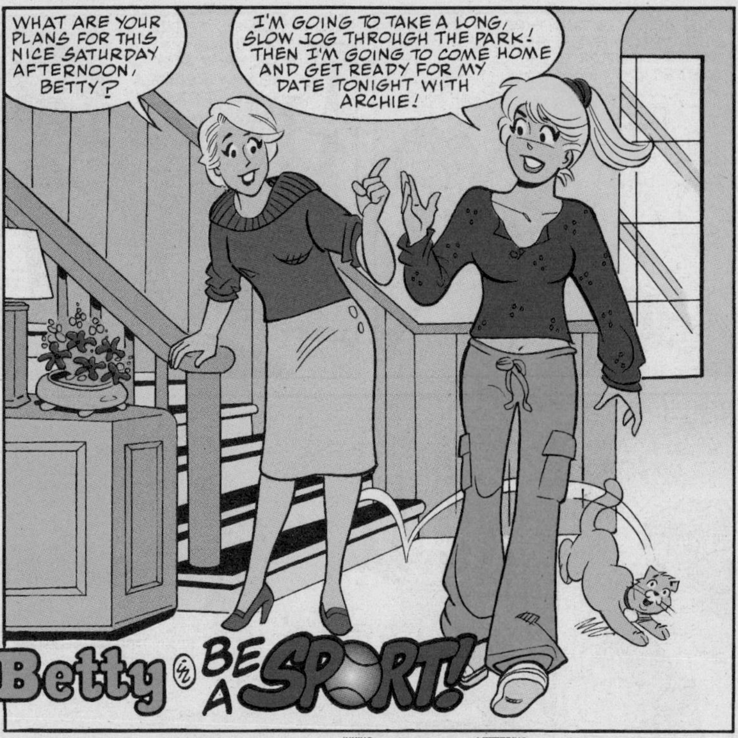
WHAT ARE YOUR PLANS FOR THIS NICE SATURDAY AFTERNOON, BETTY?
I'M GOING TO TAKE A LONG, SLOW JOG THROUGH THE PARK! THEN I'M GOING TO COME HOME AND GET READY FOR MY DATE TONIGHT WITH ARCHIE!
Betty
BE A SPORT!

SCRIPT: MIKE PELLOWSKI | PENCILS: STAN GOLDBERG | INKING: JOHN LOWE | LETTERING: JACK MORELLI | COLORING: BARRY GROSSMAN

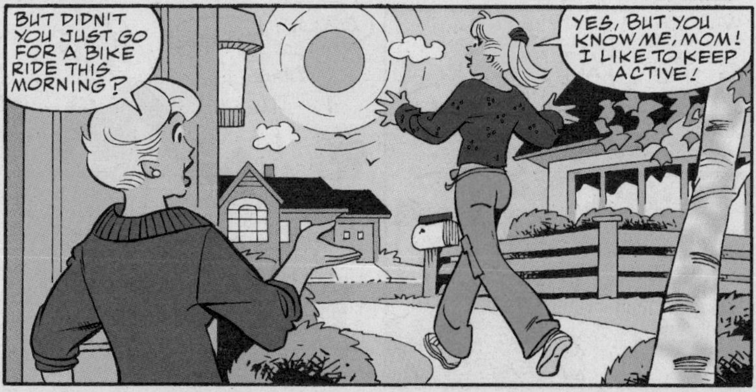
BUT DIDN'T YOU JUST GO FOR A BIKE RIDE THIS MORNING?
YES, BUT YOU KNOW ME, MOM! I LIKE TO KEEP ACTIVE!

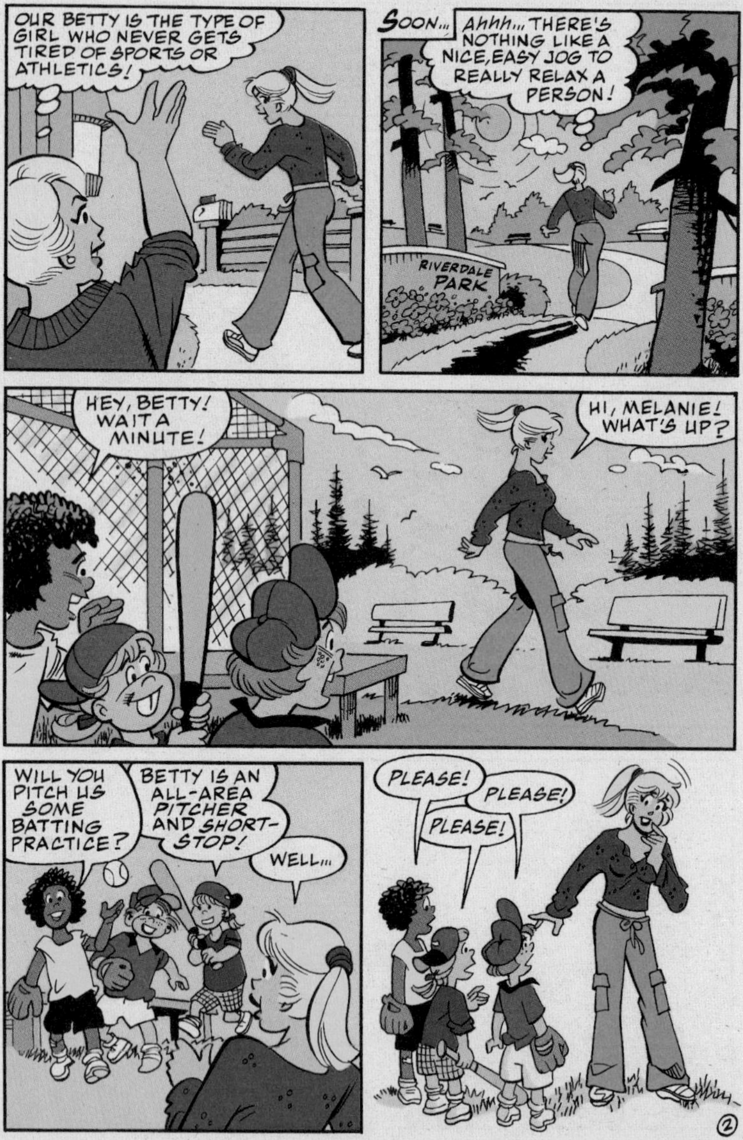

OUR BETTY IS THE TYPE OF GIRL WHO NEVER GETS TIRED OF SPORTS OR ATHLETICS!
SOON...
Ahhh... THERE'S NOTHING LIKE A NICE, EASY JOG TO REALLY RELAX A PERSON!
RIVERDALE PARK
HEY, BETTY! WAIT A MINUTE!
HI, MELANIE! WHAT'S UP?
WILL YOU PITCH US SOME BATTING PRACTICE?
BETTY IS AN ALL-AREA PITCHER AND SHORT-STOP!
WELL...
PLEASE!
PLEASE!
PLEASE!

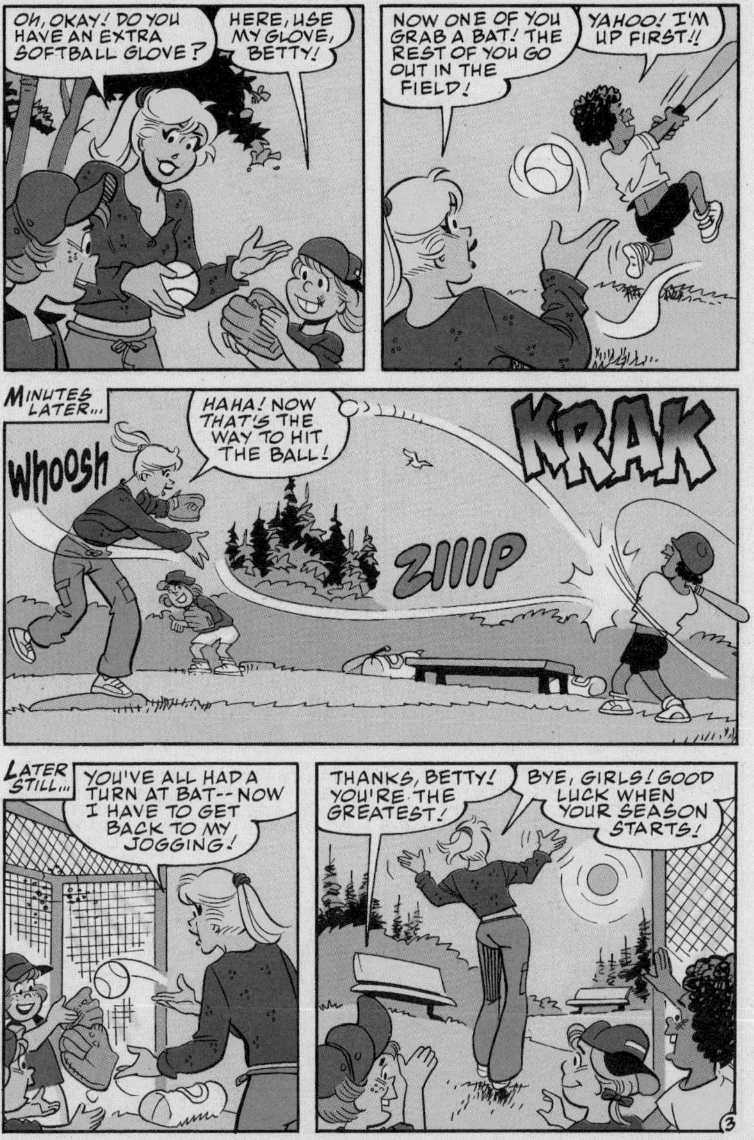
OH, OKAY! DO YOU HAVE AN EXTRA SOFTBALL GLOVE?
HERE, USE MY GLOVE, BETTY!
NOW ONE OF YOU GRAB A BAT! THE REST OF YOU GO OUT IN THE FIELD!
YAHOO! I'M UP FIRST!!
MINUTES LATER...
HAHA! NOW THAT'S THE WAY TO HIT THE BALL!
WHOOSH
KRAK
ZIIIP
LATER STILL...
YOU'VE ALL HAD A TURN AT BAT--NOW I HAVE TO GET BACK TO MY JOGGING!
THANKS, BETTY! YOU'RE THE GREATEST!
BYE, GIRLS! GOOD LUCK WHEN YOUR SEASON STARTS!

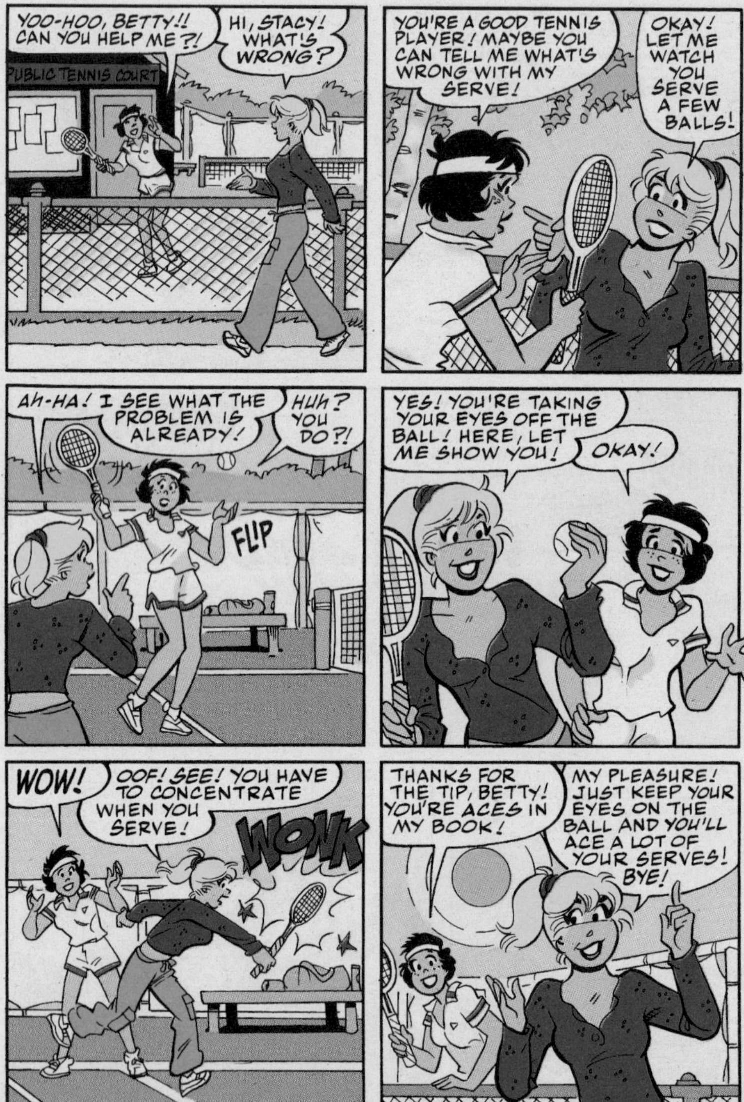
YOO-HOO, BETTY!! CAN YOU HELP ME?!
HI, STACY! WHAT'S WRONG?
PUBLIC TENNIS COURT
YOU'RE A GOOD TENNIS PLAYER! MAYBE YOU CAN TELL ME WHAT'S WRONG WITH MY SERVE!
OKAY! LET ME WATCH YOU SERVE A FEW BALLS!
AH-HA! I SEE WHAT THE PROBLEM IS ALREADY!
HUH? YOU DO?!
FLIP
YES! YOU'RE TAKING YOUR EYES OFF THE BALL! HERE, LET ME SHOW YOU!
OKAY!
WOW!
OOF! SEE! YOU HAVE TO CONCENTRATE WHEN YOU SERVE!
WONK
THANKS FOR THE TIP, BETTY! YOU'RE ACES IN MY BOOK!
MY PLEASURE! JUST KEEP YOUR EYES ON THE BALL AND YOU'LL ACE A LOT OF YOUR SERVES! BYE!

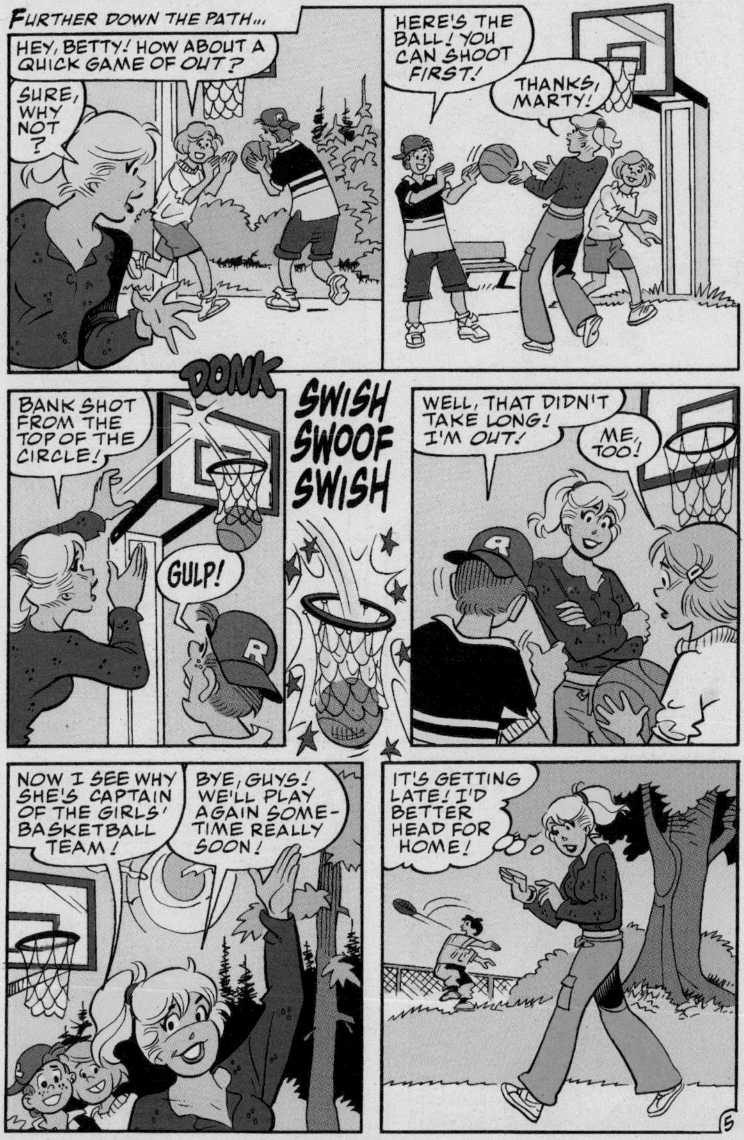

FURTHER DOWN THE PATH...
HEY, BETTY! HOW ABOUT A QUICK GAME OF OUT?
SURE, WHY NOT?
HERE'S THE BALL! YOU CAN SHOOT FIRST!
THANKS, MARTY!
DONK
BANK SHOT FROM THE TOP OF THE CIRCLE!
GULP!
SWISH SWOOF SWISH
WELL, THAT DIDN'T TAKE LONG! I'M OUT!
ME, TOO!
NOW I SEE WHY SHE'S CAPTAIN OF THE GIRLS' BASKETBALL TEAM!
BYE, GUYS! WE'LL PLAY AGAIN SOMETIME REALLY SOON!
IT'S GETTING LATE! I'D BETTER HEAD FOR HOME!
5

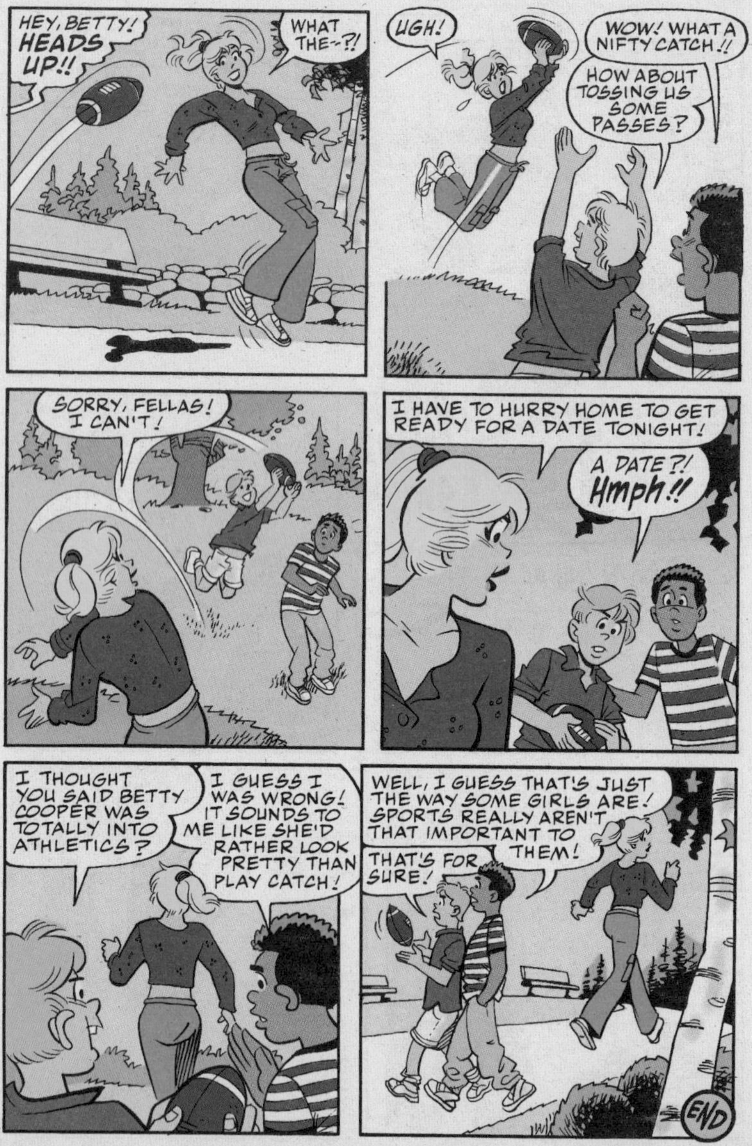

HEY, BETTY! HEADS UP!!
WHAT THE-?!
UGH!
WOW! WHAT A NIFTY CATCH!!
HOW ABOUT TOSSING US SOME PASSES?
SORRY, FELLAS! I CAN'T!
I HAVE TO HURRY HOME TO GET READY FOR A DATE TONIGHT!
A DATE?! Hmph!!
I THOUGHT YOU SAID BETTY COOPER WAS TOTALLY INTO ATHLETICS?
I GUESS I WAS WRONG! IT SOUNDS TO ME LIKE SHE'D RATHER LOOK PRETTY THAN PLAY CATCH!
WELL, I GUESS THAT'S JUST THE WAY SOME GIRLS ARE! SPORTS REALLY AREN'T THAT IMPORTANT TO THEM!
THAT'S FOR SURE!
END

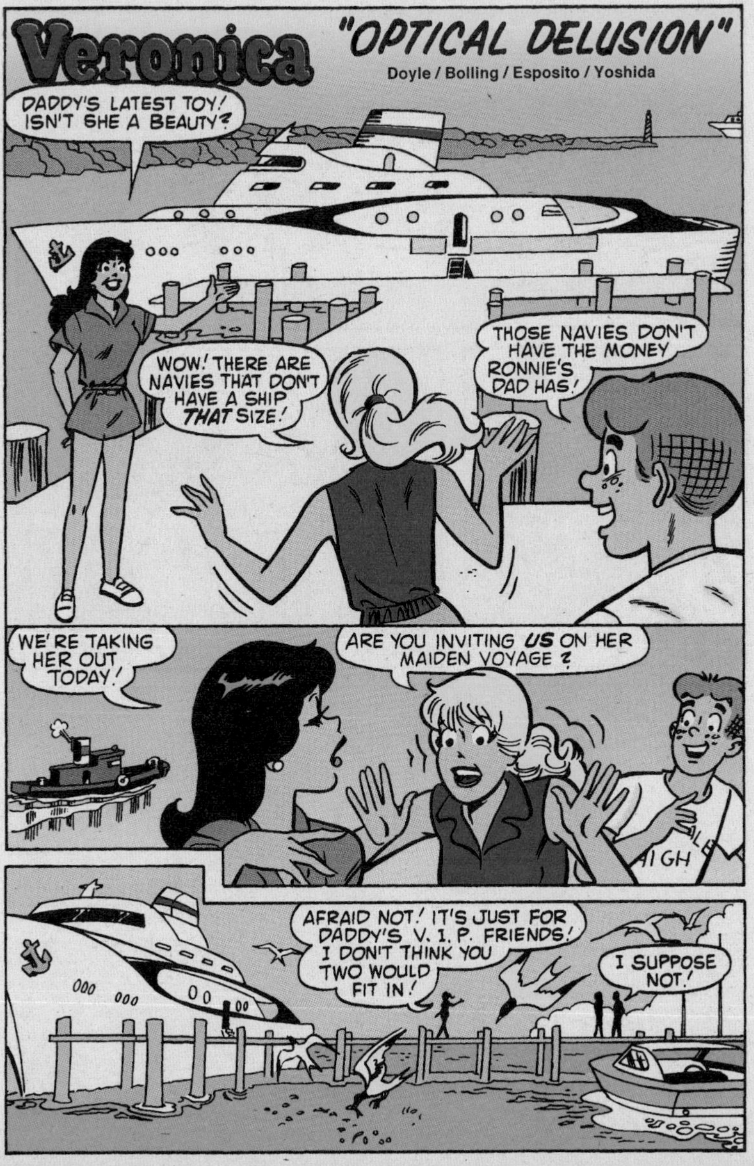
Veronica
"OPTICAL DELUSION"
Doyle / Bolling / Esposito / Yoshida
DADDY'S LATEST TOY! ISN'T SHE A BEAUTY?
WOW! THERE ARE NAVIES THAT DON'T HAVE A SHIP THAT SIZE!
THOSE NAVIES DON'T HAVE THE MONEY RONNIE'S DAD HAS!
WE'RE TAKING HER OUT TODAY!
ARE YOU INVITING US ON HER MAIDEN VOYAGE?
AFRAID NOT! IT'S JUST FOR DADDY'S V. I. P. FRIENDS! I DON'T THINK YOU TWO WOULD FIT IN!
I SUPPOSE NOT!

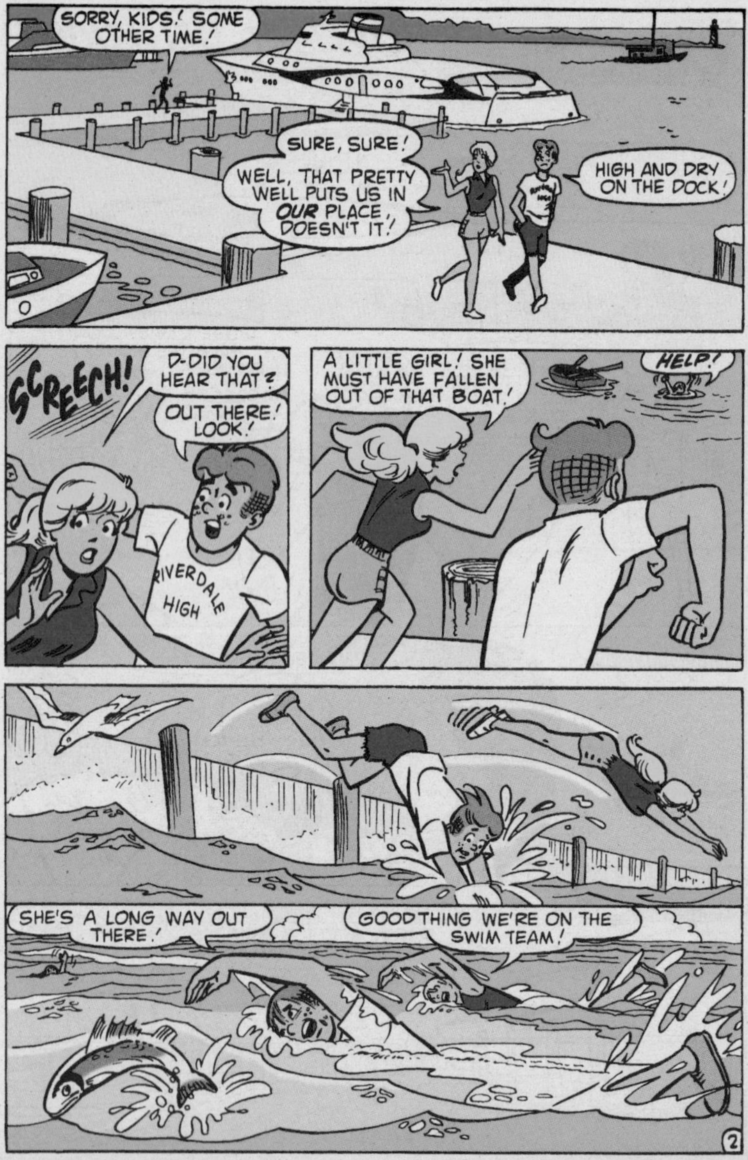
SORRY, KIDS! SOME OTHER TIME!
SURE, SURE!
WELL, THAT PRETTY WELL PUTS US IN OUR PLACE, DOESN'T IT!
HIGH AND DRY ON THE DOCK!
SCREECH!
D-DID YOU HEAR THAT?
OUT THERE! LOOK!
RIVERDALE HIGH
A LITTLE GIRL! SHE MUST HAVE FALLEN OUT OF THAT BOAT!
HELP!
SHE'S A LONG WAY OUT THERE!
GOOD THING WE'RE ON THE SWIM TEAM!
2

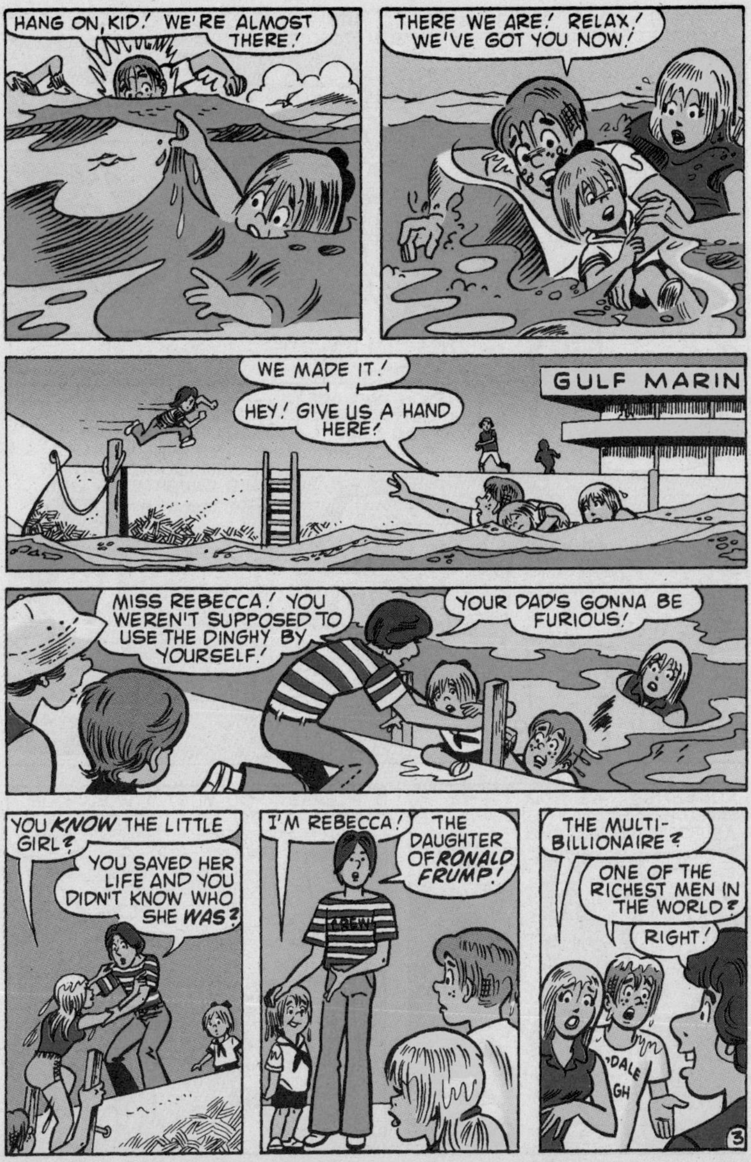

HANG ON, KID! WE'RE ALMOST THERE!
THERE WE ARE! RELAX! WE'VE GOT YOU NOW!
WE MADE IT!
HEY! GIVE US A HAND HERE!
GULF MARIN
MISS REBECCA! YOU WEREN'T SUPPOSED TO USE THE DINGHY BY YOURSELF!
YOUR DAD'S GONNA BE FURIOUS!
YOU KNOW THE LITTLE GIRL?
YOU SAVED HER LIFE AND YOU DIDN'T KNOW WHO SHE WAS?
I'M REBECCA!
THE DAUGHTER OF RONALD FRUMP!
CREW
THE MULTI-BILLIONAIRE?
ONE OF THE RICHEST MEN IN THE WORLD?
RIGHT!
3

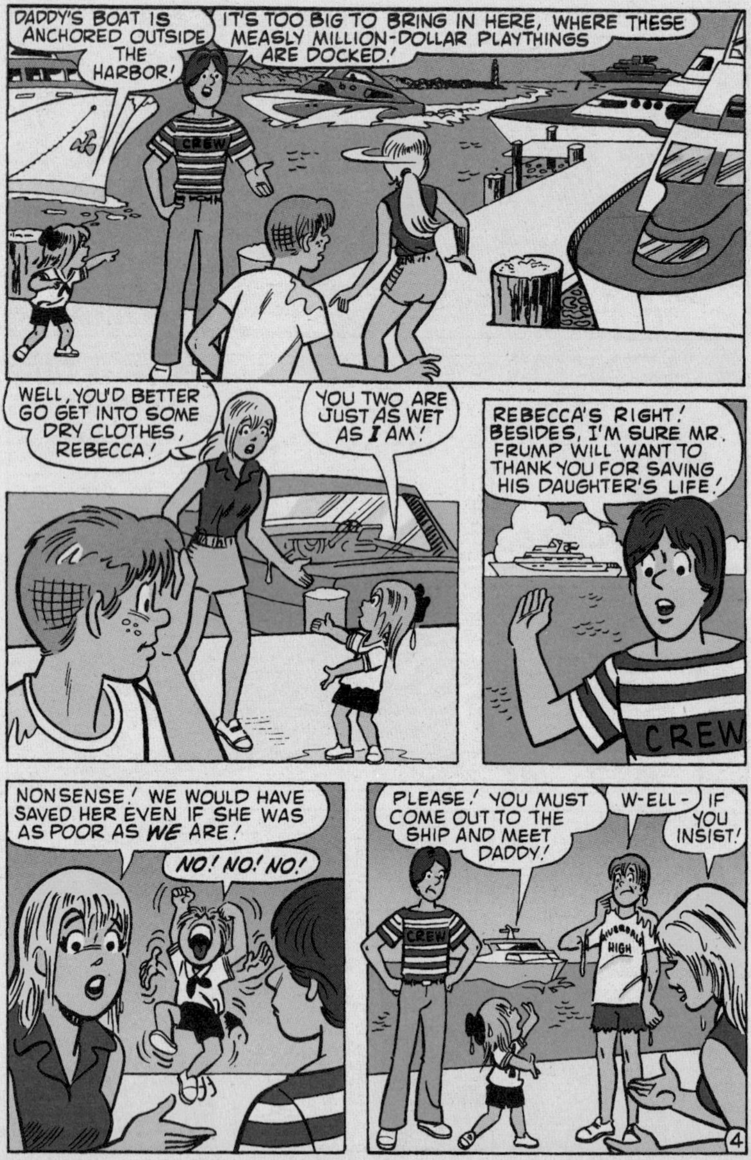
DADDY'S BOAT IS ANCHORED OUTSIDE THE HARBOR!
IT'S TOO BIG TO BRING IN HERE, WHERE THESE MEASLY MILLION-DOLLAR PLAYTHINGS ARE DOCKED!
CREW
WELL, YOU'D BETTER GO GET INTO SOME DRY CLOTHES, REBECCA!
YOU TWO ARE JUST AS WET AS I AM!
REBECCA'S RIGHT! BESIDES, I'M SURE MR. FRUMP WILL WANT TO THANK YOU FOR SAVING HIS DAUGHTER'S LIFE!
CREW
NONSENSE! WE WOULD HAVE SAVED HER EVEN IF SHE WAS AS POOR AS WE ARE!
NO! NO! NO!
PLEASE! YOU MUST COME OUT TO THE SHIP AND MEET DADDY!
W-ELL -
IF YOU INSIST!
CREW
RIVERDALE HIGH
4

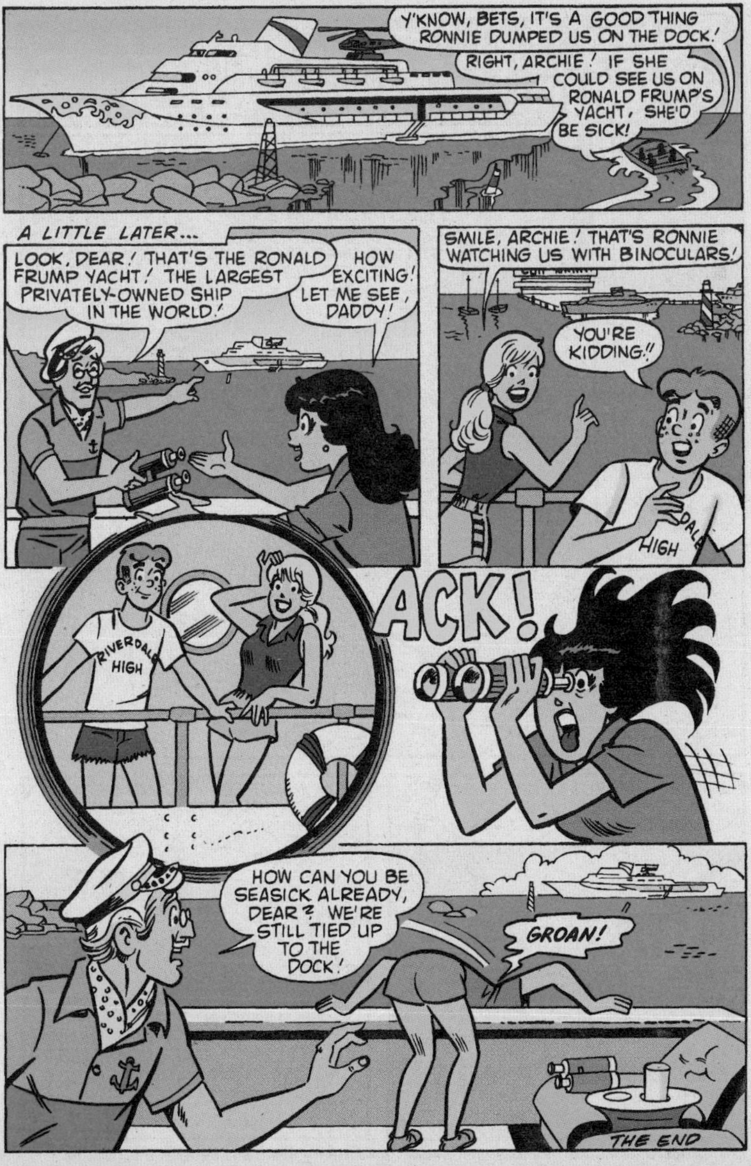

Y'KNOW, BETS, IT'S A GOOD THING RONNIE DUMPED US ON THE DOCK!
RIGHT, ARCHIE! IF SHE COULD SEE US ON RONALD FRUMP'S YACHT, SHE'D BE SICK!
A LITTLE LATER...
LOOK, DEAR! THAT'S THE RONALD FRUMP YACHT! THE LARGEST PRIVATELY-OWNED SHIP IN THE WORLD!
HOW EXCITING! LET ME SEE, DADDY!
SMILE, ARCHIE! THAT'S RONNIE WATCHING US WITH BINOCULARS!
YOU'RE KIDDING!!
RIVERDALE HIGH
ACK!
HOW CAN YOU BE SEASICK ALREADY, DEAR? WE'RE STILL TIED UP TO THE DOCK!
GROAN!
THE END

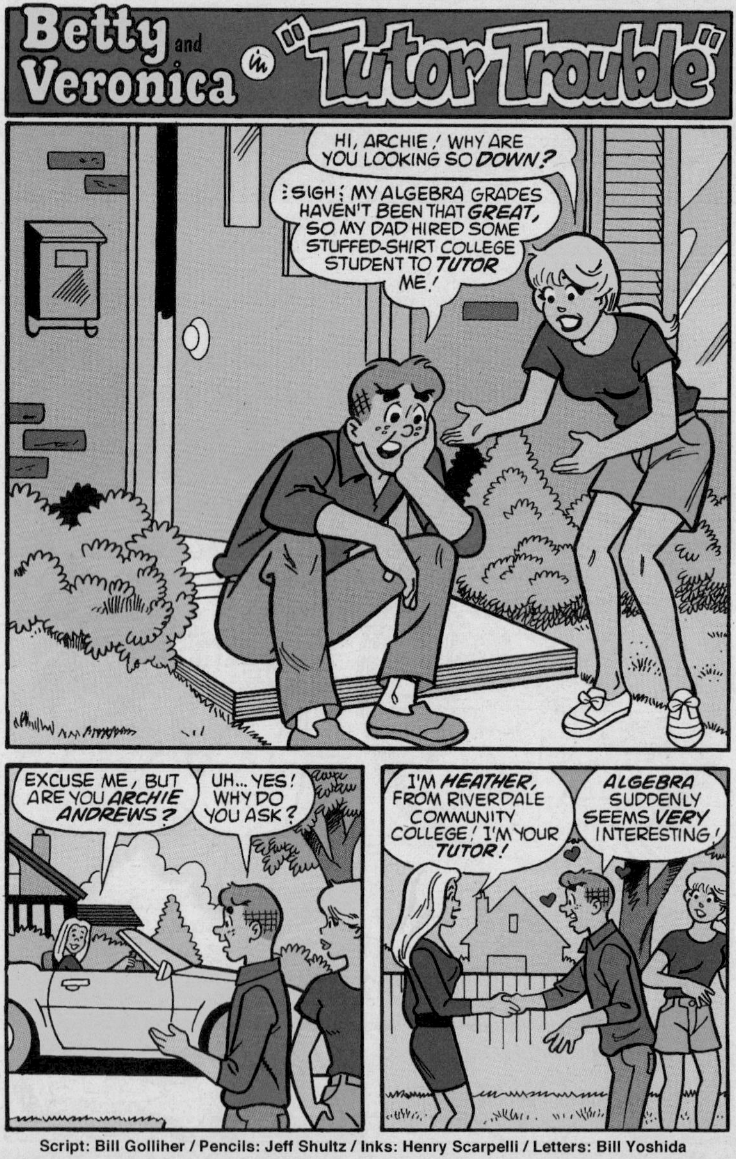
Betty and Veronica in "Tutor Trouble"
HI, ARCHIE! WHY ARE YOU LOOKING SO DOWN?
:SIGH: MY ALGEBRA GRADES HAVEN'T BEEN THAT GREAT, SO MY DAD HIRED SOME STUFFED-SHIRT COLLEGE STUDENT TO TUTOR ME!
EXCUSE ME, BUT ARE YOU ARCHIE ANDREWS?
UH... YES! WHY DO YOU ASK?
I'M HEATHER, FROM RIVERDALE COMMUNITY COLLEGE! I'M YOUR TUTOR!
ALGEBRA SUDDENLY SEEMS VERY INTERESTING!

Script: Bill Golliher / Pencils: Jeff Shultz / Inks: Henry Scarpelli / Letters: Bill Yoshida

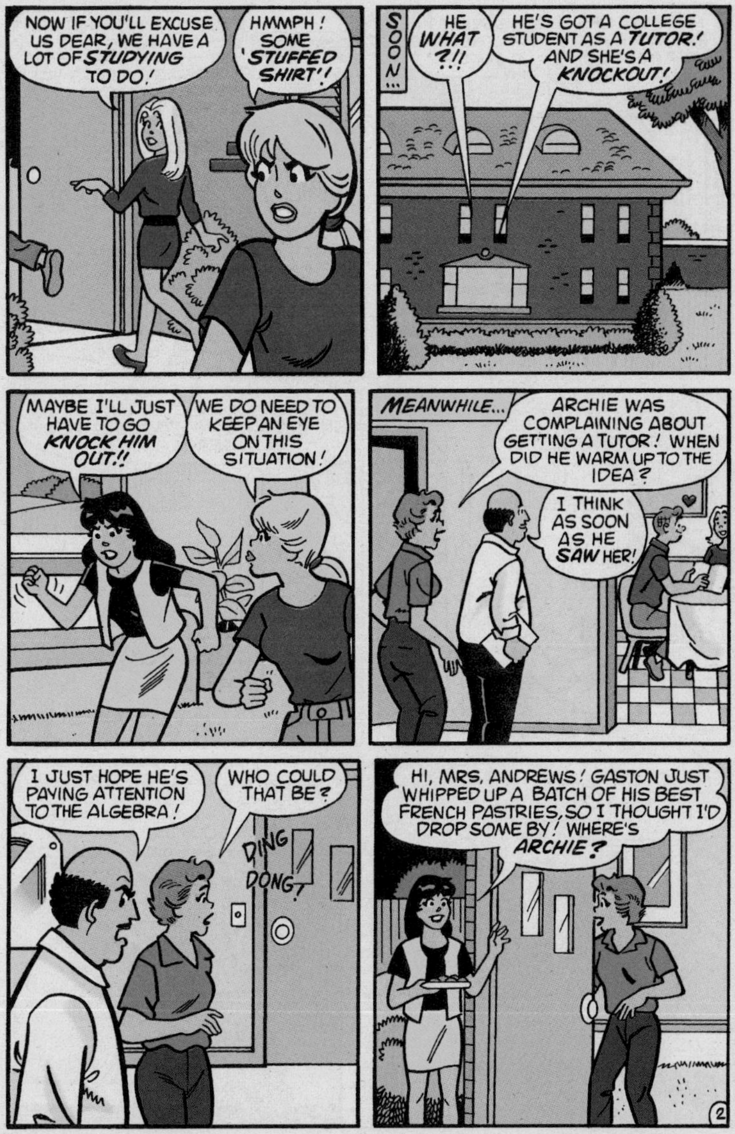
NOW IF YOU'LL EXCUSE US DEAR, WE HAVE A LOT OF STUDYING TO DO!
HMMPH! SOME 'STUFFED SHIRT'!
SOON...
HE WHAT ?!!
HE'S GOT A COLLEGE STUDENT AS A TUTOR! AND SHE'S A KNOCKOUT!
MAYBE I'LL JUST HAVE TO GO KNOCK HIM OUT!!
WE DO NEED TO KEEP AN EYE ON THIS SITUATION!
MEANWHILE...
ARCHIE WAS COMPLAINING ABOUT GETTING A TUTOR! WHEN DID HE WARM UP TO THE IDEA?
I THINK AS SOON AS HE SAW HER!
I JUST HOPE HE'S PAYING ATTENTION TO THE ALGEBRA!
WHO COULD THAT BE?
DING DONG
HI, MRS. ANDREWS! GASTON JUST WHIPPED UP A BATCH OF HIS BEST FRENCH PASTRIES, SO I THOUGHT I'D DROP SOME BY! WHERE'S ARCHIE?
2

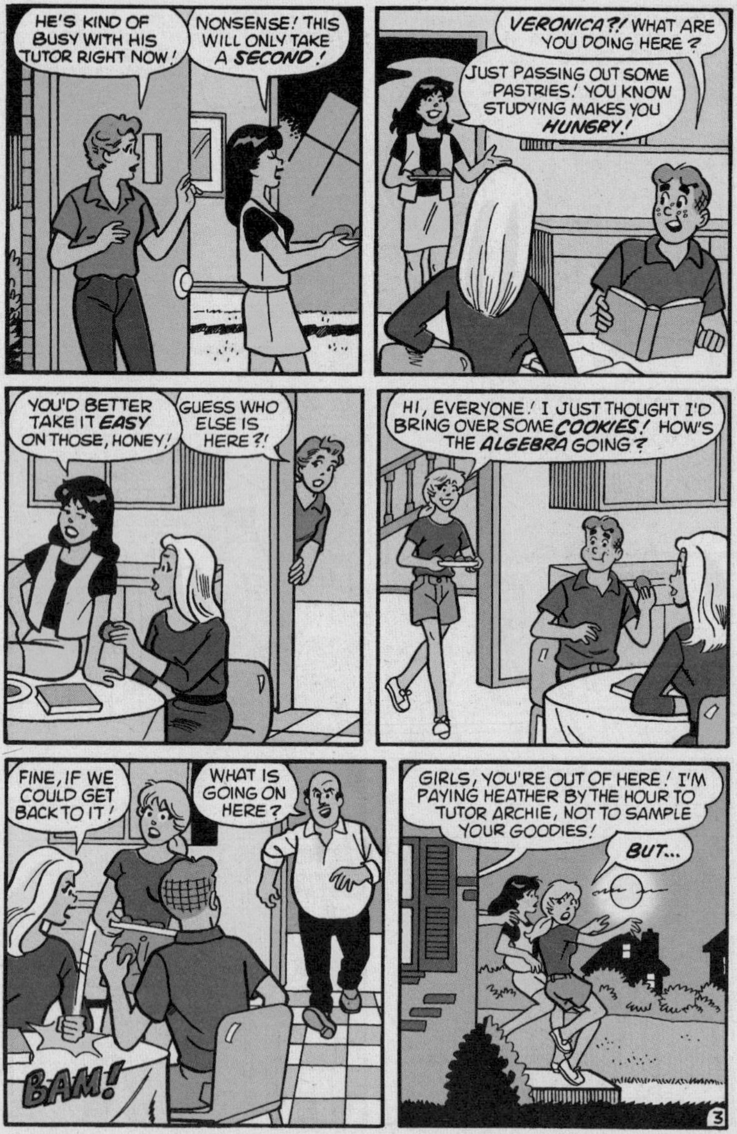
HE'S KIND OF BUSY WITH HIS TUTOR RIGHT NOW!
NONSENSE! THIS WILL ONLY TAKE A SECOND!
VERONICA?! WHAT ARE YOU DOING HERE?
JUST PASSING OUT SOME PASTRIES! YOU KNOW STUDYING MAKES YOU HUNGRY!
YOU'D BETTER TAKE IT EASY ON THOSE, HONEY!
GUESS WHO ELSE IS HERE?!
HI, EVERYONE! I JUST THOUGHT I'D BRING OVER SOME COOKIES! HOW'S THE ALGEBRA GOING?
FINE, IF WE COULD GET BACK TO IT!
BAM!
WHAT IS GOING ON HERE?
GIRLS, YOU'RE OUT OF HERE! I'M PAYING HEATHER BY THE HOUR TO TUTOR ARCHIE, NOT TO SAMPLE YOUR GOODIES!
BUT...

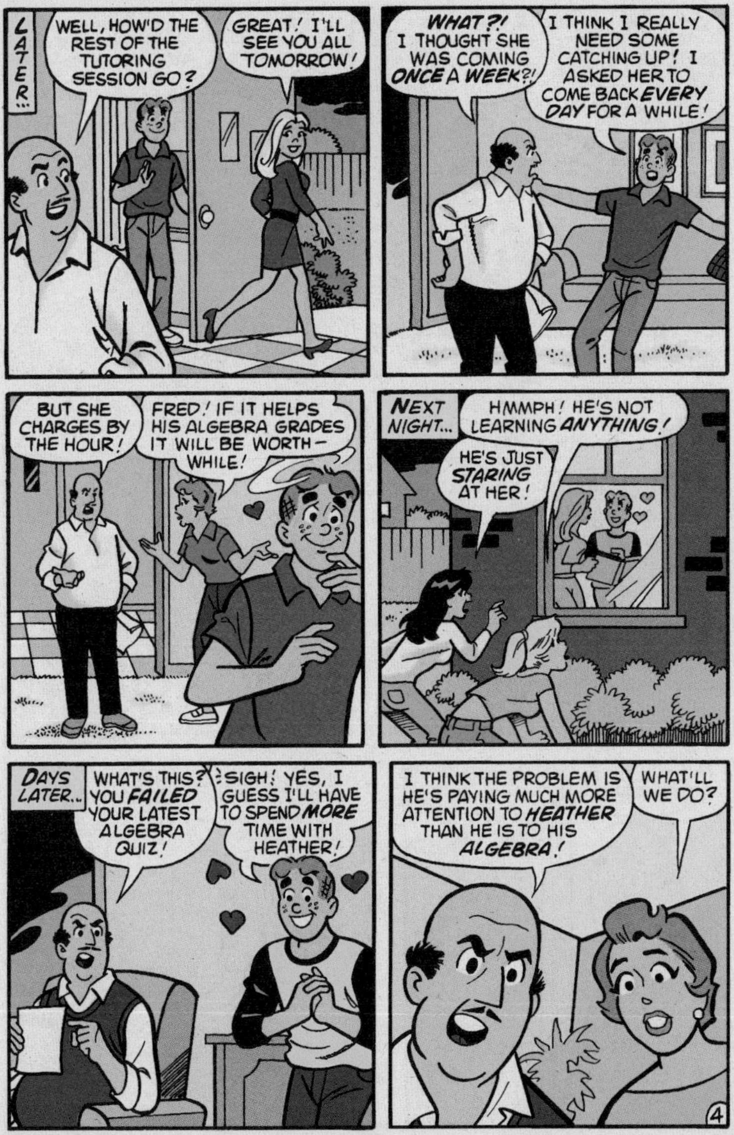
LATER...
WELL, HOW'D THE REST OF THE TUTORING SESSION GO?
GREAT! I'LL SEE YOU ALL TOMORROW!
WHAT?! I THOUGHT SHE WAS COMING ONCE A WEEK?!
I THINK I REALLY NEED SOME CATCHING UP! I ASKED HER TO COME BACK EVERY DAY FOR A WHILE!
BUT SHE CHARGES BY THE HOUR!
FRED! IF IT HELPS HIS ALGEBRA GRADES IT WILL BE WORTH-WHILE!
NEXT NIGHT...
HMMPH! HE'S NOT LEARNING ANYTHING!
HE'S JUST STARING AT HER!
DAYS LATER...
WHAT'S THIS? YOU FAILED YOUR LATEST ALGEBRA QUIZ!
SIGH! YES, I GUESS I'LL HAVE TO SPEND MORE TIME WITH HEATHER!
I THINK THE PROBLEM IS HE'S PAYING MUCH MORE ATTENTION TO HEATHER THAN HE IS TO HIS ALGEBRA!
WHAT'LL WE DO?
4

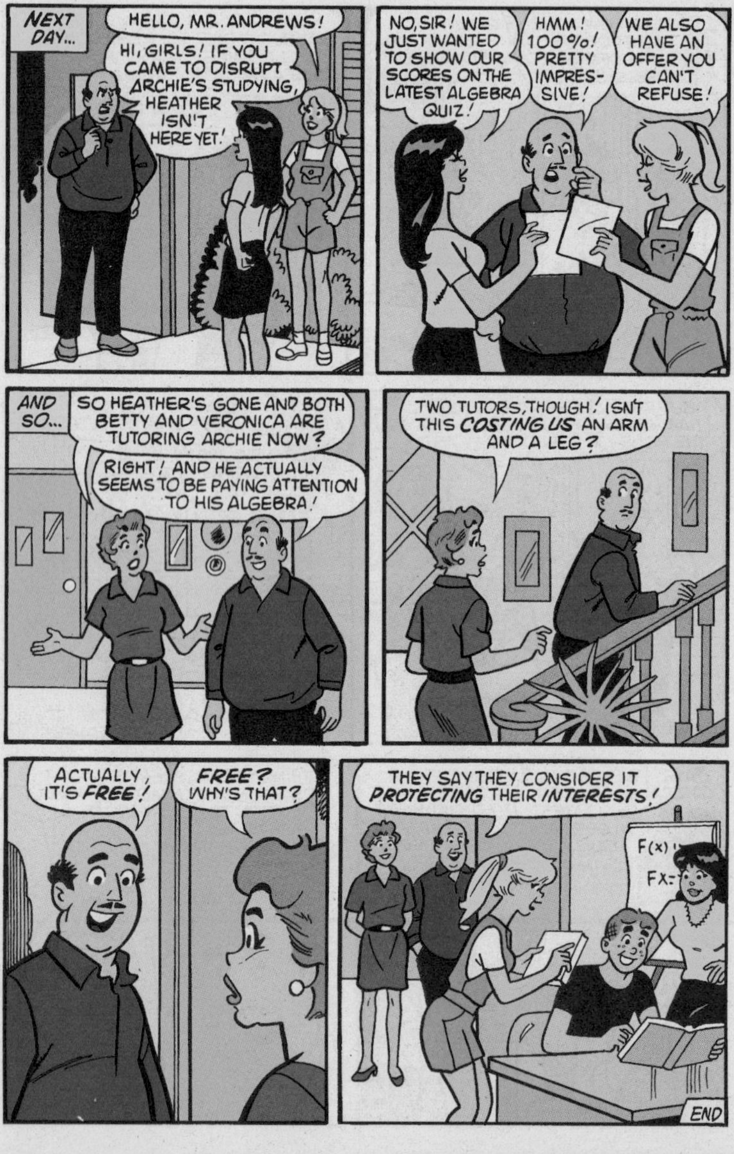
NEXT DAY...
HELLO, MR. ANDREWS!
HI, GIRLS! IF YOU CAME TO DISRUPT ARCHIE'S STUDYING, HEATHER ISN'T HERE YET!
NO, SIR! WE JUST WANTED TO SHOW OUR SCORES ON THE LATEST ALGEBRA QUIZ!
HMM! 100%! PRETTY IMPRES-SIVE!
WE ALSO HAVE AN OFFER YOU CAN'T REFUSE!
AND SO...
SO HEATHER'S GONE AND BOTH BETTY AND VERONICA ARE TUTORING ARCHIE NOW?
RIGHT! AND HE ACTUALLY SEEMS TO BE PAYING ATTENTION TO HIS ALGEBRA!
TWO TUTORS, THOUGH! ISN'T THIS COSTING US AN ARM AND A LEG?
ACTUALLY, IT'S FREE!
FREE? WHY'S THAT?
THEY SAY THEY CONSIDER IT PROTECTING THEIR INTERESTS!
END

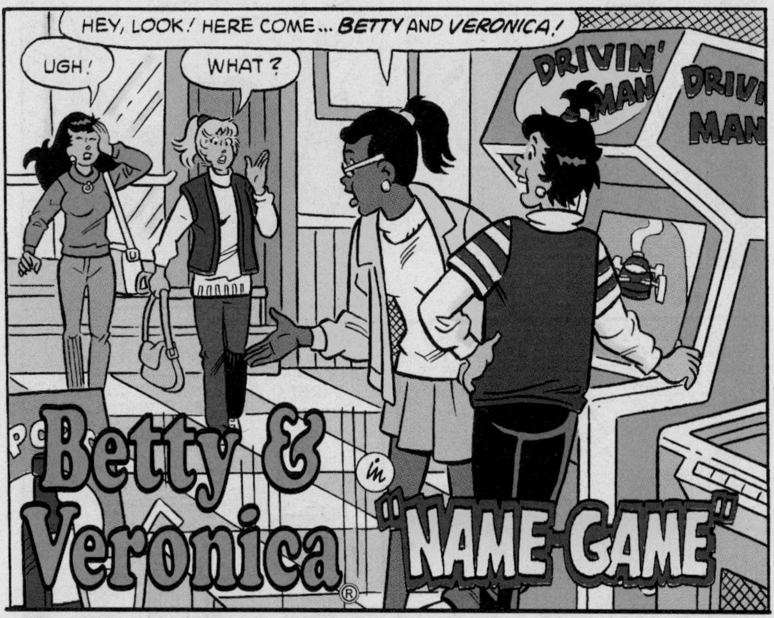
HEY, LOOK! HERE COME... BETTY AND VERONICA!
UGH!
WHAT?
DRIVIN' MAN
DRIVIN' MAN
Betty & Veronica
in
"NAME GAME"

SCRIPT: MIKE PELLOWSKI PENCILS: TIM KENNEDY INKS: RUDY LAPICK
COLORS: BARRY GROSSMAN LETTERS: BILL YOSHIDA

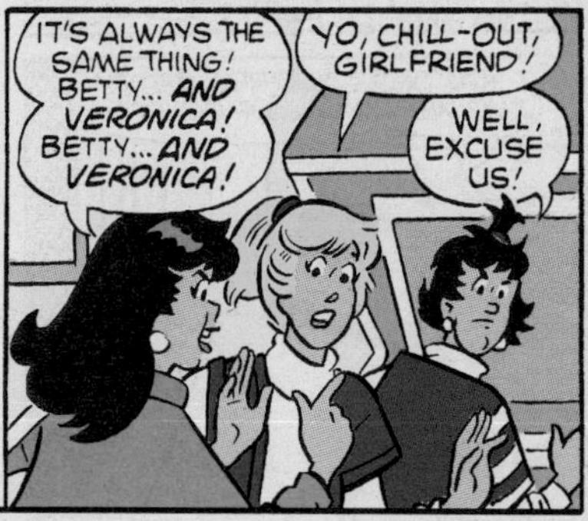
IT'S ALWAYS THE SAME THING! BETTY... AND VERONICA! BETTY... AND VERONICA!
YO, CHILL-OUT, GIRLFRIEND!
WELL, EXCUSE US!

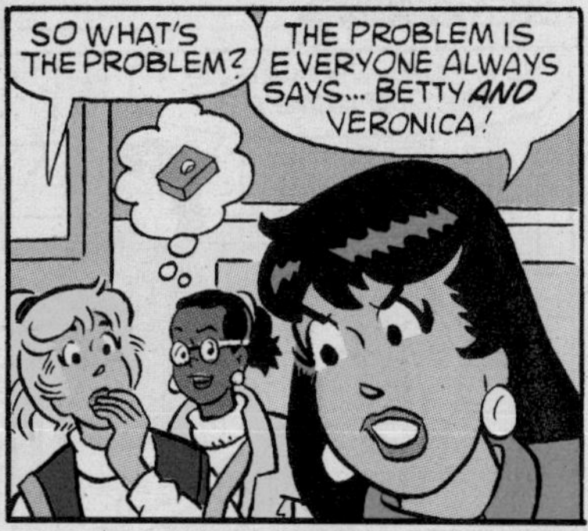
SO WHAT'S THE PROBLEM?
THE PROBLEM IS EVERYONE ALWAYS SAYS... BETTY AND VERONICA!

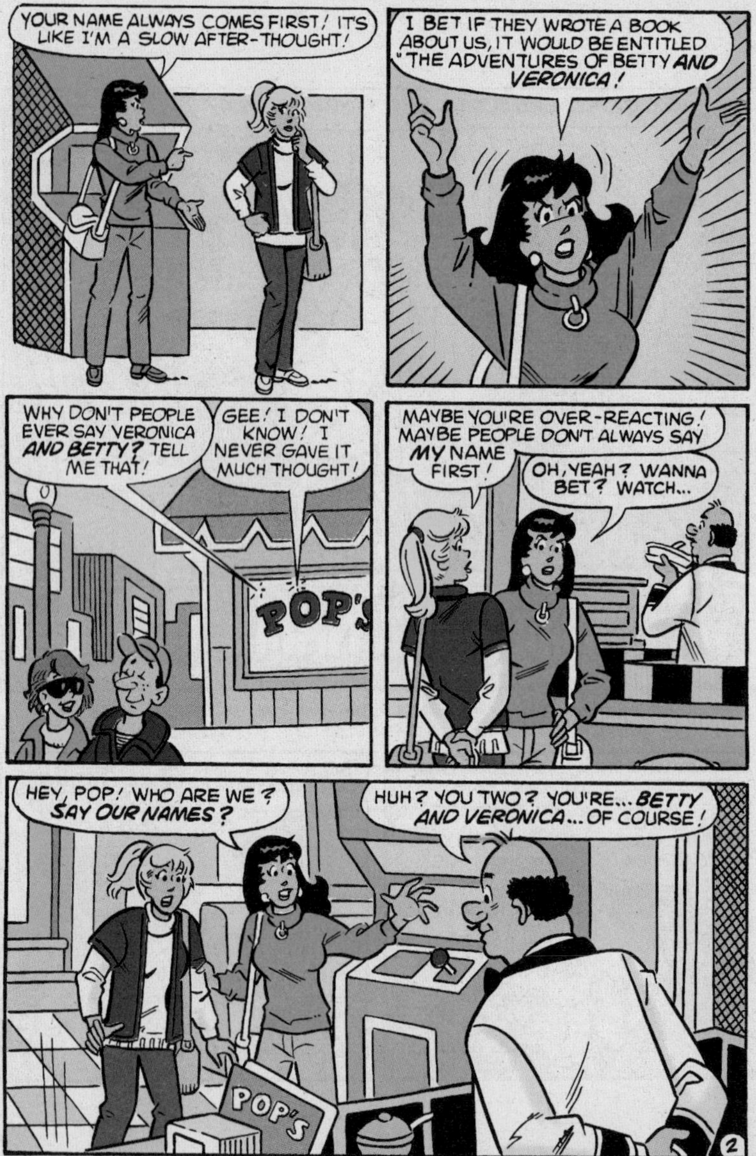

YOUR NAME ALWAYS COMES FIRST! IT'S LIKE I'M A SLOW AFTER-THOUGHT!
I BET IF THEY WROTE A BOOK ABOUT US, IT WOULD BE ENTITLED "THE ADVENTURES OF BETTY AND VERONICA!
WHY DON'T PEOPLE EVER SAY VERONICA AND BETTY? TELL ME THAT!
GEE! I DON'T KNOW! I NEVER GAVE IT MUCH THOUGHT!
POP'S
MAYBE YOU'RE OVER-REACTING! MAYBE PEOPLE DON'T ALWAYS SAY MY NAME FIRST!
OH, YEAH? WANNA BET? WATCH...
HEY, POP! WHO ARE WE? SAY OUR NAMES?
HUH? YOU TWO? YOU'RE... BETTY AND VERONICA... OF COURSE!
POP'S
2

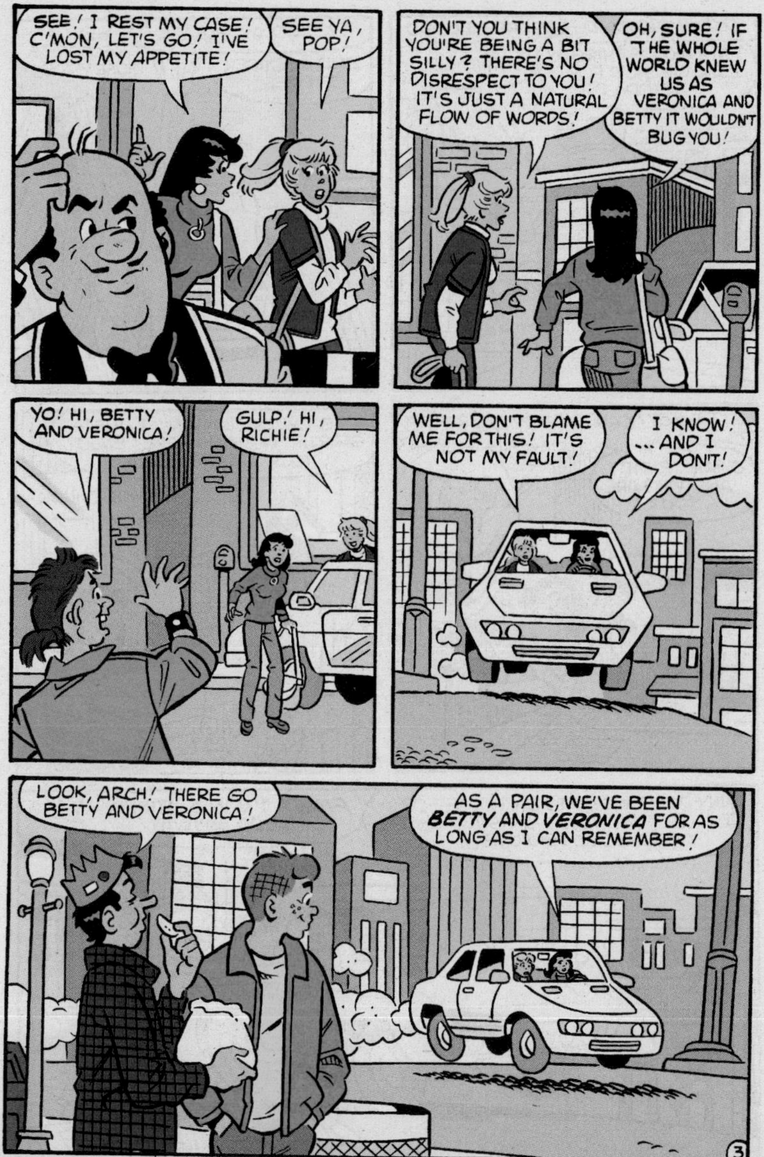
SEE! I REST MY CASE! C'MON, LET'S GO! I'VE LOST MY APPETITE!
SEE YA, POP!
DON'T YOU THINK YOU'RE BEING A BIT SILLY? THERE'S NO DISRESPECT TO YOU! IT'S JUST A NATURAL FLOW OF WORDS!
OH, SURE! IF THE WHOLE WORLD KNEW US AS VERONICA AND BETTY IT WOULDN'T BUG YOU!
YO! HI, BETTY AND VERONICA!
GULP! HI, RICHIE!
WELL, DON'T BLAME ME FOR THIS! IT'S NOT MY FAULT!
I KNOW! ...AND I DON'T!
LOOK, ARCH! THERE GO BETTY AND VERONICA!
AS A PAIR, WE'VE BEEN BETTY AND VERONICA FOR AS LONG AS I CAN REMEMBER!
3

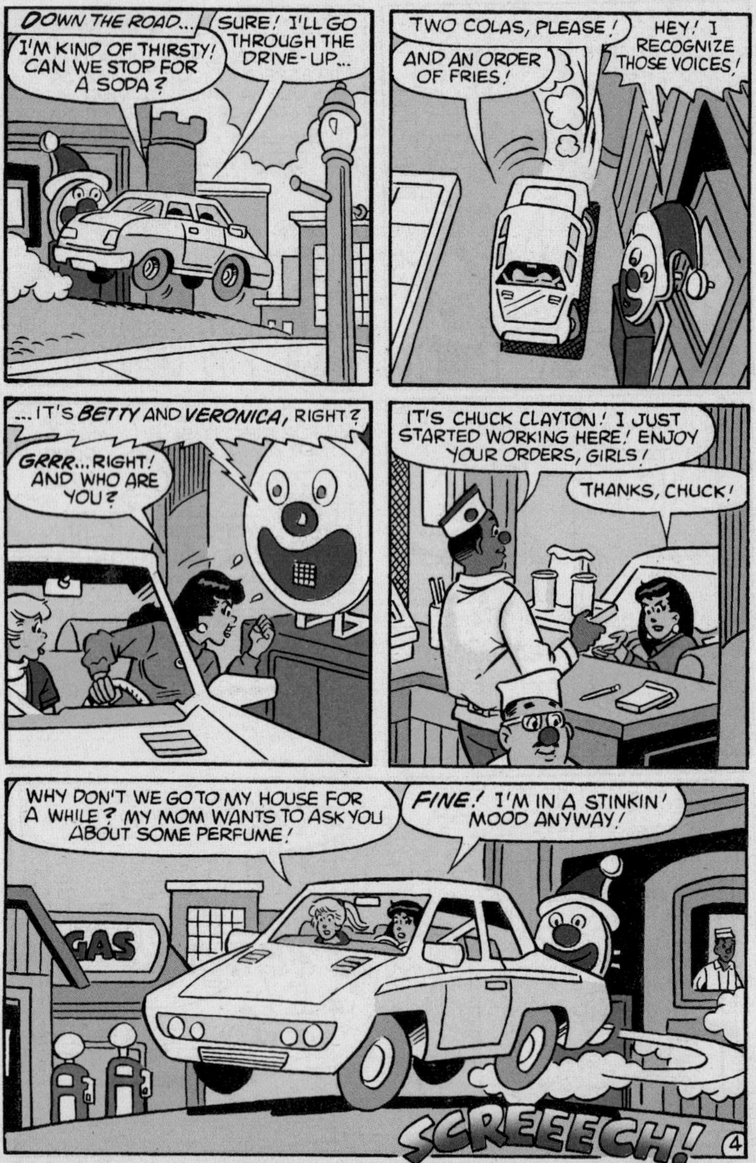

DOWN THE ROAD...
I'M KIND OF THIRSTY! CAN WE STOP FOR A SODA?
SURE! I'LL GO THROUGH THE DRIVE-UP...
TWO COLAS, PLEASE!
AND AN ORDER OF FRIES!
HEY! I RECOGNIZE THOSE VOICES!
...IT'S BETTY AND VERONICA, RIGHT?
GRRR... RIGHT! AND WHO ARE YOU?
IT'S CHUCK CLAYTON! I JUST STARTED WORKING HERE! ENJOY YOUR ORDERS, GIRLS!
THANKS, CHUCK!
WHY DON'T WE GO TO MY HOUSE FOR A WHILE? MY MOM WANTS TO ASK YOU ABOUT SOME PERFUME!
FINE! I'M IN A STINKIN' MOOD ANYWAY!
GAS
SCREEECH!

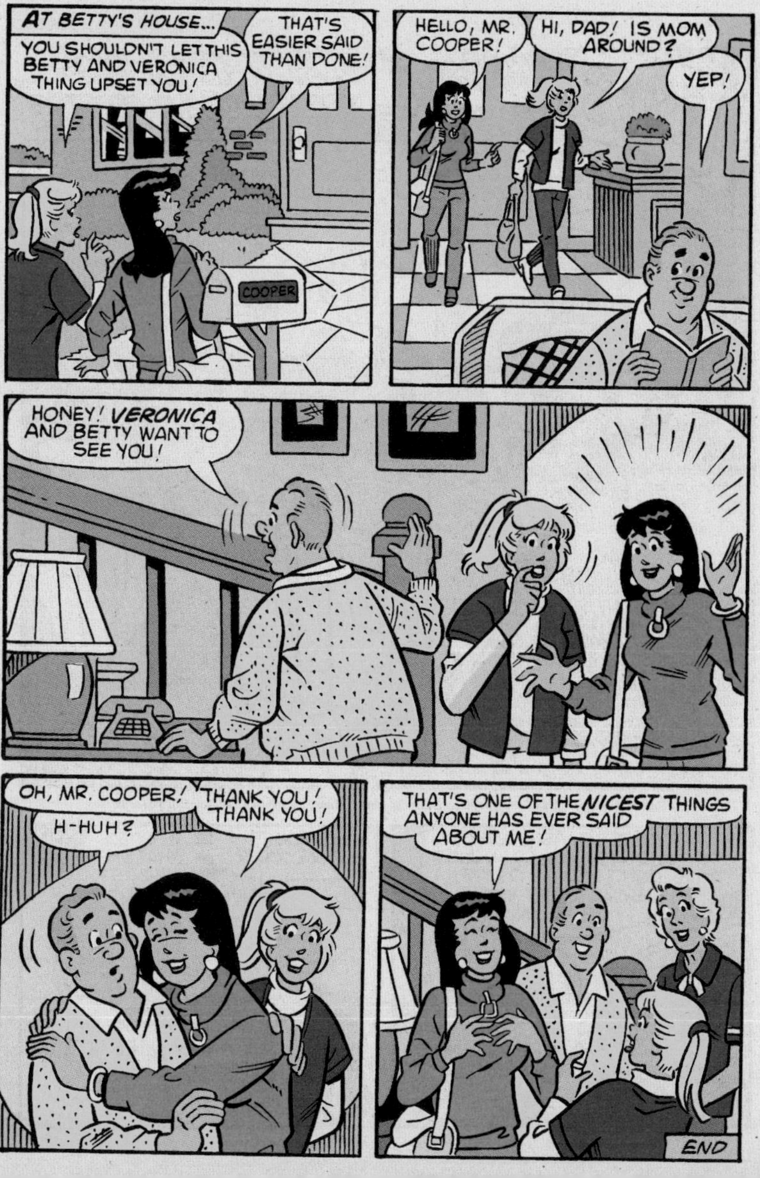
AT BETTY'S HOUSE...
YOU SHOULDN'T LET THIS BETTY AND VERONICA THING UPSET YOU!
THAT'S EASIER SAID THAN DONE!
COOPER
HELLO, MR. COOPER!
HI, DAD! IS MOM AROUND?
YEP!
HONEY! VERONICA AND BETTY WANT TO SEE YOU!
OH, MR. COOPER!
THANK YOU! THANK YOU!
H-HUH?
THAT'S ONE OF THE NICEST THINGS ANYONE HAS EVER SAID ABOUT ME!
END

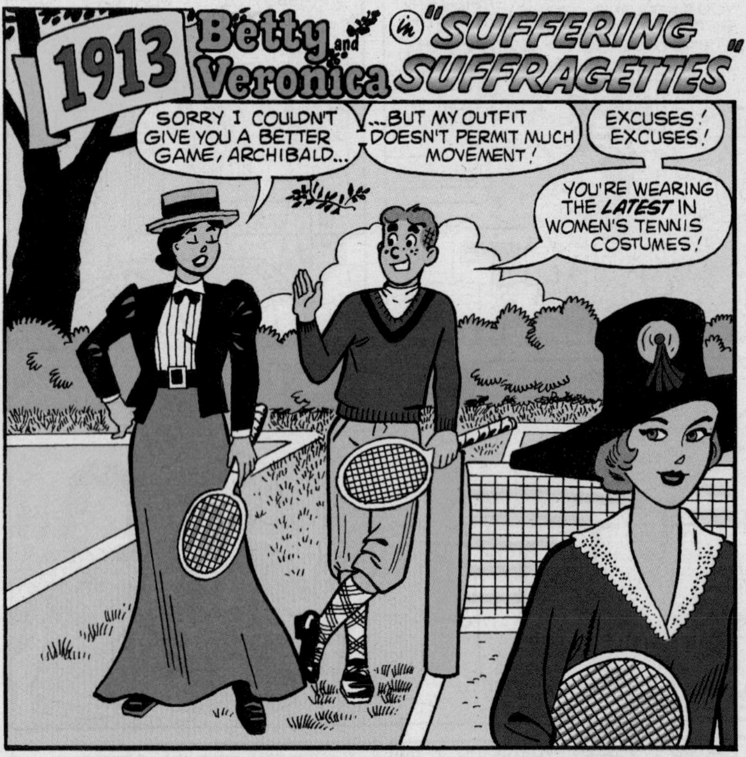
1913
Betty and Veronica in "SUFFERING SUFFRAGETTES"
SORRY I COULDN'T GIVE YOU A BETTER GAME, ARCHIBALD...
...BUT MY OUTFIT DOESN'T PERMIT MUCH MOVEMENT!
EXCUSES! EXCUSES!
YOU'RE WEARING THE *LATEST* IN WOMEN'S TENNIS COSTUMES!

Script: George Gladir / Pencils: Dan DeCarlo / Inks: Henry Scarpelli / Letters: Bill Yoshida

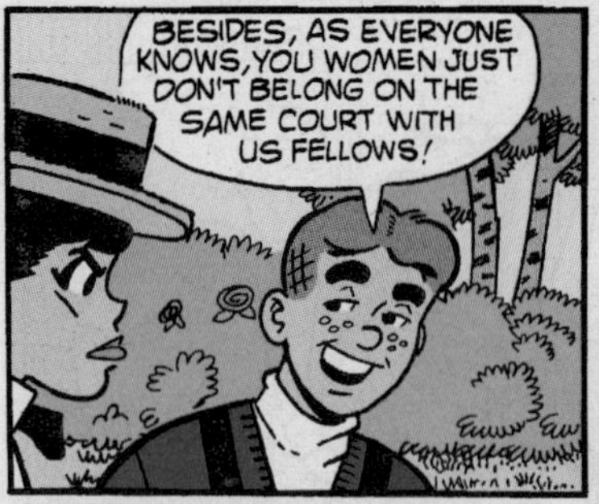
BESIDES, AS EVERYONE KNOWS, YOU WOMEN JUST DON'T BELONG ON THE SAME COURT WITH US FELLOWS!

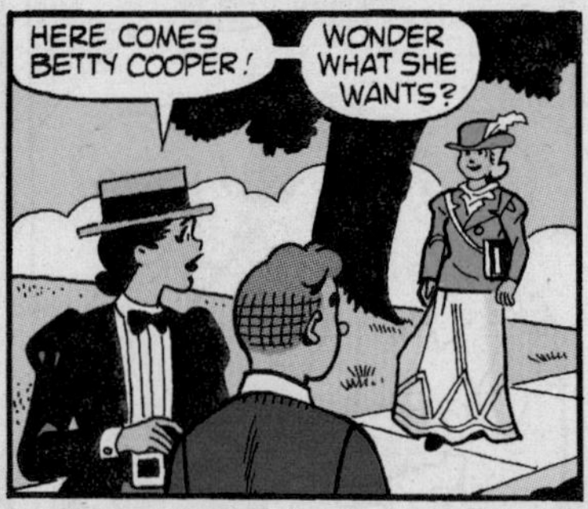
HERE COMES BETTY COOPER!
WONDER WHAT SHE WANTS?

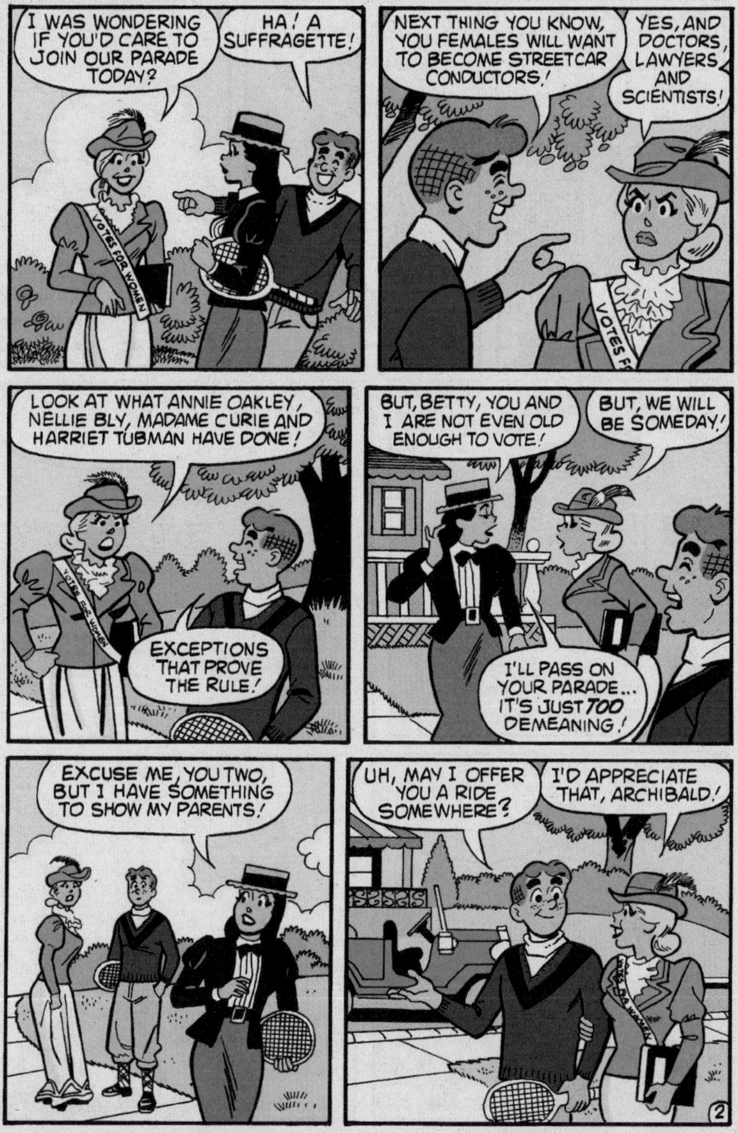
I WAS WONDERING IF YOU'D CARE TO JOIN OUR PARADE TODAY?
HA! A SUFFRAGETTE!
VOTES FOR WOMEN
NEXT THING YOU KNOW, YOU FEMALES WILL WANT TO BECOME STREETCAR CONDUCTORS!
YES, AND DOCTORS, LAWYERS AND SCIENTISTS!
LOOK AT WHAT ANNIE OAKLEY, NELLIE BLY, MADAME CURIE AND HARRIET TUBMAN HAVE DONE!
EXCEPTIONS THAT PROVE THE RULE!
BUT, BETTY, YOU AND I ARE NOT EVEN OLD ENOUGH TO VOTE!
BUT, WE WILL BE SOMEDAY!
I'LL PASS ON YOUR PARADE... IT'S JUST TOO DEMEANING!
EXCUSE ME, YOU TWO, BUT I HAVE SOMETHING TO SHOW MY PARENTS!
UH, MAY I OFFER YOU A RIDE SOMEWHERE?
I'D APPRECIATE THAT, ARCHIBALD!
2

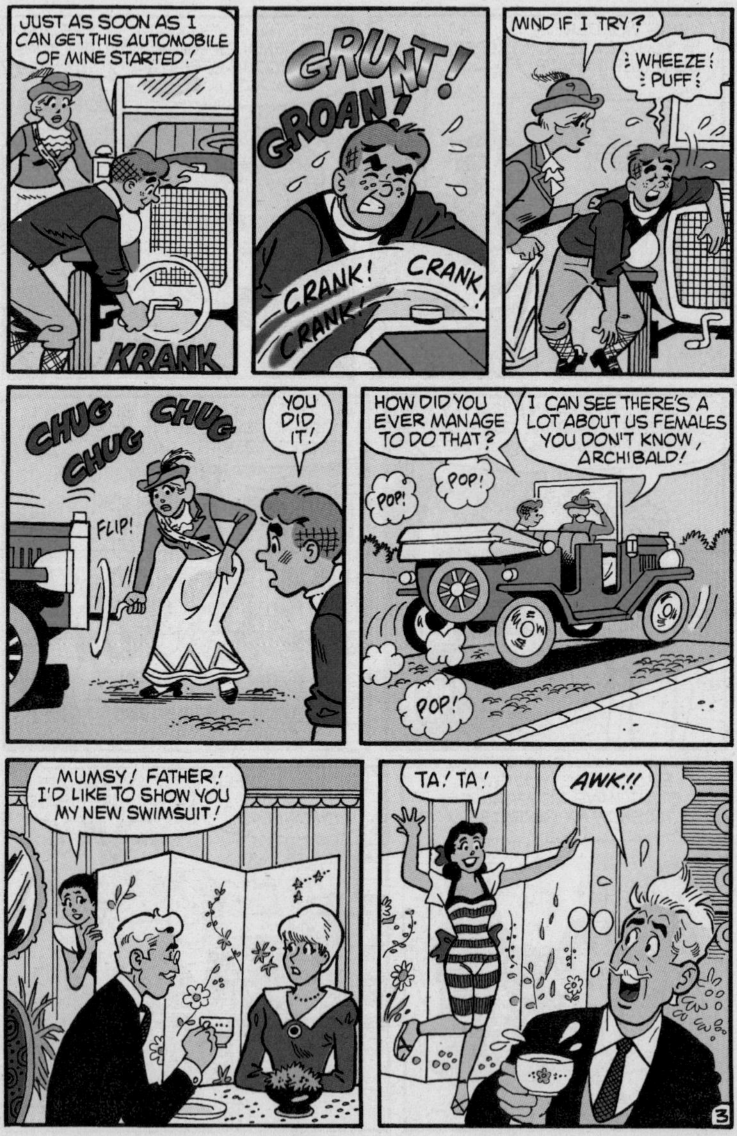
JUST AS SOON AS I CAN GET THIS AUTOMOBILE OF MINE STARTED!
KRANK
GRUNT!
GROAN!
CRANK! CRANK! CRANK!
MIND IF I TRY?
WHEEZE PUFF
CHUG CHUG CHUG
FLIP!
YOU DID IT!
HOW DID YOU EVER MANAGE TO DO THAT?
I CAN SEE THERE'S A LOT ABOUT US FEMALES YOU DON'T KNOW, ARCHIBALD!
POP! POP! POP!
MUMSY! FATHER! I'D LIKE TO SHOW YOU MY NEW SWIMSUIT!
TA! TA!
AWK!!
3

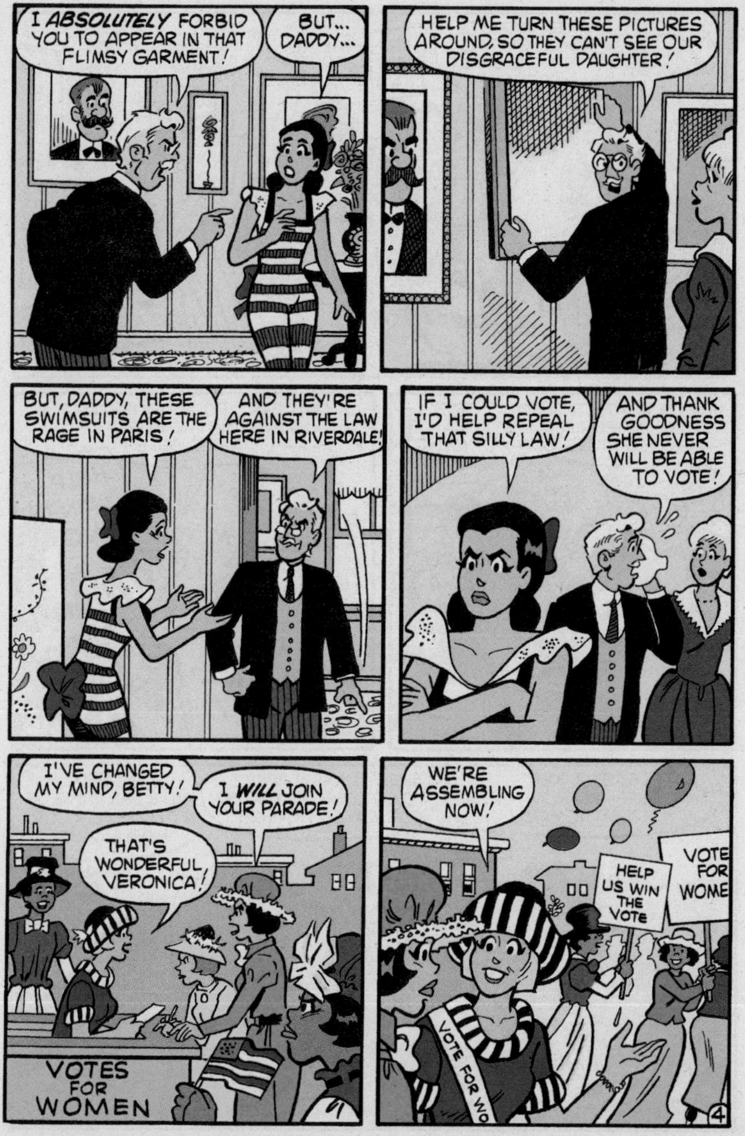
I *ABSOLUTELY* FORBID YOU TO APPEAR IN THAT FLIMSY GARMENT!
BUT... DADDY...
HELP ME TURN THESE PICTURES AROUND, SO THEY CAN'T SEE OUR DISGRACEFUL DAUGHTER!
BUT, DADDY, THESE SWIMSUITS ARE THE RAGE IN PARIS!
AND THEY'RE AGAINST THE LAW HERE IN RIVERDALE!
IF I COULD VOTE, I'D HELP REPEAL THAT SILLY LAW!
AND THANK GOODNESS SHE NEVER WILL BE ABLE TO VOTE!
I'VE CHANGED MY MIND, BETTY!
I *WILL* JOIN YOUR PARADE!
THAT'S WONDERFUL, VERONICA!
VOTES FOR WOMEN
WE'RE ASSEMBLING NOW!
HELP US WIN THE VOTE
VOTE FOR WOME
VOTE FOR WO
4

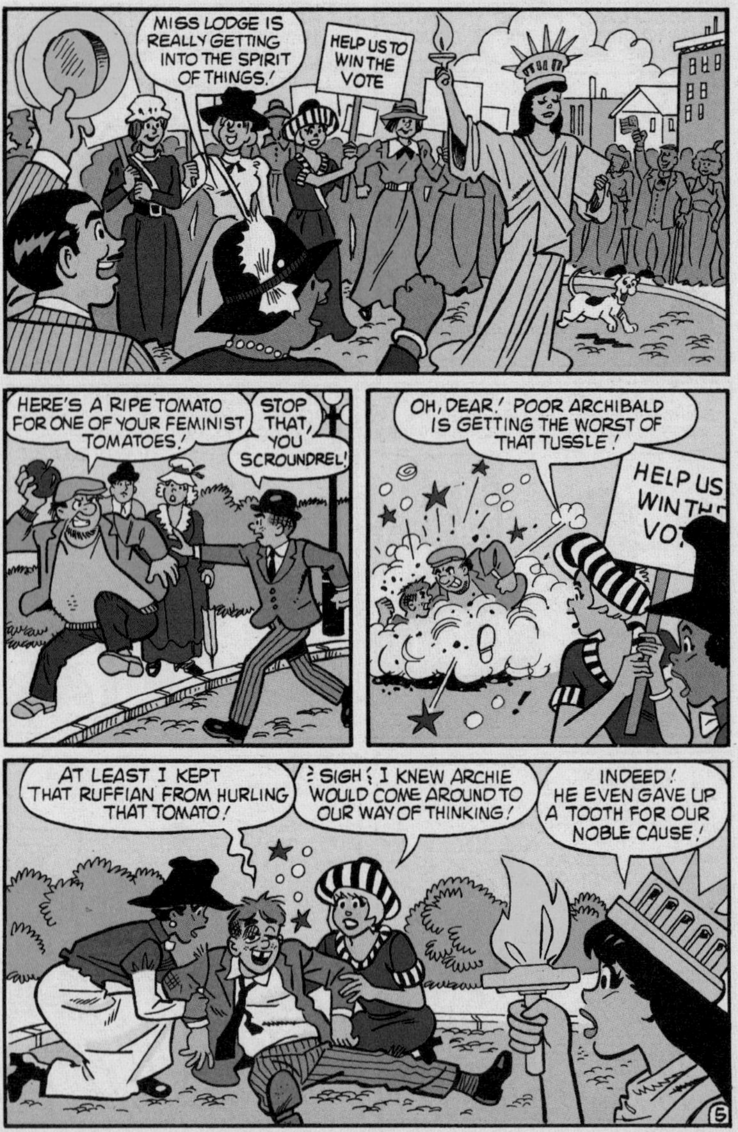
MISS LODGE IS REALLY GETTING INTO THE SPIRIT OF THINGS!
HELP US TO WIN THE VOTE
HERE'S A RIPE TOMATO FOR ONE OF YOUR FEMINIST TOMATOES!
STOP THAT, YOU SCROUNDREL!
OH, DEAR! POOR ARCHIBALD IS GETTING THE WORST OF THAT TUSSLE!
AT LEAST I KEPT THAT RUFFIAN FROM HURLING THAT TOMATO!
SIGH I KNEW ARCHIE WOULD COME AROUND TO OUR WAY OF THINKING!
INDEED! HE EVEN GAVE UP A TOOTH FOR OUR NOBLE CAUSE!
5

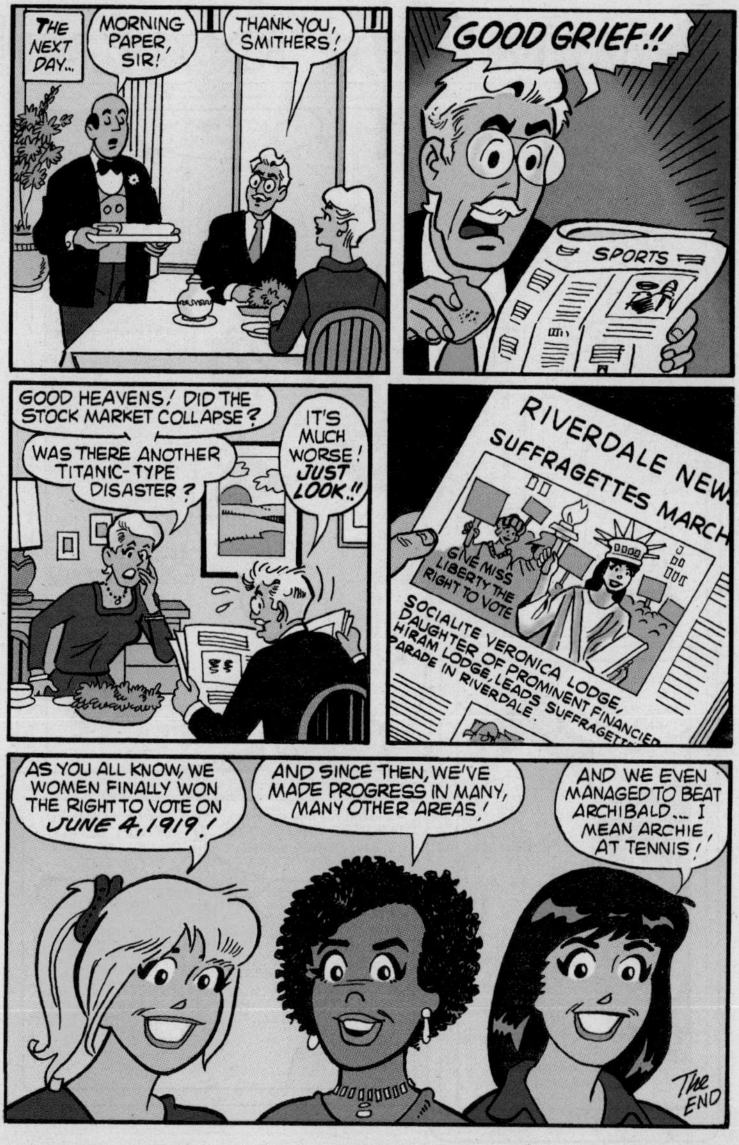
THE NEXT DAY...
MORNING PAPER, SIR!
THANK YOU, SMITHERS!
GOOD GRIEF!!
SPORTS
GOOD HEAVENS! DID THE STOCK MARKET COLLAPSE?
WAS THERE ANOTHER TITANIC-TYPE DISASTER?
IT'S MUCH WORSE! JUST LOOK!!
RIVERDALE NEW
SUFFRAGETTES MARCH
GIVE MISS LIBERTY THE RIGHT TO VOTE
SOCIALITE VERONICA LODGE, DAUGHTER OF PROMINENT FINANCIER HIRAM LODGE, LEADS SUFFRAGETT PARADE IN RIVERDALE.
AS YOU ALL KNOW, WE WOMEN FINALLY WON THE RIGHT TO VOTE ON JUNE 4, 1919!
AND SINCE THEN, WE'VE MADE PROGRESS IN MANY, MANY OTHER AREAS!
AND WE EVEN MANAGED TO BEAT ARCHIBALD... I MEAN ARCHIE, AT TENNIS!
THE END

Veronica Time Together!

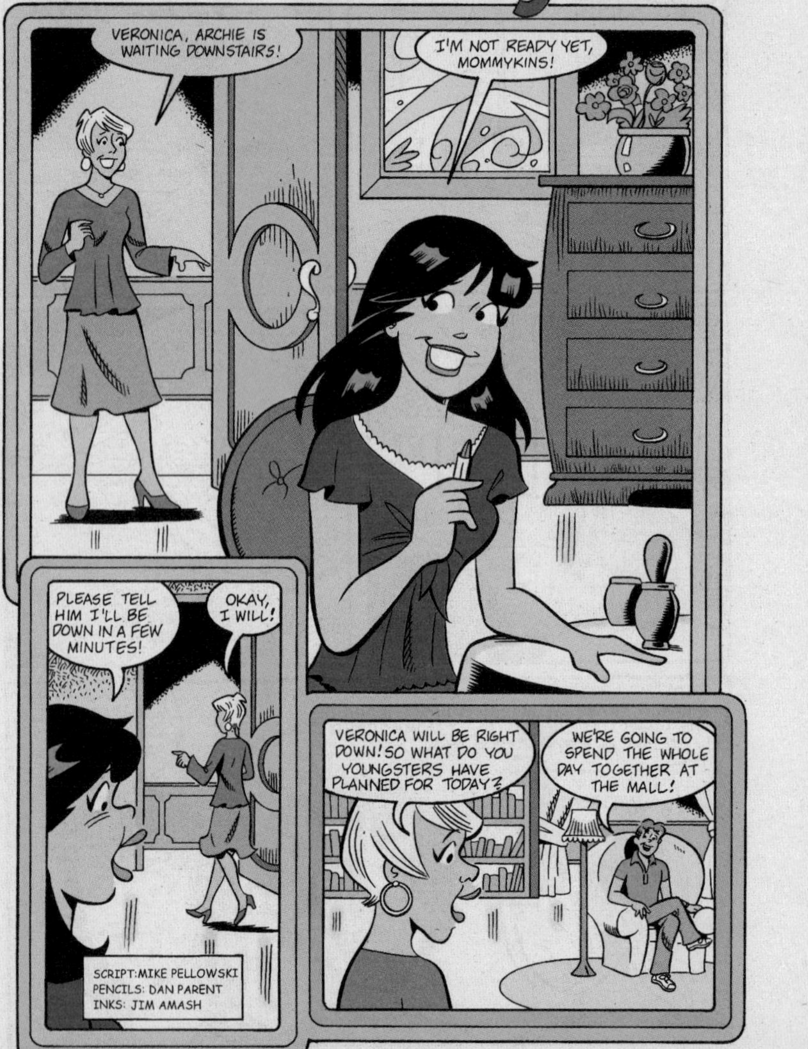
VERONICA, ARCHIE IS WAITING DOWNSTAIRS!
I'M NOT READY YET, MOMMYKINS!
PLEASE TELL HIM I'LL BE DOWN IN A FEW MINUTES!
OKAY, I WILL!
SCRIPT: MIKE PELLOWSKI
PENCILS: DAN PARENT
INKS: JIM AMASH
VERONICA WILL BE RIGHT DOWN! SO WHAT DO YOU YOUNGSTERS HAVE PLANNED FOR TODAY?
WE'RE GOING TO SPEND THE WHOLE DAY TOGETHER AT THE MALL!

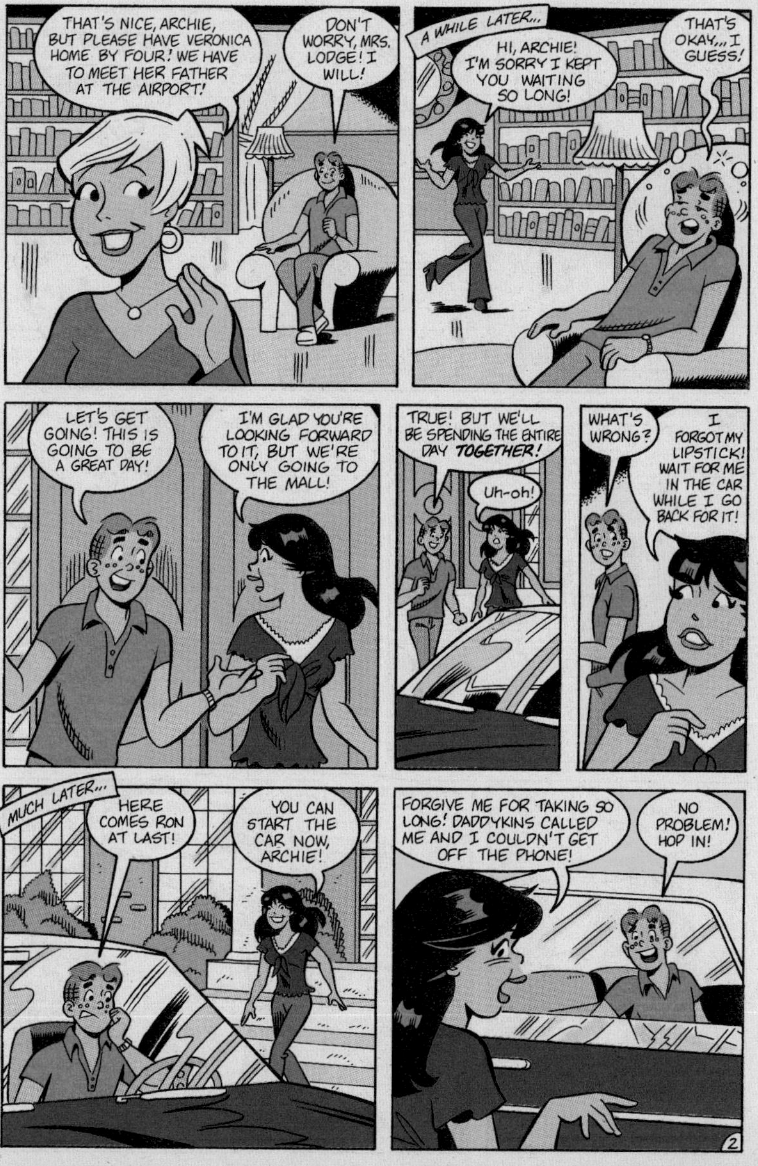
THAT'S NICE, ARCHIE, BUT PLEASE HAVE VERONICA HOME BY FOUR! WE HAVE TO MEET HER FATHER AT THE AIRPORT!
DON'T WORRY, MRS. LODGE! I WILL!
A WHILE LATER...
HI, ARCHIE! I'M SORRY I KEPT YOU WAITING SO LONG!
THAT'S OKAY... I GUESS!
LET'S GET GOING! THIS IS GOING TO BE A GREAT DAY!
I'M GLAD YOU'RE LOOKING FORWARD TO IT, BUT WE'RE ONLY GOING TO THE MALL!
TRUE! BUT WE'LL BE SPENDING THE ENTIRE DAY TOGETHER!
Uh-oh!
WHAT'S WRONG?
I FORGOT MY LIPSTICK! WAIT FOR ME IN THE CAR WHILE I GO BACK FOR IT!
MUCH LATER...
HERE COMES RON AT LAST!
YOU CAN START THE CAR NOW, ARCHIE!
FORGIVE ME FOR TAKING SO LONG! DADDYKINS CALLED ME AND I COULDN'T GET OFF THE PHONE!
NO PROBLEM! HOP IN!

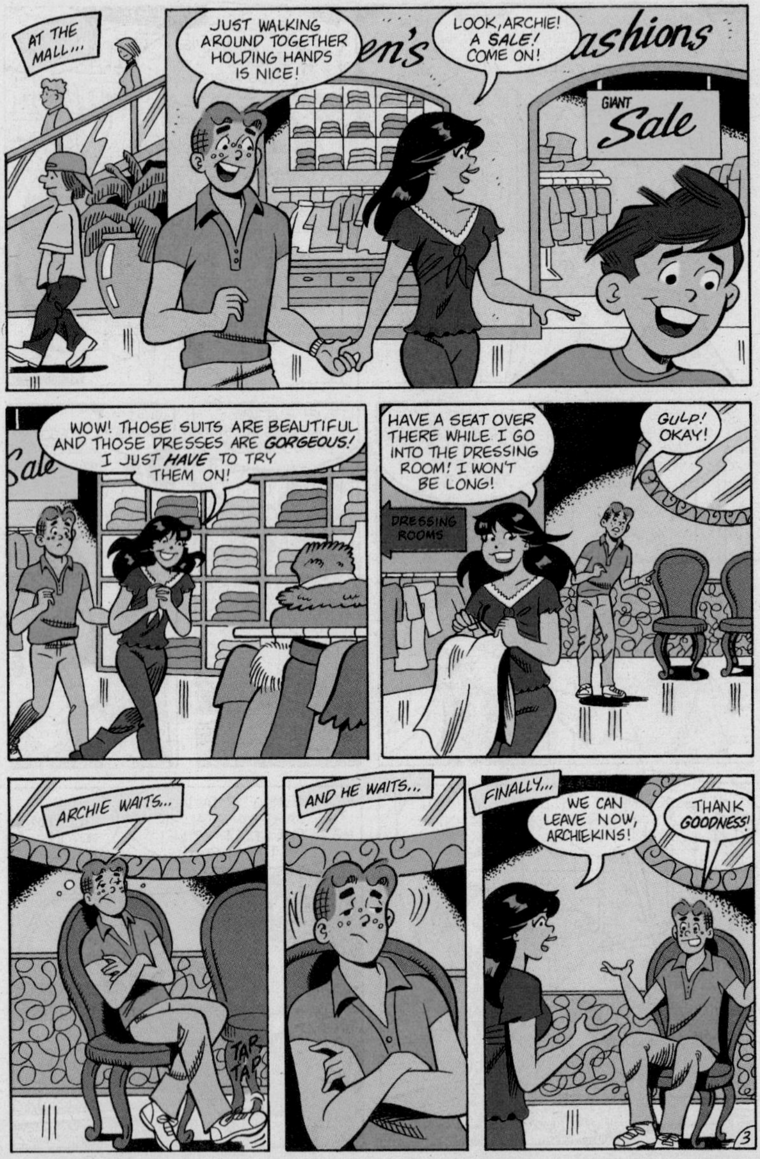
AT THE MALL...
JUST WALKING AROUND TOGETHER HOLDING HANDS IS NICE!
LOOK, ARCHIE! A SALE! COME ON!
GIANT Sale
WOW! THOSE SUITS ARE BEAUTIFUL AND THOSE DRESSES ARE GORGEOUS! I JUST HAVE TO TRY THEM ON!
HAVE A SEAT OVER THERE WHILE I GO INTO THE DRESSING ROOM! I WON'T BE LONG!
GULP! OKAY!
DRESSING ROOMS
ARCHIE WAITS...
TAP TAP
AND HE WAITS...
FINALLY...
WE CAN LEAVE NOW, ARCHIEKINS!
THANK GOODNESS!
3

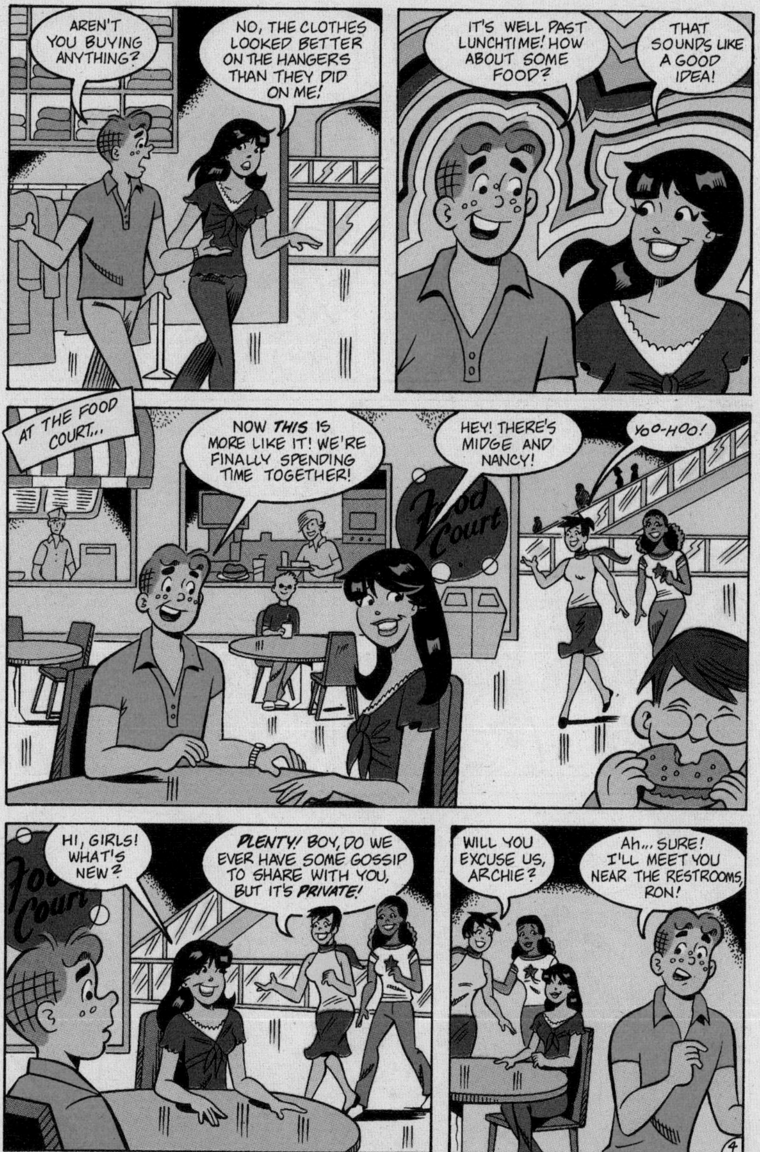
AREN'T YOU BUYING ANYTHING?
NO, THE CLOTHES LOOKED BETTER ON THE HANGERS THAN THEY DID ON ME!
IT'S WELL PAST LUNCHTIME! HOW ABOUT SOME FOOD?
THAT SOUNDS LIKE A GOOD IDEA!
AT THE FOOD COURT...
NOW THIS IS MORE LIKE IT! WE'RE FINALLY SPENDING TIME TOGETHER!
Food Court
HEY! THERE'S MIDGE AND NANCY!
YOO-HOO!
HI, GIRLS! WHAT'S NEW?
PLENTY! BOY, DO WE EVER HAVE SOME GOSSIP TO SHARE WITH YOU, BUT IT'S PRIVATE!
WILL YOU EXCUSE US, ARCHIE?
Ah... SURE! I'LL MEET YOU NEAR THE RESTROOMS, RON!
4

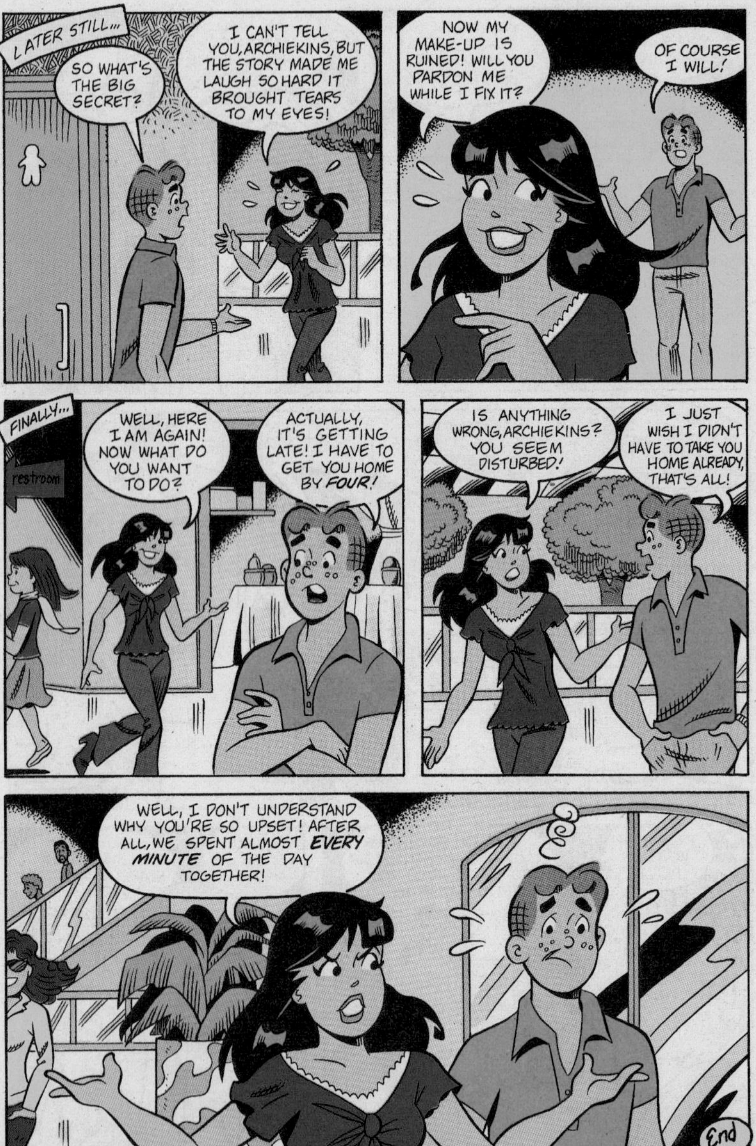
LATER STILL...
SO WHAT'S THE BIG SECRET?
I CAN'T TELL YOU, ARCHIEKINS, BUT THE STORY MADE ME LAUGH SO HARD IT BROUGHT TEARS TO MY EYES!
NOW MY MAKE-UP IS RUINED! WILL YOU PARDON ME WHILE I FIX IT?
OF COURSE I WILL!
FINALLY...
restroom
WELL, HERE I AM AGAIN! NOW WHAT DO YOU WANT TO DO?
ACTUALLY, IT'S GETTING LATE! I HAVE TO GET YOU HOME BY FOUR!
IS ANYTHING WRONG, ARCHIEKINS? YOU SEEM DISTURBED!
I JUST WISH I DIDN'T HAVE TO TAKE YOU HOME ALREADY, THAT'S ALL!
WELL, I DON'T UNDERSTAND WHY YOU'RE SO UPSET! AFTER ALL, WE SPENT ALMOST EVERY MINUTE OF THE DAY TOGETHER!
End

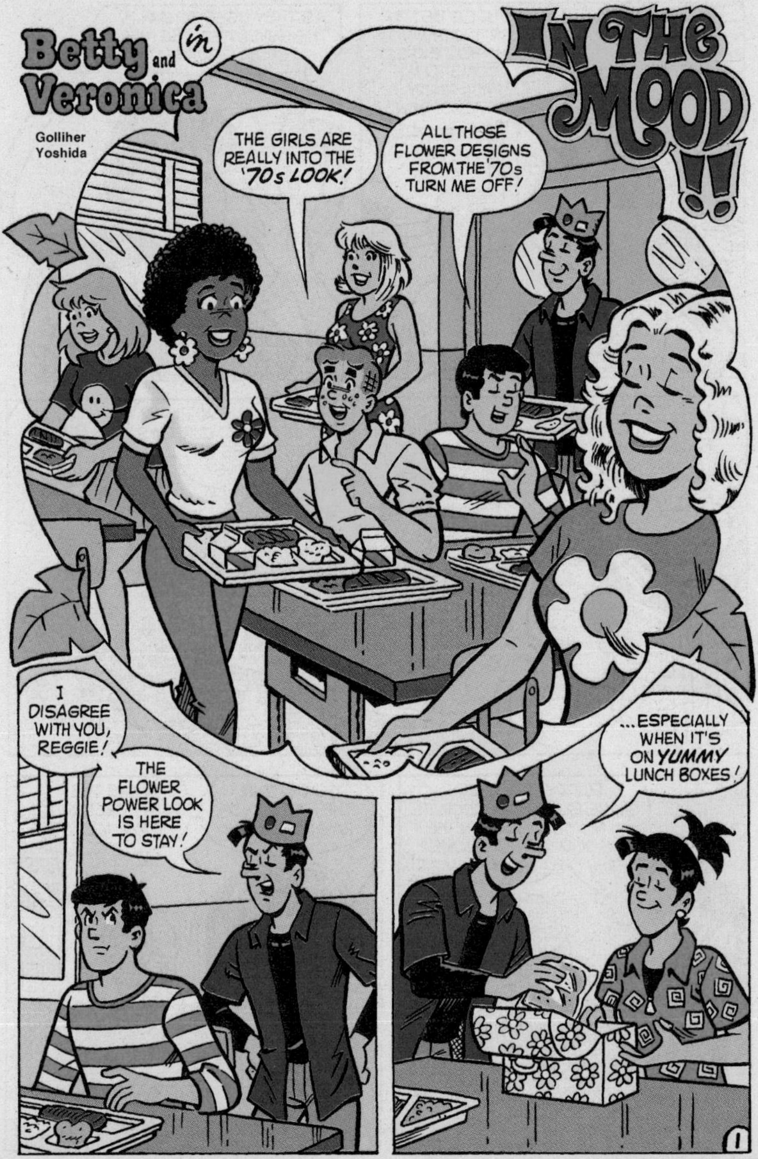

Betty and Veronica in
IN THE MOOD!!
Golliher
Yoshida
THE GIRLS ARE REALLY INTO THE '70s LOOK!
ALL THOSE FLOWER DESIGNS FROM THE '70s TURN ME OFF!
I DISAGREE WITH YOU, REGGIE!
THE FLOWER POWER LOOK IS HERE TO STAY!
...ESPECIALLY WHEN IT'S ON YUMMY LUNCH BOXES!
1

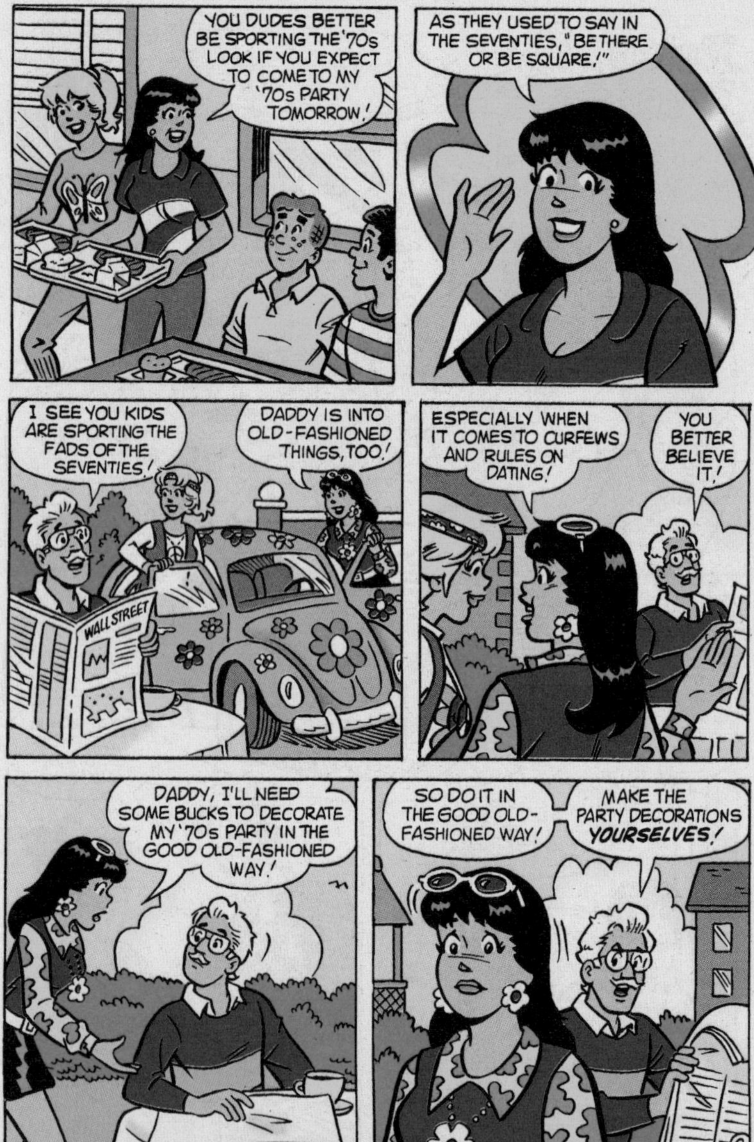
YOU DUDES BETTER BE SPORTING THE '70s LOOK IF YOU EXPECT TO COME TO MY '70s PARTY TOMORROW!
AS THEY USED TO SAY IN THE SEVENTIES, "BE THERE OR BE SQUARE!"
I SEE YOU KIDS ARE SPORTING THE FADS OF THE SEVENTIES!
DADDY IS INTO OLD-FASHIONED THINGS, TOO!
WALL STREET
ESPECIALLY WHEN IT COMES TO CURFEWS AND RULES ON DATING!
YOU BETTER BELIEVE IT!
DADDY, I'LL NEED SOME BUCKS TO DECORATE MY '70s PARTY IN THE GOOD OLD-FASHIONED WAY!
SO DO IT IN THE GOOD OLD-FASHIONED WAY!
MAKE THE PARTY DECORATIONS *YOURSELVES*!
2

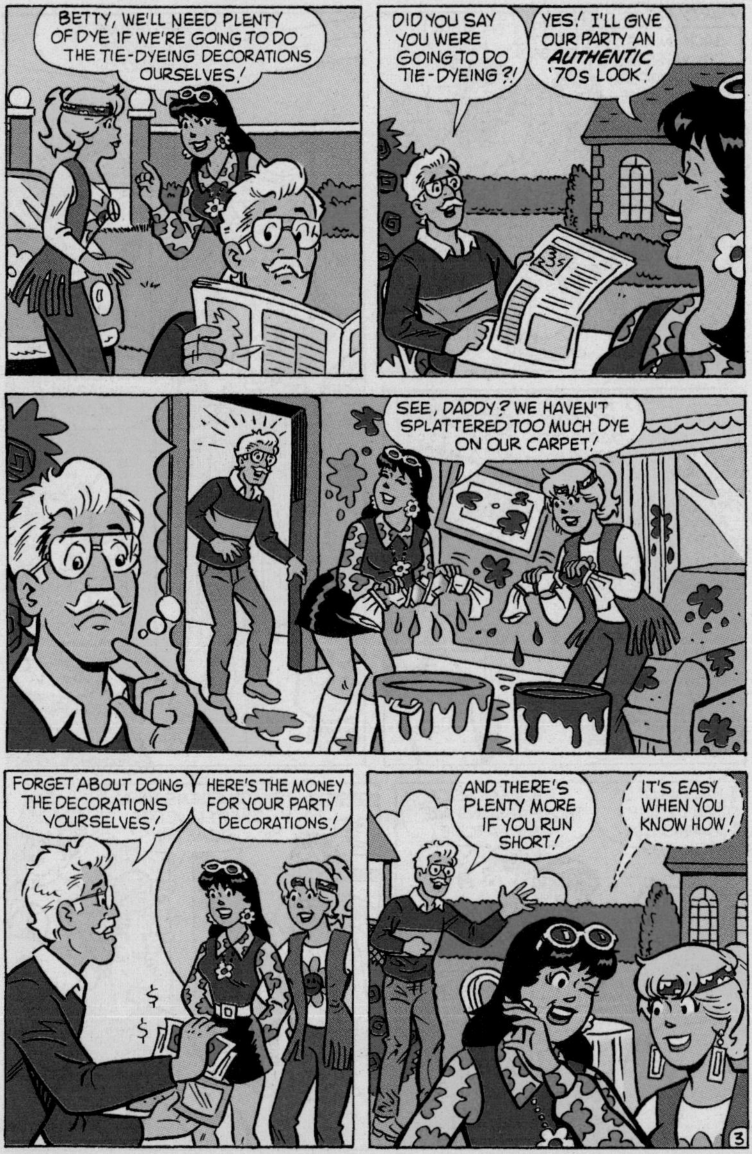

BETTY, WE'LL NEED PLENTY OF DYE IF WE'RE GOING TO DO THE TIE-DYEING DECORATIONS OURSELVES!
DID YOU SAY YOU WERE GOING TO DO TIE-DYEING?!
YES! I'LL GIVE OUR PARTY AN AUTHENTIC '70s LOOK!
SEE, DADDY? WE HAVEN'T SPLATTERED TOO MUCH DYE ON OUR CARPET!
FORGET ABOUT DOING THE DECORATIONS YOURSELVES!
HERE'S THE MONEY FOR YOUR PARTY DECORATIONS!
AND THERE'S PLENTY MORE IF YOU RUN SHORT!
IT'S EASY WHEN YOU KNOW HOW!

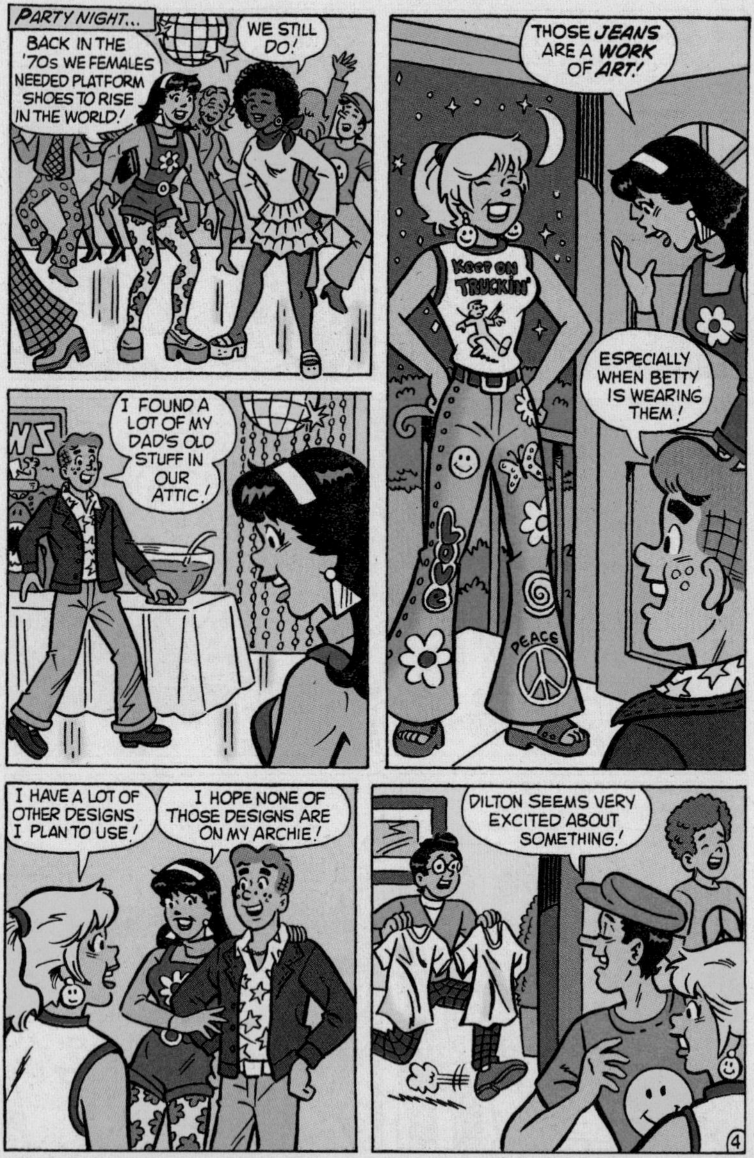
PARTY NIGHT...
BACK IN THE '70s WE FEMALES NEEDED PLATFORM SHOES TO RISE IN THE WORLD!
WE STILL DO!
THOSE JEANS ARE A WORK OF ART!
I FOUND A LOT OF MY DAD'S OLD STUFF IN OUR ATTIC!
KEEP ON TRUCKIN'
LOVE
PEACE
ESPECIALLY WHEN BETTY IS WEARING THEM!
I HAVE A LOT OF OTHER DESIGNS I PLAN TO USE!
I HOPE NONE OF THOSE DESIGNS ARE ON MY ARCHIE!
DILTON SEEMS VERY EXCITED ABOUT SOMETHING!
4

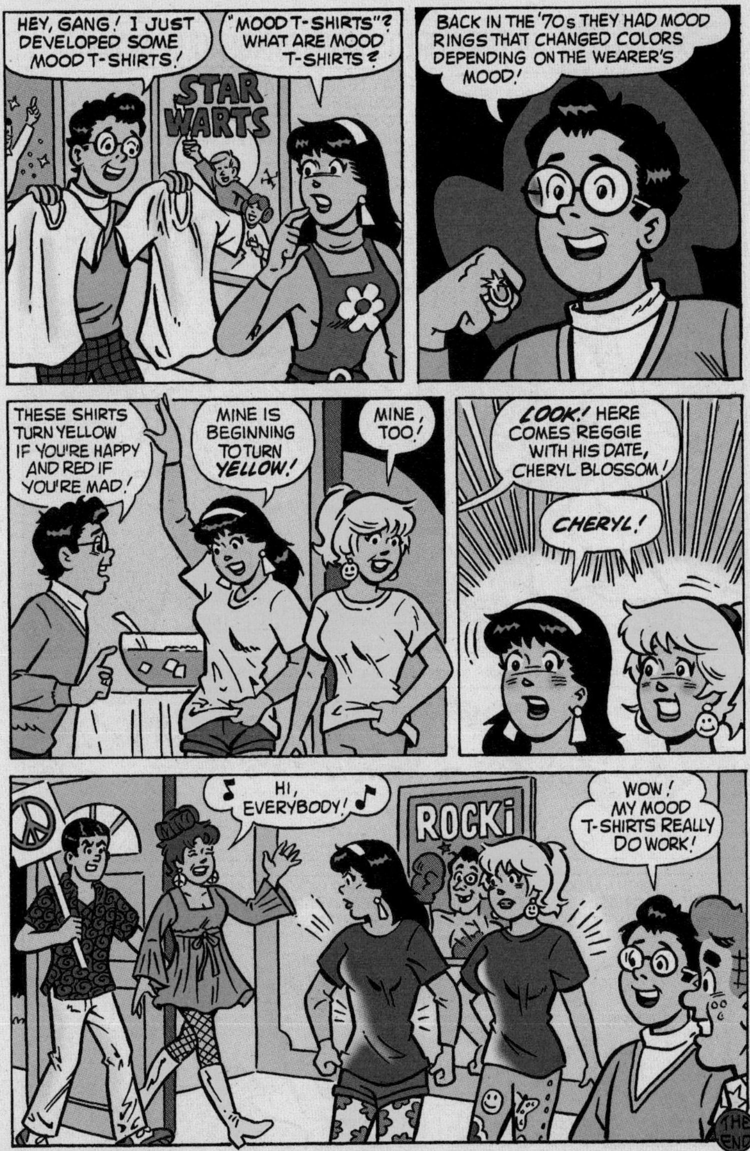
HEY, GANG! I JUST DEVELOPED SOME MOOD T-SHIRTS!
"MOOD T-SHIRTS"? WHAT ARE MOOD T-SHIRTS?
STAR WARTS
BACK IN THE '70s THEY HAD MOOD RINGS THAT CHANGED COLORS DEPENDING ON THE WEARER'S MOOD!
THESE SHIRTS TURN YELLOW IF YOU'RE HAPPY AND RED IF YOU'RE MAD!
MINE IS BEGINNING TO TURN YELLOW!
MINE, TOO!
LOOK! HERE COMES REGGIE WITH HIS DATE, CHERYL BLOSSOM!
CHERYL!
HI, EVERYBODY!
ROCKi
WOW! MY MOOD T-SHIRTS REALLY DO WORK!
THE END

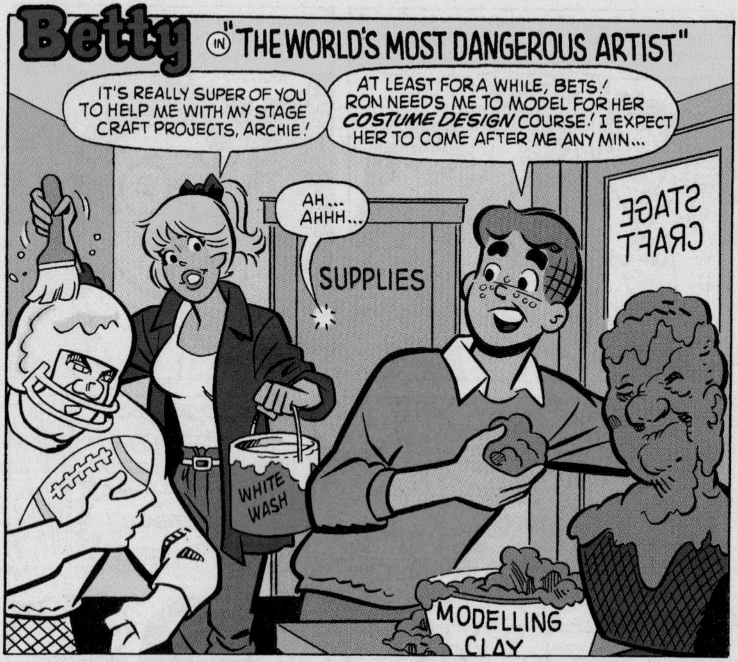
Betty
IN "THE WORLD'S MOST DANGEROUS ARTIST"
IT'S REALLY SUPER OF YOU TO HELP ME WITH MY STAGE CRAFT PROJECTS, ARCHIE!
AT LEAST FOR A WHILE, BETS! RON NEEDS ME TO MODEL FOR HER COSTUME DESIGN COURSE! I EXPECT HER TO COME AFTER ME ANY MIN...
AH... AHHH...
SUPPLIES
STAGE CRAFT
WHITE WASH
MODELLING CLAY

Script: Bob Bolling / Pencils: Doug Crane / Inks: Tim Kennedy / Letters: Bill Yoshida

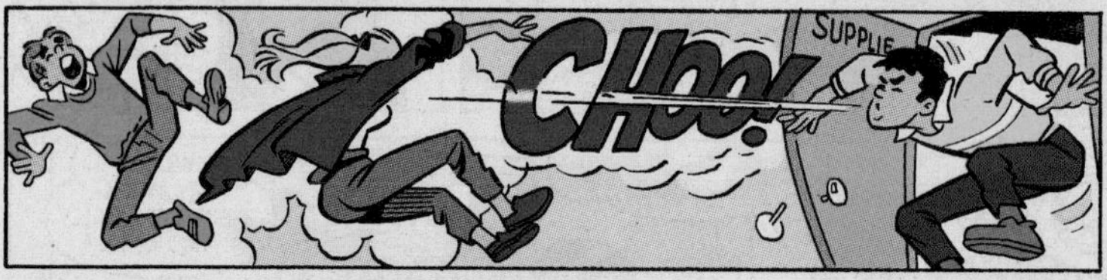
CHOO!
SUPPLIE

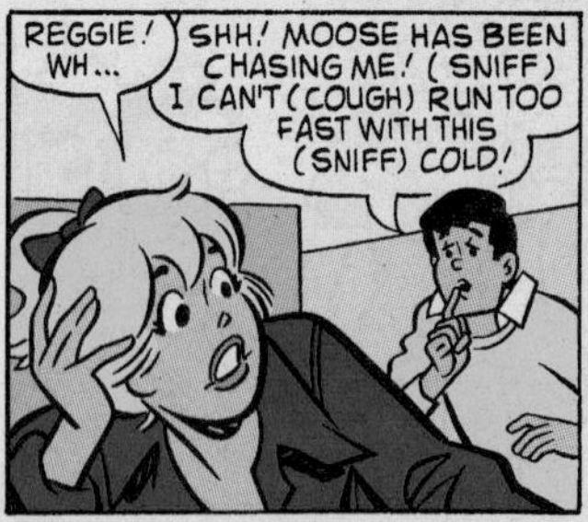
REGGIE! WH...
SHH! MOOSE HAS BEEN CHASING ME! (SNIFF) I CAN'T (COUGH) RUN TOO FAST WITH THIS (SNIFF) COLD!

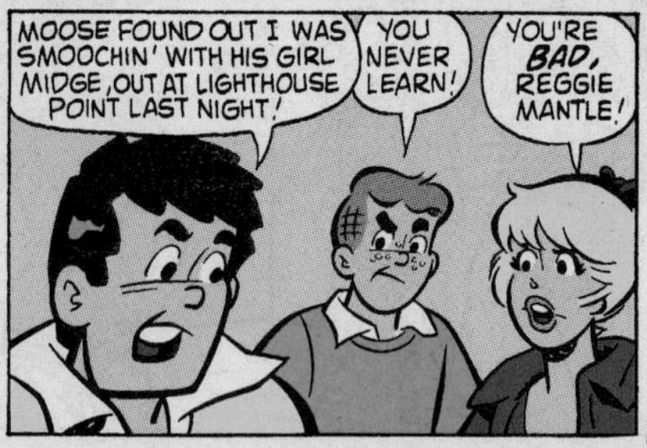
MOOSE FOUND OUT I WAS SMOOCHIN' WITH HIS GIRL MIDGE, OUT AT LIGHTHOUSE POINT LAST NIGHT!
YOU NEVER LEARN!
YOU'RE BAD, REGGIE MANTLE!

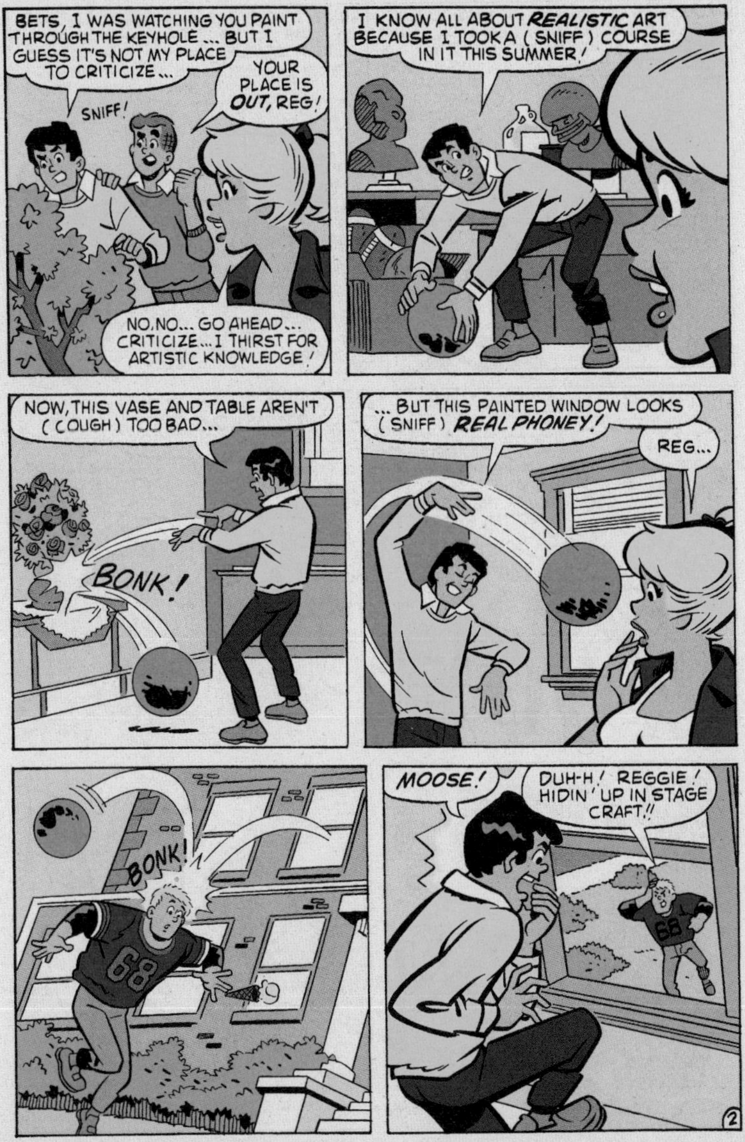
BETS, I WAS WATCHING YOU PAINT THROUGH THE KEYHOLE ... BUT I GUESS IT'S NOT MY PLACE TO CRITICIZE...
SNIFF!
YOUR PLACE IS OUT, REG!
NO,NO... GO AHEAD... CRITICIZE...I THIRST FOR ARTISTIC KNOWLEDGE!
I KNOW ALL ABOUT REALISTIC ART BECAUSE I TOOK A (SNIFF) COURSE IN IT THIS SUMMER!
NOW, THIS VASE AND TABLE AREN'T (COUGH) TOO BAD...
BONK!
... BUT THIS PAINTED WINDOW LOOKS (SNIFF) REAL PHONEY!
REG...
BONK!
MOOSE!
DUH-H! REGGIE! HIDIN' UP IN STAGE CRAFT!!
2

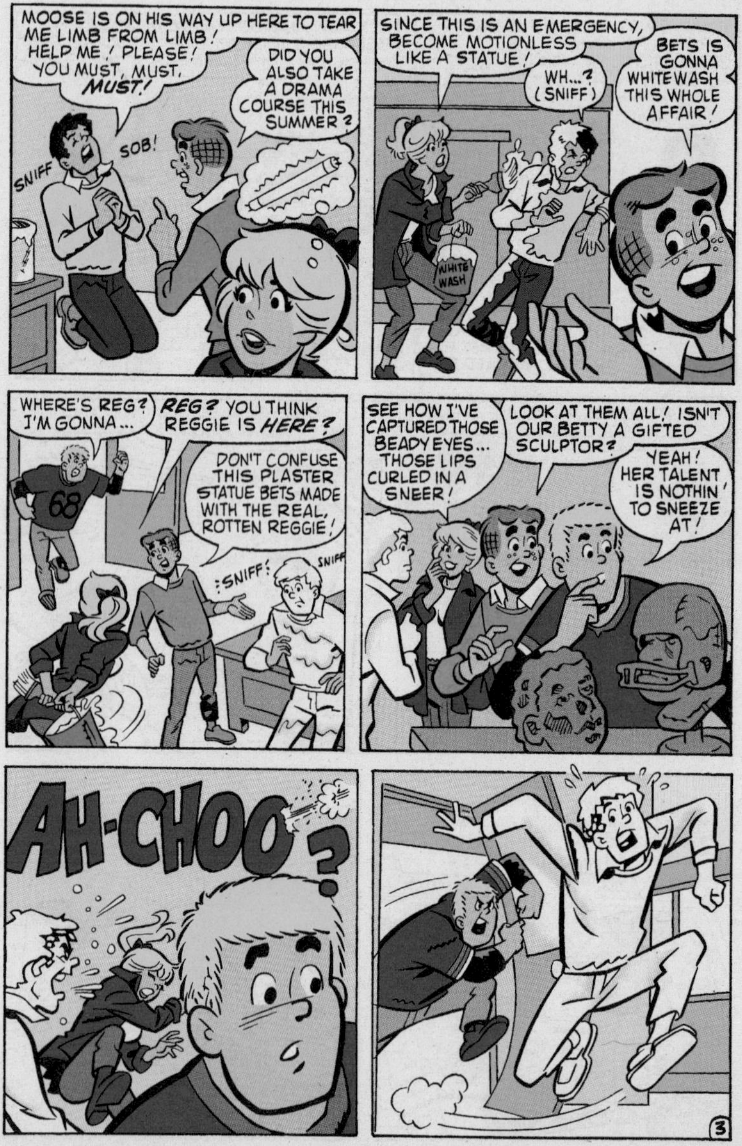
MOOSE IS ON HIS WAY UP HERE TO TEAR ME LIMB FROM LIMB! HELP ME! PLEASE! YOU MUST, MUST, MUST!
SOB!
SNIFF
DID YOU ALSO TAKE A DRAMA COURSE THIS SUMMER?
SINCE THIS IS AN EMERGENCY, BECOME MOTIONLESS LIKE A STATUE!
WH...? (SNIFF)
BETS IS GONNA WHITEWASH THIS WHOLE AFFAIR!
WHITE WASH
WHERE'S REG? I'M GONNA...
REG? YOU THINK REGGIE IS HERE?
DON'T CONFUSE THIS PLASTER STATUE BETS MADE WITH THE REAL, ROTTEN REGGIE!
SNIFF!
SNIFF
SEE HOW I'VE CAPTURED THOSE BEADY EYES... THOSE LIPS CURLED IN A SNEER!
LOOK AT THEM ALL! ISN'T OUR BETTY A GIFTED SCULPTOR?
YEAH! HER TALENT IS NOTHIN' TO SNEEZE AT!
AH-CHOO
?
3

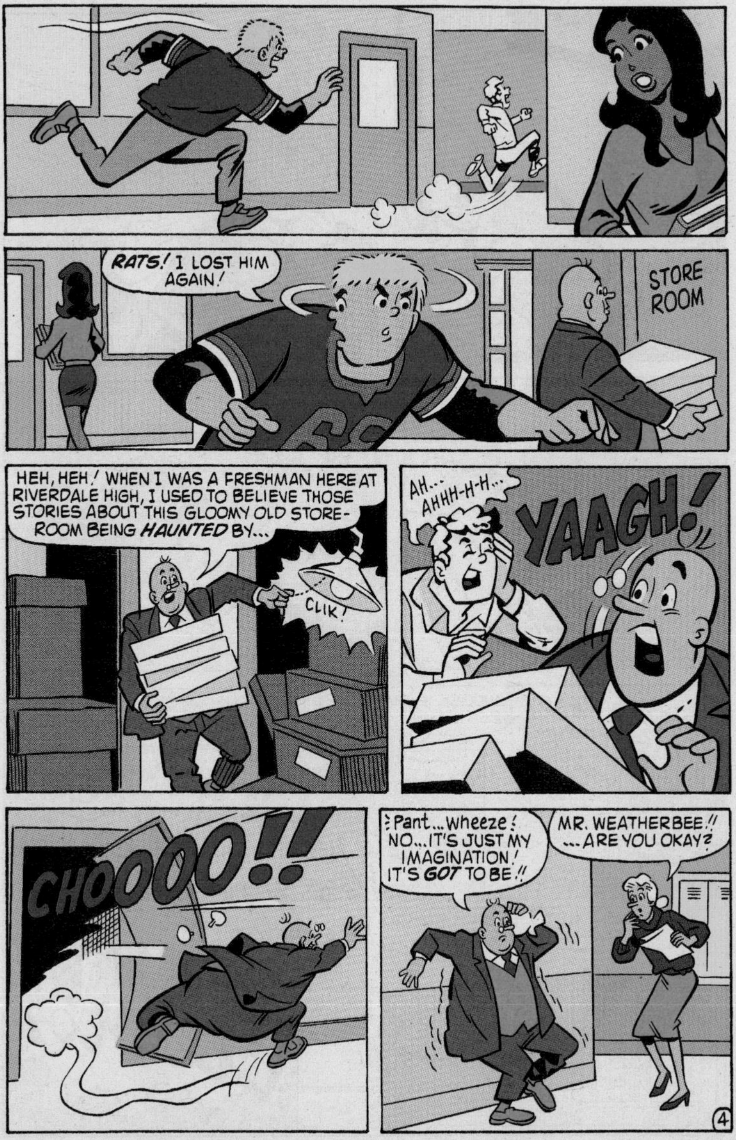
RATS! I LOST HIM AGAIN!
STORE ROOM
HEH, HEH! WHEN I WAS A FRESHMAN HERE AT RIVERDALE HIGH, I USED TO BELIEVE THOSE STORIES ABOUT THIS GLOOMY OLD STORE-ROOM BEING HAUNTED BY...
CLIK!
AH... AHHH-H-H...
YAAGH!
CHOOOOO!!
Pant... wheeze! NO... IT'S JUST MY IMAGINATION! IT'S GOT TO BE!!
MR. WEATHERBEE!! ...ARE YOU OKAY?
4

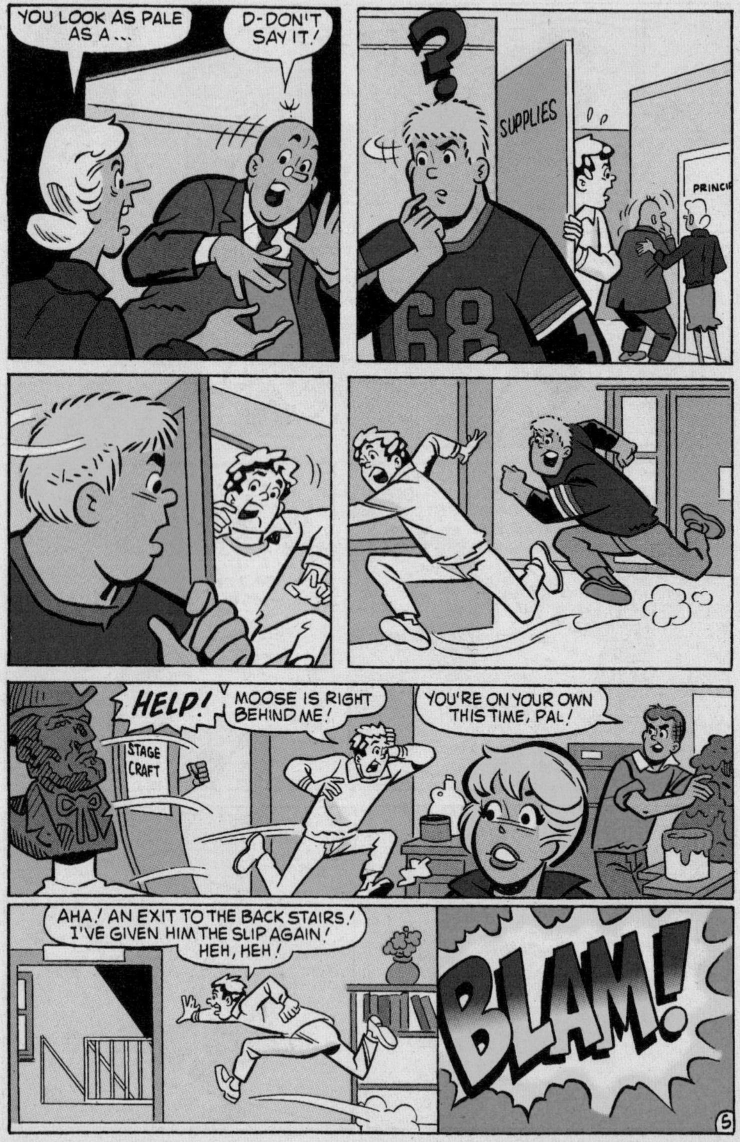

YOU LOOK AS PALE AS A...
D-DON'T SAY IT!
SUPPLIES
PRINCIP
HELP!
STAGE CRAFT
MOOSE IS RIGHT BEHIND ME!
YOU'RE ON YOUR OWN THIS TIME, PAL!
AHA! AN EXIT TO THE BACK STAIRS! I'VE GIVEN HIM THE SLIP AGAIN! HEH, HEH!
BLAM!

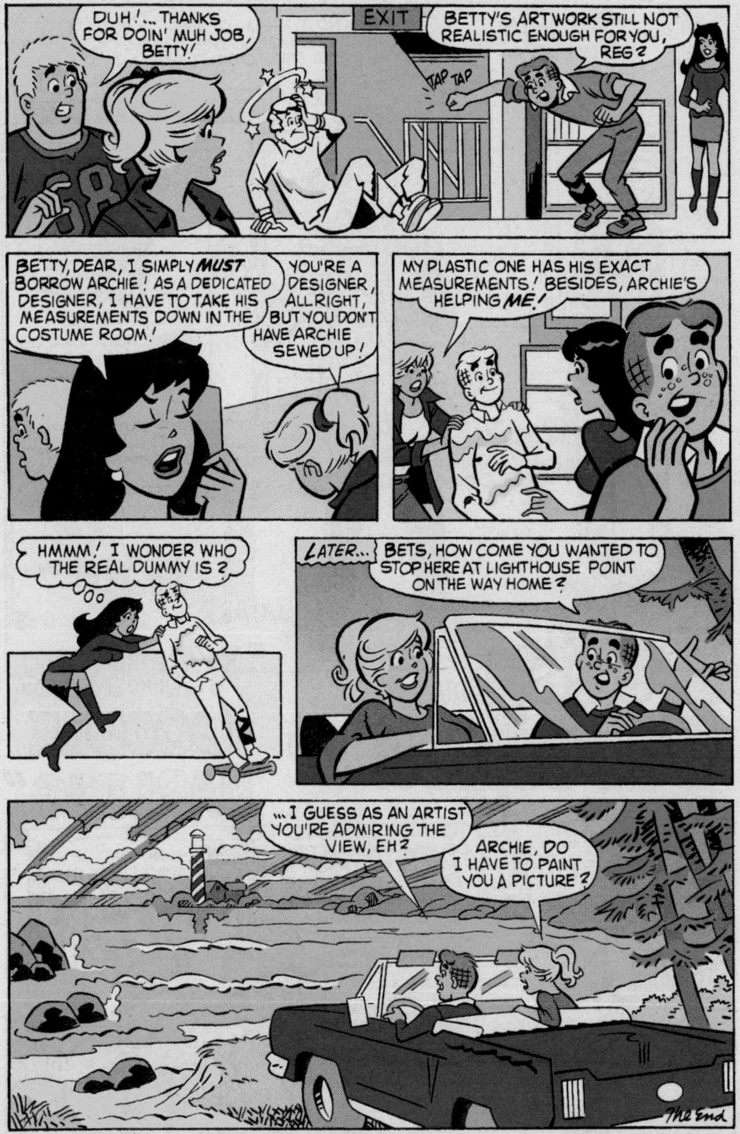
DUH!... THANKS FOR DOIN' MUH JOB, BETTY!
EXIT
TAP TAP
BETTY'S ARTWORK STILL NOT REALISTIC ENOUGH FOR YOU, REG?
BETTY, DEAR, I SIMPLY MUST BORROW ARCHIE! AS A DEDICATED DESIGNER, I HAVE TO TAKE HIS MEASUREMENTS DOWN IN THE COSTUME ROOM!
YOU'RE A DESIGNER, ALL RIGHT, BUT YOU DON'T HAVE ARCHIE SEWED UP!
MY PLASTIC ONE HAS HIS EXACT MEASUREMENTS! BESIDES, ARCHIE'S HELPING ME!
HMMM! I WONDER WHO THE REAL DUMMY IS?
LATER...
BETS, HOW COME YOU WANTED TO STOP HERE AT LIGHTHOUSE POINT ON THE WAY HOME?
...I GUESS AS AN ARTIST YOU'RE ADMIRING THE VIEW, EH?
ARCHIE, DO I HAVE TO PAINT YOU A PICTURE?
The End

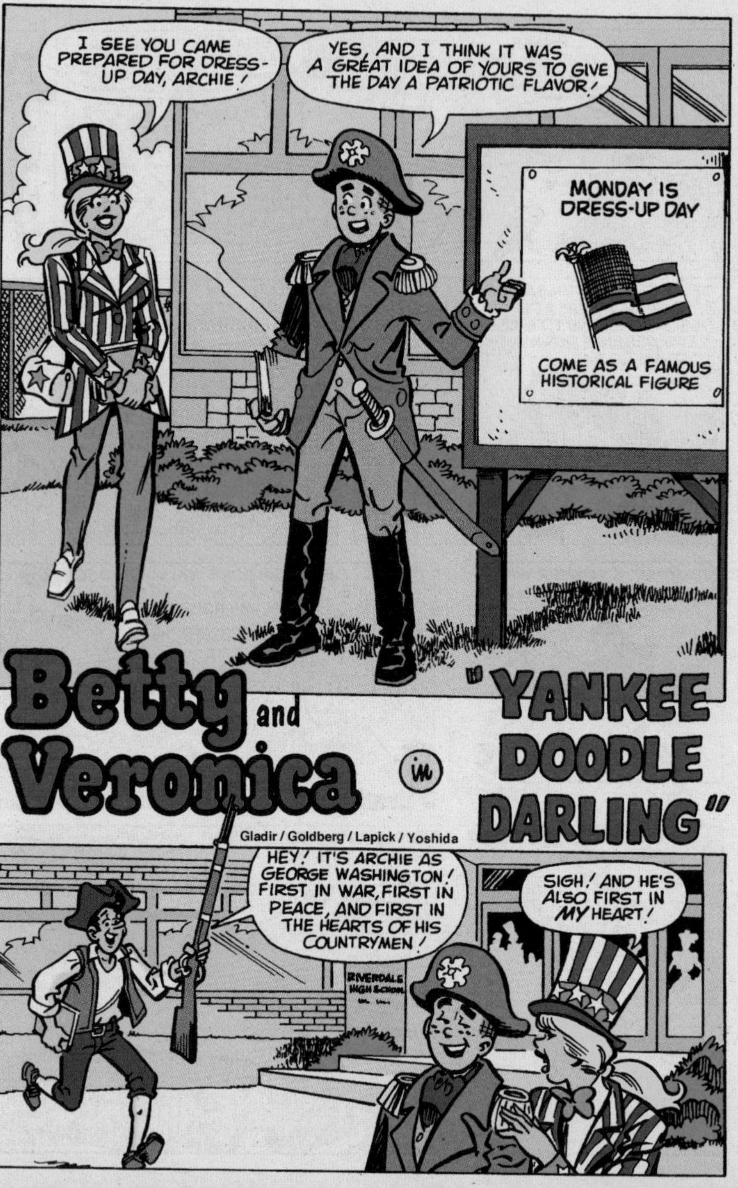
I SEE YOU CAME PREPARED FOR DRESS-UP DAY, ARCHIE!
YES, AND I THINK IT WAS A GREAT IDEA OF YOURS TO GIVE THE DAY A PATRIOTIC FLAVOR!
MONDAY IS DRESS-UP DAY
COME AS A FAMOUS HISTORICAL FIGURE
Betty and Veronica in "YANKEE DOODLE DARLING"
Gladir / Goldberg / Lapick / Yoshida
HEY! IT'S ARCHIE AS GEORGE WASHINGTON! FIRST IN WAR, FIRST IN PEACE, AND FIRST IN THE HEARTS OF HIS COUNTRYMEN!
SIGH! AND HE'S ALSO FIRST IN MY HEART!
RIVERDALE HIGH SCHOOL

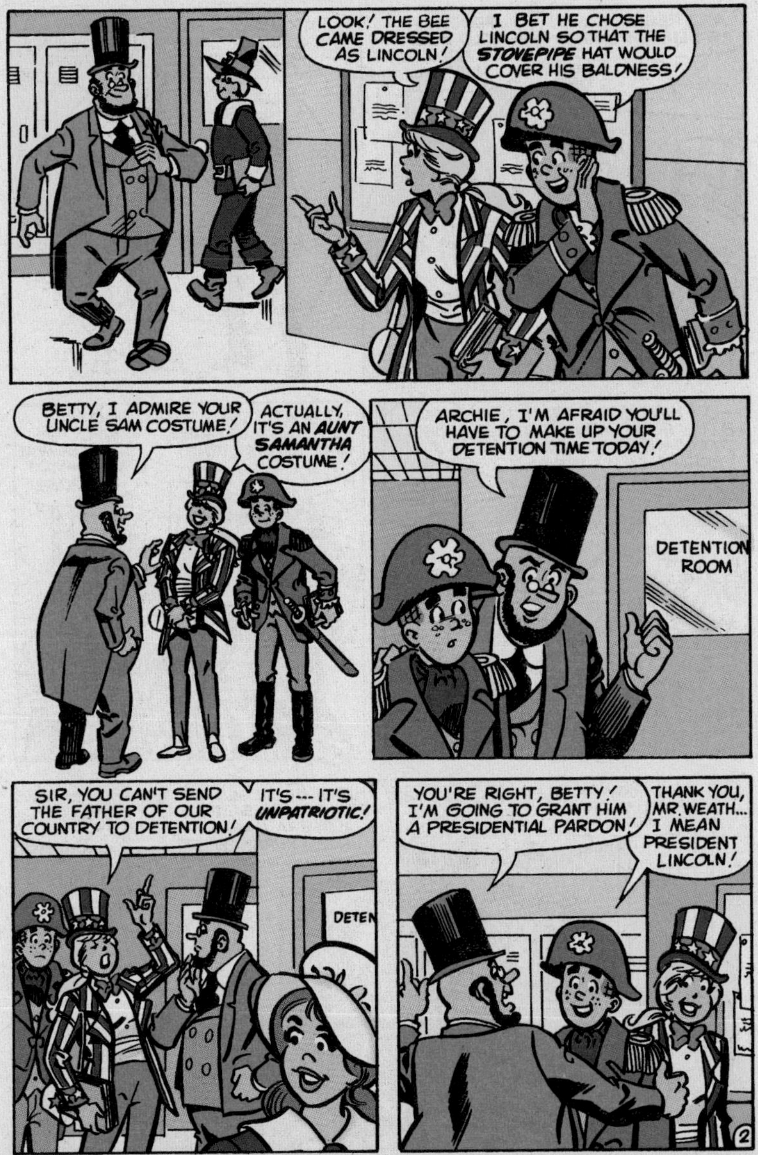
LOOK! THE BEE CAME DRESSED AS LINCOLN!
I BET HE CHOSE LINCOLN SO THAT THE STOVEPIPE HAT WOULD COVER HIS BALDNESS!
BETTY, I ADMIRE YOUR UNCLE SAM COSTUME!
ACTUALLY, IT'S AN AUNT SAMANTHA COSTUME!
ARCHIE, I'M AFRAID YOU'LL HAVE TO MAKE UP YOUR DETENTION TIME TODAY!
DETENTION ROOM
SIR, YOU CAN'T SEND THE FATHER OF OUR COUNTRY TO DETENTION!
IT'S --- IT'S UNPATRIOTIC!
DETEN
YOU'RE RIGHT, BETTY! I'M GOING TO GRANT HIM A PRESIDENTIAL PARDON!
THANK YOU, MR. WEATH... I MEAN PRESIDENT LINCOLN!
2

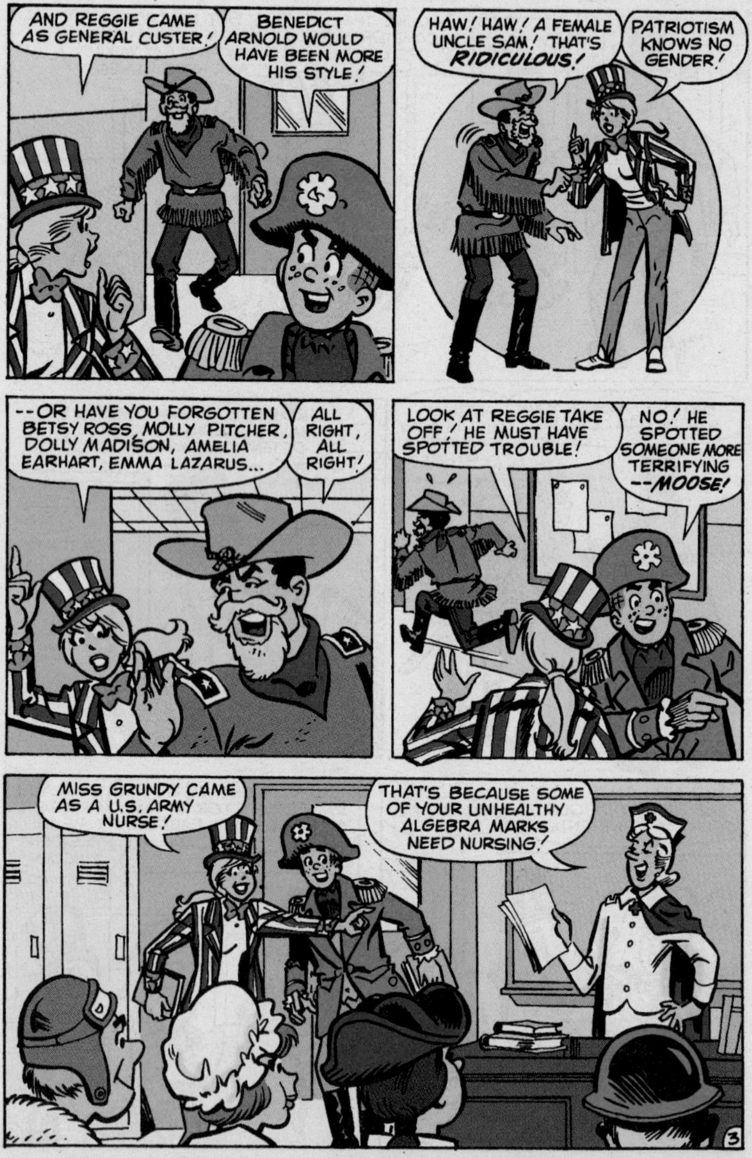
AND REGGIE CAME AS GENERAL CUSTER!
BENEDICT ARNOLD WOULD HAVE BEEN MORE HIS STYLE!
HAW! HAW! A FEMALE UNCLE SAM! THAT'S RIDICULOUS!
PATRIOTISM KNOWS NO GENDER!
--OR HAVE YOU FORGOTTEN BETSY ROSS, MOLLY PITCHER, DOLLY MADISON, AMELIA EARHART, EMMA LAZARUS...
ALL RIGHT, ALL RIGHT!
LOOK AT REGGIE TAKE OFF! HE MUST HAVE SPOTTED TROUBLE!
NO! HE SPOTTED SOMEONE MORE TERRIFYING --MOOSE!
MISS GRUNDY CAME AS A U.S. ARMY NURSE!
THAT'S BECAUSE SOME OF YOUR UNHEALTHY ALGEBRA MARKS NEED NURSING!
3

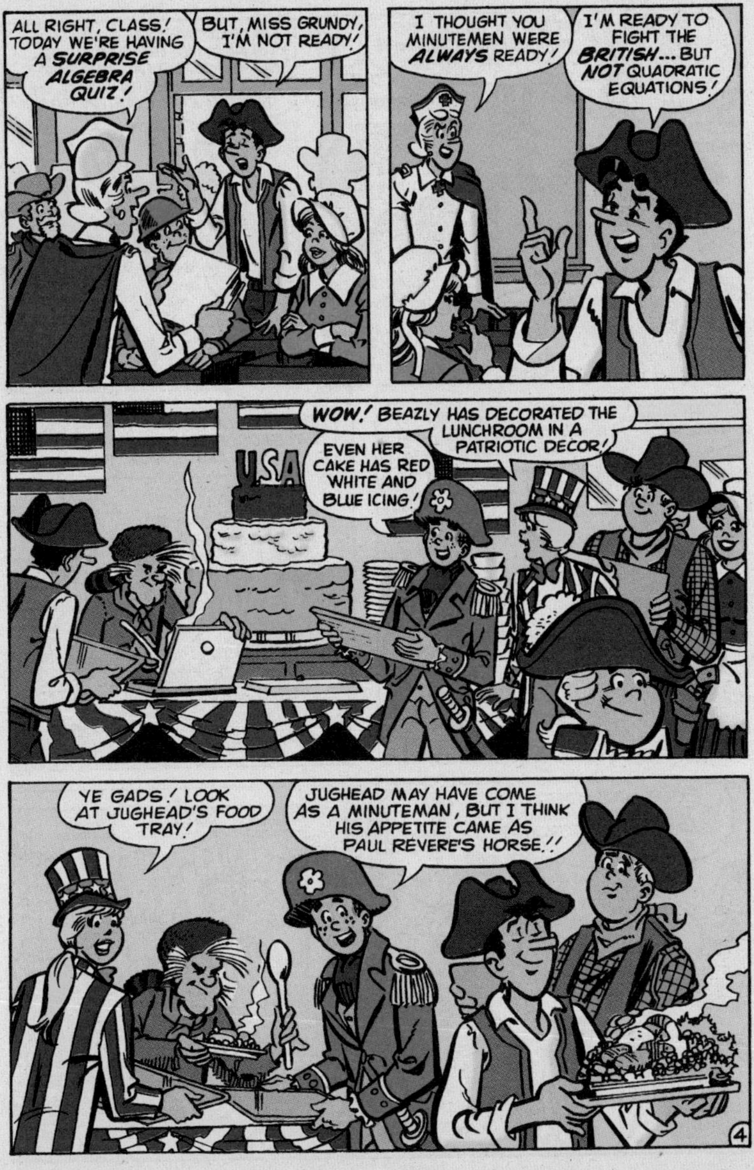
ALL RIGHT, CLASS! TODAY WE'RE HAVING A SURPRISE ALGEBRA QUIZ!
BUT, MISS GRUNDY, I'M NOT READY!
I THOUGHT YOU MINUTEMEN WERE ALWAYS READY!
I'M READY TO FIGHT THE BRITISH... BUT NOT QUADRATIC EQUATIONS!
USA
WOW! BEAZLY HAS DECORATED THE LUNCHROOM IN A PATRIOTIC DECOR!
EVEN HER CAKE HAS RED WHITE AND BLUE ICING!
YE GADS! LOOK AT JUGHEAD'S FOOD TRAY!
JUGHEAD MAY HAVE COME AS A MINUTEMAN, BUT I THINK HIS APPETITE CAME AS PAUL REVERE'S HORSE!!
4

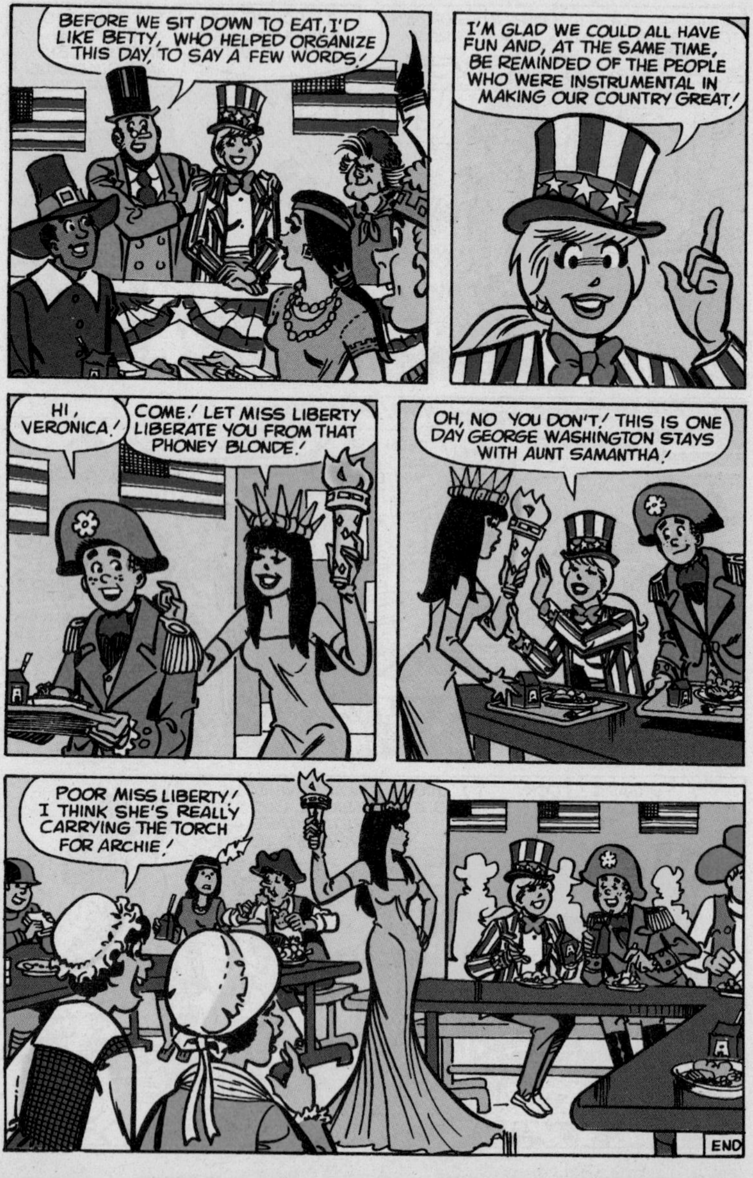
BEFORE WE SIT DOWN TO EAT, I'D LIKE BETTY, WHO HELPED ORGANIZE THIS DAY, TO SAY A FEW WORDS!
I'M GLAD WE COULD ALL HAVE FUN AND, AT THE SAME TIME, BE REMINDED OF THE PEOPLE WHO WERE INSTRUMENTAL IN MAKING OUR COUNTRY GREAT!
HI, VERONICA!
COME! LET MISS LIBERTY LIBERATE YOU FROM THAT PHONEY BLONDE!
OH, NO YOU DON'T! THIS IS ONE DAY GEORGE WASHINGTON STAYS WITH AUNT SAMANTHA!
POOR MISS LIBERTY! I THINK SHE'S REALLY CARRYING THE TORCH FOR ARCHIE!
END